THE DECEIT SYNDROME

Catch 69

By

Dr Paul Hobday

Strand Fiction

First published 2019 by Strand Publishing UK, Ltd.

Registered in England & Wales Company Number 07034246

Registered address: 11 St Michael Street,

Malton, North Yorkshire, YO17 7LJ

info@strandpublishing.co.uk

www.strandpublishing.co.uk

Paperback ISBN 978-1-907340-22-2

**The following need acknowledgement in the production
of this book, because without them it would
not have been necessary**

Sir John Redwood, Sir Oliver Letwin, Baroness Thatcher, Jeremy Hunt, Lord Lansley, David Cameron, Nick Clegg, Arthur Seldon, Lord Horder, Nigel Lawson, David Willetts, Roy Griffiths, Madsen Pirie, Alain Enthoven, Ken Clarke, Tony Blair, Alan Milburn, and a few other rather useless but self-serving Secretaries of State, the authors of *Direct Democracy* (you know who you are - still in the cabinet in 2019), the BMA, the managers who did the dirty work, the quislings in the CCGs, those who went round the revolving door of politics, management, then private company boards, McKinsey, KPMG, PricewaterhouseCoopers, Deloitte, all the right wing front organisations calling themselves think-tanks, Richard Branson, Virgin Care, Circle, Serco, Malling Health, Capita, UnitingCare, Care UK, In-Health, Vanguard Healthcare, The Practice PLC and a few other vultures, not forgetting the giant UnitedHealth and its subsidiary Optum; and all the patient transport, pharmacy, ophthalmic, diagnostic and out-of-hours provider private company cowboys, charlatans and confidence tricksters.

"To learn who rules over you, simply find out who you are not allowed to criticise"
– Voltaire

This book is dedicated to all the hardworking, devoted
and kind National Health Service staff who do so much and
put up with so much, for so little reward...

and the other good guys, obviously
Aneurin Bevan

Kenneth Robinson
Barbara Castle
Frank Dobson

Prof Stephen Hawking

And inspirations like
Dr Maurice Little
Dr Bob Gill
Dr Chris Day
Dr Youssef El-Gingihy
Dr Peter Fisher
Dr Julian Tudor-Hart
Dr Harry Keen

plus the Ash family
from Keep Our St Helier Hospital (KOSHH)
Colin Crilly
Save Our NHS in Kent (SONiK)
and the many dedicated NHS campaigners countrywide

special thanks to Janie my editor at Strand
for her enthusiasm and encouragement and without
whom this book would not have been possible.

This book is sold in aid of our NHS and all proceeds will be
used to fight for its survival and rejuvenation.

1 - LOVE AND JEALOUSY

JEALOUS GUY

I was feeling insecure
You might not love me anymore
I was shivering inside
I was shivering inside
Oh I didn't mean to hurt you
I'm sorry that I made you cry
Oh my I didn't want to hurt you
I'm just a jealous guy

John Lennon (1971)

"Oh, for fuck's sake. Okay. Once only. Never to be mentioned again. Agreed?"

Rob agreed.

"Pay attention as I'm not repeating myself. The first is pretty predictable. An old school friend who was persistent, but he didn't need to pester much as all the girls fancied him. We were still at school. Bit of a trophy really. Was a disappointment though as despite a load of practice he really didn't know what he was doing. Keen just to please himself. I only knew the theory but I could recognise clumsiness when I felt it. And I certainly felt it. I was the grand old age of seventeen so it was 1989. There was a charity version of *Ferry Cross The Mersey* for the Hillsborough disaster at number one so I can't listen to that without squirming. The track lasted four minutes seven seconds but he didn't. The second was known as 'pharmaceutical Pete'. Seems he kept the whole town supplied with whatever. He was too spaced out and up himself to care about what he was doing either, so another disappointment. Not sure what I saw in him."

So far so good, thought Rob. He did not think he was much different to all the other males he knew - whether friends, professionally or on television. He felt insecure and, in the immortal words of John Lennon it made him shiver inside when it came to sharing the love of his life. He felt childish for feeling like this even though it was all in the past and nothing really to do with him. The Y chromosome made him competitive so he knew he was not alone. He wanted to know he was the best or at minimum most appreciated. It was comforting then to learn that the first two were useless. Then came the smack in the face.

"Next was fantastic. Multiple orgasms. Probably to do with the RAF uniform. A friend of my brother and much better looking with those wings on his chest than out of his kit. I know you are thinking how fickle women are. The first time the earth moved for me... well, with someone else anyway and no need for batteries."

Rob knew this would happen. He was beginning to get agitated. Did he really want to know? Of course he did, he could not resist.

"Sorry about this next bloke. Typical stereotype. Cliché. A one night stand with a fireman at a New Year's Eve ball. The thought of another uniform I suppose but he had great muscles and not only on his thighs."

Another gulp from Rob who was pretending to take it in his stride - he dared not interrupt in case Suzy got bored and stopped. It did not seem like embarrassment would stop her.

"Fifth, I think. This was the daring of youth, pushing the boundaries, and fun in a supermarket. We'd been eyeing each other pushing our trolleys up and down the aisles and hovering around the fish counter. When eventually we accidentally on purpose collided, he winked and strolled off to the toilets. I'm not sure why but I followed him. Obviously a quickie; not something I'd do now."

Rob screamed within himself, what, not something I'd do now, with a stranger, who, crikey, blimey, no, fucking hell! He wanted to be Mr Nonchalant and it took all his might to appear as cool as a cucumber even though he was internally a red-hot chilli.

He was desperate to know more but dared not stop Suzy's flow. It was like having to suck a lemon. He had to go through with it but

2

it was agonising. What or who would she come up with next - perhaps someone he knows - perhaps someone famous? She seemed to be quite enjoying this. She seemed to glow in the nostalgia of it all. And she clearly knew the power she had over him. What he really wanted though was for her to say next time we are in Sainsbury's can we do it? But he knew that would never happen.

"Not long after that, not one of my finest moments. I still feel guilty about this. I went to a party with a new boyfriend and got off with a guy I had fancied for a while. Played centre forward for our local team. The boyfriend caught us behind a large rhododendron at the end of the garden. Strangely he never spoke to me after that. It was meant to be, as we'd had a tiff on the way to the party and I was pissed off with him. He couldn't understand why he hadn't been able to get into my knickers. The pressure turned me off. Bit of a harsh way of making my point though.

Was this the sixth or seventh Rob was puzzling. He hoped it was not going to turn out to be the Andie MacDowell and Hugh Grant scene from *Four Weddings And A Funeral*. He did not want this to go on all night. But that last one confirmed what he knew already that some women use sex as a weapon. Sometimes like a peashooter, but other times like a Kalashnikov. It is their main strength and best tactic for being in control. He felt like asking how many more but knew that would backfire. He dreaded her saying she'd only just started.

"Cliff Wessel you know about. You know what a bastard he is. No idea what I saw in him. Taking advantage of my naivety in my first year at Oxford. I was only nineteen. 1991. Rajiv Gandhi had just been murdered and Eric Clapton's son had fallen out of that New York window."

There was a pause. Suzy broke the silence.

"It must have been a boring wedding to end up with him."

"Yea, but what a boast. Getting off with the Best Man at your brother's wedding. I haven't noticed that in you though, 'this programme is boring, let's have sex?'" Rob thought he should lighten the mood.

He liked her talking about the past but she rarely did. When he prompted her she made him feel he was just being nosey, which of course he was, but Rob really believed the more he knew the more he could love her. The well known ways to impress a woman, such as showing a keen interest in her did not seem to work with Suzy. Trust him to end up with an awkward one. He used to think her too secretive, as though she had something to hide, but he did not think that now.

"Now I should have got a promise out of you about all this being confidential."

Rather too quickly Rob fired back.

"Of course. I'm insulted you would think I'll sell your story to the *Daily Mail*?"

It was meant to be light-hearted, but they both knew he was not good at keeping secrets. Suzy only felt confident of this exercise in trying to deal with Rob's jealousy now they were planning their wedding. But his jealousy did have to be dealt with. His illogical pain had brought her to tears before. She was relieved that mobile phones were not cameras in her previous life or she would worry about revenge porn. She would have been up for saucy photos then, but not now. She sometimes wondered if she was too prudish and not adventurous enough. Does it die with age? What did Jerry Hall's Mum tell her? *To keep a man, be a maid in the living room, a cook in the kitchen, and a whore in the bedroom.* None of those three appealed to Suzy, and would her Mum have also advised marrying Rupert Murdoch? Would her advice now be, *find yourself a husband richer and more powerful than Jagger who looks like a tortoise?*

Suzy Dwight was named after the Suzy who *wore her dresses tight* in *Crocodile Rock.* It was 1972 and although already a fan, Reg, her Dad had only just found out he had the same name as Elton John. He spelt it incorrectly though. The song's Suzy was spelt Suzie. He made the same mistake when Suzy's younger sister Leila was named after the Derek and the Dominos' classic. That should have been *Layla.* When his two daughters were young he often thought *I never knew me a better time and I guess I never will.* Although Suzy's Mum did not *leave us for some foreign guy* the marriage failed to last past their childhoods. Her Mum did not like music much. In fact they had little at all in common. She eventually went off with a fish and chip shop owner from Tenby.

Nevertheless Suzy's childhood was happy. She was close to her sister, but more distant from her brother as he was five years older. She was bright and strolled through her comprehensive education to study History of Art at Oxford, a few years before the worry of paying for tuition fees. On graduation she landed a job at the Royal Academy of Arts in London. After just two years she became their Art Sales Programme Curator. She met Phil when she was sent to look at some recently discovered paintings in a dusty old storeroom in his Whitehall department. They both clicked.

One of their first dates in 1998 was the march to protest about tuition fees. She knew when the politicians said the cost would be limited to £1000 a year that they were lying, devious, scheming bastards and her view of our glorious leaders had gone downhill ever since. This epithet, as she hoped all would know, was a thinly veiled reference to many politicians having morals and ethics on a par with Nazis. Expressing this view was not very consistent with her being in her posh job - although she was not as inhibited as Phil. She increasingly resented, on his behalf, the stories he told about the way the civil service, and his job, had been turned into a Government propaganda machine, and not the neutral force for good he thought he had joined. He hated doing the politicians' dirty work for them, and getting the blame when they cocked up, but then watching them take the credit when a good job was done.

Phil took her on an unauthorised tour of the Foreign and Commonwealth Office. She was in awe at the Grand Staircase and the ceiling above, the Locarno Suite and the Durbar Court. Suzy could easily understand how the elected acquired delusions of grandeur. How Prime Ministers develop Hubris Syndrome then drag us into wars that in turn raise the UK terrorist threat. She learnt that George Gilbert Scott the architect had originally envisaged a Gothic style but was overruled by the Prime Minister who insisted on Classic. Any politician working there would easily be seduced into thinking Britain did and should rule the world. Perhaps suitable for when it was built in the mid-nineteenth century but Suzy's solution, to help them avoid falling into this trap, was that the whole department should be moved to an office block in Milton Keynes. That would keep their feet on the ground. Phil did not really appreciate the joke.

Philip Hobbs was forty-five when he and Suzy married in 2001. Suzy was only twenty-nine. For some reason children never happened and they were at the start of infertility investigations in 2007 when Phil was killed in a road accident. They had just returned from a wonderful skiing trip to Megeve and he died on his first day back at work.

Suzy met Rob in 2011. He happened to be in London on a course with some time to spare before the train home so had popped into the National Portrait Gallery instead of waiting for half an hour for his train in the cold. He went straight to Room 24 as he wanted to see Michele Gordigiani's oils on canvas of Robert Browning and Elizabeth Barrett Browning. He felt a connection with them, albeit weak. Lennon had used their poetry and Rob's youngest was named after her. As he turned he saw the most amazing legs pelmetted by a short white skirt. The owner was gazing at the portrait by Ballantyne of Sir Edwin Landseer modelling one of the lions for the base of Nelson's column. For a man who was obsessed by punctuality he suddenly did not care if he missed his train.

"The dog at Sir Edwin's feet, called *Lassie,* went on to have its own show on TV," he said without looking directly at her.

He had shocked himself. He was not looking to make new friends with anyone, and it was not his style to chat up complete strangers, but she had a warm welcoming air about her and her body language was inviting.

"What? That collie?" she encouraged back.

"Yes, you obviously know your dogs?" he said, for want of something better to keep the conversation flowing.

"But do you know your American TV shows? The whole nineteen-year run was sponsored by the Campbell's Soup Company in one of the first instances of product placement. Their products are seen in all the background shots."

"Maybe Andy Warhol did more for them than *Lassie*" said a very impressed Rob, bringing them back to art.

Suzy moved off to the next portrait muttering something about a picture being worth millions of words. She stared at *Augustus Pugin* by an unknown artist. Rob knew a little about the architect being brought up near Ramsgate where he lived the last decade of his life and was buried. He was about to tell her that he was responsible for the interior of the Palace of Westminster and the Elizabeth Tower housing Big Ben but with a jolt he realised it was too risky. Where would it lead?

Two weeks later in a reversal of corny roles Suzy spotted him again in the adjacent Room 21 looking at the bust of Tennyson and spoke from behind.

"Tis better to have loved and lost than never to have loved at all."

Rob shot back.

"Ours not to reason why, ours but to do or die."

Suzy later admitted she had sought him out.

A close second in the attraction stakes to Suzy's legs were her values, as demonstrated by her sense of humour. When a *Made In Chelsea* type stood beside them and was obviously trying to impress the bimbo he was with.

"Of course Jung's link with mysticism continued with his interest in Daoism where he began to experiment with the use of I Ching."

All Suzy could say out loud was, "Oh, for fuck's sake... no! Please."

Coffee followed, then an exchange of numbers and a meeting on the fifth day of Rob's weekly course, which turned out to be the beginning of a new course in both of their lives. They had an affair for a couple of years before Rob finally left his family for her. To Rob she was his Yoko to the Cynthia he had left with the children. He was infatuated, which made him feel insecure. He knew it was safer and easier to be loved more than you love but life cannot be planned that way, not even with his obsessive tendencies.

"Neville Gideon?" Rob repeated in astonishment. You're joking... 'the' Neville Gideon? Her Majesty's Chancellor of the Exchequer?"

Now he realised why Suzy might have introduced the confidentiality clause.

"The bloke who likes to be whipped and led around on a lead, begging his mistress for mercy? Amazing. I could never have anticipated that."

By this time Rob was beaming like a Cheshire cat. How had she managed to keep this quiet throughout their five years together? Astonishing, perhaps even funny? Suzy then demonstrated perhaps her most irritating habit. She corrected Rob's English.

"You mean you wouldn't have expected that. Your use of the word anticipated is wrong. To anticipate is to prepare, to act in advance. Whereas to expect something is to think it may happen. So you could never have expected that."

After that scolding she continued.

"You know that famous Bullingdon Club photo with the prats all looking so smug after trashing a restaurant, I think that was taken the night after. If you look carefully Wessel is in it too. I was seduced by his Dad's mansion and, I am embarrassed now to admit it, there was something seductive about his unshakeable belief he would outdo his father and rule the world. After pouring the best part of two bottles of Dom Perignon into me he had no doubt sex was his right. I found out later that his mate, to the right of him in the photo, had bet him three bottles of Krug that he couldn't lay a comprehensive girl. The git."

Then it began to sink in. He hated all the posh multi-millionaire toffs who ran the country with such arrogance, like it was their birthright anyway, then to find out one had slept with his wife-to-be put them in a different league of loathing altogether. He would not find Budget Day interesting any more.

Suzy had had enough after this. She had never talked about the past for so long. There were a few others. The car mechanic who was always ready and greased up, the skiing instructor at Val d'Isere, a lot of metal in him from accidents but no steel where it counts, and an accountant from Shoreham-on-Sea, always insisted they put on Brighton and Hove Albion shirts, but Rob was not really taking any of it in. She was a bit more animated whilst describing Philip's blue eyes and muscles as a turn-on, and then she told Rob she was 'celibate after Philip's death, until you, my darling'.

Four years? He wanted to believe her.

2 - FRUSTRATION AND BEWILDERMENT

THIEVES

Thieves, thieves and liars, murderers
Hypocrites and bastards

Hey thanks for nothing!
Morals in the dust
Two-faced bastards and sycophants
No trust

Ministry (1990)

Rob usually got lost in thought and introspection on his way to work. More often than not he could not really remember the fifteen-minute drive to the surgery.

Autopilot was a great thing. Today was no different, reflecting on last night's chat it could have been worse. At least she called him Rob throughout. That exhibited her loving side. He knew that when she was trying to be assertive or was angry he was Robert. Bob was when he needed to be treated like a naughty boy. He told himself he now needed to be grown up about Suzy's past. Did retroactive jealousy really exist or was it a term made up by psychologists to broaden their empire? Was he suffering from it? But at least most were not really lovers and, he would not admit it to anyone, but imagining her having sex on a train, or upstairs at a party was quite a turn-on, even if it was with someone else. Why the hell should he still feel jealous about these ghosts from the past? Totally illogical, which upset Rob the most, as he always thought he was a rational person. It proved to him that emotions are not at all sensible, or why would he have abandoned his very loving Cynthia for his risky perhaps less loving Yoko? Getting married was to him really moving on. He was not sure whether it helped him deal with the guilt he still had, that still brought him out in a cold sweat at 3 a.m., about breaking up a perfectly happy family. Would it be another kick in the teeth for his three lovely daughters? What a fucking idiot he had been he often told himself. Still, it is progress when it is not dominating his life twenty-four hours a day - just perhaps twenty-three. He should have listened to those who had said 'been there done that', not the well-meaning follow-your-heart brigade. He learnt that following your heart means breaking someone else's.

As he arrived at the surgery, later than usual, he saw a few familiar faces treading their well-worn path to the reception desk. Rob had been a General Practitioner long enough to know most of his patients quite well. He often predicted what they wanted, or at least the type of consultation that he could expect, before they walked through the door. He could categorise them: those who just needed reassurance, those who demanded an instant cure, those who came for a chat, those who thought only a specialist for their problem good enough, those who wanted a drug, and those that regarded all drugs as poison, but also those whose teeth itched and stools glowed in the dark, and there were those who thought he could cure everything and was the Messiah despite trying to tell them, in the classic words of Terry Jones, that he was, *not the Messiah but a very naughty boy*. A naughty boy called Bob.

It was a fantastic job and a privilege to be trusted and allowed into the confidential and private lives of so many people and to deal with generations of the same family too. But this unique and invaluable aspect of family medicine was being killed off by stupid, ignorant, self-serving politicians most of whom were in the pockets of others. It made Rob so fucking angry. Increasingly patients were attending as a result of ill health caused by poverty, benefit cuts and hassle from employers. So unnecessary. So wrong.

Medical school in Rob's day was seventy-five per cent public school intake. How he managed to squeeze in was still a mystery to him. When he first turned up at Guy's in 1982 he entered an alien world. He was the only doctor from a family of builders from Margate. When one of the toffs discovered this he spoke in his 1930s BBC accent looking down his nose.

"You know T.S. Eliot wrote some of *The Waste Land* there? Appropriate, eh what, after all, the place is a wasteland."

11

"Yeah, but Marty Feldman used to work at Dreamland," Rob replied to his totally puzzled taunter.

He spotted immediately those following daddy into a money-making lifestyle. They were heading straight to ophthalmology or orthopaedics for a lucrative private practice. Their families and friends only used the NHS as a last resort. They looked at socialised medicine as almost communist. They were unmistakable with their superior attitude and disdain for the lower forms of life. They initially looked at Rob with their noses in the air as though he smelt of buses, chicken nuggets and *ITV*. Most were not in the Bullingdon Club league of course but still another stratum of the cream.

"Yeah, just like cream," Rob used to say, "thick and rich."

The group Rob befriended was more normal. He knew nothing except the NHS and that Bevan's creation was the main reason for his wanting to become a doctor. On 14th January 1977 two great things happened to him. He had gone out to buy Bowie's *Low* the day it was released and he started to read A. J. Cronin's *The Citadel*, which a spinster aunt had just given him for Christmas. She was a nurse working in Aberalaw in Wales and was the first to interest him in medicine. This is where his hatred of corrupt private medicine was first conceived, born in his time at Guy's and grew up while he was in general practice. If he had had his way it would have been strangled at birth but now it has become a delinquent monster. Yesterday two letters arrived from the same Ear Nose and Throat Consultant colleague responding to Rob's referral of two six-year-olds with identical symptoms. The opinion about the child who saw the specialist on the NHS was to wait and see. He did not think grommets would be in her best interest. The parents of the girl who saw him privately however were told that grommets would cure her almost immediately.

"You wouldn't want to leave her with an infection that is just an inch from her brain, would you?"

Cheeky bastard, Rob thought, but not uncommon. It will help fund his new Merc.

For once the morning surgery went like clockwork. He actually enjoyed most of it and bumped into his partner at the end of a four-hour session. Rob was increasingly pleased with Clive, the normal lad he had taken on six years ago. Rob did indeed think he was a lad and was quite envious of his marathon running and the boozy nights he had with his rugby mates - although playing was now a thing of the past. Clive had spent a few years abroad after qualifying. The only doubt Rob had at interview had been his tendency not to stay at any practice for too long. His CV listed five in twelve years, the last being in Hackney. And he was a smooth character. Smooth enough to survive a GMC hearing concerning an alleged BJ from a patient. But that was in Hackney. He did have a fantastic barrister, a bit like the one OJ Simpson had hired. Although fantastic was Clive's word. Rob looked at him more as a nasty bastard who, like OJ's lawyer managed to twist the truth to make out it was all the fault of the victim. Clive swore his innocence but Rob was not totally convinced but he kept that to himself. Despite that hiccup he had turned out to be a breath of fresh air for the practice.

"Fancy a quick drink after work tonight?" Clive fired at Rob.

That usually meant Clive wanted something so he always accepted with mixed feelings. Today was different though. He really needed a pint or two and to get some things off his own chest.

Clive Lister was forty-five, so seven years Rob's junior. He was more laid back about politics than Rob, which sometimes frustrated the senior man. Rob thought he should care more. Curiously, and to prove Rob wrong on this occasion, Clive didn't have a lot to say at the bar in the Bell and Jorrocks. After knocking back the first pint of Harvey's in less than two minutes Rob began to relax and put behind him the afternoon surgery, which was not as easy as the morning. Clive's uncharacteristic lack of verbosity and almost creepy display of unexpected quiet allowed Rob to sound off.

"I caught Mrs Credula with the *Daily Mail* in the waiting room today. Usual GP-hating headline: GPs MISS 99% OF CANCERS. So outrageously untrue but as Goebbels once said if you tell a lie big enough and keep repeating it, people will eventually come to believe it. Something really bad must have happened to the editor at birth.

13

Probably dropped on his head by a GP. Can't win can we, but they don't want us to."

"It won't make much difference, he has stepped down after nearly three decades," replied Clive in an attempt to re-engage with the real world, "and his successor will probably be just as good at delivering a daily dose of hate."

"And what hypocrisy!" fired back Rob, "Apparently, although he hates the EU, this didn't stop him trousering nearly half a million quid from them for his Scottish Estate!"

"We really shouldn't allow the *Daily Fascist* into our building," Clive retorted, and Rob was not sure if he was taking the piss or not.

"Their pre-war appeasement and support for Hitler was bad enough, but their anti-Semitism was a disgrace. They are not much better now. History repeating itself."

"They think we should refer everything that might be cancer within sixty seconds of it walking through the door, but yesterday they said the NHS was in a state because GPs refer too much! *Catch-22.* Wankers."

Rob realised Clive did not know what he meant by *Catch-22.* A great book. He had lapped it up as a teenager. In the war, any pilot claiming not to be sane enough to fly must have been sane, as only a crazy person would want to fly dangerous missions. Should he explain? No. He could not be bothered. Born after the Beatles split too. How depressing. Those seven years seemed like a generation sometimes.

"Be great if the public really knew the facts. We actually diagnose eighty per cent of cancers in one or two visits. Seventy-five per cent of myelomas present with back pain but ninety-nine point nine per cent of back pain is not due to myeloma. Do we refer all these just in case? Of course not, that is where our skill, training and experience come in. Politicians have no understanding of what our job involves and the media are dancing to their tune. Bastards."

"I think the public are more canny than you think. We still have high approval ratings despite the attempts to discredit us. And only the stupid and Mrs Gullibles believe their lies that we are lazy and spend most of our time on the golf course. That we should work twenty-four hours a day, seven days a week so that Harry Hedge-fund can have an appointment when he feels like it, pissed on his way back from the city, at 11.00 p.m. because he thinks he has a wart on his knob."

Rob felt a rant building up too much steam. Time to call a halt by getting another drink. As he approached the bar he realised Len the barman had already pulled two pints for them.

"I knew one would not be enough for you two tonight. One look at your stressed faces as you walked in?"

"Thanks Len. Don't tell anyone."

For years he had worked on the assumption two pints was just within the drink-drive limit. Now he was not sure. But the loosening up effect of the first pint always made Rob more confident that it was okay. One day he might learn the hard way.

"The media's the most powerful entity on earth," Clive said very slowly on his return from the bar, *"They have the power to make the innocent guilty and the guilty innocent, and that's power because they control the minds of the masses."*

"What?"

"The wise words of Malcolm X."

Rob was impressed. He does know something of the past after all. He will have to explain *Catch-22* one day and why The Beatles were the greatest group ever. But that innocent-guilty and guilty-innocent stuff could equally be applied to Clive's barrister.

"You only know what you know," Clive carried on, "as that war criminal Donald Rumsfeld said. I arrived in general practice after they started micromanaging us, and de-professionalising all of the noble professions. So I'm more used to it than you. I've known nothing different. They are succeeding in changing a vocation and profession into just a job. They can control us better that way. Politicians have always hated the medical profession. Not really sure why but I bet it's jealousy, irritation about our strength, and certainly they resent how popular we are with the public compared to them. No surprise politicians, journalists and estate agents are down the bottom of the popularity league, beneath the Waffen-SS."

15

This was the first time Rob had heard Clive sounding off like this. It made him feel a little less isolated. It still did not help him to understand what was really going on though.

"I know I must sound like a sad old git but it really was better when I started. I visited poor old Mrs Cackitt at lunchtime. She's ninety-four and bedbound, as you know. Years ago she would have had as many visits as she needed from our district nurses, bath ladies, cleaners and meals on wheels, all people we know and who knew her well. Never a stranger walking through her door. Fantastic continuity of care, kept her in her own home where she was happy. A concept our prat of a Health Minister hasn't got a clue about. It was a great early warning system in case of trouble. This kept people happy and cared for by familiar faces and out of hospital. Now look at it? Regimented fifteen-minute unpredictable visits usually by complete strangers from a private company, who are so pressurised they can't stop to talk, their travel time included in the old person's care time. Her daughter told me she often has to clean her mother herself. The carers have a habit, if she looks a bit peaky, of dialling 999 to cover themselves. She has ended up in A&E twice this month for no good reason. It's very distressing for an ill lady living out her last days. The tossers responsible for this know the cost of everything and the value of nothing. Apparently the fifth richest country in the world can't afford to look after its old folk properly. People who fought the war for us. Now I hear their latest brainwave is that your house will pay for it. A tax on dementia, multiple sclerosis and disability. Better for your kids if you shoot yourself."

Clive agreed.

"The way we look after the elderly in this country is a disgrace. Pretty well all the care homes are in private hands now. They pass from private equity outfits to opportunistic US hedge funds. It's a high-stakes financial game in which the players aim for increasingly fat rewards. It's nothing to do with looking after our old folk. But the big companies are all in trouble because they overloaded themselves with debt. Greedy bastards. Southern Cross failed because of its addiction to fancy sale-and-leaseback property deals.

16

Who suffers from their games in the end? The elderly and the taxpayer."

Rob sipped his pint, quite impressed. He introduced another hobbyhorse of his.

"And how many of the elderly we look after suffer from loneliness? That's another real problem of modern times since the scattering of the family. It's supposed to be as dangerous to health as smoking fifteen cigarettes a day. As our glorious leaders close community centres and other places where people congregate like libraries, they make that worse too. Stupid short-sighted prats."

Clive attempted to move on.

"Never mind, now those idiots in Whitehall have started scoring us in league tables, they are saved! They can all pick the number one GP of the Premier League and the rest of us will be sacked. Solves the funding problem too as only need to employ one surgeon who is so good he can do all the work!"

Rob was more serious.

"Of course the best surgeons attract the most complicated cases, thereby have higher death rates. So according to those fucking stupid politicians they are the worst, even if we know they are the best. You know the statistics? After years of funding-starvation over the decades we were spending six per cent of GDP on health. The last lot said they'd aim for the EU average and it was up to eight point eight per cent by 2009. Trouble is the EU average had risen in the meantime to ten point one per cent. Now we are back down to six point six per cent again. What's worse, we have half the beds per head of population than Germany and a third that of Japan and have cut thirty-seven thousand beds in the last fifteen years and the idiots are planning to cut even more. When we are thousands of GPs short the plan is to cut more. Unbelievable! Sixty thousand nurses short, training places cut and the bursary abolished, the EU supply drying up after that referendum, manpower planning done by a team of politicians sharing one brain cell. Hypocrites and two-faced bastards! Wages down ten per cent in the last five years, a wage collapse on a par with Greece. The difference is that the Greeks were forced to do that by the Troika, but our Government did it because they wanted

17

to. Hospital workers even pay two hundred pounds a year to park their cars! If the nurses got together and fought all this they'd easily win. Let down by their union, familiar story."

Clive's eyes had glazed over by this stage as he had heard it all before.

"My aunt was one of forty thousand nurses and midwives from the Caribbean who answered the call from the mother country to help build the NHS. Like many she had to prove herself working as an orderly for four years before she was accepted for nurse training. Then they were only allowed to train as a State Enrolled Nurse, or second tier nurse as she called herself. They were persuaded to work nights so their colour didn't offend the patient's visitors."

There was a pause for a sip of beer.

"And we now have proof of where all this is leading. Austerity has led to the increase in life expectancy coming to a halt. It has now begun to fall in some areas, for the first time in ages. Tens of thousands of extra deaths and not among the well off that's for sure."

"You know boss, your passion needs an escape value. You are like a pressure cooker sometimes. You should stand for Parliament or write a book. Get it off your chest."

Clive was serious.

"No chance of either. Daft idea if I may say so. The public can't be dragged away from the main parties in a totally unfair electoral system and I can't write anything that is publishable. If JK Rowling gets rejected what chance have I got?"

"Hmm, okay? The clinical job itself is great though, isn't it?" Clive said moving on, "You know how satisfying it is when you review someone you've just put on steroids for polymyalgia rheumatica? After months of debilitating aches and pains they bounce in like a five-year-old and think you're a miracle worker. It happened to me today. Mrs Vittne, a lovely old lady, thought I was the Messiah."

He then changed the subject quite abruptly.

"When I was in town last week I was on the Piccadilly line on my way to the Royal College, the course was useless by the way, when I remembered one of my favourite adverts. Paul Hogan was asked do you know the way to Cockfosters?"

Puzzled, he replied and Rob joined in.

"Yes, serve it warm. Boom-boom!"

"What's the troika? A type of ice pick?" asked Clive.

Rob's short drive home took him along the side of a golf course. Not infrequently he would see a golf ball in the gutter and wondered what damage it had done to a passing car. Tonight he had to brake to avoid four men crossing the road from the pub to the ninth green. They were dragging their trolleys and not paying much attention to the road. Two were on their phones. Rob assumed they wore such loud trousers so no one could possibly not see them.

He also passed his girls' school, now called an academy for some reason. He saw a new sign being put up that said:

TOMORROW'S FUTURE TODAY.

"What a load of fucking bollocks!" he shouted to himself, "What the fuck is that supposed to mean? Christ, I feel like emigrating to somewhere sane. Something must be done about these idiots."

3 - POMPOSITY AND ARROGANCE

REVOLUTION

You say you want a revolution
Well, you know
We all want to change the world
You tell me that it's evolution
Well, you know
We all want to change the world

You say you got a real solution
Well, you know
We'd all love to see the plan
You ask me for a contribution
Well, you know
We're all doing what we can

But if you want money for people with minds that hate
All I can tell you is brother you have to wait

The Beatles (1968)

July 1969

It would be two more years - in July 1971- before Jim Morrison died in the bath in his rented apartment in Rue Beautreillis, Paris. He was twenty-seven. The singer-songwriter and poet was buried in Cimetiere du Pere Lachaise, which has become a shrine for Doors fans.

The other Jim Morrison could not have been more different, although only thirty-two he was already middle-aged in every way. He was rarely seen out of a three-piece suit with waistcoat, with the Haas Neveux and Co. Swiss gold pocket watch, fob and chain given to his father by Grand Duchess Xenia. He loathed the decadent youth and the way the country was going to the dogs. It was July 1969 and *Honky Tonk Women* had just been released, the day after

Brian Jones had been found dead - also in water - in his Cotchford Farm swimming pool. Morrison the poet mourned and wrote *Ode to LA* while thinking of Brian Jones, deceased. The other Morrison celebrated and was glad and, thinking to himself, pathetic excuse for a man who did not deserve to live. The sort we must push to the bottom of society's ladder. But the bottom of a swimming pool will do.

Sir James, as the concierge correctly addressed him, was sitting quietly in his club, reading about the moon landing in *The Times*. The In And Out Naval And Military Club, in Cambridge House, on Piccadilly overlooked Green Park and was founded in 1862. His grandfather claimed to be an original member but Sir James knew he would not have been old enough. His father Charles however, belonged for years and bored Jim with tales of all the alcoholic lunches he had had there with the rich and famous. The one story that did interest him though was of a secret meeting of the Right Club held there before the war. He had been told the details on several occasions as Charles had a habit of forgetting those he had already entertained with the anecdote, but Sir James lapped it up even though he thought his father a bastard.

Sir James, or Jim as his friends knew him, still was not used to *The Times* putting news on the front page instead of advertisements. When policy changed in 1966 he had written in disgust to the editor, Sir William Haley, pronouncing it vulgar. Tradition was much more important to the fabric of society than the death of any longhaired pop star. Sir William was at Cambridge with Jim's father so he was appalled to get just a cursory acknowledgement rather than an invitation to dinner to discuss the matter. Two years ago the new editor, Rees-Mogg, had, in Jim's opinion, dragged *The Thunderer* down even further with an editorial entitled *Who Breaks A Butterfly On A Wheel* in support of Brian Jones' fellow scums Jagger and Richards who had also been jailed on drugs offences. Jim was outraged, did not understand what butterflies had to do with it, and thought all the Rolling Stones should have been banged up on Robben Island for life with all those South African terrorists to help stop the rot in society.

Jim felt very at home at the club. Equally he felt very at home in his Mayfair house, on his Sussex estate, at his house in Scotland near Edinburgh, and also his villa in Barbados where he had spent the last month. Welchtown House on the northeast of the former colonial island was usually the winter escape for Morrison but he had used it this June as a convenient rendezvous to meet some American businessmen for some arms deals. Naturally he took his mistress. His father had bought the house from his friend Sir Henry Vaughan-Warner whose great-great-grandfather owned the sugar plantation next to St Nicholas Abbey and Cleland. Their neighbours and fellow slave owners were the Cumberbatch family. Sir James' father still owned Welchtown House but was now too disabled to get to the Caribbean following his stroke.

The Sussex country estate was less of a draw when Jim found out Brian Jones had become a neighbour, but his grandfather had bought Hetherington Park and he could not possibly entertain the idea of selling it. He had no idea who owned Cotchford Farm now but hoped it would end up in the hands of someone more respectable like its former owner A.A. Milne - someone more deserving with whom he could hunt. Jim thought even Winnie-the-Pooh was more of an upright character than Brian Jones.

The interior of the Club, with its walnut-panelled walls and portraits of past presidents had not changed since his grandfather's day. Sir James was proud of his heritage and what his father tried to achieve through the Right Club. That did not mean he liked him though. In the months leading up to the outbreak of war their raison d'être was to avoid war with fellow fascists. Members of the club, even prior to its formation in May 1939, had established numerous secret back channels to Nazi Germany and fascist Italy. Their contacts and activities often amounted to treason. They were not scared of a Nazi invasion as they assumed that would mean either Sir Archibald Ramsey (who established the club) or Sir Oswald Mosley being installed as puppet leaders, and possibly the Duke of Windsor being re-established on the throne. After war was declared their main hope rested on Viscount Halifax succeeding Neville Chamberlain. They were opposed to the warmonger. It pained Sir

James every time he heard someone say Churchill had saved Great Britain from Nazi tyranny. It pained him because he did not want to admit it might be true. He had said to his friend Gerry that we needed a dose of strong dictatorial leadership, German style, but we had to settle for an ex-Harrow failure. Plato's preferred state was not democratic, but ruled by a philosopher king. Hobbs's solution was an absolutist monarch. They were right. Doesn't matter whether the ruler is called a King or Fuhrer does it? Although the only Hobbs Gerry knew was the cricketer Jack, not the seventeenth century political philosopher.

His father Charles would lament that what we ended up with was the communist Attlee and degenerate socialist ideas like the National Health Service and nationalisation, and the giving away of an Empire. Charles twisted the criticism of imperialism and colonialism in Aimé Césaire's *Discourse On Colonialism* in an Orwellian manner. Césaire stated that European empires were run for the profit of the occupiers rather than for the benefit of the colonised peoples. Morrison agreed but said that was intentional and a good thing. Morrison also agreed that the roots of Nazism could be found in the toxic soil of imperialism. To Césaire this meant not risking Nazism by getting rid of Imperialism. To Morrison this meant encouraging imperialism so that new buds of Nazism would flourish and prosper across the globe. From the name Morrison assumed the author was a French woman. Had he known Césaire was a black poet and a politician from Martinique he would not have given his 1955 book house room.

Churchill's description that, *democracy is the worst form of Government except for all the others*, proved to Jim and his father that Churchill was actually too accommodating and weak. Charles had a tour of duty with the British army in India in the 1930s. He was in tune with Churchill on only one issue that giving the Indians home rule would lead to the downfall of the British Empire and the end of civilisation. They were both late Victorian imperialists. Gandhi should have put some clothes on before being allowed to die by fasting. That would have got rid of an enemy of the Empire and a bad lower form of life.

The meeting Charles told his son all about had been in this very building and was between Sir Archibald Ramsey MP, Lord Redesdale, the 5th Duke of Wellington and Arthur Ronald Nall Nall-Cain the 2nd Baron Brocket. That had been a small clique of the Right Club. They met separately and secretly from the main executive, as they had to discuss possible infiltration into their group, hence the meeting at Charles' Club instead of their usual venues. The honesty, trustworthiness and commitment of other members were examined in fine detail. They had full confidence in their military club members. Brigadier-General Robert Byron Drury Blakeney and Major-General John Frederick Charles 'Boney' Fuller were beyond reproach. Lieutenant Colonel Graham Seton Hutchinson, who had formed the British Empire Fascist Party, was also sound. Arnold Spencer Leese was the Club's main proponent that control of money was the key to power - they could not believe that a man who as early as 1935 was proposing the mass murder of Jews in gas chambers could be a traitor to the cause. There were no suspicions either about Sir Michael Francis O'Dwyer who was Lieutenant Governor of the Punjab in India until 1919 and believed the Amritsar massacre was the correct action. There was more of a debate about Robert Cecil Gordon-Canning whose relationship with Mosley had grown a bit frosty recently despite being best man at Oswald's wedding to Diana, in Goebbels' house and in Hitler's presence three years before. And some worried that the Duke of Westminster's affair with Coco Chanel jeopardised security particularly as she was friendly with Churchill. However, they ended the meeting with worries but no conclusions. For some unexplained reason James McGuirk Hughes and Ernest Talbot had not been put on their list to discuss.

The Second Baron Redesdale had to be careful that his other, anti-fascist daughters Jessica and Nancy did not have their noses rubbed in his activities. However, Diana as Mosley's wife and Unity who was in love with Hitler would certainly have approved. They had been to the 1937 Nuremberg Rally together and smoothed the path for the Duke of Windsor's visit a month later, when negotiations took place for Hitler to install the former King as a puppet Head of State after the invasion of Great Britain. This was why it had to be top secret and anyone who was slightly suspect exposed.

1937 was the year most of the alliances between British Nazi sympathisers were formed and reinforced. Lord Mount Temple, Chairman of the Anglo-German Fellowship liaised with all those who went on to form the Right Club along with Joachim von Ribbentrop, the German Ambassador to the Court of St James, despite his Anglophobia. They all went to the Queen's Hall together to hear Arturo Toscanini conduct Beethoven's *Symphony No.6 in F Major* to celebrate the Luftwaffe's destruction of the Basque town of Guernica five weeks earlier, and the marriage of the Duke of Windsor and Wallis Simpson at the Chateau de Cande the next day. Mount Temple was the father of Edwina who married Louis Mountbatten of Burma.

Another story Jim's father told whilst reminiscing some years later, was about an early full meeting of the Right Club, which was sidetracked by the activities of Nicholas Winton, the 'Jew-lover'. He organised the Kindertransport getting children out of Nazi-occupied Europe. They were ashamed Britain was the only country allowing in Jewish refugee children. Not though for the reasons most would be ashamed, that all other countries should be doing the same, but ashamed because they thought Britain was wrong to do so thus contaminating the gene pool and was letting the side down. The glamorous blonde Nazi spy who claimed to be working for the Swedish Red Cross, who tried to befriend Winton and get him to stop, was a cousin of Charles. Winton's boss at the Stock Exchange had a visit from William Joyce who persuaded him to order Winton home immediately. They even sent two Rabbis round to knock on his Hampstead Heath door to say he should not board Jewish children in Christian homes. Their main aim was appeasement. To their dismay Winton carried on.

Jim was also pleased about his father Charles's friendship and involvement with the Duke of Windsor, his trips to pre-war Germany, and that tale of securing a promise from Hitler about being installed as Head of State in a German-occupied Britain. He had bored all his friends with the story on numerous occasions. Although keen to boast about the Royal friendship, Jim had more recently been convinced that his father was more of a minor player in direct contacts with Germany than he had been led to believe. Only two years ago at Baron Brocket's funeral he was told that Charles Morrison was just helping the Baron. Brocket was friendly with Joachim von Ribbentrop, had a contact with Hermann Goering through a Swedish intermediary, and was used by Viscount Halifax as a conduit to convey views to leading Nazis. He pushed hard for a negotiated peace settlement and tried to arrange talks with Hitler. The other staggering news Jim had learnt was that his father had accompanied Brocket to Hitler's fiftieth birthday party celebrations. His father had never mentioned this to him. He could not understand why, when he was so keen to boast about everything else.

So Charles Morrison's life-long regret was that he failed in getting Viscount Halifax, rather than Churchill, to replace Neville Chamberlain. Charles visited Chamberlain at Highfield Park as he was dying from bowel cancer towards the end of 1940. He had just come from seeing the Duke of Wellington at the adjacent Stratfield Saye House in Hampshire. The purpose of his visit was to ask the ex PM and fellow appeaser why he had advised the King to send for Churchill instead of Halifax as his successor when Chamberlain himself preferred Halifax. He did not get a satisfactory answer.

Halifax would have made peace with Hitler. The deal was that Hitler could do what he liked in Europe as long as he left Great Britain and her Empire alone. This would have allowed the elite, the establishment, the upper classes and the aristocracy to continue their lifestyles without interference, or so they thought. The country house weekends - most notably those at Polesden Lacey - the balls and shooting parties would have continued. Halifax was the preferred choice of the King and Queen. He continued with his overtures to Hitler even after Churchill beat him by a whisker to the premiership.

Charles firmly believed the Right would have prevailed across the world. No Attlee or socialism. No evil State ownership. In 1939 they were optimistic that they would get their way. Brocket's links

26

seemed to be paying off. They managed to sabotage the plot in the summer of 1938 by a group of Hitler's generals to overthrow him. They intercepted a smartly dressed German diplomat who turned up at the Foreign Office carrying a message from senior figures in the German military. The message said they would launch a coup against Hitler if the British Government would publicly state that Great Britain would go to war if Germany invaded Czechoslovakia. According to the diplomat, the Government simply had to say this and they would act. Oberstleutnant Hans Oster of the Abwehr, the German Military Intelligence Organisation, organised the plot. He and other conspirators used the diplomat Theodor Kordt to contact the British on whom the success of the plot depended. They needed strong British opposition to Hitler's seizure of the Sudetenland, but did not get it with Chamberlain, who was arrogant enough to think he could outwit Hitler in other ways, but also the only people this message got to made sure it was buried.

The Right Club was a group where everyone owed someone for covering up trouble in the past. In the Duke of Windsor's case it was the help he had had from the establishment to keep him out of court and hence the newspapers over the Maggie Meller scandal. He was in enough trouble with his father George V as it was. This renowned boudoir gymnast's real name was Marguerite Alibert. Her affair with the Prince of Wales, as he was then, as the Great War was drawing to a close, was well known in high society. A young Prince was taught all the bedroom tricks anyone could ever need and their intense affair produced embarrassing letters that the clever Maggie had kept. She went on to marry the Egyptian Prince Ali Fahmy but murdered him by shooting him twice in the back and then head in the Savoy Hotel in 1923. Clearly guilty of murder - then punishable by hanging - Maggie threatened to reveal the letters, so the judge at the Old Bailey was leant on by friends, the establishment and Curzon the Foreign Secretary to let her off and so she quietly disappeared. Others passed around young children amongst themselves and were protected by the group. Of course paedophilia existed in those days on a grand scale but was never talked about at any level of society. Many could not even see the problem with it.

Polite English society thought children should be seen and not heard. Some in upper English society thought children should be abused and not heard of again.

Jim was just getting into *The Times'* piece about Neil Armstrong's first steps on the moon when the unmistakable clumsiness of Gerry announced his arrival. Knocking one of the Club waiters out of the way in the narrow entrance doorway, a whisky went flying but Gerry did not even notice - the waiter's fault, of course.

"Jim, how are you old man?"

Morrison did not get up or even answer. He gave Gerry a look as though he had brought in a horrid smell. That treatment went over his head. Gerry plonked himself down in the leather chair next to him. Disapproving heads turned but on recognising Gerry they turned back in defeat.

"Enjoy Barbados? Welchtown House still standing? Did I ever tell you my father wanted to get shot of it when he discovered subsidence after that earthquake tremor hit the island in the fifties? Should have declared it before selling it to your father I suppose! He would have sold it at any price. Bad memories after his nephew was swept away by the sea at Bathsheba. He was eventually washed up and buried in St Andrew's Church where there are other plaques to my ancestors on the walls."

Sir James was not the least bit interested and ignored Gerry's attempts at point scoring.

"Northern Ireland is kicking off so I might be distracted for a while if I end up there, which is likely."

He eventually got to the point.

"We are making good progress though aren't we, so I won't be missed, will I?"

The thought that they were making good progress immediately antagonised Jim, as this was where they had left off at their last meeting. They had argued about the speed of progress. Jim wanted more revolution than evolution but had to compromise. He was not going to throw an olive branch by telling Gerry he would be missed.

Brigadier Gerald Vaughan-Warner DSO had served at Suez and in Aden. He had done well although still only thirty-five. He had just returned from a tour of duty fighting in the secret war in Oman. The main threat to his army career was his alcohol abuse. It was difficult for Jim to judge whether he was a true alcoholic or just could not handle it, though there were plenty of his type in public life. Last year the Prime Minister, Harold Wilson, had just managed to get his drunken foreign Secretary, George Brown, out of the way. Plenty enjoyed their drink - Richard Burton, Jack Kerouac, Oliver Reed and the Queen Mother. He stubbed one cigarette out and immediately lit another. The Brigadier's right wing credentials and pedigree were impeccable. Jim was a proud racist, misogynist, homophobe, xenophobe and snob, and believed passionately in the British class system, but Gerry was in a different league.

Gerry's father, Sir Henry Vaughan-Warner had first met Charles Morrison, Baronet Willingdon, through their mutual acquaintance the Marquess of Linlithgow in India in 1938 at the races. At first Sir Henry was appalled by the Baronet flaunting his affair with Gayatri Devi of Cooch Behar. She was only a young girl of eighteen but went on to become the third wife of the last Maharaja of Jaipur State. However, he soon warmed to him after a few late night drinking sessions and realised he was just jealous. Charles helped further though by setting Henry up with a fifteen-year-old for the rest of his stay in India.

Sir Henry was one of the UK's representatives in Geneva in 1948 where he salvaged a General Agreement on Tariffs and Trade (GATT) as compensation for failing to create a World Trade Organisation. This was called an agreement to avoid having to pass the two-thirds majority in the Senate. They were labelled treaties as soon as they were passed of course. Before that he was a junior bag carrier at The International Monetary and Financial Conference of the United and Associated Nations at Bretton Woods, New Hampshire in July 1944. Delegations from forty-four nations attended and Sir Henry knew then he was going places as he had always been told from his prep-school days. Many years later he counted up that no fewer than seven future prime ministers and presidents were in the same Mount Washington Hotel with him. The stated aim was to establish a stable post-war economy, but the USA had other motives. It pushed for the liberal and free trade policies. It saw the opportunity to transform the crumbling and stricken empires of the UK, France, Germany, Austria and Hungary to an internationalised corporate model - in short the transfer of power from the State to private institutions and corporations. American ones. The Americans could not of course come clean on this however. It had to be dressed up as the fight against communism. But they wanted to wrestle the former, now bankrupt great powers out of the way and plunder the colonies of the free or cheap labour and natural resources. To the USA this was only fair. It was their turn. They were the new rich and powerful negotiator at the table, which had missed out in 1884 at the Berlin Conference when the colonial powers met to carve up between them what King Leopold of Belgium described as, *this magnificent African cake.*

So, without realising the trap they were falling into, what was established at Bretton Woods was a future, which had the world under the spell and control of the USA. They established the International Monetary Fund to manage interest rates between member states; the World Bank, to provide loans to countries devastated by the Second World War; General Agreement on Trade and Tariffs to ensure free trade and Fixed Exchange Rates – all currencies to be valued in US Dollars, and all biased in favour of the USA. Sir Henry recognised these important steps in strengthening capitalism against communism and starting on the long road to globalisation. But like most of the other delegates he did not see beyond this. The cunning Americans had duped him like many others. He was not one of the architects of big business ruling the world but certainly was an establishment figure expected to put it into operation.

The technique was fairly straightforward. First they identified countries with resources their companies wanted, like oil. Then they arranged a huge loan to that country from the World Bank or some sister organisation. However, the money never found its way direct to governments for the benefit of the people, but to their own corporations in that country. They made massive profits whilst the population suffered, as money had to be diverted from education, health and social services to pay interest on the debt. Now for the masterstroke - when the debt could not be repaid (they would make sure of that) the IMF moved in and asset-stripped by telling them they had to sell their resources, like oil, to the corporations and at an eye-wateringly cheap price as they had little choice. Even more money was sucked out of poor countries by insisting all utilities such as the water, electricity, schools, jails and hospitals were privatised and taken over by the corporations. The African continent's re-colonisation in the form of land grab was not only by countries, but corporations like Goldman Sachs, Morgan Stanley, and US Academic institutions such as Harvard University. In Ghana, after water privatisation charges increased by ninety-five per cent, one third of the population has no access to water. Who needs a war when countries could be taken over this way? Most of this could be achieved without bloodshed but where the economic hit man failed the jackals moved in. Their job was to arrange assassinations, coups and regime replacement.

Sir Henry was a proud member of the Mont Pelerin Society with Hayek, Friedman and Stigler who kicked off neo-liberal policies which Gerry and Jim were still fighting for. The last meeting between Jim and Gerry had been tense and disagreeable. They had argued about tactics and speed of progress with the Plan, as it was known. They both knew a fair bit had been achieved but that in the early days they had been naïve. They had learnt from their fathers that playing a straight bat and honesty usually backfired. Attlee, all his socialism and especially the NHS, disgusted them. This robbed them of the rich pickings from a lucrative market in healthcare that they knew something had to be done. Of course the Americans were with them all the way and threatened Britain with bankruptcy but that did not go according to plan. They were confident they could rely on the British Medical Association to block this National Health Service. The medical representatives did their best, voting against it nine to one, but the likes of Jim have never trusted the medical profession since. They blew it by over-reacting and bringing out all their right wing nuts that said things like it is the first step, and a big one, towards National Socialism as practised in Germany. This secretly amused the authors of the Plan, as it was pre-war Germany that they so much admired. They thought commissioning a report into the NHS as soon as Churchill had been re-elected in 1951 would expose it as a disaster so they could immediately abolish it, but the Guillebaud Report showed the opposite. Macmillan had his civil servants work up a plan for a fully contributory service to replace the NHS in the late 1950s but that was stopped by, of all people, Enoch Powell. It got even more depressing for them when in 1963 Kenneth Arrow published a damning report called *Market Failure In Healthcare* in the *American Economic Review*. At this point they thought they were stuck with the NHS, as it was overwhelmingly popular with the British public by this time. They had to be more underhand.

Just last year Gerry, after hearing Arthur Seldon talk on the subject, managed to persuade him to write his pamphlet called *After The NHS: How To Introduce An Insurance-based System In The UK*. Arthur was a co-founder of the Institute of Economic Affairs, which was specifically created to help the Plan. Unfortunately the pamphlet did not get the publicity they wanted, being published on the same day as the Soviet tanks rolled into Prague, but it had rejuvenated the group a little. They needed a morale boost after the failure of Cecil King's plot the previous year. King was head of the International Publishing Corporation, and tried to persuade Lord Mountbatten of Burma to head a coup d'état against Wilson. He would become interim PM overseeing the military. For several years they had supported the illegal campaign of destabilisation by a rogue element in the security services.

Dissident MI5 officers had been plotting against Wilson for years. The CIA were convinced the KGB had poisoned Hugh Gaitskell, Wilson's predecessor as Labour Party Leader, and had installed their man. They knew some of their wealthy supporters were dim enough to believe this. It was their money that was needed not their brains. MI5 however also had dossiers on many, which made it easier to get them to part with their money, especially the ring that operated from

Dolphin Square. The general goals were well established. They were initially drafted at the first Right Club meeting in 1939. Shrink the State to a bare minimum, to serve just to rescue the starving from actually starving but no more. Some were even against that. Sell off as many State assets and land as possible preferably to each other.

The Right Club got a shock when post-war everything went in the wrong direction. Pre-war there was not much to shrink or abolish, but Attlee changed all that. Every effort was put into reversing the growing State. Universality was growing and in their eyes was toxic. A post-war generation had benefitted from free education, healthcare, social care, libraries – the list was too long. So now there needed to be years of propaganda coercing and brainwashing the public that everything now has to be paid for out of one's own pocket. Universality is dead. The aim is to get to the point where there is nothing left to govern or administer so that big business is in charge - the businesses that they owned and ran of course. Game, set and match. Total control. Democracy sidestepped. Churchill was wrong, there is a better way. It was all about economics. Fundamental lessons and theories had to be taught. The USA was several steps ahead in this game.

It was time for another visit to Washington to discuss the next steps and to get more help. Jim thought it may take another generation to achieve these goals, but Gerry was more optimistic. So he appeared to Jim to be too relaxed about their timetable.

Their British allies were fully aware that the aim of the United States was world domination, despite denials. Only Russia and China can challenge the Empire's hegemony, so both countries have to be surrounded. Base after base must be built, missiles with Moscow and Beijing in range. Back in 1969, Jim and his like could not have dreamt how well this would go for them and their American friends. They would live to see NATO grabbing one former Soviet republic after another and all of them embracing the joys of neo-conservatism. But it would not be them receiving the benefits of the privatisation, deregulation and austerity policies. They would be joining Greece, Portugal, Ireland and Spain as impoverished orphans of the family.

With the rest of the world wrecked after World War Two, the United States undamaged at home and triumphant abroad saw the door wide open for world supremacy. Only communism stood in the way politically, economically, militarily and ideologically. So the Marshall Plan was developed to spread the capitalist gospel, to counter any possibility of the devastated countries moving to the left and to open markets to provide new customers for US corporations. That was the main reason for helping rebuild the European economies. It was important to push for the creation of a united Europe, initially just as a common marketplace, and NATO against the alleged Soviet threat. Funds were used for propaganda and there was the threat to withhold money from any of the recipient sixteen countries that did not exclude the left from any kind of influential role. That helped sabotage the Communist parties in France and Italy. It was money well spent. The great bulk of Marshall Plan funds returned to the USA, or never left, being paid to American corporations to purchase American goods. The same happened after the Iraq War. Most contracts for rebuilding the country went to American companies.

"Northern Ireland, eh? Will your wife go with you?" Gerry hadn't thought that far ahead and mumbled words to that effect. "And your children? How are they?"

Jim had never asked that of Gerry before. In fact Jim had never even acknowledged Gerry had any. In one sense he did not. The two boys were from his wife's previous marriage that had ended just before the youngest, Hubert, was born. The children kept their mother's surname, although she had reverted back to her maiden name of Witney to distance herself from disgrace. The boys' father was a policeman who had caught a peer of the realm cottaging in a Bethnal Green toilet. He had followed the aristocrat from the Kray's house at 178 Vallance Road. The establishment rallied around and, to get His Lordship off the hook, the copper was accused of inventing evidence, framed as a burglar and sacked.

"Because you know you will have to use your children to take the Plan further forward, don't you Gerry?"

"Nonsense. We will sort it out well before then," he replied impatiently.

"Your eldest is five, yes? Perfect for indoctrination and training him up. So take the family with you to Northern Ireland so you can start the process. You don't know how long you will be there, but knowing the Irish, probably quite a while."

"Hmm... the kids' father may have something to say about that."

Jim was not interested in why Gerry had said that and continued.

"You know I hate children but they have to be looked at as necessary vehicles for our project. One lifetime isn't long enough to see our aims bear fruit. Hitler never thought he'd personally last a thousand years. My wife wants a screaming brat but it won't happen. I avoid her most of the time and besides I'm too knackered out by Sonia and Dorothy. This free love is the only bit of the swinging sixties I do approve of, but let's face it, it's never stopped our ruling class playing away from home has it?"

Both laughed the warm laugh of contentment. Gerry had just come from his mistress's apartment he had set up for her. They knew they had to plot. They knew they had to lie and be devious. That was how they were brought up. It was normal. They knew they had to control the media and the political agenda to fool the British public, for whom they had nothing but disdain. How could they have respect for the masses that often voted the wrong way?

"We need to do more to get the right result at the next General Election. That'll probably be next year. Wilson is a canny operator. He knows the oil we depend on is a fragile business when we are at the mercy of ex-colonial powers with a grudge. Rumour has it that with England apparently favourites to win the World Cup again, Wilson will go to the country in June to capitalise on that."

Gerry stated the obvious.

"Fortunately you cannot unscramble an egg. They cannot undo what we have done. We need the next phase to be the same. No going back."

Then after a pause.

35

"I despair sometimes at our fellow countrymen if he gets back in."

"That's the problem, Gerry!" Jim snapped back, almost spilling his whisky, "Many who now can vote are not fellow countrymen. So we may have to fix it. We've done it before. Something must be done about these idiots."

4 - INSOMNIA AND ANGER

TOSSIN' AND TURNIN'

I kicked the blankets on the floor
Turned my pillow upside down
I never, never did before
'Cause I was tossin' and turnin'
Turnin' and tossin'
Tossin' and turnin' all night

Bobby Lewis (1961)

Rob could not sleep. His mind was alive as he could not decide who he hated the most.

It was tricky as all the candidates were worthy of his loathing. The Secretary of State for Health for buggering up his job satisfaction and the NHS and for being such a snivelling little prick; his boss, the PM, for being in charge and colluding, if not dictating and running the whole corrupt show; Gideon for being another toff, and for screwing his bird, a phrase he had thought cringe-making and beneath him; Peter Bonetti for letting those goals in against West Germany and getting us knocked out of the 1970 World Cup; or the whole England squad of overpaid prima donnas with silly haircuts for losing to Iceland in the 2016 European Championships in France - his England supporting pain had been with him since the age of six. Perhaps Jimmy Savile? Kelvin McKenzie? Donald Trump, no he just despised him. In contention was that broadcaster doctor who had informed him poor sleep on a regular basis increased his chance of diabetes and dementia. Thanks a lot.

The light went on. Suzy spoke a little impatiently.

"What's the matter? When you can't sleep no one can. I can always tell from your fight with the pillows."

"There's only you and me, what do you mean no one?"

"There's Eric as well," she half joked in an attempt to emphasise her point.

"Well he shouldn't be in the bedroom, should he?" Eric was the ginger cat they both wanted when they first moved in together, and named by Rob after Eric Cantona.

"But it's cold outside."

This was not good. He should not be taking on Suzy too. If he got any angrier the night would be a complete disaster.

"Anyway you'd better tell me about it. Get it off your chest?" she continued.

"You might regret that. Are you sure?" He did not wait for an answer, "Do you know what that stupid tosser is proposing now?"

He loved the word tosser. It was Rob's favourite insult.

"He thinks everyone should self-diagnose on their own computer. He said if he could have matched his daughter's rash to a computer image he wouldn't have had to wait in A&E for so long, if at all. Prat should not have gone to A&E anyway. He should have seen his GP. Perhaps he realises he has made that difficult with funding cuts? Shows he hasn't got a clue. So as the pinprick red or purple spots of Meningococcal Septicaemia develop into the classical bruising appearance will he tuck his daughter up in bed and reassure himself she must have knocked herself? What bollocks!"

His favourite swear word.

"Smug, out of touch idiot! I wish I could punch him! I'm sure he has some sort of syndrome. Although perhaps his family should pilot it to see how many are decimated by it?"

He was warming up now and Suzy knew she just had to let him explode, but she could not resist.

"You are using the word decimate to mean destroy, a common mistake, but incorrect. Decimate, by derivation, strictly speaking means killing one in ten."

Rob ignored her, as he did not understand her point.

"What we really need is to replace politicians with computers. The programme would be easy to write. Make decisions that are always wrong, cost a fortune, build in a bit of corruption, boost their own bank balances, make sure they are never to blame and of course get a gong at the end."

Rob never missed an opportunity to tell Suzy that having contact every day with up to sixty people with problems he, as a GP like all other GPs, was more in tune with what is happening in society and what is wrong with it than most people.

As he said it again he added, "Giselle told me all about it after surgery tonight. In her sexy French accent."

Yet another mistake at this time of night as Suzy was suspicious that Rob fancied Giselle and his commenting on her accent did not help his cause. But she had just heard this on the six o'clock news - bloody *BBC* unreservedly and uncritically promoting his loony ideas.

Giselle Arouet had come over from France with her husband Derek to live in the sixth most populated French city that is London. They had met when he was on a two-year secondment in Paris from his City firm. He then had to return and she was keen for an adventure. After a few years in London's financial racket, as she called it, she wanted a proper job and started working in the NHS taking a considerable drop in income. There was nothing like the NHS in France and the concept excited her. She moved into primary care then became a Deputy Practice Manager in Tower Hamlets. As a victim of the Government's lack of interest in general practice, and despite being in such a deprived and poor area, it had funding taken away and closed.

Rob and Clive took Giselle on as manager five years ago when she wanted to get out of town. She missed the countryside, having been brought up with her sister in the small village of Veyrac near Limoges. Apparently Clive had vaguely known her whilst working in London. She had been a fantastic breath of fresh air for the practice. She had grown to despise people who did nothing useful all day but move money around on a computer screen and counted their huge bonuses. They did not make anything useful, care for anyone, help the nation nor even get off their fat arses. She had to get out and contribute to society. When she joined the NHS little did she realise she might one day just be working to give those with fat arses even more money through their vulture-like infiltration into the health market, skimming off taxpayers' money that should be going to clinical care to 'putain de share'olders!' A great French accent indeed.

Giselle could not quite understand why there was not more of a revolutionary spirit amongst the British. Where she was brought up there was real anger about the past and the present. It was only anger and action that would make the future better she had been taught. Why is there not more civil unrest? She was too young to remember the events of May 1968 when barricades were built, factories and universities occupied, cars burnt, and strikes. But she had seen the Philippe Garrel movie *Regular Lovers* and was inspired. Rob teased her by trying to convince her he wanted to introduce the guillotine and those messing up their wonderful NHS would be first to lose their heads. However, her time in England was having an effect and fat arses had become the more correct morbidly obese gluteals. But she still got as angry as Rob and if she had twigged how right wing Britain had become she might have stayed in France.

Now it was Suzy's turn.

"Well, it's depressing and frustrating that, although the picture you always paint of politicians is true and most people think so, nobody reacts or does any more than shrug their shoulders. Those ministers must have been amazed and pleasantly surprised when, as they laid a torch to the welfare state, they discovered how few rebelled. But just because we expect them to be like that and are not surprised, shouldn't mean we must tolerate it. It is odd. People have become zombie-like. Must be the diet, and I don't mean food. The daily diet of drivel on television, lies in the newspapers and the development of attention spans equivalent to that of a gnat. We are all conditioned to accept only what is in the Overton window, you know if it's not mainstream you're nutty. Jeff says the same, but having lived in the USA for about ten years says it's a lot worse there. We both concluded a long time ago we live in a corrupt, undemocratic plutocracy; so as that's not a startling new revelation just get over it and go to sleep. At least for tonight."

There was a real contradiction in Suzy's thinking as far as Rob was concerned. Here she is saying nothing can be done therefore accept it. They have had the same argument but in reverse over the starving and the poor. Rob believed it is useless giving a few quid to charity as it does not make any difference and just lets the politicians off the hook. Look at *Live Aid* and Bob Geldof. No individual could have done more but thirty years later are we not back at square one and did not a lot of the money go to arm the corrupt regimes?

Rob thought the only way forward was revolution, regime change and, at a minimum, tackling the worse aspects of capitalism. The powerful ruling class at the apex of the capitalist system had to be eliminated. Probably proper socialism that he thought had never been practised in the world without some fascist taking control like Mao or Stalin. That was always the problem. The cause might be right but the leadership was always crap and sabotaged the ideals and principles. Even Cuba is now going in the wrong direction. Unions, the Labour Party, you name it, always with leaders who sold out.

Suzy thought his way forward was irresponsible, as people would be killed. Rob thought, for the greater good. You cannot make an omelette without breaking eggs. Suzy made a big thing he thought, just as much to annoy him as to do any good, of stopping and giving to those with a dog on a bit of string and a cardboard box in the street. So why does she think we should not accept that situation yet put up with the corruption that causes it in the first place? So he was not going to let her get away with that.

"You just cannot be disinterested. You can't turn a blind eye."

"Why not, everyone else does? You know, there was a time when your fiery anger with the establishment was an attractive feature but now darling it's a little bit boring. You can't allow yourself to be eaten up by it. And the word is uninterested, not disinterested."

Rob knew she was right about becoming a bore, but he was not going to admit it. He was passionately anti-Thatcher at university, despite being surrounded by all those public schoolboys who he accused of jerking off to her.

Hating everything Tory had been the glue between him and his first wife Jenny. They met in Kennington Park on 31st March 1990 on the anti-Poll Tax march. Rob had put the event in his diary some weeks before and used the opportunity to have a few drinks with an old mate Robin from his Lewisham Hospital days, so had travelled up the previous night. Robin was still working there as a lab technician and he lived opposite the park in the coach house attached to the side of a large Georgian House on Kennington Park Road that used to be a doctor's surgery when appendices were taken out on the kitchen table.

They spent the evening in the White Bear pub (there since 1780) just down the road and enjoyed more pints of Young's than was good for them. Robin had told Rob all about the disaster in the Blitz in 1940. A public trench-style bomb shelter took a direct hit. One hundred and four were killed. Over fifty bodies were never recovered. The tragedy was covered up. The park was also famous for a mass Chartist meeting in 1848. Chartism as Robin reminded Rob being the first British national working class movement. The year he moved into his Coach House, he saw Bob Marley playing football with mates in the park. Marley had just visited the Rastafarian Temple. That was the beginning of Robin's love affair with the area. He had heard Michael Caine had filmed some of the *Ipcress File* in 1965 by the bandstand. Now though he hoped it would become more well known as a starting point for a branch of the Anti-Poll Tax march.

Robin was a fair bit older than Rob and had been working at Lewisham since the mid-seventies. He got caught up in the famous 1977 Battle of Lewisham when five hundred far right National Front members clashed with about four thousand anti-NF demonstrators. Robin belonged to the anti-Nazi League and got hit on the head with a bottle for his trouble. It turned out that Jenny's mother was probably the nurse who stitched him up. In 1979 at a demonstration in Southall against a National Front election meeting, he saw Blair Peach knocked unconscious. Peach died and it took some time before the police admitted responsibility.

A little worse for wear the next morning, Robin told Rob they were meeting a student nurse in the park by the Oval Fountain, who wanted to go on the march with them. All her mates were working and she did not want to go alone. It was then Robin admitted he really fancied her and was going to make his move. She was working in Lewisham A&E like her mother did once, but living on the Queen's Road in Peckham in a small flat opposite the London and

Brighton pub. She caught the 436 bus to work, but used it in the opposite direction on this day as it took her to Kennington Park, hence the place of their rendezvous, as good as any for joining the start of the march. Jenny was waiting at the fountain. The park was packed but soon started to empty slowly, as at about 1.30 p.m. the two and a half mile march got underway.

Robin introduced Rob to Jenny and seemed keen to impress her. Rob listened while he told her all about the right wing groups he had had battles with. How he once had a confrontation with John Tyndall their leader, where the police had to intervene. How a man called Arthur Chesterton had influenced Tyndall and had founded the organisation in 1967. The only Chesterton Jenny had heard of was G.K. Chesterton the writer and philosopher and she wondered if there was any connection. One thing Robin was good at was research and he knew they were cousins. He was feeling pleased with himself, but Rob was thinking sad git, that is not the best sort of boast to get off with a girl.

Rob stole the day, much to Robin's discomfort, by saying innocently, "Didn't he have that well-known saying *fallacies do not cease to be fallacies because they become fashions*? I believe that was one of his?"

Jenny was impressed as she recognised the quote and started to pay attention to Rob for the first time. Robin tried to wrestle back Jenny's attention.

"Arthur Chesterton was a member of the Nordic League, then the Right Club before the war, and set up the League of Empire Loyalists in 1954."

No wonder he has had so little success with women Rob thought, but he would impress Boudicca and would probably get off with Joan of Arc. Rob thought he could rescue his old friend by turning the conversation towards Jenny. He only made things worse though.

"Where do you live Jenny?" Rob was useless at small talk but he could manage that.

"Peckham, right opposite a pub on the Queen's Road."

"I used to work in a pub around there with a mate of mine when we were medical students. The London and Brighton."

43

"That's the one! Terrible place. Never did know why it was called that?"

"Ah well, I can help you there. It's after the London, Brighton and South Coast Railway. My mate Stephen and I thought it the most unwelcoming pub in London. So dead you couldn't really even tell if it was open or closed, a bit like The Slaughtered Lamb in *An American Werewolf in London* movie. That's why we chose to work there; we thought there would be no customers."

Jenny was livening up.

"Oh, that film is one of my favourites, scared me to death, when all the locals fall silent, classic!"

"Yes, just like the London and Brighton, except it was always silent and just as threatening."

Rob and Jenny got on well and for once Rob had little trouble knowing what to say, which he felt unusually tended to be the right not the wrong thing. Robin though was unusually quiet. He thought Jenny was correct - they were films, not movies.

When they finally arrived in Trafalgar Square the clashes with police made them think of Orgreave during the miner's strike. Tony Benn was addressing the crowd when the police charged down Whitehall. They lost Robin in the crowd and realised he had strangely disappeared. Before they had a chance to decide whether to start looking for him, to their horror they saw an old woman have her wheelchair knocked over by charging police horses. Rob wondered whether the BBC would reverse the footage here too, to make out the protestors and aggressive hard left old ladies in wheelchairs provoked it all. He could imagine the *BBC* bulletin: 'Mrs Thatcher condemns wheelchair users for charging at police', and the *Daily Mail* headline: 'PM to confiscate wheelchairs if used as weapons by the undeserving'.

Whether her wheelchair was pushed over deliberately or not, they were not sure. What was so shocking however was the police just left her lying there on the ground. Jenny and Rob ran up to help and got her back in her chair. Although badly shaken she escaped real injury. It was a bright day and together Jenny and Rob took her away from the chaotic crowded area, which was getting more and more dangerous. They stood chatting for a while in front of Charing Cross Station. They introduced themselves and within a few minutes knew each other's names and professions.

"When I saw the crowd turn towards the police and the riot cops just turned and ran, I knew this was different from any other demonstration I have been to," said the old lady.

Then Rosa, as they now knew her, changed the subject completely.

"I think that tribute to his wife is beautiful, don't you?"

She was pointing at the old cross. Rob realised she was talking about the lavishly decorated stone monument that he had walked past hundreds of times without really paying the slightest attention.

"It was one of twelve erected by Edward I in memory of his wife Eleanor of Castile between 1291 and 1294. I'm no royalist but I'd like to think it is a tribute to love. They marked the nightly resting place of her body on its return to London. They left her viscera in Lincoln. So they are now a year short of their septcentenary. Except of course this one isn't. It's a more ornate replica."

Rob was straining his neck gazing up at the seventy-foot fake.

"Commissioned and erected in 1865 by the South Eastern Railway Company for their new hotel. It's not even in the right place. The original cross once stood at the top of Whitehall on the south side of Trafalgar Square, although obviously not called that then. It was destroyed by parliamentary forces in the Civil War in 1647 but replaced by an equestrian statue of Charles I in 1675 following the Restoration, a few hundred yards from the site of his execution. Did you know this point is the official centre of the city when measuring distances from London?"

Her knowledge seemed to erupt up like a stream of consciousness and was unstoppable like a torrent of lava. For an uneasy moment Rob thought he still might be standing in the same spot this time tomorrow. Rob discovered later that Rosa would always turn any conversation away from personal matters and onto history and politics. After years of medicine dominating and squeezing everything else out of his life these happened to be Rob's main interests. She expressed it in a way that was not at all boring

45

though. The difference he thought between a good and a bad teacher. He was keen to find out more about this interesting woman and take the weight off his feet, so offered to buy her tea while she recovered from her fall.

"If me talking about viscera hasn't put you off, that'll be nice, thank you."

Rosa lived alone and had no rush to get back. Jenny had taken charge of the wheelchair and started to head down to the bottom of Villiers Street near the Embankment where she said she knew of a café. Although the road down to the river was not too steep Rob worried about her losing control as the wheelchair was an old-fashioned heavy monstrosity, but although quite petite she seemed strong.

"As you are both in the game you should know the Charing Cross Hospital Medical School was founded in this street in the 1820s," said Rosa, "The hospital opened in 1821 at number 28 with twelve beds. It had moved again by the time they built the station in the 1860s."

They passed the blue plaque commemorating the building where Rudyard Kipling once lived at number 43 from 1889 to 1891. This was another trigger for an opinion from Rosa.

"Do you two know Orwell called him a *prophet of British Imperialism?* Anyone who believed so strongly in the British Empire and hobnobbed with Cecil Rhodes shouldn't have any memorial as far as I'm concerned. White man's burden indeed."

"But he did coin the phrase *the female of the species is more deadly than the male* in his poem. Do you believe that?" Jenny's warmth of personality kept the conversation flowing seamlessly.

Rob was impressed by Jenny and found himself to be more of an observer of the dialogue between this interesting lady and this sweet girl, neither of whom until only this morning he had ever met, and he could not resist adding his bit.

"Yes, of course. Much deadlier."

The two women both just smiled at him. Jenny stopped opposite her destination on the corner of Watergate Walk opposite the famous Gordon's Wine Bar and tilted her head as a signal to Rob to open the teashop door.

"Over there used to be the Arena Picture Palace and a bit further up a Mr Joyce was convicted of running a brothel in 1923. Before my time, I might add."

They both manoeuvered Rosa in her wheelchair through to an empty table. Rosa recognised the nine steps down towards the Victoria Embankment Gardens.

"Down there is the York Watergate built by Inigo Jones just as Charles I started his reign. It was at the bottom of the garden of York House built by George Villiers, the first Duke of Buckingham. That is why this is Villiers Street, obviously."

Rob knew a little about this and he was not going to let an opportunity pass to demonstrate some intelligence.

"It gives an idea of how far the Thames was pushed back by the construction of the Embankment in the late 1860s doesn't it?" But he realised he would struggle to keep up with Jenny.

"If you look carefully you can see the Buckingham family coat of arms on the top of the gate. It is one of the few surviving structures in London, along with the Banqueting House, that follow the Italianate tastes of Charles," said Jenny.

Then Rosa trumped both of them.

"It was sold by the second Duke for development in 1672. Proves developers have been around forever. They were even in Jane Austen's unfinished novel *Sandition*. The vain Duke made it a condition that all the streets around should be named after him."

The conversation continued to flow easily. It was as though Rosa had been bottling it up and Jenny and Rob had taken the top off.

Rosa Davies had been in Trafalgar Square to hear Nye Bevan condemn Eden's Suez escapade in November 1956. She was seventeen and her parents were proud of her. The very next day Gerald Vaughan-Warner, aged twenty-two, was parachuted with his 3rd Battalion onto the El Gamil airfield, which they took with ease. He was awarded the DSO for the effective use of his Sten gun against the Egyptian enemy. She received abuse from an old colonel, so after that she was on every Aldermaston march from 1958 to 1964.

She was proud of being named after Rosa Luxemburg. It was her communist parents' token protest at the signing of the Nazi-Soviet Non Aggression Pact on the day she was born, 23rd August 1939. Her father was a miner in the Merthyr colliery in South Wales and felt he had had a personal kick in the teeth from Stalin, entering into an alliance with the devil. Another sell out. She was called Dorothy for her first few days. The MGM Movie *The Wizard of Oz* with Judy Garland as Dorothy Gale had had its Hollywood premiere at the Chinese Theatre the week before. Her mother had read all about it. But when the news of the Pact filtered through, her parents were stunned and thought their initial selection too trivial. Years later Rosa realised the politics of international relations was not as simple as that. That was the version the West had sold them all. She did not blame her father for being taken in by it. Rosa worked out for herself that the Soviets were forced into the Pact by the refusal of the Western powers to sign a mutual defence treaty with Moscow in a stand against Hitler. To Rosa this was worse than appeasement with the Nazis, it was collusion. It would push the Germans eastwards against Russia and communism. The Soviets had to stall for time whilst they built up their defences. When the West also refused to come to the aid of the socialist-leaning Spanish Government under siege by the Spanish, German and Italian fascists, both Hitler and Stalin concluded from this that for the West the true enemy was not fascism but socialism and communism.

"If you are a fish swimming around in the capitalist sewer, as it's the only place to swim, you can't help but be contaminated and you end up living by their rules as they are the only rules around. Then it is easy for them to call you a hypocrite," Rosa would explain to Rob.

Her socialist pedigree was impeccable. Uncle Robert Owen Davies, named after the social reformer, had been killed fighting against Franco in the Spanish Civil War two years before she was born. He had eloped with a Brigadier's wife he met through Jessica Mitford. The scandal was kept out of the papers through her husband Henry's contacts. The couple came across George Orwell in Barcelona. The police in the battle of Cable Street beat up a young cousin, Hywel Davies, in 1936 protesting against the march by the British Union of Fascists led by Oswald Mosley through east London. In 1945 Hywel campaigned for the communist Harry Pollitt who failed to take Rhondda East by only nine hundred and seventy-two votes. A Soviet Navy ship was named after Harry.

Rosa's first brush with police brutality was on the anti-Vietnam War march to Grosvenor Square in 1968. She followed Vanessa Redgrave from Trafalgar Square for this one and was one of three hundred arrested. The truncheon blow to the head made her see stars but did not knock her out. She found herself in the back of a police van with a chap called Max who took her to hospital to get some stitches. He became a very good comrade and friend. Two months after that she joined the Paris student demonstrations and befriended Dany Cohn-Bendit.

Rob was impressed by Jenny's knowledge of all these events even though she was only twenty. Like a light going on he suddenly realised how attractive she was. He had always preferred petite women. But of his two new acquaintances however, he found it easier to arrange to visit Rosa again than to ask Jenny out for a drink. Although now into his thirties and professionally successful, Rob was still shy in company, especially female company. He had regrets about his student days, always too awkward and reserved to take that final bold move to ask someone out. He had, but he was not in the same league of confidence as some of his mates who were not so afraid of rejection, although they were not rejected very often. They made it look so easy. Such missed opportunities he now thought. He believed he had been born one drink under, that is, he needed a drink to feel like normal people.

Rosa finished her tea and wondered whether her two saviours wanted another. This pleased Rob, although he did not, he took it as a sign that at least Rosa was not getting bored with them, or was not in a rush to get home and he could use it as an excuse to learn more from her. He found her fascinating and charismatic. Rosa told Rob and Jenny she was only fifty, but looked and felt eighty. She had had her share of bad luck with health. She lost her job through disability and victimisation and had no doubt if she had lived in the USA she would be dead by now. She put her survival down to two things, her mental strength and the NHS. It was not possible for any individual to save her, only society acting together to organise collective help. The society, she reminded them, that Margaret Thatcher the PM they came to demonstrate against said did not exist - the Thatcher who had destroyed most of manufacturing in Britain and was having a good bash at civil liberties.

Rosa did not go into detail about her career except to say she used to be a teacher. Rob thought that made sense. She positively glowed when talking about the unfair world. Rob had never heard such an articulate summary of what, up until then he had failed to grasp or understand. He knew he hated the right in politics but could never explain it simply in policy terms. He felt like an angry child does when he wants to throw a tantrum but is not sure what about. Rosa could put it in easily presentable sentences that were more than just slogans. She told them that it is a myth that Thatcher had liberated free markets. There was no such thing. Globalisation had developed rigged markets dominated by a plutocracy and plutocratic corporations linked to concentrated financial capital that are able to gain increasing amounts of rental income by virtue of their wealth. Meanwhile wages are stagnant. Rob thought he understood.

"We are all being conned. Eggs used to come in three sizes: small, medium and large. Now they are medium, large and jumbo, although the eggs haven't changed. What do bosses do all day that they should earn a thousand times more than schoolteachers and nurses? To say one per cent of the population owns thirty-five per cent of the wealth is deceptive. If you have thirty-five per cent you can control much more than that."

She put it in a way that had Rob thirsty for more. She elaborated blaming Britain's economic problems on the size and power of multinational corporations able to exploit their market power by pushing up prices while at the same time underinvesting.

"Communist governments take over companies. Under capitalism companies take over the government. Which is more attractive if you believe in democracy?"

Tackling the spiral of decline of manufacturing she said, required public ownership of a company in each sector of the economy, industrial democracy, curbs on imports, withdrawal from the EEC and a few more things that went completely over Rob's head.

"What are we here for today? We are all anti-Poll Tax, but how many really know why? It's a tax on people with the poor paying for the poor. Worse than that it continues their policy of the Tories fleecing the poor to line their own pockets. They don't care. They can say with a straight face, like that creepy chain-smoking minister Nicholas Ridley said, *why should a Duke pay more than a dustman?* When we are up against that sort of crap then the campaign against the Poll Tax cannot depend on the labour and trade union movement of Neil Kinnock and Norman Willis. Any successful resistance against the Poll Tax requires going beyond legal, constitutional and traditional methods of struggle."

Rosa stopped there - as good a place as any - as she could have talked all night.

"So Rob and Jenny, if you are both medical, aren't you wondering what I'm doing in a wheelchair at fifty? Well, I'll put you out of your misery then we won't be distracted by such trivia and we can concentrate on important issues like getting rid of this evil Government."

"More tea?" enquired Rob, lifting the pot and gesturing in Rosa's direction.

He poured it anyway as he realised she was not going to be sidetracked by trivia.

"I'll test you. See who gets to the diagnosis first. It was 1983. I was about forty-three and teaching in Eltham. I was getting more back pain than usual. Initially I thought I'd just overdone it and it was due to standing most of the day. But it was the first time I'd had sciatica. I put this down to a stress reaction of Thatcher getting re-elected with a majority of one hundred and forty-four. My pain was a lot worse on 10th June for more reasons than one. People started saying I was walking a bit oddly but of course I thought I would with the pain I had. Then I noticed it was trickier getting up the stairs and realised I was developing increasing weakness or rather poor muscle control in my legs. In fact I had developed foot drop. That was followed by losing some sensation, they seemed less sensitive to touch than usual."

She paused and stared at Rob.

"Got it yet?"

She did not want to embarrass either medical person so did not wait for the answer.

"I couldn't ignore all this any longer when I went into urinary retention." Much to Rob's alarm and slight embarrassment, Jenny butted in.

"You had spinal cord compression?"

"Yes, but that's not the exact diagnosis. But you get the prize Jenny as within twelve hours I had had my emergency decompression operation at the Brook Hospital, thanks to a bright on the ball junior doctor who immediately recognised the red flags as you medics call them. He used his clinical skills. He didn't have the fancy scanners we are getting now. A very good regional neuro-surgical centre. Now the bastards want to close it. Let's give Rob some help, shall we Jenny? Further clues. You know that feeling when you've been on the bike too long and your bum and all around it goes numb?"

Rob heard himself declaring in a voice a little loud for a small café.

"Saddle Anaesthesia!"

"Yes, so, come on?"

Rob felt he was back at medical school being tortured by one of the nastier neurologists.

"Yes, I know… you had Cauda Equina Syndrome?"

"Well done," said Rosa. "But why? You can assume it wasn't from a cancer pushing on the nerves, as six years later I'm still here albeit still with foot drop."

"That leaves a ruptured or herniated disc, which is the commonest cause by far but unlikely as the onset was too slow and insidious. Did you have an abscess?"

"Well done Rob. Never found out why or where this came from, but I used to joke I caught a bug by getting too near a Tory. Remember Nye said they were lower than vermin. But still I made a fair recovery. I still have some residual trouble hence resorting to this chair when I have to. Like on demonstrations."

"This is why I had to learn Latin for a medical degree. Just for this! The bundle of nerves extending down from the bottom of the spinal cord looks like a horse's tail. Cauda Equina is Latin for horse's tail."

He was directing this towards Jenny, who to Rob's astonishment actually appeared to be interested.

"I had to give up history at school for that. I'd much rather have studied our past than a dead language."

Rosa went on to describe how she had not really worked since then. She had been a Union Official and had ruffled too many feathers. The anti-union brigade used her ill health as an excuse and hounded her out of the job she loved. They had to invent a disciplinary case against her of course with false accusations but they got their way. After another cake they realised it was getting late and said their farewells. Rosa was determined to make her own way home. They all disappeared in different directions. Not before exchanging details though, to Rob's relief. The crowds had more or less dispersed. There was litter everywhere.

Suzy had just said he was boring her, or at least that is how he interpreted it.

"Make me feel better by telling me Gideon was useless in bed."

"Robert, the deal was not to re-visit this. You promised," then one of her classics, "It's like deja-vu all over again."

"I know but this was a bolt out of the blue. It's not every day someone's wife-to-be says she has been 'Poldarked' by the Chancellor of the Exchequer. What would you think if I told you I'd slept with Princess Anne?"

"Well done, that's what I'd say."

"Was there anything odd about him? Just wonder what drives him and his Old Etonian cronies. I do wonder about my prejudices sometimes you know. But I am psychologically well balanced really. I've got a chip on both shoulders."

Rob was pushing his luck and he knew it.

"Did he like pain or want tying up? Was he into water-sports or liked to be led around on a lead, beaten, smothered in chocolate or whipped?"

Suzy thought she had better deal with this once and for all.

"Robert. You'd like nothing more than to end his career wouldn't you? Is this political or now personal? Those who live in glass houses shouldn't catch the worm. I wish I'd never told you. Let's just say judging from his performance and what he wanted me to do, he liked boys more than girls. I had very, very short hair at the time, my tribute to Annie Lennox, as my favourite album at the time was *We Too Are One*. I think he had learnt most from his public school dorms. The whole family was weird. Even his father was a dirty old man who used his tongue when he decided it was his right to kiss me goodbye as I bumped into him in the entrance hall the next morning. It felt like droit du seigneur. He was Neville Morrison then though. I never did find out why he took on his mother's maiden name of Gideon, but it was just before he went into politics. The whole time I was there I had the creepy feeling I was subservient, a lower form of life, a plaything that they had the right to use in any way they wanted. Comes from centuries of power and inbreeding I suppose, and the magnificent surroundings. I'd never been to such a stately home that wasn't National Trust. I think it was called Hetherington Park."

Rob was amazed she had spoken so freely, and grateful, but he had to ask.

"What do you mean by droit du seigneur?"

"The supposed legal right of feudal lords or noblemen to have sex with local women on their wedding night. You did Latin. Jus primae noctis - the right of the first night. It's in *The Marriage of Figaro* and Orwell mentions it in *1984*, but there it's the right of every capitalist to sleep with any woman working in one of his factories."

There was quite a long silence so Suzy turned the light off. She was startled and shocked to have her dozy state dynamited.

"Do you think Philip's death was really an accident?"

"What?" she yelled. "What the fuck are you on about now? And why pick 1.00 a.m. to ask such a fucking stupid question? You and your conspiracy theories. Yes it was an accident of course, and no Kennedy wasn't shot in Dallas by Walt Disney dressed as Donald Duck, Elvis doesn't work in the Balham KFC, and Lord Lucan is not Freddie Mercury in disguise. But I do think our PM might be a lady-boy from Bangkok. You are flogging a dead cat Robert. Good night."

Rob noticed she had called him Robert twice now. That meant he was walking on thin ice but he tried to explain. He did want to demonstrate logical thinking.

"Well you did hint once he was worried about corruption and was snooping around. You said being at the heart of Whitehall he didn't have to do much digging but it was obvious what he was up to in such a small world. And then he told you that the shooting of that Brazilian in Lambeth was nothing to do with terrorism as the public was fed, but all to do with the files he had in his rucksack? Perhaps he told one person too many. Dangerous stuff, I would say."

Suzy did not know how to respond so she did not bother at first, then she found herself suddenly exclaiming totally inadequately.

"Where did you get all that crap from? I said once he had concerns, that's all. Nothing specific. You are taking two and two and making four. You're an idiot, Robert. A real jackal and hide. Goodnight. Say another word and no sex for two weeks."

She was so tired this quite daft idea was not going to keep her awake. Rob was not going to risk no sex, so he let her jackal and hide misquote go until the morning. He was reminded of Mae West's quote, *Good sex is like good Bridge. If you don't have a good partner, you'd better have a good hand.*

5 - PRIVILEGE AND DELUSION

THE GRAND OLD DUKE OF YORK

Oh, the grand old Duke of York,
He had ten thousand men,
He marched them up to the top of
The hill and he marched
Them down again.

English Nursery Rhyme (1642)

June 1939

"Well gentlemen that is enough about Winton. He will soon be dealt with. Not that it will be anything to do with us, naturally. However it is doubtful we will be condemning any unfortunate accident though, is it not?" said the 5th Duke of Wellington in his best Etonian accent and with a smile on his face.

It was seen by the others as the menacing joke it was supposed to be and was accompanied by a mixture of giggles, desk thumping and loud cries.

"Hear! Hear!"

Sir Henry Vaughan-Warner wanted to bring home just how grave this was.

"Winton is diluting the strength of the gene pool. It is essential he be stopped. He is sabotaging all we stand for. Germany has the correct ideas. Even the USA now has forced sterilisation of women with learning disabilities and genetic conditions in the majority of States. We must return to the main and more important business. We had a summary of our goals from Sir Michael O'Dywer at the last meeting. That was necessary to focus our minds, crystallise our aims and policies and make sure we are not distracted by recent events. Tonight we move to the next and main item, which will be led by Jock. Jock has studied the economic situation. An understanding is essential for our success. Indeed grasping the way others see economics and influencing how it is comprehended is the only way we can succeed. So over to Jock to emphasise my point, I think you told me you wanted to give us two lessons, one true, and then the other fictional, one for the masses. Am I right?"

Sir Archibald 'Jock' Ramsey was the Scottish Unionist MP who attracted followers after supporting Franco in the Spanish Civil War and declaring he wanted to rid the Conservative Party of perceived Jewish control. He produced the red book which was a lockable private ledger bound in burgundy calf 10¾ x 8¼ x 1½inches with one hundred and thirty-five names and a separate list of one hundred female members. He designed the Club's logo, which was seen on its badge. An eagle killing a snake with the initials P.J. that stood for Perish Judah. He was working on a parody of *Land Of Hope And Glory* but so far had only developed little more than the first line *Land Of Dope And Jewry*. He was thin and dapper and sported a neat black moustache, a beaky profile and a straight-backed commanding posture you would expect from an ex-officer in the Coldstream Guards. This was only the third meeting of the Right Club, which had been formed the month before. Sir Archibald wanted to amalgamate the right wing groups he had helped set up.

In 1935 two Nazi agents - one being Alfred Rosenberg - established the anti-Semitic Nordic League with Jock chairing the fourteen-man Leadership Council. This was modelled on the Nordische Gesellschaft and had close links with the White Knights of Britain, otherwise known as the Hooded Men, with ritual initiation based on Freemasonry and not unlike the Ku Klux Klan. Meetings of the Nordic League usually ended with a rendition of the *Horst Wessel* song, a Nazi anthem that would trigger a ripple of fascist salutes. Ramsey announced the Right Club launch when he was guest speaker at a meeting of Link, a pro-Nazi organisation with four thousand members, which met at the Crofton Hotel in Queen's Gate. Ramsey boasted that the Club already had members in most Government departments except Censorship and the Foreign Office and he was working on this. Members meant influence. They had infiltrated the police and MI5. Although the Inner Circle met on Wednesdays at Ramsey's house in Onslow Square, the official Club meetings had moved to the Russian Tea Rooms at 50 Harrington Road, South Kensington. This was at the invitation of Anna Wolkoff, a diminutive slim-waisted White Russian émigré and the daughter of Admiral Nikolai Wolkoff, the former aide-de-camp to Nicholas II.

Anna and her father held right wing anti-Semitic views and were totally sympathetic to the Nazi regime in Germany. She was a tremendous admirer of Ramsey, supporting him as chauffeur and secretary. So intense were her feelings about the Jews that she blamed them for every international problem and for destroying the Tsarist society into which she had been born. On several trips to Germany Anna had had meetings with Rudolf Hess and other top Nazis and Hans Frank who took part in the Munich Beer Hall Putsch. Anna's mother fled Russia with the Grand Duchess Xenia and the Tsar's mother at the time of the revolution. Xenia was the Tsar's sister and cousin of George V. The cousins were very close. Anna learnt of a plot to murder Edward VIII from her friend Arthur Kitson who was a monetary theorist and employed as an economic advisor by the Nazis. Kitson wanted to use her friendship with Xenia to get the documents about the assassination plot to the King. Indeed a rather botched murder attempt was made in Hyde Park after Trooping the Colour.

This third meeting of the Right Club had been in progress for an hour and hadn't even started on the official agenda. This was always distributed on the night, added to, then every copy collected up and destroyed afterwards. They had just finished Supreme de Fruits Lucullus followed by Bisque de Langouste aux Croutons. The wine met with general approval, a 1936 Chateaux Grand Barrail Lamarzelle and a white 1937 Chateau Latour-Martillac. Wine was less fashionable a decade before because of the popularity of cocktails on one side of the Atlantic and prohibition on the other, but it never lost favour in the clubs.

Sir Archibald Ramsey had run though his thoughts on economics on numerous occasions. He was only too pleased to be able to spell them out again, and again if necessary. The ideas were crucial to gaining control. He sipped his Chateau Latour-Martillac and began.

"As we discussed last time the elite in this country and across the Empire is under pressure and we must fight back to survive. Our homes and estates are under threat from an undercurrent of Bolshie sentiment, the State's death duties and envy from the poor. They must be put back in their place and the State rolled back. The revolution in Russia was more than twenty years ago and so far we have stopped it spreading here, but for how long? They are still in control. War now seems inevitable but we should not fear it. If our country comes under Germanic control Hitler will save our type. This much is guaranteed. Our links over the last few years have proved to him we are the only people to run Great Britain even if under his guidance. Amongst others, we have our Chairman to thank for this, partly because of his Anglo-German fellowship."

The Duke acknowledged the approval of all those around the table. There was a pause so Arthur Wellesley (as he was also known like his great grandfather who won the Battle of Waterloo) filled it.

"If war does come it's because of the anti-appeasers and the fucking Jews."

There was more thumping of the tables. A.K. Chesterton, another member of the Club clapped. He was on record as stating that the lamp post is the only way to deal with the Jew. He was sitting next to Lord Lymington who was employing Arthur as editor of his right-wing journal *The New Pioneer*. The Duke of Westminster, a leading member of Link who had just donated £1000 to the cause, the Marquess of Graham and Lord William Sempill continued to enjoy their meals. Brigadier-General Blakeney, 'Boney' Fuller, and Graham Hutchinson were more restless. Sir Archibald ran his hand over his receding greased down hair but was not put off his stride.

"In such a war all our enemies here in Britain will be called up and used as cannon fodder, a very neat, efficient and conveniently patriotic form of social cleansing. What have our efforts to resist rearmament been for otherwise? And our victories like when we killed off that plot coming from a few treacherous German generals to mount a coup against Hitler, what was it for otherwise? Our preferences are clear. First avoid war and negotiate with Hitler who will help us into power. If war comes though, to make sure Hitler is not defeated. We have more in common with him and the German people than those in control in Britain at the moment who are taking us over the edge. Churchill may force us into a naive and pointless fight against the Fuhrer, but he will not win."

He paused for dramatic effect.

"We cannot be totally sure of this sadly. We would be foolish to take this all for granted and not have a back-up plan. So we have to plan, a counteroffensive."

He took another sip of his Bordeaux. To murmurings of quite agree old chap he continued before anyone had the chance to interrupt further.

"If we don't get control of the country by coup d'etat, with or without German help, then we do have another path to follow. This is the economic route. I am convinced a subtle economic takeover would be effective, reasonably risk free and possibly longer lasting. This is the back-up plan. To be in charge of the money and the economy gives us power and, if we do it correctly, could make the State an irrelevance and so therefore bypassing so called democracy. This is what I intend to lay before you today." Another sip, "You remember what Henry Ford said? If Americans knew how the banking and monetary system really worked there'd be a revolution before tomorrow morning, or something to that effect. We have a fantasyland version of economics that is very convenient to the rich, us of course. It is fantasy but plausible to the gullible. You may be convinced war is on the horizon and so you may wonder why waste your time on all this, is economics really so important? Gentlemen, it is everything. Even war is mainly economics with some megalomaniac thrown in. War is profit. We have to think ahead to protect our class, our country, and ourselves. In the next decade, war or not, the Americans will be our biggest threat."

"The Americans?" butted in 'Boney' Fuller, "I thought they were our allies. Churchill had an American mother. Surely you mean Russia?"

"No, and yes, he did!" was the snapped reply.

"But you know the rumours that he had her bumped off," chipped in Graham Hutchinson. He was ignored and Jock was beginning to show his irritability.

"I plan now to hand over to Arnold Leese. You all know Arnold as a vet whose expertise is the camel, but since retirement he's become something of an economic expert. Arnold worked with Arthur Kitson on this, a neighbour who sadly died two years ago. He will spend the next few minutes running through why control of money is power. I assure you it will not be boring. In fact it will amaze you. One warning, it has been said that the camel is a horse designed by a committee. Our economic policy is a thoroughbred stallion, it is not up for any committee debate or it might evolve into a camel."

His attempt at humour lightened the mood and this just encouraged him.

"Oh, by the way, have you heard the story that when Halifax met Hitler he mistook him for a footman and went to hand him his coat?" For those in the room whose respect for Hitler was greater than for Halifax, this wasn't funny. Leese, who was ruffled to have his start delayed by the very man who wanted to get a move on, reached for the notes in his dinner jacket inside pocket.

"Gentlemen. I must defend the camel from that terrible metaphor. It is a highly efficient machine for its function perfectly adapted and finely tuned for its environment and not a misshapen horse, but I won't deviate further from our topic.

You will of course be aware of what I call simple basic economic theory. Public spending must be paid for through taxation, sales of assets, or borrowing. We on the right have always thought we can achieve our aim of low taxation and a small State by keeping Government spending to as little as we can get away with, perhaps, but not necessarily short of all the poor starving to death. The left of course want higher taxes to save everyone from that fate by state intervention. Well that basic economic theory is, of course, all tosh and codswallop. Despite that we have been feeding the public that line for well over one hundred years and will continue to do so. It serves our purpose very well.

Treating them as simpletons has been surprisingly easy. They can understand the idea by relating it to their household expenditure. If you spend more than you earn you go bankrupt and get punished. So similarly the country has to live within its means. It can't spend more than it earns. So the less the country spends the better. It can't be reckless and spend like a drunken sailor. That's what they must believe and what we must continually drum into them even though it is all baloney.

We've been working on the propaganda to complete the brainwashing in many ways. We even imported the American board game Monopoly only four years ago to reinforce this basic economic nonsense in the public's mind. It demonstrates that a good economy should reward wealth creation, and teaches that one needs to grind any opponent into the dust and enjoy taking all their money off them. I'm sure many of you have played it at Christmas? This catches the youngsters and next generation early. Something we learnt to do from our friend Herr Goebbels. But, of course, Henry Ford knew the truth.

Let me explain what that quote of Jock's actually meant for those who don't know. But I warn you it is complicated. In actual fact he was paraphrasing a chap called Charles Binderup in the US House of Representatives two years ago, shortly before the Coronation of our George VI. I have a lot of time for Ford. Like us he blames the Jews. Like Hitler he thinks they are engaged in a worldwide conspiracy to subjugate western civilisation. He certainly puts his money where his mouth is. He actually bought a newspaper called the *Dearborn Independent* to disseminate his beliefs and printed a forgery written by the Tsar's secret police in 1903, *The Protocols Of The Elders Of Zion*, that details the Jewish conspiracy to take over the world. He knew it was a forgery. He made all Ford dealerships carry it so the workers were brainwashed to his way of thinking. There are lessons there for us. He is so vocal with his anti-Jew beliefs that Hitler has a picture of Ford in his office, praised him in *Mein Kampf* and presented him with the highest Nazi award for civilians, the Grand Cross of the German Eagle, for his financial support of the Nazi regime. Hitler wants his Volkswagen to be Germany's Model T."

Lord Redesdale another founding member showed a little impatience. The next course of Poitrine de Canard Montmorency au riz sauvage petit pois a l'etuvee was being served.

"That only explains Ford's background. It doesn't tell us what he meant."

Robert Gordon-Canning agreed. Leese ignored the intervention and carried on.

"For an understanding of that we have to go back a century. I'll put it in an American context first, so you can see why Ford believed this - but it equally applies to Great Britain."

He looked down at his notes.

"The Revolutionary War in the United States was fought over the British central banking system. The fourth US President, James Madison, said history records that the moneychangers have used every form of abuse, intrigue, deceit, and violent means possible to maintain their control over governments by controlling money and its issuance. The third President, Thomas Jefferson, said *I believe that banking institutions are more dangerous to our liberties than standing armies.* You see in the US the Federal Reserve System is nothing more than a group of private banks, which charge interest on money that never existed. The Government prints a billion dollars worth of bonds, takes them to the Federal Reserve, which sticks it into an account and then the government writes cheques to the total of $1 billion. Where was that $1 billion before they stuck it into an account? It didn't exist. We allow this private banking system to create money out of absolutely nothing, all of it a loan to our government, and charge interest on it forever. The bank collects interest on the Government's own money. Our Bank of England works in the same way. Money doesn't grow on trees. It is easier than that. It comes from nowhere. This summary of a highly complex system is oversimplified but accurate."

The waiters were busy filling glasses. Most members were coming to the end of their main course but Sir Archibald had not really had a chance to eat much as Leese continued.

"A communiqué sent while Victoria was on the throne from the Rothschild investment house here in England to its associate in New

York remarked, *the few who understand the system will either be so interested in its profits or so dependent on its favours that there will be no opposition from that class, while on the other hand, the great body of people mentally incapable of comprehending will bear its burdens without complaint.* The few gentlemen include us, which is why it is vital you understand. Another Rothschild said, *give me control of a nation's money and I care not who makes its laws.* So you see, we must control the financial world, which will make the State an irrelevance.

How though to keep this secret within an elite and select group for so long? As Rothschild said, *it is fairly easy as the great body of people are mentally incapable of comprehending. When suspicions do surface, or people get too near the truth, the legislators pretend to be on their side.* Hence the Federal Reserve Act of 1913. This was a deliberate charade to pacify the American voters. They had been crying out for a banking reform and held scores of elections alternating one set of politicians with another only to find themselves with the same programs and deeper debt. Twenty years ago Charles Lindbergh pointed out the double-dealing of the so-called legislators. He tried to impeach members of the Federal Reserve, charging them with conspiracy to violate the Constitution and laws of the United States. Some say the kidnap and murder of his grandson was his punishment.

Government office-holders understood that by joining with the banking interests to exploit the people their re-election is more certain than if they serve people who elect them. By joining the exploiters their campaign expenses are paid, the support of the 'machines' and the capital press is assured, and if by chance they should lose they are appointed to the same office that should suit them equally or better. The same phenomenon is visible today. The same cast of characters emerge in key positions whichever way the nation votes. Both sides appear to have sold out. A revolving door of lucrative jobs for the boys. I foresee in the future, those in Government not looking at that as the pinnacle of their career, not even the job of Prime Minister, but of a way of laying the groundwork for a cushy little number after office, which makes millions and almost allows a dynasty to develop because of so much wealth. It is one way of replacing the nobility I referred to earlier that is being destroyed even if they are not of the same standard.

The Federal Reserve and our British equivalent is an engine that has created private wealth that is unimaginable even to the most financially sophisticated. It has enabled us as an imperial elite to manipulate the economy for our own agenda and enlist the Government itself as our enforcer. It controls the times, dictates business, and affects homes, and practically everything in which the public is interested. Hear me out. Of course the majority of people do not know about the functioning of today's banking system and it is essential it is kept that way, or capitalism would collapse. It has been kept secret for more than a century by any method necessary, even killing Presidents. Bankers assassinated Abraham Lincoln, when he realised the huge earning of banks. He saved an estimated $4 billion by printing $400 million rather than borrowing from bankers. The twenty-eighth President, Woodrow Wilson, knew the dangers. He regretted being forced into the 1913 Act. He said, *some of the biggest men in the United States in the field of commerce and manufacture are afraid of something. They know that there is a power somewhere so organised, so subtle, so watchful, so interlocked, so complete, so pervasive that they had better not speak above their breath when they speak in condemnation of it.* That included him, the President, supposedly the most powerful man on earth. Well, we know that is not true."

Leese looked down at his notes again.

"This is Wilson again. *A great industrial nation is controlled by its system of credit. Our system of credit is concentrated in the hands of a few men. We have come to be one of the worst ruled, one of the most completely controlled and dominated governments in the world - no longer a government of free opinion, no longer a government by conviction and vote of the majority, but a government by the opinion and duress of small groups of dominant men.* By small groups of dominant men, he was of course referring to the like of us, gentlemen. And the purpose of the Right Club is that we remain dominant."

More table thumping and shouting.

"Hear! Hear!"

Louder this time as more Chateaux Grand Barrail Lamarzelle had been consumed.

"I'll conclude on the economic agreement…"

Brigadier General Blakeney, who had lost the thread two glasses of wine before, impatiently muttered.

"Thank Christ for that."

"The economic crash of '29 and the Great Depression in the United States were both necessary for us to maintain our dominance. When America sneezes the rest of the world catches a cold as the old cliché goes, but we actually benefitted. We provoked all this and were able to blame the money vultures and foreign swindlers of the Federal Reserve. But we had to be careful as we didn't want the system to become too unpopular, or to give the impression, even if it was true, that it hadn't got the interest of the Nation at heart, but just us elite. As you know, Gentlemen, we succeeded by getting them to withhold currency from circulation and raising interest rates, which was all that was needed after an inflationary easy-money policy in the early 1920s. It has been done before and it will be done again. Their fear of excessive speculation led it into a far too deflationary policy in the late 1920s destroying the village in order to save it."

By this stage 'Boney' Fuller had not a clue what he was talking about but would not dare expose his ignorance.

"Yes, very good," he added.

"So by these means we can control money and the economic system and thus control governments, but it is dependent on the ignorant cooperation of the masses. That is why we must continue to feed them the nonsense of simple basic economic theory. I'm sorry to have to go into detail, but it is vital that this is all clearly understood. It has been passed down the generations to us and we must pass it onto our descendants."

Several members reached for their wine at the same time.

"So in summary, every time a government spends it creates money. The money comes from nowhere. And the UK Government can no more run out of money than the scorer at Lords can run out of runs," and in an effort to lighten the topic he added, "In a week's time Len Hutton will be batting against the West Indies at Lords. The scorer will have a problem keeping up with him."

William Francis Forbes-Sempill, whom Jock thought was not really paying attention to Leese, retorted.

"Let's hope so."

The nineteenth Lord Sempill was known by the security services to be passing secret information to the Imperial Japanese military, but the Right Club could turn a blind eye to that.

"Taxes are only necessary to destroy some private sector spending power to make room in the economy for the Government to conduct its desired spending on public goods," Leese continued, "Taxes are necessary solely to limit inflation. As a government cannot run out of money and therefore faces no financial constraints but can run out of people, skills, technology, infrastructure, natural and ecological resources we have good reason to not only protect and defend our class, but to expand it and at the same time maintain an underclass of lesser beings as workers."

With that Leese took a mouthful of his cold dinner. He wondered how much his fellow Club members had taken in. He had tried to keep it simple.

The biggest problem Sir Archibald thought he and Leese had was credibility. His analysis was so far away from safe thought that many thought it preposterous. Sir Archibald had no doubts or a lack of self-belief. Those who failed to understand had either drunk too much, like Sir Ernest Bennett the Labour MP, or were too dim. He knew that if the dim ones learnt nothing else at public school they had found out how to bluff their way in the world.

The Duke of Wellington was as pompous as they come. He rarely missed an opportunity to mention his time in the Grenadier Guards serving in the Boer War. In addition to his membership of the Anglo-German League, he was President of Liberty Restoration League, another anti-Semitic front organisation. He seized the opportunity to emphasise his Chairmanship this time by saying thank you to draw a line under Sir Archibald and Leese's contributions. He was eager to move on before Leese could swallow and say any more.

"You will have heard that last week the Duke of Windsor visited the Fuhrer again in Germany. That is now four times since October 1937. Word has got back that he has finally achieved what we always wanted. In the event of war, Hitler would be prepared to install the Duke as monarch. The Duke is of course one of us and it will help our cause. He is even quite content to be installed as our first President if, God forbid, we end up as a Republic."

There were murmurs of alarm.

"Out of the question. It will affect our way of life and all we stand for," chipped in the Duke of Westminster.

There was more thumping of tables.

"Our gratitude is to you, Brocket, for such good work with your contacts. We also must thank Charles who went to the Nuremberg Rally a few weeks before the first meeting to prepare the groundwork for this. Well done, Charles. I understand you met the Fuhrerin too, another powerful figure?"

Charles knew he needed to educate those present as to the importance of this.

"Yes, Chairman. Gertrud Scholtz-Klink is leader of the National Socialist Women's League. She is a slight contradiction in terms as her main task is to promote male superiority, the joys of home labour and the importance of childbearing. Despite her own position, she speaks against the participation of women in politics."

"Jolly good," butted in 'Boney' Fuller.

Charles finished off.

"She had her six children but is a figurehead really. Nevertheless, the more friends we make the better. She has influence over women like Hitler does over everyone else."

"Excellent, Charles."

"I also had the pleasure of visiting one of the Reich Bride Schools, or Reichsbrauteschule, where they turn out perfect Nazi brides for the SS. Gertrud played a big part in setting them up. We really should follow that example."

More table thumping. It never ceased to amaze the more moderate of the group how more intense and extreme the right wing views became in direct proportion to the amount of Bordeaux consumed. Salade a la Chauveau was quickly followed by Gateau St Honore.

The Chairman introduced the last item on the agenda.

"Like all matters I cannot emphasise enough the confidential nature of what I am about to tell you. Our Nazi contacts have informed us of attempts by them to forge alliances with militant nationalists in the Celtic territories of Ireland, Scotland, Wales and Brittany in an effort to undermine the Governments of Britain and France from within. They are keeping us informed because of course they want us to join them, and help out where we can. It will give us the opportunity to seize power. It may be bloody however and we must be prepared for armed insurrection, espionage and sabotage. The Germans will supply the arms needed. I will keep you informed gentlemen, but when the time comes events will happen swiftly. We must be ready to take power."

The last sentence added to the alcohol-induced warm glow. It was not necessary to say more. They had dined early as they had all had an appointment.

The Duke decided it was time to draw the meeting to a close.

"Just one more thing, gentleman. The other day Charles Lindbergh, the great American aviator, wrote to me and as it's short I'll read it to you:

My dear Duke,

As some of you know, for the last three years I have been living at Long Barn in Kent courtesy of Harold Nicolson and Vita Sackville-West. This was to seek refuge from the press intrusion after the murder of our son. I have been following the progress of the Right Club, and I would like it known you have my full support. Sadly my time in England is drawing to a close so I cannot join you, but your fight must go on. Peace with our friends in Germany is vital. They have the correct policies for the future of Europe. Hitler is undoubtedly a great man. The America First committee, which I represent, believes the Jews wish to involve us in war. The danger lies in their ownership of our motion pictures, our press, our radio and the US Government. They must be stopped and with your help we will be victorious. We may need to rally our troops at the top of the hill to achieve our aims.

Best wishes to you all,

Charles A. Lindbergh."

It was a bright note on which to end. There was general approval. The Club's links with the Nazi groups like the Auslands-Organisation in the USA were blossoming. Charles had been their representative at Fritz Kuhn's Nazi rally at Madison Square Garden, with twenty thousand others, on Washington's birthday that February. There was anger at the closure of the training camps like Yaphank on Long Island the previous year but the Duquesne spy ring was gathering rewards.

"Now gentlemen your carriages are waiting. We have just a short ride up Exhibition Road to the Royal Albert Hall. There is more entertainment and refreshments to be found in your loggia boxes in the Hall. Please be seated by 7.50. But may I take this opportunity to remind you about Jock Ramsey's aim to hire the Albert Hall in December for an enormous rally? We hope you will all be there."

The same group had been going to concerts together on a regular basis since the visit to the Queen's Hall in June 1937 to see Arturo Toscanini conduct *Beethoven's Symphony No. 6 in F Major*. It was Saturday 17th June and Dr Malcolm Sargent was conducting the Royal Choral Society performing *Hiawatha* by Samuel Coleridge-Taylor staring Errol Addison and Jack Spurgeon. The Club were all guests of the Duke of Wellington who was celebrating the 124th anniversary of his great-grandfather's victory at Waterloo, albeit the next day. There was no Sunday programme so it had to be a day early. The Duke had been to the first staging of the trilogy of cantatas fifteen years before, in May 1924 when the composer's son Hiawatha Coleridge-Taylor conducted it. He had been a guest of his seventy-five year old father, the fourth Duke of Wellington, in the presence of George V and Queen Mary. They all sat in the Royal box. The cantatas had been an annual event since. Little did they know that tradition was about to be cut short by the war. The fifth Duke liked the work so much he was prepared to overlook the part-Creole descent of the composer. He was after all born just three miles away in Holborn. He even felt sorry for him because of his untimely death at only thirty-seven from pneumonia, attributed to the stress of his poor financial situation. He had sold the rights of the popular *Hiawatha's Wedding Feast* for fifteen guineas. The Duke called him the African Mahler. If he had known he was illegitimate, of an illegitimate mother, he might have taken the Club elsewhere.

6 - FRIENDS AND LESSONS

LIFE AIN'T NO DRESS REHEARSAL

It's the one time shot
And there are no retakes
So let's make it happen

Life ain't no dress rehearsal
No life ain't no dress rehearsal

Chynna Phillips (1995)

A few weeks after the poll tax protests Rob had a half-day so decided to visit Rosa in her council flat in the Tamworth Block on the Market Estate in Islington.

A few weeks into his early days of General Practice the normal working week was roughly four eleven to twelve hour days with a half-day that usually did not start until about 3.00 p.m. On top of that was the on call. In his practice it was every third night and a full weekend. The two partners teamed up with a neighbouring single-hander to make the rota that was called a one-in-three. When leave and holidays were taken into account there were long stretches when they worked every other night on top of the normal fifty-sixty hour week. He had been on call the night before and had been out of bed three times. But he felt lucky that he had managed to finish most of his work by 2.00 p.m. so could jump on an earlier train than expected.

Rosa's tower block was called Tamworth after the pigs from the old market. The only part left was the Cally Tower built in 1855. Rob wanted to make sure she was well but was also keen to learn more about her fighting spirit and campaigning experience. He was surprised when she answered the door on her feet without a wheelchair in sight.

"This flat is so small I've always got something to cling onto. I just can't cope outdoors very well nowadays."

She loved her little flat. She was a new tenant when the Greater London Council built the estate in 1967.

"I can manage to get to the park though. I feel very at home in Caledonian Park mainly because of its long history of political dissent. I sit on the bench and can feel the ghosts of revolutionary heroes permeate my very soul. Perfect for me, eh? Did you know, when it was called Copenhagen Fields thousands of locals marched on Parliament in support of the Tolpuddle Martyrs? That was in 1834. There should be a memorial or plaque. I'm fighting for one."

The subject soon turned to who built her flat and the rent. She made a point of letting Rob know what she thought of Thatcher's right-to-buy scheme.

"Totally corrupt, despite the spin," she said, "Do you know so far one and a half million council houses have been flogged off? It's storing up a housing crisis for the future. Speculators have made millions out of exploiting public assets. The son of Thatcher's Housing Minister has bought forty in Roehampton. A disgrace. As I said in that cafe in Villiers Street, the rich are fleecing the poor. Gerrymandering, selling homes for votes. The scale of their election fraud is staggering. That dreadful Shirley Porter, the woman in charge of Westminster City Council and heiress to Tesco's, I've always refused to shop there to the point of being called anti-Semitic, which is ridiculous of course. I bet she's made a Dame soon, but hope she will also be sued for being the most corrupt public figure in my living memory, and that's saying something. She will probably turn out to be a role model though for some. Scandalous, but I fear a sign of things to come. MacMillan was right about them selling off the family silver. I never thought I'd agree with that old Etonian. I reckon if this bunch remains in power they'll be selling everything off... land, buildings, the NHS, eventually the air we breathe. They will probably privatise the birds in an already privatised park. And outer space."

Rob thought that amusing and made a note to use that line himself. Rosa asked how Jenny was and expressed her surprise on learning Rob had not seen her since the anti-Poll Tax riot as the media called it, and almost shocked that they were not together.

"For goodness sake Rob, ask her out! She clearly has eyes for you! Considering you two had just met for the first time that day, the chemistry between you was electric."

This startled Rob.

"Really?"

"Apologies, electricity is physics rather than chemistry, isn't it?"

A week later they did meet. Rob had got her phone number from Robin. He seemed reluctant and Rob could not understand why. Rob's shyness dragged out their eventual bonding but they officially became an item on 22nd November 1990 when they celebrated Thatcher's resignation by making love for the first time. Rob had never felt so good.

They married in May 1996 and had their first anniversary as Blair walked into Downing Street. That was an anniversary worth celebrating. There was real optimism in the air. Their three daughters arrived in 1999, 2001 and 2004 and life was complete. Their girls were perfect. Their eldest had a port-wine stain over her left eye but to them it added to her beauty. After that though, cynicism had set in with the Blair betrayal of all he - they - believed in. They celebrated the tenth and twentieth anniversary of their meeting on 31st March 2000 and then again in 2010 at the teashop in Villiers Street where they first entertained Rosa. The last time Rob had walked towards Watergate Walk at the bottom of Villiers Street to sit in Victoria Gardens on the Embankment he was sad - actually angered - to notice the tea-shop was now a Starbucks. Bastards get everywhere like the plague, he thought. He often sat opposite the memorial for the Imperial Camel Corps of the First World War. His grandfather served in it and fought in the Sinai and Palestine campaigns. He would reflect on the pointless sacrifice of that generation.

They saw Rosa less and less often as life got busier with children. Then he made the biggest mistake of his life. He was tempted to blame Blair for this too, but knew that was taking it slightly too far. Call it a mid-life crisis, or stupidity or just the desire for passion and interesting sex. Rob still cannot work out what drove him to wreck so much. He really wished he could turn the clock back. How could he hurt those he loved so much? He still felt sick if he thought about it for too long. There were great times and there could have been more. He did not listen to those whom he now understood did know better. The wise words did not penetrate because he did not want them to. He had years of torment and pain and inflicted it on others. Years of happiness lost forever. Or perhaps he could never be happy - it just was not in his nature.

He was encouraged to make the fateful decisions by the well meaning but reckless telling him 'life ain't no rehearsal'. He should have listened to Lennon when he sang, *life is what happens to you while you're busy making other plans.* He only had himself to blame. Now he blames immaturity. Who ever really grows up, until it is too late? Rob would often repeat to himself the Virginia Woolf quote to help him make more rational decisions, *growing up is losing some illusions, in order to acquire others.* Now he had to put up with listening to those who said he must see the advantages he has gained - but he was not convinced.

He left in 2013 when his girls were fourteen, twelve and nine to see if the grass was really greener. Eventually he found out it was almost dead, not green at all. He was forty-seven when he started his affair with Suzy in 2011. They were now in their sixth year together - fourth official year. But at that visit to Islington all this was in the future.

So Rosa was correct and helpful in pushing him towards Jenny on that afternoon visit to her flat in 1990. He had so much to be grateful to her for. Not only as a friend but an educator and political inspiration. He had never heard of the Ken Loach film *Cathy Come Home* until Rosa told him about it. He was only two when it was broadcast so he did have an excuse. The politicians had no excuse though that the homelessness problem it portrayed was no better. Rosa on the other hand saw the programme in 1966 when she was twenty-six. It was no surprise to her. She was still suffering and raw from the Aberfan disaster four weeks before.

She told him how the British Empire was built on the slave trade and getting the world addicted to opium and sugar. Many of the stately homes he had visited with his National Trust card were funded at the expense of the lives of slaves, and the descendants were still sitting in the House of Lords. The scandals she seemed to know all about opened his eyes. How big business and bankers killed Kennedy - a military-industrial complex, which included the CIA. Ideas in Kennedy's time like Northwoods, a false flag operation, which would have entailed fake terrorist attacks on American soil in order to whip up public opinion in support of an invasion of Cuba. How exaggerating North Vietnamese attacks on the US Navy in the Bay of Tonkin incident ramped up the Vietnam War. And in the UK how political establishment figures like Jeremy Thorpe could get off serious charges because of who they knew. The adoption scandal where young unmarried mothers had their babies taken away from them against their will by Moral Welfare Clinics run by the Catholic Church, the Church of England and the Salvation Army.

"One was just up the road from here," said Rosa, "St Pelagia's home in Highgate founded by nuns. They were all told they were sinners, up to half a million girls in total."

The Kincora Boys' Home outrage, which was never talked about, visited by the establishment and the famous. Later, Rosa told Rob about the organised child sexual abuse that went on there for years and at several other Catholic-run boys' homes in the Belfast area. How it was covered up with state collusion. Some said Mountbatten was a visitor.

But before explaining this Rosa had asked if he would be prepared to put his life on the line because just knowing about this was dangerous. She thought it had such serious implications for some important people that the truth was very unlikely to come out in her lifetime, if ever. Rob was totally shocked. Does this sort of thing really go on in modern Britain? And were people being killed to keep it under wraps? He could hardly believe it but needed to know more.

"Well, if you are willing to listen, I'm willing to tell you things you won't hear anywhere else. But it's toxic stuff. For instance, on the same theme you will find what happened in Tuam, County Galway very distressing. Nearly eight hundred babies discarded into a septic tank, a mass grave, at a state-backed Catholic institution that was a secret home for unmarried mothers between 1920 and 1961. Thirty-five thousand altogether treated this way across the whole of Ireland. The same people who don't believe in contraception and rant about abortions being a sin. A worse sin than what they got up to? I bet you cannot or do not want to believe this, do you Rob?"

As Rosa explained, it's like reaching a cliff top. Up to that point, whatever tale is told, if it seemed incredible people are inclined to dismiss it as fantasy. We all like to stay within our safe boundaries. Being blinkered is more comfortable and less complicated. Once one has seen and believed the impossible however, it is like having the veil lifted and the shutters opened to the real world. Then anything can be credible. Like flying off the cliff top and seeing the world as it is as a whole and in perspective. But people are scared and think they will plummet to the bottom of the cliff. A risk they would rather not take - much safer to dismiss the so-called conspiracy theories.

So tell people that the State kills in order to further the cause of the few in control and you are dismissed as a nutter, as they leave to go to the cinema to see the latest fantasy James Bond film. Tell people the Government has a secret plan to abolish the welfare state and our NHS and it will not be believed. Show the evidence that the Prime Minister lied to the country over the miners' strike and controlled the police and media at Orgreave and you are looked upon as deluded. Thatcher used sixty thousand police at the coking works in South Yorkshire. There was miners' blood everywhere but ninety-five of them were arrested for riot and unlawful assembly. All were acquitted though. Despite perjury, false statements, and cover-ups by the police there will never be an inquiry.

"It's time for the public to wake up and get real," she said.

So she told Rob what she knew about the Belfast boy's home and others. How the paedophile ring had links to the intelligence services.

State-sponsored child prostitution that MI5 covered up 'in the National interest' what went on from at least 1958 to 1980. Prominent businessmen, high-ranking Whitehall civil servants and senior officers in the British military were involved. It is not known how many boys were killed or disappeared.

"Have you heard of Haut de la Garenne?"

"No."

"You will... eventually. Otherwise known as the Jersey Home For Boys. The sexual abuse and murders that occurred there will make your blood run cold."

Another fresh scandal Rosa told him about was the Hillsborough football disaster just the year before. In fact it was the first anniversary, 15th April. She knew, although Rob had no idea how, that the South Yorkshire police were totally at fault for the ninety-six deaths of Liverpool supporters. Like at Orgreave they had falsified police statements, there was media collusion, and coroners being paid off, all under the direct control of Margaret Thatcher's Government and her poodles like Bernard Ingham and Kelvin MacKenzie.

There was a secondary plot and that was to take over football. It had been spotted to have potential as a multi-million pound business and rich businessmen wanted to make themselves even richer by siphoning off some of the wealth. The disaster suited them. They were going to twist the real version of events to further their cause. Blame the fans and label them as hooligans in order to introduce all seater stadia. That was deemed necessary to turn the game into a middle-class family event with expensive tickets - aided by their friend Murdoch and his television coverage - and charged for, of course. Rosa predicted the cover-up of this disaster would go on for decades.

"That makes sense," Rob said, "A mate of mine, Robin, who was on the anti-Poll Tax march, went to the FA Cup Final between Liverpool and Everton which was only five weeks after the Hillsborough disaster. He was disgusted at how many tickets went to the corporates, businessmen who knew and cared nothing for football, whilst real fans that couldn't get or afford tickets were left outside and didn't see the match. Liverpool won 3-2 after extra time. Big business again leaching and cannibalising to enrich themselves."

"I'm not that interested in football, but I am interested in injustice," said Rosa, "so I know that when England won the World Cup just before Aberfan in 1966 the whole team got just twenty-two thousand pounds and none of the wives were invited to the celebration dinner. Just the old white men in suits who still run and profit from football."

Rob had been taken to that cliff top and Rosa had taught him how to fly. She had no hidden agenda and no reason to make up all these horrific stories. He thought the world was bad. Now he knew it for sure. A line from a Lennon song came to Rob on his way home. *God is a concept by which we measure our pain.*

7 - TRAITORS AND SPIES

SOMEBODY'S WATCHING ME

Who, I always feel like somebody's watching me.
Who's playing tricks on me?
Who's watching me?
I don't know anymore… are the neighbors watching
Who's watching?
Well, it's the mailman watching me: and I don't feel safe anymore.
Tell me who's watching.
Oh, what a mess. I wonder who's watching me now.

Rockwell (1984)

1940

Sir Archibald Ramsey boasted that the Right Club had infiltrated the police and MI5. It had, but what they were all unaware of was the infiltration of MI5 into the Right Club.

The Club attracted the type that had no doubt they were right, and they had no doubt that anyone who was anyone supported them. The Prime Minister, Neville Chamberlain, was vain and the most autocratic PM in recent times. He and Stanley Baldwin were perhaps the most important of the appeasers. Neither fought in the trenches in the last conflict.

Before the outbreak of war members of the Club took comfort and were encouraged by their intelligence reports that the Secret Service were following and hounding anti-appeasers. This was on Chamberlain's orders. All Churchill's telephone conversations were monitored. MI6 helped the Gestapo with exchanges of information about communists up until at least 1937. They took comfort from the support they had amongst the establishment and aristocracy. The Cliveden Set, whose members included Nancy Astor, Lord Lothian, Viscount Halifax and Geoffrey Dawson the editor of *The Times*, was an upper class aristocratic Germanophile social network of appeasers. Dawson from Eton and Oxford forbade any mention of German anti-Semitism in his paper. A 1938 editorial stated that the warmongers - Churchill and his supporters - ought to either be impeached and shot or hanged.

It was no surprise then that the Right Club thought they were mainstream thinkers. Nazism had become fashionable amongst the upper classes in London's West End with ladies wearing bracelets with swastika charms and men combing their hair to slant across their foreheads. But this was amongst their set. They rarely mixed with others. Nancy Astor and Joseph Kennedy both agreed that Hitler was the solution to both the world's problems of communism and of the Jews. But when the tide turned and war was declared MI5 turned its attentions more towards the appeasers.

MI5 had the cooperation of the Rote Kapelle, or Red Orchestra, the anti-Nazi resistance movement in Berlin. Their resistance radio operators (known as pianists) sent, through their transmitter (known as pianos), information about the messages they intercepted from Right Club members to the Nazi hierarchy. Charles Henry Maxwell Knight (known as Max), who was a tall athletic pipe-smoker and Fleming's inspiration for 'M', ran Section B5b from his apartment in Dolphin Square. This huge development was built by Costains near to the Thames in Pimlico and was only about four-years-old. Their promotional booklet feared that with the provision of a restaurant, 'wives will not have enough to do'. With the war the underground garages had been transformed into major casualty depots.

Eric Roberts, alias Jack King was one of Maxwell Knight's first recruits as far back as 1925. Posing as a Gestapo agent, a member of the Einsatzgruppe London, he infiltrated fascist groups and despite his handicap of not being educated at a public school, managed to befriend Charles Morrison. For Morrison King was a great discovery. He believed King had a hotline to Hitler and used him, or so he thought, to communicate directly with Berlin.

Amongst Maxwell Knight's other recruits were Marjorie Amor, a roly-poly forty-year-old with a warm personality and Welsh accent. Hélène De Munck was twenty-five and targeted for all that she had in common with Anna Wolkoff, which included being born abroad, going to school in Britain, travelling widely and being multi-lingual. Both had an interest in spiritualism and, for Hélène being genuinely anti-Semitic, no acting was required there.

Also controlled by Max Knight was a double agent called James McGuirk Hughes who was integral to the entrapment operation. When he called himself P.G. Taylor he was also a key Mosley-ite linchpin. Hughes was a bald cannon ball headed man with a small moustache, who also had an apartment in Dolphin Square the home of paedophiliac atrocities.

Charles Morrison, by then Baron or Lord Willingdon, knew Anna from an earlier Right Club meeting held at her Russian Tea Rooms. At a rally in Caxton Hall, where addresses by 'Jock' Ramsey and A.K. Chesterton incited the audience to dispense cries of P.J. (Perish Judah), Anna introduced him to her friend of over ten years Enid Riddell. Charles was instantly attracted by her sheen of well-bred poise. Her slight nervousness exposed by a mild stammer endeared him further. Charles spent most of the time that Chesterton was whipping up hatred, trying to work out how to get rid of the young ex-public schoolboy Enid had brought as an escort so he could try to get her into bed. He failed that evening but he would have other opportunities, as he, Anna, Enid and the Duke del Monte, Assistant Military Attaché at the Italian Embassy, would meet regularly over a steaming plate of smolenskaya kasha, which Anna described as a quintessential Russian example of gastronomic poetry. She would tempt them with pirozhki too which were pastries stuffed with meat, potatoes or cheese and follow up with the menus star attraction tyanuchki, a sublime caramel-like dessert. It was not long before Marjorie, or Helene, or both would join them. Their discussion was nearly always treasonous.

Appeasement was their aim but none feared a successful Nazi invasion either. Mosley would be installed as a puppet leader like Vidkun Quisling in Norway, although Lloyd-George would make a suitable Prime Minister. Ramsey was Hitler's chosen Gauleiter for Scotland and their friend the Duke of Windsor would be put back on the throne. But the word invasion was never used. It would be a Grand Alliance. Alternatively, if a war were needed first, Edward would serve as President of an English Republic. They knew that a document had been drawn up for the Duke to sign promising Germany the return of her former colonies and the gift of Northern Australia. This had been delivered for Goering's approval.

Anna's father, Admiral Nikolai Wolkoff, the former Naval Attaché at the Imperial Russian Embassy in London had been part of the Russian Imperial Counter-Revolutionary Group that ran a network of anti-communist agents and hoped to overthrow the Soviet regime. Now he ran the café. Her mother fled Russia with Grand Duchess Xenia. Both got to know Arthur Rutherford's father. Her grandfather owned substantial estates in Russia and had mixed with the likes of Leo Tolstoy and Richard Wagner. The revolution had stripped the family of all that.

Anna liked to introduce herself as Miss Anna de Wolkoff and rarely allowed herself to be seen wearing anything other than an understated chic Parisian-style black dress, which conveyed her politics. She ran a couture business - one client being Wallis Simpson. Her high cheek-boned Slavic face was framed by unruly dark auburn hair. Anna was in constant fear of sharing the fate of other White Russians and being abducted by the Soviets, like the leaders of the Russian Armed Services Union, an organisation that sought to depose the communist regime in her native country. She got comfort from an illusory protection from the Right Club.

In early 1940 a cipher-clerk from the US Embassy called Tyler Kent approached Sir Henry Vaughan-Warner, having found out the English soldier was a member of the Right Club. His boss, Ambassador Joseph Kennedy who had sympathies, put Tyler in touch with Sir Henry. Kennedy wanted the Chamberlain Government to enter peace negotiations with Germany, was anti-British, isolationist and anti-Semitic. He had no doubt Britain would be defeated quickly by Hitler. In a letter to Charles Lindbergh, who had adopted Nazi views on race and eugenics, his main concern about Kristallnacht was not so much the violent acts against German Jews, as the bad publicity it generated in the West for the Nazi regime. Tyler Kent wanted to join, or at least make some contacts with the Right Club. After vetting by both parties Kent was thought to be safe. Henry first introduced him to Charles and before long he too was coming to the Russian Tea Rooms.

Anna and Tyler became firm friends for the cause. Kennedy was against Roosevelt agreeing to the First Lord of the Admiralty Churchill's request for the loan of aircraft, ammunition, anti-aircraft guns and forty to fifty destroyers. It just so happened that Kent had got hold of the sensitive communications between Churchill and the American President and told Anna and Ramsey about them. On 13th April 1940 she went to Kent's flat to borrow them and to get them photographed.

Other more formal Right Club meetings were held at the Duke of Wellington's Apsley House, Hotel Rembrandt near South Kensington Underground, and at St Ermin's, an exclusive restaurant near Caxton Hall. But they were being monitored. All Max's agents were gathering condemning evidence. Neither Marjorie nor Helene was under any suspicion at all of being anything other than good eggs. So Anna had no concerns about asking Helene to pass a coded letter through her Italian Embassy contacts to William Joyce. Anna had used this route before, taking advantage of the Duke Del Monte. But of course Helene gave it to her controller Maxwell Knight.

On 20th May 1940 Anna Wolkoff and Tyler Kent were arrested and charged with violating the Official Secrets Act. Kennedy appeared to have hung Kent out to dry. Charles and Henry started to get nervous which was intensified when a few days later others were rounded up. The detention of British fascists using Regulation 18b of the Emergency Defence Regulations began with Sir Oswald Mosley four days later on 24th May. Maxwell Knight was waiting with detectives on the seventh floor of the Hood House wing of Dolphin Square where the Mosleys had an apartment. Oswald and Diana came out of the lift and were confronted. Oswald was taken to HMP Brixton where, finding life tough without servants was granted the services of a couple of deferential sex offenders as valet and gofer. Diana flaunted her furs in Holloway.

Sir Archibald Ramsey had been taken there the day before. He was arrested outside his Onslow Square house after returning from his Scottish Estate, Kelly Castle in Arbroath. Both Wolkoff and Kent were tried in camera at the Old Bailey. Wolkoff was sentenced to ten years imprisonment and Kent received seven.

Ramsey had given his red leather-bound ledger to Kent to hide in his flat. Knight discovered it when Kent was arrested. It was forced open to reveal the names of the Right Club members. There were five levels of membership - Wardens, Stewards, Yeomen, Keepers and Freemen - with differing joining fees and subscriptions. Exposed were Enid Riddell, Molly Stanford, Anne Van Lennep, Major Philip Le Grand Gribble and Johnny Coast. There were Royal connections - Lord Carnegie married to Princess Maud, Queen Victoria's granddaughter. Sir Alexander Walker (Chairman of Johnnie Walker), William Brinsley Le Poer Trench, Francis Yeats-Brown and Sir Ernest Bennett the Labour MP were also exposed.

Dolly Newnham joined Anna in prison. Her husband Henry edited the anti-Semitic, anti-war, anti-Churchill, pro-fascist weekly called *The Truth* - this was secretly run by Major Sir George Joseph Ball, a former MI5 officer who met with Ramsey at the Carlton Club in June 1939. He was a confidant of Chamberlain, possibly was responsible for the Zinoviev letter, and worked hard to secretly undermine anti-Nazis including Churchill.

Was the Establishment rotten to the core?

Pamela, the second Mitford daughter of Lord Redesdale, was close to her sister Diana Mosley. She was married to Derek Jackson, a bi-sexual pro-Nazi aristocrat who part owned the *News Of The World*. Pamela bought a cornflower blue Aga to match her eyes and had turned down proposals from John Betjeman and Oliver Watney of Red Barrel fame. William Joyce had joined the Right Club on 1st July 1939 but had escaped to Germany at the end of August when he thought he was going to be arrested. Nicknamed 'Lord Haw-Haw' he began his Nazi propaganda broadcasts with, *Germany calling, Germany calling, Germany calling*. They began on 18th September 1939 and had at least six million regular British listeners.

Four weeks after Joyce's first broadcast. Myra Hess started her lunchtime concerts at the National Gallery that ran throughout the war, often throughout air raids. Maxwell Knight and his colleague Arthur Rutherford attended the first, which included Beethoven's *Appassionata*. Geoffrey Dawson went with Charles Morrison, but Rutherford and Morrison did not see each other. When Archibald Ramsey heard of his fellow Right Club members' attendance he could only say with exasperation, *you know she's a Jew, don't you?*

Leniency reeking of aristocratic privilege was granted to the Duke of Wellington and Lord Redesdale. Lord Sempill, being a son of an aide-de-camp to George V, found that a blind eye was turned regarding his treachery of helping out Japan. Some disappeared, others were murdered. Sir Michael Francis O'Dywer was stabbed to death in March 1940 in Caxton Hall supposedly in revenge for the Amritsar massacre - he had been Lieutenant Governor of the Punjab. Collateral damage were Marjorie and Helene, who had also to be arrested so cover was not blown.

Having heard about the discovery of the ledger Charles Morrison waited for the knock on the door. When it came Maxwell Knight was standing there. The door was one of the large studded heavy double oak ones at Hetherington Park, and the knock produced by a twelve-inch brass lion head knocker. The butler opened it. Charles used the only defence he knew and that was blackmail material he had gathered over the years. Did the establishment really want exposed the Maggie Meller scandal and how they let off a murderer so as not to discredit the Royal family? What about all those MPs he had evidence on concerning the paedophile circuit? Did Mr Knight know it was going on under his nose where he had an apartment in Dolphin Square, he asked the MI5 operative? Would Mr Churchill be happy to explain the money he had received from the Burmah Oil Company and possible involvement in the death of Lawrence of Arabia five years before? This one Charles had to explain. The new PM of only sixteen days was paid in 1923 to lobby the Government to allow them sole control over oil resources in Persia. T.E. Lawrence was about to write a book, which included some mention of Churchill's wrongdoings. What about MI5 tapping the phones of the royal family during the abdication crisis?

"I could go on, Mr Knight," Charles had made his point. Maxwell Knight left, never to return.

So Britain was at war and the Right Club had had a setback. Unity Valkyrie Freeman-Mitford shot herself in the head on the declaration of war in the English Garden in Munich. Others like John Amery, a fascist and son of the Conservative Government Minister, continued to plot for a treaty. But they did not feel safe anymore. Someone was watching them. As a challenge to the Duke of Wellington and his great grandfather, George Orwell wrote the next year that, *the Battle of Waterloo was won on the playing fields of Eton*, but the opening battles of all subsequent wars were lost there.

8 - PLOT AND CONTROL

POWER IN THE DARKNESS

And it's about time we said 'enough is enough'
And saw a return to the traditional British values of discipline
Obedience, morality and freedom
What we want is

Freedom from the reds and the blacks and the criminals
Prostitutes, pansies and punks
Football hooligans, juvenile delinquents
Lesbians and left wing scum

Freedom from the niggers and the Pakis and the unions
Freedom from the gypsies and the Jews
Freedom from left wing layabouts and liberals
Freedom from the likes of you

Tom Robinson Band (1978)

1974

The mini-skirted air hostess on Pan Am Flight 370 to London Heathrow had been told in training it was part of the job to keep the men in first class happy, but Sir James took too many liberties. He seemed to have no shame or guilt where his hands went - indeed she felt like a lump of meat and he the butcher doing what he pleased. To complain was not an option if she wanted to keep her job. And many thought it acceptable behaviour then, a bit of fun, slap and tickle. She was supposed to keep smiling. What a relief to see him walk down the steps straight into his limo, which was waiting on the tarmac ready to take him directly to his club. His last remark to her was something about his disapproval of how London Airport had been renamed Heathrow eight years earlier. To pretend now he could engage her in intelligent conversation was to ignore and deflect from his sexual assault.

Not that Sir James saw anything wrong with his actions anyway. He actually cultivated a reputation as a man who enjoyed basking in the scandalous limelight. It often paid off. He put the rumour around society himself, that he was the famous headless man. During the acrimonious divorce case of the Duke and Duchess of Argyll in 1963 Polaroid photos were used as evidence. They featured Margaret, the Duchess and former debutante of the year, in her Art Deco-style bathroom at 48 Grosvenor Street, Mayfair, giving a Turtle Head or Bodmin Dark, as the more street-wise servants called a BJ, to a naked man whose identity was concealed because his head was not captured in the frame. For years all wondered who this headless man was. Sir James wanted it to be known it was he, such was his ego and lack of shame of the man. The Duchess, whose reputation had gone through the mangle, got fed up with the speculation and threatened to reveal the headless man's true identity, Pan Am's sales director Bill Lyons. Sir James volunteered to help Bill cover up for the sake of his family. In return he used Pan Am like his own free private airline. That is how it paid off. So now he had had plenty of rest and was keen to get on with boasting about his satisfactory negotiations and then putting into operation what had been decided between him and his American friends. Gerry was instructed to meet him. The club was secure and a safe place to talk.

Three days before Jim walked back into his club the Prime Minister, Edward Heath, had asked the Queen to dissolve Parliament so a general election could take place on 28th February. Heath wanted the election to be fought on who governs Britain in a battle with the unions, but inflation was at twenty per cent and the public was feeling the effects. His Home Secretary, Maudling, had to resign because he helped a crooked architect called Poulson get lucrative contracts, and then two other ministers, Lords Lambton and Jellicoe had to quit having been caught with prostitutes. For Sir James this was all too much. There's nothing wrong with prostitutes but Heath was not right wing enough. The pinko had to go. He was not tough and had no staying power.

Tiger Feet by Mud was still at number one and his chauffeur had it playing softly in the front of his Rolls Royce so it did not disturb his boss. On the drive from the airport he rehearsed his thoughts.

"We need to build a unit like the Afrikaner Broederbond. They were strong and determined. They designed and implemented apartheid. And that South African, Eugene Terre'Blanche is what I would call a strong leader. His new Afrikaner Weerstandsbeweging - the resistance movement he formed last year - would be a good model."

All Sir James' group knew they needed their own man in place with more balls. Ousting Heath would be more difficult if he won the election. In Sir James' opinion there was little to choose between Heath and Wilson, both believed in this mixed economy nonsense. It is about time we said enough is enough and saw a return to the traditional British values of discipline, obedience, morality and freedom. When will they realise multi-nationals running the world is the future. Their sort may never accept that the State has no role, as they would at minimum want a safety net for the poor and sick. Sir James and his colleagues did not even want that. The future is where the Prime Minister is a puppet and may not even realise how controlled and manipulated he (because of course it would always be a he) would be.

Sir James had met both Heath and Wilson last in St George's Chapel, Windsor at the funeral of the former King Edward VIII about eighteen months earlier. The Duchess wanted him there as an old friend. He had taken the baton from his father who knew the Duke of Windsor intimately from their trips to pre-war Germany together. The Duke had no doubts about the loyalty of Charles Morrison. Although very young, Charles saw an opportunity to ingratiate himself with the Prince of Wales when he heard the whispers about the Marguerite Alibert affair. He had heard judges and politicians needed leaning on to prevent Maggie releasing embarrassing letters about the heir to the throne, which she had threatened when she was charged with the murder of her husband. Charles demonstrated his thuggery in a violent manner that even surprised him, but also kept the pressure on Maggie to be discreet (until she died the year before her ex-lover in 1971). She later lived her life in luxury near the Ritz in Paris only three miles from the Duke. The letters were destroyed after her death. The Duke was very grateful to Charles.

When his brother, George VI died in 1952 from smoking too much, Charles and Kenneth de Courcy saw their chance to get the Duke back on the throne, and thus help the right wing cause. De Courcy wrote to the Prime Minister, Winston Churchill, suggesting the new young Queen needed support. This was further to his plot in the late 1940s to return the Duke and Duchess of Windsor to Britain to establish regency even when George VI had still been alive. The excuse was that the King was dying. The Duchess of Windsor in a handwritten note to Kenneth de Courcy declared that *something must be done.* He proposed a caretaker monarchy to neutralise the Mountbatten influence.

In the 1930s de Courcy was secretary of the Imperial Policy Group, which supported appeasement. At the abdication of his friend, he also supported and pushed for installing Queen Mary as Queen Regent, thinking Edward VIII's younger brother too weak to be King. James was very young then but after the war accompanied his father on social visits. They were close enough to not only stay with them at Villa Windsor, the mansion located at 4 Route du Champ d'Entrainement within the Bois de Boulogne (where the Duke died in 1972), but also the Moulin de la Tuilerie, their weekend retreat to the south west of Paris. On their last meeting they were invited down to Chateau de la Croe on the Cote D'Azur. It was the mid-sixties and Charles was not in good health, so James was more use as a minder than son. Kenneth de Courcy was also a guest after a prison sentence for fraud. Charles had a stroke whilst staying with the Windsors and had to be flown home. To James' relief this affected the left side of his brain producing a paralysis on the right side of his body and speech problems. As a consequence and for the first time in his life his father did not order James about. He hoped it would stay that way.

Heath and Wilson had switched roles of PM and Leader of the Opposition a couple of years before the Duke's death. Sir James regarded Wilson then as a canny operator who could outmanoeuvre enemies so had to be watched carefully. He was more dismissive of Heath - rotten apple in the barrel.

Jim even had a smug way of walking. He always wore double-breasted suits from Henry Poole of Savile Row and for a while tried using a monocle. The gold matched his pocket watch. All this was to cultivate his image. The crest of his tailors read By Special Appointment To The Late Emperor Napoleon III. His favourite German General, Hans Krebs (who shot himself in the Fuhrerbunker in 1945) inspired the monocle. Jim had seen photos of his father sporting a monocle too. The strange thing was he did not seem consistent which eye he put it in. His mother Edwina told him, years later, it was clear glass and he wore it as a tribute to Joseph Chamberlain, often when he went to meet his son Neville to try to impress him.

Sir James was very satisfied with the results of his US trip. His new arms deal was of no concern to Gerry, so he launched straight in to what he used Gerry for.

"Very successful. The Yanks are encouraging us into the next phase, actually pushing us, but of course they want another slice of the action."

This was not quite true. The White House staff had been angry that more progress had not been made. Jim had been shouted at and humiliated.

"They are way ahead of us in demolishing the state although their public sector never matched ours for size so they had a head start. But like it or not, we need their guidance, experience and skills. I can see clearly we must adopt their phrases - everything government bad, everything business good. Competition raises standards and quality, and get our media friends to continue with the public brainwashing. Remind me to tell you about a nasty bit of work called Murdoch later."

"Did you meet Ehrlichman?"

"No, but I met his sidekick in the White House. You may have heard of him, Lyndon C. Woodward, a deputy Chief of Staff? He has just pushed through their Health Maintenance Organisation Act. I'll tell you more about that later but in a nutshell it's all about making a load of money from healthcare whilst pretending to serve the public."

Gerry lit the second cigarette since Jim had arrived. It was 10.00 a.m. He sipped his whisky and soda, clumsily spilling some, as he put it back on the nineteenth century French Rosewood and Marquetry Bijouterie table. Some of his drink trickled down one of the elegantly shaped and tapered cabriole legs. Jim clicked his fingers for a waiter. They stood ever ready by the door.

"Woodward says Nixon wants not only zero obstacles to his multinationals spreading throughout Britain, but active help, encouragement and sacrifice. And once a firm base has been established then he wants our help infiltrating Europe. Now we are in the common market he expects us to bat for him in that market. He would like a McDonalds or KFC on every street corner throughout the continent. I bet you didn't know about the addictive new type of fat they put in their so-called burgers? Brilliant. Get the masses hooked on particular types of food and the sky's the limit!"

"A bit like how we as an empire got all the Chinese hooked on opium and generations past hooked on sugar, I suppose, eh Jim?"

He told the waiter to shoo.

"Yes, but we are back talking empires, Gerry. You do understand that the cold war is not really a struggle between the USA and the Soviet Union, but between the Americans and the third world? But the Americans want their empire extending beyond the third world. All those poor countries are fighting for economic and political change and to set up their own progressive governments, but this clashes with the needs of the American power elite. So the USA, land of the free and champions of democracy, move in to crush those movements even though the Soviet Union virtually plays no role in those countries. Washington can't admit they are blocking change so they call it fighting communism. What they are really doing is fighting for their big business interests in those countries and exploiting their markets and natural resources."

He thought and hoped Gerry understood but had his doubts. After all he was only a soldier.

"So McCarthyism was really about keeping the communist conspiracy in the forefront of the public's consciousness rather than unveiling spies and traitors?"

Gerry was getting it after all.

"Nixon wants US pharmaceutical giants selling their drugs on every European street corner and to become the main supplier to the NHS as their home market is already saturated. Get the masses to believe that there is a drug for every ill and then to demand it. Then, when that market has been saturated, to extend the definitions of illness to take in a whole new population. Take depression. At the moment the medics and academics have a very tight definition of true clinical depression, so only those get treatment. Everyone gets a bit fed up from time to time. Convince them that they have a treatable condition too and hey presto, a whole new market! They may not need the treatment and some will come to harm, but so what?"

The waiter was swatted away like a fly after taking Jim's order for coffee.

"The President wants Heath replaced as we do, more union infiltration and then have them smashed, the media brought more on side and run by us, and all before the Soviets realise what is happening. We are getting there. Notice how newspapers already refer to the union bosses as barons, a lovely pejorative term and pretty cheeky really if you think about it. If any group today still thinks of themselves as barons it's the Lords and billionaires who own, run and control the papers, from Beaverbrook to Rothermere, Camrose and Kemsley to Murdoch and Maxwell.

Now it was Gerry's turn.

"You know what Stanley Baldwin said about these men? That they are aiming at power without responsibility, the prerogative of the harlot throughout the ages," then moving on Gerry said slowly, "My worry is that the Yanks just want to turn us into their fifty-first state, and we can't let it go that far."

"Hmm, they think they already have. It's been their ambition since the last war when they came out unscathed and the rest of the world was broke and a heap of rubble," murmured Jim, knowing that Gerry did really understand that, "We know all they push for has nothing to do with helping others, especially us, but is totally one hundred per cent self-interest. America first. Nixon had no thoughts of how it would affect us when he abandoned the Bretton Woods agreement of fixed exchange rates, allowing them to float against each other again and no longer convert dollars into gold. That was purely to help the US economy at the expense of the rest of us. This accelerated the end of the Keynesian nonsense though."

Great Britain wanted to remain equal partners but like a man hanging onto the cliff edge by his fingernails knew deep down it was all in vain. The Americans were staring at us just about to fall off the cliff, not showing any signs of wanting to help, even if they were not actually stamping on our fingers.

"Special relationship my arse," said Jim, "the politicians in the UK should stop kidding themselves. By now it is clear the United States want world domination. That is what it is all about."

They had to be reined in. But Jim and Gerry believed Great Britain was still able to challenge their hegemony if they had the right leader.

"We are supposed to deal only with Woodward. He should be our main and first point of contact. According to them. A bit slimy but very bright and knows all the right people. He has Gerry Ford in the palm of his hand in case Nixon falls under that Watergate bus. I went to dinner with his typically American family in Georgetown. Like having a meal with the Flintstones. He is about our age and has a young son Nelson."

"Named after our Horatio?" interjected Gerry.

"Hardly!" snapped back Jim, "He was their enemy, and I thought it was the Americans who had no idea of history. Besides which they wouldn't have heard of him. He was young but had his own ship by the time of the War of Independence, which was sent to support a disastrous attack on Nicaragua. He contracted yellow fever for his pains and took a year to recover."

Gerry knew Jim would talk about any subject rather than his family. After years of saying he hated children and never wanted any, Jim now had a three-year-old son. Gerry knew if he wanted to annoy his old friend he only had to ask how the child was. Jim was not sure how his wife conceived as he went near her only when desperate. He thought he had been tricked but would get revenge by packing the brat (as he called him), off to Eton as soon as possible. So Jim continued, away from the family theme.

"Anyway, that's off the point. It's not important who he was named after but it was Rockefeller if you really need to know, who is his godfather, one of Kissinger's mates. Will be very useful to us in years to come."

Gerry forced another word in.

"Ford has only been Vice President little more than a month."

"Yes, but why do you think he was shoe-horned into that position? Not on merit, that's for sure. Just to be used."

"If it is true that LBJ said he spent too much time playing football without a helmet, then we might end up with a brain-damaged President."

Sir James smirked and added that it would not be the first and certainly not be the last. Anyway he preferred the former President's other put down, that Ford was so dumb he could not fart and chew gum at the same time. The prudish US media cleaned that up to walk and chew gum. They saw themselves as protectors of the nation's morals. When nine-year-old Phan Thi Kim Phuc was seen running naked after being severely burned by a Napalm attack during the Vietnam War, the media would not show the Pulitzer Prize winning photograph, not because of the atrocity, but because she had no clothes on. Almost as obscene was President Nixon wondering if the photo had been fixed. Years later Facebook banned it briefly as it could not distinguish between an iconic famous war image and child pornography - nor between porn and pictures of starving children in Bergen-Belsen without clothes. No wonder Disney makes three year old girls cover their nipples.

"Not the brightest then, but who wants a bright stooge? He played the role for his masters perfectly on the Warren Commission investigating Kennedy's death. We have him to thank for his part in the cover up of the plot to get rid of the Catholic Commie. Once Kennedy was onto us, and our banker friends, he had to go and they dealt with him. Kennedy got what was coming partly because of the arrogance he got from his Dad, but mainly as he was getting worryingly too close to understanding what we were up to. Thought he could stand up to the central banking system. The final straw was signing that Bill which allowed the US Government to print its own money. He printed over four billion dollars. That's American billions, i.e. four thousand million, not our British correct version where a billion is a million million. Anyway, one week later he was dead. There was a risk of being exposed. You can't murder the most important man in the world without coming under scrutiny. Ford helped us here. If he does take over from Nixon, big business won't be able to believe their luck that they have got their man into place so easily. The only man to be both Vice President and President without being elected to either office."

Sir James needed to get to the point and end the meeting. He preferred the company and comforts of his mistress Sonia to Gerry and a week in the States made him impatient, despite the girls the administration offered him. But Gerry was looking too comfortable slouched in the leather armchair nursing his whisky. To Sir James' irritation he went off at a tangent.

"I met Enid while you were in Barbados. She sends her regards and was sorry to have missed you."

Enid Riddell was well known to both their fathers. Very well known. There was a time when she was shared between them. She had been a fellow former member of the Right Club and as young boys Jim and Gerry remembered her as a frequent visitor to their houses. Except between 1940 and 1943 when she was detained under Defence Regulation 18b.

"She is looking rather frail now she is over seventy and was still badly shaken by Anna's death."

Her friend and another acquaintance of them all, Anna Wolkoff, had been killed in a road accident in Spain the previous August in a car driven by Enid.

"Enid told me Anna, as usual, wasn't wearing a seat belt and shot out of the car like a cannonball. Poor dear. She was like an aunt to me."

"And me, but lets get on Gerry. I have an important appointment."

"I'm with Anna, though it was her right not to be forced to wear a belt in a free society. The police say it will waste their time. Another example of where the Heath Government is misguide..."

Jim cut him short before he had completed the word misguided.

"Back to business. I learnt how they are dealing with healthcare and how Nixon will reverse some of LBJ's pinko reforms. We can follow although we will have to be a bit more subtle and devious. Seldon's ideas are good and can be built on. Keith Joseph started well at the Department of Health getting in our friends at McKinsey but has been disappointing since."

Gerry stopped Jim in full flow.

"Wasn't McKinsey that sex researcher?"

Sir James looked at him with disdain.

"That was Alfred Kinsey, you idiot. McKinsey are private US management consultants. You are teasing I hope?"

Gerry showed he knew more than it appeared, by quoting Kinsey.

"The only unnatural sex act is that which you cannot perform," and adding, "That's what they believe in Dolphin Square, anyway."

Jim continued, ignoring the intervention.

"Keith Joseph seems too timid in his lukewarm attacks on socialised medicine, which is odd and goes against all we thought about him. Anyway Woodward told me about how the Health Maintenance Organisation Act came about. Apparently early in 1971 Nixon and Ehrlichman met Edgar Kaiser who runs a scheme in California. All the incentives are towards less medical care, because the less care they give them the more money they make. Obvious really. Clearly healthcare is a multi-trillion dollar untapped market and we must get our fingers in the pie, and I mean trillion in our sense not the American corruption. They are ahead of us and want not only their pie but ours too. We need to use their tactics but secure our share before it is too late."

Gerry at first thought all this concentration on healthcare was a distraction, but through the whisky could still see how it was a cog in the big wheel of their goals of globalisation. He began to realise it was a big cog. After all, every one of the four billion on the planet needs healthcare so it could be the biggest market ever - and they need it over and over again. Furthermore the private health sector sell things the patients do not even know they need, things they have never heard of, and at a price of their own choosing. The perfect market for the vendor - one the purchaser does not query.

"Woodward re-emphasised the need to get rid of the word service and replacing it with business. In their eyes service is a dirty word, except the service they got from their mistresses. Woodward also told Sir James to push much further with infiltration. He thought the group had made fairly good progress in a relatively short time getting their men in place in the media, publishers and the unions. Even the church, although there were a few annoying Archbishops around. They were pushing at an open door with the Armed Forces, the police and the judiciary. But Woodward wanted no stone unturned. Publishers needed leaning on. Small inconsequential organisations like the Women's Institute and Boy Scouts need to be controlled. The trick with the *BBC* worked well. Even though it was, to be fair, neutral. The masterstroke had been to convince the public it had a left wing bias. So the balance needed to be altered, much easier then to load it with those from the right. Then to continue to complain the Corporation was left cemented them in place and gave an opportunity to get more of our people in. And it is important to keep making the case for an avowedly biased counter-balance.

Ah yes, back to that Aussie called Murdoch. He has an ego the size of Jupiter and took over the *Sun* newspaper about five years ago. I think he'll be a pushover as long as we help him with his media interest, as fundamentally he believes what we believe. That means destroying the *BBC* as much as we can. Then there is his rival that Czech-born Jew called Hoch who now goes under the name of Robert Maxwell. Don't you remember he tried to buy the *News Of The World* before Murdoch, but the owners allowed the editor to run a brilliantly racist campaign to keep a foreign socialist Jew from getting his mucky paws on it? Murdoch is known to despise the peasants, although of course he is one himself. He thinks with a diet of tits and bums he can reduce their attention span to that of a newt, to not then question what he puts on the front page. They will then believe anything. He wants investigative journalism to be exterminated. He doesn't want people looking into what he gets up to and nor do we.

Moving on. That miners' leader, Joe Gormley, too nice and despite the current strike he's difficult to demonise in the media although they have tried their best. So plans are in line to put a man called Scargill in charge who often says stupid things. He will lead them into the elephant trap we will set up. That way they can get the public to hate him. Then the public is more likely to back the plans to castrate the trades unions. But we will neuter the unions with or without the public."

"It's actually quite a measure of our success that we have managed to get the ordinary working man, many of them anyway, to hate and despise the only body that really stands up for them," said Gerry.

"But the unions will become irrelevant within a decade or so anyway. We will use debt as a method of controlling the masses. We are taking the brakes off borrowing. In abolishing the rules designed to protect the consumer we want to persuade everyone to go into debt. This serves two purposes. It, *takes the waiting out of wanting,* good slogan eh, which makes the public feel better, but more importantly it puts them at our mercy? How can they possibly go on strike if they know the credit card bailiffs will be knocking on their doors? And once in debt we can keep them in debt for years with high interest rates. The bankers that back us are delighted of course. As with most of these moneymaking schemes to fleece the poor the yanks first thought of it, first the Diners Club Card in 1950 then American Express in 1958. We have tested the water with Barclaycard launched eight years ago and Access the year before last."

"Ah so that explains why the stigma seems no longer to be applied to debt and borrowing?" Gerry said, as though a light had just come on.

"We will be pushing this hard. Anyway back to Woodward. He was convincing about grooming businessmen, especially the young ones who had influence in the next generation."

Sir James explained further.

"The hippie who backed Mike Oldfield's *Tubular Bells* last year, a man called Branson, we need him to be onside but appear cool, or whatever the word is, to drag in the youngsters. All the professions like medicine and law and teaching need de-professionalising to neuter them too. Woodward's most interesting plan is to infiltrate all the political parties. The only problem with the bugging at Watergate was getting caught. Just make sure that doesn't happen, he said. First the Tories, all agreed Heath must go, but to be replaced by whom? Keith Joseph, although fairly intellectually sound, had proved not determined enough and a disappointment at the Health Department as I mentioned. Enoch Powell has clawed back some of his treachery over not finishing off the NHS in the early 1960s, with his 'rivers of blood' speech, but can't be controlled."

Gerry chipped in, to Sir James' horror.

"Denis is still pestering me about Margaret, you know?"

"Don't be ridiculous Gerry, we can't have a woman as leader of the Conservative Party. Totally unelectable and we'd be a laughing stock. She'd want to powder her nose, or go shopping when she should be abolishing the unions. And who would look after poor old Denis?"

He continued.

"The Labour Party take-over will have to be a ten to fifteen year plan. If Wilson beats Heath in a few weeks, he won't last that long. Rumour has it he is losing it. His mother had Alzheimer's and all those plots against him have taken their toll. We can take credit for that. But we have enough on him to blackmail him into an early retirement. One thing Cecil King's plot achieved is that we've made him very paranoid, although he is right to be. All the burgling of the homes of his aides and the bugged phones is enough to unnerve anyone. We can then get a weak temporary caretaker in, someone unelectable to buy time to see if the Conservatives deliver, then our man if not, someone like Michael Foot. Eventually getting the two main parties to be almost indistinguishable from each other is the trick, although appearing to offer radically different policies to the public so they think democracy works. The so-called Labour man would need careful grooming, the usual trick. Acts very left at first to get the confidence of the nutty extremists, so has to join CND, be anti-Europe, support the workers, you know the sort of stuff. Then once elected to carry on with our Tory ideology, but carefully wrapped up in modernising public services, which of course really means reducing and privatising them.

Meanwhile, to also gradually replace all Labour MPs by imposing vetted candidates selected by the leadership who are of course all puppets of ours? MPs will become no more than salesmen for us and the companies they represent, although the public won't know that. Those not so persuadable will soon change their minds with a nice boardroom job or an honour. They won't even have to pay for it. The genius though is to control the lot of them with what we know about them. As Woodward reminded me, Chuck Colson, Nixon's chief counsel, the one who organised the Watergate break in, had a sign on his office wall, *once you have them by the balls, their hearts and minds will follow*. It's all in a series of files."

"Files?" Gerry repeated, puzzled.

"Fill individual files with blackmail material. Sex is the obvious. We already have dossiers on so many anyway, especially the group involved in the Dolphin Square paedophile ring. It's pathetic how weak are some of our establishment. Every walk of life goes through those mansion doors."

"Even the clergy?" Gerry said.

"Especially the clergy!" Sir James smiled, "They are up to their eyes in it. Or should I say crotches?"

"We are especially strong in the security field. Maurice Oldfield got promoted last year to head of the Secret Intelligence Service because of his visits to Dolphin Square, that Elm Guest House in Barnes, and male prostitutes. Same with Michael Hanley, he ended up as our new MI5 Director General because of his involvement and visits to Barnes. No good having someone in such a powerful position without having something on them. In fact it's essential or they get too big for their boots."

"We have our teeth into your lot too. You wouldn't believe what some of your generals and top brass get up to. They may be fucking war heroes running around on the Normandy beaches of Sword, Juno and Gold, but they let off steam in weird ways, mostly illegal. It's our McCarthyism, but secret."

Tricky territory, Gerry thought. Especially with what they both got up to. However to have a mistress was normal and he felt they had nothing to fear and were not hypocritical. What was it their mate Jimmy Goldsmith once said, *when a man marries his mistress, he creates a job vacancy*? Proves it is mainstream and acceptable now. Otherwise what were the swinging sixties all about? Fiddling with little children, and worse, and certainly murdering them, was in a different league however. Trafficking them from abroad, from orphanages and council children's homes was the modern slave trade. Very lucrative, easy to run and, in many cases, carrying on a family tradition, but a brilliant way to control those in power and get them dancing like marionettes.

"Even the present Prime Minister with his yacht trips to the Channel Islands is under suspicion. It was rumoured he had visited Haut de la Garenne, the youth hostel on Jersey. There is just no proof yet but we have a team working on it. Once we have that blackmail material he will not get away with phrases like *the unacceptable face of capitalism* of our friend Tiny Rowland at Lonrho. We would have had him under better control."

Anyway there is no such thing as an unacceptable form of capitalism Gerry and Sir James believed. Capitalism should be able to invade every corner of the earth, irrespective of the consequences. Rolls Royce should be able to do what it wished. Yes, there will be casualties, but who cares?

"One more thing Gerry. Rein in those ex-army buffoons of yours, will you?"

"You mean dear old Major Alexander Greenwood, I suppose?" replied Gerry.

"He is so stupid he might discredit all of us and all we're trying to do. Trying to establish a private army with which he tells everyone he wants to take over the airports, *BBC* and Buckingham Palace. Very unhelpful. But I also mean General Sir Walter Walker, as you know, until recently NATO Commander of Northern Europe. He says too publicly what we believe. He wants Enoch as PM. I know he has been in contact with Mountbatten and has written a speech for the Queen ready for the takeover. Also the wrong people overheard Lord Carve discussing military intervention. It hasn't happened only because Heath doesn't have the whole of the ruling class behind him. He has declared five states of emergency in four years as PM. He has lost all credibility. Do you know how many times the Emergency Powers Act has been used before Heath since it was introduced in 1920? Just six. Then there's Quintin Hogg, Heath's Lord Chancellor, saying it is legal for the army to shoot unarmed civilians. These people may be right but they have to be persuaded to keep their mouths shut. Operation Clockwork Orange is all we need. You know all about that."

"Indeed. I know it well from my time in Northern Ireland. It is run there by the Information Policy Unit from the Army Press Office and works in conjunction with MI5. Colin Wallace is the Ministry of Defence press officer with whom I have had dealings. It plays a key role in the disinformation against Wilson. Wallace thinks this is responsible for the growth of paramilitary organisations as encouraged by Greenwood and Walker."

"Did you come across Major General Frank Kitson when he was serving in Northern Ireland?"

"Yes, briefly. He gave me a copy of his book *Low Intensity Operations* in which he advocates the use of the army in certain civil situations in Britain."

"Well, he needs to be careful too," said Jim.

"The campaign against Wilson and its distribution to overseas newspapers is a carbon copy of the Zinoviev letter which helped destroy the first Government of Ramsay MacDonald in 1924."

104

Gerry was solid on his own territory now.

"That was a forgery printed by our wonderful *Daily Mail* made up to discredit the Labour Party. History repeating itself. But there is a good side to these so-called troubles which is a euphemism for war," smiled Gerry, "The security apparatus designed to combat Irish Republicanism is used against the workers too. We just mustn't overdo it, that's all."

Jim had had enough and got up ready to march out of his club and without any finesse.

"I've a meeting with Andrew Doolan, my young architect, who is finishing off my new house near Edinburgh."

He left Gerry with an expression of confusion on his face.

9 - FISHING AND BRUSH-OFF

YOU'RE SO VAIN

You walked into the party like you were walking onto a yacht
Your hat strategically dipped below one eye
Your scarf it was apricot
You had one eye in the mirror as you watched yourself gavotte
And all the girls dreamed that they'd be your partner

You're so vain, I'll bet you think this song is about you
Don't you? Don't you?

You had me several years ago when I was still quite naïve
Well you said that we made such a pretty pair
And that you would never leave
But you gave away the things you loved and one of them was me

Carly Simon (1972)

Rob despised everything about Clifford Wessel. If Rob had his way he would not even have been considered for medical school. In Rob's opinion Clifford was exactly what the medical profession did not need if it was to succeed in serving patients properly and retaining public support. But to the Establishment he was exactly the right type.

Clifford was the most arrogant git Rob had ever known - God's gift to God, as well as to women. Not particularly good looking, but thought he was. He was sure all the girls dreamed of being his partner. Not exactly funny, but thought he was. Not superior to everyone else, but thought he was. Not caring about anyone else, and almost proud of that - self-centred and pleased about that. Clifford was totally money focused. The sort who could not understand why anyone would give money away to charity?

"Why? What for? It only encourages them. What's in it for me?"

He did not need to worry about status as he already had it. When they first met at a BMA conference in 1995 Cliff had just qualified.

He stormed through his post-graduate training to get his Consultant Ophthalmic surgeon post within ten years, although he had had rooms in Harley Street for some time before that. His path was smoothed by connections including a cousin who was Ophthalmic Surgeon to The Queen. By all accounts he was a real bastard to his staff - terrorised them. He was quite open about the string of women who visited him in his rooms. Everyone knew except his wife. Rob could not feel sorry for her though as the only time they met she reminded him of Cruella De Vil. She was the Claire to Kevin Spacey's President Francis Underwood in *House of Cards*. And Wessel was as ruthless as Underwood. It was rumoured he was already attending meetings amongst the powerful inner circle of the Conservative party to groom him for high office.

One measure of his almost delusional self-confidence and arrogance was when he strayed into the territory of others. He designed a new artificial hip, which he modestly named after himself. He knew very little about orthopaedics but guessed with an ageing population they would be needed by the shedload, so a real money-spinner. Clifford told Rob over coffee at conference how he was to make his fortune. He spoke to Rob like he was addressing the conference audience even though he was a few years younger. The speech sounded rehearsed and one he had delivered many times before. He addressed Rob almost grudgingly, as though it was a waste of his precious time just addressing one person, especially an inferior. He always sought the widest possible audience to get his unshakeable views across and to get his hip into every conversation. He was not quite a Sir Lancelot Spratt type - at least Sir Lancelot was not in the profession only to get rich. It seemed Cliff's ambition was to be like him in attitude though. His party piece was to impersonate James Robertson Justice with quotes such as, *a good surgeon should have the eye of a hawk, the heart of a lion and the hands of a lady*, adding, *and the bank balance of a Rothschild.*

"I've removed enough stones in my time to cobble a courtyard."

It was quite endearing at first but Rob had heard them too many times.

Cliff socialised only with those he understood, so that meant orthopaedic and other ophthalmic surgeons whose main aim also was just to get rich. He had no understanding of geriatricians, paediatricians, or general practitioners. How were they to afford to send all their sons to the best public schools, have a few spare houses and a yacht when they did not spend their week in private practice? Unbelievable. When Rob told him he was a GP, Cliff clearly meant it when, quick as a flash, he retorted.

"Oh dear, sorry to hear that."

Lord Moran, Churchill's doctor, said that GPs were would-be consultants who had fallen off the lower rung of the ladder. This was the man who made money by breaking patient confidentiality by publishing all about Churchill's ailments. It was taught at medical school in Rob's day that GPs were a lower form of life and Cliff made sure this attitude continued.

Cliff told all he had worked his way up the BMA ladder and got the position he wanted, Chair of the Private Practices Committee. In reality there was no work involved. It was an escalator straight to the top as his right. A minor role in the grand scheme of things but it helped his income. He was soon on the Governing Council - not an ordinary elected member but one of the inner circle who manipulated all the decisions of conference in their favour. He would not have wasted his precious time otherwise. But his long-term political ambitions were much wider. He rarely spoke at the podium unless he felt a vote might go the wrong way and he had to stand up to threaten and bully. When he did speak it was always pro-Government and their reforms, which in reality meant undermining and eventually abolishing the NHS.

This is how Rob managed to bump into him most years. However, Rob had decided that he would give up going. There were too many like Cliff there. There were the pompous, self-important, those who preached how medicine should be practised but were useless at it themselves, those who would not recognise a patient if one was smacked in the face by one, those who seemed to want to destroy the profession by cooperating with the enemy at every turn, and of course those out to oversee the dismantling of the NHS.

There was another group that appeared so old it sometimes seemed like the Darby and Joan Club outing. A few even remembered the pre-NHS days and pleaded with conference to put up more of a fight to save it. Rob had a lot of time for them, but the chief officers just put their views down to Aloysius Alzheimer's disease.

Rob's small group was the reason though for his persisting so long. He had never met such a bunch of people before who were completely on his wavelength and would fight for the NHS. No hidden agenda or ulterior motives. It was they who persuaded him to stay-in-the-tent-pissing-out, rather than go outside-the-tent-and-piss-in. Now though he wanted to do more than piss in. Cliff and the hierarchy who allowed the Government to get away with their privatisation outraged him. They who were seduced by being invited into the corridors of power and who now were waiting for their gongs. Treacherous bastards. Selfish gits. Only in class ridden Britain, with a corrupt honours system, exemplified by jokers like Sir Mark Thatcher. He and his group knew what they were up to. Aiding and abetting a classic privatisation tactic, used before with British Rail, all the energy companies and telecommunications, as outlined by Noam Chomsky, *defund, make sure things don't work, people get angry, then hand it over to private capital.*

In this case so many had their fingers in the private healthcare companies' pies. Rob was suspicious that Wessel was behind the private company that had taken over Hinchingbrooke Hospital in Cambridgeshire. The staff was told they were failing, as the hospital had a £40 million PFI related debt. Their plan was to cut staff, increase the number of private patients, reduce nurse-patient ratios and downgrade departments. The exact model that Stafford Hospital adopted which led to disaster. Standards dropped, but that failed to stop the company being awarded further contracts.

Last year at Conference Rob got this off his chest. He got up onto the platform to speak in a debate and told them they were like quislings and collaborators in Nazi-occupied Europe, cooperating with the enemy and other malevolent forces who have invaded and taken over our island's NHS. Before he could continue to say he was a resistance fighter who would lead the tarring and feathering of

109

them all, the microphone was shut off and he was not called again. The Chair ordered his speech be erased from the record.

So Cliff knew what Rob was like and Rob knew what Cliff was like. He always adopted a superior attitude and it was not an act. Cliff never failed to mention that he had slept with Suzy. Every time. Sadistic sod just enjoyed the taunting. As best man at Suzy's brother's wedding he was the target of the bridesmaids apparently and could have had his pick but Suzy got there first. Rob hated to admit it but he could see what women saw in him with his pewter-grey eyes, an aura of power and total self-confidence. But any attraction, Rob thought, should surely disappear as soon as he opened his mouth? But no.

Her brother Jeff regretted his choice of best man almost from the moment he asked him. It was alcohol induced. They had met through Wessel's older stepbrother Ivan. Jeff was working at Conservative Central Office at 32 Smith Square helping to draw up plans for the Poll Tax. Cliff, although a medical student at the time, was always hanging around in the background keen to assist and to see whom he could chat to that might be influential. They had been superficially close because of their love of rugby, playing for the same team. It was after a heavy drinking session, following an unexpected victory that Jeff asked Cliff. But they had lost contact within a few years, their friendship a very fallacious, rugby club, alcohol driven one. On the field he was a bastard as a player, going for peoples eyes and squeezing their bollocks in the scrum. The drifting apart did not bother either of them but Cliff made it clear that he wanted to move in higher circles and Suzy's family was not good enough. He was the first most people knew to have a phone in his car and a croquet lawn he never used. When Cruella De Vil instructed Harrods Estates to find them a suitable property, it was made clear they would not consider anything without a tennis court and swimming pool. Another first was his website set up to promote his private practice. Rob was convinced Wessel had written most reviews himself. All along the lines of *what a wonderful doctor...* but maybe a few were convinced.

Those higher circles he moved into now included the ex-Bullingdon Club mates of Ivan, who was serving his second term as the Conservative Mayor of London. Well before Cliff's stepbrother ran for office he had decided it ought to be with a different surname. He took his mother's maiden name of Humphrey. This was rather forced on him as Cliff had started bragging about being a distant cousin to Horst Wessel, the storm trooper who Goebbels had made into a martyr for the Nazi cause after his murder in 1930. So he became Mayor Ivan Humphrey. Horst Wessel's grave in St Nicholas Cemetery in Berlin had been vandalised and removed to stop the site being a rallying point for neo-Nazis, so when Cliff filed a petition asking that Horst's gravestone be restored on the eve of the Mayoral elections, Ivan was furious with his younger half-brother.

Ivan had only just recovered from the scandal involving his German father. Herman Wessel was born in Berlin at the start of the war to a mother who was awarded the Ehrenkreuz der Deutschen Mutter or Cross of Honour of the German Mother and an SS-Oberst-Gruppenfuhrer in the Schutzstaffel. The family ended up in Argentina when the Americans sneaked them away from the advancing Russians in 1945 as part of Operation Paperclip. He pretended to be a scientist who would be useful to them. They spent a few years there mixing with the likes of Adolf Eichman, Gunther Niemand and Joseph Mengele. Aged nineteen Herman left them and bluffed his way into Britain by securing a job at the German Embassy in Belgrave Square. He wrote to the Ambassador, Hans von Herwarth, pretending that his father had been associated with Claus von Stauffenberg's 20th July plot to assassinate Hitler. The Ambassador was a cousin by marriage of the Operation Valkyrie leader. Soon after his arrival he began to secretly make right wing contacts. The Nazi connections were bad enough for Ivan to fend off, but then it came to light that Herman had left his wife, Lady Sophie De Laet Waldo Sibthorp Humphrey, Ivan's mother, for his mistress, who was already pregnant with Cliff. It was when Ivan decided to run for Mayor of London that the newspapers dug further into his private life. They found that Herman was a member of the British National Party, then the November 9th Society. Ivan was tainted further, but Cliff loved it. He was proud. He even gave an interview in which he defended the Society's policies. They were anti many things: immigration, communism, abortion, homosexuality and foreign aid. They denied the Holocaust, supported David Irving, argued for state control of all media outlets and were anti-Semitic. The party claimed its name came from the date in 1923 when sixteen Nazis lost their lives at Feldherrnhalle as part of the Munich Beer Hall Putsch, but Cliff said it was based on Kristallnacht in 1938. Despite this, Ivan was still elected - twice.

Rob was unaware of all this but assumed there was some scandal involving their father. It was clearly something awkward Ivan did not want to be associated with. The association he did not seem to mind was with the thugs in the 1986 Bullingdon photo dressed in their dark navy blue tailcoats, mustard waistcoats and sky blue bow ties, which included Hubert Witney who had been PM for the last three years. So Cliff had cultivated connections a few years older than he was. Contemporaries of his at Oxford included Neville Gideon. He was in the same Bullingdon Club photo in the early 1990s.

Wessel did his bit by being Chairman of his local Conservative Association. He appointed himself although he soon got bored with parochial local politics. He had been instrumental in selecting a McKinsey woman as Conservative prospective parliamentary candidate. It was a forgone conclusion that she would be elected in Tory heartland. She was immediately manipulated onto the Health Select Committee to help push the McKinsey project of NHS privatisation. The press and media did not seem interested though in this blatant conflict of interest despite the lobbying of Rob's friends.

Rob first had the idea of ringing Cliff the day before but dismissed it as stupid and risking humiliation. Now though his fingers hovered over the numbers of his Harley Street Clinic. The idea was to see what he could find out about what was going on. Cliff was so arrogant as if he was planning to rob a bank he would boast about it. Cliff was known as a gossip and a braggart. It had crossed Rob's mind that if it went well he might eventually try to infiltrate the inner circle. However, his sensible mind quickly dismissed that idea. Who did he think he was, Kim Philby - more like Johnny English? That would be a risky tactic and doomed to failure in light of his reputation. For some reason though he felt the need to try to get some evidence on what he was rapidly realising was a plot against the NHS. He doubted he would find out much but thought he had nothing to lose.

When faced with something unpleasant to do Rob always told himself if you have to swallow a frog just do it. So he did it. After quite a wait his secretary put Rob through. Even the initial pleasantries left Rob thinking it was already fifteen - love to Cliff.

"How are you?"

He responded to the usual greeting with the Alan B'stard attitude.

"Perfect, naturally, and getting richer by the minute."

He didn't bother asking how Rob was.

To make the call more legitimate Rob heard himself saying.

"I'm ringing to invite you to my wedding. You did such a splendid job at Suzy's brother's do. I've never heard a best man's speech like it. The jokes about Jeff's divorced parents and his bride's passion for S&M were unbelievable."

Rob could not bring himself to be sycophantically complimentary but thought Wessel would interpret it as flattery anyway. He did not really believe any criticism would penetrate Wessel's ego anyway.

"You'll get a proper invite but I want you to put the date in your diary."

"Be delighted old boy. Jeff is in the USA isn't he? Went there I presume to forget his humiliations on the rugby pitch?"

"Yes he is divorced now but I don't think it was directly related to your speech, Cliff."

Wessel ignored him and continued.

"I'll be there, assuming I'm not extracting ten cataracts that day at three thousand pounds a time."

Then, not letting Rob get a word in he went straight for the jugular.

"So finally making an honest woman of the old slag are you? Second time for you isn't it? Won't be the last, I'm sure. Don't you know it's only the female wasps that sting?"

Rob was just about to offer the date when.

"How's her famous lung capacity? You've probably found out yourself but she could go down on you for hours, it seemed, without taking a breath. Must have practised as a deep sea diver, eh?"

Thirty - love.

That was his best taunt yet. He could only get two minutes out of Suzy. He had to hand it to the man, he was good at producing pain in people. He was aware of the sweat dripping down his back as he realised he would have to break the news to her that he had invited to their wedding someone neither of them could stand. This was more terrifying and worrying than anything Cliff could say. He could feel himself tensing up as he waited for the next put down. Please, please, tell me you cannot make it Rob was hoping, but he was unlikely to be put out of his misery today so he continued.

"Would be good to see you Cliff. There will be a few familiar faces. The usual suspects."

Rob tried to steer toward his purpose. He had to tackle this head-on.

"How's life generally, the BMA and your private practice?"

Cliff served an ace in response to that. Forty - love.

Rob knew he had to be devious.

"Listen, I know you are no fan of the NHS, and I'm so disillusioned I'm thinking after all you may be right. The NHS is at an end, I realise that now. I'm in my last ten years in practice and I would like to help with the transition to a better system before I finally pack it in. I think I've got a fair bit of general practice know-how to contribute."

There was silence. Rob was not sure how to continue. Was he, to Rob's surprise, taking the bait? So he just said the next thing that came into his head.

"Do you and the team need any help drawing up your plans and perhaps a GP perspective?"

Rob was aware of how transparent he sounded, but he did not know a better way of putting it. There was just a cough. It seemed clear Wessel was happy for him to carry on.

"Three million patients now belong to GP practices run by Virgin Health. That makes Branson the biggest GP in the country and patients haven't got a clue. It was a masterstroke of Blair to let them all use the NHS logo. The GPs have to refer to Branson's other companies as you know so are you worried that you might lose some business?"

Forty - fifteen.

Cliff batted that away by saying that he had more than enough business - a typical indication that he could not think beyond himself. The offer of help was noted but they didn't need any assistance. The GP committee were doing a splendid job and completely fooling the more bolshie grassroots. After all, Wessel reminded Rob, they had just voted to support the introduction of patient charges. Rob sensed he had been rumbled but was not sure so he moved on.

"Are you still friendly with Gideon?"

"We see each other at the club from time to time."

Wessel got more serious.

"Listen, he and his Government have been good to me and mine, and I'm richer than you could ever dream of as a result. I won't shit on them for you. In fact I won't do anything for you. Number one is my only concern."

Rob now thought the game was up so fished further.

"Strange how that Natalie girl who spilled the beans on his coke habit and masochism didn't get more publicity. Do you think he was part of the Westminster VIP paedo ring?"

The atmosphere had chilled. Rob knew he had gone too far.

"Not very good at this are you, old fruit? Your wife to be should know about Gideon's preferences. Bet she gave him a good time?"

Game to Cliff.

"You don't fool me Baigent. I've heard your rants at conference. What are you up to? Trying to get the dirt? If you turned from your crusade to join us, it would be like Richard Dawkins taking communion. You won't get anything from me. Besides, you're fucking paranoid. Take my advice and drop it, and get back to your little surgery. The boys in Tavistock Square will not be impressed when they hear about this. You really don't know what you're up against. We've rewritten history to make out the BMA were in favour of the NHS in the 1940s. We are still keen to give that impression, but it is only that. You had better understand how powerful we are and the influence we have. Now we are in control and things are going to change. We will win and things will never be the same again. We can rewrite whatever suits us. Watch your back old boy or before you know it a GMC complaint may land on your doormat. You won't be the biggest fish we've had to fry and the heat will finish you off. If you've any doubt check out the fate of Alex Ephialtes. Anyway, no one will give an old leftie like you any credibility."

Rob tried to salvage something.

"Only making polite conversation. See you at the wedding I hope?"

But the phone had gone dead. Rob was shaken but had tried not to show it. As with any tense upset he could not quite take in what had happened. Had Wessel just more or less admitted that there was a plot against the NHS? The comment about someone called Ephialtes who he had never heard of was immediately forgotten.

10 - DEATHS AND THREATS

MY GENERATION

People try to put us d-down
Just because we get around
Things they do look awful cold
I hope I die before I get old

This is my generation

The Who (1965)

To pee in the same urinal as Keith Moon. An honour and a privilege. Moon was to the drums what Jimi Hendrix was to the guitar. Only the night before the Who's drummer really was in the same bathroom in Peppermint Park in Soho. He had been to see *The Buddy Holly Story* with Paul and Linda McCartney and they all dined there afterwards. He then went home to the flat in Curzon Place he was renting from Harry Nilsson, where Cass Elliot had died four years before. He died in the night. Both were thirty-two. His last words to his Swedish model girlfriend were, *if you don't like it you can fuck off.*

This boys' piss-up had been arranged for weeks though and they had no idea the place would become famous overnight. The food fight was spontaneous but they still did not get thrown out. Six of them travelled up together but Rob and Jerry were at a table by themselves. The two of them had hit it off from their first encounter. Rob instinctively knew Jerry had not one neuron of prejudice in his unique brain. The others fancied their chances with a group of girls.

It was September 1978 and Rob was only fourteen. In those days no barman ever bothered to check ages. Why should they? It was business to them. No one carried ID and the police left the bars alone. There was no need to speak about the arrangement. The free drinks and other entertainment were provided in exchange.

Back then the boys' entertainment was mainly football and drinking. They had been to White Hart Lane to see Spurs lose to Swansea 3-1 in the League Cup the night before. In those days they could just turn up and pay at the turnstile, and five minutes before kick-off. With Crystal Palace playing away at Sheffield the previous Saturday, which was too far to travel, on that day it was a choice between the Chelsea Shed and the Den. They chose the Den where Millwall lost to Brighton 4-1. They were pleased to see Peter Ward who had beaten the club scoring record the year before with thirty-six goals. Jerry thought Ron Greenwood should call him up to the England squad. Although they missed seeing Bonetti, Ron Harris and Ray Wilkins losing to Leeds 3-0 they thought they had chosen the better match. At Chelsea 'Sundance' Hawley scored twice in a side still with Paul Madeley and Tony Currie. Rob predicted that both Brighton and Palace would be promoted to Division One this season.

"With Terry Venables in charge, and Dave Swindlehurst up front, we are going places mate," he said.

He bet Jerry £1 who thought West Ham would bounce straight back?

"Not with John Lyall still in charge. That Trevor Brooking plays better for West Ham than England though," replied Rob, "Don't like this new stupid American import of calling the karzi a bathroom. There's no fucking bath in there. They could equally call it the snooker room. There's no snooker table either," Rob, already having drunk too much, was slurring his words.

They were still at school together but Jerry was really the one responsible for the most important part of Rob's education. Jerry introduced him to the Beatles, the Stones, the Who, and Led Zep, plus pot, Penthouse, Mayfair, New Musical Express, his first strip joint, and Crystal Palace Football Club, also the Campaign for Real Ale and politics. Palace was Rob's local team now the family lived in Purley. They had moved up from Margate when his Dad changed jobs and area in an effort to protect his wife from prejudice. This coincided with Rob's start at secondary school. Jerry was the first in his class to have sex, always something to give teenagers street cred, but lost a few points when his corny chat up line, *your perfume drives me wild with desire* was overheard. Apart from that everyone seemed to admire him. He was more mature than his age, even shaving before arriving at school.

Jerry was streets ahead of Rob in his political maturity. Rob often found himself way out of his depth. Jerry would talk about so much that Rob did not understand but he dared not admit it. He had introduced Rob to Orwell's *1984* and had interested him by predicting Orwell was wrong on two counts. It did not go far enough, and *1984* was too early. Jerry was certain the masses would be totally controlled in everything they do, say, believe, and think, but it was more likely to be 2000 before these evil powers achieved their goal. Jerry was convinced they were plotting domination but, after the lessons of failed revolutions, they were proceeding in a subtle and devious manner. They would win by manipulation and fear. The thought police would see into our minds and turn families against one another. The Ministry of Truth would get an iron grip on what happened in the past. Those who control the past, control the future. Whosoever controls the present controls the past. They would own and control the truth. Shifting allegiances in any argument or claiming black is now white without anyone noticing would become easy. Facts would become their facts. Politicians would use this reality control but they would soon be out-played by stronger hidden forces.

"For fuck's sake read Martin Jacques in *Marxism Today*," was what Jerry fired at Rob when he looked mystified.

Peppermint Park occasionally had bands playing. One advertised for Friday was Desmond And The Tutus, which neither of them had heard of, nor Dire Straits. When they looked further down the list they began to wonder if it was a joke. Marilyn And The Monroes, Holly And The Ivy's, Toad The Wet Sprocket, Hootie And The Blowfish, Biff Hitler And The Violent Mood Swings, Scrotum Pole, Rumplforskin, and Quasimodo And The Eunuchs - all due to play soon. One of their mates said they must go to see Dire Straits. They were playing in a pub in Deptford. The common thought was they wouldn't get anywhere if they were from Deptford so they didn't bother.

Rob, in his inebriated state, then went from what seemed like talking to himself to saying to Jerry Dolan his old mate.

"He had an extra five years."

"Five years? What you on about?" Jerry slurred back.

"You know, the 27 Club. Keith Moon. Rock legends who died at twenty-seven. It's that dangerous age to be a rock star."

"Well I hope I die before I get old."

"Usual quiz… lets take it in turns and the one to dry up gets the next two rounds."

"You're on. Brian Jones."

"Jimi Hendrix."

"Janis Joplin."

"Cheap thrills… too bluesy for me."

Then they sang the intro to *Me And Bobby McGee* together.

"Jim Morrison."

Then something weird happened. Jerry said, "Amy Winehouse," but she would not be born for another five years.

It was like being on a trip. Rob came back with Kurt Cobain but he would have only been eleven and was not to die for another sixteen years. It was as though they could see the future.

"Pete Ham from Badfinger."

Back to reality. He died three years ago. They both remembered him hanging himself in his Surrey garage.

"That Echo And The Bunnymen guy who died on his motorbike… Pete de Freitus," said Rob.

"He doesn't count. You can't have him," said Jerry.

"Why not?"

"'Cos it hasn't happened yet. Not 'til 1989."

"What about Amy Winehouse then? That's even further in the future?"

All very weird, Jerry was struggling now, and then he burst out.

"Ron McKernan from Grateful Dead. He counts. 1973 if I'm not mistaken?"

"Then I think I must insist Richey Edwards is allowed into the 27 Club even though he only disappeared and that hasn't happened yet. Not for another seventeen years. Where will we be then? What will we be doing, I wonder?"

Then they both started playing air guitar to *Australia* the Manic Street Preachers track - even though the band had not even been formed in 1978 let alone the track written. Der der der der da der der der der. Officially declared 'presumed dead' in 2008, Rob knew even though it was only 1978. And it continued. After buying the next two rounds, Jerry changed the subject. This was turning sinister.

"We're finalising the plot to kill Thatcher. She'll die with half her corrupt evil and smug cabinet when we blow up the Grand Hotel in Brighton. It'll be at one of their love-in conferences. That'll knock the smug expressions off their faces. Hopefully detach their faces from their heads."

"What the hell are you talking about?" Rob was shocked. Was Jerry winding him up? "She's only Leader of the Opposition. There's no saying the British public will elect a woman?"

"We already know what she will do. She will destroy society, as we know it. Abolish effective trade unionism, dismantle our manufacturing industry and the welfare state, close the mines and sell off all our assets including council houses, then abolish the State. Plus outlaw gays, abortion and abolish the NHS. She has to be got rid of."

Into view came the faces of those at the next table, characters from *An American Werewolf In London* and *Shaun Of The Dead*; next to them Sexy Sadie, the Maharishi, no John Lennon though. Richey Edwards walked in. Rob recognised him immediately, but Jerry seemed oblivious and carried on talking.

Richey walked over slowly towards them giving Rob the opportunity to speak to him.

"I thought you had jumped off the Severn Bridge?"

"Yes, and no one survives that," Richey said and immediately drew a Glock 19 from under his leather jacket and shot Jerry in the face. The friends they came with all moved over from the bar and started laughing. Rob was splattered with blood and brain matter and started shouting.

"Arrrh, get it off me! Jenny, Jenny get it off me! I feel like Jackie Kennedy, get it off me!"

"Rob, Rob, bloody hell Rob, wake up. You're screaming in your sleep. You're having a nightmare. What is it? Get what off you? And my name's Suzy by the way, you git."

He was coming round but was drenched in sweat. Suzy tried to lighten the mood but she thought her heart was going to come out of her chest.

"Manchester United losing again? England in another penalty shoot-out?"

He sat on the edge of the bed. Suzy could not tell if he had properly woken up. He tried to compose himself.

"Do you remember me telling you about my old mate Jerry who suddenly seemed to disappear off the face of the earth years ago? Well I've just had this weird vivid dream about him. I have not thought about him for ages. He was plotting to kill Thatcher. Then in my dream was shot himself."

Suzy had her arm around him.

"Just disappeared like Richey Edwards. Think you are right. I'm going a bit mad with paranoia."

"Sounds horrible. Pity his plot didn't happen. But let's get back to sleep now. We have busy days ahead."

Then after a pause.

"Who the fuck's Richey Edwards?"

11 - INTIMIDATION AND RUTHLESSNESS

MEAN

You, with your words like knives
And swords and weapons that you use against me
You have knocked me off my feet again
Got me feeling like a nothing
You, with your voice like nails on a chalkboard
Calling me out when I'm wounded
You, picking on the weaker man

Well you can take me down with just one single blow
But you don't know, what you don't know...

Someday I'll be big enough so you can't hit me
And all you're ever gonna be is mean
Why you gotta be so mean?

Taylor Swift (2010)

The sound of the phone ringing interrupted Rob's train of thought. Mrs Sharma was exhibiting a list of worrying symptoms. Any experienced GP knew to sit up and pay attention when someone who hardly ever attends surgery shows up. He had last seen her five years ago, which was unusual for a woman her age, and that was only about her daughter. The family was well known to the practice, however, for not very happy reasons.

Mrs Sharma was a delightful third generation Indian and proud of her heritage. She delighted in telling Rob when they first met that her name meant joy, shelter or comfort in Sanskrit. Her partner, Marko Visnjic, had escaped the siege of Dubrovnik during the Croatian War of Independence. His family had died at the hands of Slobodan Milosevic and Marko remained bitter that Milosevic had succumbed to heart failure before the conclusion of his trial for war crimes. The father of Mrs Sharma's children, an unpleasant character called Ravi Sharma, had abandoned her. She and Mr Visnjic had both been subject to racial abuse and an arson attack had once made their home uninhabitable for over a month. Now, after the Brexit vote, Mr Visnjic was worried about being thrown out of the country that had been his home for twenty-five years.

Rob thought of himself as totally cosmopolitan and imagined a world, like Lennon, where there were, *no countries, nothing to kill or die for.* That is why he loved London during his training and its multi-cultural atmosphere. He delighted in seeing couples from different backgrounds together. It restored his faith in human nature. The more immigration the better as far as Dr Baigent was concerned.

Now the weight loss, clear clinical anaemia, change of bowel habit, dark mixed rectal bleeding meant only one thing, especially with her father dying of bowel cancer aged fifty-one. Why had she left it so long? He owed it to Mrs Sharma to ignore the phone and continue focusing on her. It rang again, then again.

"I'm so sorry. Excuse me. The surgery must be burning down."

"Yes?" was his abrupt answer to Giselle. No other member of staff would have dared interrupt him.

"I'm so sorry but there's this connard cologist who insists I interrupt, saying don't you know who I am? 'E said he'd come round and walk into your room if I obstructed 'im any further."

Rob had an idea who it was.

"Baigent. Simon Chisholm here. Get yourself a more compliant manager who knows her place will you? Now, you know beating about the bush is not my style and I've no intention of starting with you. I hear you've been snooping around. Asking questions about Gideon, amongst other things. Look old chap, you are out of your depth. Stick to the day job. Whatever you are up to, if you're trying to find dirt on our boys, we will come down on you like a ton of bricks. Be warned, you will be squashed out of existence. You stand no chance if your naive idea is trying to discredit our plans, or whatever, forget it. No one will believe an old leftie like you anyway. Especially from your stock. Parents met when your navvy Dad was knocking up a shack for your coolie dinge of a mother, didn't they?"

Rob refused to rise to the bait and replied calmly.

"Actually he was installing a new bathroom."

But Chisholm had not finished.

"You stand no chance of putting us off course. It's all been decided at Davos and Bilderberg when Carington was Chairman. It's unstoppable. You will be swatted away like a fly."

Rob remembered Cliff using the same phrase. With Mrs Sharma still sitting in his consulting room he thought better of replying and making this more public but also knew arguing was pointless. He could not get a word in anyway.

"You've got three nice young daughters, haven't you?"

He need say no more. The threat was clear. But he made it clearer. "Acid so disfigures."

A shiver went down Rob's spine as the phone went dead. Did that really happen? Mrs Sharma was sitting in the hot seat patiently and politely pretending to ignore what was going on. Rob tried to stay composed and launched straight back to where they had left off but he was shaken and distracted. He had had practice hiding his emotions during consultations. When he could not decide whether to leave Jenny for Suzy he went through quite a spell where he doubted he was doing his job very well. He realised he was not listening to patients.

"Mrs Sharma, you've given a very clear account of your trouble. Now if you don't mind I should examine you?"

As she disappeared behind the curtain, and Rob called for the now obligatory chaperone, his mind was racing and not on the problem his job demanded. What the hell is going on? He felt in a surreal nightmare and for the second time in twelve hours. Though the one where Jerry was going to kill Thatcher and then was shot was imagined, this was real. He was an ordinary GP who had led a respectable life and only ever done one bad thing - split his family up. He was nothing. Why were they bothering with him? He had become more outspoken certainly especially under Rosa's influence but not in the same league as some. He still worried about going too far in his conference speech. He was not a David Kelly, James Bond or some character out of the imagination of John Buchan or John le Carré. Surely people's children are threatened, only in chilling thrillers? He felt as if he had been knocked off his feet. This man had made him feel like nothing. Then the anger started rising.

Simon Chisholm. How dare he? What an arsehole. He is nothing - too full of self-importance. He seems to really believe he is all-powerful and influential, and has the right to be condescending and so unbelievably rude. But like Wessel, did he give something away? Is there some sort of secret grand plan for the future? Does he really believe he is part of some mafia-like organisation that can threaten and intimidate people? He is just a doctor like me for fuck's sake. And a public school toff educated way above his intelligence and taught confidence that is not warranted.

Rob vaguely remembered some gossip about Chisholm having big gaps in his CV where he had disappeared for a while. Some said he had been in prison. Others that he had to flee the country to escape an angry and violent husband of a patient he had abused. Rob had also been told over tea at a BMA conference that Chisholm was madly buying up chemist shops everywhere but that was hardly illegal. Rob just wished he knew the truth. But he should have picked up the clues by now.

He had met Chisholm at a mutual friend's wedding at the time they wanted to close the local maternity unit. Rob thought he would recruit Chisholm to the cause and asked if he would help fight the closure.

"Let them close it. There are far too many units around. Fifty miles really isn't that far to travel," was his terse reply.

Needless to say Chisholm was desperately trying to expand his private practice. Rob really wanted to smack him in the mouth. He would end up with a sore fist soon, what with also wanting to punch the Secretary of State. Not good for a man against violence. Or was he being too sensitive? He had to get this into proportion. His problems were nothing compared to poor Mrs Sharma. She is likely to have advanced bowel cancer and may be dead within a couple of years. Far too young. Three teenage children, just like Rob. She will probably never see them marry or have children of their own.

After Mrs Sharma had left Rob was on his own. To his surprise, embarrassment and disgust Rob felt tears well up. He never believed he was a threat to anyone, so why should he be threatened? He was only trying to do some good. His intrigue with conspiracy politics disturbed him greatly, but it was no more than an interest. What possible influence could he have, even if he managed to convince a few others? Yes he was angry about the clandestine demolition of the NHS and if he could achieve just one thing in his life it would be to try to protect the institution that made him most proud to be British. Maybe he should forget the whole thing. After all, it probably would not make any difference. Maybe others have already been down his path, discovered a fair bit, been intimidated and backed off just like he is now inclined to do. But he had to get through surgery.

When Rob felt the pressures getting too much he would walk across his consulting room and stare at the Édouard Manet on his wall. This was his mindfulness trick, although he rejected the modern hijacking of what he thought of as simple meditation. Studying *Luncheon On The Grass* for a few minutes helped him reconnect with his sensations and allowed him to see the present moment clearly. Manet finished the large oil on canvas *Le Dejeuner sur l'herbe* in 1863 and Rob had seen the original in the Musee d'Orsay in Paris. When inspectors from the Care Quality Commission complained that it was inappropriate to display a nude woman casually lunching with two fully dressed men in front of patients, Rob was prepared. He claimed medical reasons for displaying this masterpiece. He said it was to remind him that Manet died at fifty-one of syphilitic complications including tabes dorsalis or myelopathy in 1883, two years before Sir Arthur Conan Doyle completed his MD on the subject. By the time he had baffled them by also connecting Conan Doyle's character Dr Watson, who lived at 221B Baker Street with Sherlock Holmes, and had qualified in Medicine at Bart's in 1878 (although he would not hold that against him), and had played rugby for Blackheath, the inspectors had forgotten what their original complaint was about. Then Rob would finish with this consideration.

"By the way Sherlock Holmes never did actually say, *elementary, my dear Watson* in any novel."

After a few minutes engaging the gaze of the nude woman *Victorine Meurent* he felt relaxed and calm again. By now Rob was running forty-five minutes late. This always made him feel guilty but most patients more often than not understood. For those whose moaning was over the top he had a good put-down line, used to great satisfaction, but sparingly.

"I'm sorry but I've just had to explain to a couple that their toddler has a terminal illness and won't see Christmas. It's a bit tricky squeezing that into ten minutes."

They never complained again.

He called in his next patient and apologised. This was Felix Denning, a great name for a circuit Judge. Rob always enjoyed his stories which both knew he should not be sharing. Today though that would make him anxious, as he would drift even further behind if he allowed the Judge to reminisce like he usually did.

They had known each other since Rob joined the practice and were on the border of being too friendly in a doctor-patient relationship, despite Felix being about twenty years his senior. He always wore a bow tie and spoke in a gravelly voice, like the actor who introduced trailers for movies at the cinema. He lived in what was now called Pleasure Towers. Felix delighted in telling everyone that it was so named because it used to be Edward VII's retreat for liaisons with Alice Keppel. He joked he should invite Alice's great-granddaughter Camilla and Edward's great-great-grandson Charles there for a dirty weekend. He also thought Jenny Churchill had been there. Apparently the couple that lived in the house at the time had to make themselves scarce at the drop of a hat when the royal party turned up.

Today Rob dealt with the Judge's annoying recurring gout in an unusually perfunctory manner for him. He hoped it did not show, but it did.

"Anything the matter, Rob? You don't seem your usual self. You look upset."

This caught the GP off guard as he thought he had returned to his normal acting persona - to a certain extent a doctor has to perform in the consulting room. Then, without any hint of feeling he had spoken out of turn, the patient attempted to lighten the mood and spoke with a smile on his face.

"Shall we change seats, old boy?"

"No, I'm fine," was Rob's repeated knee-jerk reaction, followed by, "Well, I've had a bit of a shock, actually."

What was he doing? He knew this was totally unprofessional but he could not help himself. He had to tell someone. The temptation to share his worries came from a previous conversation the two of them had had about the deliberate decline, through starvation of funds, of the NHS. At the time Rob was quite surprised the Judge seemed so sympathetic. Now he felt a little reckless and could not really think of any other patient he would feel comfortable discussing this with.

Rob tried to keep it brief. He explained how he was worried about what was happening in what laughably was called the cradle of democracy. How he felt those in power were out of control and to try to keep it credible, used the NHS as an example of his worries - appropriate considering where they both were - how it was being undemocratically dismantled by stealth, secretly and deviously and how some are going to get exceedingly rich, whilst most people will suffer as a result of its demise. However, trying to explain his conspiracy theory simply made it sound ridiculous and paranoid, especially when he threw in the reason for looking upset was that he had had some concerns confirmed and had also been threatened. That was the shock.

The Judge listened calmly with a sympathetic face, which seemed more than genuine.

"It's the same in my field. Legal Aid has been all but abolished creating a two-tier justice system. Justice is now only available to those who can afford it. It serves as just a plaything for the rich. Another of Attlee's great achievements destroyed. And it's much worse than that," he continued, "Let me give you an example."

Rob's heart sank when he realised the Judge was now on a roll. He tried to look at his watch without it being obvious.

"One legacy of the Jeremy Thorpe trial, when somehow he was acquitted of conspiracy to murder, was Thatcher getting a law

129

passed creating the very British crime of refusing to cover up wrongdoing, at least in the jury room. Did you know that if you do jury service and your fellow jurors decide the case on the toss of a coin, or by reference to racist or homophobic comments about the defendant, you will go to prison if you tell the media?"

Rob managed to slip in one word.

"No."

"You see. There are parallels with what you are telling me. The general public don't really have a clue what is being done in their name and how the vice of control is getting tighter and tighter. You know about the NHS as a doctor, I know about the legal system as a judge, teachers know about the destruction of the education system, I could list other professions they are destroying, but it doesn't penetrate the dura mater of the brains of the vast majority of the population."

"I'm sorry, this is all daft and not the place," Rob said, "and I shouldn't be burdening you with my problems."

When he showed the Judge out Rob was not sure whether he had understood, was sympathetic, or maybe just thought he had got too much sun.

They were late finishing that night. When Rob emerged from his consulting room, Giselle was still there. He sensed she needed to talk and was right.

"Putain de bordel. Who was that 'orrible gynaecologist?" she thundered. Her French accent was far less pronounced when she was being serious.

"And obstetrician. Poor women. Do you remember about ten years ago, on the front of most tabloids, DOCTOR TO FACE GMC FOR SEX ACTS WITH PATIENTS? It was him. Mostly he abused them by spending too long with his examinations. One other trick was to mislead women about his charges when he persuaded them to see him privately. You know the old scam. In the NHS clinic, being told you need a procedure urgently but saying, 'I'm sorry, this Government isn't funding the NHS as it should, so there's a worrying eight week wait, during which time anything could

130

happen'. Like most surgeons he would pause so you could cut the atmosphere with a knife, until the patient broke the silence with: 'Could I see you privately?' I used to witness this as a student, 'Oh, no, that would be wrong really... but here's my card'. There was a stream of women who felt they had no choice and this boosted his bank balance. A few were especially targeted. He cautiously selected ones he judged could not really afford his bills, which usually turned out double his original quote by the time he had added on the extras. Ten pounds for a swab costing twenty pence and all the other crooked practices. So do you know what he did? Hinted that the bill could be reduced or even binned for a special favour. A sex act of some sort! Clearly he picked whom he thought he could approach in this way very, very carefully, the very vulnerable and weak. He gave them time to think about it and offered them a follow up appointment. The desperate, those who had overstretched themselves financially, and those he was arrogant enough to think fancied him, would come back. But the most frequent safe targets were those he knew were hiding potentially damaging medical secrets. Especially sexually transmitted diseases not caught from their partners. Chisholm threatened to tell, unless... and it often worked. Until one day, at one of those follow up appointments, when he thought he would be getting a blowjob, a husband walked in with his wife, smashed him in the face and rang up the *Sun*. Then, with the most expensive barrister in town, he got away with it, and probably still is getting away with it. The medical fraternity is a small world and many knew of his reputation and had no doubt he was up to no good. This sort of behaviour is usually spotted at medical school but little is done to root it out. Most thought it was about time too, deserves all he gets, except he didn't get what he deserved."

Rob then remembered what Clive had said in the *Bell and Jorrocks*.

"You know that old saying that if they wish, the press can make the innocent guilty and the guilty innocent. Well, Chisholm and Murdoch were mates. Here he made the guilty look innocent. The *Sun* made the innocent, that is his patient and her husband, look like the guilty ones. They went through their bins and tapped their phones and made up evidence that they were trying to extort money out of poor innocent Chisholm. Then there was a systematic campaign, day after day to discredit all his other victims, the ones that came forward due to the publicity of the first case, and their secrets were leaked. Poor women had their reputations trashed and he got off. He destroyed so many. One rule for some, eh? This made him even more arrogant so he thinks he can get away with anything. Teflon-coated, rather than white-coated. Went to Latimer, the public school and claims to have taught Hugh Grant how to act there. Once a public schoolboy, always a public schoolboy, eh? He is a racist too. Refused to have anyone other than white junior staff with English names. Gets no choice nowadays of course but makes their lives hell. Apparently he's into buying up chemist shops all over the place too."

"Do you think people like that still get into medical school?" Giselle asked.

"I think it did get better for a while. But now of course with private medical schools you can buy your way in. Not too sure they are really bothered where the money comes from. So they are increasingly full of the young-dumb-with-a-lump-sum and who cares about their ethics and morals?"

"By the way," Giselle suddenly remembered, "another of your wonderful colleagues got 'is secretary to ring to say 'e won't be coming to your wedding. No explanation or apology. Wessel 'is name. Quel con! Ring a bell?"

So a silver lining to the cloud of today. At least Rob would not have to explain to Suzy why he invited an old lover to their wedding. Off the hook!

"Shame. Wessel's the sort to make Harvey Weinstein look angelic. Has the telephone recording gadget been working the last few days?"

"Of course, you know we need it more than ever now."

"Good. Could we mark the last few days' tapes Wessel and Chisholm and keep them somewhere safe? Thanks."

132

12 - PILGRMAGE AND CHAT-UPS

GOD BLESS AMERICA

While the storm clouds gather far across the sea,
Let us swear allegiance to a land that's free.
Let us all be grateful for a land so fair,
God bless America, land that I love,

Irving Berlin (1918)

2006

"Some of y'all pissing me with what you're sayin' bout our cuntree. And you, you Limey mother-fucker had better get on your knees and apologise before you see the wrong end of my Dallas Special!"

The four at the table were stunned. The night had started out so well. Now they had a large cowboy standing over them in a very threatening manner and jabbing his finger at Pete. He was the complete article and they all knew he meant business. His white Stetson, the Old Gringo Rattlesnake boots, the trophy buckle with 1956 Champion Saddle Bronc Rider on it (clearly not his as not old enough) holding up his Wrangler Performance Jeans, the classic button-down western shirt and Texas Sheriff Star Bolo tie said it all.

Pete Moodey was touring the USA with his mate Mike. After landing in Boston they had rented a Buick from Alamo, saw the sights they wanted to, and had now arrived in Dallas. They had both taken sabbaticals from work. At thirty-six they were both getting on and thought such an adventure was now or never. Pete was now a freelance journalist, having become increasingly disillusioned as a staff writer on a local paper where he knew he was producing crap, as that is all they wanted. Nothing serious was sought or considered. He was single so could take the chance. He had saved up. Mike worked in Whitehall and was just as fed up. He took unpaid leave.

He helped his frustration by leaking stories of incompetence to his old mate. It was so easy. He was never under suspicion. But incompetence was so common it was not even news, so he searched for the conspiracies - much more fun and interesting. As he left for the break he was hearing rumours of a paedophile ring involving some famous people but did not have time to follow it up before they set off for Germany.

The first stop was Frankfurt to see England beat Paraguay in their first game of the 2006 World Cup. England, as usual at the beginning of a tournament, was unconvincing but squeezed a 1-0 win courtesy of Carlos Gamarra's own goal from Beckham's left wing free kick after three minutes.

"That was the thirtieth own goal in World Cup history," declared Mike the geek.

"I know of one," said Pete. "Poor old Escobar who was murdered after his own goal which lead to Columbia's elimination from the 1994 tournament."

"But did you know," added Mike, "that the day after his murder Alan Hansen was commentating for the *BBC* on another match and very insensitively said, *the Argentinian defender warrants shooting for a mistake like that?*"

The England victory was spoiled by the way the fans were treated. Before getting anywhere near the ground all food and drink, even water was confiscated. They then had to queue for up to an hour to buy the special FIFA water at exorbitant prices in direct sunshine of thirty-two degrees Celsius.

"Bastards!" said Pete, "They don't give a shit about the fans. They're just here to make a load of money. Taken over by big business."

"What's new?" replied his mate.

They saw the Sweden game on a big outdoor screen in Berlin and, after losing to Portugal in another penalty shoot-out in Gelsenkirchen, flew off to Boston. The flight turned into a drinking session as they both wanted to sensitively shoot Ronaldo for getting Rooney sent off.

Pete and Mike Emptage, who met at University, made straight for Gator's on N Market Street as they were keen to get to Dealey Plaza as soon as possible, but needed a quick drink first. The sight of the Kennedy slaying was the highlight and reason for coming to Texas - perhaps the only reason. The place the whole world knew about. They only had to continue down the road to Elm Street and turn right. They deliberately booked into the Crown Plaza for that very reason. They could not wait to stand on Zapruder's concrete pedestal from which he took twenty-six point six seconds of probably the most famous film in history with his Bell and Howell camera.

That drink was a must, though they thought they would be there for only ten minutes, especially when they realised they could only get Budweiser.

"Almost undrinkable gnat's piss," was how Mike described it on the plane as it was landing in Boston.

"No," Pete corrected him, "Coors is almost undrinkable gnat's piss and Budweiser is weak, almost undrinkable gnat's piss. A remarkable advertising achievement that's all, it must be they sell forty thousand million litres a year."

Mike went into geek mode again speaking in a Michael Caine accent.

"Do you know the Budweiser Trademark dispute has been a fight between two brewers, one in the Czech Republic and one in the US, on going since 1907? Since Budweis first brewed beer in the thirteenth century, at least five hundred years before the United States' Declaration of Independence, I think the Yanks have a bit of a cheek. Now not many people know that."

At least they could get Sam Adams in Boston. On chatting to the barmaid with her *Cheers* t-shirt in the Bull and Finch pub found out the Dallas equivalent was Lakewood Lager. Still gassy shit as far as they were concerned - but when desperate. So it was Lakewood Lager. They had only been in Gator's for a few minutes when, to their delight and nervous surprise two stunning girls came straight up to them. They were still standing at the bar but had already drunk half their beers when the blonde spoke.

135

"Gee, your English accent is delicious. So sexy."

The other just giggled. Mike was more confident with strangers and fired back.

"That's because we're English. We invented it. You stole it. You do a strange version, but from you it's quite sexy too."

Pete's only thought was, oh shit, now we will be stuck here talking flirtatious crap with no end result and an evening wasted. Mike did most of the early talking and seemed to be prepared.

"You Americans should really learn how to spell doughnut without skipping half the letters, and you should not take the u out of words like favour, honour and neighbour. It's rude and uncouth."

He seemed to get away with this, probably as they did not know what he was talking about. Pete cringed when Mike exaggerated a posh accent and made a note to take the piss later. The blonde introduced herself as Cheryl and her friend, who Pete thought prettier and more refined as Madison.

"After the fourth President or Madison Square Gardens in New York?" joked Mike.

That fell flat with Cheryl who clearly had not heard of either. Madison brightened up and entered the conversation by staring Pete in the eyes rather than the questioner and replying.

"After my grandmother, actually."

Pete suddenly lost all interest in going to Dealey Plaza that evening. He decided he would give this bar visit more than the scheduled ten minutes. He continued to push his luck.

"Why do you Americans call a concert hall a garden, and gardens yards? Yards should now be metres anyway?"

"We will only answer that on two conditions. One, you tell us what you are on about as we haven't a clue, and two, you buy us a drink?" said Cheryl.

They all seemed comfortable with the suggestion and sat down together to find out more about their different cultures. I've never heard of trying to get off with someone called that before, thought Mike. They paired up quite naturally. Mike would always go for the quick shag, quickly forgotten. Pete was more interested in a mind connection before a body connection. The whole meat market as he called it made him uncomfortable. Mike did not really care if they even have a mind. True to form Mike was soon talking to Cheryl about what she wore as a former cheerleader for the Dallas Cowboys, whilst Pete asked about why they were in Dallas. It was soon obvious that Cheryl and Madison were very different. So different it was difficult for Pete to understand why they were friends.

Cheryl was three years younger at twenty-seven, and was a barmaid in the nearby Rodeo Bar in the Adolphus Hotel. It soon emerged her grandmother was an original cheerleader in the Cowboys Inaugural season in 1960. They were called Cowbelles and Beaux. She was an eighteen-year-old mum, as was in turn Cheryl's mother. Cheryl's ambition was to work in a sports bar, nothing more than that. She was uninterested in politics and had only been out of Texas once, when a boyfriend drove her to Washington to see the Redskins with the sole intention of claiming her virginity, which he did and they missed the game.

Madison was worldlier. At least she had been to Washington to visit the Smithsonian Institution and some of the other historical sites. Her parents had taken her to Yellowstone National Park, which sparked her interest in the natural world. It took half the evening before she slipped into the conversation that she had studied Ecology, Evolution and Marine Biology at the University of California, Santa Barbara. Pete was impressed. He told her that is where their trip would end with whale watching - so a connection. After university she had returned to Dallas to work for the Green Party and various charities. It seemed like she had about six low-paid jobs which all added up to just covering her living expenses. She lived on her own though.

Pete seemed to amuse her with tales of their adventures. After Boston, they of course went to New York, then Philadelphia before Gettysburg. That was Pete's choice. His degree was in Twentieth Century History but he knew a lot about the American Civil War and wanted to see where Lincoln gave his famous 1863 address. After the sights of Washington, and the First President's place at Mount Vernon, they toured through Atlanta to Memphis. Graceland

137

was a must. Madison loved the story of them being thrown out of Elvis's home. As a girl who was strictly brought up and very deferential to all authority so she could not believe what she heard. Mike saw one of Elvis' favourite chairs so leapt over the security barrier and sat in it. All the alarms were triggered and four guards dragged him off and splayed him across the floor. After searching him, he was escorted off the premises and told never to return - along with Pete. Pete did not speak until they arrived back at Heartbreak Hotel.

"What the hell were you doing?" was the only thing Pete could get out.

Mike's justification was.

"I did wait 'til the end of the tour so you didn't miss anything. It was all worth it for those five seconds sitting in the same seat as Elvis."

"You were just lucky you weren't shot you fucking idiot!"

Then there was New Orleans. After Dallas Pete told Madison they planned to head up to the Texas Panhandle and join the old Route 66, or Will Rogers Highway, famous since it opened in 1926. Then on to Los Angeles, deliberately missing out Las Vegas.

"So why Dallas?" asked Madison.

"Dealey Plaza, of course and the Sixth Floor Museum. We have to see the most famous site in the States, the School Book Depository, the grassy knoll and all that. You will think this weird but that's my email address, petegrassyknoll at gmail dot com."

Madison paid no attention to his weird obsession.

"My mum was there."

That was like a bomb exploding for Pete. He did not know what to say.

"Really?"

"That Zapruder film. You will see a couple with a nine year old in the background as Jackie is climbing back onto the trunk to pick up bits of his brain. The secret service agent is trying to get on board. Frame three hundred and seventy-one. That nine-year-old is my mum with my grandparents. They were all pretty traumatised by the whole thing."

He realised he needed to get to know this lovely interesting girl more. He felt in touch with history - a famous event.

"Do you believe Oswald acted alone?"

"Well that's what the Government tell us so why should I believe any differently? We live in the best most honest democracy in the world."

At that Pete's heart sank. Now he knew he was not on the same wavelength as he had believed and could not help himself.

"You are joking? You are in the most evil empire there is!"

This caught the attention of Mike and Cheryl.

"Your honest democracy has tried to overthrow more than fifty foreign governments, most of which were democratically elected, grossly interfered in democratic elections in at least thirty countries, attempted to assassinate more than fifty foreign leaders, dropped bombs on the people of more than thirty countries and tried to suppress populist or nationalist movements in twenty countries."

"Oh no, hear we go, Pete has started one of his rants and he is only warming up," said Mike.

More worrying for Mike was the thought, is he going to sabotage my chances of a shag, yet again? He tried to put Pete off his stride by offering more drinks, asking Cheryl more about the cowboys and kicking him under the table but none of this worked.

"You are one of the worst aggressors in the modern age. You've started thirteen or more wars in the last thirty years, spending fourteen trillion dollars at a cost of one hundred thousand lives. You surround Russia and China right up onto their doorsteps with nuclear bases and weapons pointed at them and then have a hissy fit just because a few missiles arrive in Cuba. You dominate the Pacific Ocean. Then you call them evil when they protest and try to protect themselves. Just because they threaten your declared aim of world domination. You have over four thousand bases and more than one thousand more on every continent. You have secret armies in one hundred and seven countries. You even have a name for it - Full Spectrum Dominance. You are all brainwashed and your mainstream media are unquestioning and complicit."

Mike was beginning to panic.

"But this wasn't just one leader, they are all at it. It doesn't matter who is in the White House, it's the system. You could call it the Military Industrial Money Media Security Complex."

Some at the bar were beginning to look round as Pete got louder.

"Have you heard of the NED, your National Endowment for Democracy?" he asked Madison, but was really addressing all three of his tablemates. They all looked blank.

"It's an agency created by Reagan to promote political action and psychological warfare against states not in love with your foreign policies and is Washington's foremost non-military tool for effecting regime change. It does what the CIA has been doing covertly for years. It wants to spread the free economy, the minimal government neo-liberal agenda and, of course, US investment everywhere. You want world domination, not the Russians or Chinese, but it suits you to accuse them of that."

Cheryl was completely lost now and looked bored so decided to use the rest room. But for Madison it was feeling like Pete was calling her mother a whore and her father a paedophile. She had had enough.

"That dills my pickle. We have total allegiance to a land that's free, and we are grateful for a land so fair. You're a communist aren't you?"

Those on the next table stopped talking.

"That's always the response of you Yanks. And most of you don't know what communism is. You think it's socialist to share communal sewers. You blame communism for everything but it's all about economics really. When Russia became capitalist you got worried you might have a rival so destroyed their economy, and when the market economy came to China and they began beating the US at the capitalist game, it's that you find unforgivable. The difference is simple though. Billionaires don't control the Government in China, but they do in the US. Here you can change the party in power but not the policy. In China they can change the policy but not the party. Who are you to say their system is worse? They have lifted six hundred million out of poverty and have no ambition to run the world, but you threaten them. Did you know

Mao tried to open diplomatic routes and friendly relations for decades and the US Government wouldn't even reply to him. It's as though you need an enemy. In fact I'm sure you do to support your arms industry. A six hundred billion dollar arms industry needs a war."

Mike knew he had to stop this. He was feeling uncomfortable at the glances from some of the rednecks. There was a difficult period of silence but as Cheryl came back to the table Mike tried to change the subject and lighten the mood.

"Why do you call it a Rest Room? Do you rest in there?"

"Well, y'all hat and no cattle, aren't yer? It is being polite. We don't want to refer to what we really do in there. When I was little my parents called it a bathroom, but we didn't have a bath in there either."

"The language of Shakespeare is being corrupted by the linguistic equivalent of the grey squirrel," said Mike.

"Who's Shakespeare?" queried Cheryl.

"I heard someone ordering a latte to go yesterday in Denny's," said Pete, "To go where? I thought. Then I realised she meant she wanted a coffee to take away."

"And why do you say someone has passed when you mean snuffed it, croaked, is pushing up the daisies, kicked the bucket, shuffled off this mortal coil, expired, is no more, gone to meet his maker... died?"

"Eh?"

That is when the cowboys came over.

"Some of y'all pissing me with what you're sayin' bout our cuntree. And you, you Limey mother-fucker had better get on your knees and apologise before you see the wrong end of my Dallas Special."

It was obvious the Texan was a little bit worse for wear. They hoped it would slow him up. So they took a gamble.

"When I shout, look over there... run," Mike said to Pete out of the corner of his mouth.

"Waddle you say, boy?"

Pete did not need to be told twice.

141

"Well, look over there… what's that?"

Both on cue they shot through the door and headed towards Elm Street. Fortunately a nervous glance over their shoulders reassured them no one was chasing.

"That went well," said Mike.

"Yes, just like at Graceland. Everyone can remember 22nd November 1963 and what they were doing when the news broke of Kennedy's murder. Thanks to you we were close to getting murdered on 19th August 2006. Do you think that date would have the same impact on the world? And what's a Dallas Special?"

"It's a long knife… special because it's illegal."

"Oh, is that all. I ran because I had visions of being buggered like Ned Beatty in *Deliverance* and having to squeal like a pig."

13 - PROGRESS AND INFILTRATION

THE STAR SPANGLED BANNER

And the rocket's red glare, the bombs bursting in air,
Gave proof through the night that our flag was still there.
Oh, say does that star-spangled banner yet wave
O'er the land of the free and the home of the brave?

Frances Scott Key (1814)

1986

It was an uncertain relationship where the command or control had never been openly defined. But each man thought he should be running the show and the other should be subservient.

Each country wanted to run the operation although both knew which one was really subordinate. Deep down the British knew they were just a small cog in the world domination plans of the super-power but both played the game and neither missed an opportunity to push home any tactical advantage. Maybe the American thought it was a General Eisenhower-Montgomery situation but the Englishman did not want to admit that. This time Lyndon C. Woodward had scored a petty victory by manipulating Sir James into coming to the US Embassy in Grosvenor Square. Like being summoned to the headmaster's study. The attempted put down had irritated Jim but he felt he should rise above it even though it revived uncomfortable memories for him.

The headmaster's study at his prep school was that gloomy and mysterious place known as the pain parlour where abuse occurred on a daily basis - physical beatings, emotional torture and sexual assaults. Morrison certainly did not escape. Not that he thought it particularly unusual or wrong as all the boys had similar tales. Jim dealt with it and shielded it off by telling himself what you grow up with you regard as normal. It never did me any harm, was what he truly thought but was of course highly debatable - once a public

143

schoolboy, always a public schoolboy. Jim was severely scarred by his upbringing but was oblivious to the fact. His personality - a product of abuse - became so powerful, he was the type where debating his point of view rarely happened. His point of view was not to be challenged.

The two had kept in touch since the first meeting in the States when Lyndon was Nixon's deputy Chief of Staff, but this was only the third face-to-face meeting in fifteen years. Although wanting to adopt American business practices and values, and admiring how they had squashed anything liberal, Jim liked the philosophy more than the people. He hated arrogance in others and nothing exemplified that more than the eleven-metre ostentatious aluminium bald eagle situated on the roof of the Chancery Building. He had been driven up from his country home when it was still dark. His chauffeur had dropped him off right underneath this monstrosity, which did nothing for Jim's mood. The broad stripes and the bright stars of the flag were accentuated by the dawn's early light.

Lyndon had manipulated him to the embassy.

"You live right opposite Jim. What could be more convenient? We will offer some coffee or stronger."

There was no way after that that Jim was going to admit he did have to put some effort in. His mood was aggravated further when Lyndon kept him waiting whilst talking to his son Nelson. With no apology or greeting Lyndon launched straight in.

"Nelson's in Mexico. He likes your soccer and through his usual devious means got himself a ticket to the World Cup final. He's only eighteen. I'm a bit suspicious he used our Argy contacts to get the tickets. He's still in contact with those he met in 1981. I'll whip his arse when I get near him even though he's now bigger than me."

Although of course a rugger man, even Sir James knew about Argentina's 3-2 victory over West Germany two days before and he could not resist goading.

"How come he's interested in football? The USA hasn't qualified for a World Cup since nineteen fifty? That's thirty-six years ago."

Sir James was brought up to know there was only one true type of football. Rugby football. The other game the lower classes played where they just kicked a round ball about was still football though not soccer. Soccer was a vulgar word. And that game the Americans played where they are all dressed up in full body armour and have commercial breaks every few minutes was not a game, just a money making machine.

Lyndon went on, not even recognising the below-the-belt comment.

"Do you know, my son is so right wing it even scares me sometimes. He admires Galtieri and feels he was hard done by. My fault probably as Nelson met him in nineteen eighty-one when thirteen on his visit to Washington just before he seized power. We wanted to push him to replace President Viola. I was in charge of the welcoming party President Reagan wanted. Thirteen is a vulnerable age and hero-worship is easy to develop. Reagan thought Galtieri was the bulwark against communism we needed. Richard Allen, our National Security Advisor, even described him as a *majestic general*. You may not remember him. He wasn't around long as he got caught up in a bribery scandal?"

Lyndon had stayed a key player in American politics for two decades now. He was the link and channel of communication between business and politicians. After Nixon, he worked for Reagan briefly in his last year as Governor of California, then in the build up to his candidacy for President. He boasted of being responsible for writing some of Reagan's most memorable quotes, but Sir James doubted it. The most terrifying words in the English language, *I'm from the Government and I'm here to help*, were supposedly his. The reason Sir James doubted it was because Lyndon had no sense of humour whatsoever as far as he had witnessed, but it exemplified the attack on the state - everything government bad, everything private good.

Another habit Lyndon had which irritated Sir James was to ridicule his knighthood. Sir James put it down to jealousy that the Americans had no such civilised system. Lyndon wondered aloud what he could have possibly done to get a reward so young. He was even more confused to learn it was an inherited title. Morrison's father was a Baron. When he eventually died a fair time after his

145

second stroke Jim inherited the title and officially became Baron Willingdon, but he still preferred Sir James. Lyndon had done his homework.

"Hey, Lloyd-George was charging thirty thousand pounds for those, wasn't he? Another twenty thousand pounds would have got him a peerage. But I'm joking Jim. I know your father didn't get his from the old Welshman. Amazing though what he did was legal until embarrassment got the better of you all and you made it illegal in nineteen twenty-five. When are you going to join us and realise giving people this kind of inducements is corrupting, anachronistic, discredited and medieval? It props up your nasty class system," And a final dig, "It has to be outdated when you award Orders of the British Empire. What Empire?"

He hammered home the point by always calling him Jim.

"About time we reviewed our progress, Jim. You are on track but that's the best we can say. You are going the speed of a Puffing Billy. We need you to speed up, more like a greyhound. So the President wants Margaret to get her finger out of her arse and deliver more and quicker. He doesn't think we have had our rewards and certainly not been paid back for what we have done for you and your PM."

Even Jim squirmed at how crude the American could be but knew what he was referring to. It did not need to be spelled out. Besides he was aware their conversation was being recorded.

In 1981 Margaret Thatcher was two years into her premiership and deeply unpopular. Reagan wanted to help make sure she was re-elected. The CIA had played their part in her first election in 1979 and they did not want their efforts wasted. Between them, and with the help of their media friends, they had done an exemplary character assassination on the Labour leader, Michael Foot. It was so simple. Repeat over and over again that he was unelectable and the public was convinced, as it was absorbed into their uncritical minds like blotting paper absorbs ink. It was a tactic that was always successful and had been since Goebbels first put it into practice. This would not be the last time it was deployed. However, they were not prepared to take any chances.

146

It was a coincidence that the new Social Democratic Party in Britain had been formed the same month as Galtieri's visit to the USA. They were immediately attracting support and there was already talk amongst the establishment that their leader, Roy Jenkins, would become the next PM. As far as Reagan was concerned this would be a disaster only second to Michael Foot gaining power with his commie ideas. It would derail the proposed US penetration into Britain. Jenkins would align the UK too much to Europe at the expense of the US. So he had to be stopped.

There is nothing like a war to bolster up a current leader. Short of that a good terrorist attack. A good false flag operation perhaps. Assuming he wins. But what if he is a she? There was doubt in Washington as to whether Thatcher, a woman, had the guts to fight, but she was heading for a massacre at the next election unless something was done. The idea of leading Galtieri on by persuading him that if he were to take back the Malvinas by force he would get US support was not Reagans but that of his Secretary of State, General Alexander Haig.

All those in the delegation to entertain the Argentinians were instructed to call the Falklands the Malvinas to impress and convince Galtieri. Every Argentinian schoolchild had been taught that the British had stolen the Malvinas in 1833. He returned to Buenos Aires having been told that the US would back his coup d'etat and was convinced an invasion would boost his popularity. Furthermore, it could not fail with that promised American backing. But he had to oust President Viola first, who to Galtieri's irritation had just been appointed to replace President Videla by the Junta. It did not take him long - again with American help. The British seemed uninterested in their territory now anyway. The Thatcher Government had cut its defences despite warnings from the First Sea Lord, Sir Henry Leach.

Lyndon knew Haig and thought he should run for President when Reagan's second term ended in two years. They met in Nixon's White House and became good friends. Haig was Chief of Staff and Lyndon his deputy. Lyndon thought he stood a chance of a senior role in a Haig presidency, preferably Secretary of State. But

Haig would have to declare soon. There were doubts over his stability. Yes he served under MacArthur in Korea, got the DSO in Vietnam but thought a nuclear warning shot in Europe might deter the Soviet Union, and appeared arrogant declaring *I am in control here* when Reagan was shot just after the Galtieri visit.

The manufactured Falklands War brought Thatcher from third place in the opinion polls to a storming victory in 1983. This gave her the confidence to smash the unions. Reagan was disappointed that she had not moved quicker and followed his example with the air traffic controllers. He had no hesitation in sacking eleven thousand. The USA needed the British unions castrated or American business would not thrive in the UK. US advisors came over in the summer of 1983 to plan the war against the next enemy the miners. Thatcher wanted revenge for what they did to the last Conservative Government in the early 1970s. Sir James and Gerry had used their influence to help get Arthur Scargill elected a few years before. This was a masterstroke, as they knew he would charge into the trap of a full all-out strike. Building up coal stocks and politicising the police, bribing the ordinary copper with massive overtime bonuses were essential elements. In secret liaisons with Chief Constables from dozens of Forces, they had been promised everything they wanted if they co-operated against any striking workforce. They knew they were in effect becoming Thatcher's private army but she was pushing at an open door. It was one of the first examples of the police changing from the friendly Bobby on the street to help citizens to becoming the agent of the State. Duping the media was another key element. Thatcher had already provoked the miners by appointing Ian MacGregor whom Scargill called *the American butcher of British industry*. He did his bit by telling the Yorkshire miners they were less productive than women miners in the US.

So the war against the miners, won a year ago, was setting up Thatcher's next election victory. But the US wanted rewards for this.

"Your 'iron lady' has got to live up to her name by reducing the State. We want further progress with selling off more. What has she done so far? Just a few bus routes and hospital cleaners. You've only scratched the surface."

Jim was eager to correct him.

"You have forgotten British Aerospace, Cable & Wireless, the ports, freight, telecommunications, shipbuilders and Jaguar. That's more than a scratch."

"Still not impressive. I know gas is to be flogged off this year, but we insist you move faster. I've got a list: British Airways, BAA, Rolls Royce, steel, water, electricity, and the railways. Then there's your Post Office, Land Registry, parks and plenty more. The judiciary must be a priority, all linked to security, which may be as big as health. Legal Aid has to go, as I've told you before, that was another welfare provision brought in by that man Attlee wasn't it? This will be like falling off a log with the lawyers helping us there."

Then a first glimpse of a sense of humour.

"Finally we'll go for privatising the air we breathe and all your trees."

Jim kept a straight face.

"You must get on with this. Of course the big prize is your National Health Service. Socialised medicine blocks our access to a goldmine. Problem with it is that it's too efficient. There is nothing for middlemen like us to cream off. Healthcare is a trillion dollar business if exploited properly. The infrastructure has to be designed in business and profit terms. The US market is saturated, we need to expand, as I've repeatedly told all you Limeys."

Even Jim felt uneasy about something so British as Rolls Royce ending up in foreign hands. He could cope with getting his own fingers in that pie though. He tried to defend himself.

"We have people working on the NHS," he said, "We had trouble with our wets that insist abolishing the NHS is electoral suicide, so we had to tread more carefully for a while 'til we silenced them. There was a bit of a Cabinet riot. You can take comfort from our approach, I assure you. We are to adopt the Omega Project, which has been drawn up by the Adam Smith Institute modelled on research by one of your right wing libertarian think tanks. It proposes compulsory private health insurance and a system of private medical facilities, which would of course mean the end of the NHS. This is why we must be cautious and win the propaganda debate first about how the NHS is an old- fashioned, outmoded form of care. Charging for schooling is included, which I am sure you will approve of. It's all in the Cabinet papers and minutes, which are kept under wraps for thirty years. The project will be sorted by then."

Lyndon burst in, almost shouting.

"I should think so! You are too lily-livered. You shouldn't be so scared of the public or elections. You should know how to sort them out by now. Anyhow, just don't tell them what you are up to. Don't become like the French where the Government are afraid of the people. The people should be afraid of the Government."

Jim tried to reassure.

"Two bright young brains called Letwin and Redwood are drawing up more detailed plans now. They tell me it will be a project in stages or steps so, as you say, the public don't realise what's going on until it's fait accompli. They call it salami slicing. You can expect more early next year, but it'll be kept under wraps until after the election."

"Yer, I know," butted in Lyndon almost contemptuously, "It's not new. Mussolini used to go on about plucking a chicken feather by feather so that people didn't notice what was going on until it was too late."

Jim tried to explain further.

"If we rush it, I promise you Lyndon, it'll backfire on us. The public will wake up to what is happening. Privatising most services is like shooting fish in a barrel when handled right. Starve them of funds to make them shit, and then tell the public that private would be better. Trouble with the NHS is it's still popular even when we've made it shit."

Woodward wanted to move on.

"Tell me how your infiltration of the Labour Party is progressing? Is Kinnock your plant?"

"No, we are grooming the next leader. An ambitious young lawyer elected to Parliament in 1983. Although public school

150

educated he will be hip enough to con the electorate. He's even got a guitar! He will be the wolf-in-sheep's-clothing or Trojan Horse, if you Yanks know what that is, saying all the things the left want to hear but actually continuing Thatcher's, and our, policies. We've had him saying, *the Labour right is bankrupt*, and he, *came to Socialism through Marxism*, all the usual crap that will get him in pole position eventually. Obviously CND and anti-Common Market. We don't see him being in place until the nineteen-nineties and there are one or two in the way we will have to deal with first. That's fine though. We see Margaret pushing things hard from now on. Power is driving her slightly mad so she might go too far. So far and hard she might lose her popularity, so end up going, voluntarily or not. The public will be craving for an alternative but actually, unbeknown to them, electing a worthy successor with the same neo-liberal policies, but in disguise."

Sir James was reassured by the plan and thought Lyndon should be too. But not so.

"We are losing patience. We have been much more successful imposing our policies on the Third World, through the IMF and World Bank, as well as direct pressure of course. We hope to get the rest of Europe on board without the need for more arm-twisting or threats but who knows? I'm less than convinced you see things from our point of view. It might be worth one more try at gentle persuasion, so you can re-energise all your fellow countrymen into doing what is right and what will give us power forever. And I mean forever. That's what is at stake here. Hitler was not ambitious enough only aiming at a thousand year Reich."

"Well, that's the first time I've heard anyone calling Hitler unambitious," exclaimed Sir James.

Lyndon responded.

"I was joking about the thousand years, actually. The interventionist approach that replaced classic liberalism after the great depression until recently was a big mistake. It was wrong to think that capitalism required significant state regulation in order to be viable. Our neoliberalism is an updated version of the classic liberal economic thought that was dominant in the US and the UK prior to the nineteen thirties. We are returning to that, and so will you, whether you like it or not. Persuade your friends."

The glazed-over look on Jim's face only encouraged Lyndon to continue.

"The main difference is that Adam Smith in his book *The Wealth Of Nations* warned against concentrations of wealth and the use of laws to favour the affluent. We are deliberately ignoring that. He was right about the self-regulating free market but wrong about whom it should be allowed to benefit. Did you know that was published only sixteen weeks before our Declaration of Independence from you Limeys? Good year seventeen seventy-six, what?"

Lyndon was trying to mimic Bertie Wooster. The American really was unsure how much of this his British pawn had understood. Jim's facial expression remained fixed. Lyndon was quite irritated that it seemed the lesson would need to be continued and drummed in harder. But he would not let any opportunity be wasted. This was all basic stuff and was what they and the generations before had been working towards. For some it was their life's work.

"An unregulated capitalist system, a free market economy, not only embodies the ideal of free individual choice but also achieves optimum economic performance with respect to efficiency, growth, technical progress and distributional justice."

"You actually believe that, don't you?" challenged Jim.

"Well of course. All but the bit about choice and efficiency, that's crap, but needed to take people along with us. The state should have little role. As you must be aware, this requires dismantling of what remains of the regulationist welfare state. We need deregulation of business. Your spin boys employed good tactics by banging on about red tape. It is a brilliant pejorative term that brainwashes people into going along with deregulation without realising that this so-called red tape actually protects them from the likes of us! We need cutbacks in, or better still, elimination of social welfare programs. You are working on the other necessary policies, privatisation of public activities and assets, as well as reduction of taxes on business and the investing class, meaning us of course, I assume?" He did not wait for an answer, "In the international sphere, neoliberalism calls for free movement of goods, services, capital and money, but not people, across national boundaries. So corporations, banks, investors like us should be free to move property, and acquire property across national boundaries. Come on, Jim. You know all this."

"Of course. I thought you were just trying to convince yourself. We have seen off the old socialist system based on human need rather than private profit. It is dead but we have to bury it so deep it not only wouldn't stand a chance of revival, but it will be as though it never existed in the first place. Airbrushed out of history."

"What a relief. You were beginning to worry me. Talking sense at last," Woodward sighed, "And one other issue before I forget. You know how much importance we put on our boys fighting any attempts at sabotaging our plans. And you remember we decided to set up a new organisation for this, as the C.I.A. can't be trusted with commitment or competence, let alone speed? My US unit tells me they aren't getting the cooperation needed from your UK cell in establishing what is expected. What's going on?"

"You are referring to the Special Operations Team? That is going well here in Britain. What's your problem?"

Woodward was clearly passing on a message.

"There are several who are acting against us who I'm told you have let slip through your fingers. The group called Poison originating from here should have been strangled at birth, but my operatives tell me they have now reached the US and are carrying out disruptive activities on our soil. That will not be tolerated. Deal with them, will you? And have you picked up and eliminated Rutherford yet?"

This last point shook Sir James but he tried not to show it. He had never heard of anyone called Rutherford involved in espionage. He knew of Ernest Rutherford, the nuclear physicist and Margaret the actress, both unlikely to be a threat, not least because they were both dead.

"Cooperation is a two way street Lyndon. Are you sure your boys are sharing all their intelligence?"

At that, Sir James made a note to himself to get this sorted. He thought a counter-act warranted.

"Of course the successes you will never hear of. Your *New York Times* and *Washington Post* brag about getting hold of your intelligence and stick it on their front pages all the time, but we don't want it in our papers. That's why you won't have heard of Colin Wallace."

"Nope. Hope this is relevant as I've got to meet Jacques Delors, the European Commission President?"

"It is. I offer him as an example of how in control we are. Briefly, he was in the Intelligence Corps in Northern Ireland and a psychological warfare specialist. He was up to his neck in the Clockwork Orange Project which you will remember was designed to smear a number of senior British politicians in the early 1970s."

"Yes, I do remember. You told me about it when we first met in the White House when I was Nixon's Deputy Chief of Staff."

"He began to cause us trouble when he started to spill the beans on this and the Kincora Boys' Home sexual abuse scandal. He was threatening to name names, which is far too close to home. He had photos of senior figures like Mountbatten going in and out. So to cut a long story short to discredit the allegations he was making we had him framed for manslaughter and he is now safely locked up. We had him beating an antiques dealer to death and dumping the body in the River Arun. This gets another potential saboteur out of the way and silenced."

"Good. But if that's keeping it brief, then I'd hate to hear one of your long stories."

Morrison knew the US wanted to take over British industry and joked yet again about making the UK the fifty-first State. He was happy to let Lyndon continue to believe that but it was not to be allowed to get that far. It was rumoured that Mikhail Gorbachev who had succeeded Chernenko as General Secretary of the Soviet Union the year before, was helped into office by the background work of the CIA and MI6. What Sir James knew for sure was the part played by George Blake.

Blake was deliberately portrayed as a British spy who worked for the Soviet Union as a double agent. He was discovered in 1961, gave a full confession - which should have aroused suspicion alone - and sentenced to forty-two years in prison. Two anti-nuclear campaigners who thought his sentence inhuman assisted his escape from Wormwood Scrubs in 1966. But the failure to find him and stop him leaving the country made some suspect the British security forces were keen to see him escape and to plant him as a triple agent into the Soviet regime. His role was then supposed to be to liaise with the other British agents and the Americans to help destabilise the communist party. But he turned again.

He worked with Donald Maclean and Kim Philby through the 1970s to undermine Leonid Brezhnev. Ideally the goal was to get a stooge like Gorbachev put in charge. It took twenty years. In 2007 Vladimir Putin awarded Blake the Order of Friendship. Putin owed his position partly to the work Blake had done. Maclean and Philby were never recognised for their patriotism. Blake outlived them all but never had the glamour of the Cambridge spies, partly as he was not posh enough and because he was not so enmeshed in the society he turned against.

Gorbachev was a man both Thatcher and Reagan could do business with. The business expected was the dismantling of the Soviet bloc and the resulting reunification of Germany. Germany was to be allowed to take over and control Europe economically and so achieve what it failed to do in 1914 and 1939. All the former satellite states and other countries east of the Rhine were then to be fair game for US business interests.

"Well, as I feared. We have always wanted a five-year plan, we are impatient. But you are telling me that it's unrealistic and is more likely to be twenty-five years or more. Where will we both be in twenty-five years, Jim?"

"Hence the need to groom the next generation or all could be lost. Better to arrive late than not at all. You have heard of the Aesop's fable of the tortoise and the hare, Lyndon?" asked Jim.

"Okay, okay, of course. Who the fuck is Aesop?"

"An ancient Greek story-teller."

"You British, you think you are so fucking clever, but what use is knowing an ancient Greek when you really need to be paying attention to a modern American?"

Sir James smiled internally with quiet satisfaction at this. He had rattled Lyndon. He and Gerry felt confident that the youngsters who were rising through the ranks and in particular their offspring could be relied upon. Although Jim's son was only fifteen and still at Eton, he was very malleable but Jim would not talk about him. Gerry's was already showing promise to take up the baton trashing restaurants through his Bullingdon Club membership at Oxford.

"What about Nelson, will his right wing thinking be put to good purpose?"

"You bet it will."

As Woodward was showing Morrison out, he told him about Tyler Kent.

"Thought you'd like to know. It seems he is dying in poverty in Texas. It's to our shame he was hung out to dry by my predecessor, Joe Kennedy."

That was one of the few times Sir James had ever heard Lyndon admit any failings, even if several places removed.

"I never met him, but Anna Wolkoff used to talk about him," said Sir James, "Didn't he marry some wealthy woman and used her money to become the publisher of some pro-segregation newspaper with links to the Ku Klux Klan?"

"Yes, in Florida. We used that to push our propaganda for a while," added Lyndon, "Went a bit nuts claiming President Kennedy was a communist and was killed because he abandoned his communist leanings. He had an affair with a girl called Irene Danischewsky who was the aunt of that sexy actress of yours, now what is her name? Great in *Caligula* and *The Long Good Friday*."

"Helen Mirren?"

"That's right."

14 - RELAXATION AND EMPIRE

GOD SAVE THE QUEEN

God save the queen
The fascist regime

There is no future
In England's dreaming

Don't be told what you want
Don't be told what you need
There's no future, no future,
No future for you

Sex Pistols (1977)

"You are being driven by a real Prince," Rob said proudly to Suzy.

The Jeep was struggling along a flooded road and Rob was impressed how Jairaj knew where track became a ditch and how skilfully he avoided it.

"The Neem trees planted along the sides are my guides. Indian lilac to you," the Prince informed them.

"Coming here in monsoon season has certainly made it interesting," replied Suzy.

It was uncertain if they would make it to the Haveli at first but the water depth was not getting any worse and the rain was easing. It was the end of July and Rob and Suzy were to be the only guests at Chanoud Garh. No one else was daft enough to visit at this time of year. Their wedding had been very relaxing. Rob put that down to it being the second time for both of them. One of his daughters did not attend and he fully understood. It was a very low-key event. Just very close family and a handful of friends. No more than a dozen. Rob really only did it for Suzy but he would not tell her that. They were keen to get right away from all stresses and searched for weeks to find something unique and unusual. As with most rare and exciting discoveries it came as a recommendation from Stephen, Rob's old mate and regular squash partner.

Although both had been to Rajasthan before, Suzy and Philip were skiers and spent more time on the slopes than in exotic places. Rob would be less reckless this time. He had returned after his last trip to start medical school with hepatitis. The worst thing about that was in those days he was not allowed alcohol for six months, which made fresher's week a bit boring.

Stephen's advice was to visit places early in the morning and do not get on any elephants. Rob thought he was being kind to elephants, which he was, but laughed until he almost wet himself over the tale Stephen told about going for a ride on an elephant with a cold. The elephant sneezed and the snot that flew three metres in the air landed on his head. His girlfriend at the time was highly amused. Rob remembered her for having a sadistic streak. The more Stephen hurt himself, like tripping over shopping trolleys or falling down steps, the funnier she found it. When he rang her to report a broken leg skiing, she had to put the phone down as she was crying with laughter. She had to go, and did.

Just off Highway 14 from Udaipur towards Jaipur their guide had arranged for Jairaj to meet them in his 4x4. The tour guide's car would not have managed the floods. Water covered the farmland as far as the eye could see.

"Doesn't this destroy all the crops?" Suzy asked Jairaj who, although ten minutes beforehand was a complete stranger she had never seen before, was one of those warm characters with whom she felt she had developed an instant rapport.

"It's not great, but we will get a second crop," he said in an impeccable well-educated English accent.

They had both done the Golden Triangle of Delhi, Agra and Jaipur previously, so decided to spend the ten days in just two new centres - Udaipur and Chanoud Garh. They thought the Taj Mahal a bit corny for a honeymoon, and that well-known image of Princess Di sitting on her own was not a good omen. Their stay in the Amet Haveli on Lake Pichola in Udaipur allowed them to wind down after the connecting flight from Mumbai. Somehow her brother Jeff had managed to organise a surprise bunch of flowers for their room. The card read:

To my darling kid sister and her handsome doctor husband. Enjoy yourselves.

Love Jeff

"I wonder how he knew we would be here?" puzzled Rob.

"Maybe he saw, or I showed him our itinerary, who knows?"

"But he hasn't been over from LA for a while," said Rob still puzzled.

Suzy was not interested in a puzzle she could not solve so in order to keep the mood light told Rob about how her brother was named after Geoff Hurst, except her father had spelled his name wrong too. Rob had heard this tale before but did not realise it was because Jeff was born on the World Cup winning hero's birthday, 8th December, four months after that hat trick. Geoff Hurst had just turned thirty-nine, and Jeff Dwight had just blown fourteen candles out on his birthday cake when John Lennon was shot. Reg, his dad was devastated but tried to console himself that because of the time difference Lennon actually died on 9th December, not Jeff's birthday. That would have been too much.

"Jeff was very close to Philip, but now loves you too," Suzy said reassuringly.

Suzy bought some jutties at the shoe bazaar in Mochiwara Street, whilst a proud local showed Rob his selfie with Judi Dench whilst filming *The Best Exotic Marigold Hotel.* Just before sunset a boat excursion gave them spectacular views of the City Palace and the Old City Ghats where the locals were doing their washing lit up with a wonderful glow. A Kingfisher beer on Jagmandir Island and then getting the boat to go close to Jag Niwas, *Octopussy*'s palace in the movie allowed Rob to forget any conspiracy theories despite the reminder of James Bond. Maybe he was sane after all. The locals seemed to have taken Roger Moore's death hard - there were posters of the film star all over town.

They both slept better than for weeks, it being quite cool helped. Maybe that was something to do with making love, this time with some passion, not just perfunctory sex, which had started to become a problem for Rob. Being relaxed and away from so many worries certainly helped. Suzy would not admit it, but so did her fantasy of thinking of number six, the centre forward from her local football team. Why he came into her head she had no idea.

By the time of booking out they were more than ready to move on. They were driven towards their Highway 14 rendezvous via the Kumbhalgarh Fort with its great ramparts winding for twenty-two miles along the rugged contours of the Aravalli Hills like a gigantic brown snake. This really was a different world. Climbing up to the top gave spectacular views but made Rob realise how unfit he was. Note to self, more exercise when back in the UK.

From Highway 14 Jairaj drove them the final half hour through the small rural village to Chanoud Garh in the Pali province. Their welcome could not have been more kind and hospitable where they felt like the only people on earth. They entered a beautiful courtyard to be greeted by the hosts and presented with garlands of sweet smelling frangipani, spiced lime water, a cooling scented wet cloth and given a red forehead bindi.

Jairaj's family had occupied the palace for thirteen generations. Thakur Anoop Singh built it three hundred and fifty years ago and made sure the palace was always prepared for the unexpected visits of the Maharana. As one of the original noble families of Rajasthan they were still held in high esteem in the village. They were the local royalty. After completing their education and growing tired of jobs in the big cities the present generation of Jairaj, Mahiraj and Anchal Singh came back to their ancestral home to join the current elder Raj, their father, in order to rescue the building and had spent the last six years trying to restore its former glory. Despite great wealth building up through the generations it seems their spendthrift grandfather blew it all. Throughout the Haveli the walls were lined with photographs of his horses at various racecourses around India in the 1950s. What he did not lose there he lost on his stud farm. He only died in 2009.

"The dogs are very friendly," said the Prince, as a Golden Retriever, a Great Dane, a Saint Bernard, and a lot of saliva greeted them.

That is what dog owners always say as they gnaw your leg off, thought Rob. What was nice though was no barking at all. Suzy always said that little dogs make the most noise, just like little men - must be a syndrome and an inferiority complex. Rob scolded her for stereotyping and being judgmental, and then he agreed.

Tea was served on the rooftop, where the delightful father, who turned out to be a retired vet, entertained the only two guests with the fascinating history. Although the rain had stopped water lay on the roof so a bit of paddling was necessary. Mahiraj took the opportunity to note where the water drained so he knew where the next batch of leak repairs would be. The original seventeenth century palace was built around two courtyards. Now one is for the guests and one for family use.

"The marble didn't come from Makrana where Shah Jahan got his stone for the Taj Mahal. That was too expensive even for our ancestors," said Mr Singh senior, with a huge grin on his face, "And it wasn't built in memory of a wife killed off during her fourteenth childbirth."

Rob had the impression this was his standard favourite joke for guests.

"The architecture is from Jaipur but the red-brown sandstone from Jodhpur. You can see the sandstone was used when that side of the quadrangle was rebuilt reducing it from three to two storeys about one hundred and twenty years ago."

He pointed.

"Do you know why?"

Rob and Suzy both shook their heads simultaneously.

"Because you British used the place as a base for pig-sticking and insisted on having bathrooms and higher ceilings. You are taller."

Curious. Having never heard of this, Suzy decided to steer the conversation in that direction. Stones and old buildings did not interest her. She knew though that Rob would want to turn it back. It was an old game they had.

"Well my dear, didn't your old relatives go hog-hunting?"

She realised their host was possibly losing his hearing when he continued as though she had not said anything.

"This area is ideal for it. Beaters chase the pigs out from the marshland and the honour is in the first spear, the thrust that draws the first blood. It was popular amongst the Maharajas and British officers in Victorian and Edwardian times. Thought to be good military training. Baden-Powell wrote a book about it. As a vet, I can't forget what he said, *not only is pig-sticking the most exciting and enjoyable sport for both the man and horse as well, but I really believe that the boar enjoys it too.*"

Rob thought privately that that said it all about Baden-Powell. If those rumours about him and little boys were true, he probably thought the boys enjoyed it as well. While Suzy was so enthusiastic - she almost seemed to be flirting with Mr Singh - Rob was studying the amazing architectural beauty of the delicate stone filigree jharokhas jutting forward, and the chajjas projecting out above the balconies. He knew in Rajasthan one function of these was to allow women to view events without themselves being seen. Oh how Suzy would like a few of those in her life, thought his mischievous mind. He wondered again what weird practices he could introduce to spice up their sex life. Maybe voyeurism was the answer. It certainly needed a bit of spice he lamented but consoled himself with a good laugh over what happened to Stephen and his sadistic girlfriend when experimenting. When they ran out of lubricant she persuaded him to try toothpaste. The sight of him running around the bedroom thinking he was on fire had her in stitches.

Pre-dinner drinks were in the courtyard under the clear blue sky. The national bird of India, peacocks, strutted around the four Fenne Fassi trees and their rich green leaves. Anchal, who cooked for everyone, brought out some delicacies and told Suzy that servants from the village had cropped the trees wrongly. Somehow she automatically seemed to know Suzy would be interested, but not Rob. When Suzy found out her other passion was embroidery he thought he had lost her for the evening. Their conversation was almost drowned by the far-reaching musical trumpet-like noisy call of a flock of cranes, hated by the local farmers. They seemed to compete with the red beaked, rose-ringed parakeets and the fluttering of the pigeons bathing in the fountains.

The candlelit dinner with the family and the wonderful Rajasthani dishes prepared by Anchal enhanced the honeymooners' feeling that they were somewhere enchanting and very special. Their hosts were clearly proud of their country. They learned about the wettest place on earth, Cherrapunji, and one of the hottest, the Thar Desert, where it can reach fifty degrees in the summer. Plus all the varieties of mango and the tons of bananas exported every year.

"Twenty-five million tons. We are top of the world league," the elder Raj proudly exclaimed.

Then Jairaj used six metres of silk to tie and form a turban onto Rob's head, and Anchal gave Suzy a sari to change into. Mahiraj told them about the lime white wash they had to scrub off. It was several inches thick having built up over many years, layer upon layer. It was thought to have disinfectant properties and protect against smallpox and malaria. By exposing beautifully carved stone and artwork their hard work was rewarded.

The next few days were spent relaxing, sitting around and walking in the village, where all the children wanted a photograph taken. There were at least five temples. They visited the salt flats by jeep, the local school where the bilingual children put their English to shame. The family sponsored the school and helped build the hospital. The operating room had nothing but a table in it. The list of available drugs, which included snake venom anti-serum, was proudly displayed two metres high on the wall. There were numerous examples of how the villagers held the first family in such high regard and great affection. Rob's escape from the real world was temporarily suspended by the hospital tour. It put his mind back into medical mode. All were quite rightly very proud of the new building despite the difficulty staffing it. Perhaps they should move out here, he thought for one crazy moment.

Their last day was spent on the balcony watching the villagers and the hotel staff. A new stretch of white lattice fencing had been put up to stop the guests falling off. Health and Safety gone mad

Rob thought - taking the piss out of the usual moaners, even though of course they could not hear and it was only for his own amusement. One master stood over a boy who could not have been more than ten years old giving him orders in Hindi, whilst he swept away the stones that had fallen from the roof after the heavy rain.

Suzy read her book on the swinging settee. She was absorbed in Marcus Chown's *What A Wonderful World*. Every so often she broke the peace with an astonishing fact she had just learnt.

"Crikey, did you know that if you took the empty space out you could fit the whole human race in the volume of a sugar cube?"

Rob just smiled. He was chilling out by browsing through the wedding album of Anchal and Jairam, left out for the guests. Apparently the event lasted eleven days.

When relaxed Rob was convinced he noticed more and took in more of the world around him. He thought his job was responsible for changing his personality. A GP has to juggle so many problems in the head at once and make so many decisions simultaneously that he was convinced it affected being able to concentrate on any one thing. He could no longer get totally absorbed by *Mahler's 5th Symphony* at a concert, or get lost in a Sebastian Faulks novel like he used to. If a movie was not sufficiently gripping he would realise he had missed vital parts of the plot while his mind drifted. Suzy was used to them leaving the cinema with the first comment being well what was that all about? There is no way he would have noticed a detail like all the chairs having small mirrors in their backs if he was in work mode. The dripping of water and the constant hum of the fans would have driven him mad if working, but here he was not aware of them. He realised he did not even notice the seasons back home.

Rob was only twenty when he was struck by what Len Murray, General Secretary of the Trades Union Congress, said on retirement, *there are places to go, books to read, flowers to smell and trees to look at. I would like to walk through Epping Forest.* About to enter an absorbing career in medicine, this worried him. Would he not read another book, smell another flower, or look at another tree until he retired?

He also realised this was the first time he had seen the press treat a union official like a human being. He even noticed the clouds. How can you live fifty-odd years and take such beautiful objects so much for granted that you do not really notice them. You certainly do not deliberately stand and stare at them. He would do now.

Rob's holidays were rarely long enough to unwind totally. He usually remained a little agitated that he was wasting time. One thing he hated to do. He tried to convince himself by thinking of what Lennon said, *time you enjoy wasting is not wasted.* He was sure it was Lennon but Stephen his old mate had told him it was Bertrand Russell.

The peace was shattered by Rob's mobile phone ringing. Shit. I forgot to turn that thing off. No doubt I have clocked up a fortune in roaming charges.

"Hello! Oh Jeff, how are you? I'm away in India with your sister on our honeymoon. Have you forgotten? Oh, of course not."

Then a pause.

"Thank you for the flowers by the way. Dialled by mistake. Ha! Hope it costs you a lot of money."

Another pause, then.

"Have a word with your little sister, I'm sure she would love to talk. But not for too long, mind. You will use up virtually all my allowance."

Another pause.

"You are her favourite brother. Oh, sorry. Forgot. Only brother."

"Hello Jeff, great to hear from you even if it's a mistake."

A pause, then.

"Why India? Rob's friend Stephen recommended it."

The two sibs chatted while Rob started to sweat at the bill. USA to India via UK network - price of another honeymoon. Sweating turned to agitation and a little irritation at the time it took them to say goodbye.

The Dwight family were well known for their long goodbyes which started with hugs and kisses and love you, answered by love you lots too, and half an hour later they were still at it. When there were more than three of them, Rob was sure they went around each other at least five times. Even when the cars had been started up, it took another ten minutes. It would have lasted longer if people were not choking to death in the fumes. Rob would watch from the kitchen and complete all the washing up from their visit by the time they showed signs of really being serious about departing. Then, and only then, would he say his goodbyes, which he deliberately kept general - if he went around everybody separately, they might as well stay another night.

The Baigents were the opposite. One goodbye and they were off - two minutes and over and done with. Time then to get on with life. Perhaps, Rob thought this demonstrated the gulf between old British families and those with foreign blood especially the Latin component. A Dwight did not so much as wear his or her heart on the sleeve as wear it all over, with a few spare hearts in a trolley behind them. Coming from a more repressed family Rob found it all too much. He said they all knew they loved each other. It did not have to be flaunted and illustrated like a three act play then duplicated on sheets and distributed. He felt that the new fashionable habit of saying love you, love you, love you, every few minutes devalued its meaning. It no longer sounded sincere.

"What do you say when you really love someone?" he asked, "Bring back the good old British stiff upper lip."

Suzy did not know what he was talking about.

"Seems he dialled your number by mistake," she said after the call, "By the way you are incorrect to use the word virtually to mean nearly all. It should be reserved for an imprecise description that is more or less right, or close enough."

Rob ignored her, which was the only way he could avoid getting irritated.

"You mentioning Stephen reminds me, I have a squash game with him booked for the day after we get back. I mustn't forget."

Back to the tranquillity - then Suzy squealed.

"Incredible! This will impress you with your Marilyn Monroe fetish. Apparently every breath you take contains an atom breathed out by her!"

166

They retired to their room after lunch and slept, something Rob would never usually ever consider even if free to do so. They marvelled at the palatial room, the elaborately carved surrounds to the doors and windows, and the massive marble shower room with twin basins and bath. It was all superbly furnished. It never occurred to them that there was no television or pool - the first things that a guest thinks of in a western hotel. Both would have ruined this haven of tranquillity.

Before the last dinner they had the privilege to be shown the grand room with its Belgium glass, which the eldest son had made almost into a museum to display the art, heirlooms and memorabilia from this ancient family. It had a real Edwardian feel to it. Ferns in pots, real tiger rugs complete with heads and pictures of all those racehorses that were nearly the family's downfall. Rob could have spent hours there. Family portraits lined the walls, all lit with an orange glow. Antlers were hung either side of a boar's head, no doubt from a hunt. Indian musical instruments lay around. There was a picture of Jairag's great-grandfather standing next to the Prince of Wales in 1921 with a row of dead boars in front of them after pig sticking. He had come hotfoot from tiger killing in Nepal, so Jairag told them. Next to that was a group photo with the same two men together with the Viceroy of India. The caption read: *Together with HRH The Prince of Wales and Edward Frederick Lindley Wood, Baron Irwin, Viceroy of India – 1927*. Rob recognised Irwin as the 1st Earl of Halifax who would have been Prime Minister instead of Churchill if the appeasers had had their way, but he did not know he had been the Viceroy of India.

Apparently the Sandringham Museum is full of stuffed animals the royals have shot over the last century and a half. Rob was a republican, although Suzy got great entertainment out of the British Royal family - the more gossip the better. She only watched the American legal drama *Suits* because Meghan Markle was in it. Rob had some for her. He knew that the Queen Mother had shot a rhino, and George V bagged twenty-one tigers for his entertainment in India in 1911. He had done his homework on the Internet whilst

Suzy read her book on the swinging settee. More of a shock for Suzy was when he told her that when a guest of the Maharajah of Jaipur in 1961, Prince Philip had shot a tiger. This was the Maharajah whose wife Charles Morrison had seduced as an eighteen year old. His host had it stuffed and it is in Windsor Castle today. Rob then got his iPad out and clicked on a photo he had been saving. There was no mistaking it. Prince Harry crouching over a water buffalo he shot in his gap year in Africa.

"Most kids work in a pub and then have a few weeks back-packing. I'm sure that buffalo wished he'd done that?"

This sent prickles up the Royalist Suzy's spine.

"He's reformed now hasn't he? Both he and William now campaign for wildlife around the world, don't they?"

Jairag just listened. Rob did not want to spoil the atmosphere so avoided further royal criticism and went for Teddy Roosevelt instead.

"The twenty-sixth President of the United States is widely thought to be responsible for the Safari craze. His party killed over eleven thousand animals, Roosevelt two thousand alone."

"Many, I believe are in the Washington Museum," contributed Jairag.

"Yes, that's right. By the twenties it was the fashionable thing to do, but it was not thought to be cricket to shoot the animals from cars like the Americans had started to do. This particularly disgusted Edward VIII when he came across it on his East African safari in nineteen twenty-eight. He had met up with Denys Finch Hatton, an aristocratic big game hunter and lover of Karen Blixen."

"Where have I heard that name before?" asked Suzy.

"The movie *Out of Africa*. She was the Danish author. It's little known she also wrote *Babette's Feast*."

"You are the fount of all knowledge my dear," mocked Suzy.

"Roosevelt said, *nobody cares how much you know, until they know how much you care*."

"Stop showing off" said Suzy to put Rob in his place.

"I mention Edward to demonstrate I would not necessarily chop the heads off all royals. Denys Finch Hatton at least persuaded HRH to shoot wildlife with a camera rather than a gun. He died in 1931 when he crashed his de Havilland Gypsy Moth biplane at Voi airport in Southern Kenya."

Jairag did not want to be left out of the game of demonstrating and perhaps showing off his knowledge.

"Teddy Roosevelt is regarded as a racist in these parts. One of the things he said was, *society has no business permitting degenerates to reproduce their kind.*"

"He held a neo-Lamarckism view," Rob added, not to be outdone.

He regretted that immediately as he could not remember what Lamarckism was and hoped neither of his two companions would ask, but he need not have worried, neither of them seemed in the least bit interested.

They continued to marvel at the family treasures. There were dozens and dozens of group photos on the walls, either at shoots or at the races. Several Viceroys were featured and quite a few minor royals with nothing better to do.

One Governor-General, the Marquess of Linlithgow was shown with a horse on one side and a man in a top hat called Charles Morrison, Baronet Willingdon next to him. On his left was Sir Henry Vaughan-Warner. The date was 1938. In a glass cabinet was an Indian Dress Sword of the eighteenth century taken at the Relief of Lucknow in September 1857. Vaughan-Warner's grandfather, who commanded the British 32nd Regiment of Foot and was awarded the Indian Mutiny Medal and Victoria Cross, captured it. He presented the sword to Jairag's great-great-grandfather.

"That Indian rebellion forced the Government of India Act eventually completed by Lord Derby when rule was transferred from the British East India Company to the Crown," said Jairag.

"It heralded the new era of the British Raj which lasted until the partition of India in 1947. Am I correct, Jairag?"

"Spot on."

Rob remembered what Lamarckism was. The idea that an organism can pass on to its offspring characteristics that it has acquired during its lifetime. But the moment had passed. It was a magical place. They both felt rejuvenated. They felt very close. Suzy looked Rob directly in the eyes and said.

"Loving you is as easy as falling off a piece of cake."

On the way back to the airport in the tour car Rob saw a huge billboard advert for wealth management towering over some tin shacks, which read: DON'T JUST BUILD A BUSINESS, BUILD A FORTUNE. That did it. A lot of the relaxation Rob felt he had eased into over the last ten days disappeared as he felt his muscles tighten and a rant bubbling up.

"Don't these potential capitalist wankers realise that if everyone has a fortune then nobody does? Money is devalued. Of course the cream at the top does. So this really targets a small audience. By definition they need the wealth gap to get wider. If it got smaller they would suffer. What's wrong with having just a fair bit? Who really needs a fortune? How many yachts does one man need? We need a fucking revolution, that's what we really need, if only that was viable. Instead the masses are told what they want, told what they need. They really have no future."

"You mean feasible, not viable Rob," Suzy thought she might as well join in although she did not want to encourage him too much.

"How many yachts? You can have at least three if you destroy British Home Stores and steal the worker's pensions. That man got it wrong. He should have fallen off his yacht before stealing the worker's pension pot, like Maxwell, not leave it until after. It would be the honourable thing but these people would need that word explained to them. How can you give your wife one point two billion pounds to avoid UK tax because she is registered as a resident of Monaco and then sleep easy at night?"

"Because they have no conscience. No different from the politicians who lie about reining in the tax evaders. We will wait for ever before they round up their mates and relatives of course. It is estimated at least one hundred and fifty billion pounds is lost in UK revenue, but benefit fraud less than a billion. What gets most attention? All those millions and millions of lazy fat scrounging couch potatoes who watch Jeremy Kyle behind drawn curtains all day, that's who. Compare it to the Great Train Robbery."

"The good news is, although the robbers got away they are a vital part of the economy. But we did manage to catch two passengers who didn't have tickets."

"Very good Rob."

"Actually its not original. One of Mark Steel's."

So Suzy retaliated with another Marcus fact.

"Did you know you age faster at the top of a building than at the bottom?"

"Did you know Britain has become a fully owned subsidiary of the City of London? The great growth of private debt since Thatcher's time has given the City immense power over the assets and incomes of the rest of the country."

"You really are a nerd, aren't you? But I don't know what you are talking about, my darling," Suzy said, but actually quite lovingly.

The journey continued past more billboards proving the capitalist credentials of the former jewel in the crown of the British Empire. One was for the Lilavati Hospital where the Bollywood stars, politicians and the rich got their healthcare. Another was for the Babulnath Hospital One Day Surgery Centre. Medical tourism was growing in India. She then fell asleep and, as in her own phrase snored like a log. She had this weird dream about collecting Eric from the cattery, but the cat was able to talk and repeated be careful, be careful, be careful.

The flight was as usual, an uncomfortable experience. The airline handed out free copies of yesterday's *Daily Mail*. Rob told a bewildered flight attendant that he did not read political pornography but she left it anyway.

"Best to know what the evil bastards are lying about now. Got to know what we are up against," Rob told an uninterested Suzy.

The story about an airline reducing legroom further in economy so that they could expand first class did nothing to improve Rob's mood. Maybe he should stay in India. To him it was almost a perfect metaphor for the way society is going. Hard luck you poor people.

171

Tough you are stuck in one cramped and sweaty position for eight hours. The refreshments trolley might reach you. It might not. We must pull the curtain. We do not want you feeling jealous of our slumber in full-sized beds, disturbed only by our champagne and five-course meal - same aircraft but totally different worlds.

They had a strange experience at Heathrow, something that had never happened before. The immigration officer slid Rob's passport into the reader and just as Rob was expecting to have it handed back so they could get home after a long journey, the official looked him in the eye.

"Just a minute, Sir."

The man pressed a button and two other officers appeared from nowhere.

"Would you come with us, Dr Baigent?"

How did they know his name? The same happened to Suzy and they were separated and questioned about their trip for at least twenty minutes. Their luggage was searched thoroughly. Even the toothpaste was squeezed out of the tube. They were then told they could go.

15 - HYPOCRISY AND POWER

CANDYMAN

Sickly sweet, his poison seeks
For the young ones who don't understand
The danger in his hands
With a jaundiced wink see his cunning slink
Oh trust in me my pretty one
Come walk with me my helpless one

Siouxsie And The Banshees (1986)

Sean McColl never stood a chance. Not with the parents he had.

His father, Liam, was a depressive, made worse by five pints a night. Like many who felt hard done by, Liam was an angry man and took it out on his family. He had felt angry as long as he could remember. The drunken beatings his father gave his mother and older brother shaped his character - he would have concluded, if he had had any insight. But Liam was not for analysing. In fact he did not think much at all. When after yet another beating his mother's brother, Eamon McBride, burst in and shot his father dead in front of Liam he cried, but they were tears of relief. Eamon never faced justice like his great-grandfather Patrick who was deported to Australia after killing rebels involved in the failed nationalist Young Irelander Rebellion of 1848 during the Great Irish Famine. Under the law of the land both should have been sentenced to death, but those with the power to enforce this thought Ireland a better place without the victims.

Liam was fourteen, had left school and after months of brushes with the law got a job at Harland and Woolf. After too many days off sick he was sacked. One of his uncles felt sorry for him after his father's murder so took him to a place called Du Barry House. He thought him old enough to finally have his weapon inspected, as his uncle put it. Liam had no idea what he was talking about until a girl called Cathy took him upstairs to bake his first love-custard. It was there Liam met Barbara who seemed to have a lot of contacts. Barbara put in a word for Liam and sneaked him a job at Short Brothers instead. He was the lowest of the low, no more than an errand boy. It was the mid 1950s.

Sean's mother Maureen was twelve when she was taken from her school and put in the Sisters of Our Lady of Charity Magdalene Laundry in Dublin. She was one of thirty thousand made to carry out unpaid manual labour by Catholic nuns. They washed clothes for hotels, the army and the Guinness brewery. At weekends she was forced to clean the floors of the local churches. Her name was changed, her hair cropped and all possessions were taken away. From then on she was Mary, as it was more holy and she needed her morals thrashed back into her. The reason given for being taken away was that her father had died and her mother, left with six mouths to feed, had no option but to resort to prostitution. It was the only way to pay the bills and keep a roof over their heads, without all the children being taken away and the family split up more. Mary was the oldest so had to be sacrificed as potentially she could look after herself. One less mouth to feed but being taken away was not her mother's decision. Far from it, she fought it but was told as a whore she was not a fit mother. The irony was the authorities thought the other children should be left in her care. It was as though at twelve years old Mary was of value to them. The others were too young to be of use elsewhere at the moment, but their mother was told they would be back for the others when the time was right. Mary was told the move would further her education but she never saw a schoolbook again.

By day Mary worked in the laundry, was fed bread and dripping and then made rosary beads before bedtime. When the school inspectors came the nuns hid her in a tunnel, as she was not meant to be in the laundry. When caught trying to escape, as punishment the nuns handed her over to a priest. Trust me my pretty one, come walk with me he said, then he raped her. She became pregnant, was shamed by the nuns, put in a punishment cell and the baby taken from her for adoption. She finally got away aged seventeen and

174

walked the hundred or so miles to Belfast sleeping rough on the way. When she crossed the border and arrived in Newry she knew she was two-thirds of the way. She broke into the collection box in the Cathedral of Saint Patrick and Saint Colman, which to her surprise was full and left unattended. She had to get out of the country and was greatly relieved to do so. Maybe the Protestants were not as bad as she had been taught. That money fed her for a few days and a new set of clothes was obtained from the washing line of a house in nearby Marcus Street.

Like her mother her only way to avoid starvation was the sex trade. She was not surprised by any hypocrisy any more. The hypocrisy of the nuns praying to God then doing wicked things. The hypocrisy of the men who paid her and her friends, then preached about how wicked were fallen women - and as for the men of the cloth? Du Barry House was in Whitla Street, Sailortown in the docks area north of Belfast. Protestants and Catholics were not segregated and often lived in neighbouring houses. Despite being host to a steady stream of foreign sailors, Sailortown was a close-knit community. She changed her name back to Maureen. Her trade gave her a roof over her head and she was fed well by the madam who took her under her wing. Men did not like skinny ones in Belfast. But she had her life totally controlled again. Men from all walks of life were sent up to her one by one. Most were foreign sailors, often from the Baltic States. If any complained about her attitude or compliance she was beaten. Some were quite nice, but others did not even mutter a word.

After a year she had some regulars. She ate with the other girls and heard horrific tales but they were not allowed to talk about their work. She thought she had had a bad life until she met the others. Cathy had been working at Du Barry House for five years and was unusual as she had relatives in a red-bricked terraced house along the cobblestoned streets between the docks and York Street. It seemed that the relatives approved of her work - mainly as they benefitted from a cut of the money she earned. Girls did have one half day a week off, and Maureen and Cathy used to walk past all the bomb damage that was the same as when it was created by the

Luftwaffe in 1941, to her relatives for a change of scenery and tea. Maureen got quite friendly with an aunt, Barbara, who could not have been much older than Cathy. Cathy showed no signs of wanting to escape the work, but Maureen was desperate for her freedom. Like most she was trapped. Barbara was keen to help. She stored her money for her and hid the tips she was supposed to hand in. Eventually with her help and after three years she managed to get Maureen a job and she escaped the brothel. She stayed with Barbara. The work was at Short Brothers where the pay was a lot less but she got her body back. In the first week in her new job she met Liam. Neither realised they had a mutual friend in Barbara. Sean was conceived in Loughside Park and despite knowing very little about each other they got married.

It was 1962. Connie Francis had just released her *Irish Favorites* record and the previous summer George Best had been spotted by a Manchester United scout and left Burren Way, three miles south to begin a new life in digs at Mrs Fullaway's council house in Chorlton under Matt Busby's wing. A genius had been discovered.

Maureen managed to disguise her past from Liam for no more than twelve months. She was at work one day when an old client recognised her and wanted favours to keep quiet. She always used the old Irish term pruning when she had to squeeze a man's testicles hard in self-defence and she tried it on this man. Sadly for Maureen Liam saw her and he shouted at her until she told him the truth. It was then they realised about Barbara. That is when the beatings started - like father, like son. It was all right for him to visit Du Barry house as a client, but not for his woman to rescue herself from starvation by working there. But it did allow her then to be open and visit Barbara and Cathy in Sailortown. Maureen hated his Guinness habit partly because it reminded her of the laundry.

Through Maureen and those visits to Sailortown, Liam met the Murphys via a man called Rutherford and was persuaded to join the Ulster Volunteer Force soon after it formed in 1966. He boasted about them firing bricks at the peelers. William Murphy used to live in Fleet Street, Sailortown and brought his three sons back regularly to see friends and relatives. Although the youngest, Lenny, was only a teenager he was already demonstrating his pathological hatred for Catholics. It was no surprise to Maureen to learn later that Lenny became the leader of the Shankill Butchers gang, which became notorious for the torture and murder of Catholic men. She did not shed any tears when the provisional IRA shot him in 1982, as she blamed him for leading Liam astray and thereby helping to destroy their relationship. When she found out about Liam's involvement in the Battle of the Bogside in 1969 and when he boasted about being responsible for burning down some of the Catholics' houses, Maureen had had enough and attacked him. She then took the beating of her life and spent eight days in hospital. She had suspended her enforced faith whilst in the laundry - even hated it because of its hypocrisy - but this, like an addiction, tempted her back to religion. She had learned the hard way that Protestants were no better. All religions were the same.

Sean sat paralysed in fear by his parents' violence. It was to become a pattern. He was fifteen when he escaped his hell. Two years younger than Maureen was when she escaped hers. He too fled his native country and thought the London of the Sex Pistols a good bet. He had seen his father hide some UVF funds under the floorboards and stole £200. He never saw his parents again. When asked later if he missed them and wanted to try to find them, he used the Northern Ireland saying, *do you think I came up the Lagan in a bubble?*

The relief of being free was wonderful. He treated himself to the Ramones at the Roundhouse. But then the money ran out. He was soon sleeping rough in King's Cross alongside Craig, a Liverpudlian of the same age. One night a shiny polished car drew up and a man in a suit (whom he later recognised as Douglas) called Craig over. Within a minute he had got in and was driven off. Three days and nights went by and no Craig. Then the same man reappeared.

"I've put your friend up in a flat. Would you like to sleep in a comfy bed tonight, like him? You must be hungry?"

That was ten years ago. Sean was now twenty-five and still in the Dolphin Square apartment in Pimlico. All he knew though was that

177

he was somewhere in London, not far from Parliament and the Thames. It took a while for him to realise all the famous navigators and admirals he heard referred to were actually the names of the tower blocks. Thirteen altogether housing over a thousand flats. He also picked up that the tenants included dozens of MPs and Lords. The residents were referred to as 'Dolphinians'. He had been outside in those ten years but only when accompanied and to serve in another residence. He was trapped too but even worse than an Irish laundry. Like his mother he got severe beatings when trying to escape. Like his mother his punishment was rape. He was in utter despair. There was no chance of rescue. His first cousin once removed Eamon McBride's son came to London to try to find him but to no avail. Just as well as the family only wanted to punish him for stealing UVF funds.

Sean clung to little things to help him survive and stay sane. His quality of life had improved slightly since Breakfast television started four years before. Prior to that he spent a lot of time staring at the wall. His favourite *Crown Court* came off the air a year later and he was bereft. His daily cycle of pain started in the mid evenings and usually lasted until half way through the night unless he was to be lent out to friends. Then he was often used until dawn when his abusers would shower, put on their three-piece-suits and head to their chambers, or Parliament, or newsroom, or police station, or the city, or go back to their diocese or parish.

He was in his usual foetal position watching TV when the news reported Prime Minister Thatcher's announcement of a review of the NHS. Her Government's policy of starving the NHS of funds had put waiting lists at record high levels and babies not getting their heart operations in the headlines. So she did what all politicians do at a time of embarrassment, set up a review. This, she hoped, would achieve two goals. To kick the NHS as a political distraction into the long grass and soften up the public for 'another way'. The usual kites were being flown - charges for GP appointments and A&E attendances, vouchers, tax breaks for private health insurance. The Omega Project was of course not mentioned. Sean remembered her being proud of her private operation for Dupuytren's contracture only eighteen months before. In his daytime boredom he followed the story closely at the time and even persuaded one of his minders to get a medical book out of the local library to study the anatomy of the hand. He would liked to have been a doctor but Sean never stood a chance.

Sean had no friends. He never met anyone his own age. Craig was reassuring company for a few years but was taken off to a new client one day and never came back. Was he still in one of the other prisons in Fitzroy Square, or Portland Place or southwest London? Sean doubted it now. In such isolation Sean often feared for his sanity. To counter becoming a vegetable he realised he must keep his brain active. His body had and continued to take a battering. A man, who said he was a doctor, had to attend Sean regularly for stitching which would put him out of action for a few days.

He listened in on the conversations all those pillars of society had at their parties in the flat. The pattern was similar most nights although the faces changed. Douglas was ever present. He seemed to have the role of doorman, butler, minder to Sean, hirer of young girls, and sometimes older women, driver and cook. His area of expertise was in trafficking victims from abroad and from poor areas. He knew where the desperate homeless were and so knew where to find Sean and Craig. He seemed to have contacts with those who would take care of nuisances. Douglas, TV and abuse were the three constants in Sean's life. They never changed much.

The early arrivals were often the clergy. The politicians and businessmen were rarely there before 9.00 p.m. A woman called Margaret was mentioned a lot and it took Sean years to realise what they meant. She was obviously well known to the men who seemed to think, from tit-bits Sean picked up, that they controlled her. This is why he could not believe at first they were talking about the Prime Minister. He tried to remember all that was said but had to pretend not to be listening. The more the evening went on the more their tongues loosened helped by the *Dom Perignon*, weed, cocaine and amyl nitrate. He had a good memory for faces although saw more of their features below the waist than above. If he ever escaped he wanted to be able to document all that had happened and who these men were. However Douglas regularly made it clear what Sean's fate would be if he tried to get out or stop cooperating. Douglas had told him he was just in one of many of a string of flats used for the same purpose. If he disappeared he would not be missed and there were plenty to replace him.

Fairly frequently Sean would see familiar faces on his television. The contrast between what they preached on TV and how they lead their personal lives could not have been greater. Lecturing about family values, wanting pornography banned, cutting sex education - then getting their mistresses pregnant, voting for the anti-gay Section 28, wanting long prison sentences for drug suppliers, condemning teenagers for being lazy, stigmatising all football supporters as hooligans, then coming to Dolphin Square, using all the substances they had just made illegal and abusing Sean and his fellow sufferers.

Sean was treated like a lump of meat. He often wondered if they had sons his own age. If they did they clearly could not connect the two. Perhaps that is the special quality it takes to be a successful politician, to be a Premier League hypocrite, able to argue black is white and not even realise what they are doing. A lack of connections amongst a certain batch of neurons in the brain, compensated for by a set of strong connections between fighting for a cause and how much money is in it for them. He had a lot of time to think. He had a lot of time and a lot to remember.

Another of Douglas's jobs was to keep Sean trapped. He photographed Sean in all sorts of incriminating and compromising poses. Sean thought the idea of the photos was to keep him under their control. But he was wrong. Douglas did not need to go to those lengths. If Sean had strayed he would just have had him killed. Simple. The purpose of the photos of Sean, often in pain, was their commercial value. They were passed around and sold or given to regular loyal customers. His abusers were careful to make sure they could not be identified but Douglas occasionally managed to get the odd head in he should not have without anyone noticing. Douglas knew it was potentially his pension - fantastic blackmail material. He had his own darkroom.

Two days after seeing Margaret on television Sean saw a few more familiar faces being interviewed about the NHS review. They clearly had been instructed to keep on saying, *the NHS is safe in our hands*, which immediately rang alarm bells. The Terms of Reference of the review were never published and it was never officially revealed who served on the panel but Sean picked up, in idle conversation, that Major and Lawson were included. Other names he heard mentioned and memorised, but did not understand, included a Professor called Alain Enthoven who wanted the market introduced into the NHS. Letwin, Redwood and Froggatt seemed to Sean to also be designing policy. Years later Sean heard the new Health Secretary, Frank Dobson call the Tory health adviser Dr Froggatt a smack head after his conviction for heroin abuse. Several books were left around the apartment as they materialised that year of 1988 - Letwin's *Privatising The World*, the publication by the right wing Adam Smith Institute *The Health Of Nations*. Letwin and Redwood's Centre for Policy studies pamphlet *Britain's Greatest Enterprise: Ideas for radical reform of the NHS* was left as coffee-table reading amongst the pornography, although those who visited Dolphin Square were usually more preoccupied with buggering Sean across the coffee table than sitting and reading.

Sean had plenty of time to look at these. He was deprived, abused, owned and trapped but he was not stupid. His education was limited but he could read. He had trouble understanding some words so persuaded Douglas to get him a dictionary. Douglas could not see the harm in letting Sean read whatever he wanted. If he was sad enough to read those pamphlets left lying around so be it.

Over time Sean gradually understood the bigger picture. Even he in his isolation could see the plots to change society and against the NHS taking shape even though he was not even sure he understood what the NHS really was. Of more importance though to Sean was building a dossier of important names to help him get revenge if he did ever escape. He knew his life would be in danger but did he care? He had made several suicide attempts. He guessed Craig was probably dead. It had to all be in his head even though he knew that meant no proof. Even if he could get hold of some of those photos he had no secure hiding place. He remembered names well, even when he could not put them into context.

He had no idea who Mandy Rice-Davies was except that she had had a flat in Dolphin Square too. He knew better than to ask questions. So did Christine Keeler. And John Vassall whom, he overheard was a Soviet spy and caused trouble for a Prime Minister called Macmillan, who apparently was still alive. Macmillan had had to turn a blind eye whilst his wife had a thirty-five year affair with one of his colleagues, the bisexual Conservative MP Bob Boothby - British stiff upper lip in full stiffness was how he heard it described in the apartment pre-sex gossip. Sean had gathered that the press knew all about it and that it was common knowledge in Parliament and every London club. Lady Dorothy was the third daughter of the ninth Duke of Devonshire and had a daughter fathered by Baron Boothby of Buchan and Rattray Head, as he became known when ennobled by Macmillan, who raised the girl as his own.

Boothby's name had come up a year or two earlier when those sitting in the flat were mourning his loss. They joked about his nickname of The Palladium because he was twice nightly. Through one of his lovers he met Ronnie Kray who supplied him with young men in exchange for favours. The conservative press covered up his underworld associations and crimes, but when the *Daily Mirror* reported them, Cecil King the owner sacked his editor. The Krays' criminal activities continued unchecked for three more years. The Queen Mother said he was a bounder but not a cad.

Sean was fascinated to learn that Diana Mitford, whose sister Deborah was Duchess of Devonshire, and her husband Oswald Mosley were arrested and interred from their flat in Dolphin Square in 1940. He did not realise the apartments were that old. The television documentary that featured Mosley was actually about the Battle of Cable Street. Amongst those fighting Mosley and interviewed was a Welshman called Hywel Davies and an eighty-year-old Phil Piratin, one of the last communist MPs. Sean learnt so much by discreetly listening, but pretending not to.

What a way some spend their childhoods. Not a surprise they grew up like they did.

16 - CLASS AND DIVISION

THE ETON RIFLES

Thought you were smart when you took them on
But you didn't take a peep in their artillery room
All that rugby puts hairs on your chest
What chance have you got against a tie and a crest?

The Jam (1979)

James Morrison never stood a chance. Not with the parents he had.

His father, Charles, was a depressive, made worse by five scotch and sodas a night. He was an aristocrat, a Baron who wanted for nothing - nothing material anyway. Like several generations he was packed off to prep school and then Eton. He got no parental love. But you do not miss what you do not know about. Without love he found it difficult to socialise and relate to others. Like most of the boys he joined at school they eventually sought comfort from each other. But the attention he needed had to be fought for. Literally. He needed to dominate. He delighted in hitting other boys without provocation and in turn got hit as punishment by his masters and fag-master. In Charles' eyes a fight was only successful if he inflicted a scar on the face. He boasted about the damage done.

"See old Rutherford over there? That scar on his right cheek is my calling card. I almost penetrated right through. Needed twenty stitches. My record. If he becomes famous I'll be able to point it out. Look at that leg brace. A cripple should go to a school for cripples. Preferably in another country. And that other pansy with him, Eddy Sackville-West, he's my next target."

His destiny was set before birth. Entry to Cambridge was a right, no matter how dim he might turn out to be. Then the Army to defend the Empire - he did a tour of India in the 1930s. The circles he naturally revolved in brought him into contact with the right sort - the right class - right wing groups heavily moulding his politics, although there was little shaping necessary. No one broke the mould he was made from. It had been used thousands of times and will be again. He thought his type of existence was the norm. This was because of the circles in which he did not mix, or even know about, therefore he would not recognise.

At Cambridge, just after the First World War, Charles was part of a group who kicked a Negro to death in the street. His father knew the police and so he was not charged. To the mob he was just a nigger who should go home. In reality he was a Guyanese merchant seaman who volunteered to come to the aid of his mother country and travelled at his own expense to enlist in the British Army. He fought on the Somme at the battles of Delville Wood and Thiepval Ridge. His Army service ended in 1919 with three medals, two gas-burnt lungs from the Battle of Passchendaele and a shell wound in the back. But there was no gratitude. Not even a job. No blacks need apply said the signs. He ended up begging on the streets of Cambridge where he met his end at the hands of a grateful nation in a land fit for heroes.

Charles loved the violence associated with beating the enemy. By 1937 he had attended a Nuremburg Rally and made many Nazi friends in Germany and Britain. He watched in jealous awe as some lads from the Hitler-Jugend kicked an old Jewish woman to the ground. It was the club he longed to join. His violence extended of course to all living things. He loved his shooting learnt in 1938 in India with the Governor General, the Marquess of Linlithgow. He had become Baron Willingdon by then. Despite that he had the disgrace of being thrown out of the Bengal Club by the President, Milne Robertson, for molesting his wife.

James' mother, Edwina, was twelve when she was taken from her home tuition for a spell at Wycombe Abbey. It had been recommended by family friends, the Carringtons, who originally owned the estate and knew the founder Dame Frances Dove.

Rupert Carington, the fourth Baron Carrington, was a close friend of Edwina's grandparents. The fourth Baron's grandson Peter had his political career sacrificed for him when he had to resign as Foreign Secretary on the Argentinian invasion of the Falkland

Islands. He was not party to the plot to make Thatcher a war hero to get her re-elected. He did end up as Chairman of the Bilderberg group though. He died in his one-hundredth year, still not able to decide how many Rs should be in his name.

Edwina then entered Brillantmont, her finishing school in the centre of Lausanne. Her classes on deportment and etiquette took place whilst enjoying views over Lake Leman and the Swiss Alps. It was never questioned that every young lady should learn the social graces and upper class cultural rites as a preparation for entry into society and then a good marriage. The school had several visits by girls from the Nationalsozialistische Frauenschaft or the National Socialist Women's League and the Bund Deutcher Madel or Band of German Maidens who demonstrated how to fold napkins into swastikas.

Becoming a debutante and being presented to Queen Mary was the next step in finding a rich husband for Edwina since the family had fallen on difficult times. That rich husband was Charles Morrison, soon to inherit a title. She tolerated all his affairs - she had no choice - which even included two years with his cousin, the glamorous blonde who spied for the Nazis and tried to sabotage Nicholas Winton's work with the Kindertransport. Charles was quite happy to pass information to her on behalf of the Right Club. Edwina was just a convenience for Charles.

So James Morrison never stood a chance to grow up and develop as a normal well-balanced and valuable contributor to society.

Gerald Vaughan-Warner never stood a chance. Not with the parents he had.

His father, Henry was a racist and a follower of Francis Galton, Darwin's half cousin, who founded the Eugenics Educational Society and Ernst Rüdin in Nazi Germany. In his teens Henry was given the 1908 *Royal Commission On The Care And Control Of The Feeble-Minded* to read by his father Sir Edward. Sir James Crichton-Brown recommended the compulsory sterilisation of those with learning disabilities and mental illness, describing them as, *our social rubbish,* which should be, *swept up and garnered and utilised as far as possible.* Crichton-Brown was in distinguished company. In a memo to the Prime Minister in 1910, Winston Churchill cautioned, *the multiplication of the feeble-minded is a very terrible danger to the race.* Henry really felt progress was being made, at least in America. Charles Davenport's ideas led to Congress passing laws restricting immigration by ninety-seven per cent in 1924.

Hitler was inspired by US policies. The ban on Jews led to Otto Frank's visa application for his family being rejected. Henry often quoted Davenport who wrote, *can we build a wall high enough to keep out these cheaper races?* John Harvey Kellogg worked with Davenport to organise the Race Betterment Conference of 1915 and developed his cornflakes as an aphrodisiac to lead Americans away from the sin of masturbation. By 1938 a majority of States permitted forced sterilisation of women with learning disabilities and those with genetic conditions. The right of certain disabled people to marry was restricted. Henry advocated the same policies for Great Britain.

His mother left him and his father when Gerald was two. The last Henry had heard of her she had reverted back to her maiden name of Alicia D'Avignor Goldsmid and gone to Spain with a Welshman called Robert Owen Davies to support the republican cause in the civil war. Henry knew it was a mistake to introduce her to Jessica Mitford.

Henry's absence - he was not at all interested in his children - effectively made Gerald an orphan. Henry was too busy enjoying himself on inherited income and then travelling around the Empire especially to India. He often attended shooting weekends on country estates where the main topic was always how Britain needed the military to take charge.

In his early thirties he had worked hard to gain favour with the society hostess Margaret Greville. Affectionately known as Mrs Ronnie, you were nobody unless you were invited to her weekends at Polesden Lacey in the Surrey countryside. Before Henry's time she regularly entertained Edward VII and his mistress Alice Keppel. Mrs Ronnie looked upon the Duchess of York as the daughter she never had. The future George VI and Queen Elizabeth honeymooned at Polesden Lacey. A great admirer of Hitler, Mrs Ronnie was virulently anti-Semitic and met the Fuhrer when guests at the Nuremberg rally. She thought the Reichsbräuteschule, or Reich Bride Schools, just the sort of thing needed in England and told everyone so. They were to train perfect Nazi brides for the SS and senior officials. Mrs Ronnie visited the first to be established on Schwanenwerder, an island in the Havel River in southwest Berlin. It was at these weekends Henry found himself hobnobbing with royalty including Queen Victoria Eugenie of Spain and the likes of Charlie Chaplin.

Mrs Ronnie was not one to fall out with. She disapproved of Edward VIII and Harold Nicolson called her, a *fat slug filled with venom*. When she died in 1942, Henry felt bereft, especially of some important social connections. Only two months before her death in the Dorchester, Henry had taken her to one of the lunchtime National Gallery Concerts that ran throughout the war. But Henry matured in his career at conferences like Bretton Woods and then got involved with the Mont Pelerin Society.

Gerald's nanny was left unchecked with his care. His uncle abused him. Like many who felt hard done by Gerald was an angry man who took it out on others. Unlike Sir James he did not think the abuse he suffered was normal. He had felt angry as long as he could remember. To him public school at Harrow then Sandhurst was a relief. He escaped his abuser and became one instead. Once a public schoolboy, always a public schoolboy. Like his father he was convinced the only way the human race would survive was to nurture a super-race and eliminate the others.

Gerry married in 1965 taking on the two small boys from his wife's first marriage. He would beat them. He thought it would strengthen them to help them become part of that super-race. What chance had the peasants against a tie and a crest?

Gerald met James through Eddie Chapman. They soon learnt from Eddie that their fathers knew each other. They were together in India in 1938. Eddie Chapman was the only Englishman to be awarded the Third Reich's Iron Cross. He started life blowing up safes such as at the Odeon cinema at Swiss Cottage, eventually caught and jailed in Jersey. He did a deal when Jersey was occupied by the Germans to spy for them, Agent Fritz, but he became a double agent, Agent Zigzag. Chapman gained the confidence of the Germans by faking the blowing up of a de Havilland factory in Hatfield. His greatest achievement on returning to Germany was feeding them false information about the landing sites of V2s, thus getting many to undershoot their target of London, saving many British lives.

After the war Chapman reverted back to his dodgy life mixing with blackmailers and smuggling gold across the Mediterranean amongst other crimes. Charles and Henry had found Eddie a useful link to the underworld if they needed something done that was not quite legal. This included murder. He seemed to know everyone. When Eddie fell on hard times in the late 1950s he thought he could use his heroic wartime record and contribution to the war effort to avoid prosecution. His plan was to contact Gerald and James, bring them together for the first time, and get them to pass the message to their fathers that Eddie would spill the beans on their plans and plots if he did not get help.

Eddie was a seductive character. He became a hero of both young men especially with his stories of having two fiancées at the same time, each in opposite war zones, whilst still betrothed to his English girlfriend. He abandoned all of them after the war to marry another former lover.

"This is what life is all about. He will be my role-model," James said to Gerry.

They both had glorious times at his health farm in Shenley and his castle in Ireland - right up until his death in 1997 they found Eddie very useful.

What a way some spend their childhoods. Not a surprise they grew up like they did.

17 - SWEAT AND MOANING

WON'T GET FOOLED AGAIN

We'll be fighting in the streets
With our children at our feet
And the morals that they worship will be gone
And the men who spurred us on
Sit in judgement of all wrong
They decide and the shotgun sings the song

Meet the new boss
Same as the old boss

Pete Townshend (1971)

"Did you hear... that Goldman-Sachs... grossed forty-five million euros... by helping the EU... crash the Greek... economy?"

Stephen whacked the ball back, high and over Rob's head as the word economy left his lips to win the point and the third game.

"Hey... you haven't... changed from... our Brockley days... have you... still using... putting-off tactics... to win?"

Rob's words came out slowly in between gasps for breath in the rhythm of a train passing over the fishplates that join the rails. They both were covered in sweat and collapsed on the floor after that winning point. Leaning against the squash court wall they both left their damp impression. There was nothing said while they struggled to get their breath back. There was just the heavy breathing. The fishplates stopped their pulsation. The tales he had heard about the plan to asset strip Greece fascinated Stephen.

"They are all vultures. WikiLeaks exposed the IMF plan to threaten imminent financial disaster if they didn't cut pensions and working conditions. Officials were caught red-handed plotting a credit crisis, pushing Greece to the edge of bankruptcy, all to destabilise Europe. Who do these people think they are to play with peoples' lives like that? They are totally self-serving or they wouldn't have blocked the Chinese rescue deal."

"That was the Germans," Rob added, "The Greeks know they have been set up. Germany dictates to Europe completely and utterly. They demanded control of Greece's finances or its withdrawal from the Euro. They are achieving what they failed to do in two world wars."

Rob continued on the European theme. He had felt angry about the 2016 Referendum but, feeling powerless, could do no more than take the piss.

"Well now we have voted to leave the EU we have the freedom to go back to having dirty beaches, abolish some of those silly old human rights and make workers have to put in double the hours. We can have our bent bananas back and made to measure condoms! Fire safety regulations can be relaxed. They can blame the odd Grenfell Tower disaster on the residents. There will be no nanny European Court of Human Rights barring our right to stick children up chimneys if that's what we decide to do. We've got our sovereignty back. You see every cloud has a silver lining!"

"Yes, but seriously they can't name one law that was imposed on us that wasn't a good idea, and they were not genuine in making that an election issue or they wouldn't have fought Parliament having a vote on it all," countered Stephen, "Like all duplicitous egomaniacs they selected their arguments and conveniently ignored the sixteen eighty-nine *Bill of Rights* which clearly stated that laws should not be dispensed without the consent of Parliament."

"Who said that instead of giving a politician the keys to the city, it might be better to change the locks?"

"No idea?"

"Nor have I. Was it me just then?"

"Doubt it. You're not bright enough," Stephen continued the lampooning and mocked further, "And no more Health and Safety holding us back either. What does it matter if a few workers fall into the cement mixer as long as the project making the bosses rich is completed on time?"

"Interesting fact for the evening," said Rob, "Did you know the first to die on the Hoover Dam project was a man called Tierney when in nineteen twenty-two, whilst undertaking the early surveys, he fell into the Colorado and drowned? The last man to die was his son who fell off the dam's tower thirteen years to the day after his dad's death. Over one hundred more died, but it was worth it."

"So how was India? Did you take my advice to avoid the elephants and so escaped my fate of being covered in Genus Elephas snot?

"Still a little jet lagged which is my excuse for losing that game," replied Rob. "All the places you recommended were fabulous. It was a real break, but not a honeymoon in the traditional sense of the word."

"Well, second time around and in an old man, not going to be the same is it?"

"Watch it sonny! Curious incident on the way back. Have you ever been held up, taken aside and questioned at Heathrow? Both Suzy and I were interrogated for about twenty minutes, and separately. Really pissed off I was."

"Can't say I have been. Didn't you show them your Tory Party Life Membership card? You'd have been guided straight through. Teach you to be a revolutionary though, won't it? No, seriously, probably just routine stuff nowadays."

"I dread going back to work on Monday too. I have a feeling of doom about it. Recently there has always been some unwelcome news waiting for me."

"You should work in hospitals mate. Never welcoming now with all the corporate crap we have to endure. One more game?" ventured Stephen.

The Brockley days were looked back upon with affection by the four ex-flatmates. Stephen and Rob initially had to share a room when they both started at Guy's, just a short train journey away. The initial six of them drew straws. When two dropped out, they converted the living room into a bedroom so none of them had to share. Of the two who left, one moved in with the woman next door and for a few years no one knew what happened to the sixth but it later emerged he had done time in Australia after a conviction for stalking Jimmy Page of Led Zep.

The flatmates did have fun. Too much time was spent in the Duke of Albany at the expense of their studies, which they realised with the exam failures. They used to tease each other that they had bumped into Kate Bush, a local girl, in the high street Co-op and had to fight off her advances. They all selectively remembered and reminisced about the parties and regular parade of girlfriends rather than the studying and exam failures.

Rob could not regard it as a happy or relaxed chapter in life. He felt too insecure and lacked confidence. Stephen though was sure of himself, but not really in a mature way. Good enough to get the girlfriends though. But the other lads in the flat teased him that they thought the moans and groans emanating from his bedroom were really coming from a cassette he had faked, not real life. Or was it that sadistic girlfriend of his torturing him? He lived in the flat longer than Rob as he joined a London medical job rotation. Rob moved to Brighton for a GP training scheme. Stephen got his postgraduate MRCP quickly and became one of the youngest Consultant Geriatricians in the country. He arrived in Brighton to take up his post some time after Rob had left for his GP principal position on the Sussex-Kent border. So they ended up within twenty miles of each other as Stephen commuted to work from Uckfield.

In those days the standard of general practice was excellent and most jobs highly sought after particularly in a lucrative dispensing practice, which attracted at least one hundred high calibre applicants. Not so now after years of government interference, micro-management, funding and staff cuts and attempts to de-professionalise the vocation. They seemed to want to change it from a worthy career into just a job. Rob could not work out why at first, but it finally dawned on him it was really because the unpopular politicians were jealous of the popular medics. How pathetic. Now he was sure it was their privatisation tactic. Get their friends in the press and media to slag off doctors so often that the public begin to believe it. False tales of GPs earning £250,000 a year and consultants on the golf course all afternoon. Blame always directed at the doctor when tragedies occurred and, most annoying of all as far as Rob was concerned, GPs getting the blame when patients were suffering actually as a direct result of the government policy of starving the NHS of funds. Divide and rule was another tactic. Pitch consultants against GPs, against public health doctors, against nurses - all with conflicting and competing budgets.

Stephen had a good reputation amongst his colleagues and was admired by some for entering a Cinderella service when he was bright enough to do anything. The three-piece-suited private practice brigade in Brighton could not understand why he should forgo a large private practice income. How could he possibly afford the private school fees, the second home in Provence and the yacht in the Brighton marina - essentials to belonging in the right circles? Over lunch in the doctors' dining room Stephen actually overheard an orthopaedic surgeon who was looking for a new house saying, there's absolutely nothing worth having under £2 million you know.

Rob and Stephen had remained friends because of their common principles. As they walked towards the changing rooms they returned to the subject of corruption. Stephen had always thought Rob a little too paranoid and was amused by his increasing belief in conspiracies. This annoyed Rob who retaliated by putting Stephen's naivety down to his closeness to the establishment arising from his public school education. Rob often teased his old friend by saying you can take the boy out of the public school, but you can't take the public school out of the boy. To Stephen's credit though the boorishness, mixed with a dash of desperation and undeserved over-confidence Rob found in most ex-public school colleagues was not there in Stephen. And there was no way Stephen had been educated beyond his intelligence, which was another missile Suzy threw at those privately groomed.

"You all say you wouldn't subject your children to the same fate of boarding school as you found the experience dreadful, but when the crunch comes, off they go, packed off in their expensive uniforms."

On the stagger to the changing rooms Stephen continued the conversation he first initiated.

"The Troika, the IMF, the EU and the European Central Bank is capitalism at its worst. They are really going for the Greeks telling them they have to make even more spending cuts. They can only see the rules and balance sheets, not the neo-Nazi assaults in Greek Island migrant camps. They are orchestrating the destruction of Greek democracy and who will be next? The Irish? The Portuguese? The Spanish? The Italians?"

"So depressing," punctuated Rob.

"Well one thing's for sure, it won't be us. Not because we have left the EU so now we are an irrelevance, but because we're doing a grand job destroying ourselves. Our productivity has dropped so much we are now almost in the same league as Greece. Have you noticed though, the media don't ask the question, why?" said Stephen, turning towards Rob who was wiping sweat from his face.

"Bloody obvious. Years of cuts, austerity and most important lack of investment," Rob replied through the hands covering his face.

"The Europeans looked at us with sheer astonishment as we held a gun to our own head and said if you don't give us what we want we will blow our own brains out, then we pulled the trigger. Did you see that BMJ article a little while back? One hundred and twenty thousand excess deaths in this self-inflicted austerity period as a direct result of health and social care cuts. And was it reported in the media? Was it fuck? They just don't care. The equivalent of four hundred Airbuses crashing. You'll think I'm a nerd but I not only read the article and I can remember the figures. Leading up to austerity, deaths in England fell by an average of zero point seven per cent a year, but once this wonderful policy kicked in deaths rose by an average of zero point eight seven per cent."

"You really are a nerd."

Rob took out his deodorant spray ready for after his shower.

"Don't use that near me!" insisted Stephen.

Rob sprayed it at him.

"That's for being a nerd," like they had not grown up since the flat in Brockley,

"Bastard!"

Rob carried on as though he had not just acted like a ten-year-old.

"One reason I'm so fed up is there seems an increasing attitude that it's over, it's impossible now, the right wing has won. They are even getting elected in Germany. At least that's what they think, the arrogant fuckers. There is nothing that will stop this tide that is actually more like a tsunami."

"No, you must be optimistic," countered Stephen, "or they really have won. Remember what Tony Benn said, *there's no final victory and there's no final defeat. Every generation must fight the same battles again and again.*"

"But they are kicking people when they are down to consolidate their advantage," Rob replied with anger in his voice, "Even a pretence of democracy is fantasy. Take the French. In their election it was a choice between a right wing fascist and a candidate no one really wanted. No other choice. Where is the option to reject austerity, privatisation, longer hours, lower wages, a widening social divide and the theft of the younger generation's future? It's always been the case that there's no real choice in the States, just a sham of democracy, but it is also now true here."

"And in Germany the losers are driven towards the right wing AfD," his squash partner chipped in then added, "I use the word loser in sympathy for those screwed by neo-liberalism, and disparagingly when they are stupid enough to vote for nutters."

Rob was on a roll.

"But look at our last general election. Called by a woman who promised repeatedly not to call one, lied about a load of other things, acted like a robot, failed to get approval and so tried to cling to power with the support of pro-hanging creationists. Strong and stable my arse. And who knows what those Irish were up to? They paid a small fortune to advertise in the London Metro a pro-Brexit stance, and for some weird reason the money apparently came from Saudi Arabia! Work that one out? Fuck me, there's so much we don't know about what's going on. The only good thing to come out of that is that the young are flexing their muscles and many have sidelined the right wing press. Quite a youth quake. Hopefully the beginning of the end for their poisonous and toxic effluent. Social media became quite a useful tool instead of loads of people using it just to tell each other how much they love one another or they are just about to have a coffee. So useful it won't be long before they ban it!"

"Oh they are already working on that," said Stephen in a sinister tone, "Why do you think there is an all out attack on Facebook and the like?"

But Rob was still depressed by the result.

"Amongst those re-elected was that ex-McKinsey creep who gets straight onto the Health Select Committee. What a conflict of interest. Free to promote the privatisation agenda. I've sent in a formal complaint, but I'm sure it will fall on deaf ears."

"Hmmm," Stephen replied, "their party needs a rebranding. It would then become the Bosses, Bankers and Landlord's Party. It is the political wing of the vested interests that fund it."

Stephen read the *Guardian* every single day from cover to cover, and told Rob he was absolutely right but what could be done? Despite Rob's view about social media he relied on it. He abandoned the *Guardian* years ago for being too middle-of-the-road.

"You know what happens if you are in the middle of the road Stephen?" He used to tease, "You get run over."

Stephen said he agreed with Rob on two further points. First the rich made tax laws complicated on purpose to hide evasion and avoidance in the muddied waters - and second, scandals hit the headlines for a few days then disappear without trace, allowing the guilty to get away with murder, sometimes literally.

"Take the case of the *Panama Papers*. That Mossack Fonseca law firm had its fifteen minutes of fame a few years ago, but have you heard anything since? Assets were hidden, taxes dodged and thousands were obviously up to no good, but after a couple of scalps, not a dicky-bird since. In a decent functioning democracy like Iceland they got rid of their Prime Minister, but did we? Did we hell! I know they have eleven million papers to go through but they should have found something juicy by now, unless they've been shut down. Then there were the *Paradise Papers*, second only to the *Panama Papers* as the biggest data leak in history, exposing the offshore investments of, amongst many others, our lovely Royal family. The giveaway is in the name. The French term for tax haven is paradis fiscal! They all get away with it. The media are so arse licking to our Royals that they said it was nothing to do with them, it was their investors who were to blame!"

"What about the sycophantic way the press dealt with the old Duke turning his Land Rover over, breaking a woman's arm and not wearing a seatbelt?" interjected Rob".

Stephen was not to be sidetracked.

"But it will all be forgotten so they can concentrate on benefit scroungers. The media and press move on, as they have attention spans no better than goldfish and because they think the public has too. But it's more sinister than that. We have a constant cycle of repeated news each day until we have heard it one hundred times, then another lot the next day. Sound bites are drummed into us but never great scrutiny or detail, but the media can claim they covered it."

"*Strong and stable. Long term economic plan,*" parroted Rob, "They offer brain-numbing fodder to throw us off the scent. Stories like Dog Goes Up In Hot Air Balloon, New Gate Too Noisy, Man Tried To Sell Himself On eBay. Crap like that. More recently the debate about Europe, Brexit and the Trump circus have dominated every news bulletin, so issues more important to the man on the Clapham omnibus like the abolition of the NHS get squeezed out and not debated. It all stops people working out what the Establishment is really up to."

By this time they were in the communal showers so Stephen had to shout to be heard.

"Look at the MP expenses scandal. It all blew over as they wanted and yet apparently they are all at it once again, and more money is being claimed than before. So where are the investigative journalists when you need them? Actually I can answer my own question here. Most are too scared to investigate and those who are brave enough disappear or get locked up."

Rob was quite stunned. He had never heard Stephen talk like this and certainly not so readily agree with him. A great sense of relief wafted over him. It was so good to hear what he had thought for a while being articulated by someone he trusted and especially good from Stephen whom he thought ridiculed him behind his back.

"Blimey Stephen, you are beginning to sound like me!"

"Really? Oh fuck, better have a pint to get my brain back in gear then."

"Those crooked MPs who tried to swindle tens of thousands of pounds out of the taxpayer are the same bunch who want to punish and lock up benefit cheats if they collect ten pence too much in error. They were caught red handed and they think its punishment enough just to have to hand the money back!"

As they were strolling out of the changing rooms Rob's curiosity got the better of him.

"Do you really think people who get too close to what is going on are disappearing?"

But Stephen wasn't listening. The poster of Maria Sharapova marketing her sports bra distracted him.

"Blimey. Magnificent. Hard to think she was born in Russia. Sorry, ah, yes, disappearing people. Heard about one last night. No, you won't see it in the British media, too cosy with the Americans who are behind a lot of this. You know I'm trying to re-learn French?"

"No, I didn't know," responded Rob, wondering where this red herring was leading.

"Well, to help my conversation style I tune into *Franceinfo TV* state television news channel quite a lot. They did an item about this American, now living in London whose husband, an investigative journalist, disappeared a few years ago whilst snooping around Washington. She thinks he was onto something big and has either been killed or locked up by her fellow countrymen. She says the British media aren't at all interested. She was very plausible but didn't help my French as she spoke English-American of course! I'm sure a lot goes on we don't know about."

The local sports complex did not have a bar as the management thought it not in keeping with their raison d'etre. They seemed not to notice the irony of still having a vending machine dishing out pure sugar disguised as health re-hydration - isotonic with vitamins. Better for the centre's profits but much worse.

"Look at this Rob, capitalism at its very best. Take a freely available substance, dress it up and sell it as something that will transform your body, soul and mind. Brilliant."

"Yes, a real crime demonstrating how gullible the public are. The original Watergate, boom, boom!"

"Ha, ha, very good," said Stephen.

Rob read them out.

"Life, Volvic, Ugly, Evian, Highland Spring, Sibberi, Plenish, Vita Coco, Coco Pro, Coco Zumi, Coconut water, CanO Water. Hey, look at this one, Birch water promising to eliminate cellulite!"

"A million plastic bottles are bought around the world every minute, twenty thousand every second! Worth billions this industry apparently, for something that falls out of the sky, wish I'd thought of it," joked Stephen.

"No you don't. You are not that unprincipled.'

"Oh, you haven't heard about my bottled air side line then? I collect Dorset and Yorkshire air and sell it to the Chinese at eighty pounds a bottle. Kidding of course. Someone else got there first too, but if I had I'd have used glass not plastic, which now is all over the oceans' floors, billions of tiny plastic fragments polluting and killing. Most seafood has plastic in it. Pyrolysis is what is needed. It breaks plastic down into more basic molecules to form an oil called plaxx which can be used as a fuel, or to make new plastic."

Rob was keen to avoid a chemistry lecture.

"Do you remember Orson Welles selling Perrier when we were young? After that water snobbery replaced wine snobbery."

"Yer. Seen the latest con, water from the Canadian Artic ice shelf, frozen for ten thousand years?"

"What's the sell-by date on that?" queried Rob with a smile.

"Perhaps we are conned another way with our beer? They say it takes up to six times the amount of water in a plastic bottle to manufacture it. And only about four pints of water to make our pint of beer. Lesson learnt. Drink beer not water from glass bottles."

"I avoid plastic if I can, probably like you Rob because of the carbon footprint it produces. Using oil in the manufacturing, releasing tonnes of carbon dioxide into the environment, but what really convinced me was the polyethylene terephthalate from the plastic that we swallow which leaks from the plastic bottle. It is recyclable but most bottles end up in landfill or the ocean and takes about four hundred years to decompose. The French have apparently banned plastic cups and cutlery. The Norwegians recycle ninety-six per cent of their bottles. Germany, as ever, wins on a penalty shoot-out. Ninety-eight point five per cent."

"Good for them," Rob said grudgingly remembering Frank Lampard's disallowed goal, "We live with the embarrassment of a Government ruled by big business, not ethics."

Stephen continued where he left off.

"Bloody Coca Cola is trying to sabotage a recycling scheme as it'll hit their profits. Do you know they produced more than one hundred billion bottles this year? On current trends by the year two thousand and fifty the plastic in our oceans will weigh more than all the fish. Plus the gassy brown stuff is toxic, nine teaspoons of sugar in each can. I bet the Government gives in, especially now after Brexit as we are at their mercy."

"McDonald's is as bad with their plastic straws. Millions are used every day and they end up in seabirds' stomachs, and up turtles' nostrils," Rob mourned.

They always left their cars in the centre car park, as The Hung Drawn and Quartered pub was directly opposite. They understood why a pub near Tower Hill was called that and they both frequented this spit and sawdust establishment as students, but they had no idea why a pub had the same name in the Sussex countryside.

Pub names was a game they used to play in the two hours it opened on Sunday lunchtimes in those days. They were so pleased when the old World War One licensing hours were relaxed. Just two hours to drink away the Saturday night hangover. They scored points if they made the other laugh. The Nobody Inn, The Queen's Dick, The Cat & Custard, The Quiet Woman, The Gorblimey Trousers, The Abba Trois, The Auntie Semitist, The Ugly Bastard, The Nine Bob Note, The Deflated World Cup Dream, The Grumpy Old Git and The Eurovision Song Contest were the best ones they could remember. They both agreed there should be one called Lenny the Lion, and The Kenneth Wolstenholme. *They think it's all over. It is now* was their favourite quote.

Sitting supping their Harvey's bitter, Stephen didn't do what often irritated Rob, that is, flitting from subject to subject and moving away from one topic just when it was getting interesting. He continued on the water theme.

"So, there's a freely available substance, at least in the western world, but somehow a load of so-called entrepreneurs make their fortunes from it. Those in advertising don't do too badly either. It wouldn't be so profitable if, at the same time, they didn't take away all water fountains on the spurious grounds of hygiene, and ban people taking their own water into venues for sporting events and other entertainments. Not to mention airports. Then make you queue up and pay a fortune for it."

This talk made Rob thirsty for another pint, but he delayed on purpose and told Stephen about the English water companies.
"They made two billion pounds post-tax profit. Some say a lot more than this and they avoid tax too. Most of this went as dividends to their shareholders - a real scandal. A basic human right is costing the average citizen much more than it need to so that the small group who could afford shares in the first place line their pockets."

"Is that so?" said Stephen, "Let's do the sums then. Two billion pounds divided by the population of England. Any idea what that is?"

"Hang on, let me play with this new thing called the Internet," mumbled Rob as he played around with his phone, "Fifty three million, twelve thousand, four hundred and fifty six at the 2011 census."

"Okay," said Stephen, "let's say its now one hundred million with all those Turks."

201

"Better add in Wales," said Rob playing along, "I think they are included. The magic machine here says in 2011 there were three million, sixty three thousand, four hundred and fifty six of them."

"Very funny. So two billion divided by fifty-three, plus three million... gives a figure of thirty-six pounds for each. Average in each household is two point three. So the average household hands over eighty-two pounds to shareholders."

A pause.

"Now multiply that by all the other privatised companies ripping us off, whether it be gas, electricity, the railways and you can see why the rich are getting richer, and the poor poorer."

Rob was still playing with Mr Google.

"And wait 'til they add health to that and these bills will be knocked into the shade. But this really is unearned income, isn't it? They do fuck all for this. They don't earn it. Certainly don't deserve it. Basic services are now just businesses sucking money from us all for no better reason than they can. The poor used to spend less than two per cent of their income on water and sewage services, now its over five per cent. Oh, and look at this!" Rob exclaimed, "They tried to cover up the Camelford water pollution scandal in 1988 as it was just before Thatcher privatised all the companies and they didn't want the industry to appear unattractive to the city. And they wrote off all their debts. Unbelievable!"

There was a short silence - one with a cloud hanging over it. Then he made an effort to lighten the mood and demonstrate a bit of optimism.

"We need a new movement, a new political party as a conduit for everyone's anger and frustration. One that would start afresh untainted by the past and free from corruption."

"Fuck me Rob, you sound like a Blue Peter presenter. Today children we are going to save the world, cure cancer, eliminate starvation and stop all wars. In the second half of the programme we will make a nuclear power station out of an old washing-up bottle and a toilet roll holder. I'm afraid that is just as likely as a new corruption-free political party. Meet the new boss - same as the old boss. Look what happened to my old mate Alex and his grand plans with that party he started to save the NHS. Good intentions but didn't get him or the NHS anywhere. Actually it nearly destroyed him. It's a long story. I'll fill you in sometime. You should meet him. He's a nice bloke. Spent a lot of his own money making a film about it all."

"You said earlier you agreed with me on two further points. What were the others?"

"Did I?" Stephen smiled, "No impossible. Goes against the grain to agree with you on more than one thing a month, maestro. No, the best hope is to knock one of the existing parties into shape, make them democratic from the grassroots, get rid of their vested interests and make them bold and unafraid of the media and press. Hand in hand with that would have to be purges of all the freeloaders and egomaniacs."

The Harvey's had been finished some time ago and they were much later leaving the pub than usual. The conversation had flowed more freely than the beer as they were both driving. They walked out of the HDQ, as the pub was colloquially known and crossed the road back to the sports centre and stood by their cars chatting a little longer.

"Did I tell you they have knocked down The London and Brighton? Rob informed Stephen.

"What? That's the worst news tonight. Now I believe we really are all doomed. Is nothing sacred? Jenny lived near there didn't she? That's where I picked up that Charlotte. Remember her? Don't mention her to the trouble and strife, the Duchess of Fife, the wife, will you? Ellie gets very jealous."

They both laughed.

"Do I remember her? Can't forget. She was the one who used to keep south London awake with the noise she made when you were having your wicked way. Unless it was your cassette?"

"Known to bring down low-flying aircraft. Used to exhaust me," added Stephen, "But that's terrible news. It wasn't the best of pubs, but all those memories."

"London and Brighton, 1867 - 2008, R.I.P."

An eight-year-old Seat Leon stood next to a six-year-old Mini. Evidence for Rob that he and his old mate still had the same philosophy in life. No swanky Jags or fashionable Land Rovers for them.

"Did you know Thatcher said that anyone who has to catch a bus over the age of twenty-five is a failure?"

"Great, so we aren't failures then," responded Stephen, "She who spawned the young-dumb-and-earns-a-lump-sum generation of followers."

On parting it was an old tradition to exchange a trivial fact, the winner being the most boring, or to test each other with obscure medical syndromes. Stephen told Rob that Hitler's favourite flower was edelweiss.

"So that's why Rodgers and Hammerstein wrote about it in *The Sound of Music*?" Rob fired back and added that Bill Lee dubbed Christopher Plummer's voice in the film.

"Natalie Wood's was in *West Side Story*," retaliated Stephen.

"Ever had a patient with Exploding Head Syndrome?" fired back Rob.

"Not today, no."

"I'll put you out of your misery. Sufferers report an incredibly loud noise from within the head. It can wake them, be a one off, or happen throughout life."

"What's Capgras Syndrome then, oh wise one?" continued Rob.

"It's not your turn but I know this so I'll let you off," said Stephen. "It's when a patient's delusion is that someone they know has been replaced by an identical-looking imposter."

"Shit. Point to you. That's why you are a lofty consultant and I'm a lowly GP."

"Okay, what about this? You know that they claim the code-breaking skills shortened the war by two years and saved millions of lives?"

"Go on… this doesn't quite qualify as trivia."

"Well, that's not the only thing that did. Historians claim strategic bombing against targets like the railways, the German oil industry also did, plus certain SOE operations. If you add all the things up that did this then the war would have finished before it even started!"

"So instead of 1939-45, it would have been 1939-37 you mean?"

Rob claimed victory on this occasion by informing Stephen that the *BBC* pips were introduced in 1924, and the final of the six pips was lengthened in 1971 so people knew exactly when the hour was struck.

"You are such a sad bastard Rob. Goodnight. Same time next week?"

As they started their engines to drive off, Stephen wound down his window and shouted.

"So when was the emergency 999 number introduced then?"

"Okay... go on tell me?"

"1937, the same year as the twelve-sided thrupenny bit was introduced, Desperate Dan appeared in the *Dandy*, and Manchester City were relegated."

"The most important events though were A.J. Cronin's book *The Citadel*, and Bobby Charlton being born."

Rob was not sure Stephen had heard. He had zoomed off in his Mini.

18 - DIKTAT AND MANIPULATION

INTIMIDATION

Intimidation is your game
Well two can also play
From here on in the battle line's drawn
It's you who's gonna pay
You think you're right you think we're wrong?
Well time will surely tell
We'll never give in we'll keep on fighting
Gonna shove you back down your well

And we'll beat you, black & blue
Because we don't take any shit
Especially from the likes of you

Dan Fogelberg (1978)

1988

"Gentlemen… oh, and Lady," he nodded to his secretary, "welcome to our seminar. Please be seated."

The Under Secretary at the Treasury had been assigned the task of instructing senior officials from all departments in the Civil Service about the implementation of the Government Privatisation Plans. Selling off British Gas had been a success two years earlier and after the re-election of the Conservative Government the year before they declared it was to be full steam ahead. The extent of the sell off and dramatic reduction in the size of the State was to remain confidential. The public had not been softened up enough yet to accept such a fundamental change in what they saw as British values. Each official attending had been vetted, interviewed and taken through the importance of loyalty and secrecy. No one was left in any doubt what was at stake. Compliance was expected and demanded. Carrying out what was necessary would lead to great rewards for the individuals. Any degree of non-compliance or sabotage would mean more than just destroyed careers. An individual's whole future and that of their family would be jeopardised. Security passes had been checked and the audience was reminded yet again of the confidential nature of the meeting. All were searched for recording devices.

The senior civil servant put it in lighter tones.

"The Prime Minister will be furious if any contents of this meeting, or even the reason for it, leaks out and she has vowed to hunt down and end the career of anyone caught betraying her."

All present in the room knew it was much more threatening than that. Everyone had had it spelled out, in their pre-meeting briefing, the dirt that was in their file. Any treachery and life literally would not be worth living. He continued by reminding everyone that this was to be an historical meeting and that he was addressing a small privileged group of selected individuals who were to make history and be rewarded for their efforts to an extent beyond their dreams. But disloyalty would be crushed.

"Mark Twain said, *Loyalty to the Nation all the time, loyalty to the Government when it deserves it.* He was wrong, gentleman. We demand loyalty to the Government all the time, as has been made clear to each and every one of you. You will be relieved that I persuaded the Prime Minister that an oath of allegiance was a little over the top. An oath pledging personal loyalty to her in place of loyalty to the constitution of our country smacked a little bit like the Reichswehreid or Fuhrereid and I told her so. She won't completely let the issue drop however, but I've put it off, at least."

There was complete silence.

"There should be no need for such an oath. The penalties for non-compliance are too extreme to even contemplate and you all know that now. To carry on my German analogy, you would be classified as Wehrkraftzersetzer, a criminal who undermined fighting morale. That attracted the death penalty. We would not go that far, but any traitor may wish we had after we have finished with him."

He took a sip of water, "Down to business. I want to start by asking you what do you think has been the most important publication in this year of 1988?"

There were murmurings about Jeffrey Archer's *A Twist in the Tale* and *The Satanic Verses* by Salman Rushdie, but only one had the confidence to shout out *A Brief History of Time* by Professor Stephen Hawking. After a few more suggestions and playing with his audience Sir Roland eventually told them the answer he was looking for.

"No, you are all wrong. It is *Privatising The World: A Study of International Privatisation in Theory and Practice* by Oliver Letwin. I will return to this. Next. Who has heard of John Redwood?"

"The new MP for Wokingham, Sir," came a voice from the back.

"Do you know why he is a rising star?"

Silence.

"Because of his two publications, which compliment Letwin's. They are *In Sickness And In Health: Managing change in the NHS* and *Britain's Biggest Enterprise: Ideas for radical reform of the NHS*, which he wrote for the Centre for Policy Studies, one of the Prime Minister's babies. We encourage the media to call it a free market think-tank now rather than right wing, it sounds better. The policies we will be overseeing in the next few years are outlined in these publications. When our work is done, there will be little left, if anything, that the State owns or runs. This is nothing less than the transfer of everything into private hands, even taboo areas like the NHS."

He paused while the senior officials looked at each other.

"Now you know why this meeting is secret and very sensitive. The public won't and shouldn't be allowed to realise what is going on until it is fait accompli. These bright young things call it salami slicing. There is no dramatic event or announcement, just slow piecemeal change so it isn't noticed. Privatising most services is very straightforward. The path is well known. I'm sure you have heard it before. Starve them of funds so they deliver a poor service, people get angry and then the public think private would be better. The trouble with the NHS is it's still popular even when our political masters have done their best to make it grim. That is why this is our biggest challenge. We had an amazingly good propaganda campaign selling telecommunications and energy and we see it will be easier with the railways. Why do you think British Rail was forced to introduce a twenty-one per cent increase in season ticket fares only a few weeks ago? Yes, to make the public angry."

Sir Roland indicated to his secretary, the lady in the room, that he was ready for the overhead projector.

"I will now take you through the steps that lead to a successful conclusion. We have devised this pathway referring to the NHS as this is the most difficult and our biggest challenge. However the basic framework can be applied to all state services. The easier ones will not necessitate every step being activated. You will see there is no timescale. Each step will take as long as it takes. Some occur very quickly. Some will develop over years, and some will occur simultaneously."

Each step was on a new acetate sheet. He nodded when his secretary was expected to move to the next.

Step 1
Healthcare is a service. We must transform it into a business. Like any business therefore we must separate it into purchaser and provider.

"To start this process we have had to split the Department of Health and Social Security into two parts. As you know Kenneth Clarke has been the new Secretary of State for Health since July. Clarke is drawing up ideas for budget holding - starting with GPs.

Step 2
Starve the NHS of funds.

"Well, that's been the case throughout its history. But especially so in the last eight years with neo-liberal policies."

Step3
Cut training places and sell off land and accommodation.

"Slowly, but surely. Eventually this will produce a manufactured staffing crisis. We will use that to close facilities on the spurious grounds of safety. You will hear us declare frequently that the safety of the public is our number one concern."

Step 4
Run a smear campaign against the NHS, its staff, its safety and even patients. Demoralise staff by hitting working conditions and pensions forcing many to leave. De-professionalise the staff.

"Conservative party policy for years. This will undermine the public's confidence and drive staff into the private sector. Horror stories will hit the front pages on a regular basis. Anything from fraud, hygiene, waiting times to chopping the wrong leg off. This will be complemented with help from our American friends. They regularly spread misinformation about our NHS for domestic political reasons. They want to make sure the public isn't seduced into wanting socialised medicine. Hence the stories of death panels deciding who gets treatment and who is left to die. We all know this is very ironic as it is actually the US medical insurance companies who have these, not the NHS. You, gentlemen, have got to understand that the point of modern propaganda isn't only to misinform or push an agenda. It is to exhaust your critical thinking, so as to annihilate the truth. Conversely the private sector will be protected from criticism. Simultaneously they are planning spending a fair bit on showing how good they are. The power of the medical profession needs to be smashed like the miners. The pilot on nurse training is working well. No longer hands on, just robots to follow protocols."

Step 5
Facilitate a corporate takeover with private companies hiding under the NHS logo so the public don't notice who is running the service.

"You notice I still use the word service when addressing the public. Particular care is needed here as so many politicians have financial links to private healthcare companies. We must make sure there is not an obvious surge in more buying up shares, and that means you too. It amounts to insider trading."

Step 6
Reduce beds, downgrade hospitals, close A&E departments, cut GP services and as I mentioned blame lack of staff which puts patients at risk.

"This will take place over a long period, at least ten years. Our propaganda will have to be slick and convincing. I foresee a boom in glossy brochures using a lot of words to say very little. We will need a stage-managed publication process to draw the venom out of public suspicion. We will release a string of documents being clear that none is the finished article. That will give us wriggle room. They will be more interesting for what they don't say rather than what's in them. It is important that long-standing difficult problems are not mentioned and the vital detail for the delivery is left absent. This will all be backed up by a series of stage managed debates which makes the public feel they are part of the decision making process, when in fact they are only debating and choosing from our limited list of options and manipulated to agree with our already decided plan. Phone-ins and chat shows will dictate the tone we want to set. Our people ringing in to agree with us will jam the switchboards. Dissenters will be vetted and won't get airtime."

He surveyed his audience with the glare of a headmaster.

"I hope by now you are realising how well thought out this is. We will leave nothing to chance. The media will be used to carry the public along. Distractions will stop people realising what is happening until it is too late. So-called celebrities and their silly activities will hog the news. More seriously the anti-Europeans will be making a lot of noise to deflect from the NHS. Who knows, we may also have a few nutty leaders in other countries hogging airtime too, crazy enough to be entertainment value. Let's hope so. All this will help quash debate and opposition."

Step 7
Pretend to separate the NHS from Government and its obligation to care for the health of the nation, so that when things go wrong, the Government can claim it's someone else's fault (but they can still claim credit when things go well).

"This is crucial. Sooner or later, preferably later, the public will work out things are chaotic. Chaos has to be produced to justify the so-called reforms. By the time we reach this stage it will be the NHS that is criticised, not the politicians who pull the strings behind the scenes."

Step 8
Appoint a man with experience of the commercial healthcare sector to run the NHS. Preferably with American experience. Tell him how much he should ask for to run the service, and when it proves to be inadequate, say 'well, that's what the NHS asked for'. In other words, continue to pass the buck and blame others.

"By this time we will be playing numbers games with the opposition who will be saying we are starving the NHS of funds, which of course we are, but we can claim it is funded as the CEO wants. And don't forget the policy is Teflon coated as all parties are signing up to it as all parties follow neo-liberalism now. And yes, you did hear correctly, I did say CEO and not manager or administrator."

Step 9
Feed the media lines that are repeated parrot fashion to fool the public:
- **Reducing services leads to better patient care**
- **The NHS needs to be more business-like**
- **We cannot afford a full health service**

- It's the fault of the obese, immigrants and the elderly
- Patients that abuse the service wouldn't do so if they paid for it.

"Standard stuff."

Step 10
Brew the perfect storm with a cocktail of underfunding (called 'overspending'), lack of staff, services unable to cope, longer waiting lists and poor safety.

"This is probably fifteen years away."

Step 11
Get NHS Providers (Government appointed but pretending to be independent) to declare an NHS crisis admitting it cannot provide services now with the funding it has, so something has to change. The Government will repeat the lie 'we gave the NHS the money it asked for'. As it still can't cope, soften the public up to accepting less care. We sell this with the usual trick of headlining something silly to ban like dandruff treatment but hiding the real meat like varicose vein operations, cataracts, hernias.

"All these things are unpleasant but don't kill. But once we have achieved this, other procedures can be quietly added to the list. Next."

Step 12
So now tell the public we have no option but to introduce charges and to encourage Trusts to ration care, but pretend not to support it as policy. Manipulate the BMA into asking for charges to be introduced so they become the bad guys.

"It will be the end of them and the medical profession. General Practice will no longer exist, as this unnecessary tier will be absorbed into the Trusts. They are a barrier to the specialists who the insurance companies want to employ direct. The Prime Minister looks at doctors as the next enemy of the people to tackle, following her great victory over the miners. Notice I use the word Trust. By the time we get to this stage we will have freed up all the hospitals making them independent so called Trusts. Running parallel to this demolition of the NHS, Education will have been sorted. It will be way ahead of Health. We will have privatised the universities and introduced tuition fees. To start with those fees will be small and not for the poor but eventually the cap will go. Same with health charges. Once the tills are on the desks, the public will acclimatise. The atmosphere will change by evolution so that the public now expect to have to put their hands in their pockets for everything."

Step 13
Introduce universal private health insurance, initially as a top-up for services now either rationed, not available or charged for.

"The public will pay the premiums for top up services, but not the premiums for core services, at least initially. So we can still claim it is free at the point of need. However, eventually the cost of the core services premium will be slowly transferred from the Exchequer to the public. Means testing will be introduced quite early in this process. Please note gentlemen the use of the word need, not want or free at the point of use. We will be determining need by this point. For instance, you may want your hernia repaired, but you don't really need it. It's unlikely to kill you. You don't need both cataracts sorted. Many people cope with one eye."

Step 14
Final move is to a full US system with compulsory insurance possibly through the employer. By this stage we will have replaced the NHS with between thirty and sixty regions, much more manageable by the so-called Care Organisations. What is left is a very basic safety net emergency service.

"Leading characters in this plan will get very rich banking exceedingly large sums of taxpayers' money. Your co-operation will be reflected in your bonuses. The insurance industry is salivating, but has made it clear to us that they need the NHS broken into manageable chunks, hence the need for thirty to sixty regions. Each region or area will have several healthcare organisations providing all the health and social care for the population in that area. We are thinking of calling these accountable care systems. There will be care organisations based on the American idea, the bodies that manage the agreements. A working name, which may change is Accountable Care Organisations as they will be accountable for all care. We must use the word 'care' of course, but within these walls the organisations will cut costs by restricting access to care, especially hospital care and specialists as both are expensive. An idea that goes back to Nixon."

He smiled and waited for this to sink in.

"Running simultaneously to these fourteen steps will be the destruction of the medical profession. You may wince at the word destruction, but believe me when we have finished it will be unrecognisable. In Step 4 I referred to smashing their power. In Step 12 we described them as the enemy. This is for a very fundamental and obvious reason. The best strategy for profit is reducing costs. While physicians make up about eight per cent of the workforce their decisions cost a huge amount more. Perhaps up to eighty per cent of the nation's health spend. So we need to degrade their importance and employ them so we can control them. That alone isn't enough. We have several other well thought out strategies.

First, we transform them from decision makers to decision implementers. We make healthcare incomprehensible to them by making them dependent on complex systems outside their expertise. We will abolish generalists. They know too much. Specialists who will be trained for one part only will replace the Consultant General Surgeon. So we will have an upper gut surgeon, a lower gut surgeon, a thyroid surgeon and so on, so they will have a very narrow comfort zone. We make these systems and protocols user-unfriendly and change vendors frequently. This may sound Kafkaesque and, in the way our new bureaucracy evokes feelings of disorientation and helplessness, it is.

Second, we break the doctor-patient relationship, which they hold so dear. We get patients to relate to a hospital not a doctor. This is aided by mechanisms to make sure they never see the same one twice. Creating staff shortages and so being dependent on locums is one way. And third, we make them insecure and compliant by firing one occasionally and when things go wrong, hanging one out to dry. Patient satisfaction ratings will be introduced but include parameters outside of their control such as parking. The best surgeons who get the most difficult cases will inevitably have a higher complication and death rate, but this will not be factored in. This will see them slide down the league table, which will take them down a peg or two. All this, and more I won't bore you with, will reduce doctors to mere workers."

There were no takers for Sir Roland's dismissive request for questions, as he hoped, so he continued.

"We understand there will develop a revolving door between the civil service and politicians on one side and the private companies on the other. We cannot do much about that and we are not sure we want to but we must at least keep it quiet. We foresee many who currently work in the NHS setting up their own consultancy firms to facilitate this process. We will be oiling the wheels of these firms such as Kahrnl-Hannah who will be joining the likes of our old friends at McKinsey, Deloitte and KPMG. There will be a lot of money to be made here. This project is so important it will not be allowed to fail through lack of funds."

It was clear Sir Roland was drawing to a close.

"We see this taking about twenty years in total but, like most well intentioned plans, through nobody's fault it may well be longer. Better to travel slowly and get there than rush it and get derailed on the way. There will be a time when MPs will be backing their Government's general policy of hospital closures just to realise that the closure of their hospital is not popular in their constituency and may lead to their defeat. You will of course have predicted we have thought of that. That is why we separate them and Government from the policy. It will not really be Government policy but NHS policy you see. So we can see this sentence being used a fair bit in replies to concerned constituents. Next."

"I am about to meet the Health Minister to alert him to this (insert problem here, such as hospital downgrade or closure, GP centre disappearing, certain operations only available privately, etc., etc.,) - remember this process is being run by NHS managers, not the government, so I want to ensure the minister can feed our concerns into the process at the highest level."

"Luckily, politicians are experts at facing both ways at once and being able to argue the earth is flat."

Sir Roland took another sip of water. He had been expecting a few interruptions but none were forthcoming.

"I have presented the most difficult of our privatisation challenges. Others will be much easier. Attempts have been made in the past, but half hearted and not followed through. This time we will not fail. Attempts to kill off the NHS were made before its conception, at its birth, then when young, a teenager and now when middle-aged. The BMA voted against it nine to one, the Conservative Party under Churchill voted against it twenty-two times, the *Fellowship for Freedom in Medicine* was set up to quash it, and the Guilleband Report was supposed to condemn it. Under this Prime Minister the pressure has been on, with reports by the Central Policy Review Staff and this year by Arthur Sheldon and Pirie's publication *The Health Of Nations* all making the case for ending the NHS. The momentum is with us now. Remember, by the time this revolution is complete, we will have rolled back the State, dismantled the Welfare State, and changed the face of Britain forever. The post war world and its socialist ideas will have been confined to the dustbin of history. There will be no such thing as a service. Service will be a dirty word. All services will be businesses. Right down to the motorway service station. Anyone taking a break from a long journey in future will be only too aware that a stop at one of these privately owned and run businesses will have them confronted by people whose sole purpose is to get their money off them. From parking to taking a leak."

This was meant to be a humorous end and it did provoke the expected nervous giggles.

"Finally," he said, "we are known as people who, when we see light at the end of the tunnel of a job ministers give us, go out and commission more tunnel. Let me warn you now. There will be no procrastination. I've already told you this will take time, but it is not to take a minute longer than absolutely necessary. I hope that is crystal clear."

Sir Roland finished by thanking all present for their loyalty. Throughout the last decade a lot of effort had been put into replacing anyone who is not one of us, and this was paying off.

"As Ed Murrow, that distinguished American broadcast journalist said, *anyone who isn't confused really doesn't understand the situation*, now let's get on with it."

With that Sir Roland turned on his heels and marched out of the room, followed in a panic by his secretary.

He had no real concerns about any lack of cooperation. That was assured now. In the last few weeks every official in the room at interview had been shown their file. It was made clear no loyalty less than one hundred per cent would be tolerated - we will not take any shit especially from the likes of you, we will beat you black and blue. Some material was genuine, but some fabricated very professionally. It did not matter. It could still cost a career, break up a family or end a life.

If you have them by the balls, their hearts and minds will follow.

19 - DATES AND BOMBS

GOD BLESS AMERICA AND ITS BOMBS

When they bombed Korea, Vietnam, Laos, Cambodia, El Salvador and Nicaragua
I said nothing because I was not a communist.

When they bombed China, Guatemala, Indonesia, Cuba, and the Congo
I said nothing because I didn't know about it.

When they bombed Lebanon and Grenada
I said nothing because I didn't understand it.

When they bombed Panama
I said nothing because I wasn't a drug dealer.

When they bombed Iraq, Afghanistan, Pakistan, Somalia, and Yemen
I said nothing because I wasn't a terrorist.

When they bombed Yugoslavia and Libya for 'humanitarian' reasons
I said nothing because it sounded so honourable.

Then they bombed my house and there was no one left to speak out for me.
But it didn't really matter. I was dead.

William Blum

2008

Pete Moodey rarely used his Gmail account now as he was worried he was being tracked. Petegrassyknoll@gmail.com was rather stupid anyhow. He had several others all for different purposes. However, it was still open and he cleared the inbox from time to time to fit in with his tidy mind and was consistent with the need to empty wastebins around the house too frequently. This time he deleted the usual

219

ads, the invites to join escort agencies, the research and survey requests and a few obviously (bad) scams to get money off him. The last one was ten days old and was titled Madison from Dallas. He deleted it turned off his desktop and as it was late went to clean his teeth.

Something was troubling him as he rinsed his mouth. Then it struck him, Madison from Dallas. That girl from the Gator's bar they had to run for their lives from two years before? The one whose mum witnessed Kennedy being shot. The one he really wanted to get to know but ballsed it up by slagging off the USA? He went back to his desktop and hoped he had not been his usual obsessional self and deleted all from the trash box too. A relief. He had not.

Dear Pete,
I don't know if you remember me but we met in my hometown in 2006 when you were touring around the US with your buddy Mike.
We had a bit of a disagreement then you ran out of the bar! We hit it off well until you started banging on about how America is an evil empire.
As I've forgiven you and I'm in London I want to know if you are interested in meeting up? If so, I'm in the Landmark Hotel for another two weeks.
Madison.

The email was twelve days old. He was probably too late.

Dear Madison,
Hope I'm not too late and you haven't gone back across the pond already.
I'm free the next few evenings if you are!
Pete.

Almost immediately a reply.

Pete,
8.00 p.m. in the Mirror Bar at my hotel.
Madison.

8.20 p.m. and no Madison – this had to be punishment for
running out on her in Dallas? Then there she was, strolling slowly
towards him with a big grin and more attractive than he
remembered. In fact he could not believe his luck. Pete suddenly
realised he was nervous. It was nearly a year since his previous
girlfriend had dumped him. Fed up with his conspiracy theories and
obsessions. He never was that good at talking to the opposite sex -
not like his mate Mike - and the lack of practice recently did not
help. What would he say? He did not need to worry. Madison was
never going to let the conversation be dull, stilted or hesitant.

"What are you doing in England? How did you know how to
contact me? Are you going back soon?"

"Wow. One interrogation at a time!" said Madison in a quiet
voice, which reminded Pete of Marilyn Monroe as Sugar in *Some
Like It Hot*. He could not help himself wondering if he was in with a
chance here. It had been so long.

"I'm over here with my new job, but I go back tomorrow. Flight
from Heathrow at nine a.m. Don't you remember giving me your
email address? Well, you didn't really give it to me, but mentioned it
while we were talking about Dealey Plaza's grassy knoll. Easy to
remember. Not difficult for it to stick in the mind."

"Well, first I must apologise for slagging off your country. It was
very rude as a guest."

"Good. And so you should! But actually you did make me think
and you are right about a fair bit. We are so isolated in the US and
places like Texas in particular, that we need some alternative views
occasionally. You are responsible for me taking a different career
path. That degree I got at the University of California isn't wasted.
I'm into the science of global warming and now work for the US
Environmental Protection Agency. I'm based in Washington at the
HQ. Amongst other things I am part of a research team checking
out the hydrologic cycle, water flow to you. This is my third research

221

project and I'm liaising with your UK Environment Agency. They are all stewed up after the floods you had last year."

"You probably know but Summer 2007 was the wettest on record. Since records began in 1766. We were still British then, just!"

She had a magnificent cleavage. Concentrate, Pete thought.

"And what about you Pete? What are you up to?"

"Oh, I've just got worse. You thought I was bad attacking the US in Dallas. I've learnt a lot more since. I will no longer stand idly by and say nothing. That's cowardly. I doubt you will be impressed but I'm not a communist. Do you remember calling me that in Gator's?

"What has woken me up are all the corrupt climate change denial organisations, and the dark money that funds them. There are hundreds of foundations funnelling hundreds of millions of dollars to about a hundred denial organisations. Money goes through third parties so it can't be traced. This countermovement has had a real political and ecological impact on the failure of the world to act on global warming. The same groups who promote ultra-free market ideas like Koch and Exxon. So many front organisations set up to con the public. All with respectable and convincing names like the American Enterprise Institute, Americans for Prosperity, the American Legislative Exchange Council, the Cato Institute, the Heritage Foundation, the Institute for Energy Research, the list goes on. I can remember them all, as I've had to check them out. But it's come at a price. I've been threatened. For years I too said nothing because I thought it didn't really affect me. The same must be going on over here? It has made me very angry. So anti-democratic and it has helped me forgive you."

"That's good. Forgiveness is good," squeezed in Pete.

Madison hardly took breath.

"Do you know the average dog has an ecological footprint twice as big as a large car? That to have one less child saves fifty-eight tonnes of carbon dioxide compared with only zero point eight two tonnes eating a plant-based diet?

"I don't want to worry you but you sound like me. Are you for real or are you a CIA hit man, I mean hit-woman? You haven't got a Dallas Special in that bag of yours then?"

"Ha, very funny! So you remember what a Dallas Special is. But yes, I'm sure you are right now. Some of what you say makes sense."

"Some?" queried Pete, "Many of our politicians are getting back-handers to spout nonsense they don't really believe. One of our ex-Chancellors of the Exchequer who should have been locked up in a loony bin years ago is always on the TV talking crap. He even had the guts to say the national treasure David Attenborough was talking balderdash."

"Oh, say balderdash again in that great English accent, please?"

Pete did not know if she was taking the piss but he played along. He repeated the word in his best Prince Charles accent. He really wondered why she had contacted him. She was a very attractive woman and could not be short of attention. They breezed through all sorts of subjects but she never mentioned Cheryl and he did not mention Mike. In a strange way she seemed to want to push him into being provocative, asking what his latest thoughts on the US were. He did not answer the first time but could not resist when she asked again. He thought he would keep it light and nothing recent.

"Franklin Delano Roosevelt, your thirty-second President got to the top on opium money. His grandfather, Warren Delano, was the second biggest opium dealer in China. We the British were number one. Probably the last time we beat you at anything apart from the Ryder Cup in Ireland eighteen months ago. Other Americans who became wealthy from the same trade were the Astor family and Forbes. Anyone with Forbes in the name has benefitted from opium money. Harvard benefitted from opium money from the Cabot family, and Yale likewise from the Russells."

"I remember now," said Madison slowly.

She was running her hand up and down her tall glass, which distracted Pete.

"You did a degree in history didn't you?"

He was reminded of the way Faye Dunaway teased Steve McQueen in *The Thomas Crown Affair* when they played chess. She ran her fingers up and down the bishop. The windmills of his mind were turning.

"Eh? Oh, yea, I did. But I learnt none of this at university."

"Then there was your 1882 Chinese Exclusion Act when you wanted to keep all the Chinese out 'cos you didn't like the competition. Rather odd Monsieur Eiffel built you Liberty Enlightening the World only a few years later. Everyone is welcome, oh except you Chinese!"

Madison looked puzzled. He was in danger of being seen as a smart arse, rather than just the intelligent bloke he thought he was.

"Oh, the slang name is of course the Statue of Liberty. That's what you call it. Did you not know its proper title? And Bartholdi the sculptor based the face on his mother who was an anti-Semite. There is a Bartholdi Fountain in Washington. I bet you have walked past it many a time in the Botanic Gardens. Put there before the New York thing," keep it light he reminded himself, "Do you know the worst thing about your country? Well, two of the worst things actually? Forgetting the letter 'u' in words like neighbour and favour and not knowing what chips are. They are not your French fries. Chips are thick cut and served with beer that's warm and flat."

Madison laughed and ignored the repetition of his moan about the lack of the letter 'u' in words which he had griped about in Dallas. But Pete was not convinced she understood what he was talking about. One of Pete's more recent investigations was what he called the Marshall Islands disgrace. Madison had never heard of them. She had heard of bikinis though - she had just bought a rather daring one - but had no idea they were named after Bikini Atoll.

"It was your nuclear testing ground. Your wonderful country dropped sixty-six nuclear devices between 1946 and 1958, the equivalent of more than one Hiroshima bomb onto those islands every day for twelve years. You carried out human radiation experiments and gave a load of the citizens thyroid cancer. LBJ said it was safe to return there in 1968, but it wasn't. In 1952 the first US hydrogen bomb destroyed the island of Elugelab in the Enewetak atoll. Paradise turned into radioactive hell."

"Wow. Did you just make that up? Y'all be telling me that Queen Victoria was named after Victoria Island next."

"The other way round. Let's see what an American education is like. Do you know where the Frankfurter or Hamburger came from?

Or the aforementioned French fries or Belgian waffles? What about Bermuda shorts or Danish pastries?"

"Don't tease me. But they are all from New York as we invented everything!"

"Even Kennedy in his 1963 speech when he said *Ich bin ein Berliner*, according to some was calling himself a jelly doughnut… that's spelt D O U G H N U T by the way, not D O N U T."

She'd heard that before too.

"He wasn't actually. He was correct. The misconception was in Len Deighton's spy novel *Berlin Game*. Wiener Schnitzel, Rottweilers, Tuxedos, Balaclavas and Cheddar Cheese?"

"These are easy. Tuxedo was from the Tuxedo Park Club in New York. Balaclavas are the headgear used in the Crimean war, and Cheddar Cheese came from a place called Cheese. Right?"

"I expect as an American you think you invented denim, eh?"

"Of course we did. And Levi's."

"Wrong again. Denim is short for serge de Nimes, a fabric made by the Andre family in Nimes, France. And Levi Strauss came from Bavaria. You Americans didn't even invent lesbians. They were named after the Greek island of Lesbos. It's where the ancient poet Sappho wrote about her love for a group of women. Good job she didn't live on Ailinglaplap. That's one of the Marshall Islands by the way."

Pete realised it was nearly midnight. The time had flown. They really were getting on well this time.

"I suppose I had better go. You have to get up for that early flight."

"You don't get away that easily. Come upstairs and sleep with me."

20 - COMPLAINTS AND STITCH UPS

FRAMED

I knew I was a victim
Of someone's evil plan
When a stool-pigeon walked in
And says;
'That's your man!'

I was framed

Richie Valens (1959)

Getting back to work after a holiday was always a challenge, even more so after a honeymoon. The first thirty seconds of each consultation was straightforward after a normal break.

"Good holiday, Doc?"

"Yes, thanks."

Niceties out of the way then straight into the patient's problem, hopefully. Rob found people wanted more detail after a special event like a honeymoon. He did not believe patients were being nosey, just friendly. Nowadays it was realised from both sides of the table how time was precious. But this still ate into the pathetic ten minutes available. The even more pathetic Government say it is up to the GP how long an appointment lasts.

"Let's turn that one around," Rob once said to Clive, "suppose just one in every thousand constituents would like ten minutes with their MP at their surgery. Not unrealistic or unreasonable. That's what they are there for, to help us with problems and paid for by the taxpayer, just like a GP. If a GP saw just one in every thousand patients on their list each week they could give them a day each, like on TV dramas. Now the average electorate is about seventy thousand. That works out at seventy in their one surgery. If each person gets ten minutes that's going to be nearly a twelve-hour surgery. Well, it's up to the MP how long an appointment lasts.

Maybe it should be half an hour like the MPs say the GPs should offer. That'll stretch their surgery to thirty-six hours, an average working week for most. We can't do that, they'll cry! When will we be able to do our other work?"

Rob continued in his rant.

"There's a lot of competition to become an MP, so give the job to the one who is prepared to see his or her constituents, not sit on his big fat arse in meetings all day long. Especially those board meetings for companies who give them pay-offs."

Rob never minded who was the victim of his rants. Not nowadays. When younger he would keep his opinions to himself for fear of offending. Never mind that what he was subjected to was offensive. He was ashamed that he often did not tackle racism head on as a junior doctor. It was not unusual to get comments like I'm not letting that nig-nog put his hands on me. I want an English doctor. This was very rare now but there is no doubt that person would be blasted out of the water, whoever they were. That night, Stephen, his squash partner was the victim of his rant against MPs.

"You know what really annoys me, Stephen?" he said during their after-match pint.

"No, but I bet you are going to tell me!" came the reply in a resigned manner.

"When a reporter says we asked a government minister for a comment but no one was available. Hypocritical bastards! They are public servants and it's their duty to be available. They are supposed to be answerable. It's not the point that if they did volunteer for an interview all you would get is crap. They are hypocritical because all you hear from them about teachers, doctors and other public servants is that they are answerable to the taxpayer. The tossers shouldn't be allowed to get away with it. How about fining them for no show?"

Stephen then got another hand grenade thrown in his direction.

"And do you know what? If they had the TV camera aimed at them individually during their disgraceful childish behaviour at PMQs they'd soon grow up. But they somehow control that! They won't allow it. How dare they? We pay them. They should do as they are told or fuck off."

When Rob first started as a GP he could just turn up to work straight after a vacation. Now this was impossible if he was to keep on top of the day's work. So now he always spent Sunday in the office beforehand dealing with paperwork and clearing up the loose ends invariably left by locums. He also found that patients would wait for him to return. He tried to discourage this as he felt it could be dangerous to put off presentation, though it more often than not fell on deaf ears, which meant the locum was paid very well for sometimes doing the crossword, resulting in Rob's first week back being hell.

Giselle, who had left a note on his desk, anticipated this Sunday's surgery visit:

Sorry, Rob, we had another cyber attack while you were away. The computers were down in most local GP surgeries as well as the hospital for three days. All resolved now, but you may notice some data missing.

Not again, Rob thought. The cuts had left no money to buy the latest protection. Rob knew that the only people really holding the NHS to ransom were at Microsoft. They had flogged *Windows XP* across the board then dumped it. Stable platforms do not make money. A new product was needed. All good business practice, but it milked the taxpayer. Rob had had a rant about this at a recent squash game with an old mate stating, if Audi had said, 'sorry your car is five years old, we're not servicing it any more, and by the way, we have built in some obsolescence, there would probably be a revolution'. But Microsoft got away with it.

Rob was usually at his desk by 6.30 a.m. even though the staff did not turn up until 8.00 a.m. and the surgery doors opened at 8.30 a.m. This allowed him to start the day with an empty in-tray but also the chance to run through the consultation list to see what potential problems he could foresee. It was good practice to make sure the outpatient letters were there and the lab results checked. On rare occasions a delivery man knocking on the side door would disturb him but usually this was a peaceful time, allowing him to relax and get into the good mood and fixed smile necessary for good doctor-patient harmonious relations.

Oddly today, at 7.20 a.m., he heard the key go into the staff door and people walk in. He could not imagine who it was so got up from his desk to investigate.

"Hi Rob, good honeymoon?" said Clive as he strolled down the corridor towards him. He had Giselle behind him looking more concerned.

"Hello, Rob, it is good to 'ave you back," she said.

Rob did not respond. He waited for an explanation for this unprecedented event. Neither Clive nor Giselle ever appeared before 8.29 a.m. Clive broke the silence.

"Have you got a minute? We need to chat about a few things that happened while you were away. Your day will be hectic as usual so we thought we should grab our chance."

"I'll put the coffee on in the common room. It'll be more comfortable there, no? *Lobodis* okay for you two?" continued Giselle.

By the time they were all sitting, looking out at the view of the surgery garden, all sorts of things had shot through Rob's mind. This was not about the cyber attack, that is for sure. A complaint? A member of staff running off with the cash? One of them leaving? Even worse, a death?

Giselle led.

"The last two weeks 'av been very odd. Apart from the computers being messed with, some strange things 'ave 'appened. First, we 'ad a break-in. Nothing was stolen, but it seems someone was looking for something. A file, information, who knows? No money went missing, the dispensary was not entered, the *Viagra* was left on the shelf, no equipment disappeared, just some rummaging around. Principally in your room."

"It looked all right to me when I came in yesterday," Rob said.

"Well, of course we tidied up. The police came along but weren't interested. They said 'oo ever it was wore gloves and walked onto the site. It 'appened at night, and the alarm was disabled. Perhaps you should check what might be missing, Rob?"

"Okay. But I can't imagine what would interest anyone. There is nothing confidential. Practice accounts, minutes from meetings, my Local Medical Committee work. Some BMA papers."

Clive took over.

"Then we had a visit from the Clinical Governance Lead of the CCG. They wanted to see you."

Giselle butted in.

"Proof that all those stupid forms they make us fill in to inform them of availability, 'olidays, study leave and so on are just filed and never looked at, as they didn't know you were away."

"Who was it? That useless self-important wanker who doesn't know one end of a patient from another? What's his name? Yes… James Wiekser."

Rob was showing his anxiety through increasing aggression.

"He is living proof of the twenty-two and a half minute rule. Do you know what that is?"

Clive felt they were getting sidetracked and was worried about the time. They had more to get through. But he thought he should let Rob go on.

"If you meet someone new, and they went to either Oxford or Cambridge they will always slip it into the conversation and you will know about it within twenty-two and a half minutes!"

Giselle was clutching a large envelope and offered it to Rob without saying anything. Rob took out an expensive looking cream sheet of paper. It was headed General Medical Council. It seemed Rob had been reported to the GMC by the CCG for inappropriate behaviour towards a female patient.

"Oh fuck. This is ridiculous. Who the hell is Saskia Bewering? I've never heard of her."

"She only joined your list three weeks ago. She was your last patient that day the rude gynaecologist rang. I checked your notes. She only wanted a renewal of her pill. Dutch origin."

"Oh, yes, I do remember vaguely because it occurred to me after Brexit we will have to have tills on our desks to collect money from our European friends. I didn't say anything of course. Wore a tight short skirt and called me darlin'. I don't remember any sort of dysfunctional consultation though. But this is outrageous. The GMC shouldn't be involved at this stage. We should have our internal investigation first, then external local as is usual. But of course they need to wait to see if the complaint is upheld first, which it won't be. Who at the CCG decided to do this? Some fucking upstart with a clipboard who is too big for his boots and probably hasn't started shaving yet, no doubt. We all know who they are. The GMC is the worrying bit. I need the name of the little Hitler who decided to inform the GMC inappropriately," Rob looked stunned. "You can't get a fair trial from them anymore, especially since one of the Government's yes men has been put in charge. They should be looking for the Shipmans. Too much like the Stasi now."

"The letter of complaint is there too and the CCG response. She claims you sexually harassed her with your eyes."

"For fuck's sake how does that work? Were my eyes out on stalks fondling her?"

Rob looked at the fourth sheet. He was requested to attend the CCG offices for a: discussion about your inappropriate prescribing and referring away from what is considered the norm. The fifth sheet was a letter from the CCG Pharmaceutical Advisor about a discrepancy in the stock of dangerous drugs. It threatened that if he could not explain himself satisfactorily the police will have to be involved.

"I see now why you both got out of bed early. But we only had an inspection last month. There was no mention of any problem then. This is all very odd coming all at once. Tell them first of all though, that if they want to see me they will have to come here?"

Clive and Giselle both made positive friendly noises along the lines of it would all be sorted out with no great consequences.

"But even the wording is monstrous. They are stating as fact 'your inappropriate prescribing'. Who says? Gits."

Rob knew he was a good GP. He did not care about the tossers at the CCG and their concerns about him. As far as they are concerned they take an average and do not understand that fifty per cent are above that and fifty per cent below. That's what an average is. They were, in Rob's eyes, mathematically illiterate not knowing the difference between the average, the median or the mode. Unless you are on the fifty per cent line you are outside the norm they said and need to be investigated. A whole department had been set up for this purpose. Does not help patient safety or quality one iota. It always made him laugh but weep at the same time, to remember the *Daily Mail* headline: SCANDAL - At Least Fifty Per Cent Of GPs Are Below Average.

What got to him though was the accusation of sexual harassment. This was anathema to him. He was a doctor. He was trained to look and being observant was the job. But he was able to switch off and become totally asexual in the consulting room. He was not sure how he achieved this but it required no effort. Just as well. Rob knew he had to keep his emotions and prejudices under control. Especially in dealing with the CCG. He regarded those who were doing the Government's dirty work in destroying the NHS as traitors, self-serving or naïve. Although seemingly voted into their posts they were self-selecting as there were ten candidates for ten places. Many had been old colleagues for years and several were very nice, but he knew he was regarded as almost eccentric for wanting to fight for the NHS. This was serious though. It could be career destroying - and to be referred to the GMC before an internal or local investigation? Is someone out to get him? Or is he being too paranoid? But by calling them tossers, gits and wankers he felt so much better.

After Rob had returned to his room, Clive quickly guided Giselle into her office and shut the door.

"What did he mean by 'now I see why you both got out of bed early?' Do you think he knows?"

"An innocent remark, I'm sure," said Giselle in a reassuring manner, "but if he is suspicious it's your bloody fault for being a bit obvious with me. Let's cool it for a week or two and let's be especially careful. I'm still not sure if 'e found out about that week we 'ad in my flat in Paris together. You were a dick leaving the Eurostar tickets for all to see."

"Mea culpa. We have a lot to deal with here and Rob doesn't need any more shocks so let's tread carefully."

"Come on," urged Giselle, "staying in my office with the door shut doesn't help, does it? And I know you say you are not bothered about your wife finding out. You say your marriage is as good as over, but I will do anything to protect Derek and my children."

"One more thing," Clive continued, "for some reason over a pint the other night, medical school came up. I think from my hesitations Rob might have wondered about a few gaps in my CV."

"Oh merde. Putain de Bordel, Clive."

"It's fine as long as his suspicions are not aroused any further and he goes to check up. I told him about working abroad, at the Homerton and another practice in Tower Hamlets."

"But none of that is true, is it?"

Morning surgery went smoothly and for the first time in years after a holiday he managed a sandwich at lunchtime without interruption. Just as he was to start on the afternoon onslaught Giselle came in to see him.

The excuse was to tell him that Judge Denning wanted a call at his convenience. Probably another attack of gout Rob immediately thought. But why come into his room with that single message? Giselle loitered and Rob suspected she wanted to check on him. A good manager concerned for the welfare of her workers. He was correct.

"Don't take all that you learnt this morning personally, Rob. We are all behind you and will fight this with you. I'm sorry we 'ad to barge in on you this morning, but Clive didn't want to leave it any longer than necessary."

Rob remarked that it had not exactly been a perfect day and thanked her. He said he felt like a victim in someone's evil plan. Giselle left satisfied that he did not suspect a thing. Not one to ever procrastinate Rob dialled the Judge's number as soon as the door closed.

"Thank you for ringing Dr Baigent. I'll be brief. After our little chat when I last came to see you, I've been thinking. I have to admit to you now I know a fair bit about your new discoveries. I've updated myself with the help of a few trusted friends and have found out a few things you need to know. I don't want to talk on the phone so can we meet when you are free after work? I know you are busy so won't take up too much of your time. You pass my little cottage on your drive home. Why don't you pop in for a pre-prandial? Pleasure Towers and Felicity will both be delighted to make your acquaintance again."

21 - SUPPORT AND COMFORT

EVERYBODY HURTS

Everybody hurts, take comfort in your friends
Everybody hurts, don't throw your hand
Oh, no, don't throw your hand
If you feel like you're alone
No, no, no, you are not alone

R.E.M. (1992)

Rob was always amused by Felix's usual understatement and modesty.

His little cottage did indeed have a little cottage on the side but it had been vastly extended in the reign of George I into quite a mansion. Without doubt the biggest and grandest property in the village. One of Rob's earlier visits had been when he had to attend the Judge's daughter when she had a horrible miscarriage whilst visiting her parents. Unlike many of Rob's upper middle class patients, Felix never clicked his fingers and expected a home visit for problems for which they could easily attend the surgery. Even on that distressing day he rang and, after apologising, did not even ask for a visit, just requested some advice. He knew he would get a house call, but he got what he needed in a polite and pleasant manner - much more effective than some who demanded their rights.

As Rob drove down the long approach to Pleasure Towers he smiled as he remembered why the den of vice was so named. The Judge's wife opened the door as he got out of his Seat Leon. She was holding back Atticus, their rather wild and savage looking Alsatian, by the collar. On a previous visit the Judge had explained that the dog was named after Atticus Finch, the lawyer in *To Kill A Mockingbird*. He was growling. As dog owners do she told him to be quiet, thinking Atticus spoke English. And as all dog owners also do told Rob that Atticus would not hurt him, but he was not convinced.

Felicity reminded Rob of Annette Mills, the sister of John, who presented *Muffin The Mule* in the Fifties on the *BBC*. He never saw it of course, being too young, but had watched several documentaries about children's programmes, and he was startled by the resemblance when she appeared clip-clopping Muffin around on top of the piano. Perhaps it was more her behaviour and demeanour, apropos an upbringing from an earlier generation, than her appearance. More popular with Rob were *Bill And Ben*, *Torchy The Battery Boy*, *Lenny The Lion* and *Pinky And Perky* - *Andy Pandy* and *The Woodentops* were for girls. Rob's puerile sense of humour was in tune with the joke about how *Muffin The Mule* must hurt. This all sparked his sophomoric humour that found Roger The Cabin Boy, Ben Dover, Seaman Staines and Master Bates equally funny. It was a regular joke with Stephen, his old mate and squash partner. This he usually had to hide. This was not the place for those crudities.

Felicity had a superb 1950s radio announcer's voice. She spoke from another era with clipped phrases and lengthened vowels. For her Cadogan Square would forever be 'Squaur'. Felix, an Old Etonian, sounded more like Anthony Eden. According to a manual from 1869 the best accents were taught at Eton and Oxford.

He was shown into the drawing room as Felicity referred to it, to find Felix, still in his three-piece, pinstriped suit with bow tie and highly polished camel calfskin Stefano Bemer shoes, which Rob had been told before took three months to make. Rob could see the suspenders holding up his socks. He had not been out of court for long and unwound by reading *Country Life*. He suited the Queen Anne Chesterfield Oxblood red leather high button back armchair perfectly. They were made for each other. Felix moulded into it as one continuum. He reminded Rob of the actor Cyril Fletcher telling his *Odd Odes* sitting in a deep armchair as though it were a throne. He could easily have been wearing an elegant green satin smoking jacket like Fletcher on his *BBC* appearances. He was already on his second whisky and soda. The room was so peaceful apart from the slow ticking of the silver dial, Georgian, eight-day, long-case clock. The view to the lake was uncluttered.

"I have few trustworthy and honourable friends at my Fountain Court Chambers or in the Magic Circle, but there are several I could trust with my life at my club, Brook's in St James's Street. As my doctor I could kid you I walk the one and a half miles down the Strand and the Mall between the two, but have to confess I get a cab every time. I'm sure that does nothing for my uric acid level. Sorry old boy, how rude of me. What's your early evening tipple?"

Rob saw the second part of his health education patter being demolished. First no heed to exercise, then no attention paid to less alcohol. He was gasping for a pint of *Shepherd Neame Spitfire* but knew he would not get that. Rob thought spirit drinkers only stocked near frozen gnat's piss lager for the guests they thought drank beer. He did not want to risk having to drink some gassy chemical lager if he asked for a beer, although he doubted the Judge would be so vulgar, so opted for the same as his. To him it was no different than asking for some beluga caviar and being given Aldi's tinned rice pudding.

"I must be frank, Rob. My political opinions have had to be suppressed. That's been the case for years out of necessity. It's safer for me. I used to tend towards the left, my reaction against public school, and still do secretly because if out in the open it only provokes arguments and career paralysis in my field. So I pretend not to pay too much attention nowadays. I never join the right wing banter in Chambers. I was told by my father that politics is the art of getting votes from the poor and money from the rich by promising to protect each from the other."

Rob smiled.

"But I've been aware for years of who powers the engine of this country of ours but also who holds the keys to it. You are not the first I've seen to have the blinkers lifted. Usually I tell them they are talking rubbish. But I know they are not. I've been watching you for years and know you are the genuine article. Can't be too careful, so many aren't. So why is my attitude different towards you?"

He answered his own question.

"I've tolerated the hypocrisy, manipulation, lying and scheming. But they are really going too far now and I've been thinking that for some time. It's becoming too sinister and dangerous. You got me thinking after seeing you the other week and I felt ashamed of my apathy. So it has rekindled my revolutionary spirit."

Revolutionary spirit, am I hearing correctly, thought Rob? This man is a Judge and a well-respected establishment figure - probably a mason.

"I thought I'd update myself on their ideas," continued Felix, "it's relatively easy for me as I'm regarded as one of the Establishment, one of them."

Exactly, thought Rob.

"I've had my suspicions confirmed from various separate sources who all tell the same story, and I must say it's not only revived my interest but made me quite annoyed again. It doesn't lead to a relaxed and contented life, which is why I stepped away from it all, something the opposition depend upon. I am a democrat and feel the right wing is knowingly putting at risk all that the British hold dear and for their own gratification. The irony is that these are the very people that claim to be safeguarding those values. This all goes back years of course and I've been following it for a long time at a very long and safe arms length. It wasn't a surprise that when I started asking what progress was being made, people guided me into a place where we couldn't be heard. I've always thought it a bit over the top but I understand why. It now seems that their attitude is that capitalism has defeated communism and is well on its way to defeat democracy. There's a German sociologist called Wolfgang Streeck who writes that the public are resigned to this and get by through coping, hoping, doping and shopping. They are burdened by debt, put up with decreasing pay and shrug their shoulders at the erosion of services through cuts and neglect. He has optimistically authored a book called *How Will Capitalism End?* He claims it will hang about in limbo for the foreseeable future, dead or about to die from an overdose of itself. I hope he is right but don't think he is."

It was all Rob could do to keep his concentration to stop sliding off the Chesterfield leather sofa. Expensive, yes he thought, but bloody uncomfortable. He would not give it houseroom.

"I like that bit about dying from an overdose of itself," Rob interrupted, "I remember reading an article in, believe it or not, the *Daily Telegraph*, which warned the greedy that they are in danger of pushing things too far. They may kill the goose that lays the golden egg. Then the pitchforks will be out for them."

"It's possible, but it'll take a revolution and they won't let that happen. I can't see another France of 1789 or Russia of 1917. Mustn't grumble is as revolutionary as the English get," replied Felix, "What you do with what I tell you is up to you but I must be left out of it. I should also warn you that you will be walking across a minefield and you might want to consider whether you are prepared to risk losing your legs or more, or will be happier and safer in the long run just to forget it all and stick to the day job. Many have reached that conclusion. I can tell you that you are not alone in fearing for our democracy but if you and all your fellow comrades link arms against what has been a long time in the planning you will still have no chance against the tsunami of right wing domination and control heading towards us."

Rob sipped his whisky and soda and continued to listen. He tried not to drink it too quickly as another would not be a good idea and he did not want to have to refuse the judge. However he had nothing to contribute at this point.

"This goes back centuries and is in the British DNA, to use your medical language. We are an island race and that fact explains the origin of all our troubles. Although we produced Darwin, you will know what ignorance, abuse and ridicule he was up against. His work has been used and misused to support eugenics, not least by his cousin Galton, isolationism, to fight immigration and all in the misguided belief that the British are a superior race and the top of the aristocracy is la crème de la crème. Once you believe that, and believe me it's taught still in some public schools, why would you want to mix the gene pool? Not only would you want to keep Johnny foreigner out on the basis that he would lower the quality of the breeding stock, but of course so would the lower classes. They clearly are inferior and have no place interfering with the ruling classes. That has always been their view. It didn't seem to register though that all that inbreeding wasn't a good idea. Look at the Royal family or the Isle of Sheppey?"

The Judge was enjoying getting his views across, as though he had suppressed them for far too long.

"We really are the only country to have such a public school network you know. Take my old school, Loretto in Scotland, founded in 1827. The headmaster ranked the virtues of the sort of boy the expensive boarding school should produce in this order: character, physique, intelligence, manners, information, and so it became an excellent factory for churning out dumb, repressed, conformist fodder for the running of an Empire along cricket club lines. We will never get rid of the toxic class system in this country until we abolish public schools."

Felix paused - was this for effect Rob wondered? Did the Judge think he was being shocking?

"It was through Loretto that I got to know old boys Norman Lamont and the 8th Duke of Montrose. His father, the 7th Duke, belonged to the Right Club and served in Ian Smith's racist Rhodesian Government."

Once a public schoolboy, always a public schoolboy thought Rob. He also wondered what the Right Club was, but let it pass.

"You may remember Don Boyd, the film director and screenwriter blowing the lid off the sexual abuse that went on there. By the way, whilst on the subject of public schools the idea that the Battle of Waterloo was won on the playing fields of Eton is bogus. Most had no playing fields or organised sports until late in the nineteenth century, by which time sport had become a guiding metaphor and by 1914 was killing tens of thousands of its true believers in the war - stiff upper lip stuff.

The second strand of thought is, of course, that the wealth belongs in the hands of the top elite as others just misuse it. The real problem is that people actually believe this, the right wing of course and many in our Conservative Party. The governing classes, those born to rule, need all the wealth so it can trickle down to the lower levels of society who only exist to do what they are told. Problems arose when those at that level, that is the peasants, started to get too educated for their own good and began to question how the country was ruled. Why do you think they encourage a two, perhaps three-tier education system and why grammar schools are making a comeback? They know they are talking nonsense when they claim that it will raise standards all round. They want segregation as they don't want their Sebastians and Fionas mixing with the Waynes and Chardonnays. They deliberately want to herd all the peasants into what are no more than day centres for thugs and delinquents. Grammar schools are expanding to become the public schools for those too mean to fork out or those who aspire to be superior but don't have the inherited wealth behind them. They deny, of course, that we are going back to the old secondary moderns. They will be starved of funds, which are siphoned off to the grammars, so it is inevitable the standard will be poor.

This ideology is a double victory as they also make money from it. Shareholders again. Even though most parents believe their kids attend state schools, in fact the majority now go to privately owned independent academies, which have money thrown at them at the expense of the other state schools to make sure they succeed. But actually they are failing even when given all these advantages. Costs are soaring and quality plummeting. The staff is employed independently too, and that is being copied by hospital trusts that are setting up companies to employ new staff so they can get around national terms and conditions. And the other benefit for them is the re-writing of the National Curriculum to be all about the majesty of the good old British Empire, thus ensuring the next generation grow up to believe in Victorian values and vote Conservative. Those who do escape from those third world schools will not make university as they are being priced out of it and deliberately so. They fiddle statistics claiming massive tuition fees aren't putting people off, but the unreported dropout rate is high and so wasteful. They fear that class getting educated and don't mind the dropouts but they don't want people to know."

Rob nodded.

"The first and second thoughts," Felix outlined, "explain what it's all about and why, and that is carving out a comfortable easy life

241

for their type. To keep them in the lifestyle they think they deserve it's necessary to have a workforce dependent on them, under their control and with nowhere else to go. The bigger the social and financial gap between the highest and lowest in society, the more secure they are. The secondary modern masses will become the servants of the higher classes. By attacking the middle ground as being left, they are aiming to convince the masses that being of the right is actually the centre, that is, moderate. That word is so abused. In their world it means leaving things basically as they are. This shift of axis has been slowly but deliberately orchestrated over the last few decades. Eventually what used to be regarded as fascist will be considered just a little bit to the right. Very clever manipulation. This puts several layers of protection and a few barriers up against socialism ever being considered in the West again."

There was a pause. Felix stared at Rob expectantly, but he really was lost for words. So he said the first thing that sprang to mind.

"And they try to stop debate by telling people not to use, say, the NHS as a political football. It's a mechanism to help leave things where they are. Leave things where they put them. But it's stupid of course. Healthcare is political. The NHS is political."

"Quite," said the Judge "I am aware you know all this but it's vital for an understanding of the next phase. Although all that I've said was practised in its crudest form with arrogance for centuries, the proponents now have to be subtler. Although they resisted and thought it beneath them, they realised they had to plot. This has only been generally accepted by, shall we call them, the elite since social media took off in the last decade - before that the enlightened knew it but the older guard had a different view. The old fogeys thought whilst they controlled the media in the form they understood, that is newspapers, television and the like, they could control minds. And in any case, how dare their divine right to rule be questioned? I have to slip in here of course that I come from that sort of background. But not all of us remained stubbornly and unquestionably loyal. I was taken in by what I was told at Loretto and had to eventually work out for myself what was really going on.

Most of my fellow pupils of course went for the easy option of not thinking."

Felix got up slowly and moved towards his drinks trolley. He appeared very stiff. Trolley was not the word though. The cabinet looking after his decanters of sherry and whisky was an amazing antique. Rob had admired it the last time he was sitting on the sofa, whilst explaining to the Judge's daughter's husband that he had lost his baby. It was a Regency rosewood chiffonier cabinet with a mirrored up-stand and shelf retaining its original pierced brass gallery on beautiful scrolling supports, with a crisply carved bunch of grapes at the head of each. Felix's great-great grandfather had purchased it apparently at a time when the family was entering the elite. The Judge moved towards Rob clearly intent on topping up his glass. Rob politely declined which Felix could not quite understand.

"So the subtle approach had to become mainstream. Stated political aims and manifestos were now only important to get elected. They can be forgotten after that, as history can be re-written. They have to be very misleading to dupe the public and ensure election but more importantly it is what is not said, more than what they do say. We are now in the post-truth era. You will have noticed elections are now won by slogans being repeated parrot fashion. It doesn't matter what the question is, get that slogan in. Every media interview will contain the same phrase no matter who is talking. 'Long Term Economic Plan' will be familiar to you. 'A Country That Works For Everyone' is beyond banality. 'Strong and Stable Leadership' meaningless balderdash and nonsense of course but it works. Look across the pond 'Make America Great Again'.

The EU referendum took it one step further. Total lies by professional liars who knew they were lying. Three hundred and fifty million pounds extra for the NHS, promised by the very people who had spent their professional lives cutting the NHS to the bone and trying to destroy it. Within hours of victory the promise was not only withdrawn but they admitted it had been a lie. Although more recently I have heard them try to justify it again. What arrogance they have, eh? Seventy-four million Turks were to invade Britain and rape our women if we stayed in the EU. Now that clown with a mop-top denies saying that, despite video evidence. And when we escape we can have bent bananas again. A lie told once remains a lie but a lie told a thousand times becomes the truth, as Joseph Goebbels so correctly said. If these rigging tactics failed then the election has to be rigged even more forcefully.

Take the NHS as an example as I have mentioned it, 'no more top-down reorganisation'. Yet within months of being elected they unveiled one so big you could see it from outer space, according to one of the NHS bosses. One doesn't cook that up in a few weeks. It had to have been years in the slow cooker. Now though it's been transferred to the pressure cooker to get their unannounced policies that no one voted for through before too many people notice. This is all what I call my nine Ds of unfair play: deceitful, dishonest, devious, disreputable, duplicitous, dishonourable, dubious, double-dealing, and dirty. And my six Us: underhand, unethical, unscrupulous, unprincipled, unfair, and unsporting."

Rob was impressed. This must have come from years of practice as a QC. There was no way Rob could remember the nine plus six let alone recite them so fluently. It might have been said for effect but it was very true. So far, apart from this great performing skill, Rob had not learnt much that was new but to have his recent suspicions confirmed helped him feel more comfortable that he was not paranoid or fantasising. He was actually enjoying the entertainment. It was music to Rob's ears to hear a public schoolboy from generations of public schoolboys articulate what Rob could not and describe the class-based group think, made up of traditions and contagious snobbery, and quoting Philip Larkin word perfect:

THIS BE THE VERSE

They fuck you up, your mum and dad.
They may not mean to, but they do.
They fill you with the faults they had
And add some extra, just for you.

But they were fucked up in their turn

244

By fools in old-style hats and coats,
Who half the time were soppy-stern
And half at one another's throats.

Man hands on misery to man.
It deepens like a coastal shelf.
Get out as early as you can,
And don't have any kids yourself.

The Judge repeated the line about *man hands on misery to man*. What he could not understand was that parents, who were deeply unhappy themselves, went on generation after generation to send their children to the same places. He said that he could only explain it through normalisation, which is rationalising the pain by deciding that it was good for you after all, or that your parents knew best - the psychological mechanism at work.

"It's a huge thing, but unacceptable to many, to admit that an entire class has been profoundly damaged by schooling, and they demonstrate their flawed characters by governing badly and only in their own interest," he concluded.

"Shall I go on or am I boring you?"

"Certainly not Mr Denning. I almost burst into applause at that rendition."

He wanted to keep the doctor-patient relationship on a professional footing. He could not call him Judge with a straight face and did not want to risk intimacy with first names, but an attempt at a joke was in order as the alcohol took effect.

"Now the more dangerous part. How do they get away with just doing as they wish and being so undemocratic, whilst pretending otherwise? Well, I've been aware they have been building a network since at least the Second World War. Some seeds were planted before that within the appeasement movement, which was much stronger and larger than the re-writes of history will ever admit. They have infiltrated every important institution in British Society you could name. That isn't done quickly or easily and has sometimes had some false starts.

Strangely the easier targets were on the so-called left such as the unions and the Labour Party. Simple things work well. Packing out meetings, buying up tickets for events then binning them so no one turns up, changing venues, intimidate voters and then at elections excluding certain candidates from hustings, all basic stuff. The left spend so much time arguing among themselves that they didn't notice our men, as the plotters called them, being put in place.

Yes, they have been infiltrated but not by the hard left, whatever that means, as portrayed in the media, but by the right. Most of Attlee's MPs were not really of the left. The so-called news channels will go on about Trots without having any idea what a Trot is. Just used as a pejorative term of abuse. Then they will interview someone in the street and get them to say they're too left wing, they're a load of Trots. If you asked them, or indeed the interviewer to define anything about Trotsky's politics, or to define left wing, they wouldn't have the first clue."

Rob thought he ought to contribute although he recognized when someone was revelling being in full flow, was enjoying it, and didn't want it to end. He felt he was listening to himself but with the relief of knowing Suzy wasn't being bored stiff. He could do no better than:

"Yes, Leon Trotsky. Most probably they think he plays for Dynamo Moscow in the Russian league."

"So, onto astroturfing. Do you know what astroturfing is? The stuffy full definition is that it's the deceptive practice of presenting an orchestrated campaign in the guise of unsolicited comments from members of the public. Sponsors of a message are skilfully masked to make it appear as though it originates from and is supported by the grassroots. The message can be political, advertising, religious or public relations. They create an impression of widespread public support for something when little support actually exists. Fake pressure groups are used. Front organisations pretending to be independent experts promote their lies. It works. They get airtime.

There was a classic front organisation set up to sabotage the NHS. Have you heard of the Fellowship for Freedom in Medicine? Got going as soon as the NHS in 1948. Secretly backed by the international insurance industry and fronted by doctors, most noticeable Lord Horder who made his name getting a tricky diagnosis right on Edward VII. Michael Foot put it perfectly in his biography of Nye Bevan when he described Lord Horder as, *a growling conscientious objector to almost any national health service in any form whatsoever.* They called it totalitarian socialism. So it wasn't a surprise that he was President of the British Eugenics Society. After Horder's death in 1955 the FFM was chaired by a GP, Reginald Hale-White who was advisor to several private health insurance companies. He moved it close to the IEA, the Institute of Economic Affairs. The Americans watched all this very closely. They kept going until the 1970s. Even way back then the right had kidnapped the word 'freedom' when they actually are aiming for the opposite!

Then there's the Overton window. The window of discourse, which amounts to the range of ideas the public will accept. But of course those in control dictate what is acceptable and what isn't. It's actually quite a narrow range of ideas. Make sure anything slightly away from what the establishment is thinking is ridiculed as mad. Hence label even the most harmless and sensible of policies such as having a state run transport system as coming from the loony left. So we've talked about the superior race that deserve all the wealth and control the media, but to finish what I was saying about infiltration…"

He took another sip of his whisky.

"The hardest groups to infiltrate are those where you would think they were pushing at an open door. The right wing factions always think they know best and want to do it their way. So they now control all the main political parties, the civil service of course, the media naturally, the City and all the financial institutions, big business, the Church of every type, your BMA, my profession, you name it. I remember when the civil service was impartial and provided government with sound expert unbiased advice. Now their numbers have been decimated and they have been reduced to just a propaganda support wing of the ministers they serve. The trouble is that most ministers are dim and temporary and are dangerous when they are allowed to just follow their prejudices rather than evidence.

They have their SPADs, which are Special Political Advisors, who are a menace. They are temporary civil servants whose loyalty lies only with the politician they serve and their careers, not the country at all.

There's a Mark Twain quote, which says the precise opposite, but I won't bore you with it. Peter Hennessy warned everyone about this. In his 1989 book *Whitehall* he defends the constitutional propriety of the civil service, which must act as a check against free-ranging politicians. Blair politicised Whitehall. Rarely nowadays do they control the minister like they used to, and perhaps they should. No one can claim government runs better today.

There has been a trend in the last few decades to put out into the cold the very people who should be consulted when policy is considered. Obvious examples are asking the medical profession about medical issues, lawyers about legal affairs, housing experts about housing, the military about defence, and teachers about education, and don't even start me on Brexit. But oh no, they might interfere and produce sensible valid arguments against something some intellectually challenged here-today-gone-tomorrow politician has already decided.

A good civil service used to be the counter-weight to these nutters. First decide the policy then find the evidence to back it up. Ridicule and suppress any evidence that contradicts, but announce controversial policies carefully and piecemeal, if at all. Chose a busy news day. They have learnt from the mistake they made with the Poll Tax. They were hubristic enough then to just say, this is what's best we will implement it. You must have heard that arrogant politician stating that he felt the public had had enough of experts. What he was trying to do was to denigrate valid opposition to his own ideas. He knew the real experts would make mincemeat of him if there were a head-to-head.

So the answer is to keep them out of the television studios by saying the public don't want to hear them. They then supplement this with fictional truths and fake news, but that's not a new tactic. All this fuss about fake news is bogus. Newspapers have produced fake news for years. The advertising industry produces its wealth from alternative facts and false claims. The propaganda and nonsense from *Fox News* or *Breitbart* is breathtaking, but it goes back much further too. Did Jesus really walk on water, cure lepers and turn water into wine? Was everything really created in seven days and did Moses really part the Red Sea? The US President thinks so. That's why he can claim similar miracles."

He coughed.

"Anyway, I digress. Teachers apparently needed a little more leaning on, as generally they are a bright bunch. Many of the tentacles of infiltration crept in from abroad and maintain their links, especially with the USA. It was evident to me along time ago that all this originates from across the Atlantic. The Americans have been recruited to cement the cause, as they are the real professionals at this game. But it goes way beyond infiltration to full scale clandestine operations."

There was a pause but before Rob could jump in.

"Take Operation Gladio. I don't expect you have heard of it. Set up by NATO, the CIA and other European Intelligence agencies after the war to resist the Warsaw Pact. They were known as 'stay-behind' operations. Most were criminal like the bombing of the Bologna railway station in 1980. Its purpose was to keep the public worried about the Soviet threat and blame the left to keep them from electoral victory in Italy, France and elsewhere. They killed eighty-six. Now of course all these years later they muddy the waters to throw people off the scent by blaming everyone from neo-fascists and Mossad to the PLO and Carlos the Jackal. They were behind the Greek coup in 1967 by a group of right wing army officers. That dictatorship lasted until the Turkish invasion of Cyprus in 1974. Then they have the nerve to moan about Russian interference in their elections!"

Rob thought it best to declare his thoughts and make it clear, although probably untrue, that he was not on a crusade.

"My lifetime passion has been the NHS and it's that which I would fight hard to protect. But the NHS has been infiltrated to such an extent that I fear it is terminal. It's the fairest and best healthcare system in the world and I went into medicine because of it. I stayed in Britain because of it. It makes me weep but also very angry to see it being taken apart brick by brick without the public knowing, because those bastards have put up a giant cloak in front of the demolition so no one notices until it has gone. But it's been done via all the practices you have outlined. They are reducing it to a shell. Hollowed out and filled by their companies. Like a graded listed building, the frontage is kept but all behind is destroyed."

The Judge started to speak like he was in court.

"I agree with the sentiment often expressed that it is a national treasure, something to be proud of, but also something, a bit like the BBC that defines us British. That's being hollowed out too. It is the nearest thing the British have to a religion, and I mean that sincerely, not as a joke or put down, as that climate-change denier Lawson intended when he said it in the 1980s. As Bevan dreamt it encapsulates values of caring for fellow mankind, meeting the needs of everyone regardless of wealth, showing compassion, equality, respect and dignity. Although you are a lot younger than me, I believe we both grew up with those values, but in the 1980s Margaret Thatcher convinced a new generation of the unthinkable, that those principles worked against the I'm-all-right-Jack and no-such-thing-as-society philosophies that she preached and she came out victorious. I'm not a religious man but I'd join any organisation with those principles. Like many, I have the NHS to thank for saving my life after being knocked down by that car thirty or so years ago. I'll tell you how and why that happened one day."

Rob now remembered why the Judge walked with a limp.

"My younger brother Oscar lives in California and tells me how dreadful the system is there. He describes their healthcare as a few small islands of possible or perceived excellence in a vast ocean of misery. Even the islands of excellence are sold sometimes to people who don't need them. He thought he had the best most comprehensive insurance policy available, but even then found out when he needed to claim that many things were not covered. He choked on a turkey bone one Thanksgiving and had to have it removed from his throat. That was at 11.00 p.m. He slept it off in a hospital bed but the crooks told him they would not cover the night's stay, as it wasn't necessary. He could have gone home! So it cost a fortune and his share amounted to a mini-fortune. Anyway, I digress.

Getting to the dangerous part. How do they control all these people and get them to do as they wish? Well, generally by using the oldest trick in the book. Blackmail. Blackmailing those who are swallowed up by man's greatest weakness, his sexual appetite and temptation. The dossiers they have on many are truly amazing. Especially on all the paedophiles and the huge Westminster ring. It seems no exaggeration to say that half of respectable society would be shamed, humiliate, or jailed if it all came out. Disgusted partners, except where they are up to their necks in it too, would sue half the cabinet for divorce.

Now the thing is that a politician not being able to keep their trousers or knickers on isn't new. Strangely, in the old days some flaunted it despite the greater risks. Boothby was notorious, his mate Tom Driberg and his hobby of cottaging, to name just two. The 1959 Government included a bisexual or homosexual Foreign Secretary, Chancellor and Ministers for Health, Labour and the Colonies! All presided over by a PM who was rumoured to have been expelled from Eton for shirt lifting. He certainly left early. I thought it compulsory there. Felt like it was in my day at Loretto."

It seemed Felix wanted to lighten the mood but the use of that phrase shocked Rob somewhat.

"But paedophilia and the murder of innocent young lads for their pleasure puts all this into a different league. Now I've had some funny looks with my probing and have got to lie low for a while. I can't take it any further than this for you, old boy, too dangerous. It's difficult to absorb just how big this all is. They have tentacles in every area of society and those tentacles strangle anyone who gets in the way. And it's all too big for you, or any man for that matter. My advice is to steer clear. It's too dangerous."

He repeated.

"It's not only you at risk, but your family. They will stop at nothing. Remember what George Orwell said, *in a time of universal deceit, telling the truth is a revolutionary act.*" You will be regarded as a

251

revolutionary Rob, if not a terrorist and they usually are put up against a wall and shot at the end of the day."

Rob sensed that that was all Felix was going to say on the matter. It was like being invited and sitting through a well-crafted lecture. It really would have been quite enjoyable if it were not so disturbing. It was comforting though that there were others with similar worries. He took his cue and shuffled forward on the Chesterfield. Felix showed no sign of wanting to stop him. They exchanged a few pleasantries as Felix escorted him towards the entrance hall. The alcohol seemed to have loosened up the Judge's stiff joints. He opened one of the double mahogany three-panel Georgian doors. The brass kick plates were so highly polished they reflected the low sun streaming in through the side window straight into Rob's eyes making him squint.

"But if you do take this further, try to make contact with those who made one or two noises then suddenly and for no good reason went quiet. The MPs who talked about the Westminster ring, then unexpectedly found another cause. That Attorney General who hinted an enquiry was necessary then all of a sudden wanted to spend more time with his family. The celebrities falsely accused as a decoy, and the more respectable journalists who have been silenced.

If you feel like you're alone, no, no, you are not alone. But be careful. I don't want to have to find another GP at my time of life."

As they shook hands, Felix's parting shot was that this could easily take him over and he should remember what Oscar Wilde said, *the trouble with socialism is that it takes up too many evenings.*"

And so Rob left the impersonators of Annette Mills and Cyril Fletcher.

On his drive back home Rob pondered on the reasons the Judge might have invited him. He seemed totally genuine but there was a little paranoia developing. What was he really up to? Why did he spend so much time with him? He was weighing up in his mind whether to tell Suzy all about this. It seemed from their parting words that the Judge was actually egging him on and wanted him to pursue it and that his earlier words to steer clear was not his real message.

22 - HEALTH AND MONEY

MONEY

Money, it's a gas
Grab that cash with both hands and make a stash
New car, caviar, four star daydream,
Think I'll buy me a football team

Money, get back
I'm all right, Jack, keep your hands off of my stack.
Money, it's a hit
Don't give me that do goody good bullshit

Pink Floyd (1973)

Rob would often tell one of his favourite jokes when he wanted to piss off some of his more mercenary consultant colleagues.

"Two surgeons are chatting. The first says to the other, what did you operate on Jones for? Answer, five thousand pounds. No, I mean what had he got? Answer, five thousand pounds."

He also regularly repeated what he said was the motto of the private health industry.

"A healthy person is someone who hasn't been investigated enough."

Healthcare varied so much. He knew why. A satirical article Rob had written for the medical journals had been received well by friends but he could not get it into print. It was rejected by all medical publications, which was not a surprise. They did not want to upset their senior readers or advertisers. He did not even get an acknowledgement from any of the august medical journals of Britain. He wanted to compare the various types of care around the world and publicise the scandals like United Health in the US overcharging Medicare by billions of dollars by making patients look sicker than they actually were. He had loads of examples and could not understand how they got away with it.

Mrs Nuffield is forty-eight, a solicitor, and has a lump in her groin.

It is 1989 and Dr Young is a GP trainee. Mrs Nuffield sees the young newly qualified doctor, as she thinks we all need to learn and this will be a simple problem for him. Dr Young correctly diagnoses an inguinal hernia clinically and tells Mrs Nuffield she should be referred for surgery. He writes a letter to the general surgeon he used to work for at the local hospital. There is a waiting list, as ten years of Thatcher's rule had seen the predicable, deliberate, chronic underfunding, however, she is seen after a phone call from Dr Young to his old boss and has her operation.

Mrs Nuffield is forty-eight, a solicitor, and has a lump in her groin.

It is the present day and Dr Old has been a GP for over two decades. Mrs Nuffield sees the doctor she has known for years. They have a good relationship. Dr Old correctly diagnoses an inguinal hernia clinically and tells Mrs Nuffield she should be referred for surgery. The ideology of the market is dominant - very expensive and not just financially. He explains this is not straightforward. They have to use a system called Choose and Book. Dr Old will complete a pro forma, tick all the boxes, and his request will go to a central office. They will write to Mrs Nuffield who will then have to ring them for a code and password. She will then have to log on to the referral site to select her hospital. This list includes private hospitals. She is not able to pick her surgeon, just a clinic. For some reason her local hospital is not on the list of choices - something to do with it being in 'special measures', but she ticks the hospital in the next town. She ponders on the lack of information. Should she go back to Dr Old and ask him if she has made a good choice? Would he know who I was seeing anyway to be able to advise?

Mrs Nuffield selects a date and attends expecting to see a surgeon to discuss her operation. Instead she is told this appointment is for a pre-operative check. She has repeated all the things she has already had done at Dr Old's surgery. She is told her blood pressure is a little raised and needs to go back to see her GP before she can be accepted for surgery. She knows her blood pressure is fine. She has it checked regularly as her father died early of a stroke. She is also told she is overweight and must do something about that. As if she has not tried for years. The man before her was clearly in pain and being consoled by his wife, as he was told he could not have his operation if he continues to smoke.

She returns to Dr Old, who expresses his frustration for the fourth time that week and writes a note to the clinic. However Mrs Nuffield has to log on again and select another appointment. The time limit for her pre-op assessment has expired so she is told she has to attend another pre-operative clinic and sees a different nurse. At least this one passes her and dismisses her saying, she will get a date for surgery through the post. The day arrives and she walks through the door under the familiar blue NHS logo. She senses a different atmosphere however. It turns out the surgery has been outsourced to Virgin Health. When she asks whom her surgeon is to be the staff nurse announces.

"It's whoever they send us love, it's a different one every week."

Mrs Nuffield is forty-eight, a solicitor, and has a lump in her groin.
It is 1986 and Dr Smart is on his first surgical firm at Guy's. Mrs Nuffield is on an open ward surrounded by medical students. Sir Laurence Glover is holding court. All twenty nervous-looking students crowded round to hear what Sir Laurence was saying but none wanted to catch his eye. That would inevitably result in being picked out, dragged to the front and humiliated. The most pompous at Guy's did not teach, they tortured and then squashed the sweaty students under their jackboot.

"Boy, what's the inguinal canal, and how long is it?'

"Er, it's an oblique passage through the anterior abdominal wall, sir, and it's about four centimetres long."

Good, a trap. The student was right which gave Sir Laurence little chance of fully using his sadistic powers, but he could retort.

"Four centimetres? We don't use those foreign units here do we?" Moving on to the next victim.

"The deep inguinal ring is a deficiency in what? You boy!"

Silence.

Sir Laurence made him sweat.

"A deficiency in the transversalis fascia, you dunce! What are you boy?"

"A dunce, sir."

"You clearly need extra help. You will come to assist me in my Harley Street clinic at 5pm tonight. Be there."

Sir Laurence moved in the same circles as Sir James Morrison who was a patient of his. He also was distantly related to Lord Moran, Churchill's personal physician. His family had benefitted from some of the royalties from the book Charles Moran published about Churchill's ailments. He defended his breach of confidentiality. Sir Laurence also thought Moran absolutely correct that GPs were a lower form of life having fallen off the career ladder. He did his best to make sure every medical student had no doubt about this. Dr Smart hated his time at medical school, claimed he learnt nothing useful until doing his House Jobs and could not get away from the obnoxious characters that controlled the place quick enough. Mrs Nuffield's hernia was fixed though, even though Sir Laurence did not once speak to her.

Lady Nuffield is forty-eight, a High Court Judge, and has a lump in her groin.

She lives in Belgravia and has a private GP. The NHS is for the poor. Rodney, as she called him, was summoned to see her at her house in Eaton Square. She had a photograph on the wall of a previous resident at number 1, Lord Robert Boothby, sitting on a sofa with Ronnie Kray. Her man had a sherry waiting for him. After exchanging their usual pleasantries Rodney looked at her lump whilst she remained in her chair. The poodle on her lap did not make it any easier.

"I'll ask Sir Laurence to deal with this in his rooms in Harley Street, if you agree?"

"Is he the best?"

The operation was done before she joined her friends on the Queen Mary for a winter's break. As she was still a little sore, she took a private nurse with her. Sir Laurence flew out to Madeira to check on her - grab that cash with both hands and make a stash.

Mrs Nuffield is forty-eight, a solicitor, and has a lump in her groin.

She has private insurance so went straight to her private hospital. As the lump was down there she assumed she had to see a gynaecologist, so an appointment was wasted when her mistake was pointed out. A friend recommended the hernia surgeon. This was based on his blue eyes and good looks, and her friend's fantasies about his bedside manner. She wondered whether she should have asked her GP but why not cut out the middleman?

She readily accepted his advice that she needed a few tests and scans first. The room, with a view of a lake and menu with a very good wine list, were both excellent. The hospital was in the quiet countryside. The repair went fairly smoothly. The next day her surgeon sat on the edge of her bed and looked at her with his blue eyes. He explained in a concerned but kind way that one of the pre-op scans did however show an unexpected finding. There was a lump on her vocal cord. Mrs Nuffield was not sure why this part of her was scanned in the work-up for a groin hernia, but she was relieved it had been done and so did not query it. The Ear Nose and Throat specialist, friend of her surgeon, told her it was unlikely to be cancer, but we had better make sure.

So the next day she had further surgery. Mrs Nuffield had been anaesthetised and the ENT surgeon had started to explore when she unexpectedly went into laryngospasm. The stimulation of the vocal cords had provoked their protective, reflex, spasmodic closure. Her airway became obstructed. The anaesthetist noticed the rib

257

retraction, the tracheal tug, the paradoxical breathing movements and her stridor. He panicked. He had no back up. He had never seen this before. He did remember that deepening the anaesthetic might work. He got the surgeon to apply suction and then get out of the way, and forcefully applied the ventilation mask to deliver oxygen. Then he performed a jaw thrust and gave a short acting muscle relaxant. Fortunately the spasm eased and life-threatening hypoxia was avoided. Unfortunately the hospital had no crash team or Intensive Care Unit, and little in the way of good experience medical cover at night, so when Mrs Nuffield unexpectedly deteriorated again she had to be transferred to the local NHS hospital that saved her life. It was touch and go.

The lump on her vocal cord was forgotten about and left alone. It was a tiny nodule that was not cancer and would never do her any harm. They seem more common in women between twenty and fifty who smoke and sing like Mrs Nuffield. One day her voice might become a little hoarse.

Mrs Nuffield is forty-eight, a solicitor, and has a lump in her groin.

Mrs Nuffield felt a painful ripping sensation as she was taking her suitcase off the belt at Mumbai Airport. She knew straight away she had provoked another hernia. She had had a repair on the other side two years before. This was very annoying at the beginning of her holiday. For a few days she kept this from the group she was touring with but the increasing pain made it unavoidable to confide in one of them. Fortunately, she had noticed the adverts.

The Lilavati Hospital was for the rich, politicians and Bollywood, so how about the One-day Surgery Centre, at the Babulnath Hospital? She had a spare day in the itinerary. She could have a full body scan for a tenth of the price in England, so a bargain too tempting to resist. The results were quick too. Yes, it confirmed her hernia and the doctor recommended immediate surgery or it could strangulate. Unfortunately it showed up fibroids on her womb, gallstones and arthritis in both knees. She was told she should see a gynaecologist, an upper gastro-intestinal surgeon and an orthopaedic surgeon. This all puzzled Mrs Nuffield as she has no pelvic troubles, no heavy periods, no abdominal pain, and no knee pain. The experts thought it wise though to consider a hysterectomy, a cholecystectomy and knee replacements before things got any worse. Before she left that afternoon she had been given prices for all the operations and she thought them all very reasonable. She could return to India and combine it with another holiday. She did not think it necessary to discuss this with her GP to see if he thought all these extra procedures were really necessary - after all, the experts were at the hospital.

Mrs Nuffield is forty-eight, a lawyer, and has a lump in her groin.
She lives in California and trusts her healthcare to the most famous Health Maintenance Organisation, Kaiser Permanente. The British Government wants to introduce these organisations to England to take over from the NHS. She was told where she could have her hernia repair and by whom, and on admission was fully worked up. She had to have pre-operative investigations including scans, MRIs, X-rays and bloods, and opinions on her cardiac state and respiratory system. She found the prospect of an operation scary and was suffering from a headache and diarrhoea on admission. She was told she needed to see a neurologist and a gastroenterologist as a result. The nurse noticed a mole on her forehead and despite being born with it a dermatological opinion was sought. Her first blood test showed very mild iron deficiency anaemia due to her periods but a haematologist and a gynaecologist were called in too. The total bill came to $74,642. Although fully insured, or so she thought, she had to pay $14,928. Sixty-two per cent of bankruptcies in the USA are due to medical bills and seventy-eight percent of these patients are insured.

Health Maintenance Organisations (HMOs) have been called the model of choice by past health ministers based on discredited studies. These companies will decide if the NHS would fund a treatment and then perform it too. The most profitable would get the green light, but loss-making areas such as mental health would disappear. Kaiser Permanente dumped a sixty-three year old patient on the streets of Los Angeles in her hospital gown and socks. An enquiry investigated over fifty cases of dumping involving nearly a dozen hospitals. Richard Nixon would have been proud, *the less care they give the more money they make.*

Mrs Nuffield is forty-eight and has a lump in her groin.
She lives in New Orleans, is out of work and so has no medical cover. She worries that the lump may be cancer. She is not to know. She cannot afford to see a doctor. So she blocks it from her mind as much as possible and takes the risk. But the worry nags away. She wonders if her three young children will have to grow up without her.

Rob ended his article with Aneurin Bevan's words: *No society can legitimately call itself civilised if a sick person is denied medical aid because of lack of means.* He could not get it published though. No one was interested.

A frustrated Rob wondered whether trying to explain the market in healthcare might attract more interest. It certainly needed explaining to the naive public, who were often the victims. He sat down again with his laptop on his knees and bashed away. It allowed him to get things off his chest. It did not take long to write. He tried to keep the sarcasm and cynicism to a tolerable level. This is the story of two families in England PLC just after the 2022 General Election.

The Laurels live just off Lansley Road, in a house built in 1948, whilst the Hardys occupy a huge PFI hotel-like mansion in a prime site on the private road behind gates manned by Protecttherich4Security. The Laurels bought their house from Oliver's grandparents who had worked hard for it. It suits their family perfectly. It was built at cost, with no middlemen taking a cut, but the property boom years, manufactured by the property owning classes, still meant they had a large mortgage.

The Hardys have a huge loan from the Cheatem & Grabbitt Bank. They are tied into a thirty-year mortgage at loan-shark interest rates but do not see the problem as they have shares in the bank and could put it against tax. So Stanley Hardy, despite earning shed-loads of money, did not have the burden of having to pay any tax. He was smart like Donald Trump. Osborne and Crook, their accountants, who by coincidence happen to be bank directors had insisted this was a good deal.

Their large support staff occupies most of the rooms and is protected from the poor further up the street by room entry swipe cards. They park their two Jags in the private car park, which C & G Bank recently sold off to a Mr Stevens. The Hardys pay extra for this but they appreciate that charging for everything is now part of life and rightly so. It must be better if paid for as this discourages scroungers. However, their loss of control hit home when both cars were clamped recently. Although this was a nuisance, as they had to hire lawyers again, they can recycle the fine when negotiating the next contract, and claim expenses on their next tax return issued from the Cayman Islands.

The Laurels' day starts with Oliver helping Jenny with the children and getting them off to school. They have always cooperated and shared the chores. They take turns with the shopping, cooking and cleaning and run a happy house very efficiently. They wish they could earn more but Oliver's boss is very mean. Fortunately their overheads are not much. They have enough time and money to see to their children's every need, even if they have to wait sometimes.

The Hardys, meanwhile, have an early family business meeting in the Hunt room with their commissioners. Their accountant goes through the agenda, which starts with the news of the arrival of a new fifty-six-page contract for breakfast provision after the successful tendering process. This had to be renewed after a poor satisfaction survey, which singled out the muesli as not fit for purpose. It is indeed a day for celebration as breakfasts for the children can start again after a break of three months. Lawyers for a US-based cereal company had challenged the bidding process but lost on appeal.

Item 2 (from 32) concerned Governance issues raised by their four-year-old daughter, Deloitte, who was challenging the authority of her parents on a technicality, and because her copy of the Teddy Bear Repair contract had not arrived. Deloitte's own lawyers were confident of victory. Other contracts involving their son, McKinsey, (which had been awarded to the Hardys for three years, renewable once only, subject to the newly privatised Disclosure and Barring Service check, costing £950) end soon and so would be put out to compulsory tender. The school outsourcing had always caused concern as the transport contract only provided for three miles of the five miles needed and, due to a drafting error, his secondary school became available before his primary. Barry the butcher supplied the children's clothes, as his bid was lowest. Unfortunately the bedtime stories service disappointed both children when it arrived as it was in Greek. The translation service had recently been abolished because of efficiency savings.

The meeting ended with a review of all their forty-two compulsory insurance policies but this was rubber-stamped as a company called Letwin, Cheatem and Grabbitt from Jersey had brokered them. The children had negotiated a good sum for clearing away the breakfast bowls but were in deadlock over the washing up contract. However Mrs Hardy did not need to make them sandwiches anymore, as, although she liked to do that, she had been told she did not have the correct qualifications so the sandwich provision was outsourced. On inspection she ticked sixteen of the twenty boxes required but was put into special measures on the sharpness of the knives. Unfortunately outsourcing often meant the sandwiches did not arrive until about 3.00 p.m., and despite one of the children's severe nut allergy, they were often sent peanut butter sandwiches. The children's collective fees for tidying, housework and a little gardening offset the rent their parents charged them for their bedrooms. The children decided to share to save money, leaving a room empty, which room management frowned upon as inefficient.

After tough negotiations involving Kaiser Associates, Dave and Theresa Hardy signed a marriage contract six years ago, and had achieved a decent spell of continuity after Dave had passed his appraisals with her. His revalidation will be a hurdle, however, as Theresa is asking for a judicial review of Dave's plans to reconfigure the kitchen. He wants to centralise the crockery to the other side of the dishwasher where he feels he can provide a better service but Theresa thinks it'll be too far away from the sink. They both dread an unannounced inspection from the Can't Quite Cope Commission.

However, Dave wants to renegotiate the frequency of their love life and is threatening putting this out to tender producing his annual satisfaction questionnaires as evidence. He has been tempted by offers from the US who specialise in targeting the low hanging fruit. He feels his wife could have more productivity and negotiating a lower price is appropriate, but for a higher frequency. Theresa thinks she will win on quality but wants to include an interference clause.

The light bulb changing service was selected via a Choose and Book website, but they had recently received a letter after the appointment saying they had missed it and had to be re-referred. This meant that at the moment they were in the dark but they had the consolation of knowing that Light Bulb England had guaranteed five choices of appliances. They had been reassured that they could force better quality through competition, although they had found out on the MarketSolvesEverything111 website that three types are not compatible. They never had to worry about other house maintenance issues as they were tied into a company owned by the bank and were persuaded that choice was not important here. Things had been a little uncertain since the UK vote to leave the EU. But the new USA-EU Trade agreement, which was specifically designed to impose five hundred and forty-nine types of bulbs from across the Atlantic, would not now affect the Hardys. They had been told they would play *The Star-Spangled Banner* when switched on. This agreement would have put all the English bulb makers out of business but as they were not shareholders this was of no concern. Fortunately for US-UK relations the British post-Brexit Trade Minister, Dr Weasel decided to sign up anyway even though the EU had rejected the deal. It is irreversible and the Government can be sued if they do not stick to the ninety-nine year contract - so Dave's brother, Vince, who works for the US Bulb Company will do well.

The Hardys, being ambitious, are quite content with their lifestyle, which the *BBC* tells them on the news every night puts them firmly in control with lots of choice and a market that guarantees quality. They are very pleased with the new Government especially as the manifesto promised a massive top-down re-organisation review of compulsory purchase of selected residential properties. The Laurels' house fell into this category so the Hardys saw a business opportunity to asset grab and convert it into another badly needed lawyer's office. This they thought was justice, as had not they stolen their great Auntie May's private hospital in 1948?

Fortunately, as we all know this is just scaremongering. The British would never tolerate the stupid, corrupt, wasteful, expensive, inefficient and Orwellian system that the Hardys are living through. It could not possibly happen in such a fair and well-functioning democracy with reliable, truthful, balanced and in-depth media scrutiny. The *BBC* would ensure that, by living up to its Charter, and no political party would implement a policy not clearly laid out in a pre-election manifesto. They would not be so deceitful, as it might damage the politicians' reputation of being honest, open and full of integrity. Even if that were not the case, no politician would ever get away with changing the system so drastically, and why on earth would they want to?

Rob could not find a publisher for this article either. They told him, 'this is just scaremongering. The British would never tolerate this. You are way over the top describing the stupid, corrupt, wasteful, expensive, inefficient and Orwellian system that your characters are portrayed as living through. It could never be like that.

It couldn't possibly happen in such a fair and well-functioning democracy with reliable, truthful, balanced and in-depth media scrutiny. The *BBC* would ensure that, by living up to its Charter, and no political party would implement a policy not clearly laid out in a pre-election manifesto. They wouldn't be so deceitful, as it might damage the politicians' reputation of being honest, open and full of integrity. Even if that were not the case, no politician would ever get away with changing the system so dramatically, and why on earth would they want to? Sorry, but your time, and mine, has been wasted.'

23 - SEX AND TROUBLE

IMAGINE

Imagine there's no heaven
It's easy if you try
No hell below us
Above us only sky

You may say I'm a dreamer
But I'm not the only one

John Lennon (1971)

There were no lights on in the house as he parked the car on the gravel drive. That meant Suzy was probably still at work. He recalled she was to visit an artist in his studio and thought she might be late. This was her favourite part of her job. As he fumbled inside the ordinary Camden Tulip front door to find the light switch he decided again that he must get those security lights fitted. Before he managed to get the light on, Eric brushed against his leg and in shock and surprise he shouted.

"What the fuck?"

After calming down but feeling irritated that, no matter how many times he asked, Suzy never put the cat out. It would have been in all day. He dreaded what surprises he might find on the kitchen floor. Her habit of feeling sorry for Eric as he might get cold was not shaken by Rob's cries of frustration.

"He's got a thick fur coat. He's an old bruiser of a moggy with a perfect gene mix. No inbreeding genetic weaknesses of a so-called purebred there. He's tough!"

Letting him into the bedroom annoyed him too, especially as the cat made him sneeze. Then she complained when his sneezing woke her up. He sometimes felt he was below the cat on Suzy's priority list. He switched on the television for company while he changed into his slob gear for the evening. The news channel was interviewing someone who was complaining that no matter how big the scandal, whoever was at the centre of it, they only had to play for time and it would all be forgotten. Her main point was that the media never follow things up, are easily sidetracked by a good celeb story of no importance, have abandoned proper old fashioned investigative reporting and, as a consequence, people get away with murder, almost literally.

"Ride on, sister," Rob heard himself saying.

Not a phrase he would use if anyone were listening. He thought he was quite good at self-deprecation, although Suzy thought he took everything too seriously. He continued to listen to an intelligent debate, which Rob rarely found now on the broadcast media.

After reaching for a beer in the larder he looked at the screen for the first time. His concentration on the topic faded, as he could not help noticing how attractive this campaigner was, and then realised that was not going to help her cause and he felt a little ashamed. He tried to take in her arguments whilst at the same time trying to deal with the stirrings down below. They had been building up for a few days. Her prominent nipples so easily noticeable through her white blouse distracted him. How many breasts had he examined that day? Ten? Usually an even number. Rob felt almost pious that he could stay very professional in the consulting room with not even a flicker of an improper thought, and then he became a normal man when he got home. It was a live interview and he would put money on it not being repeated, as there would be complaints about her exposure from a few repressed losers.

It has been claimed the average man thinks about sex every seven seconds. Rob knew this was garbage. That would be five hundred and fourteen times an hour and over seven thousand times in an average waking day. There would not be time for anything else. It was one of those pseudo facts made up to sell papers. Fake news. How many others are there, Rob wondered. Fictional truth. Rob hated the manipulation of the public with brazen lies, so he checked this one out. An Ohio University study credited the average male with nineteen sex thoughts a day, and the average female ten. But every seven seconds is what people remember. Alternative facts.

The lady in the white blouse produced some good examples. Cash for honours, MP expenses, press phone tapping - all forgotten. Murdoch can say this is the most humbling day of his life, get his famous redhead to lie low for a while, close a newspaper, then a few years later bring her back and have the same newspaper back in circulation, just with another name. Then, thinking we'd all forgotten he was judged unfit to run a media empire, is allowed to take over Sky. Must be nice to have so much power. Pathetic and wimpy. So easily bought, these politicians. So Levinson forgotten - more than forgotten - actually some of the legislation brought in on the recommendation of the £5.4 million report repealed; MPs abusing the expenses system more than ever; people being given peerages for favours and money - short memories, everyone.

She was articulate but would anyone listen. Rob was listening but still distracted by her beauty. Did he have time to consult Dr Jackoff before Suzy got home? It was a habit that was becoming more and more necessary as Suzy seemed less and less interested. It was beginning to cause a few arguments. Too late. He heard her car pull up on the gravel.

Rob had to admit that fantastic sex was a factor in his life-changing decision. He now felt stupid, naive and immature about it. But also misled. If he had known it would die out in her, but not him, would he have been so tempted? Suzy did warn him. She had a theory that in every couple the hot spots disappear after eighteen months. It fitted with Rob's Darwinism. Once the female had trapped the male there was no further need to keep him happy. But it did make him unhappy. Was it just him? They were way past the eighteen months but Rob had no desire to go on the hunt again. He was angry too. How come he gets entwined in such an unequal relationship? One piece of advice his dad had passed on, that he did not really understand at the time, was, find yourself a woman who wants you more than you want her. That puts you in a strong position. To desire your partner more than they desire you is a recipe for disaster. Rob was even more confused when he was told W.H. Auden was wrong. His dad failed to explain and Rob had to look up who W.H. Auden was - a dead English poet.

His dad used to tell him, 'also make sure your woman is more intelligent than you. You will find that useful too'. Rob did not quite understand that one either, but great words of wisdom from a builder. Academic education is so overrated compared to life education. Too late now, 'sorry I did not listen as I now know I should have Dad'. But his mum's advice showed the insight of experience. She used to say, 'every man wants his woman to stay the same and not change from their first meeting - whereas every woman, having captured her man, wants to change him and knock him into shape.'

He had had a happy childhood, delivered by two solid sensible parents. But now he was priority number two, second to Eric. At the end of the day all men are cremated equal. In his professional general practice life it was not uncommon for a woman to complain that her partner could not keep her satisfied. Perhaps Suzy had just had some bad experiences that she could not talk about. But has not everyone had those? Or was it that terrible Catholic upbringing where they are taught sex is dirty and only for pro-creation? Mix that with his Dutch cousin Lars's opinion that all the British are sexually repressed and it would be better to get another hobby like collecting traffic cones. Not that he paid much attention to Lars since he became a Geert Wilders fan and banged on about the Islamisation of the Netherlands and thought the Quran was comparable to Mein Kampf.

Rob really did wish he had been born earlier but doubted if his personality would have coped better in the swinging sixties. He had recently heard of the Dull Men's Club and was considering joining. That would cure him. He could join the ranks of barbed-wire enthusiasts or shovel collectors and could aim to get on their calendar as Mr November. He had put 'fill your stapler' day in his diary after 'tidy the fridge' week. In another age he might have liked to be a member of P.G. Wodehouse's Drones Club - a drone being a male bee that does no work and lives off the labours of others.

Suzy told him he would soon get bored with being rich and idle. She was probably right but he would not mind trying it.

Realistically, he knew it was probably more to do with him though. Was he too demanding? Was he addicted? He must be over the quota of nineteen thoughts a day. He was different and could approach the whole sex thing differently as a doctor. But as soon as he took that hat off he occasionally worried himself. Did every normal male never really listen to the weather forecast because he was staring too avidly at the presenter's Simon and Garfunkels? When watching *Strictly Come Dancing*, although Rob never did, were the males in the audience just trying to get a glimpse of the woman's knickers and wondering if the couples went straight from the dance floor to have sex in the corridor? Why had he searched Google for a poster of Nigella Lawson? Was it to do with a wasted university life, where he was too shy and fumbling to take up the opportunities literally dangled in front of him? He could never understand why women were so attracted to medics. Same reason, he thought, that they were attracted to uniforms. Not so much *Men Are From Mars, Women Are From Venus*, than men are from fantasyland and women are from a different fantasyland and never the twain shall meet. Not unless you are very lucky. Which Twains, Suzy would joke, Mark and Shania? He certainly did not know how to talk to women with ease. Not too tricky professionally but no good socially. He puzzled as to whether this was inborn or learnt as a skill. When he got off with Suzy she made most of the running. Oh for the National Portrait Gallery.

There was a loud thump. Suzy crashed in through the door, kicked her shoes off, dropped her coat on the floor, abandoned her bags like they were red hot and greeted him the usual way.

"Okay darling?"

Same every night. Everything stayed there in the hallway too until Rob tripped over them.

"I'm too knackered to cook. Lets pop down the road."

That always meant The Poet, a pub that was so named because Siegfried Sassoon was brought up in the village and did his fox-hunting locally. The pub specialised in thirty-two varieties of gin and had Sassoon mementoes on the walls, including the score of a Wagner opera. There was no German ancestry in the family. His mother named him so because of her love of Hitler's favourite composer's operas. More interesting to Rob and Suzy was a transcript of his *Soldier's Declaration* of 1917. To them it was sad and outrageous but typical of the British establishment to bung him in a military psychiatric hospital for protesting against a jingoism-fuelled slaughter. As Sassoon became a war hero on the Western Front first, they really did not think it would go down well with the public if they had him shot. So society's elite was in a difficult position. They have learnt a lot since then. Discredit them properly first, with help from friends in the media, then you can justify any action.

Suzy and Rob sat at the table by the *Declaration*. Rob decided to tell Suzy about Felix and his observations. The Poet was unusually quiet so Rob kept his voice down. He wanted to avoid being taken for a nutter. He pondered how to start in a way she would take him seriously. She did not seem receptive to a deep-meaning conversation.

"Do you know we are one third mushroom? We share a third of our DNA!"

"Well that explains that management philosophy to best motivate employees, keep them in the dark and feed them shit. Haven't you finished that book yet?"

"Not quite, but I keep on having these amazing facts spring to the front of my brain!" Rob just decided to jump in the deep end and get onto his subject. He found it hard to summarise without sounding paranoid and gullible. But he knew he had penetrated with the theories of control and the ultimate revolting crimes used to blackmail people and get their cooperation. Not much came as a surprise to Suzy but the scale of the plotting, corruption and deceit described made her food a little more difficult to digest than usual. The conspiracies she found more difficult to believe.

"That reminds me, I forgot to tell you Jeff may come over soon," Rob was bemused.

"That's nice. But what's your brother got to do with this?"

271

"Nothing really but he too is always going on about plots and corruption, and I forgot to tell you about his call."

Jeff had been working in I.T. for Sony and living in Culver City. He felt quite awkward about leaving just a few weeks after Philip had been killed in 2007 but all the arrangements had been made. He knew he should be there to support his bereaved sister but would have lost his job and his chance of a new life in California. After the breakup of his marriage to Angela he felt like a fresh start. Suzy said he must go.

The corruption Suzy referred to was that which Jeff alleged occurred in his local hospital, and for that matter, the whole American healthcare system. In his I.T. world he had met colleagues in all industries including health, pharmaceuticals, arms, retail, energy, oil, and of course his field, entertainment. Late night drinking sessions at conferences, when people loosened up after alcohol to be far too indiscreet, is where he learnt so much. Suzy knew Rob had exchanged emails with Jeff wanting to know the dirt on healthcare.

"We live in a pretty bad world, my love," she said, with an air of wanting to draw a line under this part of the conversation and move on. But she did understand how much it all upset him so tried to bring him back to being pragmatic and get him to see there was little that would be effective.

"So what do you intend to do about all this, Rob?"

"I don't know. I do feel helpless. I read in *Private Eye* about the Save The National Health Service Party last week, so might contact them.

"Well, that's great. The world is saved then. End of all your worries. Bet they do well?"

Rob did not appreciate Suzy's sarcasm.

"*You may say I'm a dreamer but I'm not the only one*, as a great bloke from Liverpool once said. Anyway you just sound like the late great Bruce Forsyth," he said.

Suzy ignored him.

"So here's another thing I remember from Marcus's book."

She was at least making an attempt to speak Rob's language.

"A quote from John Maynard Keynes, *capitalism is the astounding belief that the most wickedest of men will do the most wickedest of things for the greatest good of everyone,*' true eh?"

"Capitalism is fascism without murder quite on the same scale, is a better definition. Capitalism treats people solely as consumers, not as citizens, nor even human beings."

He was disappointed and a little miffed that she did not even seem to want to try to produce any ideas of what to do next.

Instead she just said, "Isn't the wall colour nice? Farrow and Ball I bet. It'll look good in our living room."

This was typical of Suzy and one of her most irritating features. She could change the subject abruptly at dinner parties just when it was getting interesting. Rob thought that if someone were just about to tell them who really killed Kennedy, Suzy would ask if he had fed the cat. His friend Stephen's wife, Ellie, was the same. When those two got together, Rob had no idea what they were talking about most of the time. Trying to follow their dialogue was like sitting in the middle of an explosion in a fireworks factory. So he retaliated chillingly.

"Was Philip really killed in a road accident?"

"Oh no. Not that again. Of course he was. I saw his car. No one could have survived that impact."

"No, I mean have you ever considered he might have been murdered?

She looked at him with a mixture of bemused puzzlement and shock.

"He was onto them in the paedophile circuit, wasn't he?"

"Oh, come on Robert. That's one of your conspiracy theories too far; and far too far for your imagination, and too upsetting to talk about."

"Was it properly investigated or was there a cursory coroner's verdict? You know, an open and shut case in five minutes. That's the nitty-gritty. Who was at the funeral? Did you know his colleagues?"

"It was concluded he fell asleep at the wheel. He did a Mark Bolan and hit a tree. He was working too hard so I can believe it."

Suzy made an attempt to get off the subject.

"Besides, you are not allowed to use the phrase nitty-gritty anymore. It refers to the debris left in the bottom of a slave ship at the end of a voyage extended to include the slaves themselves."

He ignored her diversionary tactic, which she cleverly used so often.

"Was toxicology done? Very simple and very common, drug him before he left the office."

"Robert, if I started to believe all this I'd get scared. And what would I do anyway? Even if you are right, how does any individual fight this? We have one life. Accept the world is shit and make the best of it."

He knew, after being called Robert, not to push his luck if he were to stand any chance of getting what had been on his mind since seeing that gorgeous lady on television an hour earlier. He could not pursue it anyway as Tim the owner came over at that moment to ask if the meal was satisfactory.

Tim was a fascinating ex-librarian who decided he wanted to meet more people and when the cuts axed his library used this as an excuse to try being a publican. He was very good at it. It was Tim who changed the name to The Poet and educated the village about Sassoon. Suzy and Rob liked him as he was so unpretentious. When they first met and Rob was talking to him about Sassoon, Tim said he did not really like him and that his favourite poet was Ron.

"I haven't heard of a poet called Ron," said Suzy.

"Oh, haven't you? There was a lot of romantic poetry in the early part of the nineteenth century, for example Don Juan, by Ron. By-Ron... Byron... get it?"

But one topic Tim never joked about was Sassoon's war.

"Why do we commemorate the fallen? They didn't fall, they were pushed."

Tim arranged his gins like his books. He knew he was taking a risk as he assumed most would prefer Sky Sports but the most unlikely of types were to appear and ask him about poetry. Very warming Tim thought and it restored his faith in human nature. The opposite of what was happening to Rob.

As they walked towards Rob's Seat Leon his mobile phone rang. He looked at the screen. Jeff flashed up. He switched it off immediately.

"Who's that at this time of night?" asked Suzy, not really caring.

"Oh, that tosser Wiekser from the CCG. Not speaking to him."

It was Rob's turn to change the subject.

"Anyway, nitty-gritty has nothing to do with slave ships any more than that myth that the word picnic was a slave lynching party. Folklore, my love."

It was 10.30 p.m. by the time they got home so they both automatically prepared for bed. Tonight Rob's idea of preparing was a good wash and getting a condom ready. Suzy's idea of preparing was to put on her bed socks, her thick nightie and pick up her book. Where did this part of their life together go wrong he thought to himself? Newly-weds too. Maybe he put too much emphasis on it, as he was happy otherwise and pleased to be married to Suzy. She had turned sex into a mechanical bit of relief, rather than lovemaking - a quick one as she described it. He had tried to rekindle her interest but she had a closed mind.

"Do you know, Seneca said, *no man is free who is a slave to the flesh.* He was right. So my conclusion is that I think all men should have their balls cut off at thirty-five!" he exclaimed, trying to get her attention away from the Marcus Chown book she was finishing after their honeymoon.

"Twenty-five would be better," she fired back without hesitation.

She remained focused on her book with no change of expression.

"Did you know I've got a hydrogen atom in a cell at the end of my nose that was once part of an elephant's trunk?"

"Just think of the misery it would save. Men would just settle down and mow the lawn without complaining. They'd probably be content to watch *The Antiques Roadshow* and listen to the *Archers* instead of *Match Of The Day*. Many a political career would not have been ruined. Profumo, Parkinson, Thorpe, Lambton, Mellor, Yeo, Davies, Oaten, the list is endless."

"I'll chop yours off in a minute if you don't let me finish my book, Robert."

"No really. Sex causes all sorts of trouble."

"You're telling me," she said, still without looking up.

"People behave totally irrationally. Families break up over it. Look what it did to me."

Suzy realised he was not going to shut up so thought she might as well get it over and done with. She closed her book and slid her hand under the covers across Rob's thigh towards where he had wanted her to put it for the last half hour.

Without any acknowledgement of what she was doing she said, "Here's a good one. In one day your body will build about three hundred billion cells, more than there are stars in the universe."

Rob did not totally ignore her this time.

"Blimey, no wonder I'm knackered" he quipped, but continued, "There is a counter-argument, which you might find strange coming from me. Supposing Edward VIII had had his chopped off, Wallis Simpson would have meant nothing to him. He would have preferred stamp collecting like his Dad to her sexual gymnastics. Then we'd have had to put up with a Nazi King until 1972. Kenneth de Courcy would have got his way. Queen Elizabeth would not have broken all those records. Monica Lewinsky, Nell Gwyn, Alice Keppel, Mandy Rice-Davies and Christine Keeler, or Camilla, wouldn't have become famous and no one would have heard of Yoko Ono."

As the words Yoko Ono came out, she tapped Rob's upper left arm with her free hand right on his John Lennon tattoo.

"Kenneth who?"

Suzy always chatted through sex. She was unlike Rob's other women who used to concentrate on the issue in hand, so to speak. When he was young he did not mind it as it helped him last longer. Now he was older it just put him off. He was now in the era of his life when he did not want it to last longer. In fact he feared it and once the negative thoughts were in his mind it usually took too long for both of their comfort.

Rob had his one and only tattoo shortly after Lennon's murder as a tribute. It was high enough on his arm that it was rarely seen by anyone except Suzy. This is how he managed to keep it hidden from his parents for so long, until one day sitting in the garden he completely forgot about it and took his top off. It caused quite a scene as Rob was only seventeen. He was really affected by the best Beatle's death. If he had a hero, apart from Bobby Charlton, it was John Lennon. Twenty years later he was amazed to see the same image being adopted as the logo when Liverpool Airport was renamed after the Beatle.

"They've even pinched my line, *above us only sky*. Cheek!" he had protested to Jenny.

The world needed a new Lennon, he often thought. A few weeks before, a lock of his hair had been bought at auction for £24,000. Lennon had to have his hair cut to play the part of Private Gripweed in *How I Won The War*. The barber kept his cuttings. Wise man. This was just a month after the release of Rob's second favourite album *Revolver*. What a fantastic track *I'm Only Sleeping* is. But *Tomorrow Never Knows*, wow! Klaus Voormann's cover for it was great. If Rob had heard about the auction he would have put in a bid. Suzy would have thought him mad but wow, to have a bit of Lennon. The only other person who would understand was his old mate and squash partner Stephen. They were due a game in the next few days. Another Lennon fanatic, he would have put in a bid too.

Then the quick one was over. Before falling asleep he decided to see Rosa. It was about time. She might be more interested - and interesting.

24 - HAPPINESS AND UNITY

GOD ONLY KNOWS.

If you should ever leave me
Though life would still go on, believe me
The world could show nothing to me
So what good would livin' do me
God only knows what I'd be without you

Beach Boys (1966)

Pete had never been so content in his private life. So much had happened in the four years since that surprise e-mail from Madison and their encounter at the Landmark Hotel.

They were on their way back from Stratford after seeing Usain Bolt win the one hundred metres at the 2012 London Olympics. Nine point six three seconds. They had been part of that crowd of eighty thousand and were lucky to get tickets in the draw. Expensive though, but paid for ten months earlier. What impressed Pete was that Madison cheered on Bolt, and not her fellow countryman Justin Gatlin who came third.

"You really are moving away from your roots aren't you Maddy?"

"What do you mean?"

"Well, a patriotic American would have wanted Gatlin to win. Although I suppose he was a dopehead. And a huge zero point one six seconds behind. Out of sight. Of the eight finalists seven were from the colonies," he said, pushing his luck and with tongue in cheek.

"Cheeky pillock. The UK is now a USA colony of the American Empire. Revenge for burning down our White House. But what will catch you out is that it won't be long before I'm more English than you. More English than the English, as Terry Reksten said."

Pillock had become one of Madison's favourite insults for Pete. It was a word unheard of in the States and she was lapping up everything English she could.

The journey to their house in Notting Hill from Stratford was fifteen underground stops mainly along the Hammersmith and City Line, taking forty-five minutes. Madison loved everything about London. The multicultural nature could not be a greater contrast from Texas. It was alive and above all it had history and culture, two words hardly ever uttered in Dallas. They were buying a large white four storey Georgian House in Lancaster Road together, or to be more accurate, Pete was buying a little of it and money from Texas was buying the rest. Money was the one thing Texas did have.

They got off at Ladbroke Grove as usual. What they did not know was, while they were watching Usain Bolt the Special Operations Team was searching their house.

Madison loved this area too. So much interesting architecture. She could not get over the narrow streets. She visited the Portobello Market when she could. She was so excited when she discovered that their home was only a few streets away from 10 Rillington Place. The house and street where the serial killer Christie lived, and had murdered at least six women plus his wife up to 1953, had actually been demolished. The new road was called Bartle Road and with a bit of searching and snooping Madison once burst into where Pete was typing away and squealed.

"Guess what? Guess what? Guess what I've discovered?"

"A positive pregnancy test?" was all Pete could think of.

"No, nothing as boring as that. No I've found the plot where Christie's house used to be. It's a sort of memorial garden now for the residents of St Andrew's Square. Apparently they have BBQs there, according to an old man I met. It's in an empty gap between two new houses. There's a bit of original wall there too!"

"Well, I'm so pleased for you," said Pete mockingly, "The thing is, Maddy darling, I don't think you could find me a plot of land anywhere in London where someone hasn't been killed, slaughtered, raped or bombed in the last thousand years. It's not such a big deal. It didn't change the world like your famous murder in Dealey Plaza."

"It's not so much that, as the miscarriage of justice."

She had just finished Ludovic Kennedy's book.

279

"That poor Timothy Evans being hung for Christie's crimes, and his wife and child murdered. It did help change the world. You've got rid of executions."

"Yup. But in English the word is hanged. We use hanged when strung up but we use hung when for example I hung a picture on the wall."

"Pete. Zip it, as we Americans say.

"Derek Bentley was another scandal. Hanged by the State."

Madison had read about the IRA bombings.

"The Guildford Four and the Birmingham Six would have all been hung, sorry, hanged, too. A man called Michael Stone has served twenty years for a murder in Chillenden in Kent he probably didn't commit. Long before you had heard of England. Some evidence that might have helped his appeal has gone missing. Funny that. He would be dead too. There are some who still want the death penalty back. In Texas over two hundred and fifty have had a lethal injection in the last decade. How many of those were innocent? And don't you think Lee Harvey Oswald being shot was also a miscarriage of justice?

"Forgetting for a moment our delightful neighbour Christie, I love it here because it is more civilised. At least now the Government and the EU restrict the export of death penalty drugs. Poor dears in Texas are apparently down to their last few doses so they are looking for alternatives. In Utah they say they will use firing squads and in Oklahoma gas chambers. Thirty-two states still use the death penalty, my home state having the highest number by far. And if you talk to the locals, they'd kill a lot more than they do. If that new lot of pillocks get their way and the UK leaves the EU, then we will be able to bring back the death penalty here. Great only a matter of time. The world will go backwards again."

"They won't get anywhere. We won't be so stupid as to leave the EU. Mark my words."

Pete returned to the previous subject.

"I know the death penalty isn't the sort of thing for stand-up comedy, but don't you find it kind of funny, or perhaps ironic is a better word, that they are trying to get those executions done before the expiry date on the drugs? Do you think those about to be executed will be asking has that drug got any side effects and, if so I don't want it, I don't want to come out in a rash, I want a fresh new drug, I pay my taxes."

Madison did see the black humour, which Pete thought rare for Americans but she added that she doubted many on death row paid taxes.

A few days later Pete was getting fed up sitting at the keyboard so decided to treat himself and stroll down to The Elgin for a pint of the local craft beer and lunch. He felt he deserved a break. He was too conscious of the constant nagging in the media that lack of exercise would kill him. He was becoming quite a regular so was on first name terms with the very friendly staff.

The Elgin was a classic Victorian building and the only pub he knew where the bar was listed. He was sitting on a stool waiting for his ploughman's when a couple came in obviously in an agitated mood. As they were standing right next to him (he did not classify himself as an eavesdropper) he could not avoid hearing what they were saying. He told Madison about it when she returned from work that evening.

"They were from that tower block just down the road from us. They had tried to get through to the officials at our local council, the knobs at Kensington and Chelsea town hall, that the place is a potential fire hazard. There are over twenty storeys, no sprinklers or fire extinguishers, no fire escape and only one staircase. The couple were furious because they had been told they were troublemakers and have even been threatened with prosecution."

"I walk past it regularly. I have a work colleague living there," said Madison, obviously interested.

"Anyway, they think the place is being deliberately run down so they can condemn the blocks, knock them down, move the residents to places like Hastings and Bradford and then gentrify the area. The term ethnic cleansing was used."

"If that's true sounds like it's certainly a type of Kosovo style social cleansing," said Madison.

"I can't see why they would have made it up. I got chatting to them, explained it's the sort of thing I'm interested in as a journalist, and the result is that I am meeting the Residents' Association next week to see if I can help."

"Good. I've heard tales of other councils wanting to get the poor out so they can make a load of money. Let me know what happens?"

"More than tales. I checked it out when I got home. In the last few years about fifty thousand have been forcibly shipped out of London, out of their community, as a result of welfare cuts and soaring rents. Southwark, Wandsworth, Newham and Tower Hamlets appear to be the worst offenders. London is being hollowed out for the rich to move in."

"How can they be allowed to get away with being such bastards?"

Pete changed the subject. He wanted to lighten up.

"I'm more excited by what happened a few streets in the opposite direction. This is something else I found out from one of the locals. The photo taken of Carly Simon for her *No Secrets* album cover was outside the Portobello Hotel. Bet you don't know where she recorded that?"

Madison failed to react like anyone else Pete had met to his nerdy facts. She was genuinely excited to learn as much as possible.

"Trident Studios in Soho where *Hey Jude*, *Transformer* and *Ziggy Stardust* were recorded."

"Wow. Can we visit?"

They did not quite fall in love that night at the Landmark in 2008, but got close. They knew they had to see each other again. Pete made the first move and flew to Washington two weeks later. They had a blissful week together. Both had done the tourist bit before - Pete's last leisure visit was with Mike - so they decided just to take advantage of the good weather and strolled around the centre. They started at the Lincoln Memorial, took in the Vietnam and Korean Veterans Memorials, and then continued along the side of the Reflecting Pool to the World War II Memorial. After passing the Washington Monument they stopped in the Smithsonian for coffee. Almost in the shadow of the Capitol they came across the Botanic

Gardens, which Pete had mentioned that night in the Landmark. Madison had to show him the Bartholdi Fountain - one of her favourites in one of her favourite gardens. Fitted with her interests and career.

"The gardens have been here since 1820 and this fountain since 1878, so don't try to tell me we Americans have no history," she protested.

Pete was dismissive. He remembered telling her it pre-dated the Statue of Liberty.

"That's new! Bet they still have their price tags on?"

"Isn't it beautiful? Known as *The Fountain of Light and Water*. Actually I know what the price tag would have said twelve thousand dollars, but Congress offered Bartholdi only six thousand dollars. We must come back to see it illuminated. I understand it will be undergoing a restoration anytime soon so we won't get much of a chance if we leave it. It was originally illuminated by gaslight."

They then went back to her apartment where they went to bed, and stayed there for fifteen hours.

Pete was planning a trip anyway at some stage, as he needed to meet a few contacts about the corruption in the Bush administration and the Iraq War he was investigating. He had just seen Charles H. Ferguson's film *No End In Sight* about the American occupation of Iraq. Paul Bremer was in his sights. He had heard that Newt Gingrich, the former Speaker of the House, had called him the largest single disaster in American foreign policy in modern times and wanted to find out more. He was criticised for disbanding the Iraqi army putting four-hundred thousand young men out of work, the de-Ba'thification of the Iraqi civil service, leaving it without skills, spending the oil revenue, shutting down critical newspapers, granting foreign contractors immunity from Iraqi law, and turning a centrally planned economy into a market economy, locking in sweeping advantages to US companies with few benefits for the Iraqi people.

Pete told Madison all this on arrival, almost using it as a test to see if they really were on the same wavelength. To his great relief

283

and happiness she urged him to dig wherever and as deep as he had to in order to expose the truth about those corrupt criminals. But even better than that, she introduced him to the book by Thomas E. Ricks *Fiasco: The American Military Adventure In Iraq* which was shocking at the scale of the blunder and how poorly prepared for and disastrously executed the war was and the ensuing quagmire.

That was when they really clicked. He just could not believe that a Texan had such an open mind. He teased her that she must be the only one to actually have a mind, that is, not just an open one. She not only listened to a new version of the world from Pete, yet had a thirst for more and wanted to talk about it well into the night. She had more energy than anyone he had ever met. They would make love half the night and just when Pete was barely conscious, she would bring up Operation Gladio or the Marshall Islands scandal and want to know every detail. It was worse when she asked about Thatcher and the sinking of the Belgrano half way through their athletics though. The murder of Salvador Allende in Chile or the Iran-Contra affair where arms were traded for hostages and funds sent to the Nicaraguan Contras, the Pentagon Papers or the Watergate affair, The Abu Gharib Prison atrocities in Baghdad, or Bush's blatant disregard of the Fourth Amendment by getting the National Security Agency to tap phones, or worse, without approval.

Pete had it all stored in his head.

"Five years before you were born and while I was still being breastfed your fellow American, a man called Daniel Ellsberg, leaked the Pentagon Papers. The contents were, are, jaw dropping. They exposed the lies about the Vietnam war, the extent of the inhumane bombing and the very flimsy justification for that atrocity."

"Yes, I've read about that," responded Madison.

All the while she almost mesmerised Pete with a look straight into his eyes that seemed to penetrate his soul and derailed his thoughts. He regained his composure as she carried on.

"Nixon did all he could to discredit him and didn't he get prosecuted?"

"Under the 1917 *Espionage Act*. All Nixon's henchmen went for him including Rumsfeld, whose name may ring a bell even now. He had an office in the West Wing. Nixon called him a *ruthless little bastard*. There was even a plan to drug him with LSD. Charges were dismissed because of the President's illegal wiretapping and misconduct."

"Tricky Dicky, indeed. Soon after all this my great state of Texas re-elected him with two thirds of the vote. Still a record."

"But do you know the worst, most frightening revelations that haven't had the publicity they deserve?"

"No, but I'm all ears, my darling Pete."

"The US had an idiotic Doomsday plan worse than in Stanley Kubrick's *Dr Strangelove*. Its nuclear plan was to fire a warning, in anticipation of, not in response to, a Soviet attack. Thousands of nuclear warheads would hit the Soviet Union and China simultaneously. Every city with a population over twenty-five thousand would get a bomb. Moscow alone would receive forty megatons or four thousand times the power of the Hiroshima weapon."

"No wonder they don't trust us. Shows the absurd logic of nuclear deterrence. We as a species can't be trusted with nuclear weapons, can we?' reflected Madison.

Pete had not finished.

"It was estimated the American first strike would kill about three hundred and twenty-five million and a US General apparently guessed that, *if worst came to worst, we would suffer only ten million deaths*."

"Oh, what a relief, only ten million. Let's do it then," said Madison like an excited child, but with an adult's sarcasm.

"Both figures almost certainly were a fantastic underestimate. They didn't take into account deaths from blast, fire and radiation."

After a pause of thought, Madison added.

"But they didn't know in those days about the resultant nuclear winter, caused by the blanket of smoke rising to the stratosphere effectively ending human existence on Earth, did they?"

"Tom Lehrer summed it up," added Pete, "*We will all go together when we go, What a comforting fact that is to know, Universal bereavement, An inspiring achievement, Yes, we all will go together when we go.*"

Madison reflected on all the other scary things Pete had told her. She was amazed at the number of coups initiated by Washington, sometimes just because they could. When in 1987 the Fijian Government made it awkward for American nuclear-powered or weapons-carrying ships to make port calls because it wanted to maintain their island as a nuclear-free zone the CIA overthrew the Government. Pete was like a coup encyclopaedia. He knew the detail.

"The 1953 overthrow of the Iranian Prime Minister, the CIA coup in 1966 that ousted the Ghanaian President, Lumumba overthrown in the Congo in 1961, Neto of Angola in the 1970s and the CIA support for the counter-revolution against Samora Machel of Mozambique. Did you know Mandela's current wife is Machel's widow? She is the only person to have been the First Lady of two countries. He of course is one of your CIA's most famous victims. A CIA agent tipped off the South African apartheid Government to help get Mandela arrested. Then began his twenty-seven year imprisonment. Mandela was on the US Terror Watch List until 1999, long after being democratically elected President and a terrorist, for being, *the most dangerous communist outside the Soviet Union*."

"So yesterday's terrorist is today's freedom fighter and hero?" said Madison.

"Shush… you never know who is listening," joked Pete, "but it's a pattern that has been repeated throughout history."

Over the next few months and into 2009 they moved on to wanting to spend all their time together and then they became inseparable. But there was an ocean between them. On another visit to Pete in 2010 Madison spoke out of the blue.

"Why don't I move to London and we can get married?"

Pete was speechless. She had solved the problems that bothered him in one sentence. He had been a little gloomy about their future. He wanted to be with her. He hated that corny old phrase soul mate yet it was right. But she was a Texan, he a Brit. She was brought up in redneck land, he was a revolutionary socialist, or so he liked to believe. Strangely she liked the Queen; he was a republican. Most difficult of course she worked and lived in Washington, he in London.

"But what about your job, your family, your friends?"

"Do you wanna marry me or what? I won't ask you twice."

"Of course I do. Are you really prepared to give up so much for me?"

"Well, you'll owe me big time and it'll take you a lifetime to make it up to me, but if you continue to be so nice, such a great friend and of course don't lose those amazing skills you have under the sheets then, on balance, you are worth it. Seriously though, what am I sacrificing? Washington is nothing like London, my job is nice but how long will it last if those climate change deniers get control, I'm miles away from my family anyway, and you learn who your true friends are when you move abroad. True friends like Cheryl will visit, fakes won't."

Pete could feel the tears welling up.

"And Pete, I know I've got so much to learn from you. You are an amazing guy. I want to be with you. *If you should ever leave me, life would go on, believe me,* but it would be hard. I know a common language divides us but we are on the same wavelength. I believe in what you are doing, trying to expose the truth. I want to help. I can get a job at your UK Environmental Agency or Greenpeace or with your Conservative Party."

After a moment realising she was joking, they both burst out laughing. It was settled. They married in London in 2011. Mike was best man and carried out the role perfectly. Cheryl was the Maid of Dis-honour and carried out her role outrageously. She modelled herself on the movie *Bridesmaids*, which had just been released. Madison was just relieved she did not make a speech.

25 - TRAGEDY AND DEMOCRACY

DEAD END STREET

What are we living for?

We are strictly second class
We don't understand
Why we should be on dead end street
People are living on dead end street
Gonna die on dead end street

What are we living for?
How's it feel?

The Kinks (1966)

Rob really needed to see Rosa. Why had he left it so long? But he always thought this. He slapped himself on the wrists for being neglectful of old friends. But he always did this. He trusted her wisdom like no one else's and hoped she did not think he only went to see her when he wanted something. He always hoped this. They had a lot to catch up on. Again.

It took Rob a little while to find her new place. It usually did. She did not want to move from the Market Estate but Islington Council demolished it in 2010. To her pride though, not before she had the satisfaction of seeing her long fought for plaque to the Tolpuddle Martyrs put on the Cally Tower the year before.

He knew she was not short of friends. There were plenty too willing to help her move, including a former pupil called Megan who travelled all the way from Wales. She was now on the Maiden Lane in Camden and, although this was Rob's fourth visit he always managed to get lost. This time the scaffolding up the side and over the entrance did not help.

"What are they doing to these flats this time, Rosa?" enquired Rob as he made them both some tea.

"The cladding they put up the side of the tower. They are checking it after the Grenfell Tower inferno. It seems hundreds of blocks are vulnerable to burning down in no time. Several residents have already moved out."

"Are you worried?"

"Not worried Rob. Furious. But it's not the first time I've been incandescent with rage, is it? Councils across London have spent millions on the cosmetic appearance so the ugliness of our homes doesn't offend our rich neighbours in their million pound houses, and more importantly, to help maintain the value of their mansions. Our safety was not considered. You haven't heard the last of this scandal, I can tell you, unless there's another cover-up which we are all expecting."

Rob passed Rosa her tea. CND was in the news again.

"Last time I was here you were telling me about all those Aldermaston marches you went on?"

"Yes. It was on the 1972 revival where I met Walter Wolfgang. Name ring a bell?"

Rob had to confess that it did not.

"Don't you remember the old man who was thrown out of the 2005 Labour Party Conference for shouting 'rubbish!' at Jack Straw's defence of the Iraq War? At eighty-two! A man of great principle - not many of those left in politics. A German born Jew whose parents got him out in 1937 before Winton's Kindertransport. He was Secretary of the Bevanite pressure group Victory for Socialism from 1955 to when I met him in 1958. I was nineteen. I've got one of his pamphlets here... somewhere."

Rosa struggled to the bookcase behind Rob and picked out *In Pursuit Of Peace* and passed it to Rob. To his astonishment he read this written on the front: To dear Rosa, keep fighting the vermin, love Nye - 1960.

"Do you know he died four months after writing that? The day after the NHS's twelfth anniversary. He would be heartbroken at what they are doing to his NHS, but he did warn us all to be vigilant."

Rosa had picked up a selection of other rather battered leaflets too.

"Here are some collectors' items. The *Keep Left* pamphlet of 1947 written by Mikado, Crossman and Foot, and the follow up *Keeping Left* of 1950. Tom Driberg gave me those. Tom was unique. The most indiscreet man in the world. The tales he told me about his cottaging and the Krays would make your hair stand on end. And I'm proud to own this book."

Rosa passed Rob a worn copy of *Guilty Men*.

"Have you heard of this, Rob?"

Rob had to admit he had not.

"It's nearly as old as me. Published in 1940 it criticises and names the appeasers. Written by Michael Foot amongst others. You will see his signature inside."

This is exactly why Rob visited her. He was never disappointed. His enthusiasm was always refreshed. Quite selfish really, he had to admit. Mainly for his own fascination, but he did care for her. And the more he learnt about her the closer he felt. It was years before she let on about her background. He knew about her communist parents and brave uncle and cousin. What she seemed reluctant to talk about was herself. He realised why when he did eventually get her talking. It was too painful.

She was twenty-seven when it happened. She was at her grandmother's funeral in St Martin's Church in Caerphilly when rumours spread down the Rhymney Valley of something terrible at Aberfan. She had been a teacher at the Pantglas Junior School for three years but had the day off for the funeral. Excavated mining debris from the Merthyr Vale Colliery where her father worked had slid downhill and buried the school. Five of her teacher friends had been killed, and one hundred and sixteen of the children. Her class of little children was wiped out with just a few exceptions. They say they were singing *All Things Bright And Beautiful* as they were buried. Not often a funeral saves a life, but her grandmother's saved Rosa.

Rosa's fury started when she heard Lord Robens on television saying it could not have been prevented. Nobody believed him. He was Chairman of the National Coal Board. To Rosa this was a defining moment when she realised the new bosses were no better than the old bosses as Roger Daltrey was to sing five years later, although she had rather gone off The Who's frontman since he said healthcare should not be free and had clearly become right wing in his old age. Supposedly nationalised, it was not done properly or it would have been run better. What she said was music to Rob's ears. He believed a good society had been sabotaged by bad leaders in charge of what had the potential to result in change for the better, and here was Rosa saying it.

"Politicians, union leaders, those running socialist countries all fakes, stooges, traitors and in the pay of our right wing enemies, either that or just stupid."

She backed the parents who wanted, 'Buried alive by the NCB' put on the death certificates. In the end the coal board gave £500 for each child.

"Did you know that George Thomas, who was supposed to have been the perfect House of Commons Speaker, as Welsh Secretary at the time raided the charity set up for the victims' families to pay for the removal of the tips? And Robens, knowing of the disaster, still just strolled off to his investiture as Chancellor of the University of Surrey. These people really are in a different class, aren't they?"

Rob nodded.

She helped the Kinks get up to number five in the hit parade by buying *Dead End Street* as her way of protesting. Ray Davies' lyrics were influenced by the disaster. To him the reaction to Aberfan was an example of insensitivity and indifference to those seemingly of lower social class. Years later, in 2005, President Bush's reaction to Hurricane Katrina, which killed at least one thousand two-hundred and forty-five people in New Orleans provoked the same reaction in her. Because it affected mainly poor people, help was slow and lukewarm. What amazed Rosa and demonstrated how sick American society had become was the fact that over seventy countries pledged donations. First in the queue were Cuba and Venezuela who the US considered hostile nations. Britain's response to Hurricane Irma was not much better.

"The last thing I said to the class before the disaster was that if I caught anyone eating Spangles or Love Hearts in class again they

291

would live to regret it. I felt guilty about that for years as I wish they had lived to regret it."

She was twelve when Attlee lost power, although Rosa argued that they were really robbed of it. The electoral system and the fair play of Attlee led to Churchill taking over, when the Labour party had gained over a million more votes than the Conservatives and more votes than in 1945 and 1950. His Government had only managed to nationalise twenty per cent of the economy and much of that was of already bankrupt industries. But Rosa soon realised the inherent flaws. No workers' representation, chronic lack of investment, little long-term planning and the appointment of senior management from the pre-nationalisation era who had little commitment to state run industries.

"What sort of nationalisation have we got when the same old gang is back in power?"

"It was a small step in the right direction though, don't you think?" countered Rob, "I read just the other day that before the underground lines were merged into one organisation in the thirties, there was little cooperation between the different private companies running them. So, to change, for instance at Holborn, between the Piccadilly line and the Central line, passengers used to have to come up, leave the station, then go down again! Competition and cooperation are not compatible and most people prefer cooperation surely?"

"Just common sense Rob, which is lacking in a capitalist society, because common sense interferes with profit."

When Rob had last seen Rosa she had just returned from her pilgrimage to Rosa Luxemburg's memorial at the edge of the Tiergarten in Berlin. She was seventy-seven and barely mobile but she was determined. She jokingly reflected that if her parents had stuck with the name Dorothy, would her pilgrimage have been to Hollywood? This was at the site where the revolutionary socialist had been thrown into the Landwehrkanal by the extreme right wing Freikorps troops in 1919. A month later Kurt Eisner was shot by the German nationalist Anton Graf von Arco auf Valley. Anton

Arco-Valley inspired Joseph Goebbels who was in Munich at the time of the assassination. He was also the nephew of Lord Acton.

"You know what Acton, Gladstone's mate said, don't you Rob?"

He waited.

"Power tends to corrupt, and absolute power corrupts absolutely. Great men are almost always bad men."

Eisner organised the socialist revolution that overthrew the Wittelsbach monarchy in Bavaria in 1918. His followers, who included Rosa Luxemburg, were known as the Eisenarchers. Rosa told Rob all this, she said, to explain why her cat was called Kurt. Kurt was a British shorthair with a blue-coloured velvety coat and copper eyes. Rosa told Rob the breed was specially suited to life indoors. She found him through Cats Protection.

"He certainly wasn't named after Kurt Waldheim," she added.

She also enlightened him about the *Berlin Requiem*, which to his shame he had to admit he had never heard of. According to Rosa, Kurt Weill set Bertolt Brecht's poem to music:

Red Rosa now has vanished too
She told the poor what life is about,
And so the rich have rubbed her out.
May she rest in peace.

She carried on educating Rob although it never felt anything more than a conversation. She was never patronising.

"Isaac Deutscher wrote of Rosa Luxemburg, *In her assassination Hohenzollern Germany celebrated its last triumph and Nazi Germany its first'*. You know who he was don't you Rob?"

She knew he didn't but was not keen to embarrass him.

"The historian who wrote those great biographies of Stalin and Trotsky."

Rob learnt so much from Rosa.

"Life is so full of contradictions, it's surprising the human race has made any progress. Politicians never do what the public wants. Newspaper proprietors and tycoons tell the public what they want and control the politicians. Ever heard of the Peace Pledge Union? In 1935, a few years before I was born, my parents walked miles knocking on doors to get the League of Nations Union ballot completed. There was growing isolationism in Britain and people with any sense feared the national Government was becoming lukewarm in its support for the league. So they thought they'd find out what the people thought."

Rosa still had a mind as sharp as a razor. Rob wondered why he did not visit her more often, and now he or she will run out of time.

"Do you know millions voted? Shows how pathetic most are now in comparison. Even with the so-called social media making it dead easy you'd be hard pushed to get half that number. Even if asked, 'Do you mind if your partner was shot and your house burnt down?' only a few would bother voting Yes. The apathy around is mind-blowingly depressing compared to those days. We could end up with democracy being totally abolished and Orwell's world coming true and do you know what? I think we would get a collective resigned 'oh dear' from most while they carry on shopping and watching *Gogglebox*. They are seeing the NHS being destroyed and there's just a shrug of the shoulders."

Rob's jaw was dropping, as he knew she was spot on but angry that this was not articulated to mass audiences and that people failed to be ignited into action. He doubted she watched *Gogglebox* though.

"The results were amazing. Nearly eleven million voted that the manufacture and sale of armaments for private profit be prohibited by international agreement! Ninety-three per cent! I know the figure as my father used it as a sum for me to do when practising mathematics. All the other questions like remaining in the League of Nations were just as positive."

Rob was relieved that he knew the League of Nations was an early version of the United Nations. He worried about how ignorant Rosa thought him about these issues and about the past in general. He was keen to impress her.

"Of course that right wing appeaser Beaverbrook and his *Daily Express* just took the piss to try to undermine the ballot. What a contradiction though, that the whole idea was the inspiration of an aristocrat, Lord Robert Cecil, son of one Prime Minister, Salisbury, cousin to another, Balfour and descendant of a minister of Elizabeth I. And his father, Salisbury, was opposed to extending voting!

Perhaps he was revolting against his father, as often happens. He got the Nobel Peace Prize in 1937 for his troubles. Also ironic that it inadvertently placed the Peace Pledge Union in alliance with some of the fascists like Mosley, Ramsey and Anna Wolkoff championing a truce with Nazi Germany.

We sunk to a new low with that European Referendum, didn't we? The campaign was pathetic and an insult to the intelligence of the people. Politicians lied like there was no tomorrow, and as far as I'm concerned there isn't. The *BBC* were so scared and weak trying to maintain balance, as John Simpson said, it mistook the need to be impartial for not being allowed to counter what was clearly wrong. It didn't have the guts to challenge the most ridiculous exaggerations even though they could prove dishonesty, for fear of being accused of bias. Proof, if ever any was needed, that they really have caved in and surrendered their impartiality and are running scared of Government power over them. How many times since have you heard, *the British people have spoken and delivered a clear decisive and overwhelming message*. The leavers only got fifty-one point nine per cent on a seventy-two point two per cent turnout. That's hardly overwhelming. I'm waiting for the next trades union strike ballot where the union gets seventy per cent or more in favour on a ninety per cent turnout and the media say, as they always do, that it was too close and doesn't give the workers the mandate to withdraw their labour. Just wait. It will happen. I reckon as an anti-establishment vote, it didn't matter what the question was, it was going to be rejected. 'Would you like the Government to give you a thousand pounds?' 'No, fuck off'. It's the same in the USA. Put up a stuffed giraffe as a candidate and as long as he says a few anti-establishment crazy sound bites, he'll get votes. Donald Trump proves my case. So a white supremacist now occupies a White House built by slaves. Probably won't be worse than Bush and his Iraq war and pathetic response to Hurricane Katrina in 2005 where he proved segregation still rules by abandoning the poor in New Orleans to their fate."

There was a knock on the door.

"Answer that for me Rob. I think I know who it is. I'm expecting the housing association. There's a crack up in the ceiling and the kitchen sink is leaking."

But she was mistaken. It was her neighbour, Mr Ephialtes. There were a few murmurings Rosa could hear from the hallway.

"Hello Rosa. Just wanted to check you are okay for your trip tomorrow. What time shall I call for you?"

Rosa smiled in appreciation and replied.

"Well, my appointment is at ten a.m., so shall we say nine fifteen?"

"Perfect. Would you like lunch in our usual place with my friends?"

"Of course. This chemo doesn't affect my appetite, you should know that by now, Yannis!"

With that Mr Ephialtes withdrew in an impressively polite manner.

"Chemo?" Rob said in a broken anxious voice.

"Well I was going to tell you at some stage Rob. Might as well be now. I've got cancer."

"Well, I gathered that."

There was a silence as Rosa fixed him with a stare. So that was what she meant when she said as far as I'm concerned there is no tomorrow. He was so thrown off guard that he did not know how to react, so he went into medical mode.

"What sort?"

"Do you know that Mr Ephialtes is such a nice man. So helpful. His parents came over from Cyprus after the war. We've had long chats about the 1974 military coup and the Turkish invasion when the island got divided. He was very upset about his relatives being thrown out of their ancestral home in the north by the Turks. He used to work at the Hellenic Institute I believe which has something to do with research into the Greek presence in London over the centuries. He has retired now but a volunteer at the Cypriot Women's Centre in Falkland Road. More recently he has been angered by the way the EU has treated his homeland. He is a great supporter of Yanis Varoufakis who has tried to convince them that the harsh medicine of austerity, prescribed by Brussels and Berlin, was killing the Greek economy rather than curing it. Mr Ephialtes thinks this is deliberate and I agree with him. I believe his son is a doctor."

"What sort, Rosa?" Rob said more firmly.

"What sort of doctor? Something to do with guts, I think."

Rosa was doing her best to stick to her lifelong habit of refusing to talk personal.

"Mr Ephialtes filled me in with what is happening in his homeland. It was felt to be too unstabilising for Greece to tell the truth, that is it was bankrupt, so a smokescreen of the largest loan in history was pushed on his nation, but immediately passed onto the French and German banks. The loan was conditional on brutal austerity."

"Rosa, you know very well what I mean. You are well known for calling a spade a spade so let's hear it?"

"Well what else would you call a spade? A strawberry blancmange?"

She was not going to be shaken off her detour.

"Imagine what would have happened in the UK if RBS, Lloyds and other city banks had been rescued not by the Bank of England, but by foreign loans. UK wages reduced by forty per cent, pensions by forty-five per cent, NHS spending by thirty-two per cent, the UK would be the wasteland of Europe, just like Greece is today. Poor Mr Ephialtes, poor people, bastard neo-liberals."

Rosa eventually could not avoid the subject any further. When she told him she had already had a stent put in to alleviate the pancreatic obstruction, he knew she was dying. But she went back to the subject of her friend and neighbour.

"We catch the 390 bus to UCH and then we lunch at the Four Lanterns in Fitzrovia. Ta Tessera Phanaia. It's named after a small bridge in Limassol, which was in the middle of the Cypriot and Turkish communities when they lived together before 1974. Simple, unpretentious Greek cuisine. They have banknotes attached to the blue beams. Greece could do with that money now so it could put two fingers up to the EU, IMF and their banks."

Rosa knew Rob deserved more detail so stopped avoiding the subject.

"I've called it Rupert," she joked, "Not original I'm afraid. Dennis Potter was the first. I considered Jeremy, but I hate Murdoch more. Like all cancers the sooner they are cut out the better. Similarly the sooner he is cut out from this planet the better. The better society will be. Trouble is his empire is like metastases with his children just as malignant and ready to take over and spread further. My main regret is I'm seventy-eight which is enough, but Murdoch is eighty-five and on his fourth marriage and has just entertained another new Prime Minister, or should I say has been crept around and wooed by another new sycophant."

"Pathetic, aren't they?" Rob said to prevent any silence.

"Murdoch gave the game away with those *Hitler Diaries* back in 1983. Lord Dacre, the historian on his Board changed his mind and decided he wasn't confident of their authenticity, but Murdoch said fuck Dacre publish anyway, according to my friends in the know. He didn't care, as long as he made more money from increased circulation. In other words the truth doesn't matter. Only money does."

"I heard they were rubbish anyway," said Rob, "Nothing interesting, just trivia like, 'Eva thinks my breath smells' and, 'I must get tickets for the Olympics' as though he needed to buy a ticket!"

"So my dear Rob, at just seventy-eight I have reached the fourth age. You know my views on this. Old age is a term to be used only for the seriously frail, the dependent and those approaching death. Everything else is active childhood. One is not old just because the calendar says you are eighty. Look at Murdoch. He may be in his ninth decade but I wouldn't call him old. But the fourth age, or old age, is a time for reflection and withdrawal and I've reached that as I'm dying and will become increasingly dependent. You may think this is being pedantic Rob, but this new definition of old age will be important when there are one and a half million centenarians by the end of this century as predicted. There are fourteen thousand five hundred in the UK now. There were only ten in the whole of Europe in the eighteenth century."

"The lying bastards use this as an excuse to say we cannot afford a health service now that the population is aging, as you know Rosa. Sounds plausible but its just deceit. The media keep uncritically peddling this zombie theory. Not surprisingly the gullible and statistically illiterate swallow it. The truth is most is spent on a person in the last few months of their lives. The cost of death decreases with age. Those between fifty and sixty cost the most."

Rob began to regret this discussion in view of Rosa's devastating new revelation, but he knew she was tough and never was one to avoid an uncomfortable subject and she confirmed it.

"With me it'll be seventy-eight won't it Rob?"

He thought it best to finish his point.

"And in those extra years people are healthier than ever before. People over sixty-five contribute more to the economy than they take out. They don't understand, or want to understand, the difference between average, mean, median and mode. Mode is the important value. I'm sure you know that's the value that occurs most often. The modal age of death in 1948 was eighty. So demand on healthcare owing to aging has increased very little since the start of the NHS. They try to win an unsound argument that serves their purpose by deception. It's what most politicians are good at. It's what the public are fed up with."

Rosa changed the subject.

"You have heard Operation Midland has been squashed?"

"Was that the child sexual abuse enquiry into Dolphin Square where they think young boys were murdered?"

"Yes, Operation Fairbank was the umbrella investigation that spawned Midland and Fernbridge. Fernbridge got that catholic priest jailed for abuse at the Grafton Close children's home in west London, and was set up to look into the Elm Guest House in Rocks Lane, Barnes, the place that Cyril Smith visited. That became Operation Athabasca!"

To Rosa another whitewash, cover up, example of how in charge the Establishment was. Rob was aware that these were the police investigations into the VIP paedophile ring, a much more sinister scandal than those abuses investigated by Operation Yewtree. He had also heard the rumours that the Establishment had used the old trick of pushing the first investigation of Yewtree so far to discredit it so that by the time Midland and others hit the headlines the public would be inquiry fatigued and not pay too much attention to it. Implausible victims paid to come forward deliberately implicated innocent people. This helped undermine the genuine witnesses to Midland and so the inquiry collapsed.

"A hell of a lot of effort's been put into discrediting the main witnesses, victims and survivors but also death threats, threats to their families, you know the usual thing. The Establishment protect themselves as usual by hanging a few out to dry and pretending that's where the problem stopped. They all undoubtedly knew what was going on for decades. People turned a blind eye to Savile and Cyril Smith was protected and his crimes in Rochdale were covered up. He abused teenagers in Cambridge House and raped boys in the Knowl View residential school. Bastard. And bastards for letting him get away with it. But of course it is worse than that. As far back as 1983 the MP Geoffrey Dickens delivered a dossier to the Home Secretary, Leon Brittan detailing all the sex abuse and naming high profile, respected, members of society. It disappeared. So did one hundred and fourteen related files. Surprise, surprise."

"They pretend to take this seriously, but we all know it's being dealt with in such a way no one will ever face justice, and victims will never get the truth out," said Rob.

"I shall go to my grave even more angry than I was coming into this world." said Rosa, "My mother says I was the angriest baby she'd ever seen when she was first handed me. Of course I was. I sensed the world was bad and it was nicer in the womb. And that trip down that canal gave me a headache."

They both burst into laughter, which lanced the boil of tension. She had got her message across and did not want to dwell on it further. Rob had never heard her talk about herself for so long - even though it was not for long. On her prompting, Rob moved to the kitchen area and made them both teas.

"You have a good view from here," he said.

As the words came out he began to regret it. Rosa did small talk less than she talked about herself. She almost despised it. She would often say there were too many important and serious things going on in the world to waste time on trivia. She would never ask how Suzy was, or even Jenny who she had known better and for longer. Not that she did not care, but more that it was not relevant. Quite logically, she assumed if they were not all right Rob would tell her, so why waste time on it? She wanted to get back to what really mattered. On putting down her mug after the first sip she pronounced.

"We are living in an age of anger. These new social forums enable hysterical contagion, don't you think?"

Rob took a few seconds to work out what she was talking about, then agreed.

"Cliodynamics shows we have elite overproduction at the moment."

Now he was lost. She explained in an effort to put him out of his misery.

"There are periods in history, and we are in one now, when as a consequence of inequality, there are too many extremely rich people for the positions of power that extremely rich people tend to want to occupy. They think it their right. This results in them going rogue and buying themselves into power, not least by hosing money at elections. Trump is the ultimate face of elite overproduction, and like all fascists seduces supporters into believing there are simple solutions to complex problems."

Rob took a gulp of his tea, and Rosa moved on. She had guessed why Rob had come along even though he had not got round to saying yet.

"You know Rob, you have to step up the fight if you and your mates are to save the NHS and other public services from those bastards. They've nearly achieved their goal. My oncology treatment has been fantastic under the NHS, but in places where it has been privatised the care is poor and fragmented. You know this. It was you who told me the traitors at Macmillan were backing a wholesale so-called outsourcing in the north. All those specialised services that need to coordinate care are now run by different companies, which don't communicate or cooperate. In fact they compete to get money from each other. All facilitated by now being allowed to have the NHS signs all over their buildings so the public don't know they are private. And when the public do realise what a cheap crap service they are getting, they think it's the fault of the NHS, as it's got that sign above the door. The patients then start to believe the politicians who say it would be better privatised, not realising that it already has been and it's the private service that is crap, not the NHS!"

This was all making Rob feel guilty that he was not doing more and shouting from the rooftops - but also angry that most of his colleagues were doing fuck all about it.

"Why doesn't your profession speak out about the two tier cancer service that is becoming more and more common in the NHS cancer units?"

"I think many are gagged now or frightened for their careers," replied Rob.

"You know about the best NHS cancer hospital in Britain? It's now one third private. It'll soon be half, and then they will change the law to let it go completely. The staff is certainly gagged there. They cannot talk about how patients are offered two streams of cancer treatment, the basic NHS and the Rolls Royce private. We are two-tier in a two-tier Britain. So we are now seeing the first US style bankruptcies as people mortgage their houses to do the best for themselves or their loved-ones."

Rob had heard about this and tried to find out more but no one would talk freely to him about it. Even when well-known people like A.A. Gill hinted at it when discussing their cancer treatment the media had failed to pick up on it. Is it because so many have private insurance and so do not give a fuck, as Rob would put it? He knew they were in for a nasty shock. They will end up paying a lot out of their own pockets for something they realise is not necessarily the best for them, but the best for a company's shareholders.

"What do you hear in your medical circles of those American Health Maintenance Organisations and Accountable Care Organisations being introduced?"

She didn't wait for an answer.

"It's as clear as day that those Government documents the *Five Year Forward View*, their so-called *Sustainability and Transformation Plans* and the *Ten Year Plan* are nearly the last pieces in the jigsaw of their privatisation policies. The first was presented at Davos to the World Economic Forum, apparently. It has been claimed the STP stands for Slash, Trash and Privatise, or Secret Tory Plans. I gather in an effort to make it seem as though there is agreement they now call them Partnerships instead of Plans. And another name change to Integrated Care Systems, then Integrated Care Providers! They really do think the public are stupid to be fooled by that old tactic."

"You heard the late, great Professor Hawking?" Rob responded, "They didn't call him a genius for nothing. It wasn't his field but he was spot on. He summed it up in a sentence. The NHS is being replaced by forty-four US-style insurance-based private organisations. No question. The then Health Secretary, who always looked spaced out, said he was wrong. It's as easy as deciding between whether you trust a Mensa intellect or a dead slug with your future healthcare. Judgement without knowledge should be a crime. That would mean most politicians should be locked up. What a result."

Rosa thought as much and let Rob continue whilst not expressing her dark thoughts that Hawking's death had come at a convenient time - a bit like David Kelly's.

"The Accountable Care Organisations were, as you say, conceived in the USA. They involve government and private insurers awarding contracts to commercial providers to run and provide services. That is total privatisation. They are non-NHS bodies. They decide which services are available, who gets them and what to now make people pay for. Quality is generally worse, and costs higher. There has been no public consultation. They suck in social care, which of course is means-tested so this has far reaching implications for the availability of free healthcare. They won't allow a debate on this either. The ACOs, or should I say Integrated Care Providers, front a network of private companies, private providers and insurance companies. We GPs are now being forced into

Networks of up to fifty thousand to start with, and to be delivered through these Integrated Care Systems. Forced and bribed of course. Property companies are jumping on the bandwagon too. Haven't you noticed that when huge developments are suggested, they hold out the carrot of new healthcare centres? And yes, the Clinical Commissioning Groups are merging with the STPs. None of this has been voted through either by the public or Parliament."

Rosa was not surprised.

"Your BMA has been useless. They could have stopped all this in its tracks if they weren't dominated at that time by a bunch of time-expired Government old lackeys who are waiting for their turn to be called to the Palace for their gongs. I can't believe some of those old farts are still alive, let alone dictating what your profession should think and do. They stitch up your conferences and when a decent resolution is squeezed through they never act on it. I meant to thank you for letting me use your BMA identity to tune into their web-cam of the last charade. With my disabilities it gives me something useful to do. It was so obvious what was going on. The junior doctors have a very just cause but now the hierarchy of unelected officers has abandoned them. Let you all down like they always do. Left the junior doctors to their fate. Even more outrageous is their lack of support for whistleblowers. Totally abandoned. Those juniors should get in and take over. But I gather they are now leaving the BMA in droves and joining a decent union."

She had started on one of Rob's hobbyhorses, which he was happy to ride.

"They've been a disaster for the profession and the country. Ever since I've been aware they have had the pathetically weak attitude of, 'well we had better do what the Government says, as if we don't, they will find someone else to do it instead'. Most BMA leaders I've known have caved into the Department of Health even when they could have beaten them. As a result they have colluded and cooperated with the destruction of the NHS. Do you know the latest, Rosa? One committee has just voted to accept co-payments, which is charging patients. If that isn't another nail in the NHS coffin I don't know what is. Fallen straight into the Government's trap. The Health Minister can't believe his luck, or the stupidity of his opposition. Stupid or cooperating, it's probably a bit of both. How many knighthoods will emerge from that cesspit?"

Rosa nodded and agreed.

"They could have salvaged something of their reputation by putting up a fight against the market, commercialisation and all that crap."

Rob was on a roll.

"But look what they have allowed to happen. We spend less per head and have fewer doctors and nurses per head than most other OECD countries, and a lot fewer beds, and the idiots are proposing to close even more. For the first time ever, spending per head is going down. Their so-called reforms are counter-productive and remind me of what Spike Milligan said, *I've just invented a machine that does the work of two men. Unfortunately it takes three men to work it.* Sums up the market, eh? It's also known as 'catch twenty-three', an act of solving a problem by creating a larger problem. If they had put up more of a fight it might have gone a little way to take the stain away of their opposition to the setting up of the NHS in the first place when some of them called it totalitarian socialism. Outrageous, but it went some way to explain which social class doctors came from in those days."

Rosa knew all about that.

"Yes, they said some ridiculous things in an effort to sabotage Bevan's plans, but as he said, he *stuffed their mouths with gold.*"

"And professionally the BMA have overseen a great decline in my profession's standing. It capitulated time after time on new contracts and working conditions, has been out-manoeuvred and wrong-footed by politicians of all shades."

Rosa summed up.

"And as a result your status now has dropped and your influence as a profession in political circles is zilch. Consider how powerful your profession was when I was young. But I think that's been the problem. Politicians were generally jealous and revelled in trying to destroy you."

Rob was amazed how quickly Rosa grasped new situations. It had taken him years to work out what was really going on in the BMA and he was closely associated with that. Things that he was more distant from might take him forever - but not Rosa. When he was telling her about the Judge she did not bat an eyelid. Rob almost felt stupid telling grandmother how to suck eggs. But what troubled Rob most was what the hell should he do about all this and what, if anything, would make an impact?

Rosa's advice could be summed up in one word.

"Grassroots. Mobilise the troops. Get the people stirred up. Unity is everything. Division is defeat. Keep spreading the word. I can't die thinking there is no hope. I've got to believe good will overcome evil. I've got my third dose of Folfirinox tomorrow. I've tolerated it quite well. As you know it's every two weeks so it'll be nice to see you after the next few doses if you have time?"

She was the first patient Rob knew who could tell him the three drugs in the cocktail: Fluroruracil, Irinotecan and Oxaliplatin. She was amazed the last one was based on platinum and was okay about taking that as a French company manufactured it. She was less happy about taking the Pfizer drug though and was on the verge of refusing on principle, but her oncologist was very persuasive, and she thought she could not further her fight with the multi-nationals if she was dead. As Rob prepared to leave he promised he would be back soon.

"You know what, Rosa?" he said, "Everything will be okay in the end. If it's not okay it's not the end."

"Sounds like one of Lennon's, Rob?"

"Correct, Rosa."

He was preoccupied on his drive back home, thinking about poor Rosa, her diagnosis and the gap she would leave in his life. He was trying to absorb all of her wisdom, and work out the way forward. It will be another good person leaving the world. The Black Audi Q7 with darkened windows had been behind him since he left Camden. Rob was not especially interested in cars, but knew the top of this range ran on diesel so would have the same dilemma as he did with his diesel Seat Leon. He bought his car when the Government was telling everyone it was good for the environment - a good example of them not listening to the experts. Were they in the pockets of the car industry? Did they know VW and others were falsifying pollution tests? Now the Mayor of London will be penalising him if he drove into town. But he approved really of the new attitude because it was the correct attitude. But what was he thinking? Why was he pondering on such trivia?

This type of car was not one you saw all the time so he knew it was the same one - still on his tail after twenty miles. Very close behind too. This was what he should be worried about. Was he really being followed and why? What should he do? Try to lose him? He told himself not to be so ridiculous. No chance in his little car and who did he think he was, Steve McQueen? He remembered McQueen as the cop doing his damnedest to shed a pair of hit men in his Ford Mustang in San Francisco in the film *Bullitt*. Rob had read that one of the classic Highland Green 1968 Mustang GTs used had apparently turned up in Mexico after fifty years. It probably was a coincidence. He really was getting a little paranoid he thought. He tried to force his mind back into the real world and away from gangsters and the Mafia by getting lost in the programmes of *Radio 4*.

He was not far from his village when *Last Word*, the weekly obituary programme started. That did not help. But then the Audi turned off.

26 - REBELLION AND REVENGE

I WANT TO BREAK FREE

It's strange but its true
I can't get over the way you love me like you do
But I have to be sure
When I walk out that door
Oh how I want to be free

Queen (1984)

Arthur Talbot Rutherford was given his Christian names (as first names were referred to at the turn of the twentieth century) in honour of the Prime Minister at the time, the Third Marquess of Salisbury.

Robert Arthur Talbot Gascoyne-Cecil first drew Arthur's father's admiration when he learnt about his resignation as Secretary of State for India from Lord Derby's Conservative Government in 1867. He objected to Benjamin Disraeli's Reform Bill that extended suffrage to working class men. How could men from that class possibly understand the way to run a country? He also objected to John Stuart Mill's proposals for proportional representation. He was the last to lead the Government from the House of Lords and, at six feet four inches, was Britain's tallest ever Prime Minister, and the only one with a full beard.

Arthur's mother's objection (a rare event) was to the full name, as she thought two Rs, Robert and Rutherford together would sound vulgar. It was one of just a handful of occasions in their marriage when her husband actually listened to her, but the only time he agreed to her request. This was because, like his children, it was unimportant to him.

Salisbury was Prime Minister for three spells over thirteen years, resigning in 1902 to pass the bat on to his nephew Arthur Balfour. Bob's your uncle. Balfour is known for stating, *nothing matters very much and few things matter at all.* For Arthur Talbot Rutherford though, his namesake Prime Minister could not have been more wrong. His clubfoot mattered. The forceful manipulation using a Thomas Wrench, which fractured several bones in his foot, mattered. His brace mattered. His father insisted the latest advice from Walsham and Hughes, published only six years before Arthur was born, recommending two types of brace, one for day and one for night, was strictly adhered to. He could not accept a disabled child. Along with his friend Francis Galton he had helped found the Eugenics Educational Society in 1907 and so mingled with other members such as H.G. Wells, Winston Churchill, Sir Edward Vaughan-Warner and Marie Stopes. He contributed to the *Eugenics Review* once established two years later. He used his influence to help draft the *Mental Deficiency Act* in 1913, which would have allowed the segregation of those labelled feeble-minded. However, he did not regard his son as feeble-minded, but a cripple who had to be cured or shunned. That mattered too.

All this moulded Arthur into the determined character he was to become. He was to have a long unconventional and influential life. But unlike his father, he was going to be remembered by his children and grandchildren as a principled man whose guidance was worth following although he never once told them they should. Indeed he set the course of his offspring's lives just by example. An example they would worship.

As Arthur grew older his father telling him what to believe also mattered. There were only three paths to follow. Agree and comply, disagree but pretend to comply but secretly rebel or, third, openly revolt. Arthur chose the middle way and from that decision most of his life was led in the shadows. From his boarding school, which his father thought would knock him into shape he entered Trinity College, Cambridge. According to his father there was no other place to go but to follow Arthur Balfour. Rutherford was roomed next to 'Gubby' Allen, who ten years later was playing cricket for England and was involved in the Australian bodyline tour. Arthur studied modern languages, getting a First Class degree, and became a Fellow teaching French there for a further five years before joining the Foreign Office. As an undergraduate he developed a crush from afar on Guy Butler who won a gold medal at the 1920 Olympics in Antwerp in the relay. This is when he realised he was not normal, as normal was defined then, and wanted to fight convention even harder.

His father feared the Russian Revolution and gave money to help in the fight against it. He argued for more British troops to be sent to help the White Russians. He got to know the Grand Duchess Xenia Alexandrovna, Czar Nicholas II's younger sister and visited her often at Frogmore Cottage in Windsor Great Park in the 1920s until his death. Because of his chosen path of revolt Arthur found himself supporting the Bolsheviks. His father never learnt of this – one of Arthur's many shadowy secrets.

On the other hand Arthur remained unaware of his father's support for the Secretary of State for War, Winston Churchill, who wanted the Government to ensure more British help for the whites and ordered fifty thousand chemical weapons, known as the M Device developed at the Porton laboratories, to be dropped on Russia, the Bolshevik Red Army, and Bolshevik controlled villages in 1918. It was only on hearing about John Reed's death in the Wren Library at Trinity in 1920 did he come across *Ten Days That Shook The World* published the year before. This caught his imagination and made him crave for a similar revolution in Britain. When Lenin wrote an introduction to the 1922 edition Arthur took on the task of translating it into French.

He tutored Anthony Blunt and had his first real love affair with him. It was Arthur who first convinced Blunt - third cousin to Elizabeth Bowes-Lyon who had just married the Duke of York, later George VI - to take a long hard look at Marxism and to sympathise with the Soviet cause. Blunt was soon won over. By this time Rutherford had built up quite a reputation. He was often approached and had to be careful whom he could trust. Several plots to undermine the Labour Party by the establishment were brought to his attention.

After the Zinoviev letter, published by the *Daily Mail* four days before the 1924 General Election, which may have originated from

White Russians or even Sir George Joseph Ball at MI5 to discredit the left, Arthur was fully aware of all the dirty tricks.

Partly because of this Arthur developed an interest in propaganda techniques well before Goebbels. He described three types: white, grey and black depending on the level, or otherwise of its camouflaged origin. White, which does not hide its origin. Black, covert in nature, which is false information purporting to be from a source on one side of a conflict but actually from the opposing side and used to vilify, embarrass or misrepresent the enemy. Here people are not aware that someone is influencing them. Black propaganda is the 'big lie'. Grey is information of questionable origin, never sourced and whose accuracy is doubtful. This work did not go unnoticed by Military Intelligence, Section 5 or MI5.

Arthur was told, after the event, of a woman from Vienna who had been Ramsey MacDonald's mistress. She had received pornographic letters from him and wanted to cash in on them. Abe Bailey, one of Churchill's friends, put up the money to buy her off but, when the money disappeared in Monte Carlo the foreign office and MI6 had to pick up the pieces. Abe, a South African diamond tycoon, was the father of Churchill's daughter's first husband, John Milner Bailey - later also a member of the Right Club. Rutherford stored all this information for future use.

During his time as a tutor at Oxford he fell under the spell of Constance Markievicz's politics. She was a revolutionary Irish nationalist, a suffragette and of course a socialist. She was the first woman to be elected to the House of Commons in the 1918 General Election, beating Nancy Astor by a year. As a Sinn Fein candidate she did not take her seat. Arthur followed her career with admiration but despite his attempts failed to meet her. She was in and out of prison and died in 1929. Arthur needed no convincing about the right of a united Ireland.

His work on propaganda brought Arthur to the attention of Arnold Deutsch, who arrived in Britain in 1933 and set up a highly successful Soviet agent recruiting strategy. He recruited Kim Philby in Regent's Park in 1934 and Donald Maclean and Guy Burgess shortly after. Deutsch controlled the Cambridge Five spy ring until

1937 - the fourth and fifth being Blunt and Cairncross. All were at Trinity College. Deutsch evaluated the American recruit Michael Straight too but was not impressed. Deutsch's tactics were highly successful. He got all his agents to break off all communist contacts and establish a new political image as right-wingers or even as Nazi sympathisers. They must become, to all outward appearances, a conventional member of the very class they were committed to opposing.

"The anti-fascist movement needs people who can enter into the bourgeoisie," he told Philby.

By this time Arthur Rutherford was at the Foreign Office. Every day he climbed the Grand Staircase to his office near the Locarno Suite and could fully understand why ordinary mortals were seduced into wanting to become emperors. So it was easy to heed Deutsch's advice. He became one of the Establishment but secretly was ambitious for revenge on the class system and Britain's elite. He knew he was right when he learnt that MI5 had helped Benito Mussolini get his start in politics with a £100 weekly wage.

Arthur had one target always in mind that drove him for revenge, a minor bonus of his actions, Charles Morrison - the arrogant thug who had slashed his face at school. The pompous right-winger, who by this time was in the army - Arthur was reminded of him every day when he shaved. He nearly always ended up bleeding adjacent to the scar that had required twenty stitches. It was not really just Morrison but what he represented. He just used the memory of Morrison to keep his anger and passion alight and this was fired up every morning by looking in the mirror. He was a bigger, better man than to just focus on petty revenge. He knew he had bigger fish to fry, but as he preferred to say to his students, 'Il a bien d'autres chiens a fouetter,' or, 'Andere Dinge zu tun haben'.

Arthur would bide his time. He accompanied Guy Liddell, an MI5 operator who had appointed Blunt to a senior post, to Washington in 1936 as part of his Foreign Office duties. There, working as a double agent, he made contact with the unimpressive Michael Straight, who had been a lover of Blunt. Straight knew the communist sympathiser Jean Tatlock who had just begun dating J.

Robert Oppenheimer the American theoretical physicist and introduced him to Arthur. These were contacts he thought might be useful in the future.

In another twist while in the USA, Arthur, using another name, Ernest Talbot, manufactured a meeting with Henry Hamilton Beamish who, despite his father being a Rear Admiral and an aide-de-camp to Queen Victoria was a Nazi Agent passing messages back to the German Government. Arthur managed to get a fair bit of useless and misleading information sent via that route. He also spied on Camp Siegfried at Yaphank on Long Island - a summer camp, which taught Nazi ideology, and Camp Hindenburg in Wisconsin. He liaised with William Sebold, who was working as a double agent in the Duquesne spy ring, and found out as much as he could about Fritz Kuhn.

Back in England Arthur was sent to Liverpool where another summer school was collating information about Britain's infrastructure for the Reich. He organised false data arriving back in Berlin. Through Liddell and another recruit Maxwell Knight, Arthur learnt as much as he could about the Right Club. Most information came from the MI5 agent Sir Philip Lee Brocklehurst who successfully infiltrated the club. He nurtured his contacts with the Rote Kapelle or Red Orchestra, who sent him valuable information. The anti-Nazi resistance movement in Berlin intercepted messages the Right Club was sending top Nazis. Arthur also worked closely with Ian Fleming when he was at the Admiralty as the Director of Naval Intelligence, Rear Admiral John Godfrey's personal assistant.

In 1941 Rutherford returned to the USA with Fleming and Godfrey to help draw up the blueprint for what was to become the CIA. After the war Arthur exploited his knowledge of Fleming's wife Ann's affair with Hugh Gaitskell the Leader of the Labour Party. Rutherford managed to get Tyler Kent and Anna Wolkoff, the White Russian emigre, prosecuted. His father never found out that his son, Arthur, was instrumental in getting the daughter of the woman who had accompanied his friend, the Grand Duchess Xenia, out of Russia jailed. Tyler Kent worked at the US Embassy and stole the secret communications between Churchill and President Roosevelt. Wolkoff was trapped trying to pass a coded letter to William Joyce, nicknamed Lord Haw-Haw, by this time in Germany. Wolkoff was eventually killed in a road accident in Spain, in a car driven by Enid Riddell, another former member of the Right Club.

Arthur would never give up on his pursuit of Charles Morrison even though it was second division in his aims. To his annoyance Morrison had too many friends in high places to be nailed, as Rutherford would have liked. Or maybe he just knew too much. He knew and recorded his visits to the Nuremberg Rallies, to India to shoot wildlife and socialise with the Governor-General, the Marquess of Linlithgow, and his affair, while there, with Gayatri Devi of Cooch Behar. When Arthur heard a rumour that Morrison was heading for Long Barn in Sevenoaks to meet Charles Lindbergh who was living there in the late 1930s courtesy of Harold Nicolson and Vita Sackville-West, he followed him thinking he might get further evidence against him. Lindbergh supported the anti-war America First Committee and the aims of Morrison's Right Club. He learnt nothing useful but took the opportunity to call in on his old Eton friend Eddy Sackville-West who had rooms at Knole. Eddy, a cousin of Vita's, had also been a victim of Morrison at the school. He too was gay and at one point in love with Benjamin Britten. When Malcolm Sargent was bombed out in the Blitz, Eddy lent him rooms until 1944. By this time Morrison had become Baronet Willingdon. During the war, using his status as a senior British diplomat as cover, Rutherford was able to make contact with Oppenheimer again so his pursuit of Morrison took a seat further back on the bus.

In July 1942 Arthur almost bumped into Morrison. Rutherford was at a National Gallery Concert. He was studying the 1d programme and looking forward to Beethoven's *Sonata for Violoncello and Pianoforte* when he could not miss the noisy arrival of his nemesis. Morrison was with a man in uniform whom Arthur found out later was Sir Henry Vaughan-Warner and Margaret Greville a society hostess whom Arthur could see was obviously in poor health. He was later to learn she had died two months after the concert aged seventy-eight in the Dorchester Hotel. Arthur was fairly sure Morrison had not seen him. He decided this was neither the time nor the place to seek his revenge. Morrison and Vaughan-Warner felt comfortable at attending the lunchtime concert as, the Jew, Myra Hess was not performing.

By 1942 Oppenheimer the theoretical physicist was head of the Los Alamos Laboratory at the Manhattan project to develop nuclear weapons. He was invited to witness the first test at 5.30 a.m. on 16th July 1945 but found out nothing useful for the Soviets that they did not discover for themselves when the first bomb was dropped on Hiroshima twenty-one days later. Arthur knew of Klaus Fuchs, however, who was working on the project with Rudy Peierls and that he was the Soviets' main source of information. He avoided Fuchs, who was doing his job for him, and did not see the point of risking guilt by association.

Years later Rutherford, who loved playing devil's advocate, used to get his sons to write an essay with the title, 'If capitalism and competition is so good why wasn't the Manhattan Project put out to tender?' His eldest son wrote one line, 'Because capitalism can't be trusted, that's why'. He talked to his sons about Oppenheimer a lot, about the disgraceful way he was treated, and that he could quote the *Bhagavad Gita*, the seven-hundred verse Hindu Scripture in Sanskrit that is part of the epic *Mahabharata. Now I am become Death, the destroyer of worlds.* He drew parallels to the way the British treated other war heroes like Alan Turing and Gordon Welshman.

After the war Morrison's associations with people plotting at Bretton Woods and his membership of the Mont Pelerin Society were scrutinised but Arthur found nothing to bring him down as he wanted. His arms deals with murderous dictators were very suspect but no worse than anyone else's. By now Rutherford was senior enough and had enough contacts to organise Morrison's assassination, but this would betray his pacifist ideals.

Arthur continued to spy for the Soviet Union and was not suspected even after the defections in 1951 of his fellow Foreign Office workers Burgess and Maclean. When Fuchs's spying was discovered in 1950 it took the spotlight firmly away from Arthur.

His work investigating the members of the Attlee Government on behalf of MI5 put him beyond suspicion especially when he fabricated evidence that implicated Wilson and Bevan. He fuelled the groundless campaign by a Conservative MP, Sir Waldron Smithers to investigate the BBC for communists, and got George Orwell to name those he thought were too sympathetic to Soviet Russia - Charlie Chaplin, Tom Driberg and J.B. Priestley. It was all harmless thought Rutherford and put him in good light providing him with cover. He trod a fine line.

Arthur kept secret links with the Keep Left group, later known as Bevanites, of which Driberg was a prominent member. He knew of Driberg's recruitment by MI5 whilst at Lancing College, but also that he was in the pay of the KGB as a double agent. He was friendly with Guy Burgess. Through Driberg, Arthur knew Evelyn Waugh who was a contemporary at Lancing. He pretended to agree with Waugh's instinctive conservatism and his views that class divisions was a good thing. He had a brief affair with the Labour MP. Churchill said that Driberg was the sort of person who gives sodomy a bad name.

For the same reasons Rutherford was also responsible for the MI5 line that Paul Robeson was another security risk because of his left wing views and support for black civil rights. 'As a personal friend of Nye Bevan', he wrote for the Home Secretary 'he is going to give us a lot of trouble on African affairs'. This was perfect for the ears of the Foreign Office and its colonial-minded hierarchy.

When Hugh Gaitskell died in 1962 after tea at the Soviet Embassy the Establishment put around some black propaganda that he was poisoned to leave the way clear for Harold Wilson, being less pro-American and therefore more likely to reject pressure for Britain to get involved in the Vietnam War. Behind the scenes Arthur was instructed by his Soviet masters to quash this rumour. He achieved this smoothly by persuading his Fleet Street contacts to run a story ridiculing the rumour. He called in debts and got his press friends to run articles lampooning any idea of Soviet involvement and so effectively killed off any conspiracy theories. There was even a satirical cartoon in the *Daily Sketch* of KGB agents poisoning spies on park benches in Salisbury. So ludicrous nobody could possibly give any credence to the idea. Gaitskell being assassinated? Crazy. Russians poisoning people in British cathedral cities? Whatever next? Pure fantasy.

When Philby defected in 1963 and Blunt confessed in 1964 he again felt more vulnerable as the spies from Trinity were being uncovered one by one. Fortunately, like Blunt, he had insurance policies. He knew too much. He shared Anthony's intimate knowledge of royal secrets. This undoubtedly delayed Blunt's unveiling as a traitor for another fifteen years, and also meant Arthur was left alone. The valuable gems his old friend shared with him concerned a secret mission the royal family sent Blunt on in 1945. Being third cousin to the Queen paid off. He was sent to Schloss Friedrichshof, the home of Edward VIII's Nazi cousin, Philip of Hess to retrieve incriminating letters, including those between the Duke of Windsor (as he had become) and the Nazi hierarchy. Meanwhile, unbeknown to Blunt, Arthur was fifty-five miles north at Marburg Castle retrieving the Marburg or Windsor Files containing at least sixty incriminating documents including details of Operation Willi, the plan to install the Duke back on the throne in exchange for Nazi forces being given free movement across Europe.

Arthur had further protection from his involvement with the Sir Harry Oakes murder case in the Bahamas in 1943. It seemed likely to Arthur that the Duke of Windsor, now Governor, deliberately perverted the course of justice, oversaw one of the worst deliberately botched investigations in the colony's history and allowed the framing of an innocent man for the crime. Rutherford was suspicious that the Duke was involved with Oakes in massive currency speculation to finance his lavish lifestyle that went well beyond his inadequate allowance from the British Government. Was Oakes killed as he discovered Windsor's link with the Swedish millionaire industrialist and German spy Axel Wenner-Gren, inventor of Electrolux vacuum cleaners, their Nazi connections and their money-laundering scheme? Arthur's knowledge of this made him untouchable.

Despite his preference for men, Arthur married in 1941 partly to protect his career. He had seen too many acquaintances go to prison and have their lives ruined. It was an era of Eugen Steinach trying to cure unzucht zwischen mannern by transplanting testicles from straight men into gay men and others performing lobotomies. Others were forced to have hormone treatment or electrical aversion therapy. It remained on the list of mental disorders in the USA until 1973.

He deliberately aimed his attentions at Ethel, a woman fifteen years younger who also worked at the Foreign Office but as a typist. Arthur had done his homework of course. Working where he did, it was not difficult to check her out. She was perfect.

Ethel was born in Châtelon in the northern part of Auvergne. Her mother Marguerite was a cousin of Dr Joseph Claussat the Mayor. Marguerite met Ethel's father, a British entrepreneur Albert Greenaway, when he visited Châtelon and the Mayor just before the outbreak of the First World War to seek out the business opportunities of its naturally carbonated mineral water. This was the first exploited and was transported by bottles to the Court of Louis XIV. Greenaway was the nephew of the former manager at the Purton Stoke mineral spring and spa in Wiltshire, which flourished up to 1872, then dwindled to almost nothing by 1880. Albert's plan was to revive this but explore importing too if necessary. Unfortunately for the Claussat family that was not all Albert explored. On his second visit it seems Marguerite became pregnant but had a late miscarriage. The disgrace led to her family disowning her. She fled to England with Albert.

Ethel was born a few years later and was brought up bilingual despite this being deeply frowned upon at the time. It was considered deleterious to development, as there was really only space in a child's brain for one language. Marguerite was never accepted and drowned herself in the River Key at the end of their garden to the west of the village of Purton Stoke when Ethel was five.

Arthur also discovered that through Joseph Claussat, Ethel was a distant relation of Pierre Laval. This was someone to despise. A former Prime Minister of France, he began his career as a socialist but over time drifted to the far right. Worse, soon after Ethel and Arthur were married, Laval got a prominent role in Pétain's Vichy regime collaborating with the Germans. He was shot by firing squad for high treason in 1945 and ended up in the Montparnasse Cemetery.

Ethel had worked in London throughout the blitz and had seen friends killed. She was not attractive to the average heterosexual, but that was an advantage for Arthur. To Arthur she had the perfect mind and he genuinely loved her. They often conversed in French.

"C'est étrange mais c'est vrai que je ne peux pas surmonter le fait que tu m'aimes de cette façon," he told her, "It's strange but it's true, I can't get over the way that you love me like you do."

They had twins. Two boys. Silas after John Reed and Maximilien after Robespierre. As a female, upon marriage Ethel was obliged to leave her job at the Foreign Office. Arthur had rebelled against his father but his sons chose the first route of agreement and complying. They needed no convincing. They were devoted to their father and followed his philosophy. They knew their father was keeping secrets and on their twenty-first birthdays he told them everything. By this time Ethel, who loved him dearly, knew all about him, but admired his principles and honesty, so was fully supportive.

It was 1963 and Kennedy had just been shot. The twins were in their last year at University and visiting for the weekend. Arthur let them finish watching the second episode of *Dr Who*, opened a bottle of 1956 *Chateau Lafite Rothschild* and then proceeded to talk slowly and softly without interruption for twenty minutes. Arthur and Ethel had been planning this for years. Even the wine was planned. He refused champagne as he objected to being derided as a champagne socialist. He laid down several cases of the 1956 vintage hoping it would be a good investment. On his death it was rare enough to reach over £1000 a bottle. He explained why he was a communist, why he supported Soviet Russia, the real story behind his facial scar, who his enemies were, his time at Trinity, discussed the Cambridge spy-ring and speculated about the future. His career was in the twilight years now he was in his early sixties. At the end he asked for forgiveness from the three of them. They not only said that was not necessary but that they wanted to carry on his work. They were proud of him. They had been slowly and carefully prepared. At regular but infrequent intervals through their upbringing Arthur would explain the world as he saw it. They had grown into Arthur's world as they grew up in the real world. He introduced them to culture in a gentle way that allowed them to develop their own tastes.

"I think you might like this boys," was Arthur's most forceful guidance.

In August 1959 he took them, at seventeen, to their first Promenade Concert at the Royal Albert Hall, where they experienced 'Flash Harry' Sir Malcolm Sargent conducting scenes from *The Song of Hiawatha* by Samuel Coleridge-Taylor, Edvard Grieg's *Peer Gynt Suite* and works by Borodin. He told them he thought Sargent had earned his nickname partly from long-standing affairs with Edwina Mountbatten, Princess Marina, and the niece of the Queen Mother. At seventeen Arthur thought this an essential part of their education, as was the correct decorum and etiquette of not clapping between symphony and concerto movements, and to avoid coughing.

Arthur introduced the twins to the work of Edward Bernays, the father of public relations and propaganda. He explained how Bernays worked on the basis that the masses were irrational and subject to herd instinct and he outlined how skilled practitioners could use crowd psychology and psychoanalysis to control them to behave in a way that suited those who wanted to exploit them. His uncle was Sigmund Freud - Goebbels read his books. Bernays defended his ideas by claiming democracy allows a pluralism of propaganda, but fascism only a single official one. He promoted female smoking, worked with Proctor and Gamble to convince people their soap was medically superior, that eggs and bacon was the true American breakfast, and was connected with the then CIA's overthrow of the Guatemalan Government in 1954. He used subliminal images of vaginas and venereal disease to convince people that only disposable cups were sanitary. Arthur gave Silas and

Maximilien these examples of manipulation so that they would always be alert to motives.

To Arthur's delight they required no prompting to want to study history. One twin chose the twentieth century at university, the other the nineteenth century. They challenged their professors on conventional wisdom.

It was Silas who challenged the true history of the *Soviet-German Non-aggression Pact* of 1939. They were taught that it was so the two powers could carve up Poland between them. He presented evidence otherwise. He told his lecturer that the Western powers, particularly Britain and the United States, repeatedly refused to sign a mutual defence treaty with Moscow in a stand against Hitler. They were hoping to nudge Adolf eastwards. As a consequence the Soviets felt obliged to sign the treaty with Hitler to stall for time while they built up their defences. When the Western powers refused to come to the aid of the socialist-leaning Spanish Government under siege by German, Italian and Spanish fascists, Hitler interpreted this as their real enemy was not fascism but communism. Stalin got the same message and knew he was vulnerable. This was certainly not without foundation.

There was a deep fear of communism amongst the elite, upper classes and the aristocracy because it would destroy their world. Fascism on the other hand would support it. Hitler was not only preferable to Stalin but they thought they had little to fear from him. They supported his ideas and were often anti-Semitic. The powerful union between communism and the Jewish people was a world conspiracy that could only be thwarted by fascism. Hitler confirmed their long-held private prejudice.

Silas's research of the aristocracy's support for Nazism uncovered treasonous activities. It was suggested that Lord Brocket lit fires on his Hertfordshire Estates to guide German bombers on their way to London. The Duke of Westminster spent the first year of the war demanding that peace be made with Hitler. His mistress Coco Chanel tried as late as 1943 to meet Churchill for peace talks on behalf of Nazi Intelligence. The Earl of Erroll, the Casanova of Kenya's debauched Happy Valley set promised to introduce fascism to East Africa. He was found murdered on 1941 in his car outside Nairobi and Silas suspected his death was down to the British Secret Service. Other sympathisers were well known - Lord Redesdale, the Duke of Wellington, Archibald Ramsey, and 7th Duke of Montrose who was at school with Arthur. He was to use this contact to help infiltrate that circle. Lord Londonderry stayed at Goering's hunting lodge. His cousin, Winston Churchill called him a half-wit. The Duke of Hamilton argued in favour of Germany's right to Lebensraum (living space). The Duke of Buccleuch, the Lord Steward of the Royal Household, defended Hitler even after the bombing started.

The Royal Family finally gave up their hopes of a negotiated peace once the Blitz started. George VI supported Chamberlain's appeasement, together with its anti-Soviet policy; after all, some of his Russian relatives ended up down a mineshaft. From the outset the King's German family were often great admirers of Hitler. Amongst them was the Duke of Coburg who used the country house of his sister Alice for meetings between Ribbentrop and others with British politicians sympathetic to the regime. Alice was married to Queen Mary's brother.

But Silas included in his thesis European comparisons. In France most old aristocratic families were far right sympathisers influenced by the anti-republicanism and anti-Semitism deeply embedded in the Catholic Church. They supported the royalist right wing counter-revolutionary anti-democratic Action Francaise and opposed the Government of the Jewish socialist Leon Blum. After the fall of France most backed the collaborationist anti-Semitic regime of Marshal Petain. Silas did not think it relevant to mention he was distantly related to Pierre Laval. In Italy the aristocracy went along with Mussolini's fascist regime until it was no longer convenient. Silas was taught that the Soviets ruled an expansionist brutal empire, which liked to subjugate foreign peoples.

"Why should they not protect themselves?" he retaliated.

At the end of the First World War, defeated German forces were encouraged to remain in the Baltics to crush the spread of Bolshevism there. The Germans installed collaborators. Within the space of twenty-five years Western Powers invaded Russia three times during the two world wars and the intervention of 1918-20, inflicting more than forty million casualties.

The twins had been brought up to question everything. It started when they began asking why are we told 'West good and East bad, capitalism good and communism bad?'

Arthur was astonished but delighted on reading through one of Maximilien's essays.

'The objective of US foreign policy is power to ensure plutocratic control of the planet, power to privatise and deregulate the economies of every nation, and forcing untrammelled free market corporate capitalism. The struggle is between those who believe the land, labour, capital, technology and markets of the world should be dedicated to maximising capital accumulation for the few, and those who believe that these things should be used for the communal benefit and socio-economic development of the many. The US has a system in place to ensure whoever is in the White House this policy would remain the number one priority. It is a system.'

He was summoned to the Dean to explain himself.

The Rutherfords' targets were any history textbook statement that was universally accepted and where there did not appear to be a counter-argument. The Marshall Plan was described as a scheme where the United States unselfishly re-built Europe economically after World War Two, including helping its wartime enemies, and allowed them to compete with the US. This was a red rag to a bull. Silas argued that the Marshall Plan was not altruistic at all, but was all about spreading the capitalist gospel, opening markets to provide new customers for US corporations and in the process suppressing the left. It sabotaged communist parties in France and Italy and threatened to cut off aid if they gained any influence. The US controlled where and whether funds were used and the great bulk of the fund returned to the US, or never left, having been paid directly to American corporations to buy American goods. Any nationalisation or welfare programme did not find favour. It was sold to the American public as 'fighting the red menace'. But as he went on to argue, the cold war was not about the struggle between the United States and the Soviet Union, but the United States and the Third World. The US moved to crush any movement that fought for economic or political change, and supported repressive regimes in their bid to spread their free market corporate capitalism. The Soviet Union played virtually no role in these countries but as Washington could hardly say the US was intervening to block economic or political change, it had to call it fighting communism, fighting the communist conspiracy, and fighting for freedom and democracy when it was actually doing the complete opposite. This is why it was so easy for the twins to understand very early on the true motives of the US in the Middle East years later, and in places like Cuba and Venezuela. In fact in countries from A to Z - from Afghanistan to Zambia.

The Cuban missile crisis the year before scared everyone that the end of the world was being threatened, but not in the Rutherford household. Arthur knew no nation would go for mutually assured destruction. To think it possible, one of the leaders had to be MAD, and he was confident that was not the case. During that very tense week his boys were the most relaxed twenty-year-olds around. Arthur told them that the Russian leader, Nikita Khrushchev, was simply giving the Americans a taste of their own medicine by installing nuclear bases eighty miles from the US mainland. He wanted them to know what it felt like to be surrounded by nuclear weapons aimed at the heart as Russia did. All Soviet then Russian leaders since that time have faced the same problem.

Silas and Maximilien Rutherford were going to devote their lives to what their father had started. They would not mind punishing Charles Morrison in the process either.

27 - CELEBRATIONS AND FOOTBALL

THREE LIONS

Three lions on the shirt
Jules Rimet still gleaming
Thirty years of hurt
Never stopped me dreaming

Drei Löwen auf dem Shirt
Jules Rimet glänzt immer noch
Dreißig Jahre lang nur Enttäuschungen
Halten mich nicht vom Träumen ab

Lightning Seeds (1996)

It was the morning after the night before. Sir James was sixty, plus nine hours.

His birthday celebration went well although the security boys annoyed him. They marched around his Sussex country estate in an arrogant fashion way beyond their station but that is what happens when the Prince of Wales, four cabinet ministers and the PM come along. Sir James made a note to himself to shout at Frampton the new security company owner, next time he saw him at his club. His staff was busy clearing up and repairing the lawn where the helicopters had landed. Fortunately the lawn was big.

Hetherington Park sat in sixty-eight acres in the Sussex countryside and in comparison made his neighbour at Cotchford Farm look like he needed to attend the local food bank. The approach via large security gates and a long driveway offered an impressive view of the white Georgian house frontage with five Ionic pillars and two octagonal wings. The principal guests were accommodated in the fourteen bedrooms, looked after by staff in the three two-bedroomed service flats. In the grounds were four lodges and a Coach House. The Coach House was reserved for a very special guest, the cousin of his father Charles. Adela was now eighty-one, and at the outbreak of the war was a very glamorous Nazi spy who claimed to be working for the Swedish Red Cross and tried to stop Nicholas Winton and his Kindertransport scheme. Through high level contacts she evaded prosecution.

Sir James' father was long dead but his mother Edwina still lived on the Hetherington Park Estate. She was in her nineties and was neglected by James. They had fallen out over Adela. Not only had Adela had a two-year affair with her husband but also she took her son's virginity too and on Coronation Day, of all days. Rather cruelly James deliberately put Adela in the Coach House, which was right opposite Edwina's accommodation. Eddie Chapman was close by too in one of the lodges. His health was failing so he needed a companion. The second division of guests, amounting to two hundred or more had to find their own way home. Murdoch did not stay longer than necessary to make connections.

Morrison had flown back from Dirleton House, his estate overlooking the Firth of Forth and the Island of Fidra nineteen miles from Edinburgh, after dealing with some Scottish affairs. He was keen to sabotage any knee-jerk reaction demanding more gun control after the Dunblane school massacre, which had taken place three months before. It would be bad for business. He had bought the land in 1972 from the 14th Duke of Hamilton, who had relocated to Lennoxlove House in East Lothian. The Duke, who had had his house designed by the famous Scottish architect Andy Doolan, had been at Eton with Charles Morrison, James' father and witnessed his razor attack on Arthur Rutherford. The families knew each other well.

Charles and the Duke, Douglas Douglas-Hamilton were both at the 1936 Berlin Olympics and guests at a grand dinner held by Joachim von Ribbentrop, at the time the German Ambassador to Britain, and were introduced to Hitler. The Deputy Fuhrer, Rudolf Hess was there too. When on 10th May 1941 Hess parachuted into Scotland he claimed it was to meet the Duke and plot a secret peace treaty that would lead to the supremacy of Germany within Europe and the reinforcement of the British Empire without. Hess was aiming for Dungavel Castle, a seat of the Hamiltons, at the time.

With Charles' help the Duke of Hamilton was able to convincingly deny any part in the plan and any prior communications with Hess. To admit anything more may have exposed the activities of the appeasers, the pro-German faction in England and the Right Club. The whole affair remained deliberately muddied in waters stirred with a big stick held by Charles. The Duke would be forever grateful. His son, the 15th Duke, who had just divorced his second wife, was of course a guest the night before at Hetherington Park.

On arrival, Sir James had to get his PA to reprimand the gardener who lived in the East Lodge for displaying an England flag in his window. This was just too vulgar. There had been another football false dawn hyped up by the press. England had reached the semi-finals of the European Championship only to be beaten by the Germans on penalties two nights before. It was thirty years since Bobby Moore had lifted the Jules Rimet trophy in the Coupe Du Monde but Sir James didn't care. When he heard the staff radio booming out the adopted England song *Three Lions On The Shirt* he lost his temper and banned the kitchen staff from listening to the wireless. His house manager needed to be more careful when selecting employees.

Sir James had retreated to the quiet west wing of the two octagonals where the library was set up like a boardroom with his newly acquired eighteen foot nineteenth century Regency mahogany pedestal dining table dominating. He had paid £45,000 to Elizabeth Jones Antiques then demanded £10,000 off when he discovered a scratch. Being Sir James they reduced the price by £15,000 as a gesture of goodwill.

Sir James of course was at the head with Gerry to his right. Since his accident in the Falklands Gerry preferred to sit to the right of whosoever he had to engage with. He had walked into a branch of one of the very few trees there in Stanley and damaged the vision in his right eye. Sir James' PA stood behind in attendance. No guest seemed to notice the CCTV surveillance that Morrison had had installed - but that was not for security. If anyone had looked more critically, they would have noticed some of the cameras were aimed at the dining table - these were to help Sir James cheat at cards.

Lyndon Woodward wanted to get on with the meeting and was looking irritable. He did not want to meet on a Sunday being the Lord's Day, but saw no conflict between disapproving of a meeting on a Sunday and the use of cocaine, drinking the *Glengoyne* thirty-five-year-old highland malt he had found, and the call girl provided by Sir James the night before. What Morrison did not know until his wife delighted in telling him a few days later was that the escort had joined her and Lyndon for a threesome. His wife did it for revenge, whilst Lyndon did it to show who was in charge. Morrison cared not at all about his wife's betrayal, but knew he was in a power struggle with Lyndon, and decided on his own revenge. His motto could have been 'revenge is a dish best served cold'.

Hubert Witney and Ivan Humphrey were attending their first meeting and were acting like good children, only speaking when spoken to. Of course they were not to sit at Sir James' Regency table, but behind their bosses. To be seen and not heard. They were both hunted out and groomed as vehicles for the future - vehicles in which to carry forward extreme neo-liberal globalisation. They were the special advisors to the two cabinet ministers chatting in the corner. They all had carefully prepared cover stories for the press as to their engagements that day, which included Royal box tickets for the European Championship final between Germany and the Czech Republic that evening. The two ministers would turn into more than political rivals when their support for the opposing teams surfaced. This originated from their ancestry.

The Secretary of State for Industry was Adam Stanek. His father escaped from the Sudetenland to Britain just before the Nazi invasion of his Czechoslovakia, and brought his son up to hate Chamberlain and the French Prime Minister Daladier as a result. But he knew who Karel Poborsky was and that he played on the right wing. His colleague, William Hartman, the Minister for Policy Development, was the cousin, twice removed of Konrad Henlein who, when he saw which way the wind was blowing, quickly aligned himself with the slogan 'Ein Volk, ein Reich, ein Fuhrer!' and was appointed Reichsstatthalter of the Sudetenland in 1939 and SS-Gruppenfuhrer.

Anna Wolkoff visited the Sudetenland in July and because of the esteem Captain Ramsey was held in by the Nazis had an appointment with Henlein organised for the seventeenth. However, Henlein was summoned to Berchtesgarden to see the Fuhrer so she met the Deputy Gauleiter Karl Hermann Frank, who became infamous for the massacres and destruction of Lidice and Lezaky and other reprisals against the Czech population. Anna bragged he told her about the imminent Nazi-Soviet Non-Aggression Pact.

Having the SS in the family was a secret Hartman had managed to keep from his Czech friend but the other company present would have been full of admiration if they had known. The Industry Secretary had just read Martha Gellhorn's *The Stricken Field* about a people under the brutal oppression of the Gestapo and the Henleinists. If only he knew.

All had stayed over from the bash but had got rid of their mistresses in time for a leisurely breakfast to prepare them for their annual review of progress. Sir James called everyone to order and started formal proceedings. Apologies came from the Chancellor of the Exchequer who was in Japan and Clifford Wessel, another new recruit who was to be given a junior role in the fairly well developed job of sorting out the British healthcare system. Although very young he was from trustworthy pedigree. He had earned his stripes at Conservative Central Office as a medical student. Along with Hubert and Ivan he was some of the new young blood that the movement required. His arrogance got him further than it should, together with some useful blackmail material he had stolen one night from secret files in Smith Square. His apology though did not go down well. It was understood that everything should be dropped for these meetings. His inclusion was to be debated again under Any Other Business. All knew the importance of loyalty. All knew the importance of commitment. All knew the importance of secrecy. Ivan hid his connection.

Despite the air of the aftermath of a heavy night in the room, the whole group was pretty pleased with itself. Everything was falling into position, the detail had been discussed and they were ready for the General Election, which would take place within the year. Thatcher had not delivered or lived up to her promise as they thought she would, and was clearly going mad so they had to be rid of her. To completely wrong-foot the enemy however, it was no good just replacing her with someone tougher but to get the opposition to let their guard down by making them think they had won. They took their lead from the Greeks entering Troy in their wooden horse.

This part of the plan was Operation Epeios, after their leader, and Blair was known as Odysseus. Odysseus was one of the soldiers hidden inside. Operation Epeios required a weak corrupt regime to seemingly see the Tories discredited and put into the wilderness for a generation. John Major was perfect for the role. The Conservative Party is, to misquote both Voltaire and Ernst von Munster, absolutism tempered by assassination. The leader can appear to do what he or she likes if they win elections, along certain guidelines - but they are toast if they lose. But Major was controlled. The cause would be aided by a group put up to fight him on the European question to help make him seem weak, together with a few manufactured sex scandals. Murdoch had played his part well, making up stories of cabinet ministers only able to get their rocks off if dressed up in full Chelsea gear. They had Major's complete unwilling co-operation, much to his annoyance and embarrassment, with the photographs, videos and recordings of him with Edwina Currie. Wessel had provided these.

The press was instructed to leave alone the two cabinet ministers present at the meeting in return for their useful role in Operation Epeios. They were both told not to worry. They would be rewarded well and back in power relatively soon. Neither though expected to lose their contested Parliamentary safe seats. Where the opposition, enemy and general public were completely wrong footed was when they really thought they would vote in a Labour Government, when in actual fact they were going to end up with son of Thatcher in charge.

The years of planning meant there was no chance of anything other than a landslide victory for their man - their Trojan horse. Odysseus had been groomed for years. He would do as instructed. To give the air of moderation and reason, he was told to court big business and get rid of *Clause 4*, which was the Labour Party's commitment to Socialism. Drafted by Sidney Webb in 1917 and adopted by the party in 1918, it read: *To secure the workers by hand or by brain the full fruits of their industry and the most equitable distribution thereof that may be possible upon the basis of the common ownership of the means of production, distribution and exchange, and the best obtainable system of popular administration and control of each industry or service.*

They could not take the chance of Blair being ousted and clauses like this being taken seriously for the first time since Attlee and then implemented by accident. To convince more worried or sceptical voters he would promise to stick to Conservative spending plans. To woo the diehard old lefties he was to promise to get rid of the market from healthcare and then drag his feet once elected. He would also make himself and some colleagues extremely rich as a reward to never spill the beans. Odysseus was made aware that his predecessor, John Smith, had been murdered in his Barbican flat just over two years before, and did not have a heart attack as the rest of the world had been led to believe. Smith was in the way. So he knew what was at stake.

The two cabinet ministers came out of their corner and sat at the table. Lyndon was not in the mood to tolerate any self-congratulating backslapping. They had all received their briefing papers about progress which was designed to keep the meeting as short as possible. These arrived by private courier and all recipients were instructed to destroy their numbered copy immediately after reading. They had to produce the shreddings for examination, which they all thought a bit silly. No one was above suspicion. Woodward expressed what he had gathered from the papers in a forthright manner.

"You Brits are a smug lot. Operation Epeios is not enough. You can't guarantee me its success and you haven't delivered a thing yet. Besides it only deals with you, our fifty-first State."

This was a deliberately provocative insult to stir them up and make the others listen. He could see Hubert and Ivan visibly jump like he had used a cattle prod on them.

"Steady on old chap. That's hardly fair or true. We have made progress," interjected Gerry, gesticulating so forcefully he knocked his glass of water over. He did not notice. He never drank water.

This just made Woodward more aggressive. He raised his voice further.

"Operation Gladio is still useful and active, but it needs to repeat the success it had with the Bologna bomb."

There was the odd look of concern.

"We need those other left leaning European governments dealt with. Pushing them harder to adopt our neo-liberal globalisation isn't adequate. We've had some minor movement with the SPD in Germany and the takeover of the European Council to adopt our neo-liberal ideas has surprised us, almost as much as the conversion of Bill Clinton. We knew he would not be tricky because of the dirt we have on him, some actually true, but the speed of his conversion was staggering. But it's not enough and not fast enough. Europe needs to get on with amalgamating currencies."

What was not said but fully understood by all, with the possible exception of Ivan, was the scheme to fleece the poorer European countries of their assets. It was quite simple. Entice them into the Union. Load them with huge debts, and then when they default demand privatisation of pretty well everything they have. Mainly US companies would benefit, a lot of land would be up for grabs, the Germans would be happy as they would achieve what they failed to do with two world wars.

"Socialism would be confined to the trash can," said Woodward, "And it would be irreversible once they had their trade deals in place. We do need to be careful of the developing areas like China and India, which might want a slice of the action. We can't effect regime change in China but we can control India. It's a pity in some ways China reversed its isolationist communism and decided to follow us. That's okay as long as they don't overtake. We thought Deng Xiaoping was ridding the world of an evil form of communism, not that there's a good form, but we may live to regret what he did. He has turned China into a rival and we are not prepared to have our domination threatened."

The meeting was in danger of being dominated by Lyndon. Sir James wanted to get back to the agenda, although this was only in reality in his head not on paper. A bit like the minutes of their meetings - there were never any for security reasons. Gerry wanted to know about Clinton. Was he really now one of us? Lyndon took up the challenge again and Sir James sighed.

"He always was. His public statements were a front. You are a bit slow, aren't you? He is the model for your new Labour leader."

He gestured to his PA to get some refreshments.

"You know US Presidents don't actually have much power. They are nearly always front men for big business. We have a system. It really doesn't matter who the so-called Chief Executive is, or whether he or she is Democrat or Republican. Clinton has been neutered and we've promised him another term if he stays on side. We have several juicy sex scandals that are bad enough to get him impeached. We have groomed a secretive group of right wing lawyers we call the elves who could bring Clinton down tomorrow if we gave the order. One of the rising stars is a gloriously nasty piece of work called Brett Kavanaugh, one of Ken Starr's lieutenants. Starr as you know is the counsel investigating various Clinton scandals and is setting a perjury trap for old Bill. Their dirty tricks know no bounds. You probably saw the fake news we put out about the shape of his penis. This whole team of hard right operatives are being groomed to take over politics, government and the media and will be running the USA within the next twenty years. Kavanaugh is one of the true believers and is recruited to infiltrate the federal judiciary. But remember the names Conway, Paoletta and Coulter. Clinton will be allowed to remain a figurehead until we get George Bush elected, who will carry on steering the ship as we direct. He will just steer the ship as we wish until we get George Bush elected, who will carry on steering the ship as we direct."

There was an audible gasp.

"What that dumb drunkard?" exclaimed Stanek.

As a more junior member he realised he may have spoken out of turn. Up until then he had been daydreaming and trying to work out how to squeeze in a visit to Dolphin Square between his report to the PM, and hospitality drinks at Wembley.

"Yes, that dumb bastard," replied Lyndon, "He is so stupid he'll start the wars we need for infiltrating the Middle East. We sell them to the American people by calling them 'just wars', justifiable under our flag. Now the Soviet Union has gone, we don't need a Reagan. We certainly don't want a Roosevelt and a New Deal. We are unchallenged and unchallengeable. But remember in reality changing an American President is like changing the advertising campaign for a soft drink - the product is the same but it has a new image."

People were supposed to laugh. Then he put on his thunderous face again, and staring hard at Sir James fired like a machine-gun.

"Now explain why you have let Colin Wallace have the freedom to blab again? We told you to keep him locked up and warned you when you let him out of jail in 1987 he would be a risk to us. He needs to be fitted up again. He knows too much about the Kincora Boys' Home. If all he knows about the disinformation activities he organised gets out, someone will pay, heavily! It was bad enough when he got compensation for MI5 manipulating disciplinary proceedings against him."

"Yes it was slightly awkward," added Gerry.

"Slightly awkward!" shouted Woodward. "I'll give you and your fucking British understatement slightly, fucking awkward. It was a fucking disaster!"

He was not intending to stop.

"One last thing. I'm sick and tired of hearing about those irritants that are fighting us below the radar. There are as irritating as fleas in the pants. Get your Special Operations Team to earn their money."

He could tell those around the table were a little puzzled.

"The fact that I need to spell it out says it all. I've been aware of Poison and bastards like your Rutherford since the 1980s. Eliminate them once and for all, or we will. They have caused trouble in Northern Ireland too."

With that he stood up, took his jacket off the neighbouring chair and spat out in a mocking attempt at an English accent.

"Now if you excuse me gentleman, you know what is expected, get on with it."

He gestured to Sir James's PA, and ordered.

"Get my car," back in his southern drawl, and walked out.

Sir James made a note to himself to get revenge on Lyndon. How dare he take control of his meeting like that in his house? Screwing his wife was annoying too. He was not going to let the others think his authority had been stamped on, so he more shouted than spoke.

"It's undiplomatic to call the future President of the United States a dumb drunkard. You can make amends by getting Lyndon's message to your boss, and tell him in his limited time in Downing Street he should think of his legacy and reputation, with us, not the great British public. It would be prudent for you all to realise we write the history."

The meeting drew to a close after dealing with a few other operational details, including making sure Wessel got a warning never to miss a meeting again and not to be disrespectful. Witney and Humphrey both felt very privileged to be part of the future.

Stanek felt it safe now to boast to Hartman about a new communication system due to be launched in four days time - American Independence Day symbolising freedom to access from anywhere in the world.

"Hotmail," Adam told William, "will make some friends of mine very rich and allow papers for meetings like this to be sent from computer to computer putting the ordinary mail out of business."

As Lyndon Woodward was driven down the long drive, he wondered why there was a removal van outside the East Lodge, but not for long. Thirty years of hurt never stopped the gardener dreaming, but now he needed to find a new job and somewhere to live.

28 - SEDUCTION AND AMBITION

KRISCO KISSES

You feed my hunger
With a fist way past the rest
Take it to the top
You fit me like a glove
My love, you fit me like a glove
Give my friend, my be-bop
Take it to the top, my love
Krisco kisses, kisses
You can take it, take it, up, up and up

Frankie Goes To Hollywood (1984)

"Come with us you two. You need to admire Sir James' estate, you might not see it again."

So the Cabinet Ministers led their special advisors through the French doors and across the immaculate five acre lawn towards the lake, like dogs on leads with tongues hanging out and with equal obedience. Stanek and Hartman were seasoned and experienced political players with Machiavellian personalities.

Hartman thought this was something to boast about, not keep quiet. The book he chose to take to the island when he was a guest on *Desert Island Discs* was Niccolò Machiavelli's *The Prince*. He hit the headlines when he claimed he based his approach to politics on the book's themes of immoral behaviour, deceit and deviousness. Leaders should seek to be feared not loved. He said the dishonesty and the killing of innocents in *Il Princip* was normal and effective in politics. He told Sue Lawley that he would want an original 1513 Italian version. When challenged about whether he agreed with Machiavelli that violence may be necessary for the successful stabilisation of power, to eliminate political rivals, to coerce resistant populations, and to purge the community of other obstacles, he said one word.

"Si."

There was no doubt the story would have run for longer if not for the Hillsborough disaster dominating the headlines.

Witney and Humphrey on the other hand had a lot to learn about political manoeuvring although they knew what they believed in. Each had an upbringing that was sound. They came from the right stock. Their paths were laid out before they were even born. Whisked off to prep school as early as possible so as not to be a nuisance to their parents, followed by Eton, then of course Oxford. They both did well, except academically. Witney became President of the Oxford Union. His grandfather along with Randolph Churchill attempted to get the 1933 motion 'this house would under no circumstances fight for its King and Country' expunged from the records. Witney was told his grandfather thought free speech a threat to his idea of democracy. Not to be outdone Humphrey served as President of the Oxford University Conservative Association but was ousted after bad publicity of a Bullingdon Club outing, which left a restaurant trashed and put three waiters in hospital. One lost the sight in one eye but was bought off with an undisclosed sum that was conditional on a gagging clause.

Humphrey was not proud of his connection to Clifford Wessel, and was so relieved it was not known at the earlier review meeting that Wessel was his younger stepbrother, or if it was nobody mentioned it. Humphrey was thankful they had different surnames to disguise the link. He was an embarrassment as was their German father. They both graduated with poor degrees in the mid 1980s, both surviving threats to be sent down for outrageous behaviour thanks to their father's intervention.

"Rustication never did Shelley, Wilde, Betjeman nor Waugh any harm," Humphrey blustered. He would not have minded.

Both had spent the last decade working for Conservative and Unionist Central Office in Smith Square, serving their apprenticeship as errand boys. They were given hopeless parliamentary seats to fight at the 1992 election to cut their teeth. After that they were allocated a safe seat to fight as a reward for loyalty. Humphrey also had a brief internship with the Freedom

337

Association. Much of what they stood for attracted Ivan. Freedom from trades unions, freedom from the European Union, and freedom from anything other than right wing views on the *BBC*. He was young when one of its co-founders Ross McWhirter was shot dead on his doorstep by the IRA, but he remembered being stunned that something like that could happen in London, not far from where his parents had a town house.

To their surprise and some bitterness, which they could not show, both had been warned they were very unlikely to win their contested safe seats in 1997, as their Trojan horse was to get a landslide. They thought they had been misled. But they were told it would be good for them and to remember that a politician is a fellow who will lay down his life for his country. For the subsequent election, jobs for life were the reward. Witney was destined for an even safer Cotswolds constituency and Surrey beckoned for Humphrey, although someone had to be lined up to contest the Mayoralty of London.

"We've got a bit of work for you two," Hartman said without even looking at his juniors, "We will be safe to talk freely by the lake."

"Do as we instruct and we will see to it you do well," Stanek then menacingly added, "Reject us, or turn us down and your career will hit the buffers."

The two Ministers treated their inferiors like their public school fags - once a public schoolboy, always a public schoolboy.

Hartman was at Repton and made Jeremy Clarkson's life hell, forcing him, amongst other degrading things, to lick toilet seats clean. That was forgotten when Hartman joined the Chipping Norton Set. William Hartman was third generation at the same school in Derbyshire. His grandfather, Wilhelm was brought by his parents as a baby to England in the last decade of Victoria's reign. He was named after the Kaiser, the old Queen's grandson. From 1871 the newly united second Reich in Germany started to change from being an agricultural nation to an industrial one. The wealth was being invested in new technologies making farming unprofitable.

So the family sold up, moved to London and after working as a waiter, the man of the house eventually opened a restaurant and gradually built up the family's fortune. Wilhelm did not allow the handicap of initially only having limited English stop his anti-Semitic attacks on fellow Repton pupil and future Olympic champion Harold Abrahams. He in turn was subject to horrific beatings because of his German ancestry during the First World War. He soon anglicised his name to William.

Another contemporary was Christopher Isherwood who became a life-long friend. Together with Stephen Spender, Isherwood would stay with Hartman's relatives in Berlin. It was at a party their cousins the Henleins were throwing that Isherwood met Jean Ross who was his inspiration for Sally Bowles. Ross being a lifelong communist had a row with the host who had joined the Nazi party well before Hitler came to power. The Minister for Policy Development remembered his octogenarian grandfather, disabled after a stroke, spitting at his television when Barry Norman was reviewing *Chariots Of Fire* on the *BBC*'s *Film '81*. Seeing Abrahams portrayed as a hero at the 1924 Paris Olympics made his blood boil. He had lost none of his hatred.

"Bloody Polish Jew", he mumbled through the dribble.

He repeatedly told his family the story of the holocaust was an invention. The old man was still bitter at his internment in 1940 by Churchill because of his Right Club membership. If Churchill had actually known the extent of Wilhelm Hartman's activities, he may well have been incarcerated for much longer. Together with SS-Oberführer Walter Schellenberg Hartman helped draw up the *Sonderfahndungsliste G.B.* or 'Black Book' which listed two thousand eight hundred and twenty prominent British residents to be arrested after the invasion code-named Unternehmen Seelöwe or Operation Sea Lion. He fed infrastructure information back to Berlin from the secret spy school in Liverpool and planned for after the invasion. Nazi HQ was to be at Blenheim Palace and Hitler would take over Apley Hall near Bridgnorth in Shropshire as his country retreat. Blenheim Palace was chosen out of revenge for the battle defeat of the Bavarians at Blindheim by the Duke of Marlborough in 1704, and of course it was the birthplace of his descendent Winston Churchill.

Adam Stanek was first generation in England from Europe and went to Charterhouse. He knew the Dimblebys, Jonathan King and the lads from Genesis, whom King helped to success before going to jail for indecent assault of teenage boys. Stanek was feared and known as a bully. Even the masters were wary, especially the one he was blackmailing for certain indiscretions.

"We don't mind which of you takes on this work as long as it's done quickly, effectively and there is no chance of connecting it to us. Not only that, make sure you convince everyone some foreigner was responsible. You can earn your spurs this way. Then your careers may flourish. I'll outline the problem. Our friends in the sugar industry need more sabotage work done. There are further attacks on the safety of sugar and those responsible are sounding too credible. Before we know it some do-gooder will call for the reintroduction of the sugar tax Gladstone abolished in 1874. You need to know some history but the research otherwise is up to you.

If you need a master class in how to discredit someone, check out what we've done to a Dr Yudkin. He published a book in 1972 called *Pure, White and Deadly*. In it he blamed sugar, not fat for the growing epidemic of heart disease and this was very inconvenient for the food industry's long term plan and profits, even though it was spot on and dangerous because it was spot on. From the early 1960s the Sugar Association began a systematic effort to get the public to consume more sugar. So it funded research to prove fat, not sugar, was the major risk factor in coronary heart disease. The head of nutrition at the US Department of Agriculture was in on the con, publishing national guidelines recommending a low fat diet. Of course most low fat food has to be loaded with sugar or it tastes disgusting. Yudkin, who first cottoned on to this as far back as the 1950s, was a threat to a massive multinational business. So a concerted campaign by the food industry, with the help of a few crooked paid scientists, set out to discredit Yudkin's work. His book was trashed as science fiction. He was uninvited to international conferences and his papers weren't published, often due to pressure from Coca-Cola and Tate & Lyle. It worked brilliantly. By the end of the seventies he had been so discredited that few scientists dared to publish anything negative about sugar for fear of being similarly attacked. The low-fat industry with its products laden with sugar boomed. They promoted the myth that sugar gives you energy, keeps you healthy and able to face day-to-day problems. It helps you *work, rest and play*. It was, and is, worse than the tobacco and energy industry. Whereas they sought to create uncertainty and doubt about the science, the sugar industry by contrast went out of its way to villainise fat.

The chemical industry didn't do so well when pesticides were attacked so we want to make damn sure this doesn't happen to the sugar industry. A woman called Rachel Carson somehow managed to get a book called *Silent Spring* published way back in the sixties. It claimed the widespread use of toxic pesticides was a menace to nature and humanity. Caused untold harm to profits. Your job is to stop anything like this happening now. We thought we'd won. Trouble is the result, that the western world is getting fat, is hard to cover up so there are still a few scientists making nuisances of themselves.

This is where you come in. We want you to seek them out and do an equally good discrediting job. You have three months and a healthy budget, if the word healthy isn't too ironic. We have a long list of contacts for you too. Amongst other things we need to know the source of stories that are beginning to circulate and may damage the manufacturers of diabetic drugs. There will be a massive increase soon in the development of these. It will be worth billions to Big Pharma. They reduce blood sugar, which you may think is a good thing for diabetics, but a few too-clever-by-half doctors have discovered this doesn't make a scrap of difference in preventing complications. This has to be covered up or discredited. Preferably both. And so do the doctors."

Witney was feeling brave and the need to demonstrate independent thinking.

341

"But if it's that bad, why are we doing this?" he offered, but regretted it immediately.

"Oh, come on. Do you really mean that? Have you learnt nothing in the last ten years? It is big business, sonny. Big money, big profits and riches for us, with the added bonus of reducing population numbers. It impresses our American friends too who have always been protectionist about their sugar industry. They want to expand their market not see it contract. Doesn't matter that it's poison."

"Globalisation," sneered Hartman, with his first contribution since Stanek's monologue.

"But without Tate & Lyle there would be no Tate Gallery..."

Witney was interrupted abruptly.

"They had to keep the politicians sweet, if you don't mind the pun?" Humphrey saw an opportunity here to appear more in tune with his masters than Witney.

"So if we thought the battle had been won what's happened recently to undermine the industry's ambitions?"

He had his intelligent expression on - the one taught at public school.

"What these annoying egg-heads are doing is going around the world telling everyone that there is this new problem called Metabolic Syndrome. Without going into detail you don't need to know today, they blame sugar and fructose in particular for inducing insulin resistance. This all leads to a load of fatties and potential diabetes epidemic. The tragedy for them is that it actually isn't their fault that they are fat. It isn't a lifestyle choice but we have to convince the world it is. We have caused it, but we have to carry on blaming them as a decoy. Thick lazy bastards who should get off their fat arses. Anyway, we are beginning to be given a hard time over the high fructose corn syrup introduced and marketed in the early 1970s. We want you to go for these scientists with the full force of propaganda or other tactics you feel necessary, the dirtier the better. Our party coffers will be healthier as a result. That pays your wages, understand me?"

"I don't quite understand when you state it's not their fault they are fat. Surely they just eat too much?" Humphrey was genuinely interested but couldn't quite follow the science, "It is a choice and they chose to gorge and become all blubby - it is avoidable and so it is their fault?"

"Ah" jumped in Hartman, "Of course. Positive energy balance. People get fat because they overeat. They consume more energy than they expend. It's the public's own fault. They take in too many calories. Nobody came out of Belsen fat. Logical. Well accepted. Proven."

"Yes, sir. That's my understanding," said Humphrey.

"Good. You believe all that?" replied Hartman.

"Of course. Who doesn't?"

"Perfect. Another one taken in. Well, you may be surprised to learn it's all rubbish. It isn't true or proven, but is accepted as it seems logical."

Humphrey and Witney weren't sure whether this was just another wind-up or some sort of test.

"You know my roots were German. So I'm proud that the real cause of obesity was postulated by Gustav von Bergmann and then Julius Bauer, in Vienna at the turn of the last century, but their hypothesis was lost - probably suppressed is a better word - for two reasons. First with the anti-German sentiment after the Second World War there was an embracing of English, rather than German, as the lingua franca of science. Secondly, big American corporations saw more profit and control in the positive energy balance theory. Now that is the way it has to be and your job boys, is to keep it on track. I was given a similar task to earn my spurs when I was your age. I was the one who coordinated the campaign against Yudkin."

"We will certainly try to deliver, sir," answered Witney, "but what was the German Austrian hypothesis, if I may ask?"

"You may, as you won't now find it in many textbooks. In a nutshell, obesity is an intrinsic abnormality, an hormonal, regulatory disorder. Insulin is the driving force. Any medical student will tell you that when diabetics are put on insulin they gain weight. Do you know what lipophilia is?"

"No."

343

"Well, those who are predisposed to get obese have fat that is more lipophilic. The excess calories go there, depriving other organs of the energy they need, leading to hunger or lethargy. So a vicious cycle. Almost anarchy exists, like when a malignant tumour is present. The sugars like sucrose and high fructose corn syrup are uniquely fattening, not really because we overeat them but, because they trigger a hormonal response that drives the fuel consumed into storage as fat."

"But why suppress this theory, which sounds very plausible?" asked Humphrey.

"First, we need to blame the public for gluttony to deflect attention away from the fact that the food industry has changed the world's diet to include huge increases in sugars. There are massive profits in this. Secondly, the diet industry in the UK and USA is worth about ten billion pounds with one in four people obese. In twenty years' time this will be one in three, and the industry will be extracting double, that is twenty billion pounds, from an estimated one hundred million dieters."

Humphrey was struggling to understand the biochemistry, but Witney had grasped it.

"So that all explains why carbohydrate-restricted diets do work, like the one designed by Atkins. I now see why a fat person can eat as much as they like as long as they avoid carbohydrates, when conventional wisdom has it that they get fat to begin with as they do eat as much as they like."

"Precisely," said Hartman with some pride and relief that his explanation had been understood, "I'll point out a circular logic that tells us nothing about the real cause of obesity and is widely accepted, but nonsense. Why do we get fat? Because we overeat. How do we know we are overeating? Because we are getting fatter. Why are we getting fatter? Because we are overeating. And so it goes, round and round."

Stanek wanted to get them back onto what their job was to be.

"You mentioned Atkins. You are right that his diet worked and science explains why. Obesity is not an eating disorder but a fat accumulation disorder triggered not by a positive energy imbalance but by the quality and quantity of carbohydrates in the diet. But for the reasons William mentioned this had to be suppressed and discredited. We ran a good campaign accusing those of promoting such diets of malpractice. Our weapon was that they were full of fats, which we we're blaming for heart disease. We tarred them as dangerous fads and the authors as quacks and confidence tricksters."

"But I thought you said we needed to protect the diet industry?" puzzled Humphrey.

"We do, but not that type of diet," explained Hartman, "It'll be a disaster if an effective diet took hold and killed the golden goose by solving the world's obesity epidemic. We want to promote ineffective diets that work a little while on them, so they sell over and over again."

"They were on the right track and we had to derail them," Stanek continued, "They had discovered that fructose metabolism induces insulin resistance, leading to raised insulin levels trapping fat in fat cells, increasing lipophilia, and driving an increase in appetite. We had to get this argument dismissed, which has worked. Thanks to our work it is regarded as unworthy of serious attention, and you have got to do a similarly effective job."

Stanek was in a reasonably good mood and quite relaxed. He realised Witney had an attractive vulnerability about him. It flashed through his mind that he might be worth seducing. He addressed his remarks more pointedly at him.

"The great thing about sugar is it's as addictive as opium and one trade has overlapped with the other. Our Empire ran on opium in the nineteenth century, now sugar and oil are big factors. It does harm to some, but what doesn't? The world continues to revolve and in the process there are victims who fall in the cogs and the workings but that is unavoidable to keep the engine running. Most of the victims are the consumers but a lot are the workers. Probably about twenty thousand sugar cane workers along the Pacific coast of central America have died from kidney failure in the last twenty years simply because they get dehydrated. They only need to be provided with more water, but that costs more than the lives do. Good old capitalism, eh? They should at least be grateful we don't have slaves or use indentured labour like we did. I sometimes think that's a shame. Anyway none of this needs to be on the British public radar. I really don't know what those lefties mean by ethical trade. There's no such thing in a capitalist society and they need to realise that. It's only then that they will stop annoying us with fatuous moralising. Generally the more dodgy the trade the more profitable and the faster the economy grows, for the benefit of all, well some of us anyway. Look at the drugs trade. We need to keep it going which means keeping it illegal. Why do you think us politicians don't want to tackle it? The arguments to legalise all drugs are overwhelming but no politician would dream of admitting that, least of all our lot. I'll give you a lesson explaining that. It is very simple. I won't charge you."

The two juniors weren't sure whether he was being serious. He continued.

"Although there is no evidence whatsoever that prohibition works, it provides an excellent smokescreen to avoid addressing the issues that make people use drugs in the first place. Poverty and despair are at the root of most problematic drug use and that is not only too expensive to tackle, but we don't want to. We need a poor class. We need to widen inequality. Prohibition criminalises millions of otherwise law-abiding citizens which gives us power over them and black people are over ten times more likely to be imprisoned for drug offences than whites. We want them stigmatised and marginalised. It suits our needs. The market for drugs is demand-led and millions demand illegal drugs. Making the production, supply and use of some drugs illegal creates a vacuum into which organised crime moves. The profits are worth billions and we benefit from this too. There is an argument that if legalised we could run the show, but we don't want the state doing any more. Now because illegal drugs are expensive some dependent users resort to crime or prostitution to fund their habit. It is in our interests to keep these crime levels quite high to keep the public in a constant state of fear. That way we can easily justify the introduction of surveillance cameras, stop and search, and phone tapping as the public thinks it is for their protection. If only they knew. Do you have any idea of the value of the illegal drugs market? It makes up eight per cent of all world trade, around three hundred billion pounds a year. Staggering eh? Whole countries are run under the influence of drug cartels and we can wield vast political power over producer nations under the auspices of drug control programmes. Clever, eh? And we need to keep feeding the masses a wealth of disinformation about drugs and drug use and peddle myths to keep the mystery there. If they really knew that many are quite safe it might damage the market so we don't want them knowing that."

They all appeared to be walking aimlessly, but they were concentrating on the conversation.

"So do you understand why, despite it being logical, humane, safer and sensible we don't follow that path? It's the market, stupid. It makes the world go round and some heads too, when high, 'til they fall off. As a side issue I should mention the legal drugs trade. There's many a win, win situation here. Take Oxycodone. It was manufactured and promoted as a non-addictive painkiller, a strong alternative to other opiates, when the makers knew otherwise and many got hooked on it. Then the innocent patients couldn't afford it and it wasn't covered by their rip-off insurance, so they had no choice but to go onto street heroin. As a result one hundred a month die in Boston alone. A win in that vast profits are made, another win in that a consumer is hooked on a product, and a win because the street market is boosted. Win again because people die, so are less of a burden. Do you know how they got away with promoting it as a non-addictive painkiller? By publishing false scientific papers claiming that real pain neutralised the risk of addiction. Pain became the fifth vital sign and US insurance companies pressurised for the cheapest treatment that is a drug. Big Pharma invented the market for it by promoting the idea that there was an epidemic of untreated pain. As I say win, win."

End of lesson but you can apply these principles to most of our political ideology, which we trust you share. We don't even want the debate. When goody-goodies do start up, our friends in the papers very quickly close down the argument. We make it impossible to appear to be rational over this. Most believe the silly misinformation that, if legal everyone would be at it and the country would fall apart. So like the sugar industry, yes, there will be suffering and deaths, but it's for the greater good. How much do you know about the triangle trade?"

By now Stanek was walking along the lake with Witney and had separated from the other two. They had got their main message across so the business was done. Stanek continued his lecture.

"To keep it simple, sugar in one form or other went from the Caribbean to Europe. The profits there were used to purchase manufactured goods, which were shipped to West Africa where they were bartered for slaves. The slaves were shipped to the Caribbean and sold to the sugar planters. The profit here bought more sugar for Europe and so on. Everyone happy, except the slaves, that is. It was so valuable France gave away its part of Canada to get back from Britain the sugarcane islands of Guadeloupe, Martinique and St Lucia. The Dutch weren't daft either. They got over the loss of New Netherlands, New York today, by keeping Suriname."

"I'm not sure this is something to boast about sir," said Witney rather sheepishly, "but my five times great-grandfather was one of the first to use indentured labour from India in 1836. He fought the abolition of slavery, but when the game was up took the Government's compensation for loss of property. Twenty million pounds was paid to slave owners like my ancestor. Apparently that's the equivalent of over sixteen billion pounds in today's money. He came back from Barbados and built Houghton Hall, our family seat, with the proceeds. He worked for the Cumberbatch family when he first landed on the island. He followed the well-trodden path ventured by younger sons of wealthy families in those days. They were too far down the food chain to inherit vast riches so had to go to the new world to find their own. He soon had his own plantations on the Chagos Islands. Our family still benefits from his entrepreneurial spirit, just like Benedict Cumberbatch. That trickle-down wealth helped pay for his Harrow education. At Houghton Hall we still have the muzzle he used on his slave cook to prevent her eating the food as she prepared it."

Stanek saw his chance.

"Of course it's something to boast about," he said loudly as though he was in the House of Commons, "It was families like yours that built the British Empire. Perhaps we need a few more muzzles. Our friend Quintin Hogg's family, Lord Hailsham to you, owned two and a half thousand slaves in British Guiana. Born to rule, eh? Doesn't all this powerful talk give you a hard-on?"

Witney went on to explain that the plantation owner was really his stepfather's family, not really blood. But all Stanek could say to that was it was not the truth that mattered, but the appearance, so he should keep that sort of thing to himself. By now they were amongst the trees at the end of the lake. Stanek made his move.

"I'm sure you will fit me like a glove."

He grasped Witney's hand and slid it into his trousers then pushed him to his knees. Witney knew what he had to do. He had little choice if he was to be the future.

29 - UNDERCOVER AND RESPECTABLE

THE SPY

I'm a spy in the house of love
I know the dream, that you're dreamin' of
I know the word that you long to hear
I know the deepest, secret fear

The Doors (1970)

Silas Rutherford was a well-respected member of society, a university lecturer in Politics, Philosophy and Economics at Lincoln College Oxford. He thought it best to avoid Cambridge and his dad's old college Trinity. But on taking up the post he found there was a connection and no escape.

Arthur Wynn, a recruiter of Soviet spies, had been to Trinity before moving onto Silas's Oxford College. Silas thought this hilarious and delighted in telling his father. Wynn was known as Agent Scott of the KGB and created the Oxford Spy Ring, the counterpart to the infamous Cambridge Five, which of course his father knew well. Silas was not at all surprised to hear that his dad knew Wynn, but they had not met since the war. He said he knew Edith Tudor-Hart better. She recruited Wynn and most of the Cambridge Spy Ring but he had heard she died five years before in 1973.

Maximilien Rutherford was less well respected but he would not have wanted respect from those who admired his brother. In the eyes of the family though he was just as valuable as Silas. The respect coming Max's way was from his underground movement. By 1978 he had already been banned from the USA.

Max had achieved a first class degree when his brother only got a 2.1. After university he worked for a few charities, then moved onto Shelter in its early years, after watching *Cathy Come Home*, to try to help the homeless. He sought out Gerry Healy and joined the Socialist Labour League. Unlike his father Max flaunted his beliefs.

This is when MI5 started surveillance. When protesting in Grosvenor Square against the Vietnam War in 1968 he was monitored and photographed, clubbed and thrown into the back of a police van. Already in the van was a woman called Rosa Davies. She was holding a bloody handkerchief above her right ear. Later that evening they were both released without charge but not before a friendship had had its first seeds planted in ground fertilised by solidarity of beliefs. Max took Rosa to the nearby St George's Hospital on Hyde Park Corner to get her head wound stitched. As they sat waiting she told him about a few of the people she had met like Nye Bevan and Tom Driberg. The latter was a name Max remembered his father mentioning. They vowed to keep in touch.

The Socialist Labour League became the Workers Revolutionary Party in 1973 but by then Max had spent several years in the USA stirring things, as he put it. He had networked across Europe. He was in close contact with the Red Army Faction and one of its leaders Andreas Baader. Two weeks after his arrest in Grosvenor Square Max was in Frankfurt when Baader with others set fire to two department stores in another Vietnam War protest. He had met Ulrike Meinhof and was inspired by her and her writings: *Protest is when I say this does not please me. Resistance is when I ensure what does not please me occurs no more.* He then travelled to Paris to help coordinate the May protests and met up with Rosa again.

He got involved in Irish politics from the mid-sixties and had secret meetings with the IRA. It took him a few years though to be trusted and encourage them to step up their activities, directly leading to British troops being deployed in August 1969. Max played a dangerous double game of infiltration befriending the loyalist William Murphy. William's son Lenny was to be part of the Shankill Butchers, an Ulster Volunteer Force murder gang. He also cultivated and won the confidence of a thug called Liam McColl who could not keep his mouth shut. Max fed back information about these loyalists to the IRA, and later tipped off the police about ammunition stores in the family home in Battenberg Street. When in Belfast, Max would stay in Whitla Street and visit Du Barry House and a girl called Cathy. Her aunt Barbara would give him a discount she said for being a regular customer, but they both knew it was because she was a little scared of him and his importance. He always passed the discount onto Cathy. Max used intermediaries to get funds diverted to the Palestine Liberation Organisation, which had only been formed five years earlier and were considered terrorists by the US.

By April 1969 Max was in Washington to help organise another anti-Vietnam war march, and in Chicago in June. The CIA and FBI started harassing him. The FBI COunter INTELigence PROgram, known as COINTELPRO, ran covert, often illegal projects aimed at surveilling, infiltrating, discrediting and disrupting American political organisations like anti-Vietnam war protestors, civil rights activists like Martin Luther King, feminist groups, independence movements, and anything vaguely left leaning starting in 1956 with the communist party. Max was on their list. When Fred Hampton of the Black Panther Movement was murdered, whilst in bed asleep, by the Chicago Police as part of COINTELPRO in December 1969, Max knew his life was in danger too. The police said they acted in self-defence and the inquest ruled his death as justified homicide. He lay low for a while and was outraged, but not surprised, by the Kent University killings in Ohio six months later when the US National Guard shot and killed four students. He was among the one hundred thousand marching on Washington five days after, and helped organise the large student strike affecting four hundred and fifty colleges. He did not want to go the same way as Fred Hampton so thought it time to get back to the UK.

He spent the next two years with the Angry Brigade. He had met Anna Mendelssohn who had been inspired by the Paris student uprising and Jake Prescott. They carried out about twenty-five small-scale bombings, which mainly just damaged property. It served its purpose but according to Prescott was more like the Slightly Cross Brigade. Max decided it was not effective enough.

Max heard a John Lennon interview on the *BBC* accusing the FBI of spying and bugging him from the moment he moved to New York in 1971. Apart from his lyrics Lennon had first impressed Max when he sent his MBE back to the Queen as a protest against the

Vietnam War and against *Cold Turkey* slipping down the charts two years earlier. The next year he paid the fines of anti-apartheid protesters against the South African rugby team at a time when most western governments supported apartheid but pretended not to. COINTELPRO had been exposed when an FBI field office was burgled and dossiers about the programme were passed to news agencies. Max was proud of his connection to its downfall. Nixon wanted Lennon out of the way as he feared his political views. 1972 was the first year eleven million eighteen-year-olds could vote and the President worried about his influence. Deportation on the back of his conviction for marijuana possession in England in 1968 seemed a good solution. The FBI file ran to hundreds of pages and they considered setting him up for a drugs bust. He antagonised them further by stating, *the trouble with Government as it is, is that it doesn't represent the people. It controls them.* On 23rd March 1973 Lennon was issued an order by US Immigration authorities to leave the country. He declared a new country called Nutopia - *no land, no boundaries, no passports, only people* - and fought it. Eventually in 1976 Lennon received his green card.

At the height of the row Max decided to return to the States to try to meet Noam Chomsky, Pete Seeger and members of the Black Panther Party. On landing at JFK Airport he was stopped, interrogated and searched. He had articles supporting Lennon's case in his luggage and notes for an article he was writing himself. He was sent straight back to Britain and barred.

In partnership with Silas, Max founded a secret organisation devoted to exposing the corruption of the establishment, producing their downfall and then the plan was the building of proper democracy by any means necessary including violence. They wanted to poison all that was bad. So the name stuck.

Their father initially funded the group with money laundered from the Soviets just after the war. Max had little trouble, with all the contacts he had built up over the previous fifteen years, in finding recruits. The trouble the twins did have was with trusting and controlling them. They distanced themselves from the violence, and appointed a series of generals who were in charge of strategy, operations, security, investigative affairs, recruitment and funding. No agent was approached for membership until after at least six months surveillance and thorough vetting. This took a lot of manpower and was usually done by those supporting the cause but not wanting to get their hands dirty. Only a selected few knew their true identities.

Jerry Dolan was an early target despite just having left school. He came to the attention of Poison's recruitment general as he had started to make a lot of noise. Once on board he was instructed to draw less attention to himself. Jerry's skill was seeking out like-minded operators. He spent the 1980s and 1990s in the field, which meant break-ins and burglaries searching for evidence that would implicate anyone in the establishment. He adopted false identities - he was known as Nick to most - to infiltrate groups. One operation involved renting an apartment in Dolphin Square. He managed to bug rooms and photograph comings and goings. He found out about Sean McColl but his orders were to leave him in position. It did not take them long to realise Sean was related to Liam McColl. Sean was excellent bait. Jerry worked out that a man called Douglas was controlling a network that provided sex to important clients. He thought him a particularly nasty piece of work and told himself regularly, in the old phrase that 'he'd be first up against the wall come the revolution'. Jerry followed and spied on cabinet ministers, the military, civil servants and lesser mortals.

With the help of a team headed by an operative called Ian, he infiltrated the In And Out Naval And Military Club in Piccadilly, not personally but by blackmailing a longstanding member who had been a little careless in a Gents lavatory in Green Park. The operation unit's successes included the Brighton bomb, which nearly killed Thatcher in 1984. The public was told it was the IRA as Poison was not to be identified. The establishment wanted Poison to have no recognition. They killed Ian Gow, the Eastbourne MP in 1990 - again blamed on the IRA. Poison had infiltrated all sides in the Northern Ireland War. They thought the Government and media were up to their usual tricks, labelling the battle The Troubles.

This title was designed to minimise and downgrade the conflict in the eyes of the public, to make it appear less important, even trivial, so they could take it in their stride and not be bothered by it.

"Troubles," as Ian complained bitterly, "was when your cat is ill, or you have a boundary dispute with a neighbour, not when people are murdering each other daily adding up to fifty thousand casualties. It was civil war, and more than that. It spread beyond the UK borders. Remember the SAS murders of three IRA members in Gibraltar in 1988? The European Court of Human Rights found against Thatcher's Government on that one."

The Rutherfords firmly believed in a united Ireland but needed spies in all camps to help the process along. It was not long before they realised there were other infiltrators in the IRA, like MI5. They estimated that up to a third of the IRA membership was actually from the British Security Services. It was this that made the IRA realise the game was up and forced them to the negotiating table. So they were not defeated by the politicians in nice suits who claimed all the credit by securing the *Good Friday Agreement* of 1998, but beaten by undercover operations that paralysed their effectiveness. Poison had the unsavoury job of bringing this news to the IRA leadership.

Amongst the things not going as well as planned was the mortar attack on Downing Street the following year - the whole building was supposed to be destroyed - and the assassination attempts on Nicholas Ridley the cabinet minister who said giving up sovereignty to the European Union was as bad as giving it up to Adolf Hitler. It was thought more effective at first to aim to cut the heads off the right wing think tanks, which had a grip on Government policy. So key figures in the Institute of Economic Affairs, the Centre for Policy Studies, the Freedom Association and the Adam Smith Institute were threatened and blackmailed but this was unsuccessful. The monsters still thrived without heads.

There were some activities in the USA when an influential figure in the right wing Christian Pat Robertson Empire was murdered by Poison's sister organisation. The Southern Baptist minister had predicted the world would end in 1982. For one of his friends it did.

He also thought that Hurricane Katrina that killed one thousand eight hundred and thirty six people was God's punishment for America's abortion policy. They had other American targets like Al Haig, Ian MacGregor and Lyndon Woodward, a former staff officer in Nixon's White House, who they watched, followed and bugged. He was known to be a liaison between the US and UK establishment. Perhaps even a leader. It was no surprise to them when he turned up in the American Embassy in London.

The Security Unit had to dispose of an infiltrator called Robin, when he was uncovered. Multi-national companies knew Poison was out to get them and set up a sabotage unit. They recruited Robin to that unit from Lewisham Hospital in the 1980s and he fed back intelligence. For many years he played a double game, rioting in the Poll Tax demonstrations of 1990 and campaigning for the Socialist Workers' Party. He was a prominent member of the Anti-Nazi League, and as an infiltrator made them less effective. It was thought this is why some of the plots failed. He disappeared in 2000.

The Investigative Unit built up dossiers and damning evidence against the Establishment. It documented its financial corruption, blackmailing, bribery, murder and its paedophile rings. But these were just the methods the Establishment used to achieve its goal which was capitalist imperialist world domination getting the wealth and power into the hands of the chosen few. A member of Poison's Council, known to all just as Guy, headed this unit and had accumulated so much information over the years that Poison struggled with what to do with it. Just the paedophile files gave them storage and security problems. The Shirley Oaks files alone filled one tall cabinet. Guy and his team had found out at least two boys were buried on the local golf course. They had the names of sixty paedophiles that either worked in or visited the children's home. Seven hundred were abused from the 1950s to the 1980s. At least forty-eight children died in the Lambeth Care System in the 1970s and 1980s, and the Council cover-up involved destroying one hundred and forty sets of records.

By this time their father could not continue to fund them at the same level, but they had no great difficulty getting backers from all walks of life. Arthur Talbot Rutherford was so proud of his two boys. He had no regrets in life apart from the desire to be more effective in his political aims. He often wondered how life would have been different without a clubfoot, without being slashed across the face with a razor, and if he had been heterosexual. He hoped it would have followed the same path. He wondered if his father, such an admirer of the Conservative Lord Salisbury, would have been pleased or horrified. Probably horrified, but how could he possibly understand such a different world. They were certainly on different sides of the Russian revolution.

As he lay there with Ethel, Silas and Maximilien at his bedside he knew he had no more than a day or two left. He was so weak now and had lost so much weight. The cancer was feasting on him like a banquet – at least four courses - and will be consuming the after-dinner coffee within hours. Arthur knew the monster arose from the bowel, but did not want to know more. His sons were told it was a descending colon adenocarcinoma T3aN3M1. They had worked out what this meant, but their father was not interested. Arthur was more than happy to have got to eighty-seven.

Mikhail Gorbachev had become the eighth leader of the Soviet Union and this was of more interest to Arthur as he lay, hardly able to move. He had lived through all their reigns. He was pleased the old Foreign Minister Andrei Gromyko had been replaced. Known as Mr Nyet his twenty-eight years in the post was far too long. Arthur had had dealings with him when Gromyko was Soviet Ambassador to Washington in 1944 and later on in 1952 in the same role in the UK. Where were Gorbachev's policies of glasnost, perestroika, demokratizatsiya and uskoreniye leading? He was worried about the abandonment of the *Brezhnev Doctrine* just announced, allowing Eastern Bloc nations to determine their own affairs, and the deep unilateral cuts in Soviet military forces in Eastern Europe. Did he not know the United States would take advantage of this? The evil empire would take over. To Arthur it was Orwellian that Reagan, from the real evil empire should throw that insult at the Soviets.

He was becoming more pessimistic about the battle between left and right. At a very young age he made sure his sons realised that the pretence of fighting communism was a front to get US trade into every corner of the world. The horrors carried out by the US in Korea, Cambodia, Laos, Indonesia, Chile, Guatemala, El Salvador and Nicaragua were justified, they claimed because they were fighting communism. The US did not really care who ran what sort of regime as long as they could get a McDonalds on every street corner. They supported brutal dictators, mass murderers and torturers from Pinochet, Pol Pot, the Greek junta, Marcos, Suharto, Duvalier, Mobutu, the Brazilian junta, Somoza, Saddam Hussein, South African apartheid leaders and Portuguese fascists. Ask most Americans to define communism and they would not be able to. Tackle their arguments in favour of capitalism head on too. Was competition needed for Fleming to discover penicillin or for Turing to break the Enigma code? How beneficial is it to mankind that the pharmaceutical industry will only produce drugs that make huge profits? Drugs they can keep people on for life.

Arthur told them that every socialist experiment of any significance had been corrupted, subverted, perverted, destabilised, crushed, overthrown, bombed or invaded by the US. In effect it had never really been given a chance and it was his deepest secret fear that it would never be. Most revolutions - the French, Russian, Irish, American, and Chinese - had been started for the right reasons but then hijacked by the conservative elite usually after a civil war. But he predicted that if communism or the myth of communism died completely the US would invent another enemy to allow them to invade other countries. So-called terrorism was his bet.

"Before Marx, it was the Church that controlled the masses but it used the threat of the devil and going to hell. It still does use that threat. Mark my words, boys," he would tell them, "unite the masses with the aim of controlling them with the fear of burning in hell, living under the tyranny of communism, or being blown to pieces by terrorists. Or even all three."

Arthur was an atheist and often declared that if he was wrong about the existence of a God, with the state of the world as it is, it is definitely the devil who has the upper hand and is winning the battle between good and evil. Unlike others, he did not convert on his deathbed in a cowardly just-in-case moment. He firmly believed in his principles. In his time in the United States his atheism was another of Arthur's secrets. He quickly became aware that atheists were among the least trusted minority there. This lack of trust was encouraged to counter the insecurity, even threat, that atheists can bring out in the religious, putting into question their core beliefs and way of life. Plus if the atheists won it would deprive the Establishment of another means of control.

His boys, he knew, would carry on the fight. He was always staggered by how different twins could be. But they had the same values, which is all Arthur needed to know and made him proud. He had a legacy. He never asked Max in detail about what he was up to but told himself that even if he did not like the answer he would still support him. The end justifies the means.

Silas had brought his two girls from Oxford to see Arthur the week before. Mary aged seventeen and named after Mary Wollstonecraft and Vilma two years younger who got her name from Vilma Lucila Espín the Cuban Revolutionary leader. Both were showing real promise in following the family tradition of rebellion and would leave home soon. They all spoke in French at the bedside. Arthur often reverted to his favourite language when overcome with sentiment. Like their mother, Max and Silas were brought up bilingual. She had ridiculed a study from 1926 that concluded: *the use of a foreign language in the home is one of the chief factors in producing mental retardation.* Arthur would quote Emperor Charles V, *I speak Spanish to God, French to men, Italian to women and German to my horse.*

Mary was fascinated by the archaeological and anthropological collection in the Pitt Rivers Museum. Silas had taken both girls there whilst still at primary school. Mary was transfixed by the Haida Totem pole from Graham Island in British Columbia standing at over eleven metres. She organised a voluntary job herself just to be amongst such wonderful items. Vilma preferred the Ashmolean and the drawings by Michelangelo and Raphael. Both hero-worshipped their grandfather. Arthur was keen that the two girls become strong feminists. He talked to them for hours about how unfairly women had been treated over the years. Their own grandmother was forced to resign her job just because she married. He deliberately fuelled their passion with tales of injustice. Why did Crick and Watson get all the credit for working out the molecular structure of DNA when it was Rosalind Franklin's images which led to the discovery of the double helix? Why did Jocelyn Bell Burnell's supervisor get the *Nobel Prize* when it was she who discovered the first radio pulsars? And Ada Lovelace should have been more recognised in her lifetime for her work on Charles Babbage's first computer, dying too early of uterine cancer at thirty-six, the same age as her father Lord Byron. He gave plenty of other examples to get them thinking. As a child Arthur was conscious of the Suffragette movement and for the first time rebelled against the mainstream thinking of the time that a woman's place is in the home. Two events of 1913 stayed with Arthur. The first was the razor attack on him by Charles Morrison in his first year at Eton, and the second suffragette Emily Wilding Davison's death at the Epsom Derby, killed by the King's horse as she tried to attach a flag to its bridle.

Silas had the stable home and family life the whole family had accepted Max was not interested in, or at least had to sacrifice and could not have whilst on active duty. So Arthur would die in 1988 still wishing for the socialist ideal. One of the last pieces of wisdom he uttered to his sons was designed to keep them in the fight. He told them that there had been three developments of political significance in his lifetime: the growth of democracy, the growth of corporate power, and the growth of corporate propaganda as a means of protecting corporate power against democracy. The propaganda was now winning. His sons never knew the full extent of Arthur's spying activities in the 1930s and his involvement with such infamous figures. He would just throw the odd comment in - as when Thatcher exposed Anthony Blunt as a spy in 1979 and was stripped of his knighthood, Arthur was heard to mutter under his breath:

"Poor old Anthony, I should have supported him more."

Like the others, Arthur knew that Blunt was ordered to defect in 1951 with Burgess and Maclean to protect Philby, but he refused. It was then he needed support, but Arthur was reassured by the strong position Blunt was in with his royal secrets, especially the secret mission he was sent on to retrieve the Marburg files and the embarrassing letters between the Duke of Windsor and the Nazi hierarchy.

The events in the decade after their father's death made Silas and Maximilien even more determined to fight the monstrosity of the attempts at world domination by big business. Infiltration into Russia with the destruction of socialism made a few very rich. Three large yacht-standard very rich oligarchs. The God-fearing United States continued to defend its spread to all corners of the world by still claiming to fight communism, when there was not a communist to be seen, so they had to find another excuse. Then the terrorist attacks started. Arthur Rutherford's prediction was spot on. This was perfect to scare the public and justify tight surveillance. The plan worked well. The Government line was swallowed. It appeared to react, not be the cause. False flag operations became more common. The public called for more surveillance and a tough line. The American people in particular acted like the children of a Mafia boss who do not know what their father does for a living, and do not want to know, but then wonder why someone just threw a petrol bomb through their bedroom window. The twins could only agree with former President Jimmy Carter who called the United States *an oligarchy with unlimited political bribery.*

When Thomas Jefferson, the third US President, said the price of freedom is eternal vigilance what he meant was, citizens watching the Government, not the reverse - but he was also a slave owner and thought blacks inferior to whites. They knew some attacks were organised by the establishment to discredit a variety of opponents and encourage the rise of the far right. They wanted them to become more credible and brought into the Overton window so that when they called for refugees to be shot, their ideas were greeted as another opinion and an option, not an outrageous idea.

This slow seeping of extreme views into the mainstream media followed on what had been happening in the press for years. It worked well and it did not take long before spokesmen had permanent places on *BBC Question Time* and *Any Questions* as well as radio phone-ins. They were even given their own slots on talk radio shows. It became the norm to invite so-called experts on all topics to give the view that the establishment wanted to get across. These experts were put up by think tanks, like the Henry Jackson Society that had been set up as front organisations to propagate their version of the truth. There were never, of course, any declarations of interest. That would have given the game away. Like a metastasising cancer, what once would have been regarded as unacceptable, prejudiced, bigoted, racist and nasty, was listened to and sometimes accepted as a valuable contribution to the debate. The timid and intimidated *BBC* were frightened into always being balanced so that two opposing points of view had equal airtime and respect, even when an expert arguing the earth is flat is put up against one trying to convince everyone the earth is actually round. And they were well organised. They had teams of the public ready to call phone-in shows with their opinions, to drown out the reasonable. Those convinced of what the powers wanted them to be convinced about gradually became a bigger and bigger group who could spread the word in the pub and in the workplace.

A man of Arthur's time, Edward R. Murrow said, *A nation of sheep will beget a Government of wolves,* but a man of the time of Silas and Maximilien, Noam Chomsky said, *The more you can increase fear of drugs and crime, welfare mothers, immigrants and aliens, the more you control all the people. Propaganda is to a democracy what the bludgeon is to a totalitarian state.*

Silas demonstrated in Oxford and London against the Gulf wars. He continued to coordinate the UK operations but kept his hands clean. Max went there. He travelled around the Middle East encouraging revolts and got his hands dirty. He suffered. He witnessed the chemical weapons depots being bombed and the release of sarin gas, exposing one hundred thousand US soldiers to traces of the deadly poison. It was of course denied, as was the existence of the resulting Gulf War Syndrome. The twins were sixty-four by the time the ex-ally of the US, Saddam Hussein was executed by the Americans in 2006. Perhaps it was time to pass the fight onto the next generation. They both knew they would not stop fighting though. Echoing in their heads was their father quoting Martin Luther King, both from beyond the grave, *our lives begin to end the day we become silent about things that matter.*

30 - FRIENDS AND MYSTERIES

YOU DON'T KNOW ME

For I never knew the art of making love,
Though y heart aches with love for you.
Afraid and shy, I let my chance go by,
A chance that you might love me too.

Ray Charles (1962)

Rob loved being so close to history. He liked to tread where the famous or infamous had trod or where major events had occurred.

His most memorable holidays were walking through Red Square or staring at the Quadriga on the top of the Brandenburg Gate. The Colosseum, the Parthenon, the Alhambra, the Great Wall of China, and Strawberry Fields in Central Park - even Hearst Castle at San Simeon - all sent shivers down his spine. He would like to visit Pearl Harbour or Dealey Plaza one day. Victoria Falls, the Grand Canyon, Table Mountain, the Rain Forest of Guyana were all magnificent, but did not spark the same excitement without the historical factor. It was probably his main interest now more than medicine. He had to give up History at school to study Latin as everyone told him he would not be considered for medical school without it. Sic fiat.

He was at the Tolpuddle Martyrs' museum taking in the poster that explained the trumped up charges thrown at the six labourers by the landowner magistrates. They stood no chance. Betrayed by one of their fellow workers Edward Legg, and persecuted by Squire James Frampton, they were found guilty of felony and sentenced to seven years penal transportation. It was 1834 and a year after the abolition of slavery, apparently. Their crime was to swear a secret oath to help improve their lot. Their wages had been reduced to seven shillings a week and the plan was to cut them further to six. They were already near starvation. Frampton sought the help of Lord Melbourne, the Home Secretary and Queen Victoria's favourite. Melbourne recommended the *Unlawful Oaths Act 1797*. No wonder Lady Caroline Lamb left him for Byron. Rob wondered whether the descendants of either of these two wealthy men, or indeed Edward Legg, had any shame in their genes. Not quite to the same degree as Heinrich Himmler Junior but approaching.

He went outside and sat beside the Dagnall's sculpture of George Loveless. Time for a sandwich. Rob rarely went anywhere without some food in his pocket. He had been left hungry too many times but only acutely whilst busy with patients or on the wards as a junior doctor, not chronically like the farm workers of the 1830s. He pulled out his plastic box from his rucksack but then realised he had forgotten his drink. It was not like him, he must be more distracted than he thought. He felt at peace for a while then his anger returned. Nothing much has changed in class-ridden Britain he reflected. The bosses are still cutting their workers' wages and treating them like shit. Nearly two hundred years on and working folk rely on food banks to avoid going hungry. *The Tolpuddle Martyrs' Festival* had been a few weeks before in July. One day he promised himself he would go. He thought it would be good to take Rosa but would she still be alive next July? Knowing Rosa she would have been even before he was born. He walked towards the thatched cottages and into the village to visit James Hammett's grave in the churchyard. He had died in the Dorchester workhouse.

It was early afternoon and Rob needed a drink. He had noticed the Martyrs Inn on the way through the village, so he thought he should treat himself to a pint. Only one though. He was no use to anyone anymore after lunchtime drinking, let alone the driving problem. He walked in past the poster for the festival. They should take that down now, he thought. He looked around for the real ales and spotted the *Hall and Woodhouse*. The barmaid (should ladies serving beer still be called that he wondered) told him it was from the Badger Brewery in Blandford Forum only ten miles away. He took his pint to the other side of the large smart interior and sat on one of the settees by the fireplace and passed a group of ramblers sitting at a table who had left a trail of mud en route. Management did not seem to mind but he knew Suzy would have gone mad. She always took off her boots even if they were clean enough to eat off as she often said - but who would want to eat off boots, clean or otherwise, he always teased her. The problem it caused Rob is that he felt obliged to take his off too, or else have to sit in an atmosphere of being on the moral low ground – 'a lump of mud in time saves nine'.

One of Suzy's endearing features was her habit of mixing up the wording of proverbs. Quite confusing. Rob had been meaning to list them for years and a quiet spell on his own in the pub was the golden opportunity. He was going to present her with his list the next time she corrected his use of words. He started to type his favourites onto his iPad mini.

Two rights don't make a wrong
A stitch in time keeps the doctor away
A poor workman gathers no moss
Those who live in glass houses catch the worm
Don't put all your stones in one basket
You are flogging a dead cat
Count your chickens after they've hatched
There's no time like the past
Haven't two feathers to rub together
Deaf as a bat
Blind as a post
The other end of the coin
My hat goes out to you
For all the gold in China
Cut off your nose to spite your mouth
Give a man enough rope and he will tie you up
Let's cross that bridge before we reach it
As thin as a pancake
As flat as a rake...

He knew more would come to him in time. He wondered how many people knew about the Tolpuddle Martyrs. It was depressing for Rob that if you asked the average man in the street you would get blank looks. Rob thought it appalling that this important social landmark in our history probably was not even taught in schools. Worse, the politicians want to celebrate the Empire. The same bunch that altered Labour Day as a bank holiday probably suppresses the Martyrs' story. Rob remembered when he was young 1st May was known as Labour Day and linked to the International Workers' Day. The Establishment seems to want nothing to do with workers except to exploit them, he thought. Even America has a Labor Day even if they cannot spell it correctly.

After leaving the Martyrs Inn, Rob strolled around the small village green, with the memorial shelter built in 1934, and then headed back to the Methodist Chapel. He was standing in front of the arch at the front of the small church unveiled by Arthur Henderson in 1912 and 'ERECTED IN HONOUR OF THE FAITHFUL AND BRAVE MEN OF THIS VILLAGE'. He was reading the quote by George Loveless's defence when he felt the presence of someone behind him in the road.

"Have you been inside? Well worth it. This was built in 1862 and the Memorial arch you have just photographed in 1912. The original chapel is still standing, on the other side of the road nearer the village. That's two hundred years old now."

Rob was not in the mood for small talk, but this man at least knew something. He was slightly unnerved to think the man might have been watching him for some time. It was not in Rob's nature to be rude so he blurted out the first thing he thought of.

"Terrible injustice. And still going on today."

"I have to agree with you. The world in many ways doesn't seem to get any better. I'm Ian by the way."

Rob gave way to an immediate uncharitable thought.

"Oh, fuck. He's coming onto me. Act masculine."

But Rob's peace of mind, brought on by this tranquil village was shattered in a more unnerving manner.

"You are on the right track. Keep going. Pursue these bastards. This is bigger than you could possibly imagine. We will be in touch shortly. I've been assigned to you."

He then spun around towards what turned out to be his car and unlocked it. The car was old enough for him to need to put a key in the door.

"Wait, who are you? What do you mean assigned? How do I pursue it? What shall I do?"

"Can't stop. Probably being watched. Just follow your nose and instincts. We will get you help. You will meet an old friend soon but be careful. They are dangerous."

And with that he drove off. Registration plate GD55 XXL, Rob noted. A small blue Daewoo Matiz. Not a spy's Aston Martin, that is for sure. But it was an odd encounter to say the least. For a doctor Rob had a poor eye for faces but could remember numbers easily and registration plates. He wondered how much he strayed into the autistic spectrum and certainly told people he had facial dyslexia. That thought reminded him of the memo he had received a few weeks earlier. The CCG was revising the definition of autism. It was to become much more complicated to be diagnosed so fewer children would be. It did not matter that some would suffer and many would not get the treatment they deserved as a consequence. It would save the CCG a lot of money. Tossers, he thought.

This theme transcended most public services as they tried to shrink the State. The fewer police, the more they struggled to cope, so less crime reported as the public could not see the point. Then the politicians could claim they have brought crime down, so more police cuts - a downward spiral.

Meanwhile in the USA they have broadened the definition of depression so they can sell more drugs and it is not uncommon for four year olds to be given anti-depressants. More kids (five million) are diagnosed in North America with Attention Deficit Hyperactivity Disorder and given Ritalin, than in the rest of the world combined. More than ten million children are being prescribed addictive stimulants and other psychotropic drugs. What more proof is needed than mixing money and medicine only results in bad healthcare?

This all flashed through Rob's mind in the time it took to enter the chapel. So he now had anger adding to his alarm. He tried to get his breath back. What is going on? Is he being watched too? How did this Ian, if that is his real name, know who he was and that he would be in Tolpuddle? Nobody knew. He had not told anyone.

Not even Suzy. He suddenly felt unsafe in a small building on his own with only one door. But he had to look around. In front of just six wooden benches was a small table that served as an altar. Apart from the hymn numbers board there were only a couple of pictures and a plaque on the very pale yellow walls. It seemed very bare. He got up from the fourth pew back and walked briskly to the exit. A shiver went up his spine at the same time. What did he mean about meeting an old friend?

It was an impulsive act to drive down to Dorset. He had been struggling with what to do with all the information he had absorbed. Who to speak to? Who might be sympathetic, not think him nuts, and would be willing to help or at least give advice. Then he thought of Pippa. He needed no other excuse. He loved visiting her and Suzy was away at an arts fair and exhibition for two days. He could have a break, see Tolpuddle, which he had been intending to do for ages, and then flirt with Pippa. She might even help but, in any case, he knew he would have a listening ear. She would believe him. But whatever else it felt good to get out of the area. Perhaps he was subconsciously fleeing from all of this.

He had rung her the night before but was told she would not be there until she got home from work at six pm. His sat nav told him his journey would take thirty-five minutes to Kimmeridge, where Pippa lived. So he re-routed to take in Bovington Camp and see Tyneham on the way and discovered it was only five minutes extra. Both places had connections to the Martyrs. Both places fed his history craving.

T. E. Lawrence, grandly also known as Lawrence of Arabia, had died in 1935 near his Clouds Hill cottage (near Moreton), when he went over the top of his Brough Superior SS100 motorcycle. Lawrence called this bike George VII. He had other Georges starting with George I in 1922 but they were named after the manufacturer, George Brough of Nottingham, not royalty. George VIII was being built when he died. The neurosurgeon, Hugh Cairns, watched Lawrence take five days to die and pioneered crash helmets as a result. He was the grandfather of one of Rob's fellow students at Guy's, Anthony, or 'Afro Ant' as he became known. Rob visited Lawrence's grave in Moreton cemetery, but resisted the strong temptation of a pint in the Frampton Arms.

But was Lawrence's death really an accident? Or was he assassinated as he was aligning himself too closely with Sir Oswald Mosley the fascist? His last journey was to see his friend Henry Williamson who was facilitating a meeting between Lawrence and Hitler. It was awkward that Lawrence was seemingly joining the appeasers and, as a war hero boosting Mosley's cause. There were several witnesses that saw a mysterious black car run Lawrence off the road. Some say this was the work of MI5 with the encouragement of Churchill who also had other motives, including what he had told Lawrence about his personal life years before and the possible inclusion of embarrassing details in Lawrence's forthcoming book.

Lawrence's cousins, the Framptons, owned the neighbouring Moreton Estate and first rented, then later sold him the cottage. They were descendants of the Squire James Frampton who prosecuted the Martyrs. They had been Lords of the Manor since the fourteenth century and there was no sign of any shame in their genes.

The ghost village of Tyneham, which sat between the two ridges of the Purbeck Hills had always fascinated Rob since Pippa had taken him there after the public regained access. Two hundred and twenty-five villagers were displaced when the War Office requisitioned the area before Christmas in 1943. This was meant to be temporary. The promise was broken in 1948 and the villagers were refused permission to go home. Rob knew that would not have happened if someone wealthy or famous lived there. It would not have happened to the Frampton estate. Parts of the film *Comrades* about the Martyrs were shot there. Robert Stephens played Frampton.

Kimmeridge was one of his favourite places on the Jurassic coast, but he knew he was biased as it was always linked with Pippa. Her cottage was typical Pippa. Small but full of class and quality, sea views, an immaculate garden and very clean and tidy. The thatched roof worried her, and the side opening onto the main street made her put up net curtains against her sense of taste, to stop the tourists peering in. She greeted Rob with a very tight hug and her continental South of France triple kiss. She once pointed out to Rob that in Paris it is always twice, a kiss on both cheeks, but she prefers the South. And so did he.

Although they may only see each other at most once a year, their chemistry was always magical. Or was it their biology? Or even physics? He remembered what Rosa had said about the chemistry being electric between him and Jenny, but Rob recognised this more acutely. She was the only true friend from the pre-Jenny era. He had lost contact with others including Anthony Cairns whose main memorable feature was his red Afro hairstyle. The most surprising was Robin, whom he saw a lot until about fifteen years ago, despite stealing Jenny from him. Then he seemed to break off all contact. It was as though he had disappeared off the face of the earth. The relationship with Pippa however was one where there was never any awkwardness and they tuned into each other immediately. She was his oldest female friend by many years. He felt totally relaxed with her and could trust her with his most intimate secrets. He saw her several times to talk about whether he should leave Jenny. He wanted her endorsement and would still have made that crazy jump whatever she said although she did not put up that obstacle.

Their backgrounds, values, politics and humour were the same and they were on similar wavelengths from the moment they first met, after she had come to work in London having got a first at Oxford. The complete opposite were Ivan Humphrey and Hubert Witney whom she remembered for their arrogance and Bullingdon Club rampages. That was in 1984. He was still a student as she was older. Her subject was French Literature and to Rob this was much more impressive than medicine and certainly more sexy, as was she.

Her first job was with the Foreign and Commonwealth Office. She had a small partitioned room in the Locarno Suite, which had been divided up into offices and storage. The fine Victorian interior

371

was covered up but Pippa could feel the history. This was the code-breaking department during the Second World War. She started in the department producing French publications but was then persuaded to move into public relations - a move she regretted.

At first she and her boyfriend moved in with her sister, who was very proud of her flat in Brick Lane. Rob thought her boyfriend was a prat but he knew it was only jealousy really. Another flatmate was on Rob's medical firm at Guy's. That is how they met. Rob and his other mates, who included Stephen and Anthony, would meet the Brick Lane lot regularly for nights out. They got on so well that several holidays were organised. Rob never needed to be asked twice. One was in an old cottage in the small village of Beddgelert not far from the base of Snowdon. It had no electricity or running water but did have a few rats. There was no phone anywhere near and in the days before mobiles they had wonderful peaceful solitude. They visited Gelert's grave together but had to put up with the 'prat' reading out the legend.

"Pity he wasn't savaged by Llewellyn's dog like the wolf," said Anthony as they walked away.

Rob thought his contrived efforts to see her were transparent. He never fully admitted this but hinted at it years later. She did not seem to notice though. He fancied her and this is what Rob regarded as his worst missed opportunity from shyness in his university days. He just thought she was out of his league. Afraid and shy, he let his chance go by. A big mistake. There was one other thing Rob had not shared with her. He used to dream about her. One exciting but bizarre dream was of them making love in the middle of London Bridge Station. Right in the road where the taxis waited, in broad daylight but nobody paid much attention. The commuters just stepped over them. His girlfriend at the time had to wake him up as he was groaning. He told her he was dreaming he was running a marathon but she was suspicious he was not being completely honest when she rolled over onto the wet patch.

After Rob qualified he was too busy to have much of a social life, so they saw less of each other. He was invited to her first wedding to the prat – otherwise known as John. That lasted six years, until the prat proved he was indeed a prat by running off with the practice manager of a surgery he visited as a pharmaceutical representative. Pippa found out he had been serially unfaithful from even before their Brick Lane days. This shattered her although she came around to the idea she was much better off without him, and actually had had a lucky escape. Then she could even laugh about it, telling the tale of the practice manager's punishment. Her husband, when he found out about her affair, burst into her surgery waiting room that happened to be packed with patients. He emptied the feathers out of four pillows the lovers had used all over the waiting room, covering everything and everyone. Apparently he shouted.

"The manager here screws drug reps you can't trust her. She knows all your medical secrets," and left.

The astonished staff and patients were so stunned nobody said a word. Then a few people started sneezing. To Pippa's great satisfaction she was sacked.

Pippa was on her own for several years and moved away from London and changed jobs to escape her former life completely. She fled to Dorset for no other reason than it brought back happy memories of family holidays. Bad timing as far as Rob was concerned as he was in his early dating days with Jenny. Then whilst hidden away in the Dorset countryside she met Dave Thackeray at a Morris dance in Wimborne. He was the fool and was extravagantly dressed and, in his role of communicating directly with the audience, picked out Pippa. He was so warm and fun they sat together after the dance and drank their way through the different ales from the Dorset Piddle Brewery. The *Cocky Hop*, the *Jimmy Riddle*, the *Leg Warmer*, the *Pointing Percy*, the *Silent Slasher* and the *Yogi Bear*. They married two years later when Pippa realised she could trust men again - especially this one who was gentle and would not hurt a fly, or as Suzy would say, would not say a bad word about a fly. Rob realised Pippa had met her soul mate; he was so nice that he became Rob's instant and warm friend too. He was not jealous this time but pleased for them both. Being in her very late thirties she agonised over whether to have a baby or just devote herself to her gorgeous nieces, Dave and travelling. Once decided of course nothing happened, so she eventually had IVF and Jeremy was the result. He was now thirteen.

Dave was in the garden attending his vegetable patch when Rob arrived. He was so much happier as a postie. He had his local round and was usually home by 2.00 p.m. The outdoor life and exercise suited him perfectly. He never moaned about the pay drop saying, why should I get more than I do for going for a lovely walk? He had fought against the Post Office privatisation. When he lost that battle he gave his shares away. Sold them then gave the money to Unicef. When Pippa and Dave first met he was working in an Oxfam shop, having got out of the rat race before the rats ate him up. The job in advertising was one found for him straight after university where he got a degree in Physics - all to keep his father happy. He hated it and despised the hypocrisy, lies, consumerism and backstabbing. Dave wondered why there was all the fuss about fictional truth and alternative facts when the advertising industry had been at it for years and the tabloids were professionals at it. Using as a selling point bollocks like a cream had been dermatologically tested. What else would they test it on? Use a big word to fool the public. Patronising gits. Glad he had left all that behind. Or that you can get a broadband speed up to 100MB - 0.5 is up to 100MB is it not? That is fraud surely, but they get away with it. Then by calling what was known as a milky coffee a poncey name like latte, a rebranding of a drink that fooled people into believing they were being suave. Flat white? What bollocks.

He had handed in his notice two days after his father died. Then he thought he would give the advertising firm 'up-to-all' his company car back - just the spare wheel was up-to-all of the car, he teased, but they did not get the joke. He loved his father too much to upset him and once dead, as an atheist, he knew he could move on without feeling guilty. Pippa loved him for his kindness and principles. She could not now believe she had actually married a drug rep. That really was a previous life.

Jeremy came downstairs still in his school uniform. He greeted Rob reasonably civilly for a Bournemouth supporter who had just entered his teens.

Jeremy was very relaxed with Rob, having known him all his life. They liked each other. Jeremy had stayed with him and the family before he left Jenny. Their youngest daughter, Barrett, was about the same age. Dave and Pippa had really needed a break and missed travelling so much it was making them doubt whether they had made the right decision to start a family. One week without Jeremy though removed all doubt.

Rob could not help noticing the school crest on his blazer. There was a gold lion on a blue background and the motto *Fas Et Patria* at the bottom. Rob remembered his Latin. He could not help tease.

"Faith in the Fatherland? Very Germanic. But they are World Cup winners."

"Faith and Fatherland actually but I'd prefer the crest the Poppies have," Jeremy replied.

Rob was struggling to work out who the Poppies were, and it showed on his face. Jeremy beamed as he realised. He impersonated David Coleman (copied from Rob as he did not have a clue who David Coleman was) with an exclamation.

"One-nil. Got you! You don't know who the Poppies are, do you?"

Jeremy had resumed a game they always played. They tried to catch each other out and used football scores to keep a tally as to who was ahead.

"Yes I do, they are your football club. They've done well this season haven't they to stay in the Premier League?"

Rob thought he had equalised.

"Hah! Two-nil. You are mixing up Bournemouth Football Club, my team who play in the Wessex league, with A.F.C. Bournemouth. We are better. We are an older club, had a bigger record win than them, and their ground is nearer!"

Rob thought hard to try to catch him out. Two-nil down and they had only been talking for two minutes.

"Both grounds are virtually next door to each other aren't they?"

"No, the Cherries are twenty-three miles away at Dean Court and we are only twenty-two miles from here."

"Oh, come on, I demand an opinion from the assistant referee. Is that true, Pippa?"

"I'm afraid so Rob. He measured it on our last trip."

"Well, you are offside with that one. As legitimate a goal as Maradona scoring against England with the 'hand of God' seventeen years before you were born. And can you tell me what the Cherries' record victory was then, if you claim your club has done better?"

"You are on a loser, Rob," Pippa chipped in as she was busily leafing through a recipe book.

"The Cherries beat Northampton Town 10-0 in 1939, but we beat Tadley Calleva 14-1 when I was nine. Me and my Dad were there!"

Pippa looked up.

"Yes, they were. It was Jeremy's first ever football match and he thought there were always fifteen goals a game. Couldn't understand the next game being 0-0."

"You say your club is older? Bet you don't know the dates?"

Like answering questions for a teacher Jeremy answered in a robot manner.

"We were founded in 1875, but the other lot not 'til 1890. I reckon that is five-nil now."

Rob thought how like his parents Jeremy was to support the underdog. A team destined to win nothing. Admirable. Dave looking through the window and spotting that Rob had arrived, prevented Rob challenging the result. Dave came inside to warmly greet him. Jeremy had had enough, did not want to get involved in adult talk and was high on his victory, so turned quickly and ran back upstairs.

Rob shouted after him.

"After you've finished playing for England, you should run the F.A. and replace all those stick-in-the-mud old white men in charge who did not have the guts to appoint Brian Clough as England manager."

But Jeremy was too quick for him. Pippa smiled though.

"I'll get him next time. I'll tease him about Poole Town F.C. who were founded in 1880 and are only sixteen miles away. I checked it out this afternoon just in case."

"Football is becoming more and more of a passion for Jeremy, particularly after we did so well in that last World Cup. It's up there with astrophysics in his interests now, a strong challenger but not quite at that level,' said Dave.

Rob was keen to talk about something light and this was a welcome distraction.

"Getting to the semis, who would have believed it? You and I have lived and suffered through terrible England times. We have stuck with them through thick and thin. A load of fair-weather supporters jumped on the bandwagon this time, eh?"

"Looking back on it, it seems easy to see where we went wrong before. We had an overpaid dysfunctional manager who took the best players, a load of prima donnas, and stuck them on the pitch, often in wrong positions. They were never a team," continued Dave, almost in sorrow.

"Fairly basic eh? It is supposed to be a team game. Big mistake to try and build around one or two players no matter how good they were on occasions," agreed Rob.

"Enough football. I get this all the time Rob," Pippa chipped in, but still smiling.

Dave and Rob did not even notice.

"So the F.A. stumbled across Gareth Southgate by accident. I bet they never saw him as anything but a stopgap. But he has been a breath of fresh air. Someone who talks a lot of sense and has cleared out the old wood to build a young team that has a bright future," enthused Dave.

"Remember watching his missed penalty together in the semi against Germany in Euro '96?"

"Are you kidding? How could I forget? Couldn't speak for days, to me worse than the penalty misses at Italia '90. Pippa and I hadn't been together long. We visited you and Jenny and saw the match in that pub near you, didn't we?"

"Yes, the Hung Drawn and Quartered. Before children. Different times," said Rob.

The three of them enjoyed a bottle each of the *Pointing Percy* local ale in the bright sunshine on the patio.

Dave delighted in telling Rob, "It's a rich amber beer at four point four per cent made with Munich malt and oats and hopped with Perle and Saaz".

He had to explain the Perle was for bittering and the Czech Saaz hops for the aroma. He thought so anyway. Or was it the other way round? They looked out over the sea and felt very relaxed. Pippa kept jumping up to keep an eye on the meal. She was never very keen on eating out despite Rob's standing offer.

"I was just finishing planting the fuchsias when you arrived, Rob" said Dave. "Next to the tulips and snowdrops. Guess the significance of my choice?"

"Absolutely no idea" replied Rob, enjoying the beer and view.

"Well the suffragettes used the colours green, white and violet... GWV, which was their subliminal way of saying Give Women Votes. My flowers, fuchsias, tulips and snowdrops... FTS... Fuck The System."

"Very clever, Dave, but not likely to change the world if you have to explain it to everyone."

"But it makes me feel better."

Pippa and Dave were the most hospitable of all Rob's friends. When he was with them he always wondered why he did not visit more often. Unlike some friends who move on and end up with a new partner who sometimes does not fit in, these two were equal in being ten out of ten in the friendship stakes. Rob was relaxed in either of their company. There were others where he dreaded being left alone with the new other half, but never here. And a few even the old other half. Some friends were always trying to organise him into doing this or that, or to get him to lead his life as they did, or so it seemed. Not these two.

"It's so good to see you, Rob," said Dave, as if to prove his point.

"I'm afraid I always leave it too long, I'm sorry."

"No, we are as bad, but you know how time flies," excused Pippa.

As she dished up vegetarian lasagne, the other three moved to the table set up in the conservatory.

"Well, I may not see you as often as I should or want to, but you are my oldest and best friends. I feel safe with you and know I can trust you."

Pippa's warm smile suddenly dropped to a face of concern.

"Oh Rob, that's lovely but you worry me when you start off like that. Have you some news we should be concerned about, or worries?"

"Let's just call them concerns, yes that's a good word. And I'll say straight away they are not personal. Not yet anyway. It'll take a fair while to explain in detail, and unless I give you the detail, you'll think I'm just one sandwich short of a picnic. Perhaps I can test your patience on a walk tomorrow?"

What Pippa said next, probably only she in Rob's life could? Dave was not so sure so he was glad his wife had pushed the point.

"Oh come on, you can't get away with that. You will have to give us a clue tonight or we will not sleep from either excitement or worry."

Then ending in her Noel Coward impersonation, which was meant to be Ian Fleming's 'M', she joked.

"Spill the beans old fruit!"

"I knew I wouldn't be allowed to put it off. I'll try to sum it up in a few sentences, but please believe me that I'm not nutty. I have evidence for what I'm going to say and other people have confirmed some of my fears. It started simply with my frustration and anger as to what they are doing to the NHS.

You know I am passionate about what most look upon as our national treasure. You will see on a daily basis media reports of how the service is deteriorating. We are told we can't afford it. We are told we are living too long. The elderly are a great burden. Not only bollocks but cruel bollocks. Their deceit knows no bounds. You will have been aware of the re-disorganisations that this Government have put it through and the rumours, denied of course, of privatisation. Well it seems this is all very deliberate, a long time in the planning, and the last stages of a plot that goes back to the beginning of the NHS in 1948. Now that may not surprise you. But what is more sinister is that this plot is just one of many. Getting rid of the NHS is one battle in a much bigger war."

Pippa and Dave did not want to interrupt and stop Rob's flow.

"There have been secret organisations set up to run governments, and all aspects of public life with the aim to get rid of the State and have Big Business take over the world. Our cabinets over the last few decades have all been puppets. Our democracy is a sham. The media is under their total control. The press *have become lapdogs, not watchdogs*, as the Irish journalist Gemma O'Doherty has said. We have been heading in one direction since the Second World War, and it's like a secret steamroller with a definite plan and one which destroys everything in its way."

Rob's friends knew him well enough to know they should be taking him seriously. He had not lost credibility with them yet but it was getting close. It all seemed so, so huge. Taking over the world, Pippa replayed quizzically in her mind, but did not say out loud. Dave was more targeted.

"Surely no Government could get away with abolishing the NHS?"

"Dave that is exactly everybody's first reaction. I could have predicted you would say that. That is because it is incredible."

But before Rob could carry on Pippa had her question.

"So how are they able to do this and persuade people? They must need to control everyone to achieve this?"

Rob was pleased how quickly Pippa seemed to be grasping the issues without obvious disbelief.

"First, it's not necessary to persuade people about something they aren't even aware of. Something that is secret. Second, control. It's the usual approach. Using human weakness. Storing up blackmail material. You know those paedophile rings they now say were exaggerated and most victims were making it up? Well they weren't making it up and if anything we are all aware of just the tip of the iceberg. There has been a lot of effort put into discrediting them unfairly. Why do you think the enquiry set up to investigate

380

has become so dysfunctional and has got through four Chairs and sacked several lawyers? It's obvious. To drag it out for years, probably until most of the guilty Establishment figures are dead. Kick it into the long grass.

On the NHS Dave, you are of course correct. They realised they can't get rid of the NHS overtly, and their early arguments against it failed as no one believed them. So they never really tried playing a straight bat. They knew they had to plot. As early as four months after the creation of the NHS a group called the Fellowship for Freedom in Medicine was set up, secretly backed by the international insurance industry and fronted by doctors who hated the idea of easy cheap healthcare for all. This is all detail though and I'll add to that tomorrow. It's too late to explain too much more."

"Always be suspicious when people hijack the word freedom," Pippa added, "Look at the Freedom Association and what it actually stands for is freedom from unions, freedom to support apartheid, freedom to gag the *BBC*, freedom for the elite and oligarchs to do what the fuck they want."

Rob was having a moment of déjà vu. It was as though he had been listening to the judge. It was reassuring to hear this again. It helped to convince him he was not alone.

"And look at the USA land of the free, my arse. Free as long as you have loads of dough. Freedom from red tape means businesses having the freedom to exploit workers."

Dave seemed to know his stuff too.

"The Freedom Association hold a Margaret Thatcher weekend on her birthday and I gather Peter Mandelson's grandma, the wife of Herbert Morrison was a member. Morrison opposed Bevan on hospital nationalisation, so he fought for freedom from a full NHS! Now there are two infill-traitors of the first order. Neither Morrison nor Mandelson should have been in the Labour Party. They were Tories, and were both loathed by many of their colleagues, and both ended up in that ivory tower of democracy the Lords."

"Absolutely. It makes me wonder how much people like that are responsible for the sinister world we are in. There a very complicated and detailed secret tangled web and to mix my metaphors, its tentacles worm their dangerous and poisonous way into every part of our society. The society Thatcher said didn't exist. My problem is what to do about all this information I've stumbled across. Woken up to would be more accurate. It's like a snowball. It's got a momentum of its own and its getting bigger and bigger. But so many things fall into place. The eye-opening moment is one of sudden realisation. Just like turning on a light to a pitch-black room. Suzy thinks it'll just eat me up, others say it's precarious and menacing territory and nothing can be done against the tide anyway. A few have warned me off. Sleep on it then I would value your advice."

After a pause, Rob said.

"Thank you both so much for not dismissing me as a paranoid nutter."

"Don't worry, we will behind your back when you've gone to bed. We will lock you in your room and call the psychiatric service. Or we would if they hadn't abolished it," joked Dave.

"Lennon was spot on when he said honesty may not get you a lot of friends, but it will get you the right ones," added Rob.

"Good old John," said Pippa.

"Have you heard of the Save the National Health Service Party?"

Without waiting for a reply Rob continued, as he knew the answer.

"Trouble is no one has! They can't get any publicity. I've been meaning to contact them for a while, though just haven't got around to it. Let's talk about that tomorrow too."

Jeremy seemed to be taking it all in which impressed Rob. It is his generation who will inherit this mess and either sort it out or suffer from it. But after Rob suggested sleeping on it Jeremy left a decent polite amount of time before asking to be excused. He wanted to sleep, but not on this topic however.

The three adults caught up on all the usual topics over cheese and biscuits. Suzy, her work, Rob's practice, the hosts' travels past and future, and Dave's life. It was getting late. Conversation flowed with ease. Rob did not want to keep his friends up, and gestured to move when Dave decided he was keen to prolong the pleasant evening.

"Have you heard of Fritz Zwicky?" Dave asked, already knowing the answer.

"Accrington Stanley FC full-back, or a new type of glue?"

"Very funny. He was a Swiss astronomer, but worked in California."

"Where's this taking us?"

"Well, there are parallels between what we know of the universe and what we know about how we are governed, ruled and manipulated by the Establishment. Only four point nine per cent of the universe is ordinary matter, which is stuff we are aware of although even most of that is not visible. It's the same for what we know about what really goes on."

"Did Patrick Moore know about this?"

"Now, now. Don't take the piss. This is relevant. Zwicky was the first to dream up the idea of unseen dark matter, the missing bit of the universe, quite some time ago in 1933."

"Oh, what a coincidence, the same year that dark-haired matinee idol Hitler was elected, any connection?"

Dave ignored Pippa and continued.

"Dark energy plus dark matter constitute ninety-five point one per cent of total mass-energy content of the universe. Can't be seen, touched or heard and barely understood but will decide the fate of the universe. This is about the same as what we don't know of how we are controlled. About six billion years ago the expansion of the universe began to speed up and dark energy is responsible. It's pushing the universe apart."

"Six billion years ago? About the last time West Ham won the F.A. Cup," Rob said, trying but failing to follow what Dave was on about.

He thought he should make an effort though and tried to sum it up.

"So what you are saying is we know as little about how the world is run as we do the universe, and most is hidden from view."

"Precisely. Big business and sinister forces are the dark matter and energy pushing everything apart and will end up destroying society. There's so much we don't know. The little they do let us know is very controlled and carefully selected."

There was a pause whilst the plates were cleared and Dave thought a switch to *Jimmy Riddle* a good move.

"This is a three point seven per cent complex chestnut beer. It's fruity with a spicy finish from the malt, rye and oats."

Pippa had heard this before so manoeuvred back to the main topic.

"So, Donald Rumsfeld was spot on. *There are known knowns.* The corrupt politicians. *These are things we know that we know.* That they are all self-serving bastards with personality defects. *There are known unknowns. That is to say, there are things that we know we don't know.* That is, where their crimes haven't been discovered yet. *But there are also unknown unknowns. There are things we don't know we don't know.* Who's running the world, something as trivial as that?"

"Zwicky used to call his colleagues spherical bastards."

Rob smiled as he took his first sip of *Jimmy Riddle.*

"Why spherical?"

"Because they were bastards when looked at from any side. Just like most politicians! I end my analogy."

"What a tremendous relief," Rob said, "I was really quite worried that you would think me as crazy as a sack full of ferrets. That the lift doesn't go to the top floor. That I had a kangaroo loose in the top paddock. A screw loose."

"Never would we think you are rowing with only one oar in the water, or not hitting on all six cylinders," said Dave.

"Not even a few penguins short of a lawnmower? The lights are on but nobody's at home?"

Rob wanting more reassurance.

"Not even as mad as a hatter, or your rocket isn't working on all thrusters," said Pippa.

"So what if I said we are heading in the direction of a fascist state?"

Silence.

"The Italian philosopher Umberto Eco defined what was needed to qualify, and we now have quite a few of the characteristics."

"He died a year or two ago didn't he? I remember reading his obituary," said Pippa.

"But I won't pursue that one or you will think the cheese has slid off my cracker," said Rob yawning again, "Just one more bedtime thought to keep you awake. The over-arching theme, which leads to my conspiracy theories, is that they have tried to convince everyone we have a public sector crisis. The public services are not sustainable. They blame so-called overspending for the financial crisis when in actual fact it was a crisis of the private sector and neo-liberalism itself. The neo-liberal dominated institutions of politics, media, economics and the financial world have gone to great lengths to rebrand the financial crisis. Scapegoating to push their agenda,"

Rob thought he had better shut up. He did not think it wise to mention the encounter with the man who called himself Ian in Tolpuddle. Not tonight anyway.

"What an intellect!" said Dave, "Rivalled only by garden tools? No seriously, we agree, but I've never heard it put like that."

They all turned to go upstairs to bed. Clearly joking Pippa said directly to Dave, pretending it was only for his ears.

"If his brains were dynamite he couldn't even blow his nose."

"Yes," replied Dave, turning to his wife, "Thicker than a donkey's dangler."

Rob wanted the last word.

"You know when I first met Pippa she introduced me to Robert Frost with one of his quotations that she said applied to me, *a liberal is a man too broadminded to take his own side in an argument.*"

"Strange that - she told me that too" said Dave.

They both laughed.

"I objected to being called a liberal, far too right wing for me," said Rob. "But you were right in those days Pippa. Now I'm an opinionated, grumpy, old bastard."

"That's what we all become," Dave countered.

Bedtime.

31 - WARMTH AND INQUIRIES

WAITING IN VAIN

I don't wanna wait in vain for love.
From the very first time I rest my eyes on you, girl,
My heart says follow t'rough.
But I know, now, that I'm way down on your line

Bob Marley (1977)

Rob woke to the sound of seagulls with light streaming through the cottage's spare room window.

He felt very at home amongst friends and lay in bed for a while listening to Jeremy get ready for school. *Fas et Patria* indeed. He was content that he had explained himself as well as he could the night before and glad he had not drunk too much. Was his credibility still intact though? Dave had left several hours before to start his round. Great day for a walk, Rob thought.

Pippa was free after Jeremy had left so they decided to walk to Corfe Castle. She had a circular ten-mile stroll, which took in Clavell Tower and the coast. Rob wanted to wait until Pippa returned to last night's topic through her own choice, so they talked of the last books they had read, films they had seen and theatre trips. Pippa was widely read and Rob wanted to keep up. He was quite good at bluff and did not think she suspected. He was still keen to impress her.

As they approached the 1830 Tuscan-style folly near the shore east of Kimmeridge Bay, Rob knew he could shine. He had just read P. D. James' *The Black Tower*, which the Clavell Tower had inspired. He had cheated though. What had got him to read about James' sleuth, Adam Dalgliesh, was seeing a re-run of the television version, which was filmed there. He then looked it up and found that Thomas Hardy had taken his first love Eliza Nicholl to the Tower. Pippa was a fan of Hardy. She had to be where she lived. Rob found him too depressing, especially *Jude the Obscure*, which he could quote.

He only persevered because it was lightened in places with some lyrical pieces about the beauty of nature. Rob was more intrigued by the battle over where he should be buried. His heart ended up in the grave of his first wife Emma at Stinsford and his ashes in Poets' Corner.

So after dropping a few gems about Hardy, such as his wife Emma had hated *Jude the Obscure* too, he moved on to discuss the Tower and P. D. James. Then he joked that he wanted to know at what point Dalgliesh gave up Scotland Yard to manage Liverpool and Blackburn Rovers. That joke would have been better received by Dave or Jeremy the football fans. Rob felt quite pleased with himself but was thinking he would not end up in Poets' Corner, more like in Pseud's Corner. He need not have worried. Pippa warmed further to him, cupping his face in her hands, as they were either side of a stile.

"You are lovely," she smiled.

However, Rob knew this was just the way she was, had seen her do it to others, and did not read too much into it. But it made him feel great. What it also did was remind him just how much he still fancied her, but he would not dream of telling her now.

The weather was perfect. They both had all their full walking gear on, but had shed their top layers. Rob enjoyed an intimate moment when Pippa caught her jumper in her hair clips and he had to come to the rescue. She had always been a tactile woman but he did not want to give her the wrong impression by reciprocating. They passed a water bottle between them too. The gentle breeze and company made Rob feel he did not want the walk to end. Apart from the subject matter grumbling below the surface it was the perfect escape.

It was not until they sat in the garden of The Greyhound, set in the square at Corfe, that Pippa returned to Rob's concerns, which she now realised were hers too. Pippa was delicately picking at her Weymouth crab salad when she asked Rob to tell her more. For once he was not staring at Pippa but at the old castle, built by William the Conqueror and one of the last royalist strongholds in the South during the civil war. That seemed to spark his thoughts.

"Chopping King Charles' head off didn't make a lot of difference did it? Look at Cromwell. He introduced military rule, shut inns, closed all theatres, banned sports, only tolerated Christmas as long as no enjoyment was had and of course, according to the Irish, was a genocidal war criminal. He banned women wearing make-up and had Puritans roaming the streets to scrub it off unsuspecting women. Our so-called rulers are not much better now. It is a magnificent act of craziness that when Charles' son returned to become King of England, he ordered that Oliver Cromwell be dug up and his body put on trial as a traitor! He was found guilty and hanged! Brilliant. Difficult to defend himself though. The world has gone so mad you could imagine that happening today!"

He spotted the Swanage Steam Railway down the hill.

"I remember going on that with Jenny when we came down here on one of our first weekends away together."

"How is she?" Pippa ventured.

It was a sad fact of life that when a couple split up friends usually gravitate to one partner and the other loses out. It is not that one is picked. It usually goes with the longest friendship.

"I think she is hating me less. I still feel so guilty. But chats with you helped me to cope. The girls see me more now and they seem to have survived."

Then abruptly back to serious issues. Who was he kidding though? The girls were the most serious and important part of his life. They both agreed that the Labour Party under Blair was a great disappointment, that it was Tory-lite, scared of the *Daily Mail*, and had lost its principles. When Rob explained how he had heard Blair was an infiltrator, planted by the right wing, Pippa just said that made sense.

"What I've noticed, as I'm sure you have, is how the masses are fed just shit and inane nonsense by the media, by the entertainment industry and by journalists to keep them thinking about frivolous subjects like who will win *X-Factor*. That Irish journalist Gemma O'Doherty gave a lecture recently confirming this for me. She said we are fed a diet of distraction. To distract from the issues that really matter. The more people are treated like morons the more they act as empty-headed twats."

Rob grabbed his chance to impress.

"As my old friend Alex Solzhenitsyn told me the other day, hastiness and superficiality are the psychic diseases of the twentieth century. No doubt he would have found the twenty-first century worse."

Pippa smiled at him and continued.

"They are being trained out of thinking about serious matters, but given a diet of what they are told are serious matters to deflect them from what is really happening. Take the EU referendum. Never a serious debate and the politicians really must think the public is witless, gormless and vacuous to even listen to all those obvious lies. They must think blimey, we got away with that porky let's try another whopper! That blonde fat self-seeking public school, detached, twat actually stood on a soapbox and said the EU don't allow bananas to be sold in bunches greater than three. The fatter he gets the more like Billy Bunter he becomes, with the same bluster too. He knew he was lying. That condom sizes were to be standardised. The media should not have given him airtime. They are complicit."

"Didn't he also claim that all Euro-manure should smell the same, and that there was a threat to the British sausage?" Rob added.

"Probably."

"I take it from the description you give of him you aren't too keen on him?" Rob joked.

"I've got a shedload more adjectives for him too. Once a public schoolboy, always a public schoolboy."

"Funny," said Rob, "someone else said that to me the other day."

"The thought that he wants to become our Prime Minister almost puts Trump's ambition in the shade. He even makes up a name for himself for show. We have just got rid of the worst Prime Minister since Lord North lost the American colonies. Could it get worse?"

"Most definitely. It reminds me of what Khrushchev said about politicians, *they promise to build a bridge even where there is no river.*"

"The incompetent bastard called a referendum for party political reasons and took us out of Europe by accident. It didn't help that the *BBC* were so scared of being accused of bias they gave equal credence to lies, when they knew they were broadcasting lies. That was stupid as they were always going to be accused of bias anyway. The *BBC* will be attacked until it folds."

"Loughborough University found that eighty-two per cent of all referendum stories were negative, and this made all the difference when just six hundred and thirty-five thousand votes for Remain rather than Leave would have averted this national catastrophe. The Press was a disgrace."

Rob said his overwhelming feeling at the EU referendum result was sadness.

"Such a shame. The rest of Europe must think us crazy isolationists. I suppose it's the end of Schengen and that wonderful Erasmus student exchange programme. What a shortsighted loss. To have foreign students study here could only be a good thing for relations. Xenophobic wankers."

"I think those who voted Leave should have to get visas and queue at borders and those of us that like our neighbours should keep free access. It's the poor who will really suffer though. The rich leavers demanding the hardest of possible Brexits, with their offshore accounts, homes abroad and lavish pensions will be all right," said Pippa.

"Yes, let us through the quick channel. Brexiteers get compulsory body search and interrogation. Perhaps a bit of waterboarding, eh? There is a special place in hell for them, according to the President of the European Council."

Rob mischievously added with a smile then continued.

"There were lies but now there is a lack of logic. They say there should not be another referendum because that is undemocratic. No, it fucking isn't. It is democracy. It's Orwellian to claim that denying the public a vote is democratic but giving them a say is undemocratic. That's the world we live in now. Politicians getting away with talking shit."

"It's actually evil," chipped in Pippa, "and the one thing that does undermine democracy. Using their logic one general election should be good enough. No need for another ever again! Things change. The situation changes. People's opinions change. A democracy that cannot change its mind ceases to be a democracy.

"But their inconsistent hypocritical lack of logic is exposed by the same tossers' insistence at dismantling the NHS," butted in Rob.

"How so?" Pippa thought she knew what he meant but needed confirmation.

"Well," continued Rob, pleased to be able to impress he hoped, "they get the answer they want from a referendum, and it's not allowed to be reconsidered, ever. When they don't get what they want from the public they ask the same question over and over again. The public overwhelmingly support the NHS and have done so for over seventy years, but on a regular basis they want to badger the electorate and get them to believe that it isn't what they want, they need and should go for an alternative to the health service."

"Yes," Pippa agreed, "every year or so they fly the kites, we can't afford it, it's totally inefficient, it's unsafe, and the stupid gullible but complicit media parrot these falsehoods on the basis that if it's rammed down the public's throat often enough it'll be swallowed. There's no need to consult the public on the NHS. For decades they have given the same answer. The enemies of the NHS hope that if they keep repeating the question, they will eventually get their answer, not the wrong answer."

Rob finished off.

"To this I say stop asking the fucking question. It's one rule when they get their right answer, and another when they don't. Citizens of the UK will not give up on the NHS. They will have to be conned out of it."

Pippa returned to Europe.

"A better informed electorate would help democracy too. A reformed European Union would have satisfied most, but that twat of a PM we had couldn't deliver. Do you know forty per cent of the EU budget is spent on the Common Agricultural Policy? And who are the biggest beneficiaries in the UK? The Queen pockets seven hundred and thirty thousand pounds, the Carringtons seven hundred and fourteen thousand pounds, and the Duke of Athol two hundred and thirty-one thousand pounds. Perhaps that should have been sorted out."

Pippa was getting fired up.

"Then there is the grammar school debate. Fucking hell, I really thought we'd grown up as a society and got over that one, but oh no, just when you think it's safe to relax," she smiled, "advocating the brutal divisiveness of selection and segregation at just eleven. Their belief that this gives every child access to a good school place is bereft of intellectual coherence. This is worse than faith schools. What a stupid idea that is. Another one of Blair's I think. In a world where most wars are now fought on religious grounds, let's just segregate the faiths, keep people apart, fuel the misunderstandings by the different factors not meeting, integrating or even talking. That's really going to help isn't it? Crazy. How did these morons get elected?"

Rob showed his solidarity with a smile.

"I thought the right wing had milked education as much as they could but clearly, yet again, I've under-estimated the bastards. They are profiting by privatising the schools and owning academies, but after the student loan rip off, which siphons money to their own loan companies, they make a killing in the property market. So many saw this as an opportunity and became landlords and squeezed the student sponge dry, apparently thirty-nine per cent of Tory MPs are renting out."

"Their property or bodies?" enquired Pippa.

"Oh, without doubt both," replied Rob.

He continued on one of his hobbyhorses.

"The majority of parents believe their child attends a state school when in reality the majority of UK children attend privately owned schools, where the majority of services are delivered by private sector staff. They sneakily put schools into the hands of private, unaccountable, profit-making, limited companies that then dictate what is taught. There's corporate sponsorship, and the National Curriculum has been dismantled. Believe it or not history teaching has gone back to how wonderful the British Empire was. They do what they like. There's a school in Derby where the teachers were forced to wear headscarves and female pupils made to sit at the back. Lessons were scrapped in favour of prayers. And another in Essex where the pupils were told they had to smile more. Are we really becoming like fucking North Korea? This has all been done so subtly not many have noticed. Even the teachers don't realise. Then we go and scare the little darlings by introducing anti-terrorist lessons! Incredible. How about something useful like first aid? They are more likely to cut their finger and need to know what to do about that than be blown up by a jihadi."

"It feeds into their fear agenda though, doesn't it? Justifies more surveillance," said Pippa.

"Absolutely" said Rob, breaking his promise to himself to use the word yes, "Part of this crime of the century is that all the buildings, land and assets owned by us, the taxpayer, have been stolen from us and given away for nothing. We've been robbed and, of course, the same is happening in the NHS. All our buildings, land and hospitals, owned by us, have been given by politicians to their mates. Those who have allowed this should be in jail."

"Yes, I was part of the protest group trying to prevent it happening at Jeremy's school," Pippa explained, "We got nowhere of course. The costs have soared and quality plummeted which proves it's done just for ideological reasons. I looked into this to help my opposition be more evidence-based. Academies and so-called free schools suck funding from the remaining state schools. While their budget has been cut dramatically, academy schools have seen theirs increase by a whopping one hundred and ninety-one per cent."

"Fuck!" said Rob, "No wonder all this is done is secret and the public are kept in the dark."

"And despite being offered shedloads of money the private companies that run these academies still can't cope. Just the other day some abandoned their contracts as they said they weren't profitable enough!"

"I think it is the scandal of our times that this isn't debated. So there are a few state schools left, some grammar, some comprehensive and soon to make a comeback secondary moderns. The rest are academies, faith schools, free schools and public schools. Who voted for this demolition of our education system? What we had when we were young was fine. We really were the golden generation, and all this crap that we can't afford it now, absolute bollocks. They have converted pretty well everything into a more expensive, less efficient system. With private companies abandoning schools, and we've heard of them dropping non-profitable hospitals and GP surgeries like hot potatoes too, maybe there is hope, eh?"

Rob's food finally arrived. He thought he had been forgotten, but at least he did not have to talk with his mouth full.

"The majority of parents haven't got a clue about this. Kids shouldn't have a religion forced on them. Saying eight-year-old Stephanie is a Pentecostal makes no more sense than eight-year-old Stephanie is a Marxist-Leninist. If children could decide for themselves which theological ideas to accept we'd expect to see a random distribution of faiths amongst children, which is of course exactly what we don't see. Young children should be taught that imposed divisions in society are bad, and that there is nothing wrong with people you don't agree with. This is not what you get from faith schools."

Pippa nodded. They were in harmony.

"Faith schools distort moral values," she continued, "Some tell their pupils that thought crime exists, that you might go to hell and burn forever, that God only rewards true belief, not goodness, and men are more important than women."

"Terrible, except the last one is okay isn't it?" Rob teased, "Pluralism is good. We should have respect and tolerance for other cultures. But cultural relativism is bad. No matter how strongly someone believes something that doesn't make it true."

Pippa looked at Rob and fixed his eyes with hers. It was an intimate moment.

394

"Blimey, Rob. I'm impressed. So glad I know you. I mean, really know you."

There was a pause. Rob did not know what to say. If only I really had known her, was his instant thought.

"Another drink?" was what came to mind to disguise what he was really thinking.

"No, thank you."

Rob steered the conversation back to the media and took it further.

"Have you noticed there is no investigative journalism anymore. Stories are cut and pasted from Wikipedia. It's not really that journalists are lazy but just controlled and paid by the yard of copy not quality. The twenty-four hour news channels were, I've heard, developed to repeat and repeat the same boring story over and over again to people with the attention span of a goldfish. Breaking news: 'Dog Hurts Nose In Shop Doorway', 'Whitstable Mum In Custard Shortage Row', 'Boy Gets Finger Stuck In Bucket'. 'Interrupting an interview with someone interesting to go straight to our reporter at the Little Wallop Annual Blindfolded Lawn Mowing Match', or in the case of the *BBC*: 'We interrupt this programme as Nigel Farage has something to say'. All designed to divert or brainwash us. Pre-packaged news. Why do you think they have invested so much in destroying three or four real quality channels and replacing them with hundreds of rubbish ones full of crap to numb the brain? And Murdoch and Trump want more.

There is a really sinister reason for this. We have two safeguards in the UK protecting us and our democracy, fairly independent publicly funded news and the libel laws. Take these circuit breakers away, as they want to, and the fake news ecosystem can take control and bypass democracy. This is how it works. It starts with an outrageous idea broadcast widely by the ultra right media and poisonous websites like *Guido Fawkes*. Something along the lines of Corbyn raped a six-year-old boy at a Communist love-in also attended by the Devil, Jack the Ripper and Gary Glitter. This is then fed into the mainstream media. If they fail to take up the story they are accused of censorship and bias. If they do run with it the attacks can continue and spin around 'at the least he has questions to answer'. This weaponises the smear and can incite the stupid to further action, even violence. Someone somewhere with a six-year-old son will feel free to attack Corbyn. This happens now and is bad enough. Imagine how it will run riot if the safeguards are removed as people like Murdoch, Bannon and Trump want. Worse still we now have a far right nutter advising him who has attended the National Security Council. Have you heard of Breitbart News? You thought Fox news was bad. Check this out. It's racist, xenophobic, sexist, anti-Semitic and it's heading our way. Loonies like Bannon, Bolton and Trump are in charge of the asylum. You know all about this really don't you Pippa? You are in this world. It's almost your profession now isn't it?"

"How dare you?" she countered with a grin, "I'm in publishing which is not journalism! It's true I have a lot of old friends still working in TV but I'm glad I don't have much to do with that world now."

They were talking so much they were very slow over their food. Rob was struggling with his slow-roasted Dorset pulled pork sandwich.

After fleeing to Dorset Pippa got an administrative job with a publisher. She was told on application that she was too qualified for the post, but the boss thought two things justified ignoring this. One, she should be snapped up as other jobs would soon be available, and two, she had a great figure. *Jupiter Press* specialised in ethical and left wing publications and had a local office in Bournemouth. It did not take long for her talents to be used in a different field and she was given more and more responsibility.

The boss clearly fancied her and used any excuse to chat to her, usually spouting odd facts.

"Did you know Bernie Taupin's mother also studied French Literature and his father had French ancestry?"

Then he would leave her room singing.

"Into the boundary of each married man, sweet deceit comes calling and negativity lands."

She recognised the lyrics from *Sacrifice* one of her favourite Elton John/Taupin songs. It made her think more of first husband John leaving her for that practice manager than her boss's clumsy attempts at a pass. She thought him nice but that was all. She learnt a lot from him though about their world, along with his trivia. She was soon copy-editing and then head of that department, even though it was a department of only three people. It allowed the company to move into some French publications, which made Pippa indispensable. It also allowed a fair bit of work to be done at home.

Rob then told her about his conversation with the Judge. All about the syndicates, the plots, the depth of corruption and the destruction of democracy. They could both see why good people - or others - were not speaking out. If they had no skeletons in the cupboard they were soon given a few that could be used against them. More paralysing was the fact they could get no media interest or outlet. Whistleblowers get no protection despite what they are told.

"My boss is a good guy. I trust him. I wonder what he knows?"

"Pippa, it was not my intention that you should get involved in all this. I just needed to get it off my chest. I worry that it's dangerous and don't want you, Dave or Jeremy to be put at risk."

"Oh don't be so melodramatic Robert. A few discreet enquiries won't do any harm. You've only articulated what I now realise has been in my own subconscious for some time. It's bubbled to the surface now like an unpleasant fart in the bath. I've made a huge number of contacts in this job. My first thought is that there must be others out there wondering about this and also agonising over what to do. Supposing there is already an organised group beginning to plot some resistance? It'll be stupid not to link up. Dave would make a good resistance fighter. He loved *Charlotte Gray* and *The Sorrow And The Pity* was one of the first films we saw together. Besides, you as much as anyone know the Martin Niemoller poem. She spoke the first line.

"*First they came for the socialists, and I did not speak out – because I was not a socialist.*"

Then Rob the second.

"*Then they came for the trade unionists, and I did not speak out – because I was not a trade unionist.*"

Pippa the third.

"*Then they came for the Jews and I did not speak out – because I was not a Jew.*"

And then both together.

"*Then they came for me – and there was no one left to speak for me.*"

Rob almost welled up with this.

"Do you remember seeing Louis Malle's *Au Revoir Les Enfants* with me when we were still in London? Not only me of course, all your flatmates too. Powerful stuff. Must see it again."

Rob paid for lunch and they continued their walk. They were heading back to the cottage now. It was cooler than before but Rob always felt chilly after lunch and sitting around. He thought it was his age. The breeze was a little more vigorous.

"We've always thought we lived in a plutocracy, haven't we? Now I'm certain. I hadn't heard of Noam Chomsky until last year but he condemns all the plutocrats for ignoring their social responsibilities, using their ill-gotten power to serve their own purposes, increasing poverty, nurturing class conflict and corrupting societies with greed and hedonism."

"Wow, that's the second time this decade you've impressed me Rob. You need your own show!" she teased.

"Well it's spreading from America. They've been called the donor class, their money buying plenty of access. There is a fusion between money and government. Lincoln would be turning in his grave. His, *of the people, by the people and for the people* in the Gettysburg Address has become 'of the one per cent, by the one per cent, and for the one per cent' as the US is increasingly ruled by the wealthiest one per cent. Look at Bush, just a front man. And then Obama, hardly any real power. What he did achieve has been reversed by his successor."

"And where America goes we eventually follow. The one per cent will do literally whatever it takes, and I mean whatever it takes, to increase their wealth. It seems what they have is never enough.

You can never have too many yachts. That money has to come from somewhere and that is the rest of us. Unfortunately for the really poor they sacrifice disproportionately."

"From what you tell me Rob, the bastards have nothing to fear either as they are in total control?"

"Yes, even when some good people are onto them, they are closed down very swiftly. Occasionally they throw a few crumbs to make it appear we are an open and honest society. Usually by announcing an inquiry into some juicy scandal. We both know what happens there. How long did the *Bloody Sunday Inquiry* go on for? Twelve years, at least not reporting until thirty-eight years after the crime. Then they moan about the cost and use that as an excuse to avoid other investigations. What a coincidence that a government minister accidently let slip that inquiry cost about four hundred million pounds, just when they wanted to avoid setting up an inquiry into the seventh of July bombings in London. Some reports are forgotten, others are buried, and most are whitewashes. Who remembers Levinson and the phone hacking scandal now? Well the organisation Hacked Off is still plugging away but they've got nowhere. The legislation here is quietly being reversed too. A few hacks were hung out to dry by the bosses who should have gone to jail. And the MPs expenses? Well, the abuse is worse than ever."

Pippa asked about the *Hutton Inquiry*.

"Do you think David Kelly was murdered?"

"Put it this way. The government of the day was caught misleading the British public over the reasons for going to war. There's not much that is more serious than that. The man who knew everything and potentially could bring down that government suddenly is found dead. He was supposed to have killed himself but nothing in his character or the circumstances support that. We all know Blair exaggerated about weapons of mass destruction hitting the UK within forty-five minutes, Chilcot told us so. History repeats itself, doesn't it?

You remember me talking about my old friend Rosa? She told me years before Iraq that the Vietnam War was ramped up deliberately by the US exaggerating North Vietnamese attacks on the

US Navy in the Bay of Tonkin incident in 1964. Blair followed that example as others have done before him. But the *Hutton Inquiry* was an establishment whitewash. He got away with it at the time and the *BBC* was blamed. And the top brass at the *BBC* were too weak to just tell them to fuck off. The worst Hutton admitted was that the Government might have subconsciously influenced the Joint Intelligence Committee under John Scarlett. Kelly's death was probably a revenge killing by Iraqi supporters of Saddam Hussein, and Thames Valley police, who knew about the assassination plot in advance, crudely disguised it as a suicide. Many of those involved received promotions and awards. It stank. Kelly was supposed to have bled to death by cutting his ulnar artery, which wouldn't do it, and with hardly any blood loss at the scene. The poor bloke, a highly respected weapons expert, talked about *many dark actors playing game*s. The post mortem report was to remain classified for seventy years but was released when Labour lost power. The amount of co-proxamol in his stomach was only a third that was needed to kill someone and, guess what, and surely this is damning, incredibly the knife had no fingerprints on it?"

"Wow. I didn't know that!"

"Nor does most of the great British public. It really doesn't need a *Miss Marple* or *Hercule Poirot* to solve this one. Just one more example of how the establishment can get away with anything. Even murder."

"That brings us neatly back to Chilcot. What about that?"

"Slightly different. The new government was not bothered about embarrassing the old government who said at first the inquiry should be in camera. It was published thirteen years after the events so didn't change anything. The committee members were all establishment and Sir Martin Gilbert actually said he thought Blair and Bush might one day, *join the ranks of Roosevelt and Churchill.* Despite that they concluded the war was unnecessary, Hussein didn't pose any urgent threat to British interests, the intelligence about weapons was wrong, the case for war and the legal basis were far from satisfactory, peaceful alternative to war had not been exhausted, and the United Nations had been undermined. Apart from that Blair and Bush were right. Oh, and of course war preparation, planning and the aftermath were all wholly inadequate, and military action didn't achieve its goals."

Pippa had stopped to do up her bootlace and Rob had walked on without noticing at first. He soon backtracked and continued, hoping she had heard his last rant. She had because she then reacted.

"But no one making all these wrong, probably criminal decisions gets punished. Yet hundreds of thousands of Iraqis died, thousands of troops and hundreds of thousand orphans resulted from the undemocratic decisions of a few. Then the Americans moved all their companies in to profit."

Rob knew their time together was drawing to a close, so he wanted to move onto more optimistic ground.

"Hillsborough was a bit more refreshing though, wasn't it? Prosecutions are actually happening! Even the Chief Superintendent and Chief Inspector!" Pippa was not convinced.

"Well, it exposed many of the terrible cover-ups and appalling behaviour of the authorities, but no one has been punished, have they? And it took some very brave and determined people twenty-six years to get near the truth. The Establishment fought them all the way. The police spent millions of taxpayers' money even disputing things at the end that had already been dismissed. Disgraceful."

"I know. It went right to the top of Government didn't it? Thatcher was involved. The cover up was Thatcher's thank you to the South Yorkshire police for helping break the miners. Her scummy cronies Bernard Ingham and Kelvin MacKenzie still seem to think they were right to blame the football fans. People like that should not be in public life. They should be prevented from influencing others with their vile prejudiced and ignorant poison. Ingham called them *tanked-up yobs* and is such an arrogant fucking arsehole, still won't admit he was wrong or say sorry. MacKenzie says he got caught up in the smear campaign - he was the smear campaign! All his professional life has been about smearing opponents. I don't understand why any newsagent within one hundred miles of Liverpool would want to stock *The Sun*. At least the football club has at long last banned *Sun* journalists from its ground."

"So have Everton now. With a bit of luck it'll spread. Next the *Daily* fascist *Mail*, eh?" contributed Pippa.

Rob nodded.

"And as for the South Yorkshire Police. They turned into the paramilitary wing of Government, like at Orgreave. They were at fault and they covered up. Wasn't it disgraceful that all their statements were altered? Makes you wonder where that's happened before and how many miscarriages of justice there have been because of crooked coppers. Ninety-six innocent people were unlawfully killed and no one has come to justice despite the coroner saying the top cop at the match was, *responsible for manslaughter by gross negligence.* Even recently the denials of the facts were still pouring out. Do you know what Cameron said? *The families of the Hillsborough tragedy are a blind man, in a dark room, looking for a black cat that isn't there?* His Culture Secretary, admittedly in the pocket of Murdoch, still blamed hooliganism. So he got promoted to become Health Secretary. Mission. Get rid of the NHS. Great!"

Pippa really was on a roll.

"And then Foreign Secretary. Unbelievable. It was sickening that Thatcher had the balls to attend the memorial service, shedding crocodile tears when she knew the truth. It reminds me of all those Tories who had moist eyes when Mandela died and claimed he was their hero. I bet they fear photos surfacing of them wearing their HANG MANDELA badges, but they must be pleased it was in an era before social media was around. Otherwise they'd have to defend clips of them on their feet applauding Thatcher when she called him a terrorist."

"Let's just hope we will get a proper inquiry into Orgreave. But I'd be surprised, it's over thirty years ago now."

They continued to chat all the way back to her cottage. Lightening up though, onto more comfortable subjects, they returned to discussing Thomas Hardy, and Pippa said next time Rob and Suzy visited they should all go to the cottage where he was born in Higher Bockhampton. Pippa loved the thatched cottage and told Rob that Hardy's great grandfather had built it in 1800. *Far From The Madding Crowd* was written there. Rob was keen to stretch out his time with Pippa so could not say no to a cup of tea before driving home. He would still beat Suzy back home from her Arts Fair and Exhibition. But of course they were not alone. Dave was gardening after finishing his post round and just as Pippa put the kettle on, in burst Jeremy.

"Do you know general relativity is not compatible with quantum mechanics so physics is having a nervous breakdown?"

He was beaming at his new discovery.

"I prefer football," replied Rob.

"The sun is a million times the mass of the earth and most stars are the same. A galaxy has a million, million stars and the universe a million, million galaxies. It all started from a singularity with the big bang nearly fourteen billion years ago. Do you know what the multiverse is?"

"Is it when a song has several verses, like an entry to the *Eurovision Song Contest*?"

"One-nil!" Jeremy exclaimed, "What's the Galaxy Andromeda?"

"Oh, I know this one. A type of chocolate bar."

"Two-nil! It's the nearest major galaxy to the Milky Way and contains one trillion stars, and the two will collide in about four point five billion years."

"Well I'd better put my tin hat on and get home quick, don't you think?" Jeremy looked at him in pity.

"There won't be a destructive explosion. More like a merger into a supra-galaxy as everything is so far apart."

"But Jeremy, is a billion a million, million or a thousand million?" asked Rob wanting to score back. He knew he would not win with cosmology.

"Easy. It used to be the former until we adopted the American definition, which is the latter in 1974. That's three-nil. An own goal by you trying to catch me out."

"Drat! So what's after a trillion?

"A quadrillion, then a quintillion, and then I think a sextillion."

"....we eventually get to a zillion, squillion and bazillion."

"No we don't, you are making it up. Don't you find it just fantastic that we now have the first evidence of gravitational waves?"

"Okay Jeremy. You are trying to humiliate me now aren't you?" said Rob, "Explain, and I hand victory to you."

"Well, a billion years ago two black holes merged with such violence the very fabric of space and time shook and ripples spreading out across the universe. We've detected the waves from that. Isn't that just great?"

"Come on Jeremy, leave Rob alone now," said Dave wiping the mud off his hands from gardening.

"No Dave I love it. It's fantastic to see unadulterated and untainted enthusiasm for knowledge and a wonderment about how we evolved."

"You don't have to live with it Rob!" said Dave, "But I promised to take Jeremy down the road to get his copy of *Railway Modeller Magazine* before Harry at the newsagent shuts up shop so we will say goodbye," he explained.

As Jeremy was putting on his coat he had to have the last word.

"Bet you didn't know there are seven hundred million trillion rocky planets like earth in the universe?"

He smiled at Rob and disappeared out of the back door with his Dad.

After Rob had finished his second cup he walked towards his car with Pippa who hugged him in a way no one else does.

"I was going to say I think you should go home and forget about all this, but neither of us will be able to, will we? I know Dave will think the same."

That was a timely reminder that Pippa had a husband whom she loved. Rob followed with the obvious query.

"What to do now, that's the question?"

They remained with arms around each other for perhaps too long.

The drive away from Pippa's always made him feel the same - melancholy with a feeling of missed opportunity. A feeling that he should have been with that lovely woman. She gave him a feeling like no other and no one else had ever come near. But he could not wait for her love in vain. His heart said follow it through, but he knew he was way down on her line. Did she not remember she had taken Rob to Higher Bockhampton before though? And returning with Suzy was the right thing to do, but he would rather be alone with Pippa.

32 - EMBARRASSMENT AND LOGIC

NO MORE HEROES

Whatever happened to
Leon Trotsky?
He got an ice pick
That made his ears burn

Whatever happened to
Dear old Lenin?
The great Elmyra,
And Sancho Panza?
Whatever happened to the heroes?

The Stranglers (1977)

Trashing a squash ball around got Pippa out of Rob's system - at least for now.

It was unusual for the two friends to play on a Saturday but Stephen suggested it might help them both cope with Ellie's dinner party later that evening. Stephen knew Rob loved winding his wife up at these events. The last time Rob and Suzy were invited Rob disgraced himself - again. On that occasion his subject was private education. He just could not help himself. The local nobs, as Rob referred to them, were too tempting a target. He felt deliberately provocative in a group he did not like very much. He could not help thinking that he was only invited to these occasions to help their middle class attempts at demonstrating their liberal and open-minded values. He could imagine them telling their friends, we had dinner the other evening with a darkie.

He started by saying he would not now ban private education, as he would have advocated as a younger man. He had even abandoned his follow-up plan, which was just to tax it out of existence. That relied on every parent that sent his or her little Henrietta, Tabitha, Aubyn or Ormerod to public school being made to pay the same school fee to the exchequer, so doubling the cost. No, he would simply nationalise all the public schools and have entry by ballot. That would get the middle classes off their arses to fight for better education for all instead of just their little brat. It had the effect Rob wanted. It was certainly a conversation stopper. The others were left with their mouths open, unable to judge whether Rob was serious. When they realised he was, some tried to change the subject to the cost of stabling their horses. But Arabella, the just-divorced Sloane Ranger fell into Rob's trap of saying she agreed with comprehensive schools. Her cleaner went to one and she seems okay but she could not put her principles before her children. Rob asked her if she knew what 'projection' was. To puzzled looks he explained that that is when someone actually argues that they are the principled ones for not having principles, whilst you should be ashamed of yourself for being so unprincipled as to still have principles.

The silence was broken.

"Full livery is now costing us over six thousand pounds. Then there's the vet's and dental fees, not to mention insurance and worming. No wonder we are broke."

Arabella's fake accent drove Rob mad. Squaur instead of Square, Mummeeeee, thinkinnnnnng, interestinnnnng, famileeeee.

"The ends of your words go on forever. Where did you learn to talk like that? Das Reichsbräuteschule?"

Suzy was relieved no one knew what that was.

"And why the fuck should private schools have charitable status? They are avoiding paying over five hundred million pounds in tax in the next five years. Eton alone, hardly poor, over three million pounds."

Arabella tried to soften the tension.

"I think you have a good point Rob, but we do save the taxpayer money by not sending our girls to state schools and we do allow the poor in through bursaries."

Then turning to the others.

"Aren't the uniforms expensive now?"

It did not work.

"So, if I give money to help others like Oxfam, or don't have children at all can I avoid paying tax too?" countered Rob.

They cut their squash session short so they would have time to loosen up in The Hung Drawn And Quartered. They felt like boxers limbering up for a fight, which was how they both viewed Ellie's dinner parties. Stephen would often spur Rob on, much to Ellie's rage and embarrassment.

Even their shower was brief so they had time to relax. On placing the first pint of Harvey's carefully in front of Rob, who was checking the Saturday afternoon football results on his phone, Stephen exclaimed.

"Guess who I had as a new customer in outpatients yesterday afternoon? I won't be breaking confidentiality, or not much anyway, by telling you. No names of course."

"Blimey, Palace won again. This must be a mistake," said Rob.

"Neither of us were around in the fifties when this happened, but are you aware of the scandal around the old Lord Montagu of Beaulieu?'

"Of vintage car museum fame? Died a few years ago?"

"Yes that's right. You know he was gay? Well, the third Baron wasn't convicted when he first hit the headlines, some hanky-panky with a boy scout in a beach hut on the Solent. He was caught with an RAF serviceman and got twelve months in 1954 with Michael Pitt-Rivers and Peter Wildeblood. It was one of their lovers I saw today in clinic! They got off by turning Queen's evidence, an appropriate phrase, against the same law that destroyed Oscar Wilde, the 1533 *Buggery Act*! A law even then four hundred and twenty-one years old! Interesting man who despite being ninety was more articulate than me. Made my clinic overrun by an hour! He held court keeping me and the nurses enthralled. We didn't want to stop him. RAF's version of Quentin Crisp. He credited Peter Wildeblood for getting the world to accept homosexuality, and starting the de-criminalisation process. Wildeblood was a journalist who was with them. He got convicted and was sent to the Scrubs for eighteen months. The book *Against the Law* was the result. He told us a thousand men were locked up each year, often caught by undercover officers acting as agent provocateurs. The name Pitt-Rivers may ring a bell if you've been to Oxford, which obviously you have. His great grandfather Augustus' ethnographic collection formed the basis of the Pitt-Rivers Museum. And his dad George was the eugenicist and anti-Semite who was interned in 1940 under *Defence Regulation 18B*."

"I knew about Augustus. I took my daughters there on one of my first weekends with them after breaking up from Jenny. Bored rigid they were. Has an eleven metre phallic symbol there called the Haida totem pole."

"I bet you didn't describe it like that to them?"

"No. After I told them that strictly speaking it is a crest pole and not a totem pole and is carved from Canadian Red Cedar they just wanted to go home to their Mum."

"Not surprised," said Stephen who continued, "Pitt-Rivers went on to marry George Orwell's widow. Sorry, I'm digressing, but not as much as you. Of course this destroyed poor old Alan Turing. One of the most brilliant minds ever brought down by ignorance, intolerance and prejudice. The man recently voted the most iconic global figure of the twentieth century. Forced to have hormone injections. Do you believe Apple's denials that their logo, an apple with a bite taken out, was not inspired by Turing's cyanide-laced apple found next to his body? I don't."

"Does seem a coincidence too far," replied Rob. "I'm worried about you Stephen. You haven't asked how the Albion got on?" said Rob trying to be serious.

"They're not playing 'til tomorrow. My misery starts then," replied Stephen.

"Have you visited Bletchley Park?" asked Rob in an effort to make sure Stephen knew he was not being dismissive of his tales.

Stephen shook his head.

"It's been on my list for quite some time especially now they've restored Hut 8 with Alan Turing's office."

"I took Suzy there last December. She was more interested in why jasmines and azaleas were appearing by the lake in winter than going into his hut. I'm going to give up persuading her to come out with me for the day, too much hassle. Too much moaning."

"That doesn't sound too positive for a newly-wed," said Stephen with genuine concern.

"Oh, it's not that bad. It has its compensations. I got married as she said she would feel more secure. Now I realise that meant more secure in being a control freak."

"Well, you know what they say? If you put a penny in a jar for every time you make love before getting married, then take one out for every time after, you never empty the jar."

It was clear the days of bragging about women and sex were over for the two ex-Brockley lads. Now they just commiserated with each other.

"Do you know they've even got a mug chained to the radiator like Turing had? What I found fascinating was learning about some of the other unsung heroes like Bill Tutte and Tommy Flowers. They decoded the Lorenz cipher, one of the German Geheimschreiber systems, called 'Tunny' by us, and much more complex than *Enigma*. Flowers designed *Colossus*, the world's first programmable electronic computer. Bloody heroes."

"I've heard of Gordon Welshman," added Stephen, quite pleased with himself, "Another forgotten genius of Bletchley Park. What is disgraceful is the way he, Turing and Oppenheimer were treated by their countries. Instead of recognition for their part in winning the war, they were treated like criminals. Says more about the politicians and officials who persecuted them. Hawking being derided by that jerk of a Health Secretary nowadays follows the same pattern. Geniuses versus bigots, lions versus donkeys, with all due respect to donkeys."

Rob seized his chance to interject.

"Auberon Waugh said, and it makes sense, that *anyone who puts himself forward to be elected to a position of political power is almost certainly bound to be socially or emotionally insecure, or criminally motivated, or mad.*"

Stephen paused. It was obvious he wanted to move on, but not before reminding Rob that Waugh helped expose Jeremy Thorpe and his plot to murder his lover, during which his ex-lover's dog was shot. Waugh stood against Thorpe for The Dog Lovers' Party at the 1979 General Election.

"Anyway, back to my patient. He went on to explain how his case contributed to forcing the Home Secretary at the time to set up the Wolfenden Committee. Old Sir David Maxwell Fyfe fought other Tories to get the committee going despite saying that he was to launch a new drive against this male vice that would rid England of this plague. He sat at the Nuremberg Trials and cross-examined Herman Goering apparently. But all that was recommended was a policy of non-prosecution in certain circumstances. There was never any question of legalisation. Maxwell Fyfe still declared homosexuality as morally repugnant. What really was morally repugnant is that he refused to commute Derek Bentley's death sentence. You know, the case where a policeman was shot during a bungled burglary attempt. He was apparently mentally substandard, illiterate and an epileptic, ideal to serve the purposes of the Establishment. Crime solved and perpetrator punished. He got his pardon in 1998 though, forty-five years later, so that's all right. He was Rex Harrison's brother-in-law, but I digress."

Rob looked bemused.

"Who? Bentley?"

"No, Maxwell Fyfe dopey."

"Just you wait, Henry 'iggins, just you wait," sang Rob.

The alcohol was taking effect.

"Another who had pancreatic cancer," said Stephen staring into his beer.

"Who? Maxwell Fyfe?"

"No, Rex Harrison you bonehead."

"Do you think there is a connection to having six wives?" joked Rob again.

"Almost certainly. Back to my patient. He was extremely angry the *Wolfenden Report* was shelved for ten years. The third Baron, otherwise known as Edward Douglas-Scott-Montagu, was in the Grenadier Guards who seem to crop up often in these stories. He left the Bullingdon Club after a fight. Surely fighting was what they did? When I got home, quite late due to this, and having to pacify a few angry impatient patients, I checked it out on the Web. He certainly got his facts right, bright as a button mentally. Maxwell Fyfe was at Oxford with Bob Boothby too, this Lord who had that long affair with Macmillan's wife. Shows more Establishment hypocrisy. Maxwell Fyfe must have known of Boothby's bisexuality but turned a blind eye, whilst at the same time locking up thousands of men. Hypocrisy or maybe Boothby had something on Maxwell Fyfe!"

Stephen finished his monologue and there was a short period of silence. Rob then remembered what he had been meaning to ask his better-informed colleague for some time.

"This corporate takeover of public health policy, clearly every sensible medic knows the vested interests will damage the health of the nation. The shortsighted cuts are like stripping the lead off the roof to make buckets to catch the rainwater. We are going backwards and the profit motive will kill people. What do you think we can do?"

Stephen was back to one of his pet subjects.

"Well, we have to try to shame the politicians, but whether the public will realise how important this is, is another matter. Our local council has shares in the tobacco industry, public buildings including hospitals make money from selling sugar water in their vending machines, the schools are surrounded by fast food places, and the Government is giving in to the alcohol and food industries. They won't introduce a minimum price for alcohol or tackle childhood obesity seriously. The alcohol companies are following in the footsteps of their tobacco friends by bending the advertising rules. Some type of alcohol advertising occurred once every other minute during a Euro 2016 match. Some more facts for you, UK obesity rates are ten times what they were in 1972. That date is not a coincidence. It was about then that the food industry tried to get everyone on a different type of fat, compensated by loading in invisible sugar into everything."

Rob agreed.

"You won't believe this but I had some pickled herring the other day, and even that had sugar added! Why the fuck would you want to sweeten pickled fish?"

"Its no wonder sugar consumption is up thirty-one point five per cent since 1990. World diabetes has doubled. You remember nobody mentioned Yudkin when we were undergraduates. Shows how powerful these lobbyists can be and end up corrupting science. Fortunately a brave American endocrinologist called Robert Lustig has taken up his torch and calls sugar a poison. He shocked many when he called it, *an addictive toxin that creates an irresistible urge to eat.* That lecture of his *Sugar: The Bitter Truth* went viral on YouTube six or seven years ago. He is brave as it ended Yudkin's career and the food industry's front groups have funded biased research to attack him. Coca-Cola funded two thirds of the studies trying to discredit him. All we can do is to keep telling people this. It's difficult to think we have any influence though. We are up against major multinationals with no morals, scruples or ethics that have governments and the media in their pockets. They seem to be able to do what they like to maximise profits including taking people out if necessary."

This all rang a bell with Rob.

"Oh, I remember now. Yes, I read the BMJ recently believe it or not. They ran a story about how Coca-Cola funded journalism conferences to create favourable press coverage of sugar-sweetened drinks. They were peddling hard the myth that consuming their products was fine just as long as you exercised, which we all know is bollocks. For them, the energy-balance message has been a crucial one to cultivate and they've all been at it for years. They have been very successful. Many believe their propaganda that obesity is more a consequence of inactivity than it is of regularly drinking liquid candy. At these conferences, industry meetings framed as science, the journalists bought into it and spread the word in their articles."

"The tobacco industry did the same," added Stephen, "They derailed the 1993 report on second-hand smoke by placing stories in major publications about the report's scientific weaknesses."

"So we are back to as we thought," said Rob with an air of despair, "We are all controlled by a group of bastards who will lie and cheat to get things done and to feather their own nests. Those things often damage fellow mankind, animals and the environment, and if they are allowed to continue will destroy the planet. You heard Trump is to repeal Obama's legislation limiting mercury emissions from coal-fired power plants? He calls coal beautiful and clean. We are doomed."

"I can give you another example of where we have been totally conned and lied to. The end justifies the means as the saying goes. You know we were told the growing infection rates in hospitals were our fault. Our white coats, our long sleeve shirts, our ties, and our watches all spreading bugs around the place, despite us being dressed like that for over a century. So all had to go. But it's all complete bollocks. There is not a shred of evidence that this was the cause, but the real causes were crowded wards, A&E overspill, inadequate clinical staff, lack of isolation facilities, poor cleaning, a disinterest in infection control, and all constitute a rather costly challenge to put right. Lopping off all those cuffs was the easiest and cheapest thing to do. As far as the managers and politicians were concerned there was an added bonus to this cost-free approach. It demeaned the status of doctors in the eyes of the general public. We all carried too much respect and authority and this was a simple way of knocking us down a peg or two. And they no longer had to pay for washing the white coats! A win, win, win situation with us losing, losing, losing. But that's not new. Now though, we take all the bugs home with us and infect our loved ones."

"Fucking hell, I never even thought to question that," Rob was quite staggered.

"But we as professionals are quite gullible too. Quite understandably we swallow what we are taught. We tend to trust our teachers. They trust the syllabus. But this makes us culpable. Take diabetes, again we are taught to lower blood sugars and we therefore put a lot of effort into this. But that's all we are doing for our diabetic patients. We are pushing the sugar away from where it can be seen into their bodies where it can't be seen and not improving

414

outcomes at all. The corrupt organisations change the definition of diabetes and pre-diabetes to drag millions more into the net, so millions more to treat. Lantus insulin alone makes Sanofi over seven point five billion dollars and doesn't stop the complications one bit."

To hear the gospel according to all his wise teachers discredited and overturned so simply shocked Rob again, but he had heard the theories - that this teaching suited Big Pharma and they were not going to allow it to seem credible. They destroyed Yudkin and they would not let Lustig or Jason Fung, who exposed the corruption, off the hook easily. Rob moved on.

"Cleaning was of course one of the first things they privatised about thirty years ago. Been a disaster. Bring back the ward sister that's what I say. Then the individual ward was under her authority and she had responsibility for everything that happened. This included the cleaning. The cleaners were attached to the ward, trained by the ward sister, were part of the team, and took a pride in their work, chatted to the patients."

"You are right. It worked. But fucking politicians have egos and personality disorders that make them want to change things. They don't understand the 'if it ain't broke don't fix it' idiom. Their stupid motto is 'no change is not an option'. Yes it fucking is an option, and often the best. Wankers. Look what a cock up the *Dangerous Dogs Act* was. A completely useless law brought in as a knee-jerk reaction. Legislate in haste, repent at leisure. I'm waiting for them to ban all sandwiches because one poor sod choked on his BLT."

"A bacteriologist looked at the effect of this crap on infection rates. Yes, the incidence of the two the Health Secretary got his knickers in a twist about, Clostridium difficile and MRSA, did indeed fall, but other ward infections showed no change. And C diff at home was rising. There must have been a load of white coats loitering in the bushes ready to pounce."

"Remember all those so-called anti-bacterial gels at hospital entrances? They made you feel anti-social if you didn't use them even though they did fuck all, certainly doesn't kill off C Diff. Who had shares in them? And surprise, surprise they are not there now!"

"Advertising bullshit again," added Rob, "Some claim to kill ninety-nine point nine per cent of household germs. Considering organisms live in communities of ten hundred billion, that still leaves a billion!"

Stephen was on his hobbyhorse again.

"Of course no politician is interested in evidence, unless it suits their purposes. Decide on the policy and what they want to do and then look for the evidence that supports their case. The rest? Ignore at best, cover up at worst."

"Then lie when challenged," continued Rob, "When they know they are wrong they try to discredit the experts. Have you noticed this campaign to make the public distrust scientists? Like I mentioned with Turing, Oppenheimer and Welshman. It's like the Yorkshire Ripper telling you not to go near or trust Nelson Mandela as he might kill you. And they do all this with straight faces. The Health Secretary thought we should trust his scientific expertise above that of Prof Hawking. What a deluded prat. When a well-respected distinguished *Fellow of the Royal Society* and genius said the UK is heading towards a US-style health insurance system run by private companies, and the cornerstone of our society that is the NHS, is being destroyed, then that's exactly what is happening. But an arrogant privileged multimillionaire sailor's son who is a distant relation to Oswald Mosley and the Queen and failed in a business to export marmalade to Japan thinks we should believe him, and that the world famous scientist is wrong!"

"Yes, Hawking had a brain the size of a planet and no axe to grind and was in the pay of no one against a duplicitous politician who breached expenses rules avoids tax and blamed the football supporters for the Hillsborough tragedy. No contest."

Rob and Stephen had become a double act.

"And talk about a bunch of self-serving gits! Most Prime Ministers end up with reputations in the gutter right? But when in power, no matter what policy they dreamt up as their own personal 'I'm my own-man' shit, usually without any mandate, their sycophantic MPs backed it and defended him or her to the death. Once gone and out of power however, they are easy prey. The same

MPs wait until they see if they feature in the resignation honours first, then once any possible advantage of staying friends has gone, it's back to looking after themselves, attacking those who are now no value to them, attacking the policies they previously defended, thereby practising their skill at trying to prove black is white."

"There are a few honourable exceptions, Stephen. But ironically they are the ones labelled as fruitcakes by the media, when they should be going for the corrupt," argued back Rob.

"Bernard Crick in his book *In Defence of Politics* argued quite correctly that low politics was the cornerstone of democracy and essential to holding governments to account. Without politicians, democracy would be surrendered to technocrats and vested interests," said Stephen getting more serious, "The problem is that I believe that was the case when he wrote it over fifty years ago but now the politicians are the technocrats and vested interests, or at least their representatives," he concluded, "but back to your point of the media going for the corrupt. They do, but only very selectively. They leave their allies alone. The media is run by unelected, unaccountable tyrants and big business, which make them corrupt to serve their own purposes. They are in each other's pockets. They are not going to condemn their own yes men are they?"

"And yes women," said Rob, in his Eric Idle *Life of Brian* voice.

"They then hunt in packs like fucking hyenas."

"And the women hyenas," added Rob mockingly, taking another sip of *Harveys*, "These personality defects collectively are what is called The Government. It cuts nurses, cuts doctors, cuts prison officers, and cuts social care, all against expert advice. Then a few years later when it realised it had cocked up, they announce they will recruit more and want the credit for increasing staff from, of course, a low they created in the first place. Incompetent, shifty shysters. They work on the principle that no one will remember, and the media help them out for their own purposes."

"The thing is," pondered Stephen, "to answer your question, what can be done? My guess is nothing. We are all impotent and at the mercy of these ignorant gits who are stupid enough to end the world. I'm not sure the human race has made much progress in the last few millennia."

"Have we time for another quick one?" wondered Rob, "Don't forget I have to go to pick Suzy up."

"Of course. Just!"

Stephen was on a conspiracy roll but rolling back towards one of his own pet hates, the pharmaceutical industry.

"There's a small crumb of comfort to be had when truth prevails, but even then the guilty generally get away with it, so it's no consolation. Take that apparent swine flu epidemic of a few years ago. You and I knew what was going on, but the media either fell for it or were complicit. Simple but very effective moneymaking exercise. Scare the public shitless that we are all going to die of this superbug, then convince everyone, governments included, that the way out of the end of the world is to vaccinate everyone. And I mean everyone! What a money-spinner! The vaccine doesn't even have to be that expensive to make billions for the company if everyone needs a dose, or preferably two to be sure. It doesn't even have to work that well, or perhaps at all! Then we eventually learn that there are strong financial links between the drug company and Government ministers, officials at the Department of Health, the World Health Organisation, and so on. And back handers and bribes to the media too. So a manufactured crisis."

"Yes, I think they did a smaller trial run of this years ago over meningitis. Same approach. Worked like a dream. Get the media to scare people that a deadly bug is on every street corner waiting to pounce and then they fall over themselves to get their kids vaccinated. The company makes millions. The only time I have felt really threatened in the consulting room was when I told a dad his five year old wasn't at risk and according to the guidelines didn't qualify for protection. The Minister hadn't been nobbled that time. He didn't actually touch me but gave me the Alex Ferguson hair-drier treatment, shouting in my face.

We have too much medicine, as you know," Stephen continued, "Our profession used to offer false advice and useless treatments, but on the whole unknowingly and in good faith, when we didn't have the understanding of disease and lacked any effective remedies. Open the windows and get some fresh air, was the advice. Now there is an epidemic of misinformed doctors and patients and this is deliberate. The root cause is the biased funding of research, the suppression of negative study results, the gullible reporting in the medical journals and the media and of course the commercial conflicts of interest. All designed to boost Pharma profits. Good old capitalism, eh? Then they rip off the NHS with inflated drug costs and get their reps on the boards of some of our biggest hospitals. Infiltrating bastards. Another pint?"

Stephen was in a more relaxed mood than Rob had seen him for a while despite the subjects they were exploring. Sometimes the conversation did not flow easily and Rob found it an effort. Stephen often seemed distracted. Not this evening.

"I've not heard the expression 'the man on the Clapham Omnibus' for some time. Shows our age, I suppose."

"Goes back to a legal judgement in 1903," Rob added with a satisfied grin. "In Australia they refer to the man on the Bondi tram."

"Oh fuck! Look at the time! Ellie will kill me. People will be arriving in half an hour. Fuck!"

They had finished their pints but were too absorbed in putting the world to rights to realise how long they had been sitting at the bar. On the way out to their cars Rob said he had wanted to hear more about that English journalist he mentioned last time who disappeared, and his mate who started a new political party, but they both knew that would have to wait. Tradition was never forgotten though, even if their wives were to kill them.

"Okay GP, what's Walking Corpse Syndrome?" asked Stephen as he unlocked his Mini.

"What our current Prime Minister has?" queried Rob.

"It's a rare neurological disorder. Sufferers believe they are dead, do not exist, or are rotting."

"Oh, not the PM then but the Health Secretary."

Rob's turn.

"Alice in Wonderland Syndrome?"

"Haven't a clue," replied Stephen.

"Another neurological one. People can't judge correctly the size of objects in their visual field. See you later. If you're still alive, that is."

Suzy was dressed and waiting by the time Rob came through the front door to collect her. She realised she would have to drive to Stephen and Ellie's as Rob had clearly already drunk too much. He was not popular as she thought it was her turn to have a few. When they arrived it was obvious Stephen was in the doghouse too. He got home just as the first guests were arriving. So the evening did not start too well and continued to go downhill.

Stephen thought it fun to bring up controversial subjects - one after another. He wanted to see Rob in full flow. It was not long before he got his reward. Ellie knew what he was up to and tried to delay the inevitable by steering the conversation into calmer waters. At her famous dinners Ellie was known as the master, or rather mistress, of flitting from one subject to another without warning. The topic could be the heart breaking tour of Auschwitz done whilst visiting Krakow and Shindler's factory, or the Manchester terrorist attack and Ellie would suddenly cut across the conversation.

"Do you know how much vets charge for our cat's flea stuff nowadays? It's terrible."

Not quite in the same league as being gassed or blown up though. Like any inebriated person Rob thought he was being more eloquent, articulate and humorous than he actually was. He kicked off by asking all assembled whose side they were on, that of Thomas Paine or Edmund Burke? When he got no answer, just looks of bewilderment, he answered for them.

"I bet Burke, eh? Possibly in favour of liberty, but not equality. There's no way you lot would want a revolution to promote egalitarianism is there? No Lenin or Lennon here."

"I'm with you on this one old friend," said Stephen, coming to the rescue of civility, "I read *The Rights of Man* as a student. Paine's ideal society is one that resembles the modern welfare state in which the care of the poor and the elderly is a right and not a form of charity."

That's when one of the other guests fell into their trap.

"But don't you think the welfare state has had its day?"

"Who's this twat?" Rob whispered to Arabella, knowing very well who he was.

The problem was his whisper was too loud. Ellie started to worry that her dinner party would end in tears so just told the others Rob was a Trot and to just ignore him. It did not help improve the tension and atmosphere when Rob, who had had too much of the dessert wine asked if anyone around the table could actually define Trot.

"What were Leon Trotsky's main beliefs and principles? Anyone know? Let me demonstrate that all around this table are Marxists really and you don't even know it."

They were all prepared to indulge him, as he was being reasonably polite.

"Now, I believe only nutty zealots would argue against a classless society being something to strive for. Anyone disagree?"

Rob didn't wait. He was not going to give them a chance.

"And most would support a progressive tax system, not one that penalises the poor, eh? The heaviest burden should fall on the wealthiest, not those on the breadline. Agreed? Agreed?"

They were all with him so far.

"And what about education? I know you lot all pay to give your kids an advantage in life, but if that standard of education was free and available to all, my money is on the fact that you would not object. Correct? Correct? So you all believe in free public education."

Rob was surprising himself. He really was quite fluent, and believed he was winning.

"Do you like feudalism and think child labour is a pretty neat thing? No? Well, that's all in *The Communist Manifesto*."

There were blank faces around the table. Arabella's jaw was half way down her chest.

"So, on to what is happening now. Fact, the gap between rich and poor is widening, strengthening the class system. Considering the rich are in a small minority, the vast majority would say enough is enough, wouldn't you agree? Time to take back control. Now you are getting frightened, eh? Real workers, not those who just shuffle paper in the city all day long, sorry if that's you, should be admired and better rewarded."

"Would anyone like more Tarte Tatin or Coffee Crème Brulee?" said Ellie trying to break Rob's concentration, and hoping one of the other guests would stop him by asking her for the recipe.

It only served to make him more determined and louder.

"So, most caring and altruistic people wouldn't argue against all that," he continued.

There were mumbles, grudgingly agreeing.

"Well, I've just described a lot of what Marx and Engels put in *The Communist Manifesto* of 1848. Surprised? So you are all Marxists and you didn't know it."

"I'm not," said Arabella.

"But I heard you earlier suggesting that renationalising the railways might not be such a bad thing."

"Well, they can't be worse than now, can they?"

"I rest my case. You are all Trots like me. That's why the opponents have put so much energy into discrediting all this with just abuse, as, if it were properly analysed, it might catch on and they are scared stiff of that."

"The Mocha Pots De Crème must all go," said Ellie.

"Marx may have put it in more strident terms and the media will emphasise that to make it all sound extremist, but it all amounts to the same thing. For instance working men of all countries unite. The history of all hitherto existing societies is the history of class struggle. Political power is merely the organised power of one class for oppressing another. The proletarians have nothing to lose but their chains."

Stephen wanted to join in.

"In *Mein Kampf* Hitler said democracy inevitably leads to Marxism and we all believe in democracy, don't we?"

"Game, set and match," said Rob, "Let the ruling classes tremble at a Communistic revolution."

"Oh, hold on. I think that's all twaddle," said the guest who thought the welfare state had had its day "I really don't follow your logic... or lack of..."

Then interrupting himself.

"I'll have some of that Tarte Tatin, please Ellie."

As far as Rob was concerned, that debate was over. He'd made his point.

"So I bet no one here really knows who Trotsky was. His name has been turned into a form of abuse to stop debate and anyone learning what his ideas were," Rob said calmly trying not to slur his words. "You are trapped within the Overton window of your middle class comfort zone. Whatever happened to Leon Trotsky?

"Ice pick anyone? Cream, Rob?" asked Ellie.

The evening did not go well. On parting Rob got the last word.

"You complain about the cost of school uniforms? I have to get a new Manchester United shirt every year. What a rip-off."

Suzy scolded him on their way home but Rob was too inebriated to pay any attention. He was concentrating on his out-of-tune accompaniment to Tracy Chapman's *Talking About A Revolution*, which was playing.

'While they're standing in the welfare lines,
Crying at the doorsteps of those armies of salvation,
Wasting time in the unemployment lines,
Sitting around waiting for a promotion.
Poor people gonna rise up and get their share,
Poor people gonna rise up and take what's theirs."

"Shut up Rob... I wouldn't mind so much if you could sing, but you sound like a rooster with flu."

"Too pissed to care," he said. "You knowa... hic... I 'ate deese middleclass self-congratuatin' shug, I mean smug dinna parties where they are soooo insecure they 'ave to try to out doo each other. We should be glad we 'ave grown outofem. More important tings in life. Hic. All claiming they are soooo fucking poor with the burden of deir school fees, the town 'ouse, the Tuscan villa and the stab... hic... les."

423

The radio went to the next track.

"Hey… this is Ellie…listen," Rob went straight into Hall and Oates' *Rich Girl*.

"You're a rich girl and you've gone too far,
'Cause you know it don't matter anyway.
You can rely on your old man's money.
You can rely on your old man's money."

"That's like a dying cow on helium."

Rob couldn't remember much the next day.

33 - PAST AND PRESENT

DO ANYTHING YOU WANNA DO

I don't need no politicians to tell me things I shouldn't do
Neither no opticians to tell me what I oughta see
No one tells you nothing even when you know they know
They tell you what you should be
They don't like to see you grow

Eddie And The Hot Rods (1977)

Another evening. Another squash game. Another pub session.

Rob tried to reassure himself that he should get away with two pints, but knowing it was wishful thinking. More of a concern was the thought he should have gone to the loo before leaving the pub. The discomfort was growing. The journey home from The Hung Drawn And Quartered was short but down dark country lanes. There was a sharp S bend half way with potholes where he knew he had to be careful. He was going slowly because of this, but actually more so because the car behind was driving too close and blinding him with headlights. He was not going to be intimidated.

"You can wait, you tosser!" he shouted, knowing no one could hear.

After a few more bends there was a sudden thumping noise and the car veered to the left. He knew instantly his tyre had blown.

"Bloody pot holes. Bloody Council. Fucking austerity Government cutting everything. Fuck, fuck!" Then, "Double fuck!"

He then realised his Seat Leon had run-flats with no spare wheel and that he did not know how to use the spray and all the stuff to give it a temporary repair. It was one of those jobs he kept meaning to do... RTFM... Read The Fucking Manual. Pity he did not even understand what run-flats meant.

He quickly ground to a halt knowing he was in a dangerous place on the S bend. More alarmingly, the car that had been tailgating him pulled up and stopped within a metre of his boot. Maybe to help.

Maybe not. A man dressed in black jumped out. Now Rob felt scared. Was this a set up? Was he about to be robbed? Even with those thoughts he still had the *Milk Tray* chocolate advert from the seventies flit into his mind, where a stud dressed in black delivered chocolates to a gorgeous woman. That was for only a second. He was not a gorgeous woman and the man certainly was not carrying chocolates. However reassurance came mercifully rapidly when the man spoke.

"Hi Robert."

Rob held his hand up to block the glare of his headlights. He could see another man now who remained in the driving seat, but he could not work out who the friendly one was. He emerged from the glare like *ET* out of the spacecraft.

"Sorry to have to stop you like that but it's time we introduced ourselves to you."

Rob felt safe enough to be annoyed now.

"Well why couldn't you ring me like a normal person, not blow my fucking car up?"

"All will become clear. And assistance is on its way to repair your car. You will be home in ten minutes. You won't recognise me since my surgery. I couldn't get a job as good as Luiz Carlos Da Rocha, who runs the massive cocaine empire in South America, as we only know a few bent plastic surgeons but I do change my identity fairly often. My favourite was Winston Smith from Orwell's *1984*, but that became too easy for the enemy. I'm Nick at the moment but I was Jerry when you last saw me nearly thirty years ago. Jerry Dolan. You will of course be sceptical, so here's the test. Peppermint Park, Keith Moon, Crystal Palace. And now Amy Winehouse has joined the 27 Club. You know I just disappeared from our school in Purley one day, yes? I was never *summa cum laude* material, was I?"

If Rob was the sort to put on an expression of open-mouthed astonishment, this was the moment - but not he. He was however, getting increasingly concerned about the size of his bladder.

"You haven't changed much Rob. But we've been watching you and hearing you are waking up to what is happening in the real world and who runs it. Twenty-plus years later than me, but better late than never. I gave up on you then. You were too respectable, a GP, who would have believed it. But now we think you can be trusted after careful vetting. That goes on for at least six months so any strange events, tailing, following you can put down to us."

"Gee, thanks," mocked Rob.

Rob wondered whether this was one of Stephen's practical jokes. Only he knew about the squash game. He had even forgotten to tell Suzy, so had it in his mind he might be in trouble with her. Then he snapped back into reality and thought it stupid to worry about Suzy's reaction compared to being forcibly stopped in the middle of nowhere, by someone he does not recognise, claiming to be an old school friend. Anyway Stephen did not know Jerry Dolan.

"Who's we, and why should I believe you? More important, what do you want?"

"Never mind who we are. I'll fill in the detail later. Enough to know we are a large organisation fighting the evil forces covertly controlling the world now. You won't hear about us anywhere or learn of our successes. We are suppressed in the media. We are flattered though that in private they called us Poison. Apparently as they knew our aim was and is to poison their plan. So the name stuck. All the security forces are trying to destroy us. We are a threat to their goals and control and they take us seriously enough to snuff us out at every opportunity. We recruit all the time and you appeared on our target list."

"You are joking. Is this *You've Been Framed?* Did Jeremy Beadle not really die… it's you? And what corny old B category Sci-Fi movie did you take the line 'fighting the evil forces'?" Anyway what possible use could I be? I'm just a local GP, as you obviously know, who's pissed off with everything and everyone telling me how to run my life. I'm not cut out to be James Bond and I really need a piss."

Rob's mocking was ignored again.

"Okay Darth Wader, get out of the headlights so we can talk properly."

Rob was surprising himself with his confidence and daring but realised he might be in danger. Nick or Jerry turned suddenly away from the road as another car passed them, then moved to the grass

427

verge. Rob could see he was the right size for Jerry and sounded a bit like him.

"Well, at least I know I've got the right man. Your sense of humour is the same. Always the one to take the mickey. But listen carefully Robert. We have to end this little chat soon. I could tell you tales that would make your hair stand on end. Orwell was right with *1984* but he underestimated the scale. We are really resistance fighters and we have infiltrated many Establishment organisations, but we need to survive, consolidate and make further progress, as much as we can. Everything depends on it. Just one or two examples for you to convince you that you are on the right track and you should join us. Willing to listen?"

"Have I any choice?"

"Not if you know what's good for you. The first conspiracy that impressed me and got me into this world was the Airey Neave murder. You will remember we were at the Eddie And The Hotrods concert at the Rainbow when we heard about an MP being blown up. The crowd burst into song with Gloria Gaynor's *I Will Survive*, which was a bit sick. But it was number one. Remember? Now only I could know that. Anyway, we found out later that he had been blown up as he drove his car out of the Houses of Parliament two days after Callaghan had been brought down in 1979. He had lost a vote of no confidence in the Commons. As usual the IRA were blamed. They've been a very useful scapegoat over the years. Turns out it was more complicated than that. Neave believed the security forces were corrupt and had probably been penetrated by the Soviets. He was looking into the possible prosecution of senior figures in the intelligence Establishment, so MI6 and the CIA had him killed. Enoch Powell thought it was the Americans who killed him and also Mountbatten five months later in County Sligo, as he was a thorn in their side too. Blew his legs almost right off. They were behind the killing of Sykes and the attempt on Tugendhat who were deputies to Neave and helping him out. The Tugendhat dynasty continues, as his nephew is now an MP. So you see, I keep up to date. The IRA's Thomas McMahon spent nineteen years in prison for killing Mountbatten. They wanted to take the credit. They knew he visited Kincora Boys' Home. The IRA got the blame for the Brighton bomb too which nearly killed Thatcher and half the cabinet, but that was us."

Rob flashed back to his bad dream. He was at Peppermint Park and Jerry had told him then he would be responsible for that. He did not believe in premonitions but that was certainly one. Nick, or Jerry, was clearly going to continue, so Rob took his opportunity.

"Sorry to interrupt but I've got to take a leak."

He turned to face the hedge behind the car out of the headlight glare and unzipped. The man in black was not to be deterred and moved next to him whilst continuing to talk.

"Another one of ours was the mortar attack on Number 10 in February 1991. We also killed Ian Gow, the Eastbourne MP, in July 1990. We weren't to blame for the murders of David Kelly in 2003, Jill Dando in 1999, Robert Maxwell nor Diana, nor the attempt on the Skripals with Novichok in Salisbury, the Establishment dealt all those. Kelly was because he knew too much about the illegality of war in Iraq. They nearly blew that one with such an amateurish so-called suicide scene. That didn't fool any half competent pathologist, but they blagged their way through it. Dando was killed because she was investigating and getting too close to the paedophile ring. Maxwell was just money rather than his work for Mossad, and Di as she was a risk to the survival of the Royal family. They killed Robin Cook in 2005 for the same reason as Kelly. And the use of nerve agents was the old trick, an attempt to take the spotlight off an incompetent Government. It always works to invent a common enemy. The 'Argies' and the Falklands War, the Jews, someone else's football team, or in that case the Russians. Remember that Brazilian Jean Charles de Menezes shot at Stockwell Station in 2005? Do you know what he really had in his rucksack? Certainly not a bomb, but the full comprehensive files about the Westminster paedophile ring. Poor boy was an unwitting courier, but of course the files were never delivered. Total police incompetence though so CCTV footage went missing. We were so close to getting them. They would have blown Westminster apart as effectively as any bomb but the establishment rescued and destroyed them.

A couple of weeks before that the powers that be were getting into a real panic about all their mates being exposed. The files implicated so many in every branch of society that they feared democracy crumbling and revolution. Sounds fanciful in good old Great Britain doesn't it? About time that myth about us being the cradle of democracy and having the mother of Parliaments was shown for what it is. Arrogant rubbish. Just ask the Greeks. I digress. So to divert attention and allow stricter surveillance they arranged the July 7th so-called terrorist attacks. It was deliberately designed to create fear. So a bus was blown up in Tavistock Square with three more explosions on the Underground. Fifty-two people of eighteen different nationalities died. It worked as they hoped. It meant the public took the broad daylight, cold-blooded murder of in their stride without much questioning. The public must be protected. Two years later in 2007 two poor lads, one was a doctor incidentally, were set up at Glasgow Airport for the same reason. More recently, in an effort to get the Government re-elected, the Russians had a hand in the Westminster and London Bridge terrorist attacks. I'm not sure about the Manchester Arena bombing and, like you, I'd never heard of Ariana Grande. She has just a few years to qualify for the 27 Club though I suspect. I could go on but won't. I hope you get the gist Rob?"

Silence.

"You met our link Ian in Dorset the other day. At least that's his operations name. He will be in touch again and guide you."

Rob could not decide whether to feel more at ease now that the odd events of the last week or two made more sense, or more alarmed about being dragged into the unknown.

"You remember 'Deep Throat' from Nixon's Watergate scandal, done so well in *All The President's Men*? One of our first cinema trips together, the year before Peppermint Park. You will meet our equivalent. Not called 'Deep Throat' of course… that would be too corny. Let's call him Guy. Guy will seek you out and tell you more. Do as he says."

"And suppose I want nothing to do with all this? Then what?"

"Rob, you have to understand it's too late for that. You've already gone down the one-way street and like virginity it's not reversible. Ask the Judge. You are a resistance worker now like in the Second World War. We will look after you. In fact we already are. You will need us. To give you an example we know about the Saskia Bewering complaint. Organised by a colleague of yours called Wiekser. He doesn't like you, does he? But Bewering won't be causing you any more trouble. We have persuaded her to withdraw her complaint. And you may find Wiekser is a little easier on you. Here comes the guy to fix your tyre, time for us to go. Remember. We are like Bletchley Park. No one talks about what we do. No politician tells us what we should be or see. They don't like to see us grow."

With that Nick, or Jerry, got back into the car. Rob just had time to shout.

"Your plastic surgery has changed you from looking like Eric Morecambe to Ernie Wise, but you're not as funny. Use Da Rocha's surgeon next time."

The driver flew off even before the car door was closed.

"Evening Sir," said the rescue vehicle man, "Better fix your wheel and get you home before Suzy starts to worry."

Only five minutes later Rob pulled up onto the gravel drive. The security light went on. The next few minutes passed quickly as the light went out and he was still sitting in the car in the dark trying to take it all in. He was sweating. After another few minutes the upstairs bathroom light went on and he could see Suzy's silhouette bending over the washbasin.

"Wow, what a body," he thought, trying to return to normality. He certainly hadn't thought of sex during this ordeal, but he remembered what a turn on Suzy was. If it is true that it is every seven seconds, he had some catching up to do. He had not realised anyone in the garden could see all that went on in the bathroom. It was at the opposite end of the house and the light produced a small shadow on the lawn mixed in with the shadow from the plum tree.

Rob thought it time to go in. Should he say anything to Suzy? It was not a difficult decision. Not tonight.

As he walked up the drive, the shadow began to sway in the breeze. Intrigued, he stepped closer. Then closer. Then he saw what was responsible for the shadow. Something was hanging from the branch. He got closer. Yes, it had fur. Ginger fur. A lifeless cat had been hung with green gardening wire. Eric.

34 - PROTEST AND SURVIVE

THATCHER FUCKED THE KIDS

We're all wondering how we ended up so scared;
We spent ten long years teaching our kids not to care
And that "there's no such thing as society" anyway,
And all the rich folks act surprised
When all sense of community dies,
But you just closed your eyes to the other sidey
Of all the things that she did.
Thatcher fucked the kids.

Frank Turner (2008)

Alex Ephialtes could not see any good reason to get out of bed.

His wife had left for work an hour before and the children were at school. He had had another bad night's sleep. He could not remember the last time he slept right through the night. Years ago. No matter how he tried to clear his head and think straight his mind drifted back to the Party. If he knew what he was getting himself into all those years back he would not have stuck his head above the parapet.

Looking back there was his life pre July 2010 and then post July 2010. One fateful day those right wing bastards in Government published their ideas, which he could see straight away meant the end of the National Health Service. This was his life just about to be turned upside down. He worked as a doctor in the NHS, for the NHS, made great sacrifices for the NHS and all because he truly believed in it, more than anything else in the world, certainly in Britain. If the NHS was destroyed, he felt it no exaggeration to say, so would his life.

What amazed him was that no one else saw what he saw. In fact the proposals were presented in such a devious misleading way they were broadly welcomed. How could people be so dim, so naive, so gullible, so conned, so asleep, so complacent, so apathetic, so defeatist? Or were they fully aware and wanted the NHS to be destroyed? Were they collaborators, quislings and selfish traitors who saw something in it for them? Or was it that they had got so used to something so great they took it for granted? The generation that had no idea what life would be like without such a system? As someone whose family came from a country with an unfair healthcare system - one that was for the rich only while the poor suffered - he thought the British had become too complacent. They took it for granted and did not realise what a treasure they had. They certainly will be stunned when it is gone.

Was it worth getting out of bed, when only the day before he had read that an opinion poll suggested as few as twenty per cent of the under forties valued democracy? So, most of the new generation thought the will of the people unimportant? What system do they prefer? Dictatorship? Another treasure so fundamental but taken for granted, its value going unrecognised. That was what was happening to the NHS and all the institutions that were for the public good too. Society does not exist so the institutions are not needed. And all rich folk act surprised when all sense of community dies. Only individuals exist, and it is every man for himself. The best excuse for abolishing the welfare state, after years of propaganda coercing and brainwashing the public, that everything now has to be paid for out of one's own pocket. Universality is dead.

Or are there dark evil forces out there that are acting to persuade and convince the masses of the previously unacceptable and unthinkable? Democracy is an out of date concept. The earth is flat. The disabled should be wiped out. The poor deserve their fate. China should be bombed. The unthinkable is now becoming mainstream. How many millions have died fighting for democracy and all for nothing? Do people understand what is happening?

Was it worth getting out of bed when he felt so helpless? Was it worth getting out of bed when he could not change a thing and the unfair voting system meant even the majority could not change a thing? One stupid species has become dominant over all the others, is eliminating others, and is destroying the world. Pigs should take over. Every day there seemed to be bad news. The latest was the report he had just read from the Institute for Public Policy Research that highlighted the failure of politicians to recognise that human impacts on the environment had reached a critical stage. Our complacent leaders were negligent in ignoring the likely catastrophic outcomes, which include economic instability, large-scale involuntary migration, conflict, famine, and then the collapse of the social and economic systems. Could it be more depressing? Of course. Another report had humans destroying all insect life within a century at the current rate of decline threatening the total collapse of nature's ecosystems. Alex understood that we are destroying the very life support systems that allow us to sustain our very existence on the planet, along with all other life.

Alex felt beaten. Evil had won. What was the point? They had been so, so clever. With skillful manipulation they can get the masses to believe anything. *Die Religion... ist das Opium des Volkes* to paraphrase Karl Marx. Still true, thought Alex, but it has moved beyond that.

To get the masses to act like sheep required the discrediting of good things so they were thought to be bad. Democracy is discredited when a bigoted, nasty, idiot is elected US President and he appoints a Secretary of State from Exxon Mobil, a Health Secretary who wants to restrict healthcare, an Education Secretary who does not believe in Education, and a climate change denier to the Environmental Agency. Then he bans whole nations from the USA, except surprise, surprise, those he owns hotels in, and our arse-licking PM will not condemn him. What have we become? We are up shit creek without a paddle.

Is this all deliberate so people think democracy does not work, so it is not worth bothering about? How come the world elects leaders it despises? Are the leaders now just for entertainment so we discuss them and not the issues? Are they just camouflage? Alex just felt like shouting from the rooftops democracy does work, it has just never been tried. Alex too had heard what they feared, that it would lead to Marxism. So the lunatics take over the asylum. Was this the birth of a new age in which left and right often looks bizarrely similar? Alex wondered how the champions of Brexit could sound like

French revolutionaries denouncing elitist enemies of the people. He had read Karl Marx's essay *The Eighteenth Brumaire of Louis Napoleon*, in which he claims the new often wears the robes of the past. A conquest borrows the garb of liberation, a right wing reaction dresses itself as a peasants' revolt. The black swan theory where events come as a surprise, have major effects and are inappropriately rationalised with hindsight, are not surprises to those who orchestrated them. Everything is planned. That was now Alex's depressing conclusion.

Back in 2010, a few weeks of listening to his colleagues pontificating about how clinicians would be put back in charge was enough for Alex. How could they be so stupid and fall for that? Did they really believe politicians and managers would voluntarily give up their power? So he chose his moment and at one BMA meeting he let them have it. Both barrels. He laid into the complacency with an aggression he did not know he had. He said they prostituted themselves as their principles melted away as soon as the money was right. Except most prostitutes were better looking and not so hypocritical.

His fellow doctors were stunned especially coming from a youngster who had his career to think about. They were having to listen to views they had not thought of, did not want to think about, and to most of them were paranoid fantasy. There was little response, but their attitude changed. Colleagues he had known for years started to give him a wide berth. Some asked if he was all right? How was he bearing up? Was everything all right at home? Should he have a break? The medical world being small, incestuous gossip spread about an eccentric called Ephialtes. Some labelled him an extremist. But a few weeks later he got a call from a public health doctor at the other end of the county he had heard of but did not know, Benedict Arnold. He wanted to meet.

A year later the Save The National Health Service Party was officially launched. Alex and Benedict were confirmed as joint leaders and they had a membership of over four hundred after some press coverage, not the mainstream press who were not interested, but the medical comics. An Executive Committee was formed which included his mate Jim Auger, but they were mainly self-selecting, as not many wanted to commit the time. He met some good people. Established authors, dedicated NHS workers, journalists, plenty of champagne socialists and those who had offered more genuine sacrifices from generations of fighters. They did quite well and had some minor breakthroughs with a few media stories. These were achieved mainly because of a very professional volunteer press officer who had lots of contacts and was very committed to the cause. Without her they might have fizzled out.

The Party gained some notoriety with its campaign against the privatisation of the ambulance service. In Kent G4S were running them and boasted about it with the slogan, 'G4S WORKING IN PARTNERSHIP WITH THE NHS IN KENT AND MEDWAY'. Jim Auger, a sexual health specialist, produced stickers that went over the words 'in partnership with' saying 'to rip off'. For a whole week dozens of the transport vehicles drove around with, 'G4S WORKING TO RIP OFF THE NHS IN KENT AND MEDWAY', until management figured out how to get the stickers off.

Jim was suspended by the Trust and reported to the GMC. He has not worked since and was thinking of retraining as a lawyer. He was a little weary of the job. The clinical side was great, but since sexual health services were transferred to local Government, they had been cut drastically. He was fairly sure he was to be made redundant anyway. His was still a *Cinderella* specialty. Not a priority. He was amused that putting clap clinic or pox doctor into a search engine still resulted in being directed to the correct clinics, who had now given up the terms VD, STD and even genitourinary.

One story that exposed the Government's lies about funding, but started getting the word privatisation mentioned, attracted the attention of a celebrity chef. It was their lucky break. He contacted Benedict and offered money and the use of one of his restaurants as a base as it had some spare office space. Neither co-leader cared where the money came from. Neither would have even guessed a chef would be at all interested in the NHS. They knew they were taking a gamble, as they did not want to be discredited by having the wrong sort of backer, but decided they had no choice and had to take a chance. They needed money if they were to have any impact. The chef attracted the publicity they craved and allowed leaflets to be left in his restaurants. He organised a number of celebrity NHS nights, with a menu featuring vegan meals such as the big NHS 'missed steak', Caesar Salads that you 'stabbed at' and Tortillas 'not a song, more of a rap'. His healthy food, shared between two, was subtitled 'if you'll beetroot to me, I'll beetroot to you'. The chef was amused that Alex was a gut surgeon, as he put it, and Benedict from the lot who would close his restaurants down if they found one microscopic bit of mould.

The membership grew to over five thousand. Not bad for a new political party they thought. With his money they stood a few candidates in the European elections, and twelve in the General Election of 2015. They were beginning to get some attention and to influence the media agenda a little, who up until then had ignored them and ignored the demise of the NHS. The *BBC* still did - too many executives with private health insurance. The chef financially backed a film Alex and Benedict made about the wilful destruction of the NHS. It was initially well received with promises of slots to be shown on *Channel 4* and interest from other stations. Strangely all these offers were withdrawn with no explanation, and all at the same time.

The Party gained more confidence and knew it was hitting a raw nerve when the other parties sat up and started attacking the SNHSP - as it has become known. Alex joked that these initials reminded him of the NSDAP - the Nationalsozialistische Deutsche Arbeiterpartei, or Nazi party. He did not mind, he said, if they called him Mein Fuhrer. As a politically naive medic, he soon learnt he had to do and say eye-catching things to get publicity. It was clearly a joke but Alex soon realised when enemies start taking you seriously, naive throwaways like calling yourself the Fuhrer will be seized on. Opponents will play dirty and sink to any level to discredit the opposition. They mobilised their media friends and soon Alex was labelled a Trot and Benedict a hypocrite as he lived in a Georgian

House even though it was up north and only worth what the journalist's London flat was worth. Why they bothered going through their bins for dirt was beyond the two co-leaders when all they had to do was make stories up, which they did as well.

Amongst the untruths were that they practised private medicine, owned five nursing homes, had had plastic surgery, sent their children to public schools, had botoxing wives who holidayed together on the Queen Mary, had relatives who were hedge fund managers, had properties in Barbados, had defrauded the NHS and had once voted National Front. Some of these stories came from friends they had never heard of. This was the first time Alex heard the term 'milkshake duck' - someone who at first appears endearing on social media only to turn out to have a poisonous past. They consoled themselves that the fight was worthwhile even though all this took its toll. To Alex they were on step three of Tony Benn's statement about progress, *first they ignore you, then they say you are mad, then dangerous... then there's a pause and then you can't find anyone who disagrees with you.* Benedict countered that, if they don't get to step five by the end of this Parliament then the cause was lost. It would be too late. What they did not take into account was the infiltration, and this is why Alex had been reduced to a wreck.

It started with an attempt to oust Benedict. A small group on the executive, whom they thought they could trust, sprang a disciplinary case on him, claiming he had brought the party into disrepute. They had asked people outside the Party for evidence against him and trawled social media for inappropriate comments Benedict might have made to justify a kangaroo court. This split the Party and it was only then that Alex woke up to the fact that some on the executive had been wreckers from the beginning. Stooges brought in to neutralise the party. He really did not want to believe it. And there was no better way to make the Party ineffective than to manufacture an internal fight.

Only looking back did he see they should have spotted the sort of people they were. Never a group to rock the boat too much, never a group to criticise the Establishment – turns out they were actually part of it. They always blocked what Alex and Benedict thought would be effective action. When given tasks they dragged their feet. It was easy to see in retrospect. What was the saying? *Keep your friends close, but your enemies closer?* The closest was a woman from a knife manufacturing family who called herself Charlotte Corday and claimed to be a book editor in Cambridge. How appropriate then to be stabbed in the back and then the front by her. Alex had heard of astroturfing, where an organisation was set up as a front. He knew this had not happened as he had set the Party up and he trusted Benedict, but he was shocked that their baby had been poisoned from within.

These people grabbed control of the Party. They broke all the rules and violated the constitution, but could spin this as appropriate action because they had control over all the I.T., the social media, the membership lists and the governance structure. Alex and Benedict were ostracised, cut out, became persona non grata, and were denigrated at every opportunity. They were told they were no longer members of the Party they had founded. Their monthly subscriptions were sent back. They were airbrushed from the Party website as though they had never existed. White, black and grey propaganda was used against them. They were never offered an explanation. They were treated appallingly by a group of egocentric morons who were using the Party for a variety of reasons. Some were paid infiltrating saboteurs who were a necessary part of the plot to destroy the NHS. Their motto was borrowed from Vladimir Ilyich Lenin, *the best way to control the opposition is to lead it ourselves.* Some just enjoyed the political machinations for no other reason than it was fun. Some liked to use the doors it opened up to meet people of influence, and some liked the sound of their own voices and had an over-developed sense of their own importance. Other colleagues who should have known better were giving Alex and Benedict the cold shoulder. So unfair but it demonstrated the power of controlling the party apparatus. Hitler and Stalin had known this. Benedict said he had updated Lenin's quote, *one man with a gun can control one hundred without one,* to, 'one man in charge of the computer can control one hundred without that power', and reminded Alex that Tom Clancy said *if you can control information you can control people.* But, Alex reassured him that Einstein had said, *information is not knowledge.*

As the dust settled on their defeat and ousting, Alex investigated the background of some of the assassins. He could kick himself for not doing it earlier. He had been too trusting and taken in by the smooth talk and their Machiavellian actions. Several had hidden their links to think tanks like Demos, the Adam Smith Institute, the Centre For Policy Studies and The Taxpayers' Alliance. The Institute of Economic Affairs had received the minutes of all their meetings.

Alex was an experienced campaigner who was used to defeat but this organised coup shocked him. In 1992 he had joined the Dongas who were protesting at Twyford Down about the proposed M3 motorway extension. He occasionally slept at their camp, occupied road-building machinery and suffered a beating from a security guard, all to try to stop a vast cutting through the historic chalk hill. It was his first direct experience of a sham public enquiry. The motorway was going to be built and that was that. Seven protesters were sent to prison but the judge told Alex that that would not be his fate, as he did not want to destroy a promising career. Alex insisted on being treated like the others but he was ignored. So Alex knew the limitations of trying to stop what the Establishment and the elite had decided was going to happen. And the destruction of the NHS was going to happen.

Alex was a different person pre 2010. This latest experience had changed him. He hated those evil bastards. He eventually got out of bed and moved slowly downstairs. There was no rush. He made some tea. Then went back to bed. He had a choice now. Continue to fight. But there were battles to face on several fronts against the NHS wreckers, against the infiltrators, against the Establishment, against the media, against politicians opposed to him, and against politicians who agreed but argued for different tactics, and against colleagues. He knew this option would damage him, his family and friends. How far would it go? Would he risk his house on a court battle? Life would not be enjoyable.

Or walk away. He was broken. He had to walk away. A victory for wrong, a defeat for right. Another nail in the coffin of democracy and all good things. Was not that Monty Python *Life of Brian* scene so true? *Are you the Judean People's Front? Fuck off. We're the People's Front of Judea. The only people we hate more than the Romans are the fucking Judean People's Front. And the Judean Popular People's Front. Splitters.* He could not watch that part of what he thought the funniest movie ever without a feeling of regret. It was *Animal Farm* come true. Alex had the same fate as Snowball and had been driven out by Napoleon. At the beginning of the Party *all animals are equal.* It then moved on to, *all animals are equal but some animals are more equal than others.* Now it had become 'some animals are in control, and others are excluded'. Where the pigs started to resemble humans, some of the NHS fighters began to resemble NHS destroyers. Alex realised the tensions between groupthink and individuality, between rational and emotional reactions and between morality and immorality were proving William Golding as prophetic as George Orwell. Like Piggy in *Lord of the Flies*, Alex felt he had had a boulder dropped on his head by people on his executive committee he once regarded as fellow NHS fighters, but now ruinous traitors. They descended into savagery - some formerly intelligent and compassionate do-gooders regressing to a primitive state. A few were decent but too weak not to follow the herd - cowards getting their protection from the mob. Their betrayal hurt. No wonder he could not sleep.

Worse was to come. In the middle of this battle, he was summoned to the office of the CEO of his hospital. As a lower gastro-intestinal surgeon Alex had a good reputation amongst his colleagues but management was not about to start tolerating any whistleblower. Alex was not really putting himself in the same category as some real heroes trying to defend the NHS. He was aware of the junior doctors who had been suspended, then reported to the GMC, had their mental health questioned, smeared by white, grey and black propaganda - some orchestrated by the Health Secretary - denied appeals, then abandoned to their fate by their so-called union. In effect, destroyed and left with no career by speaking out against wrongdoing. Alex just wanted to alert the public as to how staffing levels had become critical all because of cuts and the diversion of money from frontline clinical services to a team of contract managers instructed to outsource as many services as possible. Apparently it took a team of civil servants three days to produce a word that they thought would be more acceptable to the public and fool them more readily, than that P word, which had to be avoided at all cost, privatisation.

The CEO did not beat about the bush. He was suspended with immediate effect. They had been examining his morbidity, infection and mortality rates and his position in the league table had dropped to below the relegation level. Alex knew that it was all lies. He also knew this day might come and so kept his own detailed notes and statistics at home. League tables were sold as a quality measure but that disguised their real purpose, which was a stick to beat those who stepped out of line. Nevertheless he was escorted off the hospital premises and all passes confiscated by G4S security. The same company that more often than not delivered his patients too late or to the wrong place. His union the BMA seemed to be pursuing him with the same vigour as the mafia management of his Trust. It seemed to Alex that they were both Establishment bodies pulling in the same direction as the Government and the darker forces behind them. The BMA's lawyers wrote him a threatening letter about his film. They claimed it was slanderous and he would end up in court if it were not withdrawn. He would be expelled from the union.

So all this was why he saw no point in getting out of bed. So isolated and demoralised, he walked away from the fight for right and a new type of politics in general and the NHS and other public services in particular. He had one life and this was destroying it. He had tried his best and could not do any more. He would take no satisfaction in saying I told you so. He feared for his grandchildren and knew the human race was in the control of abnormals in self-destruct mode. And it looked like his career was over.

A victory yet again for the Establishment.

443

35 - SLOANES AND ALONE

RICH GIRL

High and dry, out of the rain
It's so easy to hurt others when you can't feel pain

You can rely on the old man's money

Daryl Hall and John Oates (1977)

Madison Moodey was eventually awoken by a continuous but soft tapping on the door. She had no idea how long she had slept through it. She stirred, dragged herself out of bed and staggered along the hallway and took the chain off the door without thinking. It was Cheryl. A good job too as Madison was only wearing her La Senza underwear. Her hair, unusually for her, was a little dishevelled but otherwise she did not look as though she had been up all night.

"I'm so sorry Maddy, but I couldn't resist him."

"Oh, that's what happened," realised Madison.

"You look as though you were dressed to make a conquest, but I assume you've got no one in there?"

"The one in the Barbour really annoyed me, so no."

Cheryl was visiting from Dallas and the two Americans had started out in the Mirror Bar at The Landmark the previous evening so that Madison could show Cheryl where she finally made it with Pete. It went downhill from there. They moved on as Cheryl, who had only been out of the States once before, wanted to see a quaint old English pub she had seen on TV. The Thornbury Castle had a Chelsea game on, which put Madison off, as Pete hated Chelsea, so after another cocktail they moved onto The Victoria and Albert, then The Globe, then The Perseverance which had a Dickensian black exterior.

"A bit different to your Rodeo Bar in the Adolphus, eh Cheryl?" Madison proudly stated. Cheryl was not impressed.

"I think the Rodeo is nicer. But I still want to run a Sports Bar."

"You are joking?" said an astonished Madison.

But she was not. How could they be so different? It was in The Perseverance that Cheryl tried her first real ale.

"Arrhh. It's warm and flat. Where's the gas? How can they drink this stuff?"

Madison was a convert and defended it.

"I hate to tell you this but this is real beer. We sell lager that is weak near-frozen gnat's piss."

Cheryl joked that she was turning anti-American.

"It must be the influence of that commie husband of yours."

Madison assumed she was joking. It was not long before they were approached. Two very smartly dressed lads who Madison knew Pete would classify as upper class public school twats who fancied themselves. One was in tweeds and a polo shirt, the other in a Barbour Stockman waxed coat and a pair of Hunters.

"Hello, darls, may we join you?"

Impressing women was easy for them without even realising what they were doing. They seemed to assume everyone had a Porsche, an apartment in Knightsbridge and access to a helicopter whenever they decided to have a weekend shooting on their ancestral estate in Scotland. Work was dabbling in the family's diamond or art trade. They had steady girlfriends, who in the old days would have been called debutantes, but also a string of women they used and for whom they did not totally hide their contempt.

Cheryl had never met anyone like it. No cowboy boots. If one of the guys had told her he was a Baronet or a Lord she would have believed him. After a little polite banter, it seemed clear Tweed-twat was taking aim at Cheryl, whilst Madison was going to get landed with Barbour-bore if she was not careful. They quickly let it be known that they had a driver waiting outside and they could be back at one of their pads in less than ten minutes. They were invited back for a swim in the pool.

Madison ignored that.

"Maybe a bit later. I like this place," Cheryl said.

For Madison that was the signal Cheryl had given before in Dallas, which meant I am going to get off with this guy, so don't worry about me. See you later.

"We both live the other side of Hyde Park from here. I'm in Victoria Road and my friend has a delightful little house in the next street, De Vere Gardens. Both roads are in the top twenty most expensive places in England and Wales. Our borough has twelve of them."

Then it was the other's turn to show off.

"My father is a councillor for our Borough of Kensington and Chelsea."

"Good for you," Madison said sarcastically beginning to dislike them.

She did not need to ask which political party he represented.

"His project is to clean it up. Get rid of the poor areas and those dirty tower blocks full of dirty people in the north of our area. The land is worth a fortune and it's wasted on those scallywags. Most are foreign and can't even speak the Queen's English."

That was it. Madison had had enough. If all that was an attempt to get the two of them back to their pads the Barbour-bore could not have got it more wrong. Oh if only Pete was with her. She thought he probably would have hit him for that.

"Well I'm foreign too and I speak American-English. We don't recognise the word wanker where I come from, but you are the Texas equivalent you cock-sucking, motherfucker. I've got friends in Adair Tower and a work colleague in Grenfell Tower. Your nob head prick of a father ought to invest in improving their living conditions, not revel in being an ethnic cleanser. And you, you are out of the rain, you can rely on the old man's money."

There was an awkward silence when Madison picked up her bag and left, leaving the Barbour-bore on his own. He was speechless. His only arrogant conclusion was that there must be something wrong with her. She walked out of The Perseverance briskly before he could attempt to persuade her otherwise, or apologise, but she doubted he had a clue he was being offensive. Just an in-bred British bellend. She walked the few yards down Shroton Street more slowly, back past The Globe, crossed Lisson Grove and back to her flat in Hayes Place. She was sober enough to remember that Pete had started to investigate what a couple had told him in The Elgin pub about the Kensington and Chelsea social cleansing and that he had met with the Residents' Association. She could not remember the outcome but decided to have another look through her missing husband's files as soon as Cheryl was not pre-occupying her. She knew Cheryl could cope on her own. She crashed out realising the cocktails did not really mix with the *Young's Special* and thankful she had the next day off work to spend the day with her friend. She wished her luck in her imagination.

It was coming up to three years since Pete had disappeared. The two married years they did have together were the best of her life. She had wangled a job, as she said she would, with the UK Environmental Agency whilst Pete carried on with his freelance journalism. He was beginning to make a name for himself even if only as a troublemaker. He still found it difficult to get published in Britain but he had some European contacts that were interested and allowed a small but steady income stream. Madison seemed to have no problem, regrets or resentment about supporting him. She had spent many a sleepless night since going over the events of the month before he vanished. In retrospect he was agitated and more short tempered. Never with her but she noticed it with phone-calls in particular. Then he said he had to go to the US for a week to meet a man about a new story. He could not say anything about it yet but would explain all on return. She never heard from him again.

In the week he failed to return she was in total despair. That despair got worse as she realised something terrible must have happened. She explored every avenue. She contacted everyone she could think of. Madison tracked down Mike Emptage to see if he would help. She searched the house in Lancaster Road for clues. She checked out his computer. She trusted him totally and dismissed her mother's knee jerk reaction that he must have found someone else. He was not that sort of man. He kept nothing from her. He had passwords for his computer, phone or tablet but told Madison them all. She went through everything and got no clues. His articles she read and re-read and gradually became more and more convinced that they provided the answer somewhere.

The police were no real help. The Foreign and Commonwealth Office were useless. The man at the end of the phone just moaned about the twenty-five per cent budget cut and loss of jobs in his department. The American authorities confirmed he had entered the country at Washington Dulles International Airport but knew nothing more. He had a reservation at the State Plaza Hotel, off Virginia Avenue, for five days but had gone without settling the bill after three. It was when she learnt this that she feared the worst. They wondered if she would settle his outstanding bill. They had stayed there together several times. Pete loved it for its central position only one kilometre from the Lincoln monument and a nice walk on the Memorial Bridge over the Potomac to Arlington National Cemetery to visit Kennedy's grave.

The media were not interested either, dismissing her with the other near quarter of a million people in the UK who disappear every year. It is not newsworthy. The police admitted that most people are eventually found, but still claimed that up to twenty thousand are gone for more than twelve months. Too big a problem to deal with - since the cuts they did not have the resources. Sorry. What the British Police and media did not admit was that the US cell of the Special Operations Team had warned them all to avoid prying into matters that did not concern them and in particular the Pete Moodey case.

After a year on her own she decided to rent out their large house in Notting Hill and move to Marylebone. The flat in Hayes Place was small and near The Landmark. It was only after moving there she found out it was a popular area for Americans. She might have reconsidered if she had known. She first overheard two women with loud mid-Atlantic English accents in Iberica, her favourite Spanish restaurant, saying they loved the quaint little area with its village vibe. Later whilst in the Edwardian Daunt Bookshop she heard the same accents emerging from the oak gallery.

"Isn't Regent's Park cute."

Madison, who was trying hard to get rid of her Texas drawl given away by its flattened monophthong, could recognise the mid-Atlantic accent spoken along the urban corridor from Philadelphia to Baltimore. She had met this in Washington. It was similar to that spoken in New York City but with a few major differences. She would rather have that herself than the Southern accent with a twist.

Madison still worked at the Environment Agency as a hydrologist but was clearly distracted and her bosses had noticed. They had not said anything to her but were overheard by a colleague at the Horseferry Road Offices, Rashida who was one of their secretaries. Rashida Ahmed was a lovely friendly third generation immigrant about Madison's age but with two young children, Aisha and Usman, who went to the Avondale Park Primary School near their home on the eighteenth floor of Grenfell Tower. Rashida often shared a journey home with Madison as she regularly called in to see her elderly disabled mother who lived in Luxborough Tower in Marylebone run by CityWest Homes for the City of Westminster Council. Lord Hailsham had opened the twenty-one-storey block in 1971 on the site of the old St Marylebone workhouse. The plaque commemorating the occasion had been defaced in protest to Hailsham's disgust expressed about gays when he appeared before the Wolfenden Committee, and his family becoming immensely wealthy from slave ownership in British Guiana.

So they both travelled on the Jubilee line from Westminster to Baker Street. She returned home from there to Latimer Road on the Circle or the Hammersmith and City line. It was on one of the journeys that Rashida told Madison what she had overheard. This did not concern Madison too much but she was grateful to her new friend.

On another journey a few weeks later it was clear something was troubling Rashida, so Madison very carefully and kindly asked if she needed any help. Madison was told about how she was happy in Grenfell Tower until a friend of Rashida's who was also working with them as an Environment Officer brought her children around to play but would not stay as she thought the tower block a potential fire death trap. When she asked the neighbours about the risks she was told there was an action group which had been warning the Kensington and Chelsea Council for years, but not only had this all fallen on deaf ears, but the Council had threatened legal action in a bid to prevent the group criticising them, claiming defamation and harassment. They were certainly regarded as troublemakers by the officials and the private company KCTMO who managed nearly ten thousand properties for the Council, had a turnover of over £17m and paid its top management over half a million each. So Rashida was very worried about the safety of her young family. Madison sympathised and told her she had heard similar rumours but she did not say it was Pete who brought this to her attention after meeting that couple in The Elgin. She told Rashida that Pete had found out the Council was sitting on reserves of hundreds of millions.

So Madison's work was suffering as she was spending more and more time checking out the scandals Pete was investigating. She looked again at his files on Grenfell Tower. Pete had discovered the 1958 race riots had started in Bramley Road - the site of the future Grenfell Tower. The redevelopment architect Peter Deakins planned an estate with shops, a library, leisure centre and all the facilities for a modern vibrant safe community to thrive. The Council rejected his plans on the grounds of cost, but everyone knew that it was because those sorts of people would not appreciate all that.

There was a further note in Pete's handwriting about the racist murder of Kelso Cochrane in 1959. To Madison it was scribbled as though Pete was taking notes from someone like he was a reporter. His handwriting was usually perfect. The police said the motive was robbery, although he had no money on him, and they knew the murderer was a man called Patrick Digby, but did not prosecute. Strangely all the evidence was destroyed.

Through Pete's files Madison also learnt of Colin Jordan of the White Defence League, a leading neo-Nazi who provocatively set up an office in Notting Hill. He founded the National Socialist Movement in 1962 with John Tyndall who had been under the influence of Arthur Chesterton and the League of Empire Loyalists.

Madison knew Pete's files were her only hope of ever understanding what happened to him. She needed more clues and after three years had exhausted all the conventional routes for missing persons. Had he got too close to exposing big business corruption? Were governments involved? What enemies had he made? She still believed he was alive and was locked up somewhere, but in dark moments thought that was probably just wishful thinking.

Pete always stored his computer under the floorboards. Madison thought he was over cautious. When he disappeared though she decided to copy his files onto several memory sticks for safekeeping. Within days she returned from work to find her Notting Hill house ransacked. The floorboards were up and the computer gone. Hers too. Whoever it was only seemed interested in information. The police were not very helpful. They seemed to want to blame her for living there. It was the main reason she decided she could no longer stay there alone so she rented the house out.

The stories on his computer were, if true, outrageous. Many Pete had told her about. Many involved her country - the Marshall Islands, Operation Gladio, the numerous schemes to overthrow foreign governments, the interference in democratic elections, the attempted and successful assassination attempts of foreign leaders, the suppressing of populist or nationalist movements, the forced sterilisation of women with disabilities or genetic disorders. In Europe and the UK - the NATO plots, the undermining of the European Union, the shrinkage of Government almost to extinction and the destruction of the welfare states, the privatisation of healthcare and the dismantling of Britain's NHS. There was a fair bit on the Iraq War, the murder of David Kelly and the sexing up of the terrorist threat.

Pete had detailed the UK ricin scare story. The Government fed the media a story about the highly toxic ricin getting into the country and being widely available to the enemy. It was not but they let the public sweat for two years before admitting the truth. It helped them get through anti-terrorist legislation, much of which was as well thought out as the *Dangerous Dogs Act* and passed in as much haste.

451

The Bulgarian dissident Georgi Markov was assassinated in London in 1978 by being shot from an umbrella with a pellet containing ricin. Pete had uncovered evidence that the UK Government had concealed from Parliament cluster bombs being brought in by the Americans in defiance of a treaty banning them.

Pete had found out about the Lockerbie bombing when Pan Am flight 103 was blown up in mid-air in 1988. For at least a year the US and UK Governments blamed Iran, Syria and a Palestinian group. But then by October 1990 they needed them as allies for the invasion of Iraq, so it was more convenient to blame Libya - the least supportive Arab State.

There were a few African stories. Shell had infiltrated the Nigerian Government and in 1996 Pfizer hired investigators to get dirt on their Attorney General to get him to stop legal action over a corrupt drugs trial involving children with meningitis. In Tanzania the IMF made them privatise their water supply in exchange for a loan. In South Africa following water privatisation ten million had their supply cut off.

Madison's attention was drawn to the notes Pete had made on the Indian Bhopal disaster as Union Carbide and the parent company Dow Chemical had their headquarters in her home state of Texas. In 1984 in Bhopal the pesticide plant accidentally released methyl isocyanate exposing over half a million Indians, causing tens of thousands of deaths and leaving over forty thousand permanently disabled. It was considered the world's worst industrial disaster. The stillbirth rate increased three fold and neonatal mortality doubled. Pete had written about Dow Chemical spying on activists involved in the disaster. He also highlighted the corporate negligence, a theory about sabotage and Union Carbide's bad track record exposing workers to silica and asbestos. News to Madison was Dow's radioactive waste leakages and production of Napalm and Agent Orange for use in Vietnam. Some of their silicone breast implants ruptured - something she thought she should warn Cheryl about.

All this when exposed could cost the company billions of dollars. So the loss of one life in order to hide it would be amazing value.

Madison was suspicious of everybody. So many had motives to silence Pete.

An older story was how General Motors in Detroit was using its subsidiary Opel to arm both sides in the Second World War. Madison thought this a triumph of capitalism but one that eventually saw the company go bust in 2009 because they paid their managers too much, gave their shareholders too much in the way of dividends, and did not bother to improve their product.

There were suppressed studies showing how reducing the number of A&E departments caused deaths, and the effects of austerity. How ordinary people pay for the crimes of the financial elite. How the defining moment in Britain's recent economic history was not the 2008 crash as we were led to believe and how it was exploited by the right wing to justify austerity, but the destruction of the industrial base in the 1980s, which cost billions.

There was information about the World Economic Forum in Davos. How the fat cats in the snow as Pete had typed were known as 'Davos Man' and 'Masters of the Universe'. How it was an opaque forum to make decisions without having to trouble the electorate or take shareholders into account. How the *BBC* was to be headed by a banker who would start the hollowing out process. This was described as a skilful and deceitful method of fooling the public that an organisation is still there and has not been interfered with, but in reality it is just a shell where the good things and good people have been pushed out, and the vacuum filled with private companies which have their own agenda, moneymaking and propaganda. Pete had added in a comment balloon, 'Even *Songs of Praise* has been outsourced! God privatised! It had to happen!' This was an excellent tactic to use on the *BBC* and NHS, which because of their popularity, could not be dismantled overtly and with the public's knowledge, and both were hardly ever discussed in the media. By this Pete had added, 'Remember the Orwell quote: *Omission is the most powerful form of lie*'.

Then there was a list of companies who declared themselves bankrupt to avoid lawsuits. Pete had a very large series of files simply labelled Money. Madison found much of the material difficult to understand. There were pages and pages of very technical economic detail. As she expected there were several bank stories and one scandal that was simply written was about the HSBC. According to Pete's notes they had laundered hundreds of millions of pounds in drug money for Mexican drug cartels as well as funds for terrorist organisations. Pined to that note was a photo of the narco-lord Joaquin "El Chapo" Guzmann. HSBC had also used failing businesses to launder money into political donations, which was pumped into the Tory party to help them win the 2010 general election. In return, after its victory, the Government continued to favour HSBC and the business interests of its donors.

One disturbing paper written by a right wing think tank was entitled *How To Invent The Truth*. It quoted and took advice from David Irving the historian who denied the killings of the holocaust. After his publicity a poll showed twenty-two per cent of Americans thought the holocaust might not have happened. It stated: *If I have facts and you have facts whoever shouts the loudest wins*. Their experiment was *Breitbart News* and it seemed to work. It was the example to follow. Its Chairman was known as an anti-Semite, a racist, a misogynist and a xenophobe and their raison d'etre was to get their man into the White House. They took lies and paraded them as opinions.

Then there was the hit list: Aung San Suu Kyi, Noam Chomsky, Michael Moore, Oscar Denning, Bernie Saunders, Jeremy Corbyn, Chelsea Manning, Edward Snowden, Hugo Chavez, Recep Tayyip Erdogan, Kim Jong-un, Marine Le Pen, Dilma Rousseff, Park Geun-hye, Rodrigo Duterte, Prayuth Chan-o-cha, Pablo Iglesias, Yanis Varoufakis, Alexis Tsipras… the list went on and seemed to have no logic to it.

There were so many candidates amongst all this information who could have been responsible for Pete's disappearance. It was not long after Pete's vanishing that she began to think she was being watched. She worried about her phone being tapped and emails hacked. She bought another tablet to work on - one that no one knew about that was not connected at all to any network. She bought loads of memory sticks to back up her work and, together with Pete's, hid them in a safe deposit box. Her parents knew of its existence. She gave one to Mike Emptage and when he saw the contents he decided to spend a week's leave in the US searching for clues. He contacted Cheryl again but did not tell Madison this.

Life had to go on but she became suspicious of all strangers. She had been a regular at the Yoga centre opposite her flat for eight months when a girl approached her from the class and wanted to know if she fancied a drink after. She said no on two occasions before telling herself she was being silly. Why not? Stop being so paranoid. It turned out she genuinely wanted to be friendly. A little bit too friendly as Madison realised she was making a pass at her. Once that misunderstanding had been dealt with they had the drink and got on well.

Chantelle Levesque came from Colmar in Alsace so their first link was Bartholdi. She was a French TV and Radio journalist based in London and one of several UK correspondents for the French international news channel *Franceinfo*. Madison joked that Chantelle's English was better than hers. She certainly had an accent that was less obviously foreign. She explained that she had lived in London before - between the ages of three and eight - so was keen to return as she had great memories. Her father was on a secondment from the French Air Force. His job was to help integrate defence forces between the two European Union allies. They had returned to France as he missed flying too much but also as he found the lack of co-operation he got from anti-European Brits sabotaged his work at every turn.

Chantelle's faux pas had arisen as she had never seen Madison with anyone and assumed she lived alone so jumped to the wrong conclusion. To explain why she was alone, which she felt the need to do, Madison told the story of Pete's disappearance. Chantelle was shocked that no one was helping her find her husband. Madison went through in detail all she had tried to find and the list was pretty exhaustive. All Chantelle could think of was to offer some publicity and making a story of it. That was the perfect way to make a good friend. As a member of the Foreign Press Association, and in her world in general, she had a lot of contacts. Madison said she was grateful and she would think about it.

The following week at their usual yoga class, they acknowledged each other at the beginning but there were too many witnesses to say more. After exercising though, Madison approached Chantelle.

"What you said last week. Yes, I'd be grateful for your help. I've almost given up. I really don't know who to turn to, so thank you. I've compiled a dossier of the stories Pete was working on. If they are true you might make a name for yourself. Sorry, a bigger name."

"I'll have a look and maybe we can have a drink after next week's class? You know you will have to give an interview? I can get it on the French domestic channels if nothing else."

Cheryl emerged from the bathroom.

"Well, that was some night. Fun up to a point, but not to be repeated. His house in Victoria Road was impressive. Six bedrooms, five bathrooms and three kitchens. Who needs three kitchens? Oil paintings on the walls, loads of antiques and strange sculptures around the place. Plenty of champagne and coke everywhere and I don't mean the liquid type. Believe it or not I only found three books on his shelves. A work by Chesterton about a dude called Mosley, *Mein Kampf* and *The Coloured Invasion* by Jordan. Colin, not Katie. Weird eh? Useless in bed though and I told him so. He didn't seem to care. Wanted to ride 'the Hershey highway' like a lot of your public schoolboy types. Told him that's not my scene. Won't be seeing him again."

Neither Texas girl realised they would never see each other again either. Neither realised that their friendship was to come to an abrupt end.

36 - SHAME AND FAME

EMBARRASSMENT

We are a disgrace to the human race he says,
How can you show your face,
When you're a disgrace to the human race?

Madness (1980)

2012

Sir James was sitting at his large Victorian oak cartographer's desk, moulded into his traditional chairman's antique mahogany and burgundy Italian leather chair in the study of his London home.

The study took up most of the third floor with views over Grosvenor Square. His Buddha-like shape dominated the room, especially as he had had the desk elevated on a platform so he could look down on people. On one end was a small bust of Napoleon, at the other a photograph of a certain German Chancellor, Adolf Hitler. In the background behind the Fuhrer's right shoulder stood a beaming Charles Morrison. In the middle of the desk was a signed photo from the younger sister of the last Czar.

To Charles, with love, Xenia - Christmas 1950 Wilderness House.

For what he saw as a reward for his deathbed vigil, James had slipped this into his briefcase before anyone noticed and while his father was still warm. His father had boasted of an affair with the Grand Duchess but James thought it unlikely. He doubted they had met until the late 1930s when Charles contacted her on behalf of the Right Club. She would have been seventy-five in 1950 - but knowing Charles?

Sir James was more pleased with himself than usual. He had just taken a telephone call from Gerry Vaughan-Warner. Gerry needed several attempts to get connected as he had tripped over the telephone cord and ripped it from the wall. As usual he blamed his old eye injury.

The Prime Minister told Gerry that the plan to cause a rift amongst a supposedly secret plotting cabal of senior cabinet ministers had worked like a dream. Stanek had been told about Hartman's past and connections to Nazi Germany. That he was the cousin twice removed of Konrad Henlein the Reichsstatthalter of the Sudetenland, when Stanek's father was forced to leave and was responsible for the deaths of so many relatives who did not leave. To make sure Stanek was also fed some black propaganda that Henlein's family were linked to the Kuhns of Munich. Fritz Kuhn was the leader of the German American Bund before the Second World War and held a large Nazi rally at Madison Square Garden in 1939. Like Al Capone, they finally got him on tax evasion, which was a bit like charging Jack the Ripper with being rude to women. Stanek was furious.

"That's the end of their cooperation with each other and any coordinated plotting against us," Gerry had said to his friend.

Sir James always preferred to be in the countryside but at least one London home was essential. He had bought this house in Upper Grosvenor Street in Mayfair opposite the American Embassy. The two miles and ten minute drive down Hyde Park and alongside Buckingham Palace to Pimlico was just long enough for the little blue pills to work when he decided to visit one of his mistresses there. It was just a few houses along from Margaret Campbell the Duchess of Argyll, infamous for her sex scandals at number 48. When the house came on the market in 1992, Jim thought it amusing to snap it up and use it as a London base even though he nearly withdrew because of the embassy. He revelled in telling guests it was only a few doors down that he had played out the role of the headless man three decades earlier. The Duchess had had to move out years before because of her debts and Jim had no idea who lived there now, but he did know that she had opened the house at one point for paid tours. He wondered if they had the Polaroid photo on display as an attraction, or perhaps an antique prayer stool that the Duchess used to kneel on.

He had a manservant called Hammond. He gave up on female secretaries years ago as he found them distracting. It took several attempts to find the right man. Hammond however was perfect. Apart from, that is, the fact that he had originated from Germany and was called Niemand. Sir James could overlook the nationality as he recognised the good qualities that accompanied the Germanic character but he could not cope with his real name so had anglicised it himself to Hammond. This was in part a tribute to Wally Hammond the English cricket captain whom Jim had met on a business trip to South Africa just before he died of a heart attack in 1965. Quiet, discreet, never in the way, and obedient, Hammond was in the room but had no presence. Sir James could indulge himself in all the usual male bad habits and not feel the slightest embarrassment. Hammond just was not really there. He was a man with no opinions or views. So Sir James would scratch his privates, pick his nose and loudly break wind at ease.

He knew Hammond was always going to be loyal. He never employed anyone without first getting some dirt on them. Hammond had a weakness for cottaging, which his wife and grown-up children knew nothing about. They would if he stepped out of line. But Sir James's research assistant also found out that Hammond's grandfather, Gunther Niemand, was a Nazi war criminal. He was in a battalion of the regiment Das Reich of the Waffen-SS and was second in command to SS-Sturmbannfuhrer Adolf Diekmann. They carried out the Oradour-dur-Glane massacre in France of six hundred and forty-two inhabitants. After the war he was recruited as an agent for the 66th Detachment of the US Army Counterintelligence Corps. The Americans helped him escape with Klaus Barbie to South America. It got better. Gunther's brother Dieter was sent to America to help out the Duquesne spy ring. This information might prove useful too. What Sir James did not know was the South American link with the Wessel family.

One of Hammond's many distasteful jobs was to arrange some light afternoon relief for Sir James from time to time when he could not be bothered to visit Pimlico. He had set up an account with an escort agency that could get one of his two favourite regulars around to Grosvenor Square within fifteen minutes. Time for the pills to work again. Depending on his mood and how busy he was, he had a not too subtle code for them. He said either 'hand' or 'mouth' and they knew what he meant. Usually 'mouth' as this was less messy. The only effort he put in was to move off the platform to his favourite and very comfortable Regency mahogany and cane desk chair with its horseshoe shaped back which stood alone by his 1700 William and Mary oak side table with brass droplet handles and turned legs united by crossover stretcher. He removed this from his father's bedroom at the same time as the photograph of Xenia.

The girls knew they were supposed to kneel down beside him. He made them remove their jewellery, as he did not want his chair scratched. Their employer engaged in no other conversation - not even saying hello or goodbye. They were objects to him. Only once or twice a year did Sir James take them onto his 19th century William IV Rosewood Chaise Longue at the other end of the room. He was confident the rich deep brown leather would not be damaged. He was mindful of what one of Nicholas Soames' women said about having to have sex with him, *a bit like a wardrobe with the key still in the door falling on you.*

Despite all the parallels with Churchill's grandson his arrogance and self-importance never allowed it to occur to him that his girls would think the same. He thought they were privileged. He was not interested in the cost. Hammond sorted all that out, even a Christmas bonus. This all went on with Hammond still in the room, standing upright against the bookcases, eyes diverted, and awaiting further instruction. Whether Lady Morrison was in the house at the time did not bother her husband one iota.

When the blonde Hammond knew as Gail had finished and had been dismissed Sir James told Hammond, as he was doing up his fly, to get the Commissioner of Police of the Metropolis to come to see him at five pm. Sir James had them all at his beck and call - even the head of the police. There was a file on him too. Sir John Varken owed his position to Sir James, who thought he had had him promoted beyond his talents but that did not matter. He was their man and did as he was told. As usual, there were no greetings or pleasantries. He was not granted the privilege of sitting down.

"Varken, before the main business, tell me you have dealt with Rutherford?"

"It's work in progress, sir. We are…"

"Don't give me that bullshit. That means no, doesn't it? Tell me, do you value your job?"

"Sir, I will be…"

"I've heard enough. You are here because I've decided to launch Operation Famulo and I'd like you to start the raids tonight."

Famulo was Esperanto for celebrity. Sir John had been expecting this for months so he was relieved to finally get the go-ahead. He was prepared and so were his team. Now the London Olympics had finished he had planned a holiday in two days' time to Sorrento but knew he would now have to cancel. A chill went down his spine when he thought about how his wife would react. She had already booked a visit to Capri to see where Gracie Fields lived and was buried, although he would have been going to the Grotta Azzurra after it inspired Mark Twain who recorded his thoughts in *The Innocents Abroad*. Not now.

The group they called Poison, which officially did not exist, had been having too many successes and it was time for the public to be distracted again. Blaming Muslim extremists was working well now that blaming the IRA was not so credible, but it would not be long before someone sees through that decoy or the public confuses matters with an anti-Muslim backlash. They knew Poison was behind the London car bombs in June 2007 and the plot of using suicide bombers at Manchester Piccadilly in September 2009. Only three months ago Sir John thought he had thwarted a planned attack on the English Defence League in Dewsbury but they still had not convincingly linked it to Poison.

"Who have you lined up?"

"Well, Jimmy Savile obviously, but a broad church of others. In the entertainment industry there's Rolf Harris, Cliff Richard, and a couple of DJs. Oh, and Stuart Hall the commentator. Dead

461

politicians include Ted Heath, Cyril Smith and Jeremy Thorpe. Live ones Oaten, Mandelson and Laws. Chris Huhne has already discredited himself by having to resign from the cabinet for perverting the course of justice over getting his wife to take the rap for that speeding offence, then rewarded her by leaving her."

"Ah, hell hath no fury like a woman scorned, but we aren't interested in small fry like him, so don't waste my time," smiled Sir James in a menacing manner.

"Then there's that short-arsed head of Formula One Ecclestone, plus Max Mosley as well as Max Clifford and a few so-called celebrities to keep the others on their toes."

"I know we don't care whether they are guilty or not, but Rolf Harris?" said Sir James quizzically.

"I assure you he is actually guilty as hell, Sir."

"Well you do surprise me. That's the end of watching *Animal Hospital* with my granddaughter then."

"Cliff Richard is totally innocent but that'll be a great distraction. The politicians are easy prey sir. Nobody ever thinks they are innocent even if they are. Mellor, Yeo, Davies. They were so easy to set up."

"There's a few I'd like you to add to your list. People that are getting irritating or in the way. A few who shouldn't have crossed me. That Paul Burrell the former Royal Butler. He has to be punished for embarrassing our monarch."

"He is already on the list, sir."

"Got anything on Sebastian Coe? If not make something up. Add a few satirists and so-called comedians to the list. I'll leave who up to you, but that Bremner and... who's the other? Hardy? Mickey taking is very effective, more so than serious debate, so quash it."

"We have a special category for those troublemakers. Names you probably won't recognise sir like Noble, Boyle, O'Briain, Davies, Elton, Dee, Hamilton, Gervais, Brand... Armando Iannucci..."

"Yes, yes, I get the point."

"The point being sir is that tackling this bunch squashes a lot of dissent. The public pay more attention to a well-crafted joke and remember it, than an hour's speech from a politician."

"Okay, but more important targets ought to be crooks like Philip Green and that Mike Ashley. There have been rumours about Green for years. I'll leave that to you to get your boys to find some dirt on them. And don't you think we should get rid of that deputy of yours. He is snooping around too much. What about a few more from the media, some editors and producers who aren't quite on side? Check out *openDemocracy*, the *Huffington Post*, *Private Eye*... that Hislop chap, public school, should know better. Add in the odd union leader of course. I assume your attempts to discredit Colin Wallace are still on going? Wouldn't it be ironic after what he alleged about the Kincora Boys Home if he was up to his neck in it? Get my meaning Varken?"

"Yes, sir. The matter is in hand."

"Give Frampton a scare too will you? He repeatedly annoys me and has done for years with that cocksure overconfident security firm of his. Oh, nearly forgot. That communist who produced the Olympics opening ceremony."

"Danny Boyle?"

"Is that his name? You don't know what shit our American friends gave me when they saw nurses jumping up and down on beds to celebrate the NHS, when we are supposed to be discrediting it at every opportunity and getting rid of it. Set our propaganda back months, if not years."

"I'll see what I can do sir."

"And Ken Loach, of course. How did you possibly let that film of his win so many awards? Total propaganda against everything we are trying to achieve. He's a disgrace to the human race. You should have killed that one off. I'm disappointed in you. Make sure we don't see his face again."

Sir John swallowed hard.

"Don't forget to tip off our friends in the press. They can have the exclusives to help keep them sweet."

Sir James knew that throwing them a few juicy morsels so easily sidetracked the public. He was not prepared to put a lifetime's work at risk, and the work of his previous generation. Lives, yes, but not all their efforts. It mattered not what casualties there were on the way. It was for the greater good. The silence and his fixed icy stare

463

told the Commissioner his time was up. He thanked Sir James and left. Hammond escorted him to the door.

37 - NEWS AND VIEWS

A DAY IN THE LIFE

Woke up got out of bed,
Dragged a comb across my head

The Beatles (1967)

"You take a little pill of news every day - 23 minutes - and that's supposed
to be enough." ~ Walter Cronkite

2012

"The headlines today on *BBC Radio 4*:
- George Orwell's Eton tutor is named as Fifth man in Cambridge spy ring
- The College of Emergency Medicine says England's A&E departments are in chaos because of a serious shortage of doctors
- Rupert Murdoch bids to add the *Los Angeles Times* and the *Chicago Tribune* to his vast American media empire
- Police have raided several houses in their investigations into child sexual abuse
- Is racism in football alive and kicking? Why did Rio Ferdinand refuse to wear *Kick it Out* T-shirt?"

Sir Gerald Vaughan-Warner looked up from his copy of *Soldier,* the British Army magazine.

"Police raids? No, can't be ours, surely?" he thought.

He returned to the Book Reviews. On lifting up his magazine he knocked his coffee over but ignored the dripping onto the floor. *Soldier* was his favourite monthly, now in its sixty-fifth year, and he did not like distractions. After dealing with the other stories, which did not distract Sir Gerald, the newsreader eventually caught his attention again.

"There have been raids overnight as police launched what they have called Operation Famulo. The houses of several prominent people have had computers and other artefacts taken for inspection investigating sexual abuse including paedophile crimes. Meanwhile, in the aftermath of his sacking, the *BBC* Director General has issued a statement saying that he stands by his decision to back the Panorama team who named prominent people from all walks of life."

He felt a jolt run though him. First shock then, gathering his thoughts, why had he not been told? He started to pace around. Jim had promised to keep his close circle informed and to give some warning before kicking this off. Surprise turned to anger and, as it mounted, it began to cloud any chance of his making a rational decision about what to do. It was too late now to warn friends to destroy anything incriminating. He did not trust Jim not to sacrifice a few old mates. He had plenty of old scores to settle.

The cat yelped, ran off and knocked over a vase of flowers when Gerry trod on its tail.

"The headlines today on *Classic FM Radio*:
- Prince Harry to spend Christmas fighting the Taliban
- Operation Famulo swoops on celebrities
- Eton denies ex-teacher was a spy
- Row over Larry the Downing Street cat and his knighthood
- Police storm pub in Morris dancer punch-up
- Private health companies say come to us for your emergency care, not a doctor-less NHS hospital
- Seagull turns bright orange after falling into vat of Tikka Masala, Brighton fan protests our colours are blue and white
- Sales of Hobnobs are crumbling as cash-strapped shoppers opt for own-label alternatives
- The FTSE 100 Index is up twenty-six at five thousand seven hundred and sixty-one."

Rosa Davies had settled well into her new flat in Camden. So had Kurt. She adapted easily to change and never made a fuss. It was two years since her eviction from the Market Estate. She had had help from a few close friends and one had fixed up her television even though Rosa was not bothered. She rarely watched it and was critical of all the channels. She once found herself telling the checkout pensioner at her local supermarket.

"We have had two or three good channels stolen from us, only to be replaced by a hundred rubbish ones like in America."

Then she discovered she could get *BBC Wales* but still avoided news and current affairs. She did not trust what she was told. This morning however she felt in need of company so *Classic FM* was her choice. She felt it the perfect forum for bits of music like Schubert's *Symphony Number 8* as it was unfinished and nothing was ever played in its entirety so that did not matter. Her first thought on hearing the headlines was, what are they providing this smoke screen to cover? What have these folk done that the powerful feel the need to hang them out to dry? What a waste of police money as they will not investigate seriously. She did want to learn more about the spy story though, as in the early 1960s she did find herself mixing with some MI5 and MI6 contacts.

And why bother with the FTSE 100 Index when it is of no interest to 99.9 per cent of the population? Pandering to the few. How about a PDD Index? A Politicians' Dishonesty and Deceit Index?

"The headlines today on *BBC Radio 4*:
- George Orwell's Eton tutor is named as Fifth man in Cambridge spy ring
- The College of Emergency Medicine says England's A&E departments are in chaos because of a serious shortage of doctors
- Rupert Murdoch bids to add the *Los Angeles Times* and the *Chicago Tribune* to his vast American media empire

- Police have raided several houses in their investigations into child sexual abuse
- Is racism in football alive and kicking? Why did Rio Ferdinand refuse to wear *Kick it Out* T-shirt?"

Felix Denning listened with interest. He always timed sitting down to his breakfast at precisely 7:00 a.m. so he could listen to the wireless. For him this news was topical. The week before he had concluded a case where he had sent down a teacher for a relationship with a fifteen-year-old pupil. This was the first time he had had such a case. The media interest was enormous. He had to censure two of the tabloids for publishing a provocative picture of the schoolgirl. He wondered if they had doctored a photo as she looked at least twenty-five, was in a short skirt, high heels and a lacy white blouse that showed a magnificent cleavage. Magnificent was the word used by the defence. What hypocrisy the papers had, he told them, slightly nervous afterwards about their reaction. Would they retaliate? Would they be going through his bins? Hopefully Atticus would savage them if they tried.

Clifford Wessel heard the same broadcast but at 8:00 am, as his clinic at the private hospital was not due to start for another two hours. He made a mental note to delete a few things from his hard drive when he got home, but it did not worry him unduly and after that bulletin he did not give it another thought. It also reminded him to destroy the tapes that had been passed onto him labelled Wessel and Chisholm. Although, maybe he would keep the one with the conversation between Chisholm and Baigent - might be useful one day.

"The headlines today on *BBC Radio Sussex*:
- Woman smeared twenty cars with peanut butter after she mistook Crawley Town Council meeting for Transvestite Convention
- Bexhill house raided in police sex investigation

468

- Murdoch bids for *Hastings and St Leonards Observer*
- Hailsham OAP re-united with lost hat on bus ride in Eastbourne after Sussex police appeal
- Can Royal Sussex County Hospital survive staffing crisis?
- A Bognor Regis man has been posting his letters in dog poo bin for two years."

Ivan Humphrey just caught the headlines as he walked in from the garden of his estate near Burwash. He needed a cigarette and his wife banned him from smoking in the house. Ivan's attempts to get her permission for a smoking room failed miserably. She was in charge in that relationship. As he saw her disapproving face his heart sank about the relationship he felt trapped in. He was nothing to her now except as the occasional odd-job man when the real odd-job man was on holiday. Ivan did not know why she asked him to do things anyway as he could never match the standards she expected. He thought he was probably being set up to fail so she had an excuse to moan. Not that a lack of excuse ever stopped her.

He could not really come to terms with being a well-respected powerful up-and-coming political force to the outside world, but an emasculated despised nobody in his own home. His need for a cigarette was partly due to his irritability that morning and his gloom about their relationship. Wondering why his wife insisted on having the local radio station blaring out throughout the whole house did not help it. Why not just some decent classical music?

He could see Bateman's from the end of his garden. He liked the thought of having the ghost of a good solid Englishman who admired the Empire so close. All the National Trust traffic attracted to Rudyard Kipling's house did annoy him though. He felt a connection and so he recently toured the Western Front battlefields. He went to France on his own and the break from his wife was like appreciating the peace when a pneumatic drill stops. He felt driven to search for Jack Kipling's grave. He died at the Battle of Loos-en-Gohelle in 1915 and Ivan found his grave at Haisnes. A shell blast had ripped off his face. Dying just six weeks after his eighteenth birthday, his father never recovered.

Ivan's frosty iceberg of a wife had given up on sex a few years back, but he did not see why he should, so he took the chance to visit a lady of the night in Peronne. Then in Bethune. And then in Ypres. She said if she ever caught him with anyone else she would tell the press, divorce him and take him to the cleaners. Hopefully he was safe in France. Why did women hold all the cards? What really hurt was he still really fancied his wife, despite being treated like a dog.

Ivan also felt angry he had not been told in advance about the police raids although felt he had taken enough precautions. Bexhill was a bit close to home though - only fifteen miles away. He did not understand the story about the hat and did not care about the staffing levels in NHS hospitals - he never used them.

His wife brought him back to his real world away from the news by shouting.

"For God's sake Ivan, are you incapable of putting anything in the dishwasher?"

"The headlines today on *BBC Radio 4*:
- George Orwell's Eton tutor is named as Fifth man in Cambridge spy ring
- The College of Emergency Medicine says England's A&E departments are in chaos because of a serious shortage of doctors
- Rupert Murdoch bids to add the *Los Angeles Times* and the *Chicago Tribune* to his vast American media empire.
- Police have raided several houses in their investigations into child sexual abuse
- Is racism in football alive and kicking? Why did Rio Ferdinand refuse to wear *Kick it Out* T-shirt?
- A Dachshund has turned up…"

Suzy heard the news but was not really listening. It was her fortieth birthday. She had mixed feelings of excitement, tainted with the horror of feeling old, and worse - waking up on her own. She thought to herself she had enough emotion brewing to sink a battleship. It was over five years since Philip was killed but she still could not get used to it. Tonight though, Rob was taking her out to dinner.

They had been together for about a year but Rob was still living at the family home and their relationship was being carried out deviously and secretly. She hated the dishonesty and betrayal. She wondered what tale he had told his wife about tonight. On call? Unlikely as he could easily be found out. It also would expose him as a hypocrite as he was always moaning about how much anti-social hours work disrupted family life. He did know he was already hypocritical by being with Suzy. Perhaps the excuse was a late meeting at the practice – no, too easy to be unwittingly unmasked. A pharmaceutical meeting? Probably.

But she thought the sex was fantastic. The best of her life. But did she always think like this with a new partner? Especially as she had had no one but her battery-driven friend since Philip died. But they had not reached her eighteen-month cut off yet, when according to her theory, and practice, the hot spots would vanish. She had told Rob, in effect warned him, of her theory, but he said it was a self-fulfilling psychological prophecy. If you tell yourself you do not fancy someone, then you do not, no matter what the hormones try to tell you. And what about him? Was he only in it for the sex? She wondered, but thought while they both were having a good time what the hell. Except for the people they might hurt, but no one will get hurt if they do not get found out. Will they?

She sympathised with his dilemma. He says he will leave but who could possibly leave such lovely girls and break up a family? Only someone unbalanced surely. He cannot win of course because she needs him to leave if their relationship is to continue, but does she really want to be with someone who is heartless enough to abandon his responsibilities and leave his family? And if that was not a turn-off then nothing was. Nothing is more important than family, so how could he even contemplate it? What are they doing?

So Suzy did not notice the news, although her ears pricked up about the Dachshund who went missing and was discovered two hundred miles from home after six months and in the garden of the owner's aunt. That interested her more. When in a good mood, and she was as it was her birthday, her sense of humour came to the surface. This time she wanted to ring the *BBC* and ask them why they had not interviewed the dog. Bloody *BBC*. Now they are anti-canine. Or was it anti-Dachshund, or even anti-German?

"The headlines today on *BBC Breakfast TV*:
- The Fifth man is named. We bring you an interview with a man who knew his brother
- The NHS in crisis: the Government say the *Health and Social Care Act* will make it fit for the 21st century
- Police launch two inquiries Operation Yewtree and Operation Famulo. We ask where do they dream up these names?
- And in sport, a survey shows most fans would welcome gay rugby players

Now the news where you are..."

Jenny always put the television on at breakfast time. She hardly got a chance to watch or even listen though as she was always preoccupied getting the girls out of the door to the bus stop for school. Francine and Leona went to the main Girls' High School six miles away, and Barrett, being only eight, walked with her Mum to the local primary school, which the others had left just two years ago and last year respectively.

She enjoyed the walk although Barrett always moaned that all her friends were dropped off at the school gate so why not her? Jenny could not believe some of the lazy slobs who drove just five hundred metres rather than walk. She had written to her local newspaper - a very rare event - to ask if there was support for a car exclusion zone around every school. Perhaps just a mile, she argued, just think how much fitter children and their parents would be. It

472

would set a good example and allow the traffic to flow more freely. She received hate mail in return.

Jenny ran a well organised house and the girls were already self-managing. There was no chaos, fighting, rushing, shouting or waits for the bathroom that Rob heard his friends experienced. He gave Jenny the credit for this. She was so calm and so methodical.

"Cliff Richard? No way… that's outrageous!" exclaimed Jenny.

Rob preferred *BBC Radio 4*'s *Today Programme* as he thought, although biased toward the Establishment and desperate not to stray out of the Overton window, at least it had less trivia. He grew mad with any media outlet spinning Government propaganda, and most of them seemed to nowadays. It was just that he felt the *BBC* misguided and controlled as it was, needed a bit of support and encouragement to fight back to regain its rightful place as something the British could be proud of. He thought they could start by sacking a few of their time-expired presenters.

He usually listened on the way to work. The *BBC* journalist had just run over most of the people on Sir John's list with a few more late additions at the request of Sir James.

"Rolf Harris?" Rob thought, "Blimey."

Then his mind moved back to the dilemma that had tortured him for the last few months. A dilemma that hurt him. Jenny had been so sweet recently. How could he possibly do this to her? She was such a good mother but the passion had gone. She was not at fault at all. She was kind, had a great personality, loved Rob to bits and still had a fantastic body. How could he betray that?

"Says it all about me. Immaturity, I suppose," he said out loud.

It must be hormone-led he thought. It was certainly not rational. But why is it so many men risk everything like this? Crazy. And how could he do this to the girls. He should not have brought them into the world if he could not look after them properly and take his responsibilities seriously. So selfish. Was he any better than Rolf Harris he wondered? Was he any better than some of the other jerks the newsreader had named? This was distracting and it had to be resolved before it interfered with his work and he made a mistake.

His head said behave and end the affair. The grass will not be greener. His heart and his dick told him the opposite. The devil was winning.

"I'll be late tonight, Jenny. I'm meeting a rep who might help fund some research I'm thinking of doing."

The front door clicked. Jenny had never heard him talk about research before.

"The news today on *France 24*:

- Prosecutors in Paris have said an alleged Islamist terror cell was planning the biggest ever bomb attack in France since the 1990s. Police have arrested twelve people in raids during which one suspect was killed

- Police investigating the Annecy shootings near Cheuvaline last month when four were killed are reported to be investigating whether one of the victims, an Iraqi born British tourist, was targeted over a contract he was working on for the multinational aerospace and defence corporation, EADS. Other possible motives such as a financial family feud leading to a contract killing, or links to bank accounts belonging to Saddam Hussein have already been suggested

- In Britain, The Metropolitan Police have announced it will take the lead in assessing sex abuse allegations by launching an enquiry called Operation Yewtree. They are following one hundred and twenty lines of inquiry over four decades. The houses of several suspects were raided overnight and computer equipment confiscated for analysis

- Mazarine Pingeot, the daughter of the deceased French President Francois Mitterand and Anne Pingeot, has published *Bon Petit Soldat*, a diary that includes memories of her childhood which was kept a state secret. She tells how she used to sneak into the Elysee Palace through the back door to see her father

- And we have Johnny Hallyday performing in concert in Montreal for you later."

Giselle reached for the television controls on the bedside cabinet and put her television on *France Today* as usual. She found this channel far more informative and investigative than any in England and it covered stories the British media seemed to censor. She remembered hearing, whilst still living in France, how the whole world knew about Edward VIII and Mrs Simpson except the British public. The press thought they should protect their monarch. Admittedly this was nearly eighty years before but she wondered how much protection the Establishment gets nowadays.

As she increased the volume Clive woke up, fell out of bed and dragged a comb across his head. He finally looked at her. Both remained silent and neither smiled. There was a melancholy atmosphere, which they both felt and was in danger of suffocating them. The night before they agreed to end their love affair. It had lasted six months and caught them both by surprise. It was exciting and gave Clive his carefree personality back, which had been stifled by his work as a GP. But they both knew it was daft, risky and dangerous. They worked together. They were both married. They both had children. But it was more Giselle's decision than Clive's. She seemed to value her family more than Clive did. People were beginning to notice and talk. Last week they were told to move on by the farmer whose field they met in regularly. They thought hiding the car behind a huge hedge was safe. The tap on the window proved it was not. It had to end. They agreed this was to be their last night together. There were tears but they had to be grown up about it.

Clive thought Rolf Harris? You are kidding, but did not say anything. Giselle thought this would never happen in France, but did not say anything. Clive slipped into the shower, dressed quickly and said the only four words he would say to Giselle for the next week.

"See you at work."

He then left.

Giselle sat on the edge of the bed for a few minutes to gain some composure. She told herself she was going to be strong and the only way that could happen is to get on with life and not wallow in self-pity. At times like this she always remembered her father and his wise words. She tried to follow his philosophy. He was her teacher and guiding spirit. It had served her well up to now and she was sure it would get her through this. This time she was not going to think about it at all. She was to get back to her old circuit of friends, get back to the gym and get back to her family.

Derek had taken the two boys away to his parents for half term. He had the time off but Giselle did not. He still worked in the City and they started drifting apart when he could not see why she became so disparaging about that type of work. But she did not mind a week on her own. She saw it as an opportunity to spend time with Clive but did not imagine that after just two days it would come to this. She knew it was the right thing to do.

She was keen to avoid Derek's father anyway, as he continually made suggestive comments and too often invaded Giselle's personal space. His hands often wandered too and, although not unattractive as a male, he now repulsed her. On kissing goodbye he once put his tongue down her throat. She nearly threw up but never said anything. Certainly not to Derek. Like most Europeans Giselle thought the British sexually repressed. She wondered about Derek's Dad. Why and how did he turn out like that? What drove him to constantly make sexual innuendoes and comment on newsreader's breasts? Did it thrill him or did he just like to shock? Why in public would he tell his wife her tits were too small? What chip had he on his shoulder, or what hang-up lurked deep down? Was he abused as a child? She will never know and maybe he has no insight either. In addition there was something of the night about him. Something Derek refused to talk about. What Giselle had gathered from his poor wife was a patchy story of a prison record as a young man for GBH. It was now a totally taboo subject.

When the subject of sex came up amongst all the receptionists at work, as manager she did not join in, but got the impression that British woman did not do sex. What was wrong with them? Why deny a pleasure, but more important why needlessly take out of a relationship the glue that often held a couple together? Madness. Where did this come from? Was it religion? Doubtful. Was it Victorian values? If so from the recent documentary she saw, that did not come from the Queen as she enjoyed sex and was always at it with Albert. It was well known around the world, certainly in France, that if denied sex, a man has a biological need to seek it elsewhere. Maybe this is why some in Britain seem to dislike Europe - insecurity? Cannot cope with love and intimacy and do not want the stiff upper lip to sag, she thought and giggled to herself.

Clive was different and must have had his British genes diluted somehow. He was a lover who was prepared to do anything that she requested, and she requested a lot. He certainly learnt a lot. Giselle was to Clive what Maggie Meller was to Edward the Prince of Wales.

Giselle switched channels to find the BBC presenter reading off the people on Sir John's list with Sir James's late additions. It took her a while to realise the list referred to people whose houses the police had raided and longer still to link it with the story on *France 24* when they named Operation Yewtree. It became a constant loop of news as she washed, dressed and made a pot of coffee. She noticed she was low with her stocks of Lobodis, her favourite coffee produced according to fair trade criteria in Saint Brieuc in Brittany. She must get the next friend who visits to bring some over.

Giselle thought no more of the news - she was too preoccupied. She turned the television set off and left for work putting her Johnny Hallyday CD into the player. Straight to her favourite *Quelque chose de Tennessee*. She could get lost in that.

"The headlines today on *TalkSport Radio*:
- Busty blonde sues fairground as she claims accident turned her into nymphomaniac
- Houses of possible sex perverts raided by police
- Have doctors become lazy? Special report on why they won't work in your local A&E

- Rooney scores at both ends as United run riot in four-two win over Stoke
- Fifth man named - did he abuse Eton schoolboys?
- American newspapers ask Rupert Murdoch to take them over"

Sean was waiting for his favourite chat show on *TalkSport* with Andy Gray and Richard Keys. Last year both were sacked from *Sky Sports* for sexist behaviour. Sean thought this was typical. Hang a few more minor offenders out to dry and the big fish get off. He remembered watching Gray play for Aston Villa and Everton on *Match of the Day* whilst a prisoner in Dolphin Square. To Sean the highlight was seeing Gray head the ball out of the Watford keeper's hands in the 1984 FA Cup Final to win the game 2-0. Sean approved as he always thought keepers too protected by referees.

He did not ignore the story about the raid, but knew it was just another attempt by the Establishment to pretend that they were taking the problem seriously and trying to show they were doing something. Sean had enough to be bitter about but for reasons even he could not understand he was not. He just accepted his lot. He thought his life had turned around after Dolphin Square when he gained a wife and two children, much to his disbelief. He accepted it as inevitable when he lost them again. He accepted the benefit cuts that made it difficult to feed himself, and certainly not keep warm in the winters. He accepted his forced move from his council flat because of the bedroom tax. He accepted the council's attempts to move him again from North Kensington to Bradford, as he was an obstacle to them gentrifying the area. It was only because of lost paperwork that he was still in the Adair Tower. He lived in the council area with the widest gap between rich and poor. His self-esteem was so low he did not even think he deserved to stay.

Andy Gray started by applauding the stunning overhead kick from Karim Benzema in Real Madrid's four-one win over Ajax, and Richard Keys posed the question.

"Should Roy Hodgson really travel to work on the tube?"

Leonard Cohen's dusky rumble of a voice oozed from the bedroom speakers, *I dreamed about you, baby, you were wearin' half your dress, I know you have to hate me, but could you hate me less? Anyhow* was Dave's favourite track from Cohen's twelfth album in forty-four years *Old Ideas*. He had played it so often in the nine months since its release that Pippa, who was not a fan, now loved it. She always thought Cohen's music was to kill yourself to. *Rolling Stone* magazine thought the first track *Going Home* was the best of 2012 and she agreed. She was not sure she wanted to wake up to it every morning though.

They had given up listening to broadcast news after the Iraq war. They just did not trust it any more. They thought *Radio 4* good but not its news and opinion. Other radio stations just broadcast Murdoch's version. Television news was even worse. Trivial, puerile and superficial fodder for the masses designed to stop them thinking too deeply about the real issues. This was all agreed on their first date. Dave impressed Pippa with the fact that on 18th April 1930 the BBC announced there was 'no news' and the rest of the time was filled by piano music.

"What a wonderful day that must have been!" said Pippa.

"And if you research further back, only four things happened in the whole year of 1317," Dave added.

They used websites like *The Huffington Post, Open Democracy* and *Left Foot Forward* to get their view of the world, plus a subscription to the *New Statesman, Red Pepper* and *New Internationalist*. The *Daily Mash* and of course *Beer and Brewing* magazine were Dave's priority though. Recently they had learnt about several outrages that were not reported in the mainstream media. They read about the council that outsourced the care of its trees to a private company who proceeded to chop them all down two weeks into winning the contract. There was no mention in the contract that they should not do that. It made the work required after that for the remaining five years minimal so the bosses could then sack the staff and retire on the profits. They learnt about the Hinkley Point C scandal where the Conservative Government decided to get the French and Chinese to build a nuclear power station and then use taxpayers' cash to pay them double the market rate for electricity for thirty-five years - and to cover the clean-up costs. The Tories had privatised the UK's nuclear expertise in the 1990s and then the French Government bought the private company, so we could no longer do it ourselves.

"The French and the Chinese must have thought all their Christmases had come at once," Dave said.

"You do realise, Dave," said Pippa, "that the competition between energy companies is not real, it is pseud-competition. They really are just crooks who are unnecessary middle men."

"And women," Dave jabbed.

"...and women, who just read meters and collect our money. Most of the time they do not even read meters, they make us do it. They are just not needed except by the big, fat cats creaming off our money for their next yacht."

"Most people want the energy industry nationalised but the media still portray that as Marxist and going back to the 1970s," said Dave.

"But we do have a nationalised energy company. It's just owned by the French Government," added Pippa.

And after a pause.

"Plus much of our transport infrastructure is owned by foreign Governments... so technically still nationalised and benefitting overseas taxpayers, not us. Even our water."

They missed the news about Operation Famulo. This did not affect them in any way. In fact they both started the day very happy and had a very nice day.

38 - BITTER AND SWEET

VENGEANCE IS MINE

Vengeance is mine
Vengeance is mine, mine, mine
To forgive is divine
But vengeance is mine, mine, mine

Alice Cooper (2008)

Rob stood and stared at their dead ginger cat hanging lifeless from the apple tree. In just a few seconds all sorts of thoughts shot through his mind.

Is this real? Yes. Is it a sick practical joke? No. Who could do such a thing? Just cruel nutters? Or has someone got something against us? Certainly feels pretty personal. Why though? What have we done? Which patients have I messed up or annoyed recently? Is it to do with the other stuff? A warning? Time to get out? Felix and Suzy said forget it. Why did I not listen? Maybe it is nothing to do with that. Poor cat. Poor Suzy. How do I tell her? Must hide Eric and move away before she sees me.

It was the latter lightning thought that brought him back out of his semi-trance. He wondered if he was more frightened of Suzy than any other scenario. He needed some cutters. He sneaked into the garden shed without Suzy hearing and fumbled around until he found what he was looking for. Not before knocking several flowerpots off a shelf though and treading on something that was sharp.

"Fuck."

There was a loud crash. He stood frozen for a full minute. No reaction from the house. Suzy must be deaf as well as the untidiest person in the world. He cleared out and tidied up the garden shed every few months. Suzy had an annoying habit of just opening the door and throwing things in to the point where it was difficult to get over the threshold. It had got to that point again now.

"I don't have time to put things away properly," she claimed.

He did not understand her logic, or lack of. He climbed out of the shed but not before a horrible crunch when he stood on something. He was not going to investigate what. Then worse. A rake smacked him in the face.

"Oh, fuck, fuck, fuckety, fuck. He rubbed his forehead. He clipped the garden wire that was around Eric's neck and there was a thud as he hit the lawn. Rob found he was still warm as he scooped him up and walked over to the compost heap. He found himself talking to the deceased.

"Hope you scratched and bit the bastard who did this to you Eric?"

He hid their ginger moggy under the grass cuttings and hoped he would remember to dispose of the body properly tomorrow before Suzy found him. With luck she would not be planning a gardening day. He also hoped speaking to dead animals was not going to turn into a habit. What if the foxes decided to play with the corpse? That did not bear thinking about.

He decided the least painful way to deal with this, for Suzy anyway - and certainly the least complicated - would be to lie and invent a story that Eric had probably just run away. What purpose would it serve to tell her someone had deliberately killed her cat? And how frightened might she get if she knew someone was trying to scare or threaten them? More to the point Rob knew he would get the blame for starting all this, although he would probably get the blame anyway.

He had collected his thoughts more rationally now and wondered which group or individual could have been responsible. A few months ago he would have just blamed nutters. One month ago he might have wondered about a disgruntled patient. A day ago he would have had no doubt it was the lot that wanted to shut him up and stop him sniffing around. Since last night though it could be his new friends - or old in the case of Jerry - showing their muscles so he is forced to help and join them.

He decided to go to work as normal and then whilst out on some visits detour home to get rid of the cat. She would be at work at the

Royal Academy. He could not dig a hole, as Suzy would notice that. He felt irresponsible but thought the easiest thing would be to stick Eric in a bag and throw him into the woods. Back to nature. What's wrong with that? A simple spreading of the molecules. If those theories were correct, eventually everyone will have one. Nothing wrong with that as long as he recycled the bag he had paid five pence for.

Since the surgery break in Rob was slightly more nervous about that peaceful time from 6.30 a.m. that he used to love when he was totally on his own. He had also developed a habit of looking at his filing cabinets to make sure the files had not been tampered with. He always picked the post off the doormat but usually just stacked it on the reception desk to be opened later. Giselle had always insisted on dealing with the mail. What Rob did not know was that she did this to protect him from racial hate letters. Now though he put aside official-looking envelopes addressed to him and took them straight to his room to deal with himself. There had been nothing that looked important for the last few days, but there was this morning. He got slightly anxious so could not open them quickly enough. No problem though. One was from the BMA and the other from the practice accountant. A relief that nothing was from the GMC, the CCG or NHS England.

Since Clive became a partner it was unusual for Michael Browning, the accountant, to address letters solely to him, but on reading he began to realise why. Michael chose his words carefully but the gist of the letter was that money had gone missing from the practice. He had noticed some irregularities in the information provided by Giselle whilst preparing this year's accounts and so decided to go through previous records. He had checked with the Primary Care Agency and it seems not all monies coming in had been put through the books. It looked like small but regular sums had been systematically syphoned off. There were only three people with the ability and knowledge to do this as far as he knew and they were Rob, Clive and Giselle.

It was obvious that Michael had made sure his letter was just factual with no pointers or accusations at all. However the fact that the envelope was addressed to Rob only and marked Private and Confidential said it all to Rob. Their accountant could defend it easily as Rob was senior partner. Michael said he would sort it out and if the error were his there would be no invoice for the work. He finished by offering his resignation as practice accountant as he felt he should have spotted the anomaly earlier.

"Oh bollocks, that's all I need."

Rob felt he was almost heading for a panic attack. He tried to control his breathing. Sitting quietly he began to settle. A simple remedy, but now complicated and commercialised with the label 'mindfulness'. Is there nothing people will not try to exploit for money? This was not quite the final straw but perhaps the penultimate one he thought. What would he advise a patient to do? Prioritise, to pace oneself, do not try to deal with everything at once, take one's time, sleep on things, do not act hastily, to put off the less urgent things until the next day.

He decided to shelve this for a few days but perhaps give Michael a ring to find out the extent of the problem. He certainly wanted to reassure him as soon as possible he would not want to lose him. Having put the coffee on he made his way to his room. He saw immediately a sheet of A4 with a list in Giselle's handwriting. Even though written in perfect English he still read it with her accent in his head:

Number One - the Medical Defence Union wants your version of events about the Saskia Bewering complaint. This is to remind you. I did ask last week. I've copied the notes to help you (attached).

Number Two - the good news. The GMC don't want to know unless you are guilty in the Bewering case.

What do you mean, unless you are guilty? Bloody cheek, Giselle he thought. And did not his old mate Jerry, or Nick, tell him at the roadside after blowing his tyre that this would no longer be a problem?

Number Three - the CCG pharmaceutical advisor is coming to see you at 2.00 p.m. today. Two issues: the drug stock discrepancy and the so-called prescribing and referral irregularities. Do you want me there?

Number Four - a man called Ian from a Toxicology Unit wants to speak to you on the phone. He would not leave a number but will ring precisely at noon. Insists it is very important. Says it is about a patient called Richey Edwards. We have two Richard Edwards on our books but he said he was not allowed to disclose which one.

Number Five - do you want your car cleaned? The window cleaner comes today. This is his sideline for £5 a time.

Number Six - have a good day.

Number Seven - there is no 7... yet. (A French woman's attempt at an Englishman's joke).

Bisous, Giselle.

P.S. Have you taken all the telephone recording tapes away for some reason? They all seem to have disappeared. But don't worry, I'll find them.

Rob plodded through morning surgery, but his heart was not in it. He did his usual acting but wondered if patients noticed anything. Certainly no one commented which was a relief. He did his best for Mrs Sharma. She deserved as long as it took and he was guessing she was reporting back after her urgent colonoscopy. He did not know, as he had had no communication from the hospital at all. To his great relief Mrs Sharma came in clutching a letter. But the relief turned to dismay when she looked to him to have lost a lot more weight.

"I'm so worried. No one has told me anything and I don't understand this letter. Can you help?"

Rob took the single sheet. It was anonymous and not addressed to anyone. The letter from the hospital simply stated:

T2N0M0 Stage 1. Grade 2. Descending colon adenocarcinoma. No other explanation at all, but like any good GP Rob knew what it meant and how to translate it into simple English for his patient. He knew he had to put her mind at rest immediately.

"This is very good news."

485

Rob tried to explain this to Mrs Sharma. T stood for tumour. There were stages of tumour size from T1 meaning the growth was restricted to the inner layer of bowel, to T4, which was bad news and meant it had spread through the bowel. Mrs Sharma was T2. It had grown into the muscle layer only. N stood for nodes. The letter said she was N0, which meant no spread to nodes. N2 would have been terrible meaning cancer cells in four or more lymph nodes. M pointed to whether there were metastases or not. M0, Mrs Sharma's stage, indicated no metastases. M1 would have had Rob explaining to her that her cancer had spread to other parts of the body and she was going to die from it.

Then there was the grading of the cancer cells. Grade 2 meant under the microscope the cells were moderately differentiated, which meant abnormal. Grade 3 was very abnormal. All this added up to her having a Stage 1 bowel cancer. Rob was taught the Duke's system of grading at medical school but his local surgeons had abandoned this. He would have put Mrs Sharma as Duke's A. This was great news. His morbid thoughts when she first presented, left him worrying about leaving three teenage daughters without a mother now evaporated. He shelved the thought and did not mention his annoyance at the hospital for their tactless communication. He would deal with that later.

"The statistics we have, or the latest I have anyway, indicate that this type of cancer means ninety-five per cent of men will survive five years. It's even better for women like you. It's almost guaranteed. Don't ask me why women do better than men, I've no idea. Stage 2 goes down to ninety per cent, Stage 3 sixty-five per cent, and the worst stage, Stage 4 only ten per cent. Five per cent for men."

She looked as though a great weight had been taken from her shoulders. At one point Rob thought she was going to hug him.

"You need the treatment of course."

"Well, this is the other letter."

She rummaged around in her shopping bag and produced what Rob recognised as an admission slip.

"It says I'm to be admitted next week for an operation. You can imagine what I thought when I got this, before the other letter. I thought it must be bad for this to be necessary and so quickly."

The tension had got too much. Tears started to trickle down her cheeks. A combination of relief, despair, pressure, stress and anxiety all bottled up and now released.

Rob knew a few years was a long time in medicine but he still could not get his head round the change in preparation for a colectomy. When he was a houseman the patient was in for a week at least, was starved of anything passing their lips for at least twelve hours and had to endure horrible bowel preparation to empty them out. Nowadays none of that was bothered with and patients were discharged very quickly - a little too quickly for some but generally Rob approved. Mrs Sharma was pleased to hear all this. She wanted as little time away from her three children as possible.

"You need to get on the phone and tell Marko the good news," Rob said.

He would not have said this in every circumstance. This was the value of good family medicine that those ignorant politicians don't understand - and sadly her surgeon who sent those letters without explanation. Rob knew the whole family. He knew they were devoted to each other. He knew Mr Visnjic would have been there with his partner if he could. Rob knew his boss docked pay if he was not at work and the family needed every penny they could get. Without this background knowledge another doctor could have easily put his foot in it. The same sentence to someone going through a divorce, or not even married, or had a female partner, could all be damaging to the doctor-patient relationship.

"I haven't got a phone now Dr Baigent. We can only afford one between us and my husband has that."

Rob picked up his and buzzed reception.

"Hello, could you show Mrs Sharma into a private room when she leaves me and give her an outside line? Thanks."

Mrs Sharma beamed.

"You can ring from here."

She came in desperate and left very happy.

Rob was pleased with himself too and thought that this job was not that bad after all. He too had a lump in his throat. What other job does this? He buzzed for his next patient.

As he ran through his list he was conscious of the noon phone-call Giselle had told him about. He tried to work it so he was free at the right time. He did not want anyone to hear him talk as he thought he knew who it would be.

At 11.58 a.m. Mr O'Brien closed the door behind him. Rob hoped his eagerness to get the consultation finished was not too obvious. A middle-aged man who rarely comes should ring alarm bells, but the consultation about his rash seemed straight forward enough. Rob hoped he had not failed to pick up on certain signs or, as can often happen, the patient had a problem that needed courage to divulge and the rash was just an opener - the old and well-known door handle syndrome. A man, as it is usually a man, prepares to leave and puts his hand on the door handle, but suddenly turns around and speaks.

"By the way doc, can I mention something else?"

Usually something embarrassing. Then as expected at 12.01 p.m. his phone rang. He could sense Giselle even before she spoke.

"Hello Rob, I 'ave Ian from Toxicology for you."

"Thank you."

"Hello, Dr Baigent here."

"Hope you enjoyed the *Hall and Woodhouse* you had in Martyrs Inn in Tolpuddle? Great beer isn't it? As you will have guessed this is Ian, although Nick might have said I would be Guy today. I've been known as Gregor Samsa too, a character from Kafka. We met at the chapel. By now you will have heard of Poison. I admit my cryptic code, the Toxicology Unit, isn't that clever, but hey-ho."

"Nick warned me you would be in contact. If you had anything to do with stringing up my cat, I didn't appreciate it?"

"Not us, mate. You are to meet one of our contacts, victims, informers - call him what you will. Let's say it's an initiation. The purpose is to let you know how deep and ingrained their control is and hear how evil they are. It should galvanise you. Do you know Chartwell, Churchill's country residence?"

"Well I've been there but years ago. Took my parents when they were alive."

"Just past Churchill's studio down the hill from the house there's a garden with a brick wall the old man built himself. Be by that wall at noon tomorrow. Go alone."

The phone went dead. Anything you say Rob thought with deep sarcasm. He resented being ordered about but after the cat incident, even though denied, he thought he ought to co-operate. Fortunately it was his half-day so by cancelling a few appointments he should be able to do the hour's drive to Westerham in time.

After four more consultations and some telephone advice he drove home and found some old sacking in the garage. He wrapped Eric in this and put him in the boot. The foxes had clearly had a night off. Even though he had no visits he still only got back to the surgery by 2.10 p.m. He decided to dump the cat later when it was dark. Being late was not deliberate but he admitted to himself it gave him some satisfaction to keep the mini-Hitlers from the CCG waiting.

Rob had asked Giselle to put them in his consulting room and not offer any refreshments. Childish he knew, but fun and vengeance was his. His heart sank when he saw who had turned up. He was expecting just the pharmaceutical advisor. A GP who was on the Board was there too and was well known to Rob. He had never liked him. He suspected the feelings were mutual. Rob had previously described him to Clive as an Arrogant Reactionary Sanctimonious Egomaniac - or 'ARSE' for short - who thought he practised medicine better than most and lived in an ivory tower. He thought he was just after getting as much money as possible and its source was unimportant. Does not matter if it came from the privatisation of the NHS. The layperson accompanying the 'ARSE' was unknown to him but wore a twin-set and pearls. She was looking disapprovingly at *Le Dejeuner sur l'herbe* on Rob's consulting room wall.

Rob was well prepared and went immediately on the offensive. He did not say hello but stared at the woman.

"And who are you, and what's your grand title?"

He did not really listen to the answer. He was not interested, but she was the pharmaceutical advisor.

"Here is the list of my referrals for the last twelve months, the reasons and the outcomes. Tell me which ones weren't necessary. It took my practice manager the best part of a morning to prepare this when she has better things to do. She has a proper job. Anonymised and coded of course. Second - we have been through the drug stock and don't agree with you that it doesn't tally. These detailed invoices list what was supplied, including the DDAs, and you can now go and count what's in the dispensary. You will have to be chaperoned of course. Wouldn't want anything to go missing. So our pharmacist will accompany you and give you any assistance you require, within reason. She too is busy. As long as I can trust you with confidentiality I'll leave you to look at the notes first."

Next came the most satisfying moment.

"Of course before you look at any confidential material I'll have to get you to sign this."

He handed the 'ARSE' a rather official-looking document that Giselle had drawn up. It was a Confidentiality Statement. Rob always thought that this sort of crazy obsession with getting written permission for everything was a one-way street. Only the authorities asked for it. This was payback time. He was tempted to charge them for parking their car too but thought he would never get the money. Rather aggressively and, regretting immediately that he might have gone too far and was being petty, staring at the twin set and pearls he added.

"And just in case you don't know DDAs stands for those drugs covered under the *Dangerous Drugs Act*. The ones we can't use now in the patients' best interest to stop suffering after Shipman got people like you to overreact and think all GPs are potential murderers."

"I know what DDA stands for Dr Baigent. I qualified as a pharmacist in 1981," the twin set and pearls calmly stated in monotone.

Before the CCG representatives could remind him that they also wanted to investigate his 'overprescribing' Rob asserted himself.

"Now if you will excuse me I've got patients to see and a few hours ahead of me filling in your silly forms."

With that he left feeling a mixture of satisfaction and slight guilt, about treating a woman he had prejudged and had never met before in a contemptuous manner. She was only doing her job, but if Rob had his way the job would not exist. Rob had to admit that what drove him was puerile. He was angry and thought it therapeutic to let off steam. Unfortunately for them they were in the way.

The era of cooperation was over but that was not the fault of GPs. For years Rob's surgery had let the district nurses have a room as a base for administration and to eat their lunches for free, as they were regarded as part of the team. The practice actually made a loss on running costs and could have got a decent rent from any paramedical worker. Then one day a district nurse slipped on the way into the surgery, fell and broke her arm. Obviously she needed time off and the bastards at the health authority who employed her got her to sue the surgery for damages so that they did not have to pay sick pay or any other expenses. Bastards. Rob evicted them as a result. Competition, budgets and non-cooperation, not what Bevan had intended.

He really felt there were more important threats and problems in his life at the moment. He knew he was taking a risk dismissing the CCG investigation so flippantly but what the hell. This dragged his relationship with the CCG down to the same level as his relationship with the Acute Trust. With a few colleagues he had fought secondary care's closure programme, otherwise known as reconfiguration. It came from Government, of course, but they denied it saying all decisions are local now. Bollocks. The Trust's CEO's bonus depended on delivery and doing what he was told. Rob had found himself up against all the surgeons who preferred to work at the new PFI hospital rather than the older one in the poorer area, as it was nearer to their private practices. The paediatricians pretended to care about the closure of one of their units until they realised they would have a one in ten rota rather than a one in five - a good bribe.

491

Perhaps this was the answer to Rob's bewilderment. Why is the public not angrier? Maybe attitudes had changed so that most people really only put themselves first now. This attitude change was bothering Rob more and more. There seemed to be no public anymore - just individuals. If it did not affect the individual it was not important and certainly not worth fighting about. If a T-shirt was a pound cheaper it did not matter if children working in slave conditions in Bangladesh made it. The pound was worth saving. I'm all right Jack. If a flight was cheaper because pilots had poor working conditions so what? Are we all selling our souls, or at least people's secure jobs and decent wages, just for a slightly cheaper holiday? Do we care as long as we are okay? Where did this attitude come from? Who was responsible? Rob had a pretty good idea.

Rob got his own back in a trivial way by refusing to send his patients privately to the NHS saboteurs as he labelled them. The return for the private companies and bankers funding the new hospital was seven times their investment. Even when paid off by the taxpayer the multinationals would still own it. The latest figures Rob had heard were that the capital assets built amounted to £12.4 billion, but the eight companies with stakes in the PFI companies would get £80.8 billion from the taxpayer - an eye-watering scandal. The land once owned by the public had been stolen and the hospital would forever be in private hands. Of course the public did not know this, and those who were told did not believe it. The maintenance contract was a rip off - hundreds to change light bulbs. More recently he had heard from staff they were worried about the fire risk. There were areas where there was only one way out and they did not think sprinkler systems worth the extra money. When Rob raised these concerns he was labelled a troublemaker who was not grateful for a brand new hospital.

It was only after Rob had left that the 'ARSE' and the twin-set and pearls noticed he had signed his part of the form Dr Hawley Harvey Crippen.

To forgive is divine, but vengeance is mine.

39 - ACCUSATIONS AND REFLECTIONS

GET BACK

Get back, get back
Get back to where you once belonged

The Beatles (1969)

Although Rob's initial decision was to sit on his accountant's letter until another day he was in combative mood. It was not in his nature either not to deal with a concern straight away. This was a hang-up from his junior doctor days of allowing an accumulation of problems to become overwhelming. He did not have patients waiting, or forms to complete, despite what he had told his two guests. He decided to see Giselle.

Rob had had a poor night's sleep. He was tired and going into combat with an insomniac's irritability was, as he knew from bitter experience, a bad idea. The CCG visit had been preying on his mind - more so than he wanted to admit. But Bernie Taupin's lyrics had been on a continuous loop through the night too. He could not switch off his mind. Jenny guilt again. *What I got to do to make you love me, What I got to do to make you care, What do I do when lightnin' strikes me and I wake to find that you're not there.* Then the horrible memory of Jenny saying to him, 'sorry isn't the hardest word for you, is it? You find it easy. You think it makes things better but you only say it to help your guilt. Your fake sincerity stinks Rob'. He was glad when the night was over. This time Suzy did not notice his restlessness.

The Practice Manager's door was closed and as he approached it his way was suddenly blocked by Celeste Venard, the practice nurse nicknamed 'Mogadon' by the other staff. Celeste delighted in telling anyone who would listen that she was named after the character on which Bizet based *Carmen*. So Nurse Celeste got her nickname from *Carmen*, who was also called La Magador. This was altered to 'Mogadon' by the other staff because of her habit of boring people into a coma. Celeste wanted to tell Rob about the latest attack on

493

breast-feeding. Rob's heart sank, wondering how long she would rant on for.

"You need to know this Dr Baigent. I've just read that the USA have stopped the World Health Assembly from promoting breast feeding further by threatening those countries that support the policy with trade sanctions and withdrawal of aid. So they've backed down, bullied by the corporate world worried about its profits."

"No surprise there," said Rob.

As he attempted to enter Giselle's room Celeste got between him and the door.

"But it's disgraceful. The milk formula manufacturers are getting the US Government to act like the Mafia on their behalf. Children are suffering as a result."

"I agree, Celeste. Thank you for updating me."

With that Rob sidestepped her and went into his Practice Manager's room, wondering why Celeste found it so important to tell him this now. To his surprise Clive was also in her room. He was standing with his back to the door immediately in front of Giselle who was sitting. Rob had the feeling he was intruding or interrupting something as Clive suddenly took a step sideways away from their manager. He looked rather flushed and quickly picked up a large file on Giselle's desk, then held it in front of him at groin level. The thought flitted across Rob's mind that he must have been feeling the strain of all this as he is now seeing things he cannot believe. His imagination is on acid. But he gave their actions no more thought. No more thought that was until Clive spoke.

"Thanks Giselle, I'll look at these insurance quotes and get back to you."

But Rob noticed the file was not about the surgery insurance at all but labelled Staff Interview Forms. How odd.

"Ah, while you are here Clive I'd like you both to look at this. We have a problem and I wonder what you think. I'm afraid it's quite serious. I'd value your thoughts as to how to proceed."

Rob was careful not to point any accusatory fingers. He managed to control his tired irritability. Clive sat down carefully, keeping the file in front of him at waist level and then placing it on his lap as he rather awkwardly descended into the chair.

"Got something wrong with your back, Clive?" fished Rob.

"No, no. Just stiff after a game of squash."

He regretted the word stiff but immediately went on to read the letter, then passed it to Giselle. Clive was the first to break the silence.

"Crikey. Does Michael know how much might be missing?"

"He reckons about forty-K."

Rob had spoken to him before surgery. He thought it slightly odd that neither of his colleagues reacted or gasped at the potential loss of such a large sum. Giselle, being as practical as ever, suggested a meeting between the three of them and Michael's team, as soon as Michael feels he could shine some light onto how this could have come about.

"I'm sure it's probably just an accounting problem," reassured Rob, but not himself.

Both Rob and Clive were keen to agree for differing reasons. Kicking it temporarily into the long grass suited all of them. Rob as he had too much on his plate at present and Clive as he did not want to face this and wanted to get out of the room as soon as possible.

"Oh and Giselle," Rob said as he was leaving, "Could you fish out those recordings marked 'Wessel and Chisholm' for me? Thanks."

The postscript in the note she wrote to him had obviously not registered, thought Giselle.

"Of course… 'ow did you get that bruise on your fore'ead, Rob?"

On his drive home Rob was in a reflective, but surprisingly calm mood. The day had been busy, an emotional roller coaster but in a curious way quite rewarding. His usual anger at how the dimwits in Parliament were messing up a great healthcare system was turning towards pitying them - and their lackeys and patsies for putting the evil plan into action, two of whom he had met that afternoon. After being perhaps too unreasonable he also pitied them. He could not get it out of his head that they really have no idea what a good GP does and how valuable and cost-effective is such a cheap resource. He could not get over that they were deliberately destroying an effective, efficient, low-cost healthcare system, fair to all citizens and patients, and deviously replacing it with one that is more expensive, more wasteful, corrupt and more unequal whilst denying what they were up to. They were diminishing levels of trust and corroding standards of ethical behaviour.

To Rob, they just did not get that the destruction of the NHS also marks the violation of important social values. The NHS was more than just a structure for the delivery of healthcare. It was also a social institution that reflected national solidarity; expressed the values of equity and universalism; and institutionalised the duty of Government to care for all in society. Instead, they were trying to persuade the public that if they see someone having a heart attack it is important to check they are not feigning it to get free biscuits at the cardiac unit, or if an old lady falls down the stairs she did not do it deliberately to swindle an insurance company. A few years ago this would have been a good example of black comedy. Nowadays black comedy is no longer funny when it is true.

He knew the politicians were deliberately ignoring the continuity of care that patients value so much. If they realised how much damage destroying this causes maybe they would think again, but deep down he knew the tossers were on a mission. Breaking the link between patients and doctors was essential or large so-called Primary Care Networks, to be delivered through Integrated Care Systems (the American way) would not work. No chance of ever seeing the same doctor twice there. Patients needed to be aligned to hospitals on the planned route to linking them with insurance companies. It was being engineered to make it more difficult to see a doctor. Trying to make an appointment now met with numerous hurdles. First you might get through to a school-leaver following a protocol. If you were lucky you might then get transferred to a more experienced receptionist. Perhaps then even a health care assistant. A few might get the prize of a chat with a nurse. A consultation with a doctor was probably another five steps away.

Instead of denigrating general practice with the help of their friends at the 'Daily Fail' they should be investing and making sure the brightest are attracted to that rewarding area. But they were deliberately underfunding practices to make them unviable. They needed to abolish what they call an outmoded form of care. The plan to reduce the number of practices from eight thousand to about fifteen hundred was on course. One practice was closing every ten days across England, over two hundred in the last year, and the rate was accelerating. The rest were falling into the clutches of vultures like Virgin, or even more difficult to swallow, groups of GPs who set up their own companies to get rich. Hospitals were taking over the running of practices too. This was spreading like a forest fire - from Northumbria to Gosport, from Wolverhampton to Somerset. A practice in the West Country had just shut its doors to twenty-two thousand patients. Whole practices were running on just one paramedic. New residents in a south costal town could not register with a GP. It made him so angry.

Specialists usually know everything about one subject, but GPs know a lot about everything. Not it all, but that is why they are generalists and consultants are specialists. It is in the name, dummy, he would have felt like screaming on a less calm day. Lord Moran was so wrong. The brightest were needed in general practice. He was pleased with himself and his recall of the bowel cancer staging system with Mrs Sharma. It meant he could serve her well. How satisfying to be able to transform her mood from one of despair to delight in under the ten minutes he was allocated for her consultation. To his knowledge they were at minimum on the fifth version of the TNM system and he had managed to keep up to date. Multiply that through all the dozens of specialties and hundreds of types of pathology and it is not surprising he thought his brain might explode sometimes.

Rob really did think his intellectual capacity was like a bookshelf and it was full. Put another book on it and one drops off the other end. There was little room for extra problems like family troubles or politics. To Rob that explained why so many of his colleagues do not seem to be conscious of what is happening in the real world.

They are at the coalface digging away and never coming up for air. It also explained, but he admitted it was not a good excuse, his impatience and intolerance at not being able to handle problems immediately thrust in his direction as soon as he walked into the family home from work, first from Jenny and now from Suzy. He had seen so many of his friends in the same situation. So many relationships wrecked on the rocks of overwork. It had happened to him once. He was damned determined not to let it happen again. His big mistake was now on his mind only eighteen hours a day.

So, as he walked through the front door he was delighted to see Suzy jump straight up from her chair and push a bottle of *Old Speckled Hen*, lid already off, into his hand with a glass. No problems thrust into his face, just a nice welcome home.

"Where did you get that bruise?"

"What bruise?"

"The one on your forehead. You obviously didn't shave or look in the mirror this morning?"

"Oh, that," said Rob.

Then he remembered the incident with the rake in the garden shed the night before.

"Bent over at work to pick up a speculum and knocked my head on the examination couch."

He hoped he sounded convincing. Anyway she changed the subject. At least she did not burst out laughing at his misfortune. Suzy's wine glass had already been drained.

"One bird in the bush is worth two in the hand," she said.

Another mixed proverb for my list Rob thought.

They both decided they had had quite a good day but Rob could do with a good night's sleep. Suzy told Rob about the follow-up to the arts fair she had visited while he was in Dorset. She really loved her job and was like a kid when explaining it to him. The daily commute was a pain though and was the reason she had finished her wine so quickly.

"The sooner those trains are renationalised the better," she would frequently complain.

Then followed her common rant, which Rob let her get on with every time she was delayed and he now knew off by heart.

"We have the most expensive, most overcrowded and least reliable rail service in Europe and the subsidies paid to those private companies are more than it costs to run the entire system under British Rail. It's crazy that foreign governments like Germany, France, the Netherlands, Singapore and Hong Kong run our railways! Did you know that the Dutch state rail operator Abellio operates so much over here that their UK network is two and a half times the size of the entire Netherlands state railway?"

"Yes, Suzy. You told me that last week and the week before. The public wants renationalisation but the media still make out it's a communist idea worthy of North Korea. Vested interests talking again, just like with the energy industry."

They both topped their glasses up again.

"But North Korea are our friends now, right? Great summit, the best there has ever been ever!"

"I have something to add which will make you reach for another bottle."

"I'm already on my way to get one."

"I read the other day about the Potters Bar rail crash of 2002. Jarvis were the private maintenance company who were found guilty of not doing their job. Seven were killed and dozens injured. They initially tried to blame sabotage but were clearly making that up. The Health and Safety Executive concluded Jarvis failed to understand the design and safety requirements. It gets better. The CEO still got a massive bonus when he successfully reduced the company's share price from five pounds sixty-six pence, to nine point five pence! You see they get rewarded for killing people and running down companies and, as a consequence, destroying people's livelihoods."

Suzy took a large mouthful of *Muscadet*, her favourite. She was never out of stock.

"One very valid argument you never hear is the waste of expertise when something is privatised. Years of experience go on the scrapheap and cowboys who haven't got the first clue about how to run something are put in charge. What about that GP NHS backrooms contract that went to an Arms manufacturer for fuck's sake! Useful if you want to bomb a hospital but no good when it comes to administering quality and outcomes framework, working out global sums, or direct or local enhanced service payments, or whatever you call them in general practice, eh Rob?"

"A mother was telling me the other day that her child's school has to make bookings for its own sports hall through a Jarvis call centre now too! The world's gone mad and being taken over by totally unnecessary middlemen ripping off anyone in their sights."

"Okay, you've heard my railway rant before," confessed Suzy, "but I bet you didn't know that the Minister of Transport who butchered the railways in the 1960s was managing director of a road construction company?"

"When Beeching closed more than four thousand miles of railway lines?" asked Rob.

"A Tory politician called Ernest Marples benefitted when his company built the Hammersmith flyover and got the contract despite it not being the lowest tender. Then the Chiswick flyover. He had a finger in the M1 pie too. When Denning investigated the Profumo affair, his habit of visiting prostitutes was covered up. Then he had to flee to Monaco to avoid prosecution for tax fraud."

"Well, well. He could give politicians a bad name, couldn't he?" laughed Rob.

This time Rob gulped some of his *Old Speckled Hen.*

"They clearly give the Transport portfolio to the dimmest. What about that one who hired a ferry company that didn't have any ships? You couldn't make it up," sighed Suzy.

"Not sure about that," said Rob, "He has strong competition from the Defence Secretary. He wants the RAF to have a drone squadron and Gibraltarians to be given paintball guns to fire at passing Spanish ships. He is the Government's Private Pike of *Dad's Army*, telling Russia to go away and shut up."

"On a more positive note on the train home, where you think I take my life in my hands, I got a call from Jeff. This made the day even better. He has booked flights and he will be over next month.

He'll obviously want to see the family but will be staying here a few days. That's okay with you isn't it?"

"Of course."

"I thought maybe we could have a sort of party here. Hopefully Leila can join us and, now my Mum and Dad are actually talking after all these years, do you think we dare invite both of them?"

"Yes. Their split was a long, long time ago. They've moved on and have new lives since then. Not sure about the new partners though?"

"Oh, they are okay. I get on quite well with Dad's new partner in Fife. She's very nice and quite chatty if she picks up the phone before he does. Not sure how she copes with his Elton John obsession though. I'll write to them inviting them down."

"It'll be good to see them all," encouraged Rob.

"Jeff talked for quite a time for him. Went on a lot about the political situation in the States. Thinks they are all mad. I told him I was a little worried about you and how stressed you are getting for the same reasons. He says you are both quite alike and looks forward to a good chat over some proper beer in a proper bar to solve all the world's problems."

What Suzy did not tell Rob was that Jeff's RAF friend (her 'third') was asking after her and wanted to meet up for old time's sake? She did not think Rob could handle that at the moment. She had to admit it sent tingles down her spine even though she had not seen him for more than twenty-five years. Her first really great sex. Probably bald and fat now and without the uniform, so would be disappointing, she told herself.

"You mustn't worry about me," Rob said calmly.

He thought about another bottle of *Old Speckled Hen*, but knew that he would risk falling asleep on the sofa in front of some rubbish on television. Then Suzy surprised him.

"But you know I think you are right. I'm really quite worried about the direction everything is going. It's as though no leader has had any history education. Perhaps no education at all. It's about time everyone acknowledged that homo sapiens are basically stupid. Crazy that it's Latin for wise man; the correct binomial nomenclature should be 'homo fuckinus stupidus'. Amongst many other disasters we are drifting towards an ecological apocalypse. Polluting the planet. Making land inhospitable to many forms of life. The decline of bees, moths, butterflies and beetles, and as a consequence, birds. We should be dragged before the European Court of Animal Rights. If there isn't one there should be. Dolphins should take over.

Apart from that we have split off from Europe and facing a new isolationist America with a dickhead in charge. Some imperialist zealots want the British Empire back. The *Daily Mail* is scapegoating refugees like they did the Jews before the last war. Right wing parties are in the ascendance in Europe. Even in Germany where the AfD has had the sort of success that got old Adolf off to a start. Tensions between countries are being not only encouraged but also invented. NATO seems to be on its way out. There are increasing numbers of the desperate poor. People are dying in the streets of Europe and drowning in the Mediterranean. Thousands of Rohinja Muslims are being massacred in Myanmar and it has faded from the headlines. I found a charity on the web the other day that claimed the refugee crisis is like nothing the world has seen before, which considering what happened in World War Two is frightening. Sixty-five million people, roughly the population of France, have been displaced. Syria, Afghanistan, South Sudan, Somalia and have you heard of the Lake Chad basin?"

Suzy stopped just enough for Rob to shake his head.

"No, nor had I. Totally overlooked by the West."

To Rob's distress, tears started to well up in her eyes.

"Nigeria, Cameroon, Niger and Chad... who talks about them? More than half are kids under eighteen, and many are on their own. And in the Yemen. We are supplying arms that are killing thousands and at the same time sending out aid. Fucking crazy."

The tears gave way to anger.

"Those refugees we would be able to help. Yet we shut our doors and pull up the drawbridge to these poor people and somehow the public are brainwashed that this is ethical. It's as fucking moral as the first class passengers guiding their lifeboats away from the steerage passengers after the Titanic sunk. What will happen next? Where are we heading Rob?"

"Blimey. I've been saying this for ages, and all I got from you was that I'm exaggerating. Have you heard of catch twenty-four?"

"You mean *Catch-22*?"

"No, I do mean catch twenty-four. When have you known me to get my numbers wrong? You know I'm on the autistic spectrum. Catch twenty-four is the wrong of evil being triumphant over good, stupidity winning over intelligence, greed overpowering selflessness and hidden agendas ruling the world. Wouldn't you say we are there now? We live in a catch twenty-four world?"

"Very good, but are you making all this up? How many catches are there?"

"Only *Catch-22*, twenty-three and twenty-four, so far. I'll think of more."

"One good thing about the Victorians," Suzy continued, "They had an open door policy towards immigration. Based on the idea that we were the greatest country on earth so people would be mad not to want to live here and be civilized by us from savages."

"From what I gather that didn't last into the twentieth century did it?" replied Rob.

He did seem to know about this.

"By the eighteen-nineties it transpired that one hundred thousand Jewish immigrants arrived in the East End of London, fleeing persecution in Russia. This sparked off a backlash movement called the British Brothers' League set up by some Major, a Tory MP, who said they were a huge threat, would never be loyal, were undercutting wages, putting pressure on housing and making neighbourhoods unrecognisable with all their foreign clothes, habits, food and religion. Sound familiar?"

"Yes. Very. Very *Daily Express* and UKIP. These horrible racists try to poison the public by deliberately mixing up the words foreigners, migrants and refugees. As far as they are concerned they are all the same, trying to sneak into our country and sponge off it."

"There's always a backlash. And they rely on how easy it is to fall back on our tribal nature. Tribe against tribe. Us against them. It's a very powerful motivator as it speaks to our most primitive self. We all know about the Windrush Generation now, don't we?" asked Suzy.

She ignored his nod.

"Well, I read Peter Fryer's book *Staying Power - The History Of Black People In Britain* at University. As you know after the war we desperately needed workers so we encouraged people from the Empire, which we still had, to exercise their right and come to Britain. The first ship to dock at Tilbury was the *Empire Windrush* with four hundred and ninety-two Jamaicans on board. Fryer highlighted the ignorance of those who believed this was the first arrival of black people in Britain and who called for them to get back to where they once belonged. Black people were here before the Anglo-Saxons arrived! Then there was Enoch Powell of course."

"They helped make the NHS the success it is," Rob managed to add, "Makes it even more appalling the way they were treated, deportations, internment, sackings. We are a racist country no getting away from it. Yet no one has been punished for this policy of hostility, prejudice and hate."

He started to fidget as he realised Suzy was on a roll so he attempted to take control of the conversation.

"Haven't I told you about my Mum's sister who works as a nurse in Aberalaw in Wales? She came over in the fifties from Barbados with the family. I'm sure I've mentioned my slave lineage. One of my ancestors was given the name Cumberbatch as a first name. Odd eh?"

This did not stop Suzy though who just steamrollered over it.

"War and terrorism in Iraq and Syria forced millions to flee and seek refuge in Turkey, Jordan, Egypt and Europe, most notably Germany. They put our Government to shame. Worse, the manufactured hostile environment was a disgrace and now the media have forgotten about them. British citizens are still being frog-marched onto planes and sent to places they didn't actually in reality come from. Those we threw out of the Chagos Islands in the 1960s and 70s so the US could build a military base at Diego Garcia are now being thrown out of Britain. A Canadian who has lived here for fifty-six years and paid UK taxes all his life has been threatened, and a man from Bangladesh who came here in 1972 was deported the other day, forcibly separated from his family."

"Cleland in the north of Barbados," Rob interrupted, sarcastically and in a vain attempt at getting some attention, but Suzy just carried on.

"They were refugees. They were called migrants though and became unwelcome in countries that feared to admit them for security, religious or economic reasons. There doesn't seem to be much compassion about for these poor people."

"A bit like the Windrush generation then and my family," said Rob, forcing the link.

Then a change of tone from her.

"By the way, your use of the word transpire to mean happen is wrong. You should know it comes from the Latin spirare to breathe. It is best used for when a fact oozes out, like a secret."

Rob ignored her correction and tried to introduce a touch of optimism.

"There were bright spots of kindness that shone through despite all this. Look at the activities of Nicholas Winton and the Kindertransport on the eve of World War Two. He rescued over six hundred children, but the right wing tried to stop him."

"I was discussing this at work a few weeks ago and heard about another bright spot, as you put it," Suzy continued, "We took in two hundred and fifty thousand Belgian refugees when Germany invaded Belgium in 1914. One of our greatest single acts of humanity. Apparently this was largely due to a Lady Lugard, previously known as the journalist and writer Flora Shaw, through her War Refugees Committee, but I'm told her imperialist ideology was incompatible with women's suffrage which put it in peril. So you win some and lose some, eh? I came across her at work as there's a photograph of her by George Beresford in the National Portrait Gallery, and a painting by Jacques-Emile Blanche came up for auction twenty or so years ago. I've no idea what happened to it."

"Interesting but too much detail. And you call me a nerd. As for your amazing conversion, one chat with your brother and it's as though it's the first time you have heard any of this about the terrible corrupt world we live in and it's all your idea to start objecting!"

"Oh, shut up," she said jokingly, "I know I started it but I don't want to be serious tonight."

"Do you know our brains do everything on about twenty watts of power? I think you must have connected yours to a generator tonight to be producing such rational thought."

"Robert. That proves you don't listen to me as I told you that a few weeks ago. Don't you remember me telling you that a super-computer is ten thousand times less efficient than the brain as it requires about two hundred thousand watts? That the brain has one hundred billion neurons and, despite it only being two to three per cent of our mass, consumes a fifth of our energy when resting?"

"Of course I do. How could I forget such a nerdy proclamation?"

"Liar."

Then to his surprise and delight, she put her arms around him and kissed him with a passion not shown since Chanoud Garh. Her hands ran firmly down his sides and then slipped smoothly and effortlessly into his boxers. Suzy pushed Rob against the fridge and caressed him until her hands were moist. Quite roughly she then grabbed his belt and dragged him to the armchair where she pushed him down, then fell to her knees and undid his trousers. It was all over within minutes. She reached for his beer to wash away the taste and then they hugged each other in silence.

Her thoughts had drifted back twenty-five years and that RAF uniform. Suzy knew the power she had over him and had already decided it would be her turn later. If he could manage it. Now was not the time. She was too hungry.

Rob could not believe his luck. Perhaps they should talk about NATO and immigration more often, he thought. He could not remember who it was that said women need a reason to have sex men just need a place. He did not know what Suzy's reason was this time but he did not care. He was surprised though.

"Bloody hell, Suzy, was that a dream?" Rob teased.

"*A dream you dream alone is only a dream. A dream you dream together is reality.*"

"Well, that's another surprise. I've never heard you quote Lennon before. Not correctly anyway," said Rob.

For that moment at least they were both feeling quite content with life.

40 - DEFEAT AND TRIVIA

DR. ROBERT

Dr. Robert he's a man you must believe,
Helping everyone in need

My friend works for the national health Dr. Robert,
Don't take money to see yourself with Dr. Robert
Dr. Robert you're a new and better man,
He helps you understand,
He does everything he can Dr. Robert

The Beatles (1966)

Stephen had WhatsApp'd to say he would be ten minutes late so Rob was warming up by the time his old mate crashed onto the squash court.

"Sorry old son. Clinic overran and then I forgot I had to take number two to Girl Guides."

"As long as Ellie didn't give you a bollocking."

"She would have done, plus no sex for a week, if I'd have come straight here which I fully intended to do, and left them high and dry. Fortunately I had to call in at home as I forgot to put my sports gear in the car this morning, so I could pretend I'd remembered. Helped that the sweet little thing was at the door in her uniform."

Once Rob had got to 7-0 he began to wonder whether Stephen was really trying, or still had his mind on other things. But then the comeback. He had obviously warmed up. 7-5, 8-5, 8-8, Stephen was letting loose all his pent-up aggression that had been building throughout the day. 10-9. Game Rob.

"That's a relief. Can't have you coming back like that. Demoralising."

Through gasps for air Stephen pleaded for a rest.

"Just one minute. Got the usual exercise-induced chest pain radiating down my left arm and up to my neck... sure its just wind.

Where did you get that bruise? Been swinging from the chandelier again, Rob?"

Rob knew he was joking and they both burst into laughter as Stephen let rip. There was nothing ever as funny as a farting joke. Two respected members of society regressing back to student days.

"Okay, before I forget, you know you mentioned that interview you saw on French TV?"

"Ummm…"

"You know… supposedly to help you learn French? Nothing of course to do with the gorgeous presenter's sweater puppies?"

"What do you mean? Are you referring to her hooters or wazoos? Speak English old boy. Are you insinuating I only watch that channel to get a butchers of her maguffies?"

"Not insinuating at all. Saying that's what you do. Don't forget I shared a room with you once. Haven't recovered yet."

"I've never been so insulted in my life. Another great episode last night though. Made me quite boss-eyed."

"Enough Trump locker-room banter. I need to dredge your memory banks for what you remember about that interview. Anything apart from the thirty-six C that springs to mind?"

"Not really, just great chitty bang bangs, known as cha-chas, or Bonnie & Clydes in Margate I believe. No, I'm joking of course."

After a pause.

"They weren't that great!"

Then laughter.

They had debated their reasons for reverting to juvenile behaviour before and decided it was a necessary release from having to spend the day being respectable. It was their reaction and revolt against the false role they have to act out for professional reasons. It helped keep them sane.

"Actually she did have a rather unusual first name, Madison, and was originally from Texas. I wouldn't mind being her bucking bronco. Ugly as hell though. And the interviewer was very French, called Chantelle."

"Ugly? I remember you saying both were very attractive. I am afraid I see it as my duty to tell Ellie."

"Only kidding. Can't remember what she looked like."

"Anyway, that's enough for me to hopefully trace the piece," said Rob explaining his enquiry.

It was just like being back in Brockley. That banter could only be between old mates who grew up through student days together. Politically incorrect maybe, but too funny to resist. They would be horrified if anyone overheard.

They both hated their student days at Guy's. Teaching by humiliation by arrogant beau monde who would rather be in Harley Street. It might have been just about tolerable if they were taught something useful, but in those days too much was non-evidence-based opinion from the likes of the many Sir Lancelots. A frightening amount eventually turned out to be just plain wrong. And drug therapy was portrayed as the panacea for everything - especially by the corrupt pharmaceutical industry. There were a few bright moments and exceptions like the wonderful Harry Keen. They reminisced too about the Professor of Respiratory Medicine whose party piece was to ask them what the chest X-ray of a woman called Jean Ross showed. None of them got it right, but maybe it showed tuberculosis? But that was not the point. She was an old patient of his who had died in Barnes in 1973 aged sixty-two and was really Sally Bowles of *Cabaret* fame.

"Two more games then I really need a pint."

Stephen was giving the impression he had already had enough. Rob would not push it. The deal always was to never make their weekly squash games any sort of trial or ordeal or they both knew they would give up the only regular exercise they got. Rob won the next two games relatively easily, and they were both glad to get off the court. Then the usual communal shower and the usual banter about it reminding them of schooldays, and the jokes about it being fatal to bend over to pick the soap up off the floor, and the mickey taking about each other's clothing, and the usual insults about deodorants.

"I like your squash shirt Rob, but what I don't get is why we pay to advertise their products. Surely they should be paying you to have

Dare2B on your front? Another example about how we are all being conned. Anyway dare to be what?"

They walked out past the Maria Sharapova bra advert, which again distracted Stephen.

"Shouldn't be allowed, should it?" he said.

"Does Ellie still buy all your clothes for you?"

"Not my bras," Stephen joked as he sensed where this one was going.

Some well-crafted insult was heading his way - a week in the gestation no doubt.

"So you went straight from your mother buying you your wardrobe to Ellie dressing you? Have you ever been in a clothes shop?"

"No, that is what the valet is for surely?"

To survive, and to avoid losing face, batting back immediately was necessary, preferably on a different topic.

"What I can't understand is why people spend a fortune on gym subscriptions, paying for their time on a treadmill, then just stand on escalators. They are staircases. They just move. Why don't people walk up them? It's free."

"I always walk up them," Rob responded, "but do you know traffic streams of people would be more efficient if they all stood on both sides? Proven fact. Ask the new American President. Talking of which, I've been giving serious thought to what you said about the need for a new movement, a new political force, one free from corruption. I think last week I called it the Blue Peter Party. Well, you'd be the ideal leader. You could be the new Ledru-Rollin."

Stephen paused for effect as he knew what Rob had to say next and he wasn't disappointed.

"Who the fuck's Ledru-Rollin?"

"Well, I'm glad you asked. Alexandre Auguste Ledru-Rollin, who now has a metro station named after him in Paris, was a French politician who in 1848 said, *There go the people. I must follow them for I am their leader.* After the lack of any good choice we talked about in the French elections they should dig him up and stick him on the ballot paper.

"Admit it, you looked that up, didn't you? No one could remember a name like that. Anyway, is that what happened to your old mate Alex? He followed rather than led? You told me last week you'd fill me in on his attempt at a *Blue Peter* Party. How do you know him?"

"I was Senior Reg at the Brook just before I came to Brighton and he was my houseman, so he's about ten years behind us. No, Alex really was a leader. A man with good intentions but he just got shafted. By those feeling threatened by a challenge to the official agenda that the Government and media insist all us lemmings stick to. They went for him. I think it was more than just the usual squabbling and in-fighting between amateur politicians with big egos. I think his film worried them a lot. That's why they did everything they could to make sure it was not aired. But some really think it's all a big game and act like children. It's probably much more serious than that. Sabotage by the well organised Establishment, just like when they go for left wing leaders, not that we've had many recently. They never stand a chance of a fair hearing."

They started their usual amble to The Hung Drawn and Quartered.

"I still get nostalgic when I drive along Shooters Hill Road and see one of the only bits left, the old water tower. John Major realised the hospital wouldn't cope without me so closed it a few years later. Alex was in A&E when Stephen Lawrence was brought in dead in April 1993. The racism was awful there. He wasn't the first but is the most famous. Two years before a fifteen-year-old Rolan Adams, was killed just a few miles away by a gang also while waiting at a bus stop. Adams' family were sent a card saying, 'Glad a nigger is dead' and when Rohit Duggal was stabbed to death the following year graffiti appeared saying 'two-nil'. The police added insult to injury by spying on and hassling the victims' families. Alex with a surname like Ephialtes was told to piss off back to bongo-bongo land. Ignorant gits. No idea it's a Greek name and he was third generation. His Greek-Cypriot grandparents arrived in Camden after the Second World War, when Cyprus was still British. I suppose you had that hassle too?"

512

"You bet. I've heard that surname before but I'm struggling to remember when and where," interjected Rob.

"Alex was nearly in prison instead of working in A&E back then. He was arrested at Twyford Down protesting against the M3 motorway extension. Seven of his fellow dissidents went to jail, but he avoided that fate, just. I think he was almost sorry he wasn't banged up."

"Medicine is such a small world. Everyone knows everyone."

By now they had lined up the pints of *Harveys*.

"I feel a little guilty as he approached me to play my part in the fight for our NHS but I didn't take the bait. Looking back I should have, of course, but I was like a lot of our colleagues, in denial and not really believing what was happening. We all made a grave error and some will see their graves earlier as a result of our indifference. His film was very powerful and woke me up. I'll let you have a copy. You won't see it otherwise."

"Is the Party still going?"

"Yes, but it's fallen into the hands of a few quislings who are making sure it is ineffective. No, wrong phrase, not fallen at all, aggressively stolen and now they have complete control to pretend there is opposition when there is none. They produce silly arguments that they know can easily be destroyed. That strengthens the Government, which is their intention. They are pseudo competitors."

"So there's no point in making contact?"

"Certainly not with Alex, who is now suspended and a broken man. The party, well, if you feel you could mount another coup and get control back, then good on ya. A lot of effort for little reward I would say, as then they would go for you. They are evil, too evil to be ashamed of themselves. Most were lucky they weren't reported to the GMC. Their behaviour was and is outrageous. It could, perhaps should, have easily ruined their careers but Alex is too nice to use their sort of dirty tactics. Now it's in the hands of the Health Secretary's mate, drop a piece of litter and the GMC will want to hold a disciplinary hearing. Alex's friend Jim is awaiting a GMC hearing for putting stickers on the sides of G4S ambulances. And you'd be in the shit with them if they heard you referring to women's anatomy like you were earlier."

"Me? Wait 'til they get my tape recording, with me edited out of course."

They both paused to savour the beer.

"If you start another Party, you'd go the same way. As for influencing the health policy of existing parties... well it's been tried. Their policies are written by big business. They've all been nobbled and have paymasters fighting for the opposite of what we want and what they claim to stand for. They are all puppets now."

"Fuck. I never thought I'd hear you talk like this. Must be time for another pint."

There was another surprise for Rob.

"I've even given up the *Guardian*," said Stephen proudly, "Jeremy Hardy, RIP, asked what is it the *Guardian* actually guards? It guards how progressive you are allowed to be. You can go this far to the left but no further. That's why they sacked him, Mark Steel and John Pilger. It's not the *Daily Mail* we need to fear. You expect that purveyor of political pornography to produce twenty-two pages attacking and lying about the leader of the opposition. What we really should fear is the mainstream media like the *BBC* and the *Guardian* who set the agenda."

On Rob's return from the bar Stephen was looking at the messages on his phone.

"Oh shit. Ellie's organised another one of her dinner parties for Saturday week. Messaged me to put it in my diary. Says she can't trust just telling me as she says I'll forget. Bloody cheek as I told her I was going to that England World Cup qualifier with you. Or at least I think I did. Shit. Leave it to me. I'll sort it out. It might take some more drachenfutter, but that's life."

"Drachenfutter?" quizzed Rob.

"Oh, come on Rob. Dragon feed. Bet you need this regularly. You know. A gift to placate an angry wife."

"My last was after she found out the real meaning of the names I gave the kids' two pet guinea pigs. Masters and Johnson. I told the whole family Masters was after Edgar Lee Masters the poet, and Johnson as a tribute to Brian Johnson from AC/DC. When she found out who Masters and Johnson really were and what they did she hit the roof. Drachenfutter needed then certainly."

"Ever thought you'd have been better off staying with that sadist girlfriend of yours, or Charlotte? Were all your women thrown out of the SS for cruelty?"

"Funnily enough yes."

"Strange creatures women. How many have you heard say the best feeling in the world is to look at a fresh washing line of linen blowing in the wind?"

"In Ellie's case only if she has done it. I'm banned from going near the machine as somehow I do it all wrong."

"Well, I sympathise. And you know I've given up on bourgeois middle-class dinner parties. Or rather they've given up on me. Does anyone really enjoy trying to outdo each other? How do you cope? Have fun though, won't you? You know you're snookered. Do you want me to see if I can get rid of your ticket?"

"No. Really. Time to make a stand. I will be coming. Promise."

"Yeah, right! Just glad I'm not invited. You know what trouble I cause. Suzy really told me off last time. Said I was a rude bore."

"Ha ha! You are invited. Don't quite agree with your Duchess of Fife, but an invite is quite amazing after your last performance. Perhaps she regards you as the entertainment. A bit like the village idiot."

"Bollocks. Well at least I have an excuse. I'll be watching Marcus Rashford score his first England hat trick. Suzy can go though."

"I think you quite fancy that Arabella. Go on, admit it?"

"Absolute rubbish," Rob said in a less than convincing manner.

Stephen needed to change the subject.

"The other message is from our glorious Government. Go to see your local pharmacist at the first sign of a cold."

"Unbelievable. They really have no idea what they are doing, have they?"

"Well, maybe they are more sinister than stupid."

Rob raised his eyebrows.

"Well, it is stupid. No doubt. Work through this logically. They would like everyone with any symptoms of a cough or cold to go to the pharmacy. That means the entire UK population between two and five times a year spreading the bugs further, and for what? Nothing does any good. It's part of life for fuck's sake. They say go to stop it becoming more serious. How does that work then? Wankers!"

Rob took over the more cynical explanation.

"Yes, but look at the retail opportunities. The pharmacists can make money selling all sorts of evidence-free shit that people might as well rub on their goolies for the good it will do. All those ex-health ministers who are now on the boards of these chains will be rubbing their hands together."

"Quite."

"Sadly the message the public will get is that they might get serious complications and die if they don't see a health professional at the first sneeze. And what if the first sneeze is at three a.m., when 'Pharmacy Phil' is closed. Better not chance it. A&E it is! And we GPs get the blame for A&E queues stretching down the street. Then what? They decide to close a few more!"

"How depressing the whole thing is," sighed Stephen.

"I'll tell you what is even more depressing, our colleagues being only too eager to join the stampede to con and fleece the public. That crook of a gynaecologist Chisholm, who is climbing up the BMA pole, is going around buying up chemist shops, but to get them at a good price, he and his mates first spent years putting out deliberate rumours that their days were numbered. Now that they have acquired them at knockdown prices the policy changes. Now they are lobbying for pro-pharmacy policies, a familiar and common tactic. He rang me recently on another matter and was boasting about it."

"We should be allowed to put him up against a wall and shoot the tosspot," said Stephen.

"But we've got other arrogant pricks amongst us who play right into the hands of the enemy. Take that bastard criminal Paterson, who called himself a surgeon but had the skill of a blind monkey with a tremor. Morals and ethics much worse than that of a monkey too. Lopped off patients' breasts for no reason other than to make money and demonstrate how great he was. He made out he was a man you must believe, helping everyone in need. The *Mail* used his crimes to beat and denigrate the NHS, producing this headline the day after his conviction, 'Why did NHS fail to stop butcher surgeon?' No mention that he actually worked privately at two Spire hospitals and he wasn't suspended from those moneymakers until after he was suspended from his NHS Trust in Solihull. So they score by firstly knocking the NHS implying incompetence and dangerous practice, secondly making doctors out to be greedy crooks, and thirdly selling their disgusting load of shit to a gullible public."

"But it produces great sensational TV! Like the other programme I saw on *Channel 4* about terrible care of dementia patients in BUPA homes. Have you also noticed how when there is yet another scandal of abuse in an old people's home, there is rarely any mention that they are now all in the private sector? Viewers come away thinking yet another NHS failure, it would be better if they were private, not knowing they already are and that's the fucking problem."

"Well, about time *Channel 4* was privatised too!"

"It will be. There is no doubt we are ruled by morons. Morons that have to change everything. There's nothing wrong with *Channel 4*. Leave the fucking thing alone! But worse as they are arrogant morons who never take the advice of experts, as it interferes with their own prejudices. And their latest justification for this is that the public are fed up with experts."

"Fracking is a good example of the bastards deciding they want to do something, irrespective of the evidence. Probably because they've been bribed or have fingers in the pies. So then like most politicians they look for the evidence to back their case and bury the important scientific data that doesn't fit."

"So there is no gas under your estate then?" Rob teased.

"It wouldn't help if there was. These devious tossers sneaked a law through that allows companies to drill sideways under anyone's land without even informing you, let alone getting permission."

"Yes, I heard about that. What staggers me about fracking is the huge amount of water necessary, let alone the earthquakes and the contamination of the surface and ground water that can take place. Some pretty hazardous chemical are used too."

"Earthquakes?"

"Yes, Cuadrilla admitted to two near Blackpool in 2011 measuring one point five and two point three on the Richter scale as far as I remember," clarified Rob, "and another quake within a day of resuming fracking. Forty-seven minor ones in two months. They must suspend drilling when tremors over zero point five are detected. So what is their response? To get the threshold raised!"

"The point being, no matter what the evidence and facts, they have decided to go ahead and nothing will stop them. They do not act in the public's best interest. And this applies to all policies."

"Shock. Horror. We always knew that they only act in their own interests. It should be a *Catch-22*. Anyone wanting to be a politician should be automatically barred."

"Same as Groucho Marx's classic, *I refuse to join any club that would have me as a member.*"

"On top of that it's what I call the deliberate chronic confusional state. Do you remember at medical school we had to learn all the different causes in someone of an acute confusional state? In those days the list didn't include duplicitous lying politicians facing both ways at once but it should now. Now part of the plot against us is to totally confuse us all, even the professionals and experts. Once fat was good for you, then bad, now quite good again. Whole milk was bad, skimmed milk good, and then we are told the skimmed version is no better than sugary water and hasn't the ability to absorb vitamins as fat is necessary for that to take place. But that might be bollocks too. Fictional truths. Who the hell are we to believe? And who wasn't confused by the EU referendum? Add to that recipe all the fake news and no one knows what the truth is so they give up. Okay, enough of that. I'm in danger of getting boring as it's not the first rant I've had on this subject."

"You remember last match we talked about the swine flu scare and how if you produce a fear in someone, you can make money out of them?" said Stephen with his mischievous grin, "Well I've thought of a scam. You told me the other week that it was now difficult to get basic help like ear syringing as it wasn't life threatening?"

"Yes, go on," said Rob.

"Well, clearly they are softening up the public to persuade them these unnecessary strains on the State ought to be paid for, right?"

"Elementary, my dear Watson."

"So, lets set up a string of private ear syringing clinics, a bit like Kwik Fit but for ears. Then we publicise new research that says wax causes cancer and should be removed every six months. The research was on twelve slugs in the *Journal Of The Bleeding Obvious*, like research for MMR by Andrew Wakefield, which conned everyone, thanks to a stupid irresponsible media. We will have them queuing down the street. We can start modestly at fifty pounds per ear."

"That would be very funny if it wasn't so close to the bone. I can now imagine something along those lines," said Rob.

The trivia was about to start as they were down to their last mouthfuls of *Harvey's*. Stephen always knew he could make Rob laugh with his *Monty Python* quiz question.

"*Which great opponent of Cartesian dualism resists the reduction of psychological phenomena to a physical state and insists there is no point of contact between the extended and the unextended?*"

But he could only remember it completely sober. For years Stephen had said the answer provided by Mrs Yeti-Goosecreature was Henri Bergson. But Rob had done his research and looked at the sketch again. He was waiting for his chance. It was not Mrs Yeti-Goosecreature but Mrs Scum. Stephen said the first thing he would do on arriving home was to check this on YouTube. His response and retaliation was the first thing he could think of.

"*I never forget a face, but in your case I'll be glad to make an exception.*"

"Another of Groucho's no doubt?" asked Rob.

"And Henri-Louis Bergson's dates?"

He knew Rob would not get this one.

"1859 to 1941."

Rob raised his glass to finish off.

"Here's to our wives and girlfriends… may they never meet."

They strolled out to their cars and agreed on the same time next week. It was always Stephen's job to book the court.

"Well, the Ledru-Rollin metro station is on Line 8, one down from the Bastille."

Rob wasn't impressed.

"That proves you looked him up. You couldn't possibly be that sad."

"Okay. Who lives at Faversham apart from Bob Geldof? None other than the granddaughter of Czar Nicholas II's sister, Xenia! Bet you didn't know that?"

Rob felt well prepared this time. He had two more trivial facts up his sleeve.

"In the nineteen sixties the top brass of the *BBC* were against Sooty having a girlfriend as they didn't want to introduce sex into the programme. The Director General overruled them as long as they didn't touch."

"Poor Sooty," responded Stephen. "Soo was very attractive though. He must have been frustrated. But having a hand shoved up his jaxsy was probably good enough!"

"So what's Stendhal syndrome smart-arse?" Rob fired, as he approached his Seat Leon.

"Having physical symptoms like palpitations, dizziness or fainting when exposed to artwork."

"Bollocks. How did you know that?"

"'Cos I think we all suffered from it in the flat in Brockley when Anthony brought his copy of *Penthouse* along."

"Now I have several relatives with this one, fish odour syndrome. The name gives away what it is, but what's the biochemistry behind it?"

"Don't know and don't care."

"The body can't break down trimethylamine which results in the strong body odour."

"Do fish have it?"

That was ignored.

"Did you know after their supposed suicides, the German Government had the brains of the Baader-Meinhof gang removed for study? Then they lost them. They could have been stolen! Beat that," said Rob.

"Maybe Andreas Baader was the Abby Normal one Marty Feldman stole for Gene Wilder to put into *Young Frankenstein?*" continued Stephen.

"Wasn't Madeline Kahn great in that?"

"Frau Blucher was more my type. Another trivial fact… the same actress played Charlotte Diesel in *High Anxiety.*"

"Yes, after some of the girlfriends you brought to Brockley that wouldn't surprise me. With the notable exception of that Charlotte of course."

"Fuck off Robert."

41 - INFATUATION AND IRRATIONALITY

I'M ON FIRE

At night I wake up with the sheets soaking wet
And a freight train running through the middle of my head
Only you, can cool my desire

Bruce Springsteen (1984)

There is no doubt Clive made the running. He had missed her so much.

They had only managed to behave themselves for seven months after trying to go back to just a professional relationship. Giselle coped and put up a tough life-goes-on exterior. She had managed to kill this relationship outside of work and put her association with one of her bosses firmly back in the box labelled career.

But Clive found every one of the two hundred and eleven days a torment. It dominated his life and affected all his decisions. When he saw no hope he considered leaving. He slept badly and woke with the sheets soaking wet and a freight train running through the middle of his head. He knew only she could cool his desire. But it did also occur to him to remove Giselle from his life by getting her sacked on some trumped up charge. His ruthlessness sometimes alarmed even him. For months he almost pleaded with Giselle to rekindle their personal relationship. To sit across the practice meeting table and be so formal made him dread any contact.

After making Clive suffer enough she became persuaded that he really was serious about a proper committed relationship. He said he would leave his family. She did not want to be responsible for that. She told him they could see how it goes. She was undoubtedly in charge. Derek did not light her fire but he was a good father. She was not even going to think about the possibility of breaking up two families although Clive seemed not to care about this.

Now they had been full on but still secret for over three years. If Clive was honest what he really missed was the sex but he was not honest. She was so fantastic. Clive joked he ought to take French citizenship now he knew what the British have been missing. She turned him on by her very presence. She had power over him like no other woman. He had never experienced anything like it and he thought he had had enough experience in his time. He worried he had developed more of an obsession and infatuation than a love.

It was this that nearly caught them both out that afternoon. He was the one who insisted she play with him despite their agreement to cool it some weeks back. He said he was desperate and would not be able to concentrate on evening surgery without a little light relief. He was like a little boy begging for Mummy's attention but the analogy stopped there as it conjured up the revulsion of incest. She later cursed herself for giving in to his weakness. It was not the first time but she was determined it was the last.

Clive had tried to convince her that PST was a medical condition and the male equivalent of PMT. He told her that pre-sexual tension messed with the male mind as much as pre-menstrual tension caused trouble for females. The frustration leads to illogical, irrational, panicky and impetuous thoughts and decisions, and when relief came the mind cleared like fog lifting. He told her that Kennedy had shocked the old Etonian PM Harold Macmillan, stating that if he did not have a woman for three days he got a terrible headache. Clive thought three days was pushing it. The French Giselle was torn between this conflicting with her views on the English being sexually repressed and Clive just being a nuisance. She deflected attention away from this by pointing out that Kennedy was not really a good role model, being a compulsive womaniser who could only last a few minutes and was bought the Presidency by his Nazi-sympathising father by vote manipulation in Texas and Illinois.

It was later that evening and they were both sitting in Clive's car by Furnace Pond. This was not far from The Poet but safely out of the practice area. They dare not be seen together. Giselle was on her way to her evening class, so she had the perfect cover. Clive was more careless and usually did not think that far ahead. He was a risk-taker and he knew one day it would backfire.

"Apparently Siegfried Sassoon used to ice-skate 'ere," said Giselle.

Trying in vain to impress Giselle that he knew all about the war poet he added rather superfluously.

"That would now be well over one hundred years ago then?"

It did not impress her, as it was obvious. To her it was basic stuff that any child should know, especially a fellow countryman. She was already preoccupied and distracted looking forward to her class. Clive just could not understand how anyone would be interested in economic theory. For Giselle it demonstrated that Clive, or nothing else for that matter, could or should dominate her life to such an extent as to squeeze out normal existence and a sensible daily routine.

Giselle credited her father, Francois Arouet, for her level-headed approach to life. He had explained to a fifteen-year-old Giselle soon after her first boyfriend dumped her that life was a cake cut up into equal pieces. No one piece was bigger than another. Those pieces were family, relationships, education, career, health, friends, money and a few others. One piece must not spill over or grow out of proportion to dominate the others. If it did it acted like a cancer. For instance too much studying should not push out family, the career should not affect health, and above all a relationship with a boy, which at the time may preoccupy the mind all day, must not be allowed to swamp the other areas. Life must go on. He sometimes changed his cake analogy to say all these things are equal sized boxes. The boxes will always be there. What is chosen to put in those boxes will change. Relationships will change. Careers will change. The education box as a child will be full of school but later in life it was important to put something else in it. Education should never stop. Sometimes a box like the relationship box would be empty. So be it. She applied what her father taught her to life and it had served her well. In her relationship box at the moment was Clive. Her husband, Derek, was in the family box. The surgery was in the career box and economics in the education box.

It was her father who had taught the two girls humanity, compassion and forgiveness. They were brought up in a small village in southwest central France called Veyrac. It was ten miles outside Limoges where they went to school. She loved that city with its Gothic Cathedrale St-Etienne de Limoges, which took six centuries to complete, and the mediaeval timber-framed houses lining the Rue de la Boucherie. Giselle showed more interest than her sister Francoise in the Musee National Adrien Dubouche with its decorated porcelain, but what really changed her life was when their father took them the five miles along the D6 to the village of Oradour-sur-Glane. This had an unforgettable impact on the fourteen year old.

On 10th June 1944 a Nazi-Waffen SS company massacred six hundred and forty-two of its inhabitants and destroyed the village. After the war General Charles de Gaulle decided the village would not be rebuilt, but left as a memorial to the cruelty of Nazi occupation. The family's visit to the destroyed village, and in particular the church where two hundred and forty-seven women and two hundred and five children died was a turning point in Giselle's life. No one was really held to account for the atrocity. Some forced conscripts - the malgre-nous - from Alsace and Lorraine were granted an amnesty.

Soon after this lesson, Francois took his two daughters to Bertolt Brecht's *Mother Courage And Her Children*, perhaps the greatest anti-war play of all time. It follows the fortunes of a cunning canteen worker called Anna Fierling who over the course of the play loses all three of her children to the very war she tried to exploit for her own advantage. This made both girls pacifists. What helped to make them feminists was Mary Wollstonecraft's 1792 book *A Vindication Of The Rights of Woman* making the case for women's co-education alongside men as equals and Betty Friedan's call to arms in *The Feminine Mystique*, against everything domestic and trivia being the woman's domain, and everything important men only. Both girls admitted they could not plough through the whole of these texts. Their father said this was not necessary. He just wanted them to know of their existence and the arguments they were putting forward. Another Christmas present was Naomi Wolf's *The Beauty Myth*, which recognised the dark truth that however clever, funny and dynamic women might be, there was always something trying to make them feel bad about the size of their thighs. Francois wanted his girls to help create a world where this attitude was no longer acceptable.

And it was Giselle's father, not her mother Marguerite or friends, who explained the facts of life to her when she was eleven. He had done it beautifully. He had put a lot of thought to this. It went well with Giselle's older sister Francoise, who had been named after Francoise Hardy, three years before. His tender loving and almost heavenly description had no hint of the dirty fornication that should only be for procreation that his catholic mother had tried to poison his mind with. She actually told him that he would go to hell if he touched himself. She could not possibly let the word masturbate cross her lips or she might be struck down. Anything below the waist was sinful. He should seek a pure virginal woman and that children born out of wedlock are illegitimate bastards. His sister was banned from washing her hair during menstruation. He thought such evil lies were almost another form of catholic child abuse and produced most of the sexual hang-ups people had.

He was transferring none of those noxious ideas onto his daughters. He told them that sexual intimacy and sexual pleasure are two of humanity's most cherished experiences and combined with an intense love there was nothing better. He surprised them by quoting, *if equal affection cannot be, let the more loving one be me*, by the English poet Wystan Hugh Auden from his 1957 *The More Loving One*. From this the girls learnt that giving was far better than taking. He quoted a study that showed that sex made people happier than religion did. People with a good sex life lived a longer more enjoyable and fulfilling life.

"It is key," he told both Francoise and Giselle, "without that, your husband just becomes an odd job man and, believe me, that will kill your relationship and you will both grow old miserably."

Her father filled her culture box not only with the theatre but also with the music of the French composers Camille Saint-Saens, Gabriel Faure, Debussy, Ravel and Berlioz and added details.

"Did you know Debussy was one of the first people to have a colostomy? He died during an aerial and artillery bombardment of Paris by the Germans."

He took the girls to see Debussy's grave in the Cimetiere de Passy in Paris.   He spoke of the authors Victor Hugo, Proust, Zola, Flaubert, Jean-Paul Sartre and of course Voltaire. Then there was Johnny Hallyday. Giselle was still grieving for him like the rest of France. And the art of Degas, Rodin, Renoir and Manet were all part of their childhood. She warmed to Rob Baigent instantly when she arrived at the practice and saw *Le Dejeuner sur l'herbe* on his consulting room wall. When in Paris she would go to the fifth floor of the Musée d'Orsay to stare at it and ponder its meaning. Was Manet really depicting the rampant prostitution present at that time in the Bois de Boulogne? Now her education box was glowing.

She was all consumed by the economics she had learnt so far and put this fascination down to tackling a subject of which she had no prior knowledge and no preconceived ideas. It all seemed extraordinary. If what she was being taught was all the truth, how does capitalism survive or at least free-market capitalism? She wondered how much her tutor was straying from the approved curriculum.

William Felt was an odd eccentric, but popular with her fellow students. She could not work out his politics. He seemed to produce statements from both ends of the extreme political spectrum, but perhaps it is true then that that is where they meet. He told his students there were grounds for optimism. Streeck is right. Capitalism will eventually die from an overdose of itself.

At the first class Giselle attended, with some apprehension, Felt casually slipped into the conversation that he had named his house 8115 Soweto, which was Nelson Mandela's address, and also called his two dogs Vilakazi and Ngakane after the junction where the house was located. After a while he had to change the house name to Soweto 8115 as the post office was getting confused, and his wife, who refused to yell out Vilakazi and Ngakane not least as she could not pronounce them, called the dogs Jo and Hanna. She joked that the next dog would be called Burg so she could round them all up with one shout, Johannesburg.

He returned to the topic several times during coffee breaks in his tutorial. Mandela had lived there until 1962 just a short distance from Desmond Tutu. It was the only street in the world housing two Nobel Peace Prize winners. Easily visible still are the bullet holes in the walls and the scorch marks on the façade from Molotov cocktail attacks. Then William would entertain by talking about his upbringing and old television shows like *Sooty* and the *Black and White Minstrels*. But then shocked his students by bringing the two stories together by reminding them that *Sooty* was a derogatory term for black people when he was young.

William opened her eyes to what was really happening in the world, not the shit the politicians and their collaborators in the media peddle. Some argue that the destruction of Britain's industrial base by Thatcher was the biggest economic disaster to hit the UK, but globally 2008 was the second largest economic crisis in history after the Great Depression, and the financial meltdown was only prevented from turning into a total collapse of the global economy by a fiscal and monetary stimulus on an unprecedented scale. The whole catastrophe had been created by the free market ideology that has ruled the world since the 1980s. Free market policies had resulted in slower growth, rising inequality and more instability, unbeknown to most people, and it was masked by huge credit expansion. US wages had stagnated and working hours increased, conveniently fogged over by a credit-fuelled consumer boom. These problems were even worse in the developing world. The bottom line is that the free market produces a tiny cadre of winners and an enormous army of losers. The public had been conned by the 'rising tide lifts all boats' and 'trickle-down economics'. Both were crap and those in control knew it. Soundbites used to con the public. In the neo-liberal world the flow defied gravity. The trickle-up was to the huge boats of the rich, which had sunk the life rafts of the poor.

In 1819 opponents of legislation to regulate child labour argued that it was destroying the very foundation of the free market. Children needed to work and factory owners wanted to employ them, so what was the problem? Regulations more recently on car and factory emissions were opposed as serious infringements on our freedom to choose - nowadays denigrated by being called the 'nanny state' or 'red tape'. Always be suspicious when you hear those phrases. It means leave us alone to exploit who and what we want. Do not regulate us - we should be free to do what we want no matter what the consequences. The Americans fought the Civil War over free trade in slaves and the British Government fought the Opium War against China to realise a free trade in opium. William taught this all in such a way that Giselle felt the scales falling from her eyes. It was so obvious. Why had I not worked this out for myself she puzzled?

He explained what had gone wrong for most, more recently, but spectacularly right for the top one per cent, was not helped by what he called the 'principle of shareholder value maximisation'. That is, professional managers should be rewarded according to the amount they can give to shareholders. Profits need to be maximised by ruthless cost cutting - staff and wages mainly - but also investment. The trouble is that this does not do the company much good in the long run. Usually productivity, quality and reputation suffer. Look at what Kraft have done to Cadbury's chocolate. Look how General Motors squandered its world domination of the car industry. It constantly downsized and cut investment on the altar of these crazy ideas. This made managers and shareholders happy while debilitating the company until it finally went bankrupt in 2009. This is why short-term individual shareholders are unreliable guardians of a company's long-term future. Long-term large investors like Governments produce stability and opportunities for investment. Look at Renault in France or Volkswagen in Germany. Why do you think the British car industry went down the tube?

William became Giselle's myth-buster.

"The Government was telling us the UK welfare state is large and bloated out of all proportion so needs to be drastically cut and shrunk," he told the class, "This was a lie produced for ideological reasons, no less devious and criminal than the lies used in Nazi Germany to con the public. In reality the UK welfare state is not large at all. At twenty one point five per cent of GDP it is barely three quarters of the welfare spending in comparably rich countries in Europe. In France it is thirty-one point five per cent and Denmark's is twenty-eight point seven per cent. It is about the same as the OECD average at twenty-one per cent which includes countries such as Mexico, Chile, Turkey and Estonia - countries which are poorer and have less need for welfare provision as they have younger populations with stronger extended family networks. The public services now formed the lowest proportion of the workforce for seventy years at about sixteen per cent. Very nearly the fifteen per cent of the USA the Government wants to emulate. In Scandinavian countries it hovers around thirty per cent - that is double. In China it's fifty per cent."

The second myth William exploded was that there is an inherent virtue in balancing the books. He told them this was not his theory but an old Keynesian idea. Whether a balanced budget is a good or bad thing depends on circumstances. In an overheating economy deficit spending would be a folly but today it may be good, even necessary. William shot down established wisdom put out by Government and uncritically peddled by the media like sitting ducks at a fun fair shooting range.

"We are told welfare spending is consumption, a drain on the nation's resources and thus to be minimised," he said scornfully, "So we are fooled or rather actually lied to and conned into believing we must accept cuts in benefits, child care, free school meals as we can't afford them. *There is no magic money tree* the sheep are instructed to repeat as often as possible. And either these sheep are gullible or, of course more likely, they know perfectly well it's idiot fodder. Taking the public for idiots is worse than calling them gullible. But a lot is investment that pays back through increased productivity in the future. Every pound spent on healthcare is rewarded by four pounds back towards GDP, so it is crazy to starve the NHS of funds… unless of course you have another motive."

At last week's class William talked about tax and the myth it is a burden.

"Would you call your Netflix subscription a burden?" he asked them, "Of course not because you recognise you get a service that you want for your money. So why call taxes a burden when you get in return an array of public services, such as education, health and old-age care, flood defences, roads, the military and the police?"

William claimed that the burden was when you had to repair your car after crashing down a pothole because the council tax did not stretch to road repairs any longer; or you had to regularly drive to the refuse tip because the bins were only emptied every fortnight; or even could not find a public convenience any longer as they had all been closed down.

"That was a burden," he said, and everyone agreed with him, "The concept that public toilets that don't make a profit are not worth having and should be closed down is an idea only from the idiotic mind of a cretin," he said quietly. "The question should be whether the Government is providing services of satisfactory quality, not what the level of tax is. If tax were really a pure burden highly taxed Swedes would move to Paraquay for the ten per cent tax rate. But of course they don't because they enjoy excellent services, where the South Americans get little."

None of this would interest Clive and Giselle knew it.

"The quality of the service provided is deliberately overlooked by those who want to cut, slash and reduce the State. Take the company that won the contract to look after all the trees in a northern city. No one thought that they'd cut them all down to save yearly maintenance and run off with the money. Or maybe they did? And which councillors were on the board of the tree murderers? It saved the Council long-term payouts and they could blame someone else for the vandalism. As no one thought this a possibility, it wasn't in their contract to not cut them down, so they got away with it."

This all fascinated Giselle. William seemed to think in a way no one else did. In comparison, although she admired some of Clive's talents she considered him a little shallow. When she came away all excited and wanted to tell him about her latest discovery she could see his eyes glaze over.

"Perhaps the trees were diseased," he said.

"What, all of them?" she replied exasperated.

He would fiddle with his phone to try to find out the latest football scores hoping she would not notice - but she always did. She wanted a meeting of minds not just bodies.

Giselle had homework for tonight. She had been given Ha-Joon Chang's book called *23 Things They Don't Tell You About Capitalism*. She had understood from this how wages are largely politically determined, and the wage gaps between rich and poor countries exist not only because of differences in productivity but mainly because of immigration control, or labour market control. This is why the speed and scale of immigration needs to be controlled - the boundary of the market is politically controlled. So much for truly free markets. And what easier way to control immigration than by turning the public against immigrants? Run a load of stories about them being spongers and rapists. That does the trick. Easy. She felt a bit guilty, as she had only got to chapter four. She was looking forward though to learning how and why the washing machine had changed the world more than the Internet.

Earlier in the day she had reviewed her notes from last week. She was desperate to be able to join in intelligently with the conversation William always had at the beginning of class. The purpose was to re-visit the previous week's lessons as a sort of revision. First, another gem she had never heard before. GDP was the wrong measure of the nation's progress. It fails to measure real wealth, just the cash value of the economy. A better measure would be the access, or not, to good warm housing, healthcare, technology and healthier food.

The second concept she had to keep rehearsing in her mind to understand and remember was the conflict between the stories told by Keynesian social democracy and by neoliberalism. How when the world fell into disorder because of the self-seeking behaviour of an unrestrained elite, characterised by the Great Depression, and that elite captured both the world's wealth and political system, working people became impoverished. Their reaction was to unite, strip the elite of its ill-gotten gains and power and pool the resulting wealth for the good of all. Public projects for the public good generated the wealth that would guarantee a prosperous future for everyone. But when the world fell into disorder as a result of collective tendencies of an over mighty State, it was claimed that collectivism crushes freedom, individualism and opportunity. Heroic entrepreneurs would restore order with the power of the markets freeing society from the enslavement of the State.

William thought the present neoliberal elite had captured the pendulum and was preventing it swinging the other way but the people would rise up eventually. At the moment the people do not behave as a cohesive force, so at a time when the free market has produced its enormous army of losers they, looking for revenge, turn to Brexit and Trump. The trouble was the right wing had also captured Keynesianism and redefined it thus preventing it returning in its full glory. They now had reduced it to two ideas: lowering interest rates when the economy was sluggish, and injecting public money when recession threatens or unemployment is high.

Other measures, which John Maynard Keynes regarded as essential components had been discarded. Raising taxes to dampen the boom-bust cycle, the fixed exchange rate system and capital controls used to prevent speculators sucking money out had been forgotten. Nixon's decision in 1971 to suspend the convertibility of dollars into gold destroyed the system of fixed exchange rate on which much of the success of Keynes' policies depended. People rising up depended, according to William, on the single and simple idea of altruism. That was why the right wing had invested so much in trying to destroy the concept.

Human beings are unusual in that we possess an unparalleled sensitivity to the needs of others, a unique level of concern about their welfare and a peerless ability to create moral norms that generalise and enforce these tendencies. But we are also supreme cooperators. This is why Thatcher needed to introduce the I'm-all-right-Jack attitude claiming there is no such thing as society and encouraged selfishness. Looking after number one was all that mattered. We have been conned into accepting a vicious ideology of extreme competition and individualism that pits us against each other. The politicians have used the media and economists to encourage us to fear and mistrust each other and weaken the social bonds that make our lives worth living. It has changed our perception of ourselves and so in turn the way we behave.

William told the class that with the help of this ideology and the neoliberal narrative used to project it we have lost our common purpose. This in turn has led to a loss of belief in one's self as a force for change. This, he went on to say, is why there is a lack of fight for the things we hold dear that we see being destroyed before our very eyes like the NHS. By coming together to revive community life we can break the vicious circle of alienation and reaction in which we have been trapped by the intolerant forces that have filled the political vacuum caused by society's disintegration.

This was the only time Giselle had heard anyone produce a way out of the misery, hopelessness and troubles in front of them. No one else had a clue what to do. Most were in despair running around like chickens with their heads cut off. To Giselle it gave hope. Giselle had to read these notes over and over again in an effort to retain the facts. It all fascinated her. It was a new dimension to her life. She was bursting to share this with whoever would listen. But Clive was not one of them. This is why she thought their future together was in doubt.

Neither Clive nor Giselle had ever seen Furnace pond frozen so maybe climate change was having an effect. They were both tired of hiding their relationship, but the deal was that, all the time that neither was prepared to leave their families, it was this or nothing. And both would have to abandon their children at the same time. For Giselle at least, risking her two boys was unthinkable. Giselle still enjoyed the time they had together but really she could cope if it ended. Clive could not though and put a lot of effort into persuading Giselle it was worth the pain. His relationship box was overflowing and had polluted his other boxes. He had one go at trying to persuade her to skip evening class so they could spend the evening together but knew really there was no chance. He tried to disguise his irritation but could not resist a jibe.

"This economics is the best thing since sliced bread, as far as you are concerned, isn't it?"

"Oh really. What a corny old cliché. Who now uses that phrase about sliced bread?

"Came in in the nineteen thirties, if you are interested?"

"What did?"

"Sliced bread."

"No, that doesn't interest me," said Giselle.

"Did you know it was banned in the US in 1943 as sliced bread required heavier wrapping which was not good in wartime."

"Boring. But what was the best thing before sliced bread?"

Clive felt sufficiently reprimanded but glad she could still attempt a joke.

"That's nearly as cringe-making as describing someone's politics as to the right of Genghis Khan! The number of times I 'ear someone saying that, thinking they are funny," said Giselle.

"First said by Senator Barry Goldwater, apparently."

Clive tried to be seen to be knowledgeable to make up for his perceived earlier crassness.

"'E wasn't even a political figure of either left or right, just a savage barbarian. If 'e really killed more than Stalin, who killed more than 'itler, and more than Mao who killed twice as many again, seventy million at the last count, perhaps the quip should run "e's even to the left of Genghis Khan'," continued Giselle.

Clive wanted to demonstrate some medical mastery.

"A DNA study has shown that sixteen million men can probably claim descent from Genghis Khan."

"Do you think they are all in UKIP?" Giselle joked and then continued, "In fact 'e was a genocidal maniac but allowed religious freedom, 'is Empire was technologically advanced, encouraged free trade, created courts and, believe it or not, was an advocate for women's rights, 'e was no democrat or enlightened liberal, but far more than the unfeeling brute 'e is often portrayed to 'ave been."

"How on earth did we get onto this subject?"

Clive was getting a little exasperated knowing their time together was running out. He was wriggling in his seat, which to Giselle meant only one thing.

"Okay, I'll leave Ivan the Terrible or Attila the Hun to another day then, no?" she teased, "Anyway I was going on to say no more of that in the surgery from now on, no? We were so close to being caught when Rob walked in on us today. We can't take the risk. We agreed a few weeks ago to cool it and be especially careful, but neither of us 'ave stuck to that. I'm to blame too to a certain extent. I was weak. But getting me to put my 'and through your flies is what schoolboys and schoolgirls do, not supposedly respectable GPs in the middle of a working day. And your effort with that file was embarrassing. I'm really shocked at either how unobservant Rob is, or 'ow 'e kindly just turned a blind eye."

"What did you expect me to do, show him my stiffy? It's what you do to me. I can't help it."

"Well you're going to 'ave to learn to control yourself. You will 'ave to put up with your so-called PST. Pre-sexual tension, my bottom. More like pretty stupid tosser. My job is at more risk than yours if the merde hits the fan. Not to mention our families."

After a fair pause Clive said the obvious and what they both knew they had to discuss.

"I think it's about to. Now Rob has found out about the money, unless we do something very clever, we are probably quite vulnerable. But let's stay calm," he continued, "we have been clever. The money has been laundered so many times it should be almost impossible to trace it back to us. That's what we pay those crooks for. So let's just see what Michael comes up with."

"Almost impossible," Giselle said with sorrow, "I don't know why I let you talk me into this. My father would be 'orrified," she said.

She saved the news that Clive would not want to hear until last.

"I've got to go away for a few days. Derek's Dad has been done for GBH again and I've got to help his Mum sort out a few things."

Before Clive had time to moan she undid her safety belt, lent over Clive's lap and finished off what they had started in her office.

Her father would have approved of her being so clever - but only if she got pleasure from it.

The PST fog cleared.

42 - ADAM AND EVE

THE CONSPIRACY SONG

Please let me tell you
They own our home, they own our banks
We take out loans to buy them tanks
They own our children, they own our pet
They owned Elvis and Bernhard Goetz
They own our rugs and our flower pots
They ain't nothin' they haven't got
They own the papers and the TVs
The water works, record companies

Let me remind you
They own the talk shows
They make the rules
They own Geraldo and Donahue
They own the state, they own the church
They pick the winners on Star Search
They own the Christians, they own the Jews
They own the Moslems, Mormons, too
They put the holes in our socks
They put that snake in my mail box

From the halls of Montezuma, to the shores of Tripoli
We are all tools of the conspiracy

The Dead Milkmen (1992)

Rob had several clues.

An American from Texas called Madison whose husband was a journalist and had disappeared, a French journalist called Chantelle, and a story about them on French television. After an hour-long Internet search Rob had found nothing. No leads at all. A frustrating wasted hour that left him in a bad mood. If there was one thing he hated it was wasting time. And money. And wasting food. And drink.

In fact there was a long list of things. Only one thing dragged him out of a bad mood, Monty Python humour. Well, two things if you included sex. Being given a load of money helped too. *What had the Romans ever done for us,* he thought to himself, *apart from the aqueduct, the sanitation, the roads, irrigation, medicine, education, health, wine, public baths... peace.*

That hour would have been only fifteen minutes if he had had a good Internet connection. Where he and Suzy lived was a big black hole for Wi-Fi and mobile phones.

"Fucking privatisation!" he fumed, as it buffered again.

Friends had heard several times about how on holiday in Sri Lanka he got a better phone signal and Internet in the rain forest than in England. He knew the Government bullshit about covering ninety-five per cent within a trillion years. Even if it did happen it would never help them. They would always remain in the five per cent, as there was no profit in it for the companies. Proof it was a business to them and not a service. In Finland and Estonia it is a basic human right. Frustration.

Rob was frequently bewildered about privatisation and why this train had not crashed before now. When will the public reject this ideology once and for all? Had selling off the railways been a success? What about the energy industry, or telecommunications, water, security, post office, or parts of education and health and all the other vital services? Clearly not. What about British Airways, buses and airports? Are they run better and cheaper? The privatisation of the everyday had gone too far. Switch on a light, catch the bus, post a letter, turn on the oven, drink a glass of water, register for an apprenticeship, use a train, park the car - it is all provided by the private sector, and often by crooks like from Carillion. Have an operation, take an exam, send your child to school, use a road, call the police, go to prison - private companies involved in it all.

He then began to question why he was looking. What was the point? Even if he finds out about this mystery it probably has no links to his concerns. But it was a hunch. Something Stephen said about the journalist investigating all sorts of conspiracies that were flashed up on the screen. He did not know if the French had a service like iPlayer to look for programmes already broadcast but if they did he could not access it.

Then he remembered Pippa. She had French contacts. Maybe one of her Paris work colleagues could help out. Or maybe she could access French television from her offices at JupiterPress. He first thought of Giselle, but on reflection did not want to involve her. It would be too much trouble to explain. Pippa knows the essentials already. He impatiently fired off an email to his old friend, so rushed it was full of spelling mistakes but the facts he knew were all there.

Pippa replied the next day, quite hopeful, but wondering if this was just a wild goose chase too. She mocked his bad spelling and grammar by replying in cockney rhyming slang:

Better use of yer time than sitting on yer kyber havin' a butcher's would be to have a J. Arthur, me old China or you'd end up crackered.

Would yer Adam an Eve it.

But I'll get on the dog and bone if I find anything.

Love to the trouble-and-strife.

Two days after that she rang.

"We've found her and the story. It was broadcast twelve days ago. Quite a long interview and well presented. That French journalist is good. She has promised to follow it up, especially some of the scandals they hinted at. It's on a disc. I'll post it to you Rob. The good bit is that at the end there are contact details."

"As always you are a star, Pippa!"

"Yes, Rob I know but next time please do better homework. I would have found it a lot quicker if you'd have told me it was *France Info*. That's a fairly new French domestic rolling news channel."

"Oh, I would if I'd known. But I only did it as I love being told off by you."

The next day Suzy picked the mail off the doormat and put it aside. She was never quick, or that interested in opening letters.

When Rob got home from work he dived straight for the mail before even saying hello.

"Ah, it's here. Suzy, we must watch this together. Must say I'm impressed by the speed it got here."

"Rob, it's too early in the evening for any of your porn. Besides, I thought we had agreed we have passed that stage."

Rob wasn't sure if she was serious or not, as some of Rob's fantasies had been a sore subject in the past between them.

"No, you don't understand. This is that story I mentioned, about the investigative journalist who disappeared three or so years ago. It might help us understand. I doubt if there is a link but you never know."

Rob poured them both a glass of *Luc Belaire Rose* and they put the disc in the player.

"Nathan Ake of Bournemouth scores three minutes into added time for a stunning victory over Liverpool. What a fantastic game that was!"

"What? Pippa must have sent the wrong disc. This must be one of Jeremy's. He told me he never watched the other Bournemouth team... wait 'til I see him."

Then to their relief it went to what they wanted.

"Ce soir, nous racontons l'histoire incroyable d'un journaliste d'investigation anglais qui a disparu aux Etats-Unis, il y a trois ans, et des tentatives, jusqu'à présent vaines, de sa femme de le retrouver. Au jour d'aujourd'hui, personne ne semble vouloir l'aider. Elle soutient qu'elle était sur le point de découvrir des scandales dévastateurs impliquant des personnes importantes. Nous relatons toute l'histoire. Chantelle Levesque est la reporter..."

"Oh fuck. Your French is better than mine. Can you get the gist of it?" said a frustrated Rob.

Before he had finished Suzy had picked up the sheet of paper that was with the disc that Rob had discarded.

"Looks like Pippa has translated it for us. You were right to keep calling her wonderful."

Rob recognised Pippa's handwriting, but also Suzy's jealousy as she read.

"Tonight we tell the incredible tale of an English investigative journalist who disappeared in the USA three years ago and his wife's attempts to find him. So far in vain. Until now, no one seems to want to help her. She claims he was on the verge of uncovering some devastating scandals and exposing some important people. We bring you the whole story. Chantelle Levesque is the reporter…"

Then Madison appeared and was talking in English or rather American English. She was subtitled for the French audience rather than spoken over so this part was easy to follow. She gave a clear, calm account of how a Texan ended up in London married to an Englishman who was investigating all sorts of wrongdoing. How he vanished and the efforts she made to find him, and how she was not helped and on occasions even obstructed in her efforts to solve the mystery. She wanted to carry on with his work as a tribute to him, but was now getting threats herself.

The angle the programme emphasised was the efforts made to obstruct anyone finding out what happened to Pete rather than just the sinister disappearance of a journalist. Investigative reporters vanishing were certainly not too unusual nowadays. The murder and dismembering of Jamal Khashoggi by the Saudi Government in their Istanbul consulate did not stay in the news for long. Trump's reaction essentially was that countries that do enough business with the United States are free to murder journalists with impunity. There was a passing comment that the number of journalist murders was increasing, and few were being brought to justice. There are no free speech safe havens. The Maltese journalist Daphne Caruana Galizia was blown up by a car bomb for digging up dirt on the most powerful figures in the EU's smallest state. The *Panama Papers* she discovered implicated the Prime Minister, and her uncomfortable questions about money laundering, organised crime, and the sale of Maltese passports went too far.

Then it was back to French with another reporter listing the contact details for the programme. Whilst talking and explaining that the French television company intends to investigate as many of the topics as possible that Peter Moodey was looking into, and would

542

like to hear from anyone with any information, the list of titles of topics rolled in the background.

Was Pearl Harbour the ultimate false flag operation?
The Marshall Islands Nuclear testing sites.
Operation Gladio.
The CIA coups.
Operation Condor.
Operation PBSuccess in Guatemala in 1954, Haiti in 1959, Brazil in 1964, Uruguay in 1969, Bolivia in 1971, Operation Fubelt in Chile in 1973, Argentina in 1976, El Salvador in 1980, Operation Just Cause in Panama in 1989, Honduras, Grenada, Dominican Republic, Columbia, Venezuela, Nicaragua and Peru in 1990.
British Guiana 1953-64: CIA and the British undermine and get rid of democratically elected Dr Cheddi Jagan.
The Iran-Contra affair.
1975: Henry Kissinger launches a CIA-backed war in Angola.
1975: The CIA helps topple democratically elected Australian Government.
Cointelpro.
The assassination of foreign leaders.
The interference with elections.
The illegal wars: Iraq, Afghanistan, Iran, Yugoslavia, Cuba, Libya, Latin America.
Human rights, civil liberties and torture.
Worldwide paedophile rings.
Conspiracies.
The Clinton Elves.
Did the Mob kill boxer Freddie Mills?
WikiLeaks.
The media.
Operation Chaos: President Johnson greatly boosts illegal spying on US citizens.
The David Kelly murder.
The Jeremy Thorpe – Norman Scott affair.
The Westland scandal.

Suez.

Approved school unethical drug experiments.

Roger Casement and the Black diaries

Rainbow Warrior.

Rainbow Warrior.

Kurt Waldheim.

Operation Paperclip.

The Secret Oman war.

Mau Mau terrorism.

Australian Immigration and the Nauru Detention Centre.

The secret dismantling of the welfare state…

The list continued to roll as Chantelle carried on with her interview of Madison. The journalist focused on all the obstructions put in Madison's way and more recent threats. It was almost as though the channel had decided it was on a mission to carry on the investigations as they were the main stories, and if they found Pete, or what had happened to him as a consequence, then that was just a bonus. It was to be two fingers up to the bastards.

The list had completed and was starting another cycle as the credits and closing music ended the show. Rob played the last part again and stopped three or four times to absorb the list. Much he was familiar with, especially the British scandals like the David Kelly affair and the Westland scandal that happened when he was a student at Guy's, but a lot like Operation Paperclip or Cointelpro he had never heard of and was clueless about. But the last one referring to the welfare state caught his attention.

"These are flagrant crimes. Absolutely outrageous," concluded a stunned Rob.

"You mean blatant? That is an offence that is glaringly obvious? It's best to use flagrant to emphasise a serious breach of law," said Suzy, reverting to her teacher's voice.

"Exactly. That's what I said. I refute your correction," dismissed Rob.

"Ah! Got you again. It's a crime to use refute to mean deny as you just did when its correct meaning is to disprove, or to demonstrate falsehood."

"Are you deliberately trying to annoy me?" smiled Rob.

"Yes."

"I thought we'd need Pippa's help with this," Rob carried on, "but I'm not too sure now. We have understood enough. I think I should meet Madison and the programme makers."

"Rob, you are a GP not Jason Bourne. Leave it to the professional. My hat goes out to you for your determination but don't forget what they say? Give a man enough rope and he will tie you up. What could you possibly achieve? You may end up as Richard Kimble instead."

"Who's Richard Kimble?"

"The fugitive, silly. Played by Harrison Ford, remember? Talking of which, that movie he was in *What Lies Beneath*. Could be an omen - you don't know what lies beneath all this and I think it's too dangerous to try to find out."

"The problem is we are beginning to learn what's behind all this. We are all tools of the conspiracy. They own us and everything about us. They make the rules. They pick the winners."

Then to lighten the mood before bedtime.

"I'm not sure that's the correct use of the word omen," he continued, trying to get his own back, "More like a prophecy or a warning. An omen is a phenomenon that is believed to foretell the future."

"Wrong again, Robert. I've a horrible feeling our futures may be determined by all this."

43 - ASSASSINATIONS AND DOSSIERS

BROKEN LEGS

Are we fools and cowards all
To let them cover up their lies?
Cause we all watched the building fall
Watched the scales fall from our eyes

We want answers
Scream from the roofs
We want justice
We want truth

Thrice (2008)

Rob left Giselle to make the arrangements with Michael.

She seemed a little off with him today, but he was not to know she was panicking internally as she still could not find the tapes he had requested despite quite a hunt, nor that she had to sort out her in-laws and was plucking up courage to ask for a few days off. Both agreed she should try to fix up a meeting for the following week as long as that gave their accountant enough time to find out something meaningful.

An unexpected home visit came up, so by the time Rob had got back he was a few minutes late starting afternoon surgery. He hated that. He prided himself for his good time keeping. Not only that, he always preferred to run through the patients due to come in to make sure he had all the lab results and out-patient letters at his disposal. No time for this today. He blamed his distractions on the CCG. That is why he had not noticed Felix Denning was down to see him again. He was third on Rob's list but at the risk of annoying other patients Rob called him in first. He felt he would not be able to concentrate on the first two, as he would be preoccupied wondering what the Judge wanted. Had he more news for him? More advice perhaps? Or was his gout playing up again?

The Judge had clearly come straight from court. He was in a smarter three-piece pinstriped suit this time. He had been wearing Gieves and Hawkes suits from Saville Row all his professional life, but clearly this one had seen better days. Rob mischievously wondered whether he had had it made when the company was founded in 1771. He had heard the history at a previous consultation and had to pretend he knew about the firm when he clearly had never heard of them, or that would have led to the history of the company too and another delay to his surgery timing. Apparently Felix shared the company's expertise with the likes of Churchill, Nelson, Wellington, Mikhail Gorbachev, Charlie Chaplin and David Beckham. Rob noted he still had the same expensive camel calfskin Stefano Bemer shoes on. Rob's most expensive suit was from Marks and Spencer.

"Several things," Felix said on sitting down, "But don't worry, it won't take long. First, are you okay?"

"Yes I'm fine, but to be fair you warned me it would get sticky. I must have missed the full-page advert in *The Times* telling the whole world I was treading where I had no right to tread."

Rob's trusting nature was his default setting and he trusted the judge without question. He had no real justification for this confidence, just instinct that he was prepared to rely on.

"I've been approached by a group called Poison and am having to meet one of their men tomorrow."

"Thought that might happen. Which National Trust property have they selected this time? For me it was at the top of Vita Sackville-West's tower above her writing room at Sissinghurst Castle. Very irritating. I had to pay an entrance fee."

"So you are more involved than you let on? You know about Poison? Crafty. But I suppose you had to be careful."

"Well I nearly told you that evening you called into Pleasure Towers but then that would have committed you. There would have been no going back. I really meant it when I said you should perhaps try to forget the whole thing, but actually I'm pleased you haven't. We need people like you."

"We? You belong to Poison?"

It was clear to the Judge that Rob was startled.

"No one actually belongs to an organisation like that, just has sympathy, spreads the word, works for the cause, and gives them money. I bankroll them a lot. Laundered naturally. Of course it doesn't exist really. But we are made up of perhaps thousands of small local cells with minimal contact between them for obvious security reasons. One thing I do know is that you had the privilege of a visit from Nick. Was it last night? You are honoured. He was one of the early members the organisation, which as I say, doesn't exist, at least thirty years ago. I knew the founder and his two sons. One was very good to Felicity and me after my accident. Names aren't necessary you understand. Gave me protection for a while. Although of course you will have guessed by now it was no accident. I'm glad it was some time ago when my hit man was obviously an amateur. Nowadays I'm sure they would have done the job properly."

"Your medical records simply state you were knocked down by a car?"

"Yes, hit-and-run. Had to mount the narrow pavement in Milford Lane near my Chambers to get me. By luck, Oscar my younger brother was walking to meet me and found me lying in the lane unconscious. That was just before he moved to California. I'm sure you have the full gory and gruesome reports from Bart's in my records."

"A compound fracture of right tib and fib, a fractured skull, a ruptured spleen and a tension pneumothorax of the left lung, in surgery for four hours. You were lucky."

Rob was taken aback that his old school friend Jerry, now known as Nick, should be so famous. But he felt comforted by what the Judge was saying. It helped him to believe he was not mad, paranoid, fantasising, and just as important, not alone. It seemed to confirm though that he was entering a risky game with high stakes.

"Secondly, have you made any effort to contact those people I mentioned? The former Attorney General?"

"No."

"Or any MPs?"

"No."

"Trustworthy journalists?"

"Don't know any. Surely, like Poison, they don't exist either?"

"Probably just as well. I'm not sure what I was doing even suggesting it. It shouldn't be for you to stick your neck out. We would be of course asking you to go over old ground, but it might help. I'm not encouraging or discouraging you, you understand. Be careful who you discuss this with."

He moved on.

"Thirdly, can I have more anti-inflammatories for my gout? I see they have been labelled kidney-killers now. Is that true?"

After the Judge had left, Rob got up and stared at *Le Dejeuner sur l'herbe* - straight into the nude's eyes.

Rob was relieved to be driving home. He was almost salivating over his reward to himself - a pint of *Spitfire*. It was a nice evening. Hopefully Suzy would be home, surviving her commute, and they could sit outside while he listened to her latest rant about the railways. He knew it off by heart now. 'We have the most expensive, most overcrowded and least reliable rail service in Europe... it's crazy that our railways are run by foreign governments like Germany, France... Jarvis and the Potters Bar rail crash... bla-di-da, la-di-da...' and so on. She usually arrived home at least half an hour before he did despite the much longer journey from London. He pondered on her saying of the day, 'a train is as strong as its latest link'.

As he approached the S bend he had negotiated a thousand times before he thought about the events of the other evening. He was passing the same location, which now took on a new significance and he would always remember on every journey home. But before he knew it he found himself in a queue of cars - unheard of on this quiet lane. Because of the bends he could not see what the problem was. Shit, the *Spitfire* ale will have to wait Rob thought. Although he was in no rush as there was nothing important to get home to he was still in work mode, which meant he was still in rush mode. He told himself to calm down. It did not matter if the journey home took a while.

The narrow country lanes were all tree-lined. He thought he could just about see a blue flashing light some distance off through the leaves. Then the faint sound of a siren. Police? Ambulance? Was it coming from behind him? Yes. The man in the Vauxhall had turned his car engine off. The woman in front of the Vauxhall was standing by her Mini on the phone. This did not look good. Should he turn around? No, he decided. Calm down and continue listening to *Radio 3*. The presenter was premiering a new recording of three of Elgar's First World War pieces written to words by the exiled Belgian poet Émile Cammaerts. This should relax him. Practice what you preach, Rob told himself. A traffic jam can in no way compare to the trenches.

The ambulance approached from behind, just about squeezing past. It thumped down a pothole but continued. The siren was deafening. Bit unnecessary that, Rob thought. Quite annoying too as it drowned out a sizeable section of the middle piece *Une Voix Dans le Desert*.

Twenty minutes passed very slowly. He wished he had turned around, but knew there was no room anyway. Then he saw a policeman walking from car to car towards him. He was clearly letting people know what was going on. When it was Rob's turn he learnt there was a car in the ditch. The driver was being stabilised before being loaded into the ambulance. Only after that might the traffic start moving. The policeman told all in the queue that they were not permitted to try to turn around because of a mysterious oil-like spillage along the other side that would need investigating. Rob now understood why people had not tried. In Rob's experience impatient drivers usually give a queue no more than five nanoseconds before reversing. It was another twenty-five minutes before he heard engines in front of him starting up. Poor bloke took a bit of stabilising, he thought, and then wondered why he assumed the driver was male. He also realised, a little late, that perhaps he should have offered his services.

The cars started to crawl forward. Rob continued to snake. Having got fully around the S bend he saw police behind their tape in front of a car. He saw a blue car on its roof. As he got closer he saw it was a Daewoo Matiz. Closer still the number plate was clearly readable, GD55 XXL. It did not take long to register, not with Rob's almost autistic skills with numbers. Last seen by Rob in Tolpuddle - Ian's car. If Ian was in it presumably he was the one needing stabilisation and was on his way to hospital as the policeman said. Rob wound down his window as he slowly passed. He thought he would push his luck.

"Hi, I'm the local GP incidentally."

"Congratulations," said the man in blue sarcastically.

"I know you can't say much but I just wondered if any of my patients were in that car?"

Rob thought he sounded plausible and with no negative signs coming from the young copper continued.

"How many in the car? Do you know their names?"

"Sorry sir, you can read about it in the papers. I can say there were two people in the car though. Now move along."

Having got clear of the jam, Rob was in another world for the last few minutes of the drive home. An accident? Surely not? Have they, whoever they are, finally got some revenge on Poison? Has Ian lost another of his nine lives? Why did the police refer to it as a mysterious oil-like spillage? He finally gathered some speed and knew that pint was now only minutes away. As he drove onto the newly laid gravel, (a job he had ambitiously done himself which nearly finished his back off for good) he almost had to do an emergency stop as there were already two cars parked. Suzy's was by the house, but behind was unmistakably an old 2CV - or deux chevaux-vapeur as her fluent French-speaking friend called it, 'two steam horses to you, Rob' she would explain. Only one person drove one of those in the whole world now, as far as he knew - Pippa.

After a tricky day this lifted Rob's spirits but what was she doing here? He walked in briskly leaving his car unlocked. He knew he should not - not with his doctor's bag in the car. Fuck it, he thought.

"Mrs Thackeray, great to see you!"

And he was genuinely delighted.

Suzy and Pippa were at the kitchen table. Half of the *Muscadet* bottle had already disappeared. Rob helped himself to a glass after embracing and kissing Pippa three times as usual.

"I've been apologising to Suzy about just dropping in like this. I hate it when people do that to me. How did you get that bruise? Whatever you did I'm sure you deserved it."

"Suzy punched me again. I'm glad you are here as the police are on their way and I need the support."

"I will punch you Robert if you don't shut up," stormed Suzy.

Being called Robert was the warning that she did not think that was funny.

"Great to see you. You know you are always welcome. Anytime."

Rob could not think of anyone else he would say this to and actually mean it.

"It's just that I want to fill you in on a few things I've discovered and didn't want to do it on the phone or e-mail. Besides it would take all night."

"Wow. That sounds ominous but encouraging?" queried Rob.

Suzy was getting hungry.

"I've already offered Pippa the guest room for the night as I've insisted driving a hundred and sixty miles back tonight isn't sensible especially in that old car."

"Hey, don't be rude about Edith."

"Eh?"

"My deux chevaux-vapeur. Named after Piaf."

"She has no excuse," Suzy continued, "I've also made sure she has had too much *Muscadet* to drive, so no choice. She has no work tomorrow and Dave has Jeremy under control. I've told her not to look at the teeth of a gift-horse. So I've ordered a take-away. I'm off to pick it up. I'll take your car to save moving them all around."

Rob had a half-second semi-subliminal fantasy of a threesome flash involuntarily into his mind. He pulled himself together.

"Great. Avoid Willow Lane though as there's been an accident. That's why I'm late. We are lucky here, Pippa. We have plenty of alternatives when it comes to takeaways."

"It's the Chinese at Golden Green, so opposite direction. And Rob, that is not the correct use of the word alternative! It is not a substitute for choices. If there are two choices then they are properly called alternatives. If there are more than two - and we have more than two takeaways - then they are choices."

And with that she picked up Rob's keys and was off.

"What was that all about?" puzzled Pippa.

"Oh, she delights in correcting my grammar and word usage. I think she considers English must be my second language. Don't worry. I'm used to it. Trains must have been bad again."

Pippa did not want to get involved in their niggles.

"It's so good to see you Pippa. You've brightened up an otherwise shit day. You are wonderful to drive all this way just for us."

"It's more than that though, isn't it Rob? You really got me thinking and disturbed. I couldn't sleep either."

"Oh, Pippa, I'm so sorry."

"No, don't apologise. This could all be so very important."

Although anxious to hear what Pippa came to tell him, he thought he would let her know about the events of the last few days first. He talked briefly about the ambush on the S bend and encounter with 'Nick', the trouble at work, and the accident he had just witnessed. He then thought he would tell Pippa about the cat.

"Then there's Eric. I found him strung up in that apple tree,"

He gestured out of the kitchen window.

"That really worried me, poor little... oh fuck, fuck, fuck. He's still in the boot! I was distracted tonight so I forgot to get rid of him. Suzy doesn't know and has just taken my car to collect the Chinese. Fuck!"

"What's your cat doing in the boot of your car?"

Pippa was not really following what Rob was on about and could only just suppress a laugh.

"It was strung up," Rob repeated, "It's dead. It was murdered. Not sure who by but Poison deny it."

"I'm sorry Rob, but what do you mean your cat was murdered. What poison? You are not making sense."

553

Now Pippa did laugh.

"Ah!" he cried clenching his fists in despair.

He felt like Basil Fawlty having a panic attack when Sybil discovers his latest cock-up.

"Was it a crime of passion by a jealous tabby or are the Mafia involved. Do you think it is linked to Jimmy Hoffa's murder?"

She took Rob's smile as a sign of encouragement.

"Or did the neighbour's tomcat shoot him? If so where did he get the gun?" she mocked, "Was it a blunderpuss and was the kitty tigger-happy?"

Rob could forgive her jokes as he could forgive her anything.

"Pity Schrodinger didn't own the cat 'cos it then could be alive and dead at the same time."

Pippa realised she had gone too far.

"Eh?" said Rob, clearly puzzled by this one, "I think it was a warning. No, I know it was a warning. I came home last night to find him... assassinated.

"Assassinated?" Pippa repeated loudly with mirth almost choking on her wine.

He pointed out of the kitchen window again.

"So I wrapped him in a sack intending on disposing of him today."

"Assassinated isn't usually the word to use about a dead cat or are you thinking Lee Harvey Oswald was involved?"

"I'll never be able to eat those apples again."

His panic kicked back in.

"Suppose she puts the takeaway in the boot. She will open the lid and see poor dead Eric staring at her. Fuck. What shall I do?"

The colour had drained from his face.

"I don't think there is anything you can do except hope, darling Rob. Hope she puts the meal on the back seat."

"She never puts things on the back seat. She always uses the boot. Fuck. Fuck."

Rob was pacing up and down and getting a little irrational.

"If you go after her you'll only make things worse. You will make her suspicious and wonder what the hell you are up to."

"You are right. She'll be on her way back now anyway. When we hear the car on the gravel, we'll know whether she has found him or not. We could play innocent and just claim he must have got trapped in the boot and suffocated."

"And how did Eric manage to wrap himself, after suffocating, in an old sack, may I ask?" said Pippa, trying to suppress laughter, "And it couldn't credibly be suicide, could it Rob."

She could suppress it no longer. She had to try to calm him down. She picked up his glass of *Muscadet* and put it in his hand.

"Drink. This actually brings me onto subject number one anyway," said Pippa, "How much does Suzy know? How much are you protecting her? You obviously haven't told her about your cat."

"At the moment she only knows I'm a paranoid jerk who has gone conspiracy-theory mad."

"Oh dear, I was afraid of that. You have to tell her everything. It's only fair."

"You are right. You tell her everything while I go down the pub," he said with a straight face.

"No seriously, when she gets back explain all or what I say won't make any sense. Another reason you have to do this is that you didn't tell her you had visited me, did you? I'm sorry but I assumed she knew and the cat's out of the bag now. Oh sorry, unfortunate phrase."

"I wish he was in a bag and not in the boot," Rob continued.

She smiled again. Rob wondered how anyone could be so deliciously seductive and attractive in such a serious situation. Rob took another gulp of *Muscadet*. Then on hearing a car on the gravel they both moved swiftly to the kitchen window to see if Suzy opened the boot.

"Oh shit, oh shit. Please no."

Rob was almost praying which showed how worried this atheist was. They nervously watched Suzy open the passenger door and take the large brown paper bag off the seat. Suzy laughed again as she realised Rob was watching through the fingers covering his face.

"There you are. She hasn't discovered him."

"We don't know that for sure. Would you put your evening meal next to a dead cat?"

"I think our local Chinese uses dead cats but point taken. She looks too calm though. But you need to tell her."

They demolished a Meal-for-three like locusts whilst covering all the small talk Rob could think of, such as Jeremy, his football, Dave and his postie job, Dave's beer and her work with JupiterPress. The French department, which sounded grand as she was the department. It was getting such a good reputation that she might start having to go to Paris on a fairly regular basis.

"You know my manager has an apartment in the eleventh arrondissement, Popincourt, don't you? Have I mentioned it? She rents it out quite cheaply for friends. Rue de Crussol, about four metro stops down from the Gare du Nord. It's close to the Bataclan too and she was staying there the night of the massacre in November 2015. Very scary."

"Thanks Rob but I only go if my boss fixes up nice hotels for me close to our sister publishers."

Pippa could tell Rob was dreaming up any subject possible to avoid coming clean with Suzy. So she kicked him under the table. Suzy put the coffee on and they retreated to the sunroom. Rob braced himself, took a gulp, then systematically went through the events he had just told Pippa. When he finished, there was silence for an unbearable twenty seconds. Suzy then asked if Pippa knew all this, and wanted to know why Rob had visited Dorset without telling him.

"I told you this wasn't worth it. We should get out now before someone gets hurt."

"Someone already has, Suzy." Suzy looked at Rob with alarm. "It's Eric. He's an ex-Eric. I'm afraid he's been killed."

Suzy looked stunned. Partly because of Eric. Partly as she was beginning to get frightened.

"Oh no. How? What do you mean killed? When? Where is he? And how can our cat be part of your silly conspiracies?"

Having heard the worst Suzy now regretted the word silly.

Rob explained.

"Even more reason to stop all this now."

"You had better hear what I've found out first. It probably won't change your mind but we all need to share the complete picture. When Rob first told me what he knew I had the same reaction as you, Suzy. Remember Rob, I said go home and forget it, but I did add I didn't think you would."

"And I said I didn't think you would either, so we were both right. Or wrong, whichever way you look at it."

"I was very careful. I spoke to my boss at JupiterPress. I buttered him up with a drink. He is putty in my hands and I don't think he suspected anything. He told me about a book he was offered a few years ago which produced all sorts of conspiracy theories and another more recently about politicians who couldn't keep their trousers on. There was a disturbing chapter about paedophilia in that one. However both books were abandoned when the Managing Director got involved. My boss thought it was purely a commercial decision. Intrigued, when I was in the office on my own, I went through the rejection file. I found the first easily but had to hunt harder for the second. That file was under Confidential. I had to laugh. Who labels their files Confidential? Might as well have a flashing neon sign pointing to what I wanted."

Rob thought they had moved onto coffee too soon.

"Would you like some Southern Comfort, Pippa?"

He knew it was a weakness of hers.

"Does a one legged duck swim around in circles?" she replied in a flash.

"Anyway, the files had contact details. I rang the conspiracy book author who told me to fuck off and leave him alone. I then Googled him and found newspaper reports. He had lost his job after being accused of stealing from a supermarket apparently. That was within a month of his book being rejected. More worrying was the death of the other author. She had been killed, this time only a few days after being rejected. Her car was found upside down in a ditch. She was alone. The coroner blamed alcohol."

"Shit. Do you know anything more about them?"

"The man used to work for the Department of Education in London but was sacked in 2006. That was in the press too. This Internet is great for that sort of thing. Apparently he was accused of sexual harassment. Doesn't quite tie in with stealing from a supermarket, but still."

Suzy was looking disturbed. She looked on the verge of tears.

"What's the matter, Suzy?" Rob asked.

"Philip was at the Department of Education then. I vaguely remember him being annoyed about them hanging several good workers out to dry. And Philip died the following year."

"The other file had an address quite close to me. The widower lived at Lyme Regis so I went and knocked on his door one day."

"You did what?" Rob exclaimed.

"It was a nice day and I felt like visiting the seaside," Pippa said, trying to lighten the atmosphere, "The husband invited me in. He was calm and was very economical with his words. He reminded me of Sir Mark Rylance as Thomas Cromwell, or in *Bridge of Spies*. He told me his wife had been brought up in Ireland. She was a victim of the laundries. You must know about the Magdalene Laundries in Ireland?"

"Yes," said Rob, "I've seen *The Magdalene Sisters* movie. Don't you remember Suzy? You couldn't bear to watch it."

"Oh yes, those horrible places for fallen women run by those depraved nuns."

"She was more or less a prisoner in one. In fact the same one where a mass grave containing over a hundred and fifty corpses was discovered about twenty-five years ago. She eventually escaped but there was a ten-year period in her life that she refused to talk about. He suspected abuse. She had been bitter all her life and after the children left home she got increasingly obsessed with researching corruption, particularly that driven by sex. The happiest he had known her was the day she finished her book. The saddest was when it was rejected. She was a teetotaller. He couldn't understand the accident. It occurred in a place she had never been and he had no idea why she was there. To him it was very puzzling, but he didn't seem to want to take it any further."

"Intriguing. And worrying. Fits in, doesn't it?"

"I haven't finished yet," continued Pippa, "That ex-Attorney General you mentioned."

"Oh no. Don't tell me you knocked on his door too?" said Rob.

"Certainly not. What sort of person do you think I am? I got a friend to break into his house."

"You did what? Oh, I don't believe this. Pippa, that's outrageous. But more than that, it's dangerous. If I had known you would risk such a thing I wouldn't have told you about this. I only came down to Dorset to ask your advice. Not to get you thrown in jail."

"When you see what I've got you'll change your tune."

She got up and unzipped her small overnight bag. Her skirt rose up as she bent over. Rob tried to avert his gaze. He really wanted to look but dared not. If Suzy had caught him it would rekindle her suspicions about the two of them. He could not be certain Suzy had not seen the kick under the table. She pulled out a dog-eared dark blue paper file about two centimetres thick within a transparent plastic folder. It was not labelled. She then put on gloves and took the file out.

"This file is amazing. I assume it's the old Attorney General's insurance policy, very useful to have ammunition against old colleagues and enemies. I also assume nobody else knows of its existence or someone else would have got hold of it before me. He should have been more careful. It wasn't under lock and key. Just in his filing cabinet next to domestic bills. It didn't take long to find, according to my chum. This dossier is dynamite. No way does this need sexing up. In here are names of Westminster politicians involved in all sorts of naughty stuff. Sexual, financial, insider trading, bribery, blackmail, bungs to newspaper men, phone-tapping, back-handers to top union officials, illegal arms dealing, the backing of illegal regime change, records of attempted coups and wars we didn't even know about. You couldn't make it up. The records go way back to when he was first sent to Parliament at the second election of 1974. He studiously kept records of all the dirt he heard about, whether there was evidence of not. I doubt if he will miss it for some time. What he will do when he does discover it has disappeared is difficult to judge, but what can he do? It doesn't seem likely he had a copy, a very silly oversight but perhaps an indication that he didn't need to use it and had forgotten about it. He is too old to have transferred it onto computer, I would say."

"Very ageist."

Pippa passed Rob another pair of gloves, which he slipped on then started to flick through the file. The gloves gave him another split-second unworthy thought. He had already exceeded the male quota of thoughts for that day.

"Wow. So many recognisable names."

"The scales are falling from our eyes. We can't allow them to cover up their lies any longer. I feel we should scream it from the rooftops. In these files are the answers and the truth. I wonder if we can help the victims get justice."

44 - DIRT AND SCANDAL

UPRISING

The paranoia is in bloom, the P-R
Transmissions will resume

Rise up and take the power back, it's time that
The fat cats had a heart attack, you know that
Their time is coming to an end
We have to unify and watch our flag ascend

Muse (2009)

"Three heads are better than one," said Suzy.

Rob, Suzy and Pippa were wearing the gloves brought along by Pippa, but none of them were entirely sure why. It seemed a sensible precaution. They planned to sit in silence as they took a third of the folder each proposing to carefully and quietly read through - except they did not. Every few minutes there would be a gasp and then a declaration. The material was so hot they could not resist moving through quickly, keen to know what was next. Rob was first to break the silence.

"Your MP is in there, Pippa. I think there's an explanation as to why he was a serial rebel then suddenly fell into line and has been a good boy ever since. He has stopped visiting that children's home now. Funny that, eh? It was like watching a wild horse being broken. Like a lot of MPs he's become no more than a salesman, and front man representing his corporate bosses. He has no interest or respect for his constituents. He doesn't need to, being in such a safe seat."

"There are some good MPs, you know Rob," countered Suzy, "Take Jo Cox. If there were six hundred of the likes of her what a great and fair democracy we would be living in. We wouldn't be sitting here in the early hours of the morning."

Nobody could disagree with that.

"Bloody hell!" exclaimed Pippa, "Here's a good one. Remember old Jeremy Thorpe, that odd Liberal leader who wore trilby hats and was terrified of his mother? That trial when he was tried for conspiracy to murder his gay lover, Norman Scott. Says here the judge was as bent as a corkscrew. That's how he got off. Establishment looking after their own again. Says here his hit men were so incompetent they shot his Great Dane instead. The compliant press sat on his story for years. Called Rinka apparently."

"Who is?"

"The dog."

"I thought Rinka is a Japanese model?"

"Oh… dirt on George Carman his barrister. Says he had a drink problem, and George Best screwed his wife! *News Of The World* stuff this!"

"Except the *News Of The World* has changed its title to the *Sun On Sunday*.

"Here it says that Thorpe and Parliament knew all about what Cyril Smith got up to too, and no one thought it a problem."

"There's a fair bit on Jeffrey Archer in this document," said Rob.

"Boring," retaliated Suzy.

"Oh my God. Not only did gorgeous George Best seduce his second wife but when Carman found out he tried to hire a gangster to break Best's legs! It says here the only reason it didn't happen was, unbeknown to Carman, the gangster was a friend of Best. He told Carman that if anything did ever happen to his friend he knew who to come after!"

"Odd. More gossip than political, eh?"

"Not when you read on. The hard nuts knew the Krays who had several MPs and Lords in their pockets like old Boothby. Carman defended Jeremy Thorpe and showed Jonathan Aitken up for what he was, a liar."

"Going back a bit there's some stuff on the Profumo affair here and Lord Denning's report. A best seller, it says. Amongst those who had his liaisons with prostitutes covered up was Ernest Marples, Macmillan's Transport Secretary. We were talking about him the other day. A corrupt crook. That's why some called it a whitewash, like most Government reports into something embarrassing."

"That was in the news not that long ago when Christine Keeler died."

"Something here on the Westland affair," said Rob.

No one was really listening. They were all too absorbed in their third of the documents, but he continued anyway.

"This 1986 scandal was all about whether an American or European-led consortium should take over our last remaining helicopter company. Thatcher wanted her rival, Heseltine, discredited so ordered the leak of a confidential law officer's letter. She, Powell her private secretary, and that horrible shit Ingham were up to their necks in it. They got a senior civil servant called Colette Bowe to give it to the press. They kept her quiet for thirty years. Seems Thatcher lied to Parliament about it. Said she knew nothing about the leak. Led to Leon Brittan being blamed and hung out to dry."

"Ruthless bloody lot."

"Ha, ha! Cecil Parkinson," Pippa jumped in, "He's another ruthless sod. Remember he got his secretary pregnant? When he told her Thatcher said *don't worry about it, Anthony Eden was worse*."

"What did he get up to then?" asked Suzy

"Apparently shagged the wife of David Beatty, who was the son of Admiral Beatty who shat on Jellicoe making sure he got the blame for the Battle of Jutland failure in World War One. Ended up marrying Clarissa, Churchill's niece. A good career move eh?"

"Of course when secrets are out they are no longer blackmail material but there's a few things here that wouldn't have improved his reputation."

Pippa was back to Parkinson.

"He apparently never met his daughter, never even sent her a birthday card, and he gagged the press with an injunction. Only the rich can do that."

Rob remembered the incident well. It was 1983 just after Thatcher was returned to power and Rob was a student at Guy's. Parkinson had to resign as Trade and Industry Secretary and they all had a drink in the Spit, as the Guy's student bar was called, to celebrate. 'Only twenty-one more Tory Cabinet Ministers to go' was the toast - not appreciated by the right wing bunch at his medical school.

"He deserved all the stick he got in *Private Eye* and on *Spitting Image*. I remember two great front covers. One was when Parkinson objected to that semi house-trained polecat Norman Tebbit's version of events in his memoirs. It showed each man saying to the other 'you shouldn't have put it in'. The other was when Hague promised to 'bring unity to the party', the cover showed Parkinson adding 'she sounds like a goer'."

"Oh, very good Rob. How do you remember such things?" admired Suzy.

"That's all fairly trivial stuff compared to this," said Pippa.

There was a danger Rob had lightened the mood and Pippa unconsciously decided to spread the gloom.

"What about this scandal? Old news now and not implicating anyone we know but horrible. In 1967 a Home Office Psychiatrist called Dr Pamela Mason gave permission for drugging up pupils at two so-called approved schools without their or their parents' knowledge and against their will. At a Yorkshire school, Richmond Hill, they were all given an anti-convulsant called beclamide to see if their behaviour improved. They were planning to give girls at a school in Leeds haloperidol but that didn't go ahead."

"What was an approved school?" enquired Suzy.

"It was half way between a children's home and borstal. Instead of wondering why they ended up classified and written off as delinquents and looking at their backgrounds and other social factors at fault, they just drugged them up. A twentieth century version of the nineteenth century straitjacket, the well-known liquid kosh."

"Appalling. But do you think anyone cares nowadays?" said Suzy.

It was now Suzy's turn to try to shock the others but they were beyond that.

"Here's a lot on MPs cash for questions. This lobbying lark is truly corrupt. These supposed safeguards have made no difference.

They are still all at it. That revolving door should be banned, Ministers setting up contracts with firms and then ending up on the Board. Disgraceful. It says here that Churchill got five thousand pounds to lobby for Burmah Oil in 1923 which oddly enough is what Chartwell cost him the same year".

"Fuck me. There's a handwritten note next to this that Churchill hated his mother, had her bumped off and T.E. Lawrence knew all about all this, so Churchill had him killed too when he was about to publish. He had other motives that meant MI5 was happy to do the dirty. Lawrence was an appeaser who was planning to meet Hitler. No one is going to believe any of this, surely?"

"That's confusing. I thought Baldwin and Chamberlain were using the Secret Service against anti-appeasers, not those on side."

"All right for some, eh? To buy your house out of lobbying money, hardly hard work," said Pippa, stifling a yawn.

Rob had discovered a section on the unions.

"Here's a list of union leaders bought off by the Establishment. It's very long. Several examples of industrial disputes where all the workers were really up for the fight, but then being sold down the river by their so-called leaders who end up in the House of Lords as their reward. It seems infiltration by secret right-wingers has gone on for years. It has had the desired effect of neutering workers' opposition to the deterioration of their working conditions and pay."

"Yes, didn't they achieve that with Scargill? Put someone daft in post, get him to say silly things then label him an extremist."

"Here's a foreign section," said Suzy.

"The sinking of Greenpeace's Rainbow Warrior, remember that? Sunk in 1985 by the French foreign intelligence services whilst moored at Marsden Wharf in Auckland, because they wanted to protest about France's nuclear test in Mururoa Atoll. Caught in the act, they ended up paying Greenpeace over eight million dollars and money to the family of the man killed. It says here that Mitterrand himself authorised the bombing. They tried to blame MI6 first. Says Thatcher was infuriated but didn't push it further as Mitterrand would have had to resign because of a Watergate-like cover up. Also says here it severely pissed off New Zealand because most Western leaders failed to condemn the violation of a friendly nation's sovereignty. This ended up with them cooling relations with us. So damage done all round."

Rob put in his bit.

"So hypocritical. The US and we are prepared to go to war over state sponsored terrorism but it seems only when it's convenient. And we have sponsored our fair share, haven't we?"

Suzy continued.

"This is disgraceful. France threatened New Zealand's access to the European Economic Community market and New Zealand exports to France were boycotted. We, that is Britain, just sat on our hands and failed to condemn this terrorist act. Now we are leaving the EU, we think that will be conveniently forgotten after that betrayal and it'll be easy setting up new trade deals with them? Jacinda Ardern is the only really decent world leader I can think of."

They were beginning to flag a little so Rob offered to get some drinks and make some coffee.

"Got any biscuits?" was Pippa's plea.

Suzy though was on a roll.

"Something here in the same foreign section about the Iran-Contra affair. The background to this is pretty convoluted. Reagan allowed secret arms sales to Iran, which broke an embargo, and funded the Contras in Nicaragua, which Congress prohibited, with the money. They probably used drug-trafficking money to fund them too. The Contras were anti-communist rebels fighting Sandinista who were a democratic socialist party. The Sandinistas started redistributing wealth. Outrageous. Reagan couldn't cope with that. When rumbled, Reagan made a load of documents disappear impeding a proper investigation. There were a few convictions but George Bush pardoned them when he was President."

"So let's get this right. Reagan broke the law, defied embargos, ignored Congress, used drug money, shredded documents, all to topple a democratically elected Government in another country and got away with it, and Clinton impeached for a blow-job?" Summed up Rob.

"But this is why it is in this file" continued Suzy, "Because what was lied about was Britain and Thatcher's involvement. We played a central role in supplying the arms via a British arms dealer who worked for the White House. And the UK Ambassador knew all about it, as did Thatcher's private secretary, Gow, who was later killed by the IRA, apparently. Maybe he was killed by someone else for another reason, eh?"

Rob didn't think this the time to tell them that Poison had claimed that victim.

"And we probably supplied Blowpipe missiles to the Contras via Chile. Don't forget Thatcher and Pinochet, that murderous Chilean dictator, were good mates. Blimey, the friends she kept!"

"More cover ups and lies here. Thatcher sold arms to Iraq and Saddam Hussein throughout the eight-year Iran-Iraq war when more than a million people on both sides died. When war was declared Western Government imposed an arms embargo, which we ignored selling arms to both sides! Slightly embarrassing when we found ourselves up against our own weapons including the supergun in the first Gulf War. This proves the point about inquiries, years after the event are either useless whitewashes or ignored. The *Scott Report* called the Government slippery with the truth, riddled with incompetence and willing to mislead Parliament. Who paid a price? No one of course, they can get away literally with murder."

"And a shed-load of money to fund a country estate and a peerage."

"Then they still feel they deserve respect."

While Suzy was reading her documents, Pippa, who had been through hers and thought Suzy's far more juicy, took a few sheets to lighten her load - still foreign issues. The next bit of US foreign policy was Operation Condor. The Americans provided arms and support to help eradicate any socialist ideas or Soviet influence in South America. They backed political repression and state terror. They propped up governments, which were often undemocratic military dictatorships. Their paranoia was in bloom.

"What a great example of democracy is the mighty US of A! Just look at this list. With their help military coups took place in

Paraguay in 1954, Brazil in 1964, Bolivia in 1971, Uruguay in 1973, Chile in 1973. Remember that one? Pinochet deposed the democratically elected Salvador Allende and murdered him, and another coup in Argentina in 1976. This is odd. A summary of Allende's post mortem report. What did the Attorney General keep that for? Anyway perhaps this is the reason. They all claimed he committed suicide but he was shot in the head first by a small gun, then by a larger weapon - something like an AK-47. Very clever suicide I'd say. Bloody amazing, the whole story."

"Henry Kissinger was up to his neck in it," Rob added, "Tom Lehrer said that political satire became obsolete when Kissinger was awarded the *Nobel Peace Prize*. Much better to give it to Bob Dylan."

"No, he got the one for Literature, dummy," Suzy corrected her husband.

"I know really, it's just that all this stuff would win a prize if in a novel."

Rob had produced the refreshments, which gave them all new vigour. Pippa took her coffee without taking her eyes off her latest discovery.

"This file is very diverse. Look at this about Kurt Waldheim. When we were young he was a well-respected Secretary General of the United Nations who became President of Austria. It seems all those in the Establishment knew of his service in the Wehrmacht, in which he rose to the rank of Oberleutnant, years before it became public. If this had been leaked earlier he may not have achieved such lofty heights. The CIA had known about it since 1945. He denied all knowledge of war crimes of course but he was stationed five miles from Salonika where the Jewish population were rounded up and sent to Auschwitz. On the other hand it seems possible that he was framed by Mossad, the Israeli intelligence agency, because he criticised Israel's war in Lebanon."

Rob had a special, almost morbid interest in the Nazi period. He had read much about Germany after the war and loved visiting the country. He sought out and enjoyed the Third Reich tours that took place in most cities.

"Post-war Germany's Justice Ministry was dominated by Nazi-era judges and lawyers who did a good job in shielding their former comrades from justice. Believe it or not seventy-seven per cent of senior officials in 1957 were former members of Hitler's Nazi Party, higher than during the Third Reich! Many had handed down unjust death sentences during the Holocaust. Everyone knows the excuses; 'we were only following orders', or 'we knew nothing about the atrocities', or 'by staying in post we prevented even worse crimes'. In fact there's been a study I was reading about only recently by a Professor Safferling who said he never found words of regret, only justifications, a bit like today's politicians. Someone started going through the files a few years ago and discovered a total of twenty-five cabinet ministers, one president and one chancellor had been Nazis. I hope their time is coming to an end. There are apparently thousands of files still to be trawled."

"I think the latest generation of Germans need great praise for exposing and now openly discussing what happened," said Suzy.

She went on to add that she had heard somewhere that for years after the war German school history lessons ended in January 1933 and started again in 1945.

"I think they've turned a corner especially with the admiration heaped on Angela Merkel for taking in refugees. Shame she gets so criticised inside Germany. Our pathetic shameful Government could learn a few humanitarian lessons from her. Imagine that. I'm saying many Germans are more considerate to their fellow man than the British. No one would have believed that fifty years ago. Who's that famous German writer who came out about ten years ago?"

"Err, Gunter Grass?"

"Yes, that's him. Drafted into the Waffen SS."

"What about Pope Benedict? He belonged to the Hitler Youth," Rob interjected.

Rob had read that the US surveyed Germans in their zone up to 1952 and found about a third still thought the extermination of the Jews and Poles and non-Aryans was necessary for security, that Jews should not have the same rights as Aryans, that Germany would be better off without Jews and the Nuremberg trials had been unfair.

"One in four still thought Hitler a good bloke," he added.

He also knew about Operation Paperclip.

"The US had a programme designed to bring German scientists, engineers and technicians to America after the war partly to deny this expertise to the Soviet Union and us, their supposed allies. Truman ordered no Nazis but that would have excluded most of the rocket scientists like Wernher von Braun. So they were bleached of their Nazism by creating false employment and political biographies. The Soviets did the same for the same reasons. Their plan was called Oso... Osoavy... Osoaviak something... yes Osoaviakhim... I think?"

"I'm whacked. I can't go on with this tonight," Suzy said quietly.

The other two were so engrossed they did not notice.

"This file marked Marshall Islands is empty but I've never heard of them," said Pippa.

"It's where the Americans tested their nuclear bombs. We used Australia, the French Algeria and the Soviets Kazakhstan."

"Strange though as it has an article about Operation Grapple, which is our H bomb testing on Malden Island in the Pacific between 1956 and 1958."

After a pause.

"There are claims here that our tests in 1957 were a bluff, and we even fooled the Americans. So much so that they started co-operating again."

Then another silence.

"I didn't know this did you? There are two broad categories of nuclear weapons. The A bombs which use nuclear fission, and the hydrogen bombs which uses nuclear fusion. The A bomb acts as a trigger for the H bomb which are thousands of times more powerful. I never did do physics at school."

Pippa really was engrossed.

"There's a paragraph written here in longhand in the margin about Klaus Fuchs. Born Germany 1911. Left for England 1933. Worked with Rudy Peierls on the Manhattan project. Exposed as spy 1950. Then this bit I don't understand. In pencil, so possibly added later it says, was Rutherford his contact? I wonder who Rutherford was?"

"You didn't do physics did you? Ernest Rutherford split the atom," said Suzy.

"But it says his initial was A."

"And," added Rob, "Ernest died before the war."

"How on earth do you know that?" said Suzy

"It's the sort of stupid thing I do remember. My autism gene. I blame my six single nucleotide polymorphisms in an intergenic region between CHD9 and 10," said Rob.

"Seriously?"

"No, I just made that up. Can't remember where I left my car keys though?"

"This is a note about a near nuclear accident in 1983. A Soviet officer, Stanislav Petrov, averted Armageddon it seems. All hushed up of course. The early warning system alerted him to an incoming American nuclear attack. Fortunately he decided it was an error and didn't respond. A close shave."

"I'm surprised we haven't found anything about the Pentagon Papers?" Pippa said to herself, "That stuff about Vietnam and America's first strike policy and all that."

Then a war none of them had heard of but it involved Britain in their lifetime.

"Looks like we had troops fighting in Oman for a few years in the late sixties and early seventies. We were involved in a war that the Sultan of Oman was fighting against guerrillas in the mountains of Dhofar in the south of the country. We were trying to prop him up. We were worried about maintaining the flow of oil through the Hormuz bottleneck, as it boosted our export trade. We British controlled the Sultans throughout the nineteenth and twentieth centuries. Officially the Sultanate of Muscat and Oman was an independent state. In truth it was a de facto British colony. So yet again we supported a tyrannical ruler and so we were responsible for the terrible lives of the Sultan's subjects. So that's why they revolted, don't blame them."

Pippa looked like she had just seen the light.

"Ah, that makes sense now. I was reading recently how the Sultan was a real bastard. He banned all sorts of things from radios to sunglasses, even playing football."

"What? That's outrageous."

"It would be funny if it wasn't so terrible. He executed people and had to call for British support to protect him from his own people. We suppressed several uprisings. Slavery was still legal. The Sultan owned about five hundred and we supported him! We were booted out of neighbouring Aden in 1967 and British rule was replaced by a Marxist State. We feared the old domino effect and worried that the Strait of Hormuz would fall under communist control. We committed atrocities. No wonder Britain needed to fight this war in total secrecy. We kept a medieval slave-owning barbaric despot in power."

"Ah… the conclusion. Looks like we won as MI6 staged a coup and stuck the Sultan's better-behaved son on the throne. So James Bond was real after all. Perhaps we should have thought of that a few years earlier and saved some lives. No wonder those in the Middle East are so suspicious of the British. If this was taught in schools we might not repeat it. You can't learn from history if you don't know it."

There was a short period of silence and a few yawns. Not for long though.

"Our Secret Intelligence Service helped the CIA get rid of the Iranian President in 1953 to install the Shah as a puppet and the two teamed up again to get regime change in Syria. The SIS tried to assassinate Nasser, and were up to no good in South Yemen, according to this."

"Amazing this one. Straight after the war in which remember the Japanese were our enemies we fought alongside them and the French against the nationalist forces of Viet Minh in Indo-China. The idea it seems was to help the French recover control of their pre-war colonial possession and suppress the Vietnam people's attempts to form their own Government. The British army, navy and RAF were involved. We even rearmed Vichy troops! It says Parliament and the public knew nothing of this."

Rob went on to read an extract from what looked like a speech that was drafted but not delivered. It had pencil alterations in the margins.

"'Between 1918 and 1939, British forces were fighting in Iraq, Sudan, Ireland, Palestine and Aden. In the years after the Second World War, British servicemen were fighting in Eritrea, Palestine, French Indochina, Dutch East Indies, Malaya, Egypt, China and Oman. Between 1949 and 1970 the British initiated thirty-four foreign military interventions. Later came the Falklands, Iraq four times, Bosnia, Kosovo, Sierra Leone, Afghanistan, Libya and, of course, Operation Banner the British army's thirty-eight year deployment to Northern Ireland. For more than a hundred years, not a single year has passed when Britain's armed forces have not been engaged in military operations somewhere in the world. The British are unique in this respect, the same could not be said of the Americans, the Russians, the French or any other nation. Only, we, the British are perpetually at war'."

"Some speech eh? Do you think it was suppressed?"

"Wouldn't be at all surprised."

"Remember hearing about Chappaquiddick and President Kennedy's younger brother Ted?" Pippa said excitedly, but then almost in sorrow concluded, "Oh, how disappointing. Nothing new. Just says an Establishment cover up, which we were aware of anyway. 1969. Six married men entertain six single women. They get pissed and go off with each other, one can guess but no one will ever know the truth about that night. One gets driven off, or drives off a bridge by accident and drowns. Panic. Looks bad for a Senator who may have left her for dead and who wants to run for the Presidency. It seems the scandal was the usual. An Establishment cover up to protect Kennedy. They had all the local judiciary in their pockets. The inquest was initially held in secret. The Kennedys were so arrogant they really thought they were above the law and could get away with murder. His older brothers had told him 'never get caught with a dead girl or a live boy'."

"Do you know?" Pippa said, "I had a holiday on Cape Cod once with an old boyfriend, post John. We stayed along Nantucket Sound in Hyannis Port where the Kennedys had their compound. We found all the locals very protective of the Kennedy family. Whoever we asked where the compound was we were greeted with an icy stare and told 'I have no idea'. Absolutely ridiculous, of course they knew. In those days I was fascinated by the dynasty and insisted we caught the ferry across to Martha's Vineyard to visit the famous Chappaquiddick Bridge where it all happened. That was before the fantasy of Camelot was so tarnished. Apparently the bridge has become a tourist attraction but we found it deserted and wired off. Have you been to New England, Rob?"

By now Suzy was asleep in the chair.

"It's on the list."

"I've fallen out of love with the land of the free but those States of Connecticut, Massachusetts, Vermont and Maine are spectacular. We drove all around there through New York State ending up at Niagara Falls. Boston has a unique feel to it. We had to visit the *Cheers* bar of course, had some *Sam Adams* in the Bull and Finch pub, and the revolution stuff including the Boston Tea Party ships and museum."

Rob could feel his totally irrational jealousy brewing, which he knew he had to fight. Why was it not me who went on a wonderful holiday like that with Pippa and drank *Sam Adams* with her?

"You obviously know the nutty right wing Tea Party was named after that - the lot who think the poor don't deserve any healthcare?"

Pippa shook her head and elaborated.

"Well, of course I have heard of them, but don't know much about them."

Unusual for Rob to find such a gap in Pippa's knowledge. The Boston Tea Party was a political protest of defiance because the British Tea Act symbolised a violation of rights by no taxation without representation. So they dumped an entire shipment of tea sent by the East India Company into the harbour in 1773 in the build-up to the First Revolutionary War near Boston in 1775 and independence one year later.

"Started the American dream, eh?" said Rob. In another attempt to impress Pippa he said, "The American dream is only believed by those asleep."

"Ha, ha, time for just one more then you need to carry Suzy up to bed."

"I'm not asleep, I'm just resting my eyes and living the American dream," Suzy suddenly interjected, surprising the other two.

"Okay, I've got this last one."

Rob was still full of enthusiasm.

"How government officials burned the records of imperial rule as the British Empire came to an end. It says here the love of secrets is 'a very British disease'. That government secrecy is not just an occasional necessity but the fiercely protected norm."

Members of the Privy Council were first asked to swear an oath of secrecy as far back as 1250. That oath has remained unchanged for nearly eight hundred years. Secrecy has become a habit enshrined in legislation. Like the 1911 Official Secrets Act. Most of the thirty-seven former colonies were unaware that their files were either back in England or had been destroyed. The Kenyan files about the Mau Mau terrorism were overlooked when compensation claims started.

"Did you know this? The British were responsible for massacres at Chuka and Hola, torture which included slicing off ears, burning, boring holes in eardrums, flogging, rape, execution and, oh no... castration. They put over a third of a million in concentration camps. Listen to this. One victim was Hussein Obama, the former President's grandfather, who had pins forced into his fingernails and buttocks, and crushed his testicles between metal rods. It's surprising Barack would talk to us at all. No wonder they tried to hide the files. Apparently thirteen files went missing. They were trying to protect the guilty. There's a handwritten note in the margin, 'Frank Kitson awarded MC in Kenya. Vaughan-Warner there as very junior officer', then underneath the word 'Guilty' with a question mark. I wonder what that means? I know Kitson was Commander-in-Chief of UK Land Forces in the 1980s, but no idea who Vaughan-Warner is. Like all so-called terrorists the Mau Mau are now regarded as freedom fighters and independence heroes who sacrificed their lives in order to free Kenyans from colonial rule.

At the bottom of the Secrecy file is a note marked, 'more trivial but a policy worth pursuing?' Extending secrecy to contracts of employment. And compensation is linked to not talking about it. There are comments here about how it would be best to slowly introduce as many gagging clauses as possible to control and stop whistleblowers. The example it gives is when doctors and nurses know that staffing levels are so low they are dangerous, 'we don't want them going on about it to the media. Let's gag them'."

By 2.30 a.m. they had finished.

"Right, that's enough," said Rob with some authority.

But Suzy had woken up.

"The big question is what do we do with this?" said Suzy, "The first thing is to make sure we have copies. I suppose the easiest way is to scan everything, although that'll take a while, and get ten memory sticks to ensure we have enough."

"I wasn't going to mention this but I've a rendezvous to meet someone from Poison tomorrow."

"Great. I'll come," said Pippa, with the enthusiasm of a kid being invited to Euro Disney.

"No you won't. I've been told to go alone."

"Tough. Try stopping me. Besides you'll need a bodyguard," smiled Pippa.

"What do you mean you weren't going to mention that?" butted in Suzy, demonstrating her peeved voice.

Rob ignored her.

"I suppose you could be useful."

"Oh, thanks," Pippa said with a lovely touch of sarcasm.

Rob continued.

"I've watched enough spy movies to know that you could come as long as it's separately of course in your tin tortoise. There's no need to say keep your distance because you will have trouble keeping up with me in that thing. You can just keep an eye on me. Ian set this up and now he is most likely dead, probably murdered. I must admit I feel a little vulnerable."

Suzy feeling slightly sidelined and out of the conversation butted in again.

"Is that decided then? No consultation or asking the wife what she thinks? Well, I'll tell you. I'll be worried sick. What's the meeting for? Who with? Who exactly is Ian? And you casually say he's probably dead, with no more alarm than he's probably a Liberal Democrat. Rob, you are not telling me everything. What is in it for you? Or me? You are not James Bond. More like Austin Powers or Inspector Clouseau."

Pippa yawned and Rob was a bit too dismissive.

"I've got a short surgery in the morning then I'll come back for you. You should follow me in your car. We'll make arrangements before we go after my return from morning surgery."

"Where are we going?"

"Churchill's country house at Chartwell. Ever been there?"

Pippa nodded.

"Oh, the one bought with Burmah Oil money, of course."

Even though it was the middle of the night Rob announced.

"Now I'm going to bury the cat."

"Not a phrase you hear every day," said Pippa.

"What other time would you bury a murder victim but when it was dark and no one was around. That's what they do in the movies, isn't it?"

45 - MYSTIFY AND DEMISTERS

POWER TO THE PEOPLE

Say we want a revolution
We better get on right away
Well you get on your feet
And into the street

Singing power to the people
Power to the people

John Lennon (1970)

A few days before Pippa's visit Rob went on another trip to London.

He quite enjoyed the journey. The train was one place where people could not get to him. But he would hate to have to spend up to two hours every day like Suzy stuck listening to idiots talking crap on their mobiles and vibrating headphones leaking a familiar shussdiddyshussdiddyshuss. Were they really listening to music or testing Gestapo-torturing techniques?

He always switched his phone off and listened to *Radio 3* through his expensive headgear, which drowned out everything else. So much so that on one journey he missed the announcement that the train was dividing and ended up heading towards Dover. It was not so much that he appreciated the classical music, some of which he would admit he did not like, but more to drown out the inane drivel some talked, so loudly too. He did not mind the teenager talking to her boyfriend, but he detested the smart-Alec businessman showing off to complete strangers about the latest deal he had done, and 'getting my people to liaise with your people'. Rob was convinced this showed a personality defect - an unresolved inferiority complex from his younger years? And he was sceptical about whether anything he heard was really true. He certainly doubted their value to society - just sitting at a computer moving money about. What products did they make? What service did they provide? Useless twats most of them. He had listened with interest to a University lecturer on *Radio 4* who had concluded that most people's jobs were worthless. The most valuable were those cheap low-paid jobs most people were fobbed off with, so low paid the taxpayer had to subsidise the mean multinationals whose main *raison d'être* seemed to be to exploit the workers and to avoid paying tax.

At Waterloo Rob followed a prize plonker as he continued to talk all the way, even through the ticket barrier. He took the Jubilee line the few stops to St John's Wood and then the three-minute walk to the hospice. Rob had had plenty of dealings with hospices. He had been on the development board of the one built only ten miles from his surgery and now used by his patients. St John's Hospice on the Grove End Road seemed particularly well organised. It cost nearly £6 million a year to run and an inpatient bed was £4,500 a week. It had nineteen beds and Rosa had been in one of those for eight days. Like most hospices it was a charity, which was a sore subject for Rob. He had always fought for these places to be integrated into the NHS, but in today's climate he knew he was rowing in the wrong direction. Soon it would be the other way round. All the NHS beds would be private or charities.

The last time he had come this way was to go to Lord's. Stephen had got tickets for the last day of the England vs Australia Second Ashes Test. Very memorable. England won their first Ashes test there since 1934, by one hundred and fifteen runs. 'Freddie' Flintoff took five for ninety-two, was man of the match and announced his retirement. Spotting Wessel in the members' pavilion was the only thing that marred the day. One thing Rob would have been sure about was that Clifford Wessel would not have become a member of Marylebone Cricket Club legitimately. He was wearing the red and gold tie, known as egg and bacon - probably stole that too, Rob thought. But life was so simple then for Rob. A cricket match with friends then home to a loving wife and three beautiful daughters. Why did he let that go?

After visiting Rosa the week before when she had just arrived at St John's, he could not resist going to Abbey Road to see the iconic

EMI recording studios. His heroes had walked through the door. John Lennon, Paul Robeson, Edward Elgar. He had to stroll across the Grade II listed status zebra crossing - an act that sent tingles down his spine - to the annoyance of the locals. He had to add his bit of graffiti, even though he knew it was whitewashed every three months. The previous year he had dragged Suzy off to the Drouot auction house in Paris when Beatles aficionado Jacques Volcouve sold his large collection of memorabilia. He was tempted by the five alternative shots for the *Abbey Road* cover, but Suzy thought €10,000 a little excessive - some with different footwear, some walking the other way. Great stuff. There were eleven alternative photos for the cover of *Sgt. Pepper's Lonely Hearts Club Band* for the same reserve price. How Rob would have loved them on his wall.

Rosa told him on his first visit that she nearly asked to be transferred when she heard that a previous Secretary of State for Health who was key to the NHS privatisation policy of the current Government had opened a new wing. The very thought of the man nauseated her much more than her chemo drugs. She had already checked that this hospice had not signed up to the scheme linking it to one funeral chain. There was enough pretend competition in that business where dozens of supposedly independent firms, trading under different names were actually all owned by the same company. She told Rob it owned a load of UK crematoria too.

Rob reported to reception, then knocked on Rosa's door and entered. To his surprise she had visitors, Mr Ephialtes and a woman on the opposite side of the bed who seemed a little older than Rob, probably in her sixties, but still stunningly attractive. Her bright ginger hair looked completely natural, but it was the short skirt and legs that caught Rob off guard. Mr Ephialtes rose from his chair immediately out of politeness and shook Rob's hand as Rosa introduced them.

The redhead turned out to be one of Rosa's pupils from the Pantglas Junior School in Aberfan. Megan. Most of her friends had been killed. There was a lifelong bond that resulted between them all because of the 1966 disaster. Megan had been especially keen to stay in touch and was distressed to see Rosa looking so ill. She was so appreciative of the fight that Rosa put up on behalf of the victims and survivors. Especially against Robens and Thomas.

"For years I've been trying to persuade Rosa not to feel bad for telling us off about eating Spangles and Love Hearts in class!"

While she was talking, Rob felt an unexpected and shocking wave of emotion wash over him. He assumed the gravity of Rosa's situation had finally hit home. Any tears that were about to sneak out against his will were, to his relief, halted by a change of subject and another sneaky glimpse at those Welsh legs.

"I understand you are a GP?" said Mr Ephialtes.

"Yes, how did you know?"

"Rosa was expecting you this afternoon so she briefed us!"

"Do you know my son Dr Alexei Ephialtes? The medical world is very small."

Rob began to feel clumsily stupid. Why had he not realised earlier? Of course, Stephen had talked about him at that last squash game. He set up but was almost destroyed by the Save the National Health Service Party for his efforts. He knew then why the name was familiar. It fell into place.

"Well yes, actually we have a mutual friend but I've never met your son. What is he doing now?"

"I'm very proud of him. He's a consultant surgeon. But he is in a bit of trouble actually. Perhaps we could chat later about it, perhaps on the phone? I'd like some advice from someone who knows the medical world. I'm just an ignorant second-generation immigrant from Cyprus. Would you mind? We don't want to bore Rosa do we?"

Rosa was not going to allow that to happen.

"Bore me? Don't be so daft Yannis. This is real life. Talk about it now. It's what I exist for, a fight. What do you want to talk about instead? My death? Once you all start with small talk about the weather I'll want to die. Nothing to battle for, then nothing to live for."

They all laughed and any tension disappeared. Although the words death and die seemed to shake the room, at least they had been mentioned.

"Very well. Alexei is a consultant gastrointestinal surgeon currently suspended by his Trust for criticising the Government's underfunding and privatisation of the NHS and saying that the Trust is deliberately running at dangerously low staffing levels. He helped set up a party to fight the so-called reforms and that has gone wrong too. He even made a film, but no one would show it. I get calls from his wife worried about him just wasting away at home. He feels his career and therefore his life have both been destroyed."

"He's not the first I've heard being hung out to dry. All this crap about how NHS workers should be able to whistleblow without it affecting their careers. It's bollocks. But actually worse than bollocks, as the duplicitous GMC paradoxically say they will investigate any doctor who should whistleblow but doesn't. And worse than that, the BMA won't help members unless the lawyers think they have a greater than fifty per cent chance of success. What sort of trade union is that, especially one as rich as the BMA?"

"So it's what I feared. That is precisely Alex's experience. The Trust wants revenge for dropping them in it. The medical director won't speak to him and the GMC are to hold a hearing, not for not whistleblowing, but for some fabricated figures about his patients' mortality in the so-called league tables. The BMA pretended to help initially but withdrew their support when it got a bit embarrassing for them. Alexei thinks they were leant on."

Mr Ephialtes looked quite sad and desperate.

"I fear he will have the same fate as his friend, Jim Auger, who you may have heard of? He was, as you say, hung out to dry by those who should have helped him. What do doctors pay their subs for if the organisations, which are supposed to represent them, are supping with the devil? Jim has given up medicine altogether and last I heard from Alexei is retraining as a lawyer whilst working as a postie in Fife."

Rob felt he had to try to help.

"I do know a few people who might be able to shed some light on this so I'll ask around for you. I don't think I'll be much use though I'm afraid, as it is a case of us against them now. If I can pass on anything useful I can contact you via Rosa?"

"Thank you, sir."

Rosa chipped in.

"This is the sort of Establishment elite stitch up I've been fighting all my life. Aberfan, as Megan knows, lying MPs, illegal wars, corruption in high places, the Westminster paedophile ring, Hillsborough, the miners' strike, the secret Oman war. The list is endless. It is worth it. We have had some victories, but they are getting more cunning and devious. It has to be fought, but we will get nowhere unless we break their stranglehold on the supply of information to the populace."

Megan listened and was clearly shocked.

"What on earth is this all about? I didn't have a clue this sort of thing went on. Is this all true? Of course I know about Aberfan and how badly treated we were by the Establishment, but to do this sort of thing to doctors. It's quite upsetting,"

Then after a pause.

"I've nothing but praise for the NHS. The staff is so dedicated. They ought to have, no, they deserve our support. What can be done? What can ordinary people like me do to help?"

Rosa was livening up.

"It's people like you that hold the key. But it has to grow into a mass movement. Very few know what is going on. It's no good us living in this echo chamber, preaching to the converted. All that does is make us feel we are achieving more than we are. It makes us feel we are the loudest voice when actually no one is paying any attention at all."

"Yes, exactly. Even when our voice is heard it isn't listened to. Don't we need another Cato Street Conspiracy, but a successful one?" asked Yannis, "I can't see anything less will be any value."

Megan needed that explaining, so Yannis started.

"I'm fascinated by British history. Rosa and I discuss the British Empire sometimes for hours. It was Rosa who told me about the Cato Street Conspiracy last month while we were travelling on the 309 bus."

Rosa then took over and told Megan about the plot in 1820 to kill all the British Cabinet Ministers along with the Prime Minister. It was a reaction against the Peterloo massacre of people demanding reform of parliamentary representation and the resulting *Six Acts* aimed at suppressing any meetings for the purpose of radical reform.

"Ah, yes of course," spoken with a beautiful Welsh accent, "I saw Mike Leigh's film at Vue Cinema in Merthyr. Brilliant. I love Maxine Peake."

"But it failed as the police had an informer. Five conspirators were hanged at Newgate Prison and five deported to Australia," Rosa continued, "I don't believe violence is the way forward not least because this monster, even if you chop its head off, will grow another."

"I agree,' said Rob.

"Coming from a long line of pacifists I feel like killing them but couldn't do that. Perhaps a smack in the face. No, but really, we need to wake people up and get the public angry, but angry about the right things. At the moment they are angry just about being left behind and the masses are thrashing out in an uncoordinated irrational manner akin to a tired little toddler who has lost his teddy. The result? Just a backlash against the Establishment, which results in a different form of the elite in charge, and bizarrely being voted in, like turkeys voting for Christmas. But the message is such that if an immature, irascible, bullying, narcissistic nutcase can galvanise people, then we can too!"

Yannis looked in despair.

"And how do you propose to wake them up? Why do you think Murdoch much prefers to rule the world through control of the media than become a politician? It's because he is much more powerful setting the agenda and telling people what to think. They have debased and devalued knowledge, truth and facts. That is why they say don't listen to experts, all necessary to push the populism agenda. With knowledge, truth and facts they wouldn't get anywhere!"

Rosa was proudly listening like a tutor listens to her best students. Although Megan was looking at her watch, she too had an opinion to share.

"I am at least aware of *Fox News* and all the lies they tell. Look what it said about Ahmadinejad. Everyone believes he said he wanted to wipe Israel off the map and he is a holocaust denier. I bet you all do. But neither statement is true. Then across the world there are the security measures put in place as they tell us we are just about to be blown up and so surveillance is necessary, the more the better. The more there is, the safer we will be. Those strict rules about liquids on planes, well I studied chemistry at university, thanks to Rosa, and I know about the near impossibility of manufacturing a bomb from liquids on a plane. You would need to spend at least an hour or two in the toilet. But you never hear that. Homeland security is a right wing concept fostered following the 9/11 attacks to answer the effects of at least fifty years of bad foreign policy especially in the Middle East. The amount of homeland security is inversely related to how good foreign policy is."

"One correction," Rob said with a smile and an attempt to lighten up the conversation, "It is not 9/11. If you do have to abbreviate a date, which is the height of laziness, it has to be 11/9, at least in this country. We, quite correctly, put the day before the month. The Americans are, not for the first time, wrong."

Megan was in no mood to be teased, and her face was matching her hair.

"I'll be off then Rosa. I can't afford to miss my train back to Merthyr Tydfil."

"How long does it take?"

"Three and a half hours with a change at Cardiff Central."

And with that, a kiss and a promise to return the following week Megan disappeared.

"I must be off too Rosa," followed Yannis.

After a brief farewell he left Rob alone with her. Rosa had been invigorated by her guests and was just warming up.

"Yannis is going to look after Kurt for me when I'm dead," said Rosa, as the door closed behind him.

As the visitors left a nurse popped her head around the door to ask if Rosa wanted anything.

"So, how are you, Rosa. Really?"

"Comfortable, thank you. I'm in a race against time, as clearly my days are limited. What I am pleased about is that the pain relief isn't clouding my mind. In fact I feel at peace and can look back on my life now and see it all coming together and making sense. So there are messages and thoughts I want to pass on. What I'm annoyed about is that I will never see Paris again. I have such fond memories of 1968 with a man called Max."

Rob thought if Rosa wanted to tell her who Max was, she would, so he left it.

"I'm not afraid of dying. I came into a world that was a mess and will leave it the same. We have made little progress on that score for centuries. But go back a few millennia and are we really any more civilised? I don't think so, although we like to kid ourselves we are. Plato was better than most of today's thinkers, and the oldest road in Europe at Knossos in Crete built by the Minoan civilisation well over three thousand years ago is still in better condition than the M25. I exaggerate slightly.

Once you realise that we are only one example from billions of one pathetic species that has the upper hand on all the others but doesn't deserve it, you feel more at ease. And by leave, I mean leave. No pretence of clinging on in some other form or strange after life, so as not to miss what is going on, used as a comfort blanket. When that great actor John Hurt died I felt we not only had pancreatic cancer in common, but our lack of belief in anything more than this existence. He said, *Vroom! Here we go! Let's become different molecules!* And that is all that will happen to me. I will mix with the atoms of Lennon & Lenin, Bowie and Byron."

Then almost to herself she added.

"Pancreatic cancer got Alan Rickman and 'Flash Harry' Sir Malcolm Sargent too. I was at his last Proms appearance in September 1967 two months after he had surgery for his and two weeks before he died. He continued playing *Beethoven's Seventh Symphony* through an air-raid, you know?"

At that moment another nurse popped her head around the door to see if Rosa wanted anything. Only tea.

"Very attentive here aren't they? So Rob, I assume you have been following recent events? Let me give you my first message. I have this overwhelming urge to make sure what I know is passed on. It needs some background.

In 1610 the *Case of Proclamations* established that the Monarch could only make laws through Parliament. It took a combination of parliamentarians and the Dutch monarchy to overthrow James II and produce the *1689 Bill of Rights*, which set out the rights of Parliament and limited the powers of the monarchy. It set out the constitutional requirements of the crown to seek the consent of the people, as represented in parliament. It clearly stated that laws should not be dispensed with without the consent of Parliament.

Leaving aside the lies told about giving the NHS all the money saved, a fundamental reason those who wanted to leave the EU gave for their case was to bring back democracy to Britain, and make Parliament sovereign again. But the hypocritical bastards then wanted to deny the House of Commons a vote on leaving arguing against their own previously stated beliefs when it suited them. They wanted to use the royal prerogative, which would have set the executive against Parliament. We are back to the civil war again between parliamentarians and royalists. And when the decision went against them they laid into the judiciary. Dangerous eh?

The Polish are going down that anti-democratic road now, seeking control of the judiciary. So the message is, as you know by now, that we have to stem the advance of the new elite. We need to create a democracy fit for the twenty-first century in which the power of the people predominates over the people in power."

"*Power to the people*, as John Lennon sang," said Rob.

"Quite. That man saw it nearly fifty years ago. That's why the establishment went for him."

The Lennon fan could not resist.

"Got to number six in 1971."

"Those really in power range from organisations you have heard of like the Bilderberg Group, the World Economic Forum and the Federal Reserve, to those, especially in the US you probably wouldn't recognise like the Bohemian Club and the Trilateral

587

Commission. And individuals like Rockefeller, Gates, Page and Zuckerberg. Oh, and Pope Francis of course."

Rob made a note to look up some of these organisations on the way home.

"Nothing should be off the table, the monarchy, the House of Lords, the power of the media, the relationship between the four UK countries and our outdated voting system. At the 2015 election we had a majority Government voted in by only twenty-five per cent of the electorate and then they fiddled expenses too in order to get that. At the 2017 election they get their majority by throwing money, which they said the country didn't have, at Irishmen who believe in creationism and got only zero point nine per cent of the vote. So we have the tail wagging the dog and a Government with the support of less than three out of ten people. The Labour Party got forty per cent of the votes and two hundred and sixty-two seats. In 2005 it got only thirty-five per cent of the votes and three hundred and fifty-six seats and a majority of sixty-six. Is that really democracy in action?"

Rob was taking it all in.

"The second message is that none of this will get us anywhere if we don't look internationally. We are in a new era of nationalism. Just look at the leaders of Russia, India, China, Turkey, and the USA. English nationalism is growing, as it is in France, and it is mutually reinforcing. And by their very nature, nationalisms are likely to clash sooner or later. By far the most serious will be the clash between China and the USA. But don't conflate patriotism with nationalism. The first is, as Orwell said, *devotion to a particular place and a particular way of life*, but the latter is a poisonous force often used by the right that disregards the national interest. But they play the same game as demonstrated by the Leninist nationalist leader of China at Davos when he defended an open globalised international economy.

Which brings me onto austerity. Up to 1972 every section of society in the West experienced similar and sizeable increases in the standard of living. Since then with neo-liberalism, the bottom ten per cent have had real falls, but the elite top ten per cent have done very well. We have talked before about where this came from, the

State haters, the right wing, the pre-war movement, but have you heard of James McGill Buchanan? He said, *economics is the study of the whole system of exchange relationships. Politics is the study of the whole system of coercive or potentially coercive relationships.* Apart from agreeing with that, I hate all he stands for. He thinks there is a conflict between economic freedom and political liberty. He sought what he called conspiratorial secrecy for a hidden programme for suppressing democracy on behalf of the very rich. He was influenced by Friedrich Hayek, a very mediocre economist but worshipped by Thatcher and Reagan. Needless to say Buchanan was a member of the Mont Pelerin Society and a Fellow of the Cato Institute. The latter was originally called the Charles Koch Foundation, one of the richest men in America, and the man who funded Buchanan via his University in Virginia. Koch thinks even people like Milton Friedman and Alan Greenspan are sell outs as they only sought to improve the efficiency of government, rather than destroy it altogether.

You will see the link here with what's happening in the UK, to the welfare state and to the NHS. Buchanan saw stealth as crucial. For example, in seeking to destroy the social security system he would claim to be saving it, arguing that it would fail without a series of radical reforms. Exactly what our governments have been doing the last few decades. They have been following Buchanan's programme to the letter. The destruction of the state through austerity, the dismantling of public services, tuition fees and control of schools, and the bonfire of regulations leading to tragedies like the Grenfell Tower disaster. Free schools stand in the tradition of sabotaging racial desegregation in the American South. It was he who first proposed privatising universities and imposing full tuition fees, the original purpose being to crush student activism."

"This makes perfect sense and to hear you talk is like having the window of British politics demisted," said Rob.

"And of course it has been misted up on purpose," Rosa shot back, "It is all obvious, but no one admits or talks about it. It's totalitarian capitalism and Buchanan's disciples are now all over the world implementing it. Any clash between freedom, that is allowing the rich to do as they wish, and democracy will be resolved in favour of so-called freedom."

"I read somewhere," said Rob, "that one of the first rules of politics is know your enemy. I've only recently realised that those we thought were on our side are indeed our enemies, and we are only just getting to know them. They've been very clever and we've been very slow."

"Then there is the pound," Rosa was moving on, "For the hundred or more years up to the First World War the pound was stable at just under five dollars. Germany, France and Britain all took their currency off the gold standard to print money to pay for the war. The cost of that war saw the pound drop to three point six six dollars. In 1940 it was pegged at four point three dollars, which is why as kids we always used to call five shillings a dollar and the half a crown half a dollar.

The cost of the Second World War saw the pound drop to two point eight zero dollars and when the Bretton Woods system disintegrated in 1971 the pound became free-floating. That happened as the Americans printed more dollars than it had gold to back the printed money to pay for the Vietnam War. Now one reason I'm telling you all this is that you'd think there has been a steady significant decline in the value of our currency to the US Dollar. That's because it suits some to want to make you believe that. Actually that is not true. The inflation-adjusted exchange rate has shown the pound versus the dollar weakened by only zero point two two per cent per annum in the last one hundred and sixteen years."

How Rosa kept all those figures in her head amazed Rob. And to think it would not be long before that brain in that skull he was looking at loses its blood supply and so life stops functioning and the world loses something wonderful.

"My point being that all this is a big game. Things are steady really, but crises are caused by changes in the make-believe world of financial capitalism. Grown men playing boys' games. They invent all sorts of entities, call them fancy names like hedge funds and derivatives, then sell bits of paper to each other and the public, and many in this wild west buying and selling become billionaires, getting bonuses greater than what most people earn in ten years. These banksters produce nothing of true value, just weapons of mass financial destruction. And we creep round these crooks letting them get away with paying little tax because for some bizarre reason we don't want them leaving the country. I'd stick these people on Devil's Island!"

"This is so refreshing to hear, Rosa," said Rob, "There was one of these pompous characters on the train coming up here boasting loudly on the phone for all to hear about his latest acquisition. I was thinking the same about how little these bloated arseholes contribute to society, but not as eloquently as you. They are thieves really."

"Quite," agreed Rosa, "One of the biggest cons of the last forty years is that the UK economy is really like your household budget and the way things are we can't afford our public services. I say forty years, but the right wing first decided to use it as a tool before the Second World War. Let me prove this to you.

The UK is worth about eight point eight trillion pounds. The national debt is one point six five five trillion pounds, probably more, but the Government isn't honest about this. Our GDP is one point nine five eight trillion pounds. My figures are probably a little out of date but it doesn't matter, the principle is the same. Now, knock a load of noughts off to reduce those figures to domestic proportions. Your assets are eighty-eight thousand pounds. Your income is nineteen thousand, five hundred and eighty pounds. All your debts amount to sixteen thousand, five hundred and fifty. That is your mortgage, your credit cards, loans, etc. Would that worry you? I don't think so. Most people would love to be in as little debt as that and even if repayment on that debt were three per cent it would only cost you five hundred pounds a year to service the loans. Now why can't the media do their job and explain this confidence trick to the public? It's a disgrace that it suits them and their masters not to. The alternative is that they are too thick to work out for themselves what an old lady like me has known for years."

"That is amazing, Rosa, so simple. Proves it's such crap to insist we must pay down the national debt and destroys the we 'must balance the books mantra'."

"We really must get this message across, but in simple terms. That's the tricky bit," said Rosa, "Einstein said, *the definition of genius is taking the complex and making it simple.*"

"Then you have just proved you are a genius," complimented Rob.

"But he also said, *everything should be made as simple as possible, but not simpler.* Can I try applying this to Modern Monetary Theory which is making nonsense of neo-liberalism and see if it works on you?"

"Oh dear, a test of my intellect. Bound to fail," worried Rob.

"It shows you that a government does not need to raise taxes or borrow for its spending. That's counterintuitive the conventionists and narrow minded would say, eh?"

"In the recent election, the main thing the commentators would bang on about is how are you going to pay for this, or that, no real discussion about the value of a policy," said Rob.

"Here we go. Let's play them at their own game by going back to using the household as a way of understanding national finances. Mum gives the children one hundred gold stars for doing chores, but taxed them one hundred for living in the house. The tax gives currency value. If she gives them eighty, but taxes them a hundred, the children are indebted to her by twenty, and she has a surplus of twenty. Conversely if Mum gives one hundred, but taxes eighty, her debt, or the Government's, is twenty and the children can save their surplus or spend it. With me so far?"

"So far so good. But as you are quoting people I'm reminded of what the mathematician Ian Stewart said, *If our brains were simple enough for us to understand them, we'd be so simple that we couldn't.* Absolutely. Shit. My new year's resolution was to stop saying absolutely when I mean yes."

Rosa continued and Rob took a deep breath.

"So Government spending equals non-government sector income, Government deficit equals non-Government surplus, and Government surplus means non-Government deficit."

"Okay. Still with you."

"Now going back to the children's surplus. Mum could keep their twenty gold stars for them, and promise a return of twenty-five. She has just issued a bond. Neo-liberals would say the children are financing Mum's spending, but it's actually just a safe, interest paying place for them to lodge the stars they want to save."

"So the UK Government doesn't need our bond money to finance spending any more than Mum needs her children's gold stars to finance hers," Rob offered nervously.

"Precisely, Rob. You've got it. But you can see how tricky this is to put into a sound bite for today's rolling twenty-four hour news, when the attention span planners aim at goldfish-like viewers."

"I see. Whether Mum issues bonds or not depends entirely on demand from her children, not on her desire to spend more. Yes?"

"Yes, Rob. So if the Government pursues a surplus, like that last idiot Chancellor wanted to do, it pushes us into debt. What he didn't understand is that when the Government spends that helps us increase our wealth. He had been sucked into his own nonsense inarticulate theories and propaganda and was fooled by it. Trouble is it was believed by everyone else."

"Hmmm."

Rob forced the image of Suzy and that rat together out of his head.

"Nearly finished Rob, I promise. The thing is I have a lot of time to think in this hospice bed. Now microeconomics is where the children want to exchange gold stars between them, trade is when they exchange with children next door, and a gold star borrowing service is called a bank. None of this negates the fact they must obtain the stars from their Mum in the first place."

"And you can see where the banks lost their way, lost sight of their original purpose, and became greedy corrupt organisations."

Rob was pleased with himself but knew he would never remember this.

"So neo-liberals by cutting spending are robbing the public of their wealth and at great human cost and suffering. Proof it's just ideology."

"So governments actually pay for their spending by spending!"

"You are brighter than you look, Rob! Spending should be based on need to provide employment and not fake notions of affordability. Our nation's spending is not limited by money or finance but by availability of real resources like labour, raw materials, real goods and services."

"What about inflation?" Rob puzzled, "I can hear them all now saying this is fantasy and we will have runaway inflation."

"Not if the Government spends to maintain the nation running at full capacity, i.e. full employment, and no further."

Rosa was aware the illiterate economic arguments that she had just destroyed were circulating pre-war but she was unaware that they had been presented to the Right Club by the fascist anti-Semitic veterinarian Arnold Leese in 1939 who as early as 1935 was suggesting sending Jews to gas chambers. All the time Rosa was talking Rob was coming to the sad conclusion that, compared to his old friend he was an intellectual lightweight.

"What also really sticks in my throat," Rob added, "Is that apparently these rich elite need tax cuts and huge bonuses to incentivise them and keep them in the country, but the poor, and I include NHS workers in that group, need the big stick to get them to work harder. The country can't afford them and there is no magic money tree they say but you have already demolished that argument. Easy to forget the rules like supply and demand when it suits them. One of the great contradictions, those in the city need huge wages, although there is no shortage of the 'hooray-Henrys', but they don't raise the wages of say neo-natal nurses when there is a genuine shortage. There isn't a shortage of people wanting to become MPs either so they should be paid less. A few years ago I said the Royal family should be put out to tender. The Baigents would do the job for a lot cheaper."

Rosa smiled and was clearly beginning to tire but Rob had inspired her onto one of her pet hates, the class structure in England.

"We will never get fairness and equality when a third of MPs went to private schools and one in ten of those Eton, that's not the real world. That compares to seven per cent of the population. There was hope some years back but now with how they are destroying the education system, and making higher education for the rich, I can see that getting worse."

Rob told Rosa medical school intake was still a quarter privately educated, and now the rich pay for expensive admission courses and for personalised coaching to get the perfect personal statement.

"Oxbridge intake is still at least two-fifths from the private sector, and they recruit more students from just eight top schools than almost three thousand other English State schools put together," Rob added.

"All education should of course be free, but when you say that to people they sigh that it would be nice but we can't afford it. Economic illiteracy and political gullibility. Same old water runs up hill argument being peddled again. We are out of step with Scotland and the great majority of European countries. The simple truth is that this is pure ideology as the fees that students pay have to be funded from public sources in the first place, and up to half will never be recovered from graduates. Many will never earn enough for repayments to kick in. A fair number will emigrate and their loan will have to be written off. As it is the students pay massive interest rates in comparison to everyone else, over six per cent. And they rent their accommodation from a new rich landlord class. Do you know a quarter of Tory MPs are landlords? It won't be long before the student loan book is sold off to vulture capitalists. Allowing degree awarding powers to be bought and sold is not a good idea."

"Those same MPs voted down a proposal to make homes fit for human habitation. So they are happy that the people who voted them into office live in squalor or unsafe housing like Grenfell Tower. To me that makes them not fit to be MPs. You probably know," Rob went on too say, "there is now a private medical school at the private University of Buckingham, fees thirty-six thousand pounds a year - four times the cap of nine thousand pounds per annum at the moment! Don't tell me that's not social exclusivity."

"They have made it difficult to even protest against this sort of thing now. Did you hear about the management at the five-star Conrad London St James' Hotel calling out the Met Police's armed response unit to deal with Unite union officials? They were only speaking to employees outside the staff entrance. Then Bayer got a court order to ban a protest outside its AGM saying it was a terrorist threat. That was just about their bee killing neuro-active pesticides that destroy hives and so threaten the food chain and supply. They are the terrorists. Have you noticed that their big exclusive economic conferences never meet now in accessible places like Seattle, as they used to, its always half way up a mountain at places like security safe Davos-Klosters? Bastards."

"Bastards," Rob echoed.

"You will come back won't you Rob. I've got so much more to say. I've just scratched the surface and I'm not sure I've fed you the most important stuff, just what is on my mind at the moment. I should have prioritised in case I run out of time."

As Rob walked out of the hospice, he walked past Vilma Rutherford who was at the reception desk. He was totally distracted on the rainy walk back to St John's Wood tube station. His mind was buzzing with Rosa's economic lessons. He was not paying attention to the traffic and a taxi had to screech to a halt as he crossed a side road without looking.

"Wanna die, mate?" shouted the cabby.

Ironic considering the building he had just left and the optimism Rosa had just instilled made him making him keener than ever to live and spread the word.

"Could you imagine full employment, and the consequences on the nation's health, wellbeing and happiness?" he said to Suzy later.

But he was right. He really could not remember how to explain it all to her. On the Jubilee line he had wondered who Max was and shed a tear. His fellow passengers looked away.

46 - RENDEZVOUS AND STORIES

STRAWBERRY FIELDS FOREVER

Living is easy with eyes closed
Misunderstanding all you see
It's getting hard to be someone
But it all works out
It doesn't matter much to me

The Beatles (1966)

Welcome to the *Messenger On-line*. The UK's fastest growing regional news network.

The local paper had a good website that seemed to keep up with everything that happened hour by hour in the area. They reported traffic jams, cats going missing and beautiful baby competitions and the occasional more serious event. Rob was up early, as he wanted to know their take on the overturned Daewoo. Was Ian, if that was his real name, alive or dead? It caused a fair hold-up for some time so it would be strange if there were not at least some report. Bread and butter stuff for this news outlet, so it would certainly show inconsistency if nothing appeared. But the doubt he felt demonstrated his growing scepticism.

He cursed how long it took the page to download but he and Suzy lived with that. They had no option. The Wi-Fi connection was pathetic and there was no prospect, ever, of an improvement while the private sector profit machine had a firm grip on delivery. There was absolutely nothing in it for them to deliver a better service to Rob and Suzy's house. When Suzy's sister's children visited they moaned and moaned to the point where they did not want to visit any more. That is how important it had become in their lives.

There was a huge advert for the new local Academy with a mission statement that should put any parent off: 'It is our mission to continue to authoritatively provide access to diverse services to stay relevant in tomorrow's world. We are a leader in education - a diverse collection of extraordinary people, distinctive brands and best in class destinations'. What the fuck does that mean?

After negotiating past more rubbish, he flicked through the pages. But there was nothing. Not a dicky bird, as his Mum used to say. Why? He had no time to dwell on that question, but the answers that sprang to mind troubled him. However he had to get to the surgery.

On the drive he pondered on what annoyed him most. The trivia the editor thought more important than what Rob wanted to know. Like the destruction of the local NHS, like the closure of clinics and the nearest A&E, and like the privatisation of clinical services. Very little coverage. The companies running the patient transport service were a joke and a disgrace. The homeless in the streets or the mental health service cuts. Or was it the way the journalists just seemed to shrug their shoulders as though they were helpless or it did not matter. He must read about traffic delays and accidents every single time he logs on, but no report of a more serious incident this time.

Suzy got up with Rob. It was clear she had shed a tear. Rob hoped it was just for Eric and not from worry about where this all might lead. But he did not ask. She got tearful when tired. Pippa was left to lie in. After all it was past 3.00 a.m. before they got to bed and there was nothing she had to do. His surgery clinic, fortunately, went smoothly and Rob could leave promptly. Giselle seemed to have everything under control and told him Michael, their accountant, was on holiday for two weeks so could not meet until the end of the month.

On his return Rob even had time for a quick coffee with the two women in his life at this time. They sat at the kitchen table but they were all a little agitated and jaded - each one had different but also overlapping reasons.

Rob broke the tension.

"Well, as we discussed last night, really just a few hours ago, I suppose if you are still up for coming it would be better if we travelled and arrived separately. We shouldn't be known to each other while at Chartwell. It's been suggested I meet whoever it is in the garden by the famous wall he built."

'He' was clearly Churchill. Churchill and Chartwell were almost the same thing now more than fifty years after his death.

"In the old kitchen garden. I took it to be more like an order. If my memory serves me right, if you were to stay up at house level, and then walk along the very top of the garden, past the croquet lawn and the new toilet block, you will find some seats. It's much higher so you should be able to look down on me from a good vantage point, and enjoy a great view over the Weald."

"Rob, I'll never look down on you!" Pippa said.

"Amongst all the other visitors you won't be noticed. Just keep an eye on me."

"What about a photograph?" asked Pippa, already knowing the answer.

"Now that's why I have my doubts about you coming! It's too risky. He probably won't be alone. He might have a minder, even if, like you at a distance. The chances are then you will be spotted. You have already put yourself at risk, what with breaking into houses and all that nonsense. I got you into this. How could I live with myself if something happened? And anyway, what would we do with a photo?"

The gravity and helplessness of the situation was slowly sinking in.

Pippa was one car behind Rob on the A25 in her 'flying dustbin' as Dave liked to call it. As they went through Westerham village, her thoughts were mainly on how nice the countryside was. I could live here, she said to herself as they drove past the old fashioned shops, the antique houses and the bronze Nemon sculpture of its most famous resident on the village green. It simply had *Churchill 1874-1965* on the base, which was Yugoslavian stone - a gift from Marshal Tito. The Croatian sculptor also produced the statue of Churchill in the lobby in the House of Commons and a huge one of Winnie and Clemmie that is down by one of the lakes on the eighty-two acre estate. On the other hand Kimmeridge is fine.

At Quebec House she saw Rob turn right and she indicated her intention to follow him. Whilst waiting for the stream of oncoming traffic to pass she had time to read the sign. General James Wolfe, the victor of the battle of the Plains of Abraham, killed in action taking Quebec off the French, lived here. He was born in Westerham in 1729. Now, the village's second most famous resident. Too keen to read, she was not quick enough to make the turn and was hooted by the car behind.

It was breezy but bright. She was glad she had brought her coat. She followed Rob uphill, along a narrow country road. After a mile or so of travelling through fairly dense woodland she wondered how much further, but it was not long before the National Trust car park signs came into view. They both turned left and downhill. The car between them had turned off so they were next to each other. She slowed right down so it was not so obvious they were together. Pippa saw Rob park and carried on past him for another hundred metres. She sat in the car whilst Rob fed the pay machine. He had given her his NT parking permit, which was just as well as she had no change. He joked she should stick it on the windscreen to help hold the 'biscuit barrel' together. Rob had suggested she follow on and enter only after about ten minutes. His rendezvous was in twenty minutes time.

After five minutes Pippa was getting restless so started to head towards the main entrance. She passed the restaurant and found herself outside the shop. Walking down the steps towards the main entrance she nearly got sidetracked by a plant sale. Another coach was pulling up. Pippa thought she ought not to get caught behind that lot. She could see Rob queuing. That was not in the plan, but he was not there for long.

After a slow stroll around Winston's swimming pool Pippa walked up past the water garden and through the rose garden. From here she could see how nice the house was. She continued past the house onto the terrace lawn. When she spotted the croquet lawn she was reassured she was heading in the right direction. She went along Butterfly House walk, the urn garden and pets' graves to reach her vantage point where Rob had suggested.

Pippa did stop and admire the small tombstones. Jock, Churchill's ginger cat with a white crest and white paws outlived his master by ten years. She had read there was always to be a marmalade cat called Jock at Chartwell. They must be on their fifth or sixth by now she thought.

All four bench seats were taken but she could easily see him. She stood to admire the view of the Weald of Kent. He was feigning an interest in all the plants in the flowerbeds by the wall that Churchill built himself. A few trees obscured her view of the Marycot but at this time of year the leaves had fallen so she could see the outline.

It got to ten past twelve and still no sign of being approached. By twelve twenty Rob was getting annoyed he was wasting his time. He had read the inscriptions set into the wall of the Rose Walk commemorating Winston and Clementine's Golden Wedding several times, and strolled off through the roses and lavender to see the chickens in their enclosure. As he approached the arch in the kitchen garden wall for the third time, he spotted the curious sight of a wheelchair being pushed by a nurse in uniform across the grass, past the studio and then onto the path towards him. In the chair was a small thin twisted shape covered by a blanket - child-sized but obviously not so once. The nurse pushed the chair slowly past Rob as by then he was sitting on one of two benches by the plaque in a deliberate show of defiance and protest about their tardiness. She made no attempt at making any eye contact. Nor did the man, for he could now make out it was a man. The nurse then stopped, feigning having to adjust her passenger's blanket and said very quietly without turning her head towards Rob.

"Sean wants you to follow us to the end of the path and meet us in the Marycot. But give us thirty seconds. I have to get this thing down a few steps."

Rob did as he was told and, when close to them at the end of the path, he obeyed the gesture to sit on the bench. Sean was next to the seat in the Marycot. Without any warning the nurse left and strolled along the path, past Winston's painting studio and up in the direction of the house. Sean called out.

"See you later, Nurse Nightingale."

Rob let out a quiet nervous chuckle, as he knew no one could seriously be called that, surely. So then they were alone.

The Marycot was a little brick house built for Winston's youngest daughter Mary. There was a note on the wall stating that Mary had baked scones for Charlie Chaplin and Albert Einstein there.

Rob got a Northern Ireland greeting.

"Bout ye? Dr Baigent, my job is to pass on my story, vet you and then convince you to help us. We hope you won't wind yer neck in."

Rob said nothing. He could see Pippa sitting on a bench several hundred metres away at the top of the hill by the house. Feeling safe he was wondering why he had allowed her to come.

"You don't need your qualifications to tell I'm ill. Very ill in fact. I was diagnosed with MND three years ago aged fifty-two. I'm pretty weak, and my gub's killing me, but unlike Stephen Hawking I have retained my ability to talk. He had amyotrophic lateral sclerosis though. I was pleased the great man exposed what the Government is really up to with the NHS before he died and its US style privatisation. Unfortunately, also unlike him I haven't got such a good wheelchair and, as to date, there hasn't been a film made about me. I may make one more Christmas who knows? I'm spending my last days sharing my experiences. I'll give you a brief history but the detail is on this."

He had a memory stick in his hand and clearly had been clutching it for a while. He gestured to Rob to take it from him, having looked around to check nobody was at all close to the Marycot.

"I'm Sean and that is my real name. Have you seen the *Magdalene Sisters* film? Fifteen years old now but tells it how it was."

Rob nodded. He first saw it at the cinema with Jenny. Pippa and Suzy had talked about it in the early hours. He remembered her being pregnant with Barrett and not happy about that, as she wasn't exactly planned. The film appalled Rob. Then story after story came out. The Australia disgrace too.

"My mother was a victim of those laundries. My father was in the UVF. The violence between them was relentless, regular and bloody. When my father turned on me I left home for London, having stolen money from a UVF stash he had. I never saw my parents again. You know about Dolphin Square?"

"Yes, lots of accusations then a backlash with ferocious denials," Rob said, somewhat provocatively.

"What do you expect? Imagine the worst and double, treble it. People have no idea. I was a prisoner there for over ten years, 'til past the age of twenty-five, and believe me I was just one of many. And Dolphin Square was just one of many. Children, adolescents and men disappeared. Many were murdered. The Establishment was to blame and cover-ups were easy. George Orwell totally underestimated the way things would turn out."

At that moment a little girl, no more than five years old, ran along the path and appeared at the door.

"Shoo!"

Sean forcefully waved her away. She burst into tears, turned around and ran away. Her excitement at seeing a playhouse totally shattered and changed to horror. A bit unnecessary, Rob thought to himself.

Sean continued.

"I met and was the victim of many famous people. It's all on the stick. That's the ammo that needs spreading. These people need exposing for what they are then bringing down. Getting them jailed is too much to hope for. They close ranks. I thought I would be murdered too when they finished with me. To my surprise, when I was no longer in demand and was not the attraction I had been, a bit old, but they just let me go. I had warnings of course to keep quiet.

A bloke called Douglas ran the place on behalf of all the nobs. Douglas had so much on me. Photographs everything. Not that I really cared. Any threats meant nothing to me. I'd already tried to kill myself several times. They would have been doing me a favour. How could they possibly blackmail a shadow of a man who was already in the gutter? I just didn't have any life left in me for any risk or conflict and they knew that. They could have disposed of me in any way they liked. On the other hand we had little evidence or proof. Douglas though had set up a hidden camera and had caught on film most of the people coming to Dolphin Square. Thatcher knew all about what was going on and had all the evidence that had been gathered by MI5 destroyed. Or so she thought. There was one file, called the Westminster file that those in power all used against each other. It would have been funny if not so tragic. Some of Douglas's photos ended up in that file. When one nob thought he could blackmail another, out came a counter claim. Their currency was devalued. Several cabinet ministers played this game of poker only to lose."

Rob was taking it all in. He was already worried about having the memory stick in his possession. Out of the corner of his eye he noticed Pippa had disappeared from her vantage point not far from the croquet lawn. Then to his alarm he saw her treading the path Rob had half an hour earlier. She was coming towards them past the chicken enclosure through the lavender. What the hell was she up to? The tension he felt building up eased somewhat when she turned off to the right and then back up an avenue of trees.

Then Sean went off at a tangent. He sensed Rob was distracted.

"Never thought much of Churchill. Quite an effective war leader as he was basically a dictator himself, fighting other dictators. But victory in 1945 was mainly thanks to the Russians and Americans. Have you heard of Rolf Hochhuth's play *Soldiers*?"

Rob had to admit he had not.

"No, most people haven't. They did their best to suppress it. It alleges Churchill connived in the death of the Polish Prime Minister Wladyslaw Sikorski, in a 1943 plane crash, to appease Stalin and was highly critical of his support for the indiscriminate firebombing of German cities like Dresden. He was a terrible peacetime politician. A late Victorian imperialist, a man against the workers who helped break the general strike, and a terrible Chancellor of the Exchequer, even worse than the one we have now. He made the Great Depression deeper and longer-lived by trying to control the value of money by overseeing Britain's disastrous return to the Gold Standard. He contributed to three million deaths in the Bengal famine of 1943 by refusing to send grains there, saying it was, *the Indians' own fault for breeding like rabbits*. He despised Gandhi. He said how nauseating it was to see *a half-naked seditious lawyer posing as a fakir*.

When Gandhi was on hunger strike he said we would be rid of a bad man and an enemy of the Empire if he died. People wonder why Churchill's warnings about Hitler were ignored in his wilderness years. It was because he was saying the same about Gandhi. That discredited him. He was a man who said, *socialists were like the Gestapo* - a true relic of the dark days of Empire."

There was a period of silence. Rob felt brave enough to take the initiative.

"What happened to you after you escaped?"

"One of the Peers of the Realm who obviously had a slight conscience got me a job packing goods in a supermarket. A supermarket owned by a cousin of his. He paid for six months bed and breakfast for me in Vauxhall then said I was on my own after that. Probably cost him no more than a pound for each buggering he gave me. A few others were set up like this but most just vanished. Some were kept men or rather boys. It was difficult re-building a life and fitting in. I was socially totally inept. Couldn't communicate with anyone and used to hide away.

Then the only good thing that has ever happened in my whole life occurred. This girl started sitting next to me on the park bench in Vauxhall Pleasure Gardens in her lunch breaks and started chatting. I'd been going there for months to get away from workmates to be alone. I found it very peaceful. She approached me first with an opening, 'you sit on the same bench at the same time every day. Don't you sometimes crave for a different view?' It took three months before I gained any confidence to converse properly. Do you know those gardens?"

"Can't say I do," responded Rob, curious as to why he was wandering off the subject.

"I read a lot in captivity. Becky Sharp from *Vanity Fair* went there. Dickens mentioned them in *Sketches by Boz*. And Thomas Hardy set scenes there. They date back to before the Restoration of 1660."

He then got back on track.

"I had saved a fair bit by practising the only trade I knew, as a rent boy. She didn't know of course, but I had enough to smarten up and get her a ring. We got married when I was thirty-one. Best few years of my life. We had two boys born in 1997 and 1999."

Much to Rob's relief Pippa was back on her bench.

"And before you ask, no, the good times didn't last and it didn't have a happy ending. You can't live the first thirty years of life like I did and then become normal. The strain of living with someone, having two small children was all too much. Obviously I had a gargantuan hang-up about sex, which caused a hot-blooded beauty a fair bit of distress. I developed a drug habit to try to blot out the past. Looking back that was very ironic. I would have thought they'd have drugged me up in Dolphin Square but they didn't. How stupid to give myself another problem when I had my freedom.

Then I got bolder. It had faded how ruthless they all are. Life came back into me and I got angry and wanted revenge. But more urgent was my need for dosh to feed my drug habit. I approached a newspaper to spill the beans but word got back to Douglas. They are all in it together. My eldest boy came home from school to find his cat strung up in a tree. When they thought I hadn't paid any attention to their warnings, they murdered my younger son. He was found in a ditch having been abused and strangled. Some innocent local got the blame. Someone they wanted to get rid of. Never has the phrase killing-two-birds-with-one-stone been more appropriate. My wife blamed me and went off to Australia with my only son and I haven't heard or seen them since. He's now a man.

I was evicted from our apartment as the bedroom tax was voted in and the council said I didn't need two bedrooms. Telling them I was terminally ill cut no ice and they added insult to injury by sticking me on the nineteen floor of Adair Tower in North Kensington. A couple of years ago we had a fire that left twelve flats uninhabitable and sixteen people were treated in hospital. There were no sprinklers, no alarms, the security cameras didn't work, and it was only after that the Council fitted fire doors. It's the same with most Council owned tower blocks. Our lives aren't worth spending money on. The few who have bought flats there get nothing for their four thousand pound service fee. We warned them that a bigger tragedy was likely, but they ignored us. This is how we are treated, with contempt by the same class of nob that held me prisoner for all those years. They think they are above the law. The Grenfell Tower and all those deaths. As Bevan said they are lower than vermin. So I continue to be a nobody in their eyes. I have nothing left and so nothing to lose at all."

There was another quiet spell while they both reflected on what Sean meant by this. Obvious. He was dying anyway. Rob felt sorry for Sean. What a terrible existence. He did not stand a chance.

"Have I passed the vetting?" Rob half joked.

"There's no vetting. I only said that to keep you alert."

Sean pressed a button on the side of his chair.

"What do you want me to do then?"

"Isn't it obvious? Spread the word. You're a GP. You know and come into contact with loads of people. Copy that stick hundreds of times and distribute. Be careful though and don't bother using the obvious routes. We tried to load it onto YouTube and all those web things I don't understand. Blocked of course. See if you can find a publisher or journalist with a bit of integrity. You won't get anywhere with the ordinary press. Stay clear as all the editors are in their pockets. Their heavies will be at your house before you know it and it won't be for a cup of tea. Living is easy with eyes closed, but you have no eyelids now."

It was clear Sean was drawing things to a close. His nurse was approaching down through the avenue of trees. Rob realised now what the button was for. He was signalling his nurse. This was obviously one of many performances Sean had done. It became clear to Rob he was one of many. There was nothing special about him. Quite polished, Rob thought.

"We won't meet again. Do your best. My life was shit. I'm not sad or bothered it's coming to an end. I'm totally scundered. I'd like to help prevent others going through what I went through, though. Good bye."

Nurse Nightingale wheeled him away. Rob sat quietly playing with the memory stick in his pocket. He reflected on the sad life he had just learnt of. Rob hated to admit it but he did not expect Sean to be quite so intelligent - embarrassing preconceived prejudice.

There were flashes of a cultured man. It started to anger him. What a waste. He did not stand a chance - not with his background. What if he were born to a well off, stable, loving family and had gone to a good school? The sky could have been the limit. But he did not even get off the ground - the throw of the dice.

After a few minutes the little girl, who had obviously seen the wheelchair man wheeled off, timidly but very sweetly curved her head around the door. Rob thought he had better try to extinguish her bad experience of twenty minutes earlier.

"Come in and play with this Lego. Or do you like the dolls more?"

She pointed to the dolls and without saying anything ran over to them. Conditioned or what, he thought? Rob reflected that in this sad world he had better not hang around in the Marycot with a little girl. A grown man on his own will be looked upon with suspicion. After a while he strolled up the hill towards Pippa. He had seen Sean and his nurse disappear out of the exit so thought it safe to now get together and talk.

Pippa was acting a bit like a puppy expecting a treat.

"Well, how did you get on and what did you discover?"

"He told me his horrible life history which was disturbing and awful, but more important he's given me a file on a memory stick. He says it's got everything on it."

Rob did not wait for a response.

"Let's sit here for a while in the sun."

They had reached the Marlborough Pavilion with its murals of the *Battle of Blenheim* - a major battle in the War of Spanish Succession in 1704.

"The first Duke won these battles and so down the generations. The seventh Duke was this Churchill's paternal grandfather."

Rob was trying to impress again, but he would not admit he checked all this on the web straight after looking at *Messenger On-line*.

"That's how Churchill was born at Blenheim Palace."

Trying to lighten the tone after what he'd experienced this morning he added.

"His Mum was at the birth there too."

Pippa was not impressed by that attempt at humour. In fact she ignored him. About thirty Canada geese flew over in formation.

"Look an RAF flypast in honour of you and Winston."

Rob was trying to blot out his poor joke, but this was not much better.

"Let's go," said Pippa.

They took a final look at the upper and lower lakes then walked up past the goldfish pond to reach the cafe.

"Fancy a cup of tea?"

"Yes," said Pippa, "But I'd rather get out of here first. And look at the queue!"

"I know a place on the way back. Do you know what impresses me most about the village down the hill?"

"Can't imagine. The Grasshopper on the Green public house?" said Pippa.

"No that's second most impressive. They have a great log fire and serve *Gods Wallop* and *Summer Pearl* Ale. I'm trying to be serious," said Rob, with a smile across his face.

"You saw the antique shops as we drove through earlier? Well the one on the right was where John Lennon bought the poster for *Pablo Fanque's Circus*."

"So he bought a poster, so what?"

"Oh Pippa. You know *Being for the Benefit of Mr Kite* on *Sergeant Pepper*? Well that gave him the inspiration. Except it didn't! For years I thought it was that shop. I used to go in there as a schoolboy so I could breathe the same air as Lennon. Then I found out I'd been misled. The shop was actually in Sevenoaks. Never have found out which one."

"Bet you felt silly?"

"You are the only one I've told. They were filming for *Strawberry Fields Forever* at Knole Park, just up the road in 1967. So I should have realised my old schoolmate was bullshitting. But that poster and album impresses me much more than Churchill. Do you know Churchill didn't write one number one song?"

"Ha, ha! Good painter though. You know that old joke from the Mel Brooks film, *The Producers*? Franz Liebkind with his German helmet on! *Churchill... his rotten paintinzs. Hitler, now there was a painter. He could paint an entire apartment in won afternoon. Zwei coats. Better looking than Churchill, better dresser, he had more hair. He told funnier jokes. And he could dance the pants off Churchill."*

"Very good and well remembered. Not so sure about the German accent though."

47 - TEARS AND SHOCKS

I'M SO TIRED

I'm so tired, I haven't slept a wink
I'm so tired, my mind is on the blink

I'm so tired I don't know what to do
I'm so tired my mind is set on you

You know I'd give you everything I've got
For a little peace of mind

The Beatles (1968)

Pippa followed Rob back carefully as she was not too familiar with this part of the world. She feared falling asleep at the wheel as the tension and the late night was catching up with her.

When needing to sleep, Pippa always claimed her bones ached. Dave told her in his considered opinion, as a qualified Morris Dancer, bones cannot ache. She tried to distract herself from the aching bones by playing CDs. Dave joked that the CD player he installed into her 2CV had more power than the car.

Carly Simon was blasting out *You're So Vain*. Every time she listened she heard something different. She loved Klaus Voormann's opening bass line. She had only recently discovered that Jagger contributed backing vocals. The volume was not turned as high as usual though. Ever since she read that too much noise affects the cardiovascular system and biochemistry and can aggravate depression. She made a note to herself to ask Rob about this. Then there was the surprise to a non-mathematical brain that eighty decibels is twice as loud as seventy decibels, and ninety decibels four times as loud, one hundred decibels eight times and so on. She had read that more than a minute's exposure to one hundred and ten decibels could cause permanent damage. Sounds at an AC/DC concert reached one hundred and thirty decibels. It was a great distraction however from the day's events.

After just ten minutes Rob pulled into a lay-by so Pippa parked behind him.

"Bit of cake too?"

"Sounds good," responded Pippa, "but I must get back to Dorset before Jeremy goes to bed."

The village consisted of no more than a road through it, or so it appeared. The street was lined with shops and more than its share of antique shops at that. But it was not difficult to find the coffee shop that Rob had previously noticed, about fifty yards from their cars. They chatted as they walked past a sewing shop and then Laptop Doctor. Rob stopped mid-sentence.

"Hang on a minute... I'll be no time at all."

He turned on his heels and walked back and into the shop. Pippa was left in the street wondering what he was up to. She did not have time to get irritated, which would have been reasonable as she had only just told Rob she needed to get back home, as he really was no time at all.

"We are going to need these," he showed her at least ten memory sticks.

"Eh?"

"Happy shopkeeper. I bought his entire stock. I'll explain over that cake I promised you."

They were in the cafe longer than Pippa intended, but she was riveted by what Rob told her. She was appreciating how important this was - more important than bedtime. He went into the detail of Sean's life and his account of all the troubles, and explained about the information he had been given on the memory stick.

"I can't wait 'til we get back to look at that," she said.

"I've got my laptop in the car... let's look at it now."

"We can't do that! It's too public here."

"Not here you muppet. Let's sit on that bench on the green. No one is near that. My battery will probably cope."

"Yeah, but what about the laptop battery?" she quipped.

Was she flirting with him? Rob was never sure. He was hopeless at reading signals from women.

What they found astonished them both. They never expected such a comprehensive amount of information or detail. Spread between several files were lists of places, dates, and names, and what was difficult to stomach, was what these pillars of the Establishment got up to. Another list was of boys who were used. Some information was very sketchy, perhaps no more than a name and a guess at age, but other poor characters had a mini biography written about them. One of these was Sean. Another a lad called Carl. Nothing could prepare them for what they saw when Rob clicked on the third file. In this one were at least several hundred photographs.

The colour drained from Pippa's face.

"I think I'm going to be sick."

She did retch, but that was all - much to Rob's relief.

Quite a few of the men were headless, but the boys and in some cases girls as young as, they guessed, five were clearly shown. The look of terror on the children's faces was horrific. Rob surprised himself when, overcome, he started to cry. Much to Pippa's amazement the tears turned into sobs. She put her arm around him and he leant over to be cradled like a baby. He tried to compose himself.

"Those poor children."

It came out almost as a stutter. Everything was catching up with him.

"I now think I'd give everything I have for a little peace of mind. I'm so tired."

Rob was embarrassed by this unexpected outpouring of emotion, but it was like lancing a boil. All the pent up tension, trauma, surprise and shocks of the last few weeks.

"Lets go home to Suzy," Pippa said in her motherly voice.

Blowing his nose Rob was adamant.

"No, I have to check out the rest. I'd rather spare her this and I'm so sorry I've exposed you to it. You don't have to look. I won't be long. I need an overall picture to help decide what to do."

But Pippa knew she had to play her part. She had to be brave for both of them. More photos showed people in public life they recognised back to the 1970s. It was a *Who's Who* of every part of society.

"I suppose this is what the police would call child porn, and what would their reaction be if they caught us with it? There's no way they'd believe us. I feel dirty and vulnerable. I understand why a victim would want to spend ages showering. I'd like to get rid of this by loading it onto someone else as soon as possible."

Pippa was puzzled as to how the photos came to be taken. Who would give permission?

"They are so incriminating," she added.

"Not sure why they'd allow it?"

"They had no choice, and most were unaware. Sean told me his minder, an evil bastard called Douglas, had hidden cameras. There is a large market for such images. I bet these aren't the only copies."

"Look at that horrible sadistic pervert," Pippa exclaimed, "he is actually smiling into the camera as he does his worst to that kid."

"There are some by windows too. It might be possible to identify where they were taken from what is outside."

The final file turned out to be a recording of Sean sitting in front of a camera telling his tale.

"I might be dead by the time you see this," was his opening line.

The talking went on for twenty-five minutes. The account they both watched was painful, articulate and above all believable. He outlined his childhood in Northern Ireland, exactly as he had done to Rob, but in much more detail. How he was caught and imprisoned for more than ten years. What was done to him. As he related depraved acts he spoke in a monotone as though detached from events. It was hard enough to listen to let alone talk about. He spoke about his life after, the threats to himself and the murder of his son, and how, now, his dying wish is not revenge but justice and to stop what he said he knew was still going on. He emphasised repeatedly that those in the paedophile ring are a small part in a large picture. They are criminals and a disgrace to humanity, but also victims as they were being blackmailed into going further than they might go otherwise and doing things they would not do otherwise. They deserved no sympathy however. Some seem to use Dr Josef Mengele and Klaus Barbie as their role models.

The bigger picture was the dismantling of democracy.

"These are dangerous, ruthless, evil people and everyone should be on their guard. They control society, and are dictating everything we do. Through the media they now set the agenda and dictate what we think. There is almost certainly one living near you and mixing in your circle. They cannot now do me any more harm. Not that I care about anyway. I'm waiting for the knock on the door. But they are destroying any chance we have of developing a civilised society. Spread this message. If this does get distribution I will be vilified and ridiculed as a deluded fantasist. No effort will be too much to discredit the tale of these atrocities. Not quite in the same league as holocaust denial, but the parallels are there. Do what you can to stop them."

And with that the camera was switched off.

Back at Rob and Suzy's house, Pippa said her goodbyes with her usual triple kiss and hug. She needed to get back to Jeremy, Dave and her work. Rob appreciated why she was in a rush but he had not quite finished.

"I think we had better be careful how we communicate. Yesterday I went out and bought these. Cheap pay-as-you-go phones. We should use these to keep in touch and give no one else the number."

"Bit over the top, isn't it Rob?" said Suzy.

"Like in Jed Mercurio's *Line of Duty* police drama, when they changed cells and threw them in the bin every few days," added Pippa.

"Oh Pippa. Cells are where you put criminals. I've never heard you use an Americanism before?" joked Suzy, "But I must go shopping and get us some food. Are you sure you won't stay?"

Pippa repeated her reasons, thanked Suzy again for the offer and they both waved her goodbye as she got into her car. Rob was quite pleased to be left alone with Pippa but was not going to be distracted.

"Remember the phone tapping, poor Millie Dowler? The bastards are capable of anything."

"Okay. I'll take it. Thanks. What next then?" Pippa asked.

"Well, I'm copying this stick and think I should post one to every paper, radio station and TV channel, don't you?"

"It's a start, and not too risky as no one will know where they came from. So good idea."

"What I don't understand is why Sean and or Poison didn't do this themselves. Why do they need to use us? Surely we are an unnecessary middleman and therefore needlessly increasing the risks?

"Puzzles me too. The only clues I had from Sean was that they probably have, but need to spread the incriminating material like napalm across Vietnam, not just a single bullet. And he more or less said we are wasting our time with the mainstream media, but what else can we do? I suppose the revolt has to come from a mass movement of people, all united in their anger and not just the victims. But I have also wondered if we are being set up in some way?"

"Well, give me one for my boss."

"No, don't be daft, you can't be seen as the source. Give me his address and I'll make sure he gets one," said Rob.

"Don't forget to use different post boxes," smiled Pippa.

"Yes, yes. I've seen the movies and read le Carré. And drive very carefully, if you can drive a tin snail that is. You got very little sleep, your mind must be on the blink?"

"Got the Beatles' *White Album* to listen to. That'll keep me awake. Certainly wouldn't risk Leonard Cohen. Sad when he died though. Dave was knocked sideways."

As Rob waved goodbye and watched her car disappear, he had his usual melancholy feelings. He soon switched moods by thinking of The Beatles, the album that Pippa was referring to. Beatles records always lifted his mood. If he had corrected her and said that technically it is not called the white album, just *The Beatles*, she really would have thought him a geek - so he was glad he held back. She might have been interested to know that of the thirty tracks only sixteen featured all four Beatles and it was released five years to the day that Kennedy was assassinated. Or maybe not. A geek indeed.

Unusually for Rob he watched the local news on television and had the local radio on in the background whilst he set about making copies of the files. He addressed small envelopes as planned and put first class stamps on. He knew using several different post boxes was going to be a pain.

There was nothing about the car accident the night before. No mention of a car in a ditch, on its roof and a long hold-up for other traffic. There was though a story about a cat that had a Hitler moustache.

When Suzy arrived home from the shops he had fallen asleep on the sofa with both the television and radio still on. She did what she always did when she walked into a room where Rob was relaxing. She turned everything off. It was the sudden silence that woke Rob. It annoyed him when he was listening to music as she always turned the volume down. Suzy also knew she had the power to annoy him or get her own back about some issue if it suited her mood. But he did not mind this time. He gave Suzy a sketchy outline of the day's events, but did not go into detail. He told her he was sending files anonymously to as many media outlets that he could think of, files that were just a list of names.

"I think we are living in a time of massive under the surface revolution. The only problem is that a real revolution grows from the people in an attempt to improve the lives of the people. This revolution comes from the top elite and is designed to control the people. It's great change that is being done so subtly that no one notices until it is too late to reverse. Typical of what they are doing to the NHS, but that's just one strand of a gigantic wave of changes. Wholesale secret imposed reform as they call it. Nobody will be aware until it is complete. We should now all be wary of any politician who uses the word reform. In some senses this is why it's bigger than Henry VIII, bigger than Hitler, Stalin, Mao, and the Khmer Rouge. This lot has learnt from their previous mistakes."

He almost felt stupid saying all this. He thought he would get Suzy's usual response that he was a paranoid conspiracy theorist who should grow up. He was in for a surprise. Suzy did not think it was an exaggeration.

"Yes, of course it is. All those movements started in one country. This neo-liberal right wing take over is multinational. It's globalisation spreading to every corner of the world. Extreme right wing groups are becoming accepted, that is normal, even convincing the easily taken in, it is desirable. The AfD is the third largest party in the Bundestag now. The right has waged an effective campaign to pretend to occupy the so-called middle ground. Through the media they emphasise the Overton window, and ridicule anyone outside it."

"What do you think of this as an analogy? Thought of it in the bath where I get all my best ideas. Got to do something, apart from wash that is, now you no longer think bathing together is fun."

"I never…"

Rob carried on with his example before she could protest properly.

"Imagine mainstream opinion to be a tent pitched in the middle of a field. You come home one night to find the campsite owner has moved it five metres to the right. When you ask him what he is up to he says indignantly, 'what yer talking about? That tent is in the middle. You are imagining things. If anything it's too far to the left. Would you like me to move it more to the middle ground?' The next night it has been moved another five metres to the right. When challenged again the campsite owner says, 'I did move it to the middle like you said. In fact I've had complaints from the other campers that it is still too far to the left'. And so it goes on until it is to the extreme right of the field. 'Any more complaints that your tent is not in the centre and I'll throw you off the site', the owner says. The owner could be Murdoch. Those who move our tent for him are his lackeys, like the Secretary of State for Health, and other politicians in his pocket. Other campers are the public who don't notice. The tent is the *BBC*. Every time Murdoch re-sites it he removes a couple of guide ropes, making it more and more unstable. He has moved his ninety thousand pound campervan onto the site and plays his music very loud from it all day and all night."

"Is that it?" says Suzy, "Quite good, but what do you think of mine?"

She sits up like she is to make the announcement of a royal birth.

"It's my analogy to demonstrate what nonsense the phrase 'Brexit means Brexit' is. The question was should the UK remain a member of the European Union? That doesn't define Brexit does it? It doesn't say whether we should stay in the single market or customs union, or try to remain part of the economic area, does it? My analogy is that it is like the referendum question being, 'should we go on holiday this summer away from Europe?' When the answer is yes then we are faced with the alternatives Canada, the USA, India, Syria, Siberia and three mystery destinations. Some want to stay at home still so hide the suitcases and talk about how nice Scarborough is."

"Holiday means holiday."

"You voted for this so it's got to happen. You have to select one of these and you can vote but blindfolded, the family is told."

"But then we won't know where we are going and you aren't telling us how much it will cost. What about visas? Will we need swimwear, skis or anti- malarials?"

"We will deal with all that after we've got there."

"Got where?"

"Can't tell you that. We can't show our negotiating position before we get to customs, can we?"

"We are going to make a success of it whether you like it or not."

"Very good," praised Rob, "I think I follow you."

"Their soundbites expose that they all talk crap and in code. Take 'we will slash red tape'. Analyse that. All it really means is that we will abolish straightforward rules that protect the public so we can do what the fuck we like. Sod the consequences. The rich bang on about freedom, but that's the freedom to screw everyone else and is incompatible with democracy."

"Back to my topic, though," Rob said, trying not to be too dismissive, "I think Syriza in Greece is a movement whose supporters thought it had pitched its tent very firmly to the left of the field. It did this in the dark when they had nowhere else to live. The Germans had confiscated all the luxury tents. At sunrise the Greek people felt catastrophically betrayed as they found their new tent was actually quite to the right, not far from the Trump, *Breitbart* and *Fox News* campervans. All along they had had a freezing night sleeping amongst the right wing bourgeoisie who had flogged off their groundsheets and sleeping bags so they could afford the campsite fees demanded by the owner, some blokes from Brussels, Berlin and Washington. As Yanis Varoufakis revealed, when the EU bailed out the Greek economy in 2010 it was designed to save the French and German banks, and Merkel and Sarkozy knew this and knew it would end in tears. They saved private banks by saddling north European states with massive debts and it'll be the French and German taxpayers who will pay the price when the Greek debt is inevitably written off."

"Complicated but I think I get it," said Suzy, less than convincingly.

"Varoufakis and his family were threatened with violence when he denounced the bailout as unworkable."

"Nevertheless," Suzy said, "Surely Syriza may be all that remains to rally the left for a last ditch fight against a fascist takeover and dictatorship?"

"Podemos in Spain is not much different. It is portrayed as being far left to dampen down protest and revolution as people think they have an alternative to get into power democratically. They haven't and it isn't. It too shows familiar signs of wanting to get into bed with those it claims to oppose. This has always been the case with our Labour Party, which has and always will act to defend the interests of capitalism and in the USA with Bernie Sanders. Labelling him a socialist gives comfort to those who want socialism, there probably are one or two in America, but he is nothing of the sort. He's an old-fashioned liberal democrat of the kind that, once in power, started most of America's wars."

"What about Le Pen in France and that 'Captain peroxide' Geert Wilders in the Netherlands?" Suzy asked.

Rob was actually quite surprised she was genuinely interested. By now she had usually switched off and told him he was being boring. Encouraged he continued.

"Their electoral net is being spread much wider by deftly appealing to fear, nostalgia and resentment of elites. Just like Trump did in the land of the free. And like the AfD in Germany. All these have been cynically clever by outflanking the left on some issues like gay rights, women's equality and anti-Semitism. They claim them as their own by depicting Muslim immigrants as the primary threat to all three groups. They have steadily filled an electoral vacuum by those who ignored voters' anger about immigration, like UKIP did here. The great irony is that the free market has produced millions of losers and in seeking revenge they turn to the very people who support the free market in the first place.

That Pim Fortuyn guy, Wilder's ideological predecessor, the one who was murdered nearly twenty years ago, was clever. He didn't go all religious like in the States, quite the opposite. He won over the far right by claiming he was defending secular progressive culture from the threat of immigration. The Danish People's Party is curious. Very anti-immigrant, it stole the Social Democrats' policies of better healthcare, better elderly care and more subsidised housing. Like most right-wingers they have hijacked the word freedom and use it when they mean nothing of the sort. A common theme of these parties is that they seduce their natural enemies. Le Pen's father called the holocaust a detail of history. Despite that his daughter has now got a Jewish following by claiming to be the only movement to defend them. She tells people you either defend the interests of the people or the interests of the banks. The Dutch far right successfully seized the mantle of radicalism by claiming to be the only lot who dares to challenge an out of touch political elite. Sound familiar? Trump? It's all such a dilemma."

"Hmmm."

Suzy was getting more and more disturbed. She came to Rob's conclusion before he did.

"The real worry with all these right wing parties emerging is that Europe's capacity for murderous violence is always lurking beneath the surface. Remember Anne Frank was betrayed by the Dutch not the Germans. It'll scare me if Europeans get their manhood back. Too much dangerous testosterone. We all know what testosterone does, don't we Rob?"

"Shall I show you?" he said trying to keep a straight face.

"You certainly won't. This is the most serious conversation we have had for ages. I didn't know you had it in you."

"Bloody cheek. It's just the first time you have listened properly," he exclaimed while throwing a cushion at her, not having totally lost hope that she might be receptive.

"Anyway, it's not a dilemma, in this context, as you put it. Don't confuse the use of the word dilemma with problem. If you have a problem, as we have with this, it means we don't know what to do and there may be many solutions. If you have a dilemma you have a choice of two courses of action, neither attractive. So we, or the world, have a problem, not a dilemma."

"Fuck me, you are pedantic. And which word have I used incorrectly there, fuck or pedantic?"

She ignored him.

"As a result of Europe dividing, the EU disintegrating and the emergence of the right wing, we might see trouble come back that we thought we'd eliminated for all time. That was the point of a united Europe, to keep the peace. All through history Europe has treated foreigners badly. Thirty years ago if you had been told there was to be genocide in Europe you wouldn't have believed it. But it happened in the Balkans."

Rob took over.

"The right always needs a scapegoat, whether it's the Jews, immigrants, Muslims, fat people… now it's the elite which is ironic as they often are the elite, they just pretend not to be. Immigrants can never do right. If they are unemployed they are a burden to society and if they work they've stolen our jobs."

"Did you hear of that new law in Denmark? They've gone nuts. Any refugees with more than twelve thousand pounds will have it confiscated to fund the cost of accommodating asylum-seekers. Of course these refugees are rolling in it, turn up at the border in a stretch-limo and furs. I think not. Plus they are forcing immigrants to put their children into day care for twenty-five hours a week from the age of one so they grow up with Danish values, and the sentences for crimes committed in their ghettos are double that of elsewhere. This is the latest spasm of xenophobia and racism to afflict European politics. Anti-liberal populism is gripping the heart of Europe. The bottom line is that European countries are rich. There is enough food for everyone. Where has compassion for our fellow man gone?"

"Yup, a good note to finish on," said Rob yawning and fidgeting.

"You seem a bit uptight. Usually having a rant makes you feel so much better. Is this really getting to you?" enquired Suzy with concern.

"Well, to drop a hint, you no longer suffer from PMT, but I still get problems with PST and always will."

"Oh no, I thought so. I've told you there is no such thing as pre-sexual tension but if there is, you are not the only one it creates problems for."

"Shall we Netflix and chill?" said Rob hopefully.

A pained expression spread across Suzy's face.

"Okay," she replied with a distinct lack of enthusiasm.

"I'll fix some drinks. That might help," said Rob with hope. He walked to the kitchen to hear the distant shout.

"You know I hate horrid American phrases. You can only fix something that is broken, and how can a drink be broken anyway?"

He returned to find her stretched out on the sofa fast asleep. For some reason the image of Les Dawson sprang to mind and his joke, *my wife is a sex object, every time I suggest sex, she objects.*

48 - SCARED AND ROBBED

CRIME OF THE CENTURY

So roll up and see
How they've raped the Universe
How they've gone from bad to worse
Who are these men of lust, greed and glory?
Rip off the mask and let's see.

Supertramp (1974)

Rob was pleased to have a few days when, compared to the previous week or two, not much happened.

He was visibly winding down and trying to relax more. The previous night he slept right through for the first time in ages. A good chat with Suzy helped. After she woke up on the sofa with a stiff neck, they went for a walk down the country lane by their house. They both agreed they should unwind like this more often. Neither mentioned the elephant in the room. They speculated about their next holiday and Rob said he had seen that Blondie was touring and should he get tickets? They had not been to a concert since a poor experience at the Proms but thought they should get out more and try again.

Their visit to the Albert Hall was a concert to mark the fiftieth anniversary of the death of Sir Malcolm Sargent, chief conductor of the Proms from 1947. Sir Andrew Davis recreated Sargent's five hundredth Prom from 1966. It included Beatrice Rana's Proms debut performance of Schumann's *Piano Concerto in A minor*, and one of Rob's favourites - Elgar's Overture *Cockaigne (in London Town)*. The concert was excellent but neither could believe how poorly behaved the audience was. They sat next to a big fat businessman who was texting about the Pharma Industry's Company of the Year Awards Ceremony throughout Berlioz's *Overture Le carnaval romain* and his wife who tapped her foot to the music when not munching sweets. And the biggest sin of all, as far as Rob was concerned, clapping between movements. Proms audiences, in Rob's experience, rarely indulged in pseud show-off talk about the music.

In front of them on their last visit Rob overheard – indeed he could not avoid overhearing at the volume they were talking to make sure all those around knew he was somebody.

"The poised allegretto was warmed by the expressive portamento," and, "The scherzo enjoyed a vigorous fugato on the lower strings," to be capped by, "The conductor and the pianist allowed the gestures to disrupt the rhythmic continuity to a degree I don't remember previously encountering," followed by, "The Marcia funebre had an air of ascetic solemnity about it."

His companion, a fair bit older chipped in.

"It all reminded me of Toscanini back in '37, but he rushed the Scherzo."

Rob was getting more and more irritated and felt the urge to retaliate with some nonsense.

"Suzy duck, what yer think of the cadenza and the pianissimos? I thought the adagio outdid the rondo with its harmonic quirkiness but the middle movement felt a bit perfunctory with a suggestion of paradisal innocence. And what a witty moment in the finale, eh? I haven't laughed so much since Herbert von Karajan fell off the conductor's platform conducting Wagner's *Tannhauser* and the Horst Wessel song at Hitler's birthday party in '35."

The younger man turned round and snarled at them.

"You are being discourteous to the grandson of Lord Sempill let me tell you. He actually met Toscanini when his Lordship took him to a concert at the Queen's Hall in 1937, the hall that was destroyed by the Luftwaffe in 1941. But I wouldn't expect your type to know things like that. I think you should apologise."

"Sorry about my husband. He is music critic for *Gramophone* magazine and has been since his de-Nazification. He can't tolerate pretentious twats."

Rob felt satisfied and even more so when he could point out that the bronze bust of Sir Henry Wood, in front of them at the Henry Willis organ, was rescued from the wreckage of the Queen's Hall. It was hit by a single incendiary bomb hours after Malcolm Sargent had conducted Elgar's *Enigma Variations* and the *Dream Of Gerontius*.

Rob wondered, again out loud to Suzy, whether he was one of those knobs with an inherited Albert Hall seat. He told her, not for the first time, that three hundred and thirty people still owned over twelve hundred seats at the Albert Hall bought in 1867 to help fund its construction.

The last time they had seen Blondie was at the Roundhouse in 2014 as part of the fortieth anniversary tour. Forty years. Rob could not believe that Debbie Harry was sixty-nine. When she kicked off the set list with *One Way Or Another* Rob thought he had gone to heaven. The Roundhouse was special to Rob. His first visit was to see the Ramones aged thirteen with Jerry. He loved *Judy Is A Punk*. He could not believe he was in a venue that had hosted Jimi Hendrix, The Doors and Led Zep. His last visit was with Jenny to see Patti Smith five years before they broke up. He bored Suzy about how before becoming an Arts Venue in 1966 it was originally built in 1846 as a turntable engine shed, then was a gin warehouse for decades.

All this did keep their minds off the elephant however.

"Michael 'as cancelled I'm afraid," said Giselle, as Rob walked in to face morning surgery.

"Have you re-arranged?"

"Yes, it won't be for another ten days, 'e's busy."

"That's a shame. I'm obviously worried about the missing money. We've got to solve this mystery. Have you come to any conclusions or had any ideas about this?"

Confidently Giselle said she had not as yet.

Rob was surprised to see Mrs Sharma on his list, and first. From his memory he thought she was due to have her hemi-colectomy operation yesterday. It soon became clear what had gone wrong. The usual problem when funding is cut. No beds. She was upset but not blaming anyone. She just thought he should know. Rob did not let on what shot through his mind - 'and the stupid wankers want to cut beds further'. *We are going to move patients into the community. The best bed is your own bed*, they would say, trying to excuse their ideology.

"I'd love to perform a hemi-colectomy at home, in his own bed, on the knob-head who thought that one up, and with a blunt knife!"

Rob shouted at the television when he heard the BBC health correspondent parrot the Government line as though it was from the Messiah.

"Rob, you know you won't sleep if you get that worked up," said Suzy calmly.

"When I get haemorrhoids I now know who I'm going to name them after!" he shouted at nobody in particular.

Only the day before he had had to calm down the relative of a patient who was in a similar predicament. The wife seemed to think it was Rob's fault that the repair of his aortic aneurysm in his chest was cancelled for the second time.

"Don't you realise he is sitting on a time-bomb?" Mrs Albert sobbed, "It could rupture anytime. We sit at home in dread. Every time he gets a twinge I panic. He would drown in his own blood in less than a minute."

As far as the efficiency of the hospital was concerned this was worse than the cancelling of a hemi-colectomy. Rob knew the vascular surgeon. For a case like this he had had it explained, at one of Stephen and Ellie's dinner parties, that it takes months to coordinate the diaries of the expert team. The problem this time was not the lack of an ordinary bed, but the lack of a place in intensive care. And guess what, the tossers want to cut intensive care beds too. Unbelievable.

Mrs Sharma was much more relaxed but worried as Marko lost money taking her to the hospital and they cannot afford for that to happen again.

"Is there anything you can do to prevent another cancellation, Dr Baigent?"

He wished he could. Shooting the Secretary of State sprang immediately to mind, but although that would give him satisfaction, he knew there was just another jerk to replace him.

At the end of the morning Rob went through the computerised results and letters - a few action points but nothing worrying. Scattered amongst his emails were the usual communications from the surrounding Trusts from dumb bureaucrats with nothing better to do, telling GPs not to admit patients unless necessary, as they cannot cope.

"Of course, we all admit patients all the time who don't need to be in hospital. We round them up off the streets."

Rob thought of replying, 'well people love being sent to hospital as the food is free and so nice, sorry, we do as the consumer wants now', but he knew they wouldn't get the point.

His paper in-tray had reduced in size considerably since he started in general practice and since computerisation. It was easier and quicker assuming the computers worked properly, but the total workload was much greater. The outsourcing of the computer maintenance contract often resulted in days without access when there was a breakdown, which meant the service Rob's surgery could offer ground to a halt. Another bunch of incompetent bastards fraudulently winning a contract on the basis that they could provide a Rolls-Royce service on the budget of a shopping trolley. Rob tried but failed to get Mrs Sharma's surgeon on the phone. That used to be easy too. Now to speak to any hospital staff you were redirected to a central operator to take all details in case a bill for advice was to be generated.

In his paper tray were a couple of drug industry sponsored dinners which he always refused, a circular from the Local Medical Committee and five England tickets for the next qualifier against Slovakia. He did not socialise much with Michael the practice accountant, but they both had a common interest in going to Wembley to watch England lose. Suzy and Eileen, Michael's wife, were unusual in that they liked the odd game so, as the match fell on Michael and Eileen's wedding anniversary, Michael and Rob were plotting to surprise them both. Whether they would really appreciate it was another matter. But that was why the tickets had been sent to the surgery, not home. The other ticket was for Stephen. He never brought Ellie as she thought football was for the plebs and could never admit to her dinner party set that Stephen was a Brighton and Hove Albion fan. He thought he would just let Michael know via email.

Hi Michael,
Tickets have arrived so it's on!
We can make the final arrangements when we meet up at the practice soon -albeit rearranged.
Sorry to hear you are so busy!
Regards
Rob

The next email was for Stephen.

Dear Superstar Geriatrician,
I hope you have got out of that dinner party of Ellie's as the ticket for the England game has arrived!
I forgot Suzy was coming too, so she can't bail you out!
However she doesn't know as it's a surprise.
Remember Michael and Eileen? They were at the Wales game. They are coming too. An anniversary treat for them.
See you for squash as usual.
Yours truly,
A poor GP

Rob retreated to the common room to escape the phone for twenty minutes to have a bite to eat. Whilst chewing yesterday's sandwich for lunch he picked up last week's BMJ to browse through. God, this is boring this week, he thought and went quickly to the obituary page. No one he knew this week. On flicking back the name Wessel stood out. He looked closely. Queen's Birthday Honours rewards several longstanding loyal BMA servants. 'It's now Sir Clifford Wessel', said the article. Oh, no fucking hell. I do not believe it. Talk about bringing the honours system even more into disrepute. How corrupt, he thought, but it got worse. 'Top gynaecologist gets a knighthood for services to women's health'.

Rob feared the worst. Yes, 'it's now Sir Simon Chisholm'. Giving that parasitic creepy broflake a gong for services to women is like giving one to a fox for services to chickens, he thought as he nearly choked on his stale sandwich. It was then that Rob decided he would definitely turn down any offer to make him Lord Baigent. The House of Lords is not for him.

Before starting afternoon surgery Rob thought he had better check his emails again. A terrible habit he was trying to deal with. An unusually prompt reply from Michael.

Who said I'm too busy!
You can tell from this quick reply I'm not!
Accountants work hard in January and July, and play games on their desktops the rest of the year (but don't tell my partners or Eileen I said that!)
Giselle said you were so overwhelmed with work that you had to cancel our meeting. Never mind.
Pleased the tickets have arrived.
Will catch up soon.
Regards
Michael

Odd, Rob thought. He was about to buzz Giselle to find out if there had just been a misunderstanding when he remembered she had gone off early to help sort Derek's parents out. His Dad had just been sent to prison again for GBH. Derek, apparently, was too busy in the City saving the country. Then the phone buzzed. One of the practice's long standing receptionists, Jean, one who was there before Rob, one who had never been up to the job, spoke in her squeaky voice.

"Mr Kuze on the line. Would like a bit of advice about his rash?"

Click. She put him through before Rob could remind her of the policy she had been told over and over again, to put these sorts of non-urgent queries into one of the telephone booking slots. After a brief chat it was clear Rob should see Mr Kuze so he put him on the list at the end of surgery.

Rob thought through the last few consultations on his drive home. He often did this to try to make sure he had thought of everything. He always was nervous about the last consultation of the day. He worried it put him and his patient at risk as he was usually tired, hungry and too keen to get away, a potential cocktail for mistakes. His concerns about Mr Kuze fortunately were not justified. He had a straightforward case of lichen planus. Classic purplish flat-topped bumps on his inner forearms. Even the Wickham's striae in the mouth. So satisfying this job, sometimes. There are things one only has to see once and they are never forgotten, was a frequent comment amongst other fellow GPs.

He passed the spot where Ian ended in the ditch. There was still a length of police tape hanging off a tree. Why was this not on the news he asked himself again? As he entered the drive and the gravel made its familiar crunching noise, he saw a police car outside. There was no one in it. He felt a tightening of his muscles, then just as he was beginning to relax, oh no, the girls, or Suzy? Is this one of those life-changing moments? This all flitted through his mind in a nanosecond. Suzy saw him coming and opened the door to reassure him straight away.

"It's okay. Nothing serious. Everyone's all right. We've been burgled, that's all."

Rob put it down to the more traumatic recent events that Suzy seemed quite relaxed about having intruders in the house. A few months ago it would have been the end of the world. He greeted the two policemen who were both drinking tea.

Suzy had a habit of offering everyone tea - the postman, the bin men, window cleaners, delivery men and even passing ramblers. Some looked at her as if she were mad, especially the deliverymen who only made a decent wage by rushing fifty visits a day. No time for them to drink tea. Rob still dined out on the story of when Suzy's kindness was misinterpreted by one caller who thought he was being propositioned. Suzy only realised later why he became all hot and bothered and ran off.

"What's the damage?" he said, to no one in particular.

"Just our computers. But they or he did force your filing cabinet."

"Or she," Rob teased.

He was in a surprisingly calm state considering.

"Can you think of any reason why someone would target your computers or files, Sir? Or can you think of anything they might have been looking for?"

Rob had a momentary panic about Sean's memory stick, but he was sure nothing was left on his Apple Mac. Not that he was going to mention that of course.

"No officer. I don't see why this should be anything other than opportunists. I assume a large Mac is still worth something on the second hand market. More than a Big Mac anyway."

"Your wife tells me you are a doctor. No personal medical files in your house, sir?"

"Certainly not."

"To be honest sir, this is why we attended. We now don't have the resources to investigate thefts and house break-ins routinely but if we do get time we like to check out anyone with medical connections for two reasons, medical notes and drugs."

Suzy had read that the Met were so stretched individual police officers were dealing with up to twenty-five cases of rape each, and could not possibly do the job well, so she was surprised to get two men to their house for a non-violent crime. Many sexual offences were not even recorded. Cases of corruption, war criminals, fraud, and money laundering were way down the list. Suzy recalled Rob telling her this was probably deliberate. If there were no police available to investigate the Westminster paedophile ring those who make these funding decisions go free. Suzy thought that far fetched.

To Rob's relief it seemed that Suzy had dealt with everything and the policemen left, not understanding Rob's Big Mac joke. Rob had a cursory look through his filing cabinet but could not see anything obvious missing. He took the opportunity to take out his insurance policy for house contents.

"When were we stupid enough to set up a two thousand pound excess on home contents, Suzy?"

"Don't you remember? You said it was worth it. We would never be robbed you said and you were buggered if you were going to give those slimy crooked rip-off merchants a penny more than you had to."

Suzy thrust a bottle of cold *Becks* into Rob's hand. She was already halfway down a bottle of white *Chateauneuf-du-Pape*. Well it was eight pm Rob told himself. Explains why she is taking this in her stride. Just as Rob was clearing his head of the jobs associated with a break-in she said ominously.

"A few more things I'm afraid."

Rob braced himself again and took a large gulp of beer to prepare.

"I'm pretty sure I was followed today. I made several trips out and this red van was always behind me. There aren't many red vans like it. I made sure I stayed on main roads but was scared in the lanes near home. They made no attempt at subtlety. I think they wanted to be seen. In other words they wanted to scare me. They certainly succeeded."

Then she asked herself.

"Who are these men?"

Straight away she knew it was a question neither of them could possibly answer.

"It goes from bad to worse."

Rob was now scared on her behalf.

"I tried to get the registration but couldn't read it mirror image. Then I thought, even if I did, would I really go to the police? The only thing I did notice was it had a large dent on the front wing and along the side. The headlight was smashed. There was a fair bit of blue or black paint, obviously from another car it had hit."

Rob instantly thought of Ian's blue Daewoo but he did not say anything to Suzy.

"Then, in the mail this morning. How many memory sticks did you post?"

She did not wait for the answer.

"Because ten came back all in the same envelope. So either they were intercepted before reaching their destination, or all the people you sent them to are in league with each other, or both."

"Oh, shit. Have they still got something on or have they been wiped?"

"How would I know dummy? Someone's nicked our computers!"

"I met our postie on the drive on my way out this morning so he handed me the mail. I just chucked it on the back seat of the car to deal with later. Just as well or all those sticks could have fallen into the burglar's hands. Maybe that's what they were after?"

Rob was still thinking straight.

"Only if the burglars are nothing to do with the lot who returned the sticks, or why would they be searching for something we had already given them, Suzy."

Suzy had finished the bottle by this time. Rob tried to make light of it.

"No chance they did me a favour and stole my copy of *Jude the Obscure* is there?"

"Rob, I'm scared."

She was clearly not as calm as he had first thought and with all of today's events he was not surprised.

"Let's get away for a while. We don't know if we are in danger but I feel it. We've had threats, a cat killed. I've been followed. We don't really know why or who. Friends like Pippa have been dragged in and we owe it to her not to put her at risk. We are into something we don't understand."

"I think I understand it all right. It's just I don't know who's behind it, what their aim is, what they will do next or what to do about it."

"Oh what a relief! That certainly sounds like you understand it!" she said sarcastically, but humorously.

"Point taken. But this will make a good book to write in retirement."

"Well, I want to live to get a retirement. Forget your Dan Brown fantasies, what about going away?"

"You know I can't. I've got fully booked surgeries all week."

Suzy was thinking that was dedicated but feeble. What's more important, their sanity or even their lives, or that of his patients? He would not be able to see them if he was dead. Or was she just being over dramatic? Yes, perhaps be rational she told herself. Why would they really be a target? Then Rob was saved by the bell. The landline rang and he answered.

"Yes… yes… yes. Okay. Thank you very much for letting me know. Could I take your contact number to find out about the arrangements? Thank you Mr Ephialtes. Goodbye."

Rob had written down a telephone number.

"Poor old Rosa. She's dead."

"Let's go to bed. To sleep," said Suzy.

49 - DYSTOPIA AND DISBELIEF

I WON'T BACK DOWN

Well I know what's right, I got just one life
In a world that keeps on pushin' me around
But I'll stand my ground and I won't back down

Hey baby there ain't no easy way out
Hey I will stand my ground
And I won't back down

Tom Petty (1989)

The contact details at the end of the programme were fairly straightforward but they were Paris numbers.

Between patients the next day he rang, half expecting to not find someone who could understand him. So he had Giselle in his office to help if need be. He thought he might as well use the practice's phone in case the call got a bit expensive. He did not explain to Giselle in advance as he hoped it would not be necessary to involve her, and he was right.

"Bonjour. *Franceinfo TV*."

"Parlez-vous Anglais?

"Oui. Yes."

With the relief of this he told Giselle not to waste her valuable time, that she would not be needed. He explained that he had seen their programme, was aware of some of the conspiracies they said they would be investigating and was keen to contribute. Then, rather recklessly, added that he had access to files. He was put through to the office and repeated himself. He added that he would like to meet Chantelle and if possible, Madison. He was told that would not be possible but if he would like to leave his contact details a reporter would get back to him. Rob knew a brush-off when he was the victim of one. He remained polite though, gave his details, then as sensing the phone was to be put down on him, thought he would take a further risk.

"I know about Poison."

There was a period of silence, and then the man just repeated that someone would get back to him.

The next patient was Mrs Sharma just ten days after her last visit to tell Rob about her cancellation. He stood up to greet her. His knee reminded him of the twist he had given it playing Stephen the evening before. She was looking good. She had had her colectomy and did not need a colostomy. She was wondering if all the antibiotics were necessary. Of course Rob had no discharge note so assumed they were prophylactic only.

"Surely they aren't a good idea if they are not targeting something specific? Not only that but you'll get the blame for overprescribing as the hospital only gave me two days' supply."

They both laughed and it was nice to see his patient now as relaxed as he felt. Rob was impressed too. She obviously had been aware of the campaign to reduce antibiotic usage. The same campaign that put the boot into GPs. This time it was not only the usual GP-bashing *Daily Mail* but also the broadsheets and full media. Totally swallowing false government propaganda. Their real targets should be the farmers but they will not go for their friends, he thought.

Mrs Sharma had just left when the phone buzzed. It was Giselle saying there was a call from a reporter from a French television station. A London call, not Paris.

"That was quick," thought Rob.

He felt some remorse for thinking bad of them. To his astonishment it was Chantelle. Wow, what a fantastic sexy French accent, Rob thought, even better than Giselle's. She was abrupt however and straight to the point. They were to meet the next evening in a pub called The Thornbury Castle in Enford Street, Marylebone.

The arrangements suited Rob. It was his half-day and once at Charing Cross it was just four stops on the Bakerloo line and a five-minute walk from Baker Street Station. He paused at the statue of Sherlock Holmes to put his umbrella up and wished he too had a deerstalker and Inverness cape as it was raining stair rods.

Rob had read most of the Arthur Ignatius Conan Doyle books as a teenager. He had devoured the fifty-six short stories and four novels making up the *Canon of Sherlock Holmes* in weeks. Rob knew *Strand Magazine* had added the deerstalker. Holmes' character was defined in the books by his pipe, magnifying glass and Stradivarius. The geek Rob also knew he was originally to be called Sherrinford, not Sherlock. *Realise that everything connects to everything else.* Dr Watson disapproved of Holmes' cocaine habit. Conan Doyle's MD subject was tabes dorsalis. Manet suffered from this. He painted *Le Dejeuner sur l'herbe*. A copy hung on Rob's consulting room wall. *Learn how to see*, was the other part of Leonardo da Vinci's quote and the wisdom that Rob was only now beginning to understand.

He headed down the Marylebone Road towards the landmark, which he knew was opposite Enford Street. As always he was early. One thing that stressed Rob was being late for anyone. By the time he got to The Thornbury the rain had stopped and it was beginning to turn into a fine evening and so, after collecting a pint of *Three Sods Session IPA*, Rob decided to sit outside under the blue awning. It then dawned on him he would only recognise Chantelle if she looked like she did on television. In Rob's experience people rarely did. Maybe it was what he called his facial dyslexia, as no one else he knew seemed to have this trouble.

They were supposed to meet at 7.00 p.m. After twenty minutes he had finished his pint and free paper he had collected at the tube station. He always regretted picking up such undiluted crap. Even the correspondence pages were clearly false, written by a team of bigots to propagate the paper's editorial line. One typical one, which he had seen before, and as usual signed only *name and address supplied*, was moaning about how much time NHS staff had off sick. *It was a disgrace at taxpayers' expense and wouldn't be tolerated in the private sector.* What bollocks, but he wondered how low an IQ was needed to be taken in by such bias. Of course the paper's campaign to privatise the NHS was clear although never openly admitted. Rob wondered how much more to the right the new Tory ex-Bullingdon Club editor would move the time-expired rag. He took heart from the recent election when newspapers seemed to be losing their toxic influence and social media was replacing them.

Rob began to wonder if she was going to turn up. However it was only ten past seven, so he thought he could get another pint. As he was walking out with a *Clouded Minds Luppol* in his hand he saw her on the opposite side of the road, trying to cross. She was with another woman of similar age. It was Madison. Jackpot, Rob thought to himself. He approached them, they all introduced themselves and to his surprise they exchanged kisses. No English reserve here. They were both carrying sports bags and from their flushed appearances had just left the gym. Either that or... Rob thought, bringing his tally to how many times an hour a man thinks of sex up to the average.

They thanked him for travelling up to London. He then realised, and they confirmed, they lived just around the corner. After settling down with drinks and, to Madison's insistence, sitting where they could not be overheard, Rob was curious to know why they now appeared so eager to meet him.

"Who says we are eager?" said Madison, but Rob sensed she was teasing.

"Poison," fired back Chantelle, "We have been trying to find out more about that organisation since we went on air. We keep hitting brick walls, as you say. As soon as you mentioned that word we knew we needed to meet, se presser le citron, we want to squeeze you like a lemon."

Rob was brutally forthright.

"Can we trust each other? I've found myself in some worrying situations recently and I don't want to get any more threats to me, my wife or any pets I have left."

Both women ignored the last reference to pets. They just subconsciously dismissed it as unimportant. Rob knew it was an unnecessary detail - a mistake.

"You can trust us. But I understand your nervousness. We too have learnt that many people aren't what they seem, and there are too many front organisations and double-dealers around. You have seen Chantelle's work on television and me pouring my heart out over a missing husband. Why would we be up to no good?" said Madison, "But why are you here, Dr Baigent?"

"Because I think your husband was unearthing the truth about the corrupt way the world is run nowadays," Rob replied.

Rob addressed the questioner.

"We all know it has been corrupt since the beginning of time, but my belief is that it was more cock-up than conspiracy. Now I think the powers that be, whoever they are, are very well organised. Obviously Pete was not alone in thinking such thoughts but must have uncovered so much information that he had to be silenced."

He sensed Madison shudder at that.

"I'm sorry. That was indelicate. I've no knowledge about your husband and his fate. I only came to know about him from your programme."

"It's okay, I am fully aware he is probably dead. My quest is to find out why it was so important to eliminate him. Is the stuff on his laptop so dangerous? What is going on and who is responsible? But above all he couldn't have been the only person uncovering dirt. If he was, then it makes sense to silence him but if there are many more snoopers then they must be killing the others too or they are wasting their time targeting just Pete?"

"You won't learn that from me. I'm only a beginner but I started thinking the same way when I went down one very narrow avenue, my particular field, healthcare, and the more I found out the more I fell over parallels in every other field. It goes way beyond abolishing the welfare state and society. I now think the aim is to abolish all governments. By the time they have finished they won't be needed. They are well on their way. The public services workforce is the smallest it's been since the last war. Big business will run everything and micro-manage us all. My wife and some of my friends will go as far as me with thinking the world is unfair, run badly and deviously for the good of the few, but they all part company with me, and frankly think I'm paranoid and nuts, when I take it that one step further, perhaps two or three steps actually, and claim there is a secret well-established and planned conspiracy which started no later than the 1930s. The name of the game is to set up in total power a very small select elite which will lead a life very different from the other ninety-nine per cent of us who will be controlled and manipulated in a way that makes George Orwell's *1984* seem like a children's bedtime story."

They both continued to just stare at him. This was a little unnerving so his rambling continued.

"When I read Margaret Atwood's *The Handmaid's Tale* as a student, to me it was just a dystopian novel like *A Clockwork Orange* or *Brave New World*. It could never come true. I don't believe that any more. The US could easily be taken over by a totalitarian theocracy. But more likely now, from what I see, the world by business."

Rob thought he had better stop there to gauge their reactions. He wondered whether by showing his hand this early, he would lose credibility, but he had decided on the train journey to London that there was little point in coming if he did not say what he believed. First he just had to be sure he could trust them. He wanted to and so convinced himself early on that it was okay. It was in his nature as a GP to trust people until proved otherwise. But he could not help noticing they had been glancing at each other throughout his monologue. Then the reassurance.

It was Chantelle who broke the silence.

"I think the Republic of Gilead taking over the USA as in *The Handmaid's Tale* is more of a documentary than a prophecy. Fundamentalist Christians are stripping women of their rights. Look at some of the fascists appointed to the Supreme Court. The book describes a coup d'etat that is entirely believable. Sudden coordinated attacks killing the president, members of Congress, Justices blaming Islamic fanatics and declaring a state of emergency, suspending the Constitution, freezing assets and bank accounts, sacking women then hunting down anyone they perceived as ungodly or a threat. If you dissect this line of events, you can name plenty of countries where one or more of these events have happened. Certainly the USA, Turkey, the Czech Republic, Spain, Russia, Hungary, Poland, Austria, Italy, some Asian and South American countries. But also my country France, the state of emergency and now in the UK the Democratic Unionist Party have strong influence. Evangelical Christians believing in creationism, the death penalty, anti-abortion, anti-family planning, anti-gays, anti-same-sex marriage very similar to the USA. This is becoming a global movement.

Rob, we both thought we were probably either wasting our time with you, or putting ourselves in great danger. At best we thought you might shed some light on Poison. We are still not one hundred per cent sure but what you have said so far is in line with our thinking. Well, mine at least. I have spent most of my journalistic career exploring this and was pushed out of a good job, I think, because of it. I was an investigative reporter on the Paris-based weekly *Marianne*, which led a strong anti-Sarkozy campaign. I wrote the article calling him insane, an aggressive piece of journalism, which is uncommon in France even if you English and Americans are used to it. From 2007 I thought the editorial board supported my investigations, but I think someone leant on them when I went further and attacked him for screwing Greece.

But I did okay. I got my last job working for *Le Monde Diplomatique*. You will not have heard of it. It is a left-leaning anti-capitalist newspaper but only published monthly. It was one of the first to criticise the neo-liberal ideology of Reagan and Thatcher. Most of your press was supportive and uncritical of them. How many papers in your countries would support a general strike? None of course. But *Le Monde Diplomatique* supported the 1995 general walkout against Prime Minister Juppe's plan to cut pensions. That's an example of how we have a free press and you don't.

The reason I am telling you this is so you can check my work. The relevant article as far as you are concerned is exactly suggesting what you said earlier. No governments will be necessary when big business rules the world. Murdoch and Bannon recognised politics was a waste of time and didn't give them the power that the media did, but even they will be left behind as those in charge of the massive multi-nationals will be even more powerful and rule the world without the nuisance of having to be elected. I wrote this just before I left for my present TV job."

Rob had a cocktail of competing emotions. Satisfaction that someone else was thinking the same; alarm that they were thinking the same; panic and despair that they were thinking the same. Chantelle apologised for going off at a tangent, but insisted it was relevant. Her researcher, she said, had this theory about where the world is heading.

"Very briefly," she told Rob and Madison, "The universe is thirteen point seven hundred and nine nine billion years old, give or take twenty-one million years, the earth four point five billion years old, life began on earth about three point eight billion years ago, Homo sapiens developed about two hundred thousand years ago and some left Africa about sixty thousand years ago. The Chinese claim the first civilisation five thousand years ago, the Greeks the first democracy two thousand five hundred years ago, and the first Great Britain Parliament sat over three hundred years ago in 1707. Her theory is we are now entering a completely new post-democracy era receding back to when a handful of the absolutely powerful ruled and controlled the masses."

"You are implying, or she is, that this is as big a milestone as the development of democracy, that is, its loss?"

"Yes, although democracy has never really been put into practice, has it, so it was a phoney era."

"The origin of life is pretty irrelevant for the ninety-nine per cent of all species that have ever lived that are now extinct," Madison added, exposing her environmental credentials.

"This new era will see the species Homo sapiens eventually destroy itself, maybe soon, or maybe in another few millennia, depending on whether destroying the insect eco-system or global warming get us first," Chantelle finished.

"A little friend of mine called Jeremy tells me that the Andromeda Galaxy with its one hundred billion stars will have a head-on collision with our galaxy, the Milky Way, in four billion years' time, so we are all fucked anyway," Rob concluded, but regretting using the 'f' word.

There was a silence and then Rob went to buy more drinks while Madison went to the bathroom. On his return, Rob had remembered the survey he had seen which showed the majority of the young thought democracy overrated anyway. He shared it with the others, but they already knew. Chantelle felt free to talk frankly.

"You do realise that this all needs widespread coverage to a sceptical population before it is too late, and they need convincing, but that very act will make us all vulnerable and exposed, and probably crushed as they, whoever they are, must have expected and prepared for this big-time. They must have teams of counter-espionage workers and spies, and multiple units and cells of troops who are there to destroy any opposition. We are just a little flea of irritation to them, but they won't allow us to risk their grand scheme, even if our risk to them is minuscule."

"So what do we do?" said Rob.

He was trying in vain to tease out of them their ideas.

"We have no great plan. Our only weapon is the media outlets we have and we wonder how long it will be before we are shut down, especially if we carry out our threat to broadcast about all those topics we had up on the screen during Madison's programme that are on her, or rather Pete's, laptop."

"I assume you have made loads of copies?"

"Of course. So many hidden in so many places and with friends we can trust. But we know we are putting them in danger."

It was then that Rob decided to tell them both about the files that Pippa had had stolen from a former Attorney General. He first went through the topics and then one or two in more detail, especially the paedophile rings that they both seemed particularly interested in, although he emphasised he was recalling this just from memory. He realised they were trying to tie up what they knew with the facts that Rob was giving out.

"This all fits. Entirely consistent with what I already knew, and what we were exploring via our investigative reporters at *Franceinfo* and my previous papers, and what Pete had found out."

Quite sensibly, they were all thinking it would be wise to protect themselves. For the same reason that the two women had revealed, Rob told them he had multiple copies in lots of places with lots of people although this was stretching the truth. This they all knew helped to keep them safe. They could not destroy all the evidence just by destroying three people. And if Rob had made a catastrophic error of judgement in trusting Madison and Chantelle, and they were with the enemy then coming after him alone would not stop the condemning evidence of crimes and wrong doing coming out. But Rob had not made an error.

Madison started to cry.

"I never really had any doubts about Pete and what he was up to but this eliminates even the tiniest bit of uncertainty. You don't know what a relief that is. There has been the odd moment when I just wanted to run away from it all."

Chantelle put her arm around Madison. She then sat up straight in a determined manner.

"This makes me feel stronger, empowered, not only to find out what happened to him, but to play my small part in spilling the beans on these bastards and stopping this shit. I felt so alone but Chantelle has become a good friend and hopefully you will help, Rob?"

"I'll do my best. It's something you get sucked into and now I feel I have no choice anyway. I get the impression, maybe wrongly, that we will get further and it'll be less risky, if this was explored in France, Chantelle?"

"I'm not so sure. I think most countries are now under the control of the elite. I think the agenda is the same. There is one almighty game plan. The mainstream media is controlled. It's only mavericks like Pete here and our new TV station over there who are independent enough of the whole gigantic conspiracy. But on balance, you are probably right, we stand more chance in France than here."

Rob agreed.

"The UK has become almost a one-party state as they are all singing from the same hymn sheet and under too much American influence. It has decided to go it alone and make enemies of its closest neighbours in Europe. No one in Britain can be trusted now."

"So I have to say I've already fed it all to my ex-colleagues on *Le Monde Diplomatique* and think they should have your files too, if you agree?"

"Certainly," Rob did not hesitate.

He fumbled in his inside jacket pocket and slid a memory stick across the table.

"Thank you, and in return have this."

A small cellphone was pushed across the table.

"This is how we should communicate. No other way. This phone has the link to just one of my mobiles. If it rings you'll know it's me. It can only be me. But the name that comes up will be Sarah. And if mine rings, if it isn't you, then something serious has happened."

"Wow," exclaimed Rob, "No beating about the bush here then. I'll add it to my collection."

"What is this beating about a bush?" Chantelle queried.

"Oh it's a quaint old English saying, Pete used to say it a lot. Prevarication. It's avoiding coming straight to the point. Pete said the English were experts at never being direct. Beating about the bush is the preamble to the main event of getting birds out of the bushes before a bird hunt. Grouse murderers still use beaters today."

"My wife gets mixed up. She would say beating up the bird or some such incomprehensible exclamation."

"Check out my latest investigation. Broadcast last night. All about forced adoption in England. A hot topic in France. Not reported in the UK. Heard that before, by any chance?"

On leaving The Thornbury and saying goodbye to Madison and Chantelle, Rob felt he had been given new vigour to follow this through to the end. He would not back down now.

On the journey home Rob reflected that her flogging a dead cat was not so funny now after Eric's demise. His death though he could cope with. He found it harder to see Suzy upset.

His train pulled out of Charing Cross on time and crossed the Thames on the Hungerford Bridge. Rob's thirst for history got him to check how long there had been a bridge at that point. His phone told him Isambard Kingdom Brunel built the original in 1845. Claude Monet painted a later version in 1899. He wondered how he could get hold of Chantelle's latest expose. Rob admitted to himself he was just distracting himself from facing the real horrible world. He used history and the past as a comfort blanket.

With a sudden jolt he realised that he would never see Rosa again. No more of those stimulating educational experiences. No more soundings off. Stephen was great to talk to but even when they were serious he did not learn much. Just that Hitler's favourite flower was edelweiss and that the Ledru-Rollin station was on metro line number eight. Would it now be back to inane boredom at dinner parties? Perhaps he needed to pursue these new contacts that were so stimulating? Or would the most exciting discussion be whether Larry the Downing Street cat could successfully beat up Palmerston the Foreign office moggy? Would the cats outlive the Ministries?

After staring out of the window at nothing he texted Jenny to let her know about Rosa.

50 - GOODBYE NOT AU REVOIR

THE INTERNATIONALE

Let racist ignorance be ended
For respect makes the empires fall
Freedom is merely privilege extended
Unless enjoyed by one and all

Billy Bragg (1990)

Rob always meant to introduce Suzy to Rosa but for some strange reason never got around to it.

Rosa was from his life before Suzy. Rosa was from his life with Jenny. But Suzy wanted to accompany him to the funeral nevertheless and he was pleased. She had heard so much about her.

They were both in reflective moods. After two stops on the train journey Rob put his headphones on and plugged into his laptop. He wanted to see Chantelle's latest programme to check on the quality and impartialness of the *Franceinfo* channel's reporting. He had managed to get Pippa to record it onto disc at her work where they have good satellite links and it arrived that very morning as they were leaving the house. Once playing he gave a separate earpiece to Suzy.

"What's the point? You know my French is only school level," Suzy protested.

"Oh ye of little faith. Pippa thought of that. She has managed to get the commentary translated and over-dubbed for us. Great to have all those facilities at work eh? They've sacked all our NHS translators. Cost too much."

"This documentary tells the horrific tale of the thousands of children unjustly removed from their families. It chronicles the families' terrifying experiences of children taken at birth, the threat of future removal whilst mothers are pregnant and the warning of removal directed at women who have not yet had children, solely on a suspicion of future harm to the child. The setting for this documentary is not a lawless, tyrannical country where child rights do not exist. These tragedies are unfolding in a State which is bound by European legislation and is one of France's neighbours, the United Kingdom."

It seemed odd having a man's voice come from Chantelle, but it did not detract. There were shots of children being forcibly removed from their parents by heavy-handed private agency workers with G4S security as back up.

"Bloody hell," said Suzy.

Chantelle continued.

"This film shows the unthinkable. Every year Great Britain sets quotas for the number of children it must remove from parents in order to facilitate adoptions. If these quotas are not met, the local authorities have to pay financial penalties and their budget is cut. Private sector companies, sometimes listed on the stock exchange, are often tasked with placing children with adoptive parents. Children are advertised by these agencies, their details completely exposed and publicly available, with descriptions which include saleable qualities such as positive personality traits."

For about ten minutes case studies were shown to demonstrate the policy, with horrific scenes.

"I can't believe this sort of thing goes on in my name," said Suzy.

"You can understand why it's not reported here," added Rob.

As if to back up Rob's point the next part of the commentary explained why. It was shocking.

"This Human Rights scandal in the heart of Europe stays hidden inside Britain's borders. The law prevents parents and journalists from telling these stories, with the threat of jail if they break their silence. They don't even have the right to mention the name of the child that's been stolen. In an attempt to save English families from this terrible tragedy, several brave wealthy Brits are helping families unjustly threatened with the removal of their children to escape Britain, and resettle in other countries like France. Of course they have to remain anonymous."

The main man giving an interview had a familiar voice to Rob – a gravelly tone, like that of a voice-over for a movie trailer. The camera avoided his face, but occasionally focused on his feet, or hands on his lap. Rob was trying to place the voice. He wore a bow tie and an expensive three-piece pinstriped suit. Then his twitching feet came into shot. Highly polished camel calfskin Stefano Bemer shoes. A dog barked in the background. The penny dropped.

"Bloody hell. It's the Judge!" shouted Rob too loudly forgetting he had headphones on. Several passengers turned towards him with disapproving stares.

"Shush Rob. Stop shouting. What Judge?"

Now in soft tone so that Suzy could hardly hear.

"Felix, my patient. The circuit Judge from Pleasure Towers."

She managed to get the gist.

The mystery man talked about how Britain's child protection sector was unethical, lawless and profiteering. He said he had evidence of abuse and sexual trafficking. He implied some well-known establishment figures were involved and this is why the story has not been covered in the UK.

After the interview Chantelle finished.

"More than two million children are trapped inside social services across England and Wales, their parents locked inside an administrative machine gone mad. Introduced by the Thatcher Government the *Children Act* gives child protection services the power to remove children from parents on a mere suspicion of maltreatment, present or future. A suspicion is all that's needed for a child to be taken away from their parents forever. There is a disturbing and skewed presumption that struggling families and single mothers can never provide stable homes or make good parents. This is occurring despite European legislation. How much worse might this become after UK citizens are no longer under the protection of the rest of Europe?"

Chantelle and her investigative journalism impressed Rob, just when he was convinced it had died out - maybe it had in the UK.

"I thought a funeral would be enough for one day, but that too?" said Suzy.

650

She was apprehensive, as she knew Jenny would be at the funeral and was not sure what sort of reception she would get. She took comfort in thinking punch-ups at funerals were very rare. She did not think she would know any other mourners, who were all beginning to gather at the Islington Crematorium. Rob and Suzy were early.

"Better late than not," said Suzy.

They wanted some fresh air and exercise so walked the mile from East Finchley Station up the High Street. As usual with any building Rob was more interested in its history than its purpose. The Art Deco detail and crematorium glass dome had him date it in the 1930s so he was pleased with himself to read it was opened in 1937.

Rob told Suzy he had no idea what to expect. Although he had known Rosa for nearly thirty years and knew her politics and passions, she never talked much about personal issues. He knew little of her family. So he was interested to see who else would turn up. He need not have worried about a lack of people. There seemed to be large contingents from Maiden Lane and the Market Estate, from Wales and Aberfan in particular. He recognised Megan from her bright ginger hair as she walked in with others. Again she was wearing a short skirt as though she knew her legs were good and she owed it to the world to display them.

Sitting behind were a group who were speaking in German, and behind them a man who could not have been more than forty in an ordinary suit with several medals pinned onto his chest. Even Rob knew he was breaking etiquette. His civilian clothes were not smart enough, he had them on his right chest not left, there was no metal bar and he had a pocket-handkerchief when this really was not the done thing. If there was one thing that annoyed Rob it was people who thought they were more important than they were or wore medals they did not deserve. Who was this man? It was at times like this that Rob wanted to impersonate Peter Cook's character, Sir Arthur Streeb-Greebling, the narrow-minded upper class English duffer and 'tear a strip off the cad', but a funeral was hardly the place.

This was not going to be any ordinary funeral though. Megan alone was seeing to that. And unseen by all, the man with the medals was noting all the attendees. The proceedings were brief with a man called Silas Rutherford delivering the eulogy and only two pieces of music. Rosa requested no religious content. To those who knew her that went without saying. There was to be no service. She was not going to allow the last thing she had any influence over, her 'goodbye' as she put it, to be hijacked by the corrupt funeral business.

Rutherford reminded all present of her admiration for Jessica Mitford's exposé of the abuses of the American funeral homes industry *The American Way Of Death*, told how commercialisation and profit was taking advantage of the bereaved. Rosa admired Decca, as she was known for her renouncing of her privileged background and communism. She was also known as the red sheep of the family. She had no time for the fascist sisters, Diana and Unity.

Like Decca, Rosa insisted on the simplest and cheapest farewell. Rosa had found an orchestral version of *All Things Bright And Beautiful*, which she wanted in commemoration of the disaster at her school. The children were singing it as the slagheap buried them. The event ended with of course the *Internationale* but with Billy Bragg's lyrics. All who knew Rosa well were aware of her favourite lines.

Let racist ignorance be ended
For respect makes the empires fall
Freedom is merely privilege extended
Unless enjoyed by one and all

Silas Rutherford explained he had known Rosa since 1968. They met through his brother who had helped her after getting injured at the Grosvenor Square demo against the Vietnam War. She was an attractive twenty-eight year old teacher and he a lecturer at Oxford and three years younger. Silas said he was keen on Rosa but she was out of his league and was too devoted to politics to have any interest in men. Long-term anyway, he added tantalizingly and suggestively. It was the sixties, after all. There were a few men she had the time of day for. It later turned out Max had beaten him to her when they were in Paris together two months later. Normal mortals might have been jealous. Silas and his twin had been taught by their father that jealousy was silly and just be proud and happy for each other.

There were few nowadays who could claim to have met Nye Bevan, Tom Driberg and Bob Boothby. No one was left in any doubt about the contempt Rosa had for anything that was not in tune with her socialism. According to Silas one of the last gems Rosa had thrown out was, 'If the Americans really believed in capitalism to the exclusion of everything else, why didn't they put the Manhattan Project to develop the atom bomb out to tender?' He had heard his father say the same and he knew they had met but who stole this witticism from whom? To her it was proof, if any more was needed, that if something needed to be done quickly and efficiently the market was not the place to do it. Central planning by skilled, incorrupt experts properly funded could not be beaten. So to Rosa it was a great irony that this was used to manufacture nuclear weapons - something she had fought all her life - but not adopted to do good for mankind.

She thought it hilarious that the British Government had just hosted an Anti-Corruption Summit, likening it to Heineken hosting an anti-alcohol event, or Hugh Hefner an anti-pornography gala. According to Silas, Rosa really did want a political eulogy. She wanted everyone to remember how angry she was that the bailout of the kleptocratic banks cost £1.3 trillion of taxpayers' funds in 2008-9. That over four hundred former government ministers and civil servants since then have passed through the gilded revolving door into lucrative private sector jobs. That accountancy firms like PWC, KPMG, Deloitte and Ernst & Young were crooks and she was not too sure about funeral companies either. Carillion shafted the taxpayer before going bust with £2 billion worth of debts. An ownerless unaccountable company denuded of any purpose except to enrich its directors and keep its shareholders happy. If John Cleese can say 'fuck' at Graham Chapman's wake, why can she not be outrageous too?

Even more rage was saved for the inequality of wealth and the widening gap. How only one per cent of the population, or four hundred and eighty-eight thousand people owned fourteen per cent of the country's assets which amounted to eleven trillion pounds. Seven point three million people or fifteen per cent had no assets or were in debt. This Rosa thought should provoke a revolution, something she had waited all her life for, and now knew would never happen in the shrug-the-shoulders Britain. We had a lot to learn from the French she said. Quite recently, when threatened with redundancy, the workers took the boss hostage. That's the way to go she encouraged.

Silas said that Rosa was angrier than he had ever seen her about Grenfell Tower inferno. It was, she said, a consequence of all of this. Seventy-one deaths produced by capitalism, profit, greed, exploitation, neglect, lack of care and caring, racism, the class system, ethnic cleansing from London, lack of respect for life, contempt for the poor, and incompetence and meanness.

Rosa said her final message was that everyone should read Jane Austen. Right through to her last unfinished novel called *Sandition*, which to her delight describes a property speculator, one of Rosa's pet hates, as a chancer who overreaches in the hope of spectacular returns, the quack among entrepreneurs. She wanted to be cremated with her copy of Mary Wollstonecraft's *A Vindication of the Rights of Woman* and Simone de Beauvoir's *The Second Sex*. A mixing of these molecules would make her more content.

And to show her sense of humour she parted with one final question, what if the hokey cokey is not what it's all about? And with that, Silas indicated through the laughter that that was all they were going to get. The end.

Rosa had told Rob the last time he saw her that she could not decide whether to have William Blum's *God Bless America. And its Bombs* or Martin Niemöller's poem printed in her memorial pamphlet. So she just had a line telling everyone to look them up and learn them both. Typical Rosa.

Rob saw Jenny slip into the back while Mr Rutherford was speaking, and by the time everyone was filing out she had gone. To Rob's astonishment, he also caught the back of what he thought was Felix Denning limping out just a few people behind her. He had Atticus on a lead next to him. His knee-jerk thought was to chase after him and ask him about Chantelle's film he had just seen but this would have appeared unseemly, and anyway, it could wait until the next consultation.

Right at the back there were two mysterious-looking men who seemed to be taking in all around them. Rob's mind raced with possibilities. Before he could work out what to do about the men, he spotted Mr Ephialtes heading towards him in a determined fashion. Rob was expecting to just exchange a few compliments about Rosa. Instead he reached out and held onto Rob's elbow, looked him in the eye.

"You should know that Alexei, my son is dead. He hanged himself."

Rob was stunned, and was completely lost for words, but his years as a GP came to the rescue and he found something appropriate to say. Mr Ephialtes did not want to talk however and just turned and left.

Just as Suzy and Rob had said their goodbyes and started to walk towards the High Street, Silas Rutherford, who to Rob appeared at least mid-seventies, called out to Rob and started to walk briskly in his direction.

"Dr Baigent? Rosa wanted you to have this," and passed Rob an envelope together with her copy of Bevan's *In Pursuit of Peace*, well-thumbed and dog-eared and with Nye's inscription to her on the inside page.

"Thank you for an excellent send-off and humorous eulogy. It warmed us all," Rob said as he slipped the envelope into his jacket pocket, "She was a marvellous woman. So principled. I will miss her."

The Baigents strolled towards the tube station in silence. Eventually Suzy asked who that man was, the one whose son had just killed himself. Rob explained. They had both forgotten about the envelope in his pocket. On the walk to the station Suzy's curiosity got the better of her.

"What was that you were singing in the shower this morning Rob? The words have been haunting me all day."

"Wasn't aware I was singing. If I was you are not supposed to listen."

"The bit I remember was, *there's no one to hear me, there's nothing to say, and no one can stop me from feeling this way.* That's very telling as you sounded like you meant it."

"Oh, that. The Small Faces, *Lazy Sunday Afternoon.* My Dad used to play it. I grew up with it from about the age of four.

"I suppose it could have been worse. You could have been singing Ozzy Osbourne's *Suicide Solution* like my Dad used to when Mum left."

On leaving Charing Cross and going over Hungerford Bridge, Rob did the honour of giving Suzy an unwanted history lesson.

"This bridge became a railway bridge in 1864. Brunel's original was just a footbridge. But the chains from the old bridge were re-used in Bristol's Clifton Suspension Bridge."

A man opposite made a point of demonstrating he was turning up the volume on his headphones, presumably to drown Rob out. The lesson was lost on Suzy anyway. She was fast asleep.

51 - KIND PEOPLE

BOUND AND GAGGED

You can run but you can't hide

I'm keeping her bound and gagged
Her clothes soaked in gasoline
Hands tied behind her back
Where no one can hear her

Creature Feature (2007)

Jeremy always loitered on his way out of school.

He was never in any rush as his regular bus home was twenty minutes after the final bell of the day. Most of his close friends lived in the opposite direction, so he was often alone - not knowing the other boys on his route who seemed so much older but were only in the year above.

Today was no different. He was in a world of his own, reflecting on the French class he had had that afternoon. He feared languages, as he got very nervous performing in public. Especially when he regarded himself as no linguist despite his mother's skills and desire to pass them on. Teenage boys were merciless in taking the piss when friends, let alone outsiders, got things wrong. Not as bad though as teenage girls according to his mates who had sisters. He often wondered what it would be like to have a sister. He would prefer a brother so they could talk about football but his Mum and Dad said that would never happen. His French teacher criticised his accent, saying it was like someone from the cast of *Eastenders* trying to speak French, and all the other boys laughed at his expense.

Like a lot of teenagers, for the first time in his life he started to worry about his health. He had heard of Autism and Asperger's so he had checked them out. He dismissed the idea of Rett syndrome and childhood disintegrative syndrome as well as semantic pragmatic disorder, multi-dimensionally impaired disorder, schizoid personality disorder and schizotypal disorder. He wondered about attention-deficit hyperactivity disorder but in the end concluded he had hypochondriasis, which he did not think was terminal. Not yet anyway. Jeremy was unusual in that most of his friends worried about physical health problems, not mental health. Top of the list were twisted testicles, prominent breast buds and torn traumatised frenula.

As he strolled down the street towards the bus stop, he wondered what it would be like to live on Mars. He had asked his Dad and was told he would miss the football and if he really wanted to know ask David Bowie, whoever he is. He knew he should educate his father so told him that the earth will eventually become too hot to live on, a bit like Venus is now. This is because the sun increases its luminosity by ten per cent every billion years. Mars will move into the habitable zone so we all had to pack our bags and go there. He hoped the journey would be better than his bus ride home. It all ends anyway in seven billion years when our sun star has consumed all the hydrogen fuel in its core and dies.

Jeremy was keen to get home to see if his belated birthday present had arrived. When he asked for *Manifestations of Dark Matter and Variations of the Fundamental Constants in Atoms and Astrophysical Phenomena* by Yevgeny Stadnik, a PhD thesis, Pippa began to get seriously worried about her son. She had been proud to see him devour Stephen Hawking's *A Brief History Of Time* as the only other person she knew who had finished it was Dave. But this was so esoteric and arcane it was eccentric for a teenager who should be rebelling by now. She would have preferred him to ask for all the *Fifty Shades* series - it would have been more normal and certainly cheaper. At least he had his football.

Whilst daydreaming about his present a red van pulled up alongside Jeremy that took him from being in a world of his own to the world he actually lived in. It had a magnetic strip on the side saying School Transport. A woman in the passenger seat wound down the window. She showed him some sort of official-looking ID badge. She seemed nice.

"Jeremy, we've been asked by your Dad, Dave, to collect you to take you straight to the hospital to meet him. I'm afraid your mother has had an accident and is in A&E. She's okay but desperate to see you. It's a short journey as you know, The Royal Bournemouth now they've closed Poole, so jump in."

A shiver went down his spine. He could not bear it if anything happened to either of his parents. He always thought them invincible. How could he possibly cope? What would he do? His mind raced but he had no hesitation or second thoughts about opening the door and getting into the back seat. He wanted just one thing, to be with his mother and know she was going to be all right. Nothing else mattered. Not even Stadnik's book or the Poppies. He was slightly surprised to see another man in the back of the van as he got in, but did not think much of it.

The radio was on and playing *Don't Wanna Know* by Maroon 5 with Kendrick Lamar. He liked that track but would not admit it to his mates. He did not understand the lyrics about past lovers. He was not a lover of lyrics, just the music. The familiarity made him feel secure. But he was worried. He fired question after question at the driver wanting to know what had happened. The lady was very nice. She told him again his mum was okay. She even offered him an apple and blackcurrant smoothie, which he accepted with thanks and drank down immediately. It did not taste quite like he remembered but he did not think anything of it.

She asked if Jeremy had had a nice day. Jeremy thought it all right, but all day he was itching to get home to get his book and, if there was time after homework, to look up more detail about the multiverse he had recently read about.

"Do you know about the multiverse hypothesis?" he asked the lady.

"We live in just one of many universes, in fact an infinite number. We know for sure our Earth is in one solar system among two hundred billion stars and a trillion galaxies, and that's just a small patch of what's out there. There are infinite parallel universes. We are in all those but playing out different scenarios. In one you might be driving a different car. In another it might break down. In another I might have been late out of school and you would have missed me. In another you pick up another pupil. Another where you decide to go to the seaside as my Mum was not in an accident. I wish I were in that one. The alternatives, I mean choices, are infinite. But they are not really choices either, they all really happen simultaneously. Do you know about Schrodinger's cat? It is both dead and alive."

But before Jeremy could hear any reply he had fallen into a deep sleep. In his dream there is a parallel universe in which he decides not to get into the van. In another he declines to drink the smoothie, which had been drugged. He was shouting.

"Don't you understand, we only know about and are aware of the five per cent that is matter? Twenty-five per cent is dark matter, and the rest, the other seventy-five per cent is dark energy... we know so little..."

Middle East 2014
Alan Henning and David Haines - British aid workers beheaded by Daesh or ISIS in revenge for the UK joining the US-led bombing campaign against ISIS.
American journalist James Foley - beheaded by ISIS as a response to American air strikes in Iraq.

2015
Maximilien Rutherford - disappeared in Syria. The Special Operations Team had finally caught up with him.

Sean McColl was quite calm. He knew the end was near. He was still in bed. He now rarely strayed far from it. It was impossible for him to move around his small flat. He had lost so much weight and muscle bulk. He was totally dependent on carers but the privatised company often did not send one, and when they did arrive it was a ten-minute flying visit - never the same person twice either.

His bed was positioned to let him see out of the window at ten stories up in the Adair Tower. He wished however he had had it moved. The carers said it was not their job. Now it gave him a clear but unwelcome view of the burnt out shell of Grenfell Tower, a constant reminder of a tragedy where so many people burnt to death. He thought it was inevitably more than the authorities ever admitted. They claimed it was seventy-one, as though that was okay then. How many more will die from the cancer-causing chemicals and toxins found around the Tower? He had never experienced such a putrid smell.

Sean did not fear death, but he was fussy about the way he died. He had a fear of being burnt alive more than any other ending. He knew of those who suffered in history like the residents of North Kensington. The Oxford Martyrs, the Canterbury Martyrs, Thomas Cranmer, Joan of Arc, Giordano Bruno, the slow roasting of an SS guard to death at the end of World War II by a lynch mob, those burnt to death more recently by ISIS, and of course sati in India. But not Guy Fawkes. The view from his window gave him night terrors.

Comparing his life with others who had suffered more bizarrely comforted him. Not because he wanted others to suffer but he just thought his existence, because that is all it was, could have been worse. He knew there was only one life and, once dead that was it, so he had blown it, or others had on his behalf. The saying 'life ain't no rehearsal' had always felt like a kick in the teeth whenever he heard it. Although it did not apply to Sean, he preferred Mae West's version, *you only live once, but if you do it right, once is enough.* He had not done it right but once was definitely enough.

So his latest bedtime reading was about famous kidnappings. First the baby Lindbergh case. In 1932 the baby of the famous aviator was kidnapped. A man called Hauptmann went to the electric chair for his murder. One investigator was called Schwarzkopf, the father of Norman the commander of Operation Desert Storm in Iraq. There is doubt whether the right man fried. Having lost a child Sean felt close to this one. But he had no sympathy for Lindbergh after reading about his belief in eugenics. Did he organise the kidnap of his own baby as the child was disabled and he could not accept this? Was the intention just to put him into an institution, but the kidnap was bungled and the child ended up dead? He was an anti-Semite, an admirer of Nazi Germany and he accepted a medal from Hermann Goering. He wanted the US to negotiate a neutrality pact with Hitler. He had seven further children with three mistresses in Europe. He lived for a while in Kent. Sean did not like the aviator at all.

Then the kidnapping and murder of the Italian Prime Minister Aldo Moro by the Red Brigade, a left wing paramilitary organisation, which wanted Italy out of NATO. Sean knew differently. He had heard it discussed while in captivity in Dolphin Court. Moro was killed as part of the US Operation Gladio to discredit the left. Steve Pieczenik, working in the State Department at the time, was overheard saying, *we had to sacrifice Moro to maintain the stability of Italy*. The same man claimed the US Government, Israel and Mossad destroyed the Twin Towers as part of a false flag operation. More recently, he had accused the Clintons of effecting a silent civilian coup, which was dealt with by a counter-coup of the intelligence services supplying information to Julian Assange and WikiLeaks. It worked. Hillary was defeated in the presidential race.

His book continued with the kidnapping of Patty Hearst, the granddaughter of William Randolph Hearst the publisher, by the Symbionese Liberation Army, a left wing terrorist group. Sean could not find Symbione on the map, then found out it was not a country but came from the word symbiosis. They wanted political symbiosis of all left wing struggles. Sean first paid attention when the Ramones mentioned the SLA in a track. They played *Judy is a Punk* at the Roundhouse. That was when Sean had just arrived in London before he ran out of money and was rescued by Douglas. Patty became sympathetic towards her captors, called herself Tania and robbed banks. She pleaded Stockholm syndrome but the court did not agree.

John Paul Getty III had his severed ear sent to his father with a ransom demand. The billionaire miser only paid the $2 million that was tax deductible, the rest was a loan to his son. The ear was in poor condition as it was delayed three weeks in a postal strike.

Frank Sinatra's son was kidnapped two weeks after the Dallas killing of Kennedy. The amateur group demanded $240,000 even though Frank Senior offered $1 million.

The Achaeans waged the Trojan War against the city of Troy after Paris took Helen - considered to be the most beautiful woman in the world - from her husband Menelaus, King of Sparta. Not a very exciting story thought Sean.

More relevant to Sean was poor Elisabeth Fritzl. He could empathise and identify with her. She had been kept captive by her father and abused for twenty-four years in their home in Amstetten, Austria. The abuse resulted in the birth of seven children. She escaped in 2008.

His sympathies were also with the three women kidnapped by Ariel Castro in Cleveland and kept captive for over a decade until 2013. Then the wrong woman, Muriel McKay, who was the wife of Rupert Murdoch's deputy - the kidnappers were after Anna, the media tycoon's wife. Muriel was fed to the pigs on the Hertfordshire farm owned by the kidnappers in 1970. Then there was Shergar the racehorse, in 1983, probably kidnapped by the provisional IRA to raise money for arms. He could run but he could not hide.

He was calm, as he really did not want to face further deterioration and become dependent on anyone. So death would be a release. He had heard the click of his front door opening. He knew it was not a carer. He turned to face the wall. He became aware of someone moving about then entering his bedroom. The next and the last thing he knew was a pillow being pushed against his head with so much force he could not move. He did not want to though. He had no desire to resist. Sean's miserable life was mercifully over.

"Is that Kensington Carers?" The man with gloves spoke softly into the telephone. There was a pause.

"Just to let you know Mr McColl wants all care cancelled. His family is taking care of him from now on. Thank you."

52 - DOOM AND GLOOM

LONDON CALLING

London calling, yes, I was there too
An' you know what they said? Well, some of it was true!
London calling at the top of the dial
After all this, won't you give me a smile?

Clash (1979)

"Any questions for Lev?"

"Yes, how much does the CCG and the taxpayer pay you to come here to spout the Government's propaganda and how much do you think this contributes to patient care?"

Every few months the CCG organised a compulsory education event, often at the local private hospital that was touting for business. There was a marked increase in the fidgeting, a few embarrassed raised eyebrows and the atmosphere soured as Rob made his point. GPs generally were not rude people and, even if most in the room agreed with him, few would actually say anything. Rob would often spend the last five minutes of a talk crafting a carefully worded comment or question, but this just came out. He shot from the hip.

Clive, who was sitting next to him whispered.

"You really should increase your Tourette's medication."

But Rob was fuming. His mood had not been improved by learning as he left the surgery that Mr Albert had died suddenly at home. Clearly his aortic aneurysm had burst. Murdered by the cuts-induced lack of beds.

The Chair who said that fees were a commercially sensitive issue and none of his business rescued the guest speaker. Lev Bronstein was from the NHS Confederation, which Rob regarded as a front organisation set up to promote and carry out the Government's privatisation and cuts agenda, whilst allowing the Government to distance itself and pretend that the ideas came from these experts, so the public should listen. Clinically led was the spin – and the public included GPs of course.

What angered Rob was that the GPs present seemed as clueless as the general public at the wanton destruction going on. The NHS Confederation had been doing its worst since its original version got off the ground, strangely enough at exactly the same time the ridiculously wasteful and ideological market was introduced into the NHS.

"Funny that," Rob had been heard to say, cynically.

Its members are those organisations that commission and provide NHS services. Its current Chairman is the latest ex-Health Minister, ex-MP sleazebag going through the revolving door of jobs they set up for themselves. This is not to be confused with the NHS Support Federation who are the good guys fighting to save the NHS. This had been founded by the only good teacher Rob had had at Guy's, Professor Harry Keen. A wonderful man Rob remembered. Qualified on the first day of the NHS, 5th July 1948. So kind to everyone. An uncle, by marriage, to David and Ed Miliband.

"Pity they didn't pay more attention to him on the NHS," Rob said to Suzy as he read Harry's obituary in 2013.

Rob got frustrated with his colleagues who did not know one organisation from the other, which he aligned to not knowing one's arse from one's elbow. In Rob's eyes three groups all shared the blame for the present sorry state of affairs - the politicians of course, but also two strands from his profession, its so-called leaders and the troops. But it was not as in the First World War lions led by donkeys, more like lemmings led by sheep.

In his professional lifetime he had witnessed doctors who fancied themselves as amateur political movers and shakers, and they certainly were amateur, being outmanoeuvred at every step by the professionals. Some were naive do-gooders, some cooperating quislings. Some well meaning maybe, but most just got turned on by mixing with those with influence and the well known, and by walking the corridors of power - to be able to boast to friends and family about that meeting with the Minister - but a walk down the corridors of power was as far as it ever went. They achieved and influenced little, as they were wrong-footed on their walk all the way, never seeing the bigger picture. Just dealing with what to them seemed like individual, relatively insignificant decisions one by one - salami slicing - and never looking up to notice where they were being led. Outwitted at every turn and led by the nose to downgrade their profession, castrate it, and to cooperate in the destruction of the NHS.

Then the third group, the troops – the group that he and Clive belonged to – just going along with it. Moaning yes, but not prepared to put up a fight. They all claimed to be too busy with the day job. Being at the coalface did not allow them the time to mess around in talking-shops or spend days in meetings. They could not or would not see that the coal mine was collapsing on top of them. They did feel they were being buried alive, but by the workload. They failed to connect the politics with their working lives.

So in less than thirty years the medical world had travelled from a highly regarded profession to just another bunch of workers - highly trained experts, to dispensable technicians. Consultants were now two a penny and knew everything about one small part of the body and nothing about the rest. Goodbye the holistic approach to the whole patient. GPs were no longer family doctors with continuity of care throughout their patients' individual lives, often caring for four generations, but had been turned into strangers to all who walked through the door. With no continuity or familiarity there was no trust. With no trust complaints escalated, egged on by the media and Government who were only too pleased to see rivals for the public's affection kicked when they are down, tripped over by them, but tripping over their own feet too.

It was so obvious to Rob now that the two main requests of the insurance industry before it took over the healthcare of the nation was the need for less care and cheaper downgraded staff. This would allow the companies to maximize their profits - their top priority and duty to their shareholders, which went way beyond quality or safety. It was all on the Nixon tapes. Rob told whoever was listening.

"We've been turned into box-ticking robots who are told how to treat, what with, who by, whether we are allowed to investigate or refer, to whom, and micromanaged by overpaid little 'Stalins' who haven't got a clue what a GP's job should be. Getting rid of individual GP lists, promoting dual registration, abolishing practice boundaries, selling off confidential patient data, all designed to help the transition to American Accountable Care Organisations, all insurance-based. Then there is the shift work in hospitals so no one takes responsibility for anything. And don't start me on the educationalists," Rob would say when on one of his rants, "A bunch of prima donnas in their ivory towers who are no good at being proper doctors themselves but they think they can tell others how to practise. We only have ourselves to blame too. It isn't just the politicians and our glorious leaders," he was convinced, "we have all been complicit in the destruction of our greatest social asset."

He thought that perhaps so many generations down the line from the beginning of the NHS we had got too used to it, too complacent and no recall of what our world was like without it and that we do not value it as we should. It has all been so tempting for those from Thatcher's I'm-all-right-Jack-sod-you generation to think the grass may be greener elsewhere and to wonder why they should subsidise those who loaf on their settees every day, with drawn curtains, watching *Jeremy Kyle*, to conclude that everyone should pay for their own healthcare and to turn it into an ideological commodity. The American attitude was creeping in like *Triffids*.

Suzy had told him about that old Murdoch journalist who has a head like a ginger acorn and now presented for the *BBC* questioning why the young should pay more tax for good healthcare when it is the old who use it.

"Selfish ignorant short-sighted right wing bastard," she said, "Even the way they pose the question exposes their bias. Why is tax always a tax burden? Without tax you'd have no services at all. And what is all this about a Brexit dividend? Again this exposes what they think about that disaster."

Rob was proud. He had delighted in telling Clive the story. Both remembered the time when altruism was unquestioned. We should look after our fellow man and those more fortunate should help those less fortunate without blinking. Thatcher closed their eyes tight to that. Everyone should stand on their own two feet, even those without feet.

One of his friends actually said once.

"Do you really think all your protesting does any good at all, Rob?"

To Rob that summed it all up and the passivity of society and the masses today - just passive grudging acceptance of their lot and an almost disdainful attitude to anyone who puts up a fight. But he did hit a raw nerve. Certainly attracting why-rock-the-boat-it's-embarrassing glances. Looked upon in the same way a five-year-old when he or she throws a temper tantrum at a friend's birthday party because the cake has not been shared out equally. An embarrassment to the parents - they should be grateful there was a cake at all and if darling Felicity ate most of it good for her.

"Why can't we be a bit more like the French?" Rob would ask, "Burn the barricades and take a few bosses hostage."

Nowadays Rob tried to avoid the typical dinner party *Guardian* readers, good at moaning and putting the world to rights, but actually too comfortably off themselves to be bothered to stick their heads above the parapet in a meaningful way that would actually make a difference. Except at Stephen and Ellie's. Patting themselves on the back for putting money into an Oxfam charity tin when it is waved under their noses, but making sure as many people as possible saw them. Feeling pious for reading *Ethical Consumer*. A rich person giving money away may feel smug but should not be congratulated unless he or she has given enough away to negatively affect their own lifestyle - a rare event indeed.

Not only that but sharing the dinner table with rich neighbours who just happen to be funding their third home in the Dordogne from creaming off taxpayers' money as management consultants to the NHS. They were often in the revolving door of in and out of the NHS, private healthcare companies, management firms and sometimes politics. Rob once accused a fellow guest at Stephen and Ellie's of being a vulture whose job it was to go into a place and set fire to it then sell extinguishers. They were paid to solve problems they created in the first place.

Celeste Venard, Rob's practice nurse had cornered him a few days ago to tell him about a study that had shown a definite positive relationship between management consulting expenditure and organisational inefficiency - the direct opposite of its supposed aim. He began to think her nickname of 'Mogadon' may not be fully deserved after all. Telling the assembled group about this did little to improve the atmosphere, but he was dismissed as a leftie.

Rob did not mind that but what did upset and alarm him was harder to swallow. These people honestly could not see the problem with getting rich at someone else's considerable expense, and he did not mean only financially either. They thought everyone should play the game of seeing how much they could leach from each other and how much taxpayers' money they could syphon off - the ultimate *Monopoly* game. What made Rob want to puke all over them was that it was often the same people who bemoaned paying taxes, and about poor public services, and complained that their public school fees and horses were keeping them poor. If only Rosa was with him to help make his case. She was far better at articulating.

Then there are the rest - the white-van-man and the genuinely hard done by. The army of losers produced by the free market. These people want to give someone a damn good kicking to help assuage their anger, but not realising that those they lash out against are almost certainly the wrong target. Some even say they cannot be bothered with politics, it is boring - not understanding that it is politics that is responsible for their predicament. The politicians have not only successfully disconnected themselves from blame, but have turned it around and claimed that they are their champions.

So it was no longer left and right in politics but now the fault line was between the somewheres and the anywheres. The somewheres live in small towns, they like tradition, and hate immigration. The anywheres are the city-dwellers, more liberal and internationally minded, with more qualifications. Giselle told Rob the same was happening in France where globalisation had benefitted the second group who voted in Macron, whilst the somewheres had lost out and joined the far right and the far left.

"It's all in a book by Christophe Guilluy called *Le Crepuscule de la France D'En Haut*, or to you Rob *The Twilight of the French Elite*," Giselle had said.

Unusually, Clive had suggested several more times that they adjourn to the pub. He had never done that before. What the hell? Then the request for questions. Clive feared what was coming next, as Rob stood up.

"Yes. The Adam Smith Institute has said doctors are low tech prescribing machines, anaesthetists are like coffee baristas, we are all overpaid, and the *Telegraph* has stated that the high tech takeover will make doctors as redundant as coal miners in a generation. When are you all going to start the fight back or are you all just a bunch of lemmings who are taking the gamble that it won't come in your professional lifetime? Have any of you even heard of the *Naylor Review*, which outlines plans for the mass transfer of NHS assets on the cheap into private hands, and land to property developers. Or understand how STPs are destroying our NHS? Or know about the thirty million pounds being paid in just this area to vultures who are doing the Government's dirty work for them?"

"Thank you Dr Baigent. I'm afraid we are running behind schedule. Time for tea," the Chairman stood up to thank the hosts.

"And a question for you Wiekser. Is the rumour true that you've done a deal with UnitedHealth's subsidiary Optum to act as a referral gateway operator, like in Ealing? Are they now responsible for all the financial decision making and do you deny you've given them access to all medical records?"

But he was drowned out at the end of his question by the rush for refreshments, which seemed more important to most.

"Come on Clive, this is a waste of time."

Clive followed, shrugging his shoulders towards the Chair. He spotted James Wiekser heading in their direction. They walked down the stairs towards the exit.

"You seem particularly pissed off today Rob," said Clive.

He was hoping for a civil reply and explanation. He got it.

"Well, apart from all that wanky-shit we've just been exposed to, Jean the receptionist told me, in her detached way as I was leaving the surgery, that poor old Mr Albert's aneurysm finally let rip. His wife stood helpless while he exsanguinated on the kitchen floor. Married fifty-two years and a preventable death. Caused by the cuts. That's one reason I'm so angry. I must go to see his widow, but a pint first. I don't think she will take consolation from me telling her at least he outlived Einstein. His burst at seventy-six. Did you know he had had his reinforced with cellophane in 1948. Kept him going another seven years. You thought E=MC2 stood for kinetic energy equals mass times the speed of light squared didn't you? Well it actually meant Existence equals Multi-layered Cellophane squared."

James Wiekser caught up with them, slightly out of breath. Rob knew he was in for an ear bashing but did not care. He thought he would get his attack in first.

"A bit of the old dyspnoea, James. You ought to lose some weight. Too much time behind a desk trying to decide which service to cut next, perhaps?"

"You risk a charge of bringing our profession into disrepute, Rob."

"Dr Baigent to you. You have a fucking cheek. If anyone is dragging us down its you lot of arse-lickers, creeping amongst the NHS destroyers and ripping off the taxpayer in the process."

"You cannot talk to me like that, and you were disrespectful to today's speakers."

"Fuck off. They don't deserve respect for privatising our health service. Did you bother to check this parasite out before you hired him for the afternoon? Did you know he is a paid adviser to Virgin, G4S and Serco? And how much do you take from this private palace of death? You shouldn't run these events from a private hospital."

Wiekser knew he would not get anywhere but his challenge had made the point to other GPs in the room that he would chase dissent and not tolerate those who stepped out of line.

"We have to keep within budget. We are over-spent. We have no choice. We can't afford the NHS anymore."

Clive added his contribution.

"Not overspent. Underfunded. If you had any self-respect you'd be fighting for more investment, as that is what it is, an investment. And when you don't get it, resigning."

Wiekser turned and muttered whilst walking back towards the conference room.

"We will see what the GMC has to say about this."

Wiekser had also just been accused, as he saw it, of taking backhanders. Maybe though he now had enough evidence to finally get that thorn in the CCG's side. Rob wondered what Jerry had meant that night when he said Wiekser 'would be a little easier' on him. If that were true he had yet to see it.

Behind the reception desk a G4S security guard was chatting up a stunning lady with beautiful blond hair while she filed her nails. There were leaflets advertising the services of the private hospital on the desk. A poster with most of the ugly mugs of his orthopaedic consultant mates posing in the grounds stared out at him.

"That must be photo-shopped. James has had his wrinkles airbrushed out. Either that or he gets free botox here," said Rob to Clive as they reached the bottom of the stairs.

"They are almost drooling at the money heading their way Rob," said Clive.

Then a sign for, 'NHS-paid patients. Selected procedures - those listed on the NHS e-referral web portal - are available to patients accessing treatment through Patient Choice'. Rob knew what they meant by selected procedures - those that make a profit. It was not really patient choice either, but private company choice if they thought you would make them money. Leeches. At least their advert claiming, 'Cancer patients who go private survive longer' had been banned.

He thought they should be taken to task for making a big deal of all the screening blood tests they offer, as most of these are a con and produce meaningless findings – and for many of them, if the results are abnormal you would be dead anyway. Cheating bastards. Worrying more of the worried well. And when an abnormal test result turned up they would not know what to do with it so they hand over the problem to the patient's own NHS GP. How many unnecessary abortions had there been because of the private sector's misuse and misreading of antenatal screening tests?

Another poster proclaimed, 'Have a PSA blood test to see if you have prostate cancer. Yearly checks recommended'.

"Lying bastards. Totally evidence free. Have a blood test so we can take your prostate out unnecessarily and make a mint out of you, would be nearer the truth. Then make more money by trying to treat the erectile dysfunction caused by unnecessary surgery. Thieving dangerous unscrupulous bastards."

Once through the front door they saw a G4S ambulance trying to get a trolley into the back. It looked like the trolley size was incompatible with the door of their new van. The two G4S staff were trying to force it, jolting the patient around. 'G4S working in partnership with the NHS' was one of the most annoying slogans. Designed to pretend the ambulance service had not been privatised. Rob had heard about Jim Auger's stickers. A load of incompetent crooks who could not even fulfil their 2012 Olympic contract.

"Hello Dr Baigent," a weak voice was heard from one end.

"Rob, someone is saying hello," said Clive, "The patient on the gurney," continued Clive who did not know whether a male or female was calling.

Rob walked over and immediately recognised Mrs Nuffield the forty-eight year old solicitor who had self-referred for a hernia repair. Rob knew about it only because she had left an insurance claim form at the surgery for him to sign.

"Hello, Mrs Nuffield, what's happening to you?" said Rob, faking as much concern as possible.

She had a drip running and a monitor beeping. A rather pissed off nurse was with her raising her eyebrows at her colleague's incompetence.

"It went a bit wrong, doc. I thought the surgery was straightforward but then they couldn't stop the bleeding. They say there is something wrong with my blood now. Something to do with clotting. And the whole thing is infected. They tell me they can't deal with it here so I'm having to be transferred to the NHS hospital to sort out the mess. Pity. The surgeon was so nice. Lovely blue eyes. He said I should call him Nigel."

Rob did his best to make her feel at ease and better about her predicament and complications. He wished her well and resisted saying why did you risk your life with these charlatans in the first place?

As they walked away he said to Clive.

"Would you let old Carnicero operate on you, especially in a place with no back-up facilities? No medical cover at night at all. Patients have no idea the risks they are taking."

"I'd run a mile. He's too dangerous."

"I had to sign her insurance claim. She had all sorts of investigations she didn't need, poor love. Seems that they missed her clotting problem though, doesn't it? My duty, according to the Government and GMC is to whistleblow of course."

"Yer, right," said Clive sceptically, "and wave bye-bye to a career? There's no support for whistle-blowers. The BMA and Government completely shat on that heroic Dr Day."

"But perhaps this is the evidence we need to stop Nigel Carnicero after all. What is outrageous is that these private places are not under the same scrutiny as NHS facilities. They get away with bad practice and the public don't know."

"Of course. Government policy is private good, public bad. They want to denigrate the NHS and boost the private sector. It's not only ideology, it's money in their back pockets too."

They continued their walk to the car park. They noticed quite a few cars had been clamped. Rob muttered almost to himself.

"Yes, private good, as loads of money to me. Public bad, as in loads of my money spent on someone else. Sums up their attitude, eh?"

Then he said more clearly.

"I suppose we'd better take both cars in case we get a call."

That afternoon practice patients were covered by the new private company that had taken over the out-of-hours contract. Rumour was that it was undercutting the existing service by several million but commercial confidentiality kept this secret. The old service was cut to the bone so all the local GPs feared how this lot would cope. At least the old service was theirs allowing more continuity of care, and an ethos that meant you took pride in a good service, as you did not want to let your fellow colleagues down, let alone the patients. How this new bunch of charlatans actually coped was by being desensitised to the suffering of patients, letting them wait, fobbing them off, not turning up to see them at all. And, of course, putting off doing what they should have done, and avoiding doing anything useful by passing the buck back to the GP at the next day's surgery, by which time harm had already been done. So unlike before, both Rob and Clive half expected a call saying the service was too busy, could they deal with it.

Once before when this happened Rob found himself shouting down the phone at the ex-supermarket manager who ran the show.

"Of course you are too busy, you don't employ enough doctors and nurses. You are always too fucking busy. Your service is crap. Sorry, I shouldn't have used that word service, you are just a business, with only one aim, lining your own fucking pockets."

A few days later Rob got a letter from Healthcare 24 'a service you can trust', saying they no longer wished to offer Dr Baigent shifts working for the service as they had doubts about his suitability. Since it had hit the headlines that one night the service had only two doctors covering for 1.4 million patients he did not want to work for them again anyway.

After a very short drive they both pulled up in the pub car park, Clive carefully leaving his car several spaces away from Rob.

"So I assume you are thirsty?"

Clive knew he was pushing at an open door, this time the door of the Bell and Jorrocks. As always happens they went in promising to only have one pint, after all it was the middle of the afternoon, but staying for two. Len the barman who was also a patient greeted them.

"Hello doctors, good to see you so early in the day," he said with a touch of jovial sarcasm.

Len was an odd character. Totally deferential when in the surgery, but when someone was on his territory you knew who was boss.

"Cured all of your patients, have you?" he said cheekily.

"All except you," Clive shot back.

That was a reply Rob would not have used.

"So the *Daily Mail* is right. You GPs do only work a few half days a week for a fortune," Len said, but could not finish with a straight face.

As Rob was handed his change, he noticed two men in the corner who looked familiar. Patients perhaps? He did not give this another thought as he was keen to carry on his aggressive tirade against the medical insurance industry.

"It's worth five billion pounds now. We all know private medicine over investigates, over treats, and people get surgery they don't need. In the US they reckon at least a third of all healthcare activity brings no benefits to patients, but plenty to shareholders."

Clive knew the facts but seemed calmer about it.

"They have managed to brainwash the public that if you pay for things out of your own pocket, it must be better. Rarely is that true. And in medicine every link in the private chain provides another financial incentive to do more to you and we've both seen how dangerous that can be. Carnicero is a good example."

Rob had also given this speech to Suzy before.

"I just can't believe the idiocy of dragging us down the American route, can you? I've thought long and hard about this and tried to figure out why anyone would think this a good idea. Applying logic, they are either stupid or evil. Stupidity you can forgive. There is usually no malice and it just requires education. But why put the village idiot in charge of healthcare. Evil can't be forgiven though. The evil reasons are easy to identify. One, I can get very rich from someone's misfortune. And the more ill they are (or I make them) the richer I can become. Two, altruism and the selfless concern for the wellbeing of others is a naive socialist idea that should be strangled at birth. It removes incentives for people to help themselves and it inconveniences me. Three, reciprocal altruism, where someone benefits at the giver's expense, is even worse and just plain stupid. In other words why should I help pay for someone else's healthcare? What's in it for me? That was the *BBC* ginger acorn-head's point. This is catch twenty-four where greed overpowers selflessness, stupidity wins over intelligence and evil is triumphant over good. Hidden agendas ruling the world."

It was only a few weeks before that the two of them had been in the same seats in the Bell and Jorrocks putting the world to rights with Len smiling at them. Now Rob regretted not explaining to Clive what *Catch-22* meant at the time. He thought Clive was following his logic, but was not quite sure as he appeared a little distracted. So he did not bother explaining catch twenty-four either.

"This explains why that stupid, ignorant, bigoted, racist, chauvinist, misogynist, anti-disabled, homophobic, wanker of a new American President has buggered up Obamacare. In order to help out the undeserving tens of millions of fellow citizens, perhaps saving many lives that don't deserve to be saved, they say to themselves our insurance premiums have gone up. Well, fuck that, why should I pay more? But of course being evil or stupid aren't mutually exclusive. If they think after getting rid of Obamacare the insurance companies will put their premiums back down then they are stupid too. The companies only agreed to what suited them. More customers to rip off. That's why some nicknamed it the 'Health Insurance Profit Protection and Enhancement Act'."

"You wouldn't vote for him then?" Clive teased.

Rob smiled but did not rise to the bait. This was too serious and made him too angry.

"No, but I think Suzy's brother over in the States may shoot him though. It's his right under the *Second Amendment* 1791 to carry and use a Kalashnikov AK-74."

"Only the Americans can turn a disaster into a business opportunity. The more injured the better. Hospital managers licking their lips at the prospect of new business."

"Does it really make a scrap of difference who you vote for nowadays anyway? And the public's willingness to put up with politicians is evaporating so much that they'd rather have a known liar in the White House because he says he isn't a politician. A man who actually believes what he says even though it is crap and often contradictory. Better than those who don't believe what they say but have to pretend or they might not get to hold influential positions or make a mint. Like climate change deniers or those who pretend the US has a good healthcare system, so good it has to be imposed on the rest of the world.

So a minuscule shift in the right direction in the USA has been wiped out with the end of the *Patient Protection and Affordable Care Act*. They spend thirty-six per cent on administration. Seven hundred and fifty billion dollars a year of healthcare expenditure is wasted through fraud, overcharging and unnecessary treatment. Just that would run our entire NHS properly for five years! Only the other day over four hundred individuals, many of them doctors and nurses in more than thirty States were charged with false billings. One drug treatment centre owner recruited addicts from other States filing fifty-eight million dollars in fraudulent claims, a problem that is heading in our direction with the commercialisation that's going on. Sixty-two per cent of US personal bankruptcies are due to medical bills and seventy-eight per cent of these even had insurance. The insurance companies control everything and often dictate who your doctor is. In the UK the price of private health cover has quadrupled in the last decade. Complaints have surged.

And back to the politicians responsible. Here so many MPs have a financial interest in private healthcare companies. Why don't the public care about this? They rise up to kick the Establishment, which explains recent incredible and shocking election results, but they still fail to get it. It's all gone wrong since the top elite decided to use neo-liberalism to rip off everyone else causing a huge increasing wealth gap. They fail to get it as the elite who control their minds have fed them all the usual scapegoats."

There was a pause.

"I know you think I'm a conspiracy nut, but I truly believe what we have been talking about is all just one small cog in a much bigger machine."

Clive was not very reassuring.

"I'm sure some of it is true. But don't you think you take life a little too seriously? You know what they say? More smiling, less worrying. More compassion, less judgment. More blessed, less stressed. More love, less hate."

"Are you on drugs?" Rob joked, "You sound like Mother Teresa."

Clive faked a chuckle.

"Newton's third law of motion. For every action there is an equal and opposite reaction."

Rob was not about to drop his serious face.

"From what I've learnt it is all a massive right wing plan which originated before the war and was outlined and put into action at the Bretton Woods conference in 1944. All top secret of course with decoys left, right and centre to put the public off the scent."

He considered telling Clive about Rosa, his fount of knowledge, inspiration and the one who had taken his blinkers off, but decided that was unnecessary detail. Besides there were others who contributed, like Felix who he knew he should not mention. Rob went on to tell Clive that he had met an American recently whose English husband had disappeared three years ago.

"He was a journalist and had found out a lot about all this. From what I gather he has uncovered all sorts of terrible scandals that are all linked. I saw a news item on French television. It seems the British and American media aren't interested."

Rob knew he was not explaining it very well, but how could such a huge conspiracy, bigger than anything the world had seen, be explained easily, and even if it was, how could it be thought credible by anyone? His thoughts were confirmed when Clive responded with trivialising the chat.

"French TV eh? The porn on our channels not good enough for you?"

It was also fairly evident that Clive probably thought Bretton Woods was a park near Basildon.

Bob thought he had better move on.

"Sorry Clive, I know you have heard all this. What I really must discuss with you is this practice money problem. You must be as worried as me. Any thoughts?"

"Not really. You know money and practice finance isn't my thing. I never have got to grips with it."

"Strange we aren't seeing Michael this week as planned. He and Giselle seem to be blaming each other for cancelling. I'm sure there is a simple explanation for that, but not to where the money has gone?"

The conversation flowed less easily as Clive seemed in a reflective mood, or so Rob thought. He had changed quite abruptly from being jovial to looking anxious and avoiding eye contact.

Rob had had enough that day and, although the afternoon pint relaxed him, he thought he would like to get back home early. But he should call in on Mrs Albert first. He could still beat Suzy to make the house welcoming and get the dinner on so they could settle down to an evening of escapism in front of the last series of *House of Cards* - they were both annoyed that Kevin Spacey had deprived them of the cancelled final series by his actions. But it all depended on her train getting her back at a reasonable hour.

On leaving, Rob initially could not see his car, as it was obscured by a red van parked in front.

"See you tomorrow," said Clive.

"Oh," Rob said, "Did you see Gatlin finally beat Bolt? Do we really need any more evidence that cheats actually do prosper? And you know Newton's fourth law? Anything that can go wrong will go wrong. But Mrs Newton had a better version. Anything that can go wrong is Mr Newton's fault."

Clive smiled then turned to walk briskly in the opposite direction towards his car, which was next to a black Audi. He got in quickly and drove off as fast as he could, trying to pretend to be blind to the commotion occurring the other side of the car park.

It all happened in the blink of an eye. As Rob walked between the two vehicles and clicked his remote control to open his Seat's door, he saw that the van had a dent in the front wing, blue paint on it and a smashed headlight. Suzy's description. But it was too late. A large man approached from the other side and quickly pulled a sack over Rob's head whilst another, who had jumped out of the passenger side of the van, bear-hugged him from behind restraining his arms and making resistance useless. Rob was pushed head first through the van door where a third man thrust his covered head down into the gap behind the drivers seat.

Totally bewildered, Rob did not make a sound. Too late he realised the two mystery men in the corner of the pub were at the back at Rosa's funeral.

53 - GUILT AND BLACKMAIL

THANK YOU

So thank you for showing me,
That best friends cannot be trusted,
And thank you for lying to me,
Your friendship, the good times we had you can have them back

Simple Plan (2004)

Clive headed out on his journey straight home.

He was shaking, wondering how he had got himself into such a mess. But he was told of one more job. One more meeting where he would get the incriminating evidence against him returned. He felt guilty, as Rob had always been good to him, but assumed and was promised he would come to no real harm. He had been told they just wanted to scare him, to stop his subversive damaging unpatriotic ramblings. He would come to no physical harm.

Clive reflected on his lack of choice. Once they threatened to tell his wife about Giselle and the police about the money disappearing from the practice he had to cooperate. From what Rob said about Giselle and Michael's stories not adding up, was he onto them? Was he naive enough to believe that it would stop here - that they would now leave him alone? He would soon find out.

He pulled into the picnic spot, relieved that there were no other cars there. Would they turn up? A few minutes passed and then he saw a car indicate to also turn into the parking area. Hopefully it was them, so he could get home. He knew he would face questioning over Rob's abduction so the less time unaccounted for the better.

To Clive's discomfort and alarm it was not what he needed to see, but Mr and Mrs Vittne. They were a pleasant retired couple that had been on his list since he joined the practice. It was she who had polymyalgia rheumatica and thought Clive was a brilliant doctor once he had given her the steroids she needed. The response was always so dramatic that the patients started to believe in miracles and the fortunate doctor got the credit. He came just once a year for his hypertension monitoring so Clive did not know him so well. They had come to walk their dog.

"Hello, doctor," said Mrs Vittne, "getting some fresh air?" she continued.

"Yes, just wanted to stretch my legs on the way home."

"Well, you've nice weather for it. I can now walk the dog again thanks to you. Good evening."

Fortunately they were a fairly formal couple that still looked at their GP with some respect, so did not think it their place to get friendlier. He could think of other patients who would have stood talking all evening. Clive realised bumping into them might not be so bad as they could verify where he was at a certain time. To help with that, Clive said, more loudly as they were turning their backs to walk off.

"Mrs Vittne, do you have the time? I've just realised my watch battery has gone."

"Yes, it's five forty-five."

"Five forty-five. A quarter to six. Thank you," Clive repeated, to emphasise the point.

It would not be too clever though if he was still there when they returned from the dog walk, or saw him with anyone, he pondered. To his relief another car pulled in just as Mr and Mrs Vittne turned the corner behind a row of thick conifers. It was one lone man. He wore reflector sunglasses. He parked next to Clive and wound down the window. He obviously had no intention of getting out.

"Dr Lister, I have this for you."

The man gave Clive a large A3 brown envelope that clearly contained documents.

"One question. Did Baigent mention an English journalist disappearing a few years back? Married to an American."

Clive thought the safest route was to lie.

"No, not that I remember."

"I will make contact again soon to see if your memory has improved."

"I've done all you asked of me. You promised Dr Baigent will come to no harm, so I hope you meant it. Will you leave me alone now?"

"We may have one or two little jobs for you, but nothing too compromising. You are one of us now, whether you like it or not."

With that he drove off.

Clive thought it time to leave before the Vittnes got back. He had four miles of his journey home to find a quiet spot to check what he had been given and to dispose of it. On the drive he realised that if he put a foot wrong and Rob got suspicious of his loyalty, or worse, any part in what had just happened in the pub car park, their friendship would be over, the good times forgotten, his lying would be exposed.

He knew of a turning into a farmer's field where he could park discreetly behind a hedge. It used to be a regular meeting place with Giselle, at least until rather embarrassingly the farmer, who fortunately was a patient at a neighbouring practice, moved them on. They used to sneak off together at lunchtime. They were at it like rabbits and in the open air too - at least for that first six-month period - to be resumed again later. In the early days they took daring, quite stupid, risks. It occurred to him Giselle might have liked dogging, but that was not his cup of tea. As he approached a tractor was coming out. He had to drive straight past. He recognised the farmer.

"Damn!" he exclaimed out loud.

There was the first place they had met though. A place they had abandoned as too muddy. One afternoon they both returned to surgery to be asked, separately by different people fortunately, where they had been to get so much mud on their shoes that had dirtied the surgery carpet. The early days of passion often made people take risks, and often made them blind to suspicion. Or was recklessness part of the thrill?

He turned right down the farm track. It was as muddy as ever. He parked and attempted to get out without sinking too deep in a combination of manure and mud. His laptop was in the boot. He just hoped it had enough battery left.

"Bollocks," he said as he sank.

He had an old towel in the boot and returned to the car with that and his laptop. He opened the brown envelope. This seemed what he wanted. The true and the forged altered practice accounts and bank statements. He had no idea how these people knew about what he and Giselle were up to and how they could possibly know about the new off-shore bank account they were siphoning money into. He had no chance of finding out either, as he was clueless as to who they were. He just knew he was at their mercy now and had dug himself into a much deeper hole than originally intended.

Then there was the smaller envelope that contained photos. One of him and Giselle in a restaurant, one walking along Beachy Head, one of Clive leaving Giselle's house and then several of them in that field, some naked buttocks - his. It was obvious what they were doing. One was clearly at Furnace Pond, and that must be recent. The only other one not showing both their faces was when Giselle clearly had her head in Clive's lap, and he was obviously enjoying something. He put the memory stick into his laptop. This took his breath away. It was almost pornographic. No, it was pornographic. There was no doubt it was Giselle and him filmed in her bedroom. Someone had gone to a lot of trouble to set this up. Who were they? How did they know? It was not often they met at her house, only usually during the day when the children were at school and Derek was on a business trip from the City. Clive knew he had to watch it until the end to make sure he knew exactly what material they had on them both. It took over ten minutes before the camera went dead.

"I didn't realise I was such a stud," he said to himself.

He knew damn well he always thought he was, even if the women in his life did not. He knew he could not take any of this into his house so he left the documents and photos in the boot to be shredded at the surgery the next day.

After pulling out of the track onto the country lane he turned into the first lay-by. There he got two flat stones, just bigger than the memory stick, sandwiched the stick between them and put it under his front wheel. He then ran it over and crushed it out of existence.

Having wiped the stick already he wondered why he had really needed to do that. Of course he also wondered if it was the only copy. He had heard tales of clever geeks being able to revive erased material though. He did not know if it was true. But was it just to make sure no one would be able to see what he had just witnessed, or was he trying to make a bigger statement to himself - to exorcise his guilt?

54 - MISSING AND MOURNING

YOU'RE MY WORLD

You're my world, you are my night and day
You're my world, you're every prayer I say
If our love ceases to be
Then it's the end of my world, end of my world,
End of my world for me

Cilla Black (1964)

Dave's face said it all. He had not looked like that, not even when his Dad died.

As Pippa opened the front door and saw him staring straight at her with sad eyes, she knew something was wrong. She had never seen such horror radiating from her husband. He always greeted her with a broad smile and a hug when she returned from work. He usually had several hours after his round to chill out and relax. This was out of character and frightening. She did not bother to close the door.

"What's the matter?"

In the time it took her to say these words she had lived several nightmares. One of their remaining parents? A friend? A financial disaster? Dave is having an affair. Nothing could prepare her for the truth.

"Jeremy hasn't returned from school. He's probably fine, but I can't get hold of him. His mobile is off and I've spoken to that little lad who came around here once, the only contact I had and he said he walked towards his bus stop as usual. He wasn't aware of any problems. He'd been telling him all about the Multiverse. But that was over three hours ago."

The colour drained from Pippa who plonked herself on a kitchen chair. Dave sat right next to her and put his arm around her. He knew saying he is probably fine was what he hoped for but he had no evidence. He said it as much for Pippa's sake as his own. She was trembling and she could feel her heart racing.

"I'm trying to stay calm, rational and logical. I'm sure there's a good explanation, but I've spent the last hour wondering what's the best thing to do. And now I think we need to ring the police."

Terror hit. If Dave thinks that is necessary... oh, God, Dave, no! Dave is a solid unflappable rock at times of crisis, and now he is not.

"How will we survive if anything has happened to him? He's my world. He's my night and day. It'll be the end of my world."

Dave looked shell-shocked.

"It's Wednesday, the only day he definitely doesn't have any after-school activities and I know he wanted to get home early to get his homework done before the Bournemouth Cup game on TV. Yes, let's get the police now. What about going out to drive around?"

She knew the last suggestion was impulsive and desperate and Dave did not need to respond.

He did not know if you were supposed to dial 999 in these circumstances or ring the local police station. As he picked up his mobile he realised how much he was sweating and shaking. It was the first time in his life he felt genuine nausea from a shock. He decided on the easy route.

"Hello, Giselle speaking."

"Hi Giselle, do you know where Robert might be?"

On leaving that morning Rob said he would be home by five pm or even earlier if the CCG sponsored teach-in was as boring as usual. The surgery closures were usually a mixture of clinical lectures and health service organisational updates. In Rob's view they were designed to keep them away from their patients and prevented them from doing something useful. This one, he had told Suzy, was particularly irritating, as it was not only hosted by the local private hospital but it was to be chaired by Rob's nemesis Wiekser overseeing talks by management consultants.

"Fucking bloodsuckers," he said to her as he finished his Shredded Wheat.

He had just switched from a lifetime of Weetabix as he was convinced they were getting smaller and contained more sugar. Some time ago he realised these companies must take their customers for fools as everything from chocolate bars to drink cartons and toilet rolls have been getting smaller and smaller, and the prices have still gone up to maximise their profits. There was even a word to describe this con now - shrinkflation. How much could he boycott without starving to death? He thought Nestle had given up its aggressive marketing of breast milk substitutes which had Rob avoiding their goods in the 1980s - even KitKat, Nescafe, Vittel, Perrier and After Eights - but now he was having to think about abandoning his Shredded Wheat switch because of their palm oil links. Their producer was guilty of ecocide in Guatemala where violence and intimidation was used against environmental activists and they were linked to the destruction of critical Sumatran elephant habitat in Indonesia's Leuser ecosystem. Proof to Rob that you cannot lead a pure life in the sewer of capitalism. Which cereal manufacturer can be trusted? Even his cat food had to be changed from Go-Cat. This all drove Jenny mad before Suzy took over her headache.

"I doubt I'll stay for the bit when they tell us we must prescribe less and refer less or patients will suffer! They are all complicit in destroying the NHS, by being quislings and cooperating with those privatising bastards. Cheeky tossers now keep a register and you get a formal letter ticking you off if you don't attend! Fuck 'em!"

He knew it was not good to start the day so wound up, but nothing did wind him up as much as the secret deceitful dismantling of the NHS.

Giselle told Suzy what she knew.

"'E left at lunchtime as planned to go to the 'alf day release at the 'palace of death' as 'e calls that new private hospital. I don't think 'e wanted to go. 'E was moaning a lot. Maybe 'e just skived off somewhere. I didn't see 'im after that. 'E didn't come back to the surgery and I left at 6.45 p.m. Clive 'ad joked that they should just go off to the Bell and Jorrocks together. I doubt very much that they did but as I drove 'ome past their favourite watering 'ole I thought I saw a car like 'is parked outside, but I'm probably wrong. Obviously 'e 'asn't come 'ome yet?"

Actually she was fairly sure it was Rob's car but found herself backtracking slightly just in case Rob was up to something he should not have been. Not that she would lie to defend him, but neither would she go out of her way to drop him in it either.

"No, and even if he'd have gone for a drink afterwards he usually calls me. More because he would be keen to know if we've got any food than out of concern for me admittedly, but it's not like him to be so late."

"I'm sure 'e'll turn up. Don't worry. Let me know if you want any 'elp?"

Suzy got the impression from Giselle that she thought she was making a fuss and she should just relax. He would turn up.

"Oh, and Giselle... who is Sarah? It's just that a phone in Rob's desk that I'd never seen before went off earlier and the call was from someone called Sarah. Is there something I should know you are not telling me, Giselle?"

Giselle said she had no idea. After putting the phone down Suzy began to get slightly irritated - first with Giselle. She was not especially helpful or sympathetic. Was she telling the truth? Then with Rob for being inconsiderate, especially bearing in mind recent events. If he were still in the pub she would kill him. If he was having an affair with a girl called Sarah she would chop his nuts off first, barbeque them, then kill him. Back to Giselle - I wonder why she did not suggest ringing Clive, as he must have been with Rob all afternoon she pondered. Probably innocent - probably thought I would have already done that. She had thought of it but could not find his number.

Suzy ate her meal alone in front of *Channel 4 News* at seven pm, although it was the eight pm repeat on *Channel 4+1*. She thought it would take her mind off what was probably just an unnecessary worry. By eight forty-five pm she tried Rob's mobile - the only one she thought he had until this evening - for probably the eighth time.

She was considering going to the pub to see if it was Rob's car Giselle had seen.

Maximilien Rutherford had been missing for over four years. Silas had given up hope. He knew it would end this way one day. If he is dead he was just surprised Max had lasted this long. They were both seventy-two years old when they last spoke. He might have been last seen in Syria but Silas knew he could have travelled anywhere, disappeared from anywhere, and been abducted by anyone.

He had made so many enemies. The top suspects were ISIS, but ranging from the Ulster Volunteer Force, neo-Nazi groups in Germany, the CIA, MI5, right wing groups in the UK, and individuals wanting to pursue a vendetta against him. Any of these could have caught up with him. Drug dealers, the Sinaloa Cartel leader El Chapo or his rival Beltran Leyva before he died all wanted him dead. Their banks were on the list too. HSBC had been exposed laundering drug cartel money and funds for terrorist organisations and Max had played his part in that. Max had discovered that a failing business was used to launder money - over four million - into political donations to the Tory party. To Max, the Tory Party, terrorist organisation, same thing.

He was a thorn in the side of so many. He ridiculed his opponents, which made him more of a target. He declared most terrorists, as opposed to freedom fighters, to be dim. If they had any sense they would not be killing the odd civilian, renting vans to drive down the pavements of London's bridges or targeting teenagers at pop concerts but going for infrastructure. It took a strong stomach to realise that the politicians and the Establishment shed their crocodile tears at these deaths then moved on. It did not really affect them or their plans. What really would make an impact would be blowing up and disabling airports, rail stations, motorway bridges, and perhaps Parliament, although he had his doubts about the latter. Maybe that would get the public on their side. He thought Guy Fawkes had the right idea for the wrong reasons. He toasted him as the last man to enter Parliament with honest intentions - but he was not burnt on a bonfire but hung, drawn and quartered.

Silas had no doubt where his duty lay, to carry on with his father's work and to make sure Max did not die in vain, if indeed he was dead. Although knowing the dangerous game he had encouraged his daughters to play, he fully supported the activities of Mary and Vilma. They were now both in their forties and had families of their own. However, they would not be put off following the family tradition whatever he might try to say.

Mary, when meeting anyone especially the powerful, would challenge them head on with Tony Benn's questions: *What power do you have? Where did you get it? In whose interests do you exercise it? To whom are you accountable? How can we get rid of you?* Vilma tackled all those she thought were not playing their part in fighting or speaking out against injustice by quoting Martin Luther King, *In the end we will remember not the words of our enemies but the silence of our friends.*

"I told the Kensington and Chelsea Council about the honk a week ago, and all I got was what do you expect me to do about it? I've never experienced such a putrid smell. It's intolerable now and I think someone needs to break the door down."

"Do you know who lives there, Sir?" asked the policewoman.

"Yes, a man called Sean. He is very ill and we've seen no one go in or out for at least a fortnight. Not even carers."

"So you haven't seen this Sean at all in that time?"

"That's right."

"So, to repeat, the flat in question is on the tenth floor of Adair Tower and you are the tenant in a flat on the same floor, Sir?"

"Yes. Will you send someone?"

"We will do our best. Can't promise it will be today though."

55 - FIRE AND WATER

THE SOUND OF SILENCE

Left its seeds while I was sleeping
And a vision that was planted in my brain
Still remains
Within the sound of silence

Simon and Garfunkel (1964)

G. Lestrade, known to all by his middle name of Stanley was looking forward to an afternoon sorting out his vegetable patch. Since he retired his wife Vera had a new man in her life but his need for routine had not changed. Thursday was always gardening day whatever the weather.

Stanley was a more relaxed man and almost human. For the first time in years she was optimistic that she would be able to live out her days with him without killing him. But his day had just taken a turn for the worse. He had noticed small circular spots with a greyish white centre and dark edges on his tomato plant leaves. Septoria leaf spot, if he was not mistaken. He had not checked on them for a few days so the leaves were already turning yellow. He knew they would fall off soon. He blamed the long spell of warm but wet weather they had just had. He went to get his bottle of fungicide down from the shelf when he noticed smoke.

PC Lestrade took his police pension as soon as his thirty years was up. A job he had loved, but towards the end, began to hate. He revelled in it when he could be the friendly bobby on the beat, there to help the public and be their friend. He had no ambition other than that. He hated it though when the job changed to that of surveillance snooper working for a government against the public. He was in the Met. He and his wife brought up their two children in a house in Pepys Road, but at the Brockley, not New Cross end. He enjoyed the banter over the garden fence with the medical students who lived next door.

He was one of the first on the scene at the King's Cross underground fire in 1987. He witnessed the thirty-one bodies being taken away. He had the smell of burning in his nostrils for weeks, or so it seemed. He had never experienced such a putrid smell. This traumatised him and he felt he was just recovering when the Marchioness disaster happened less than two years later. This pleasure boat, built in 1923 and used at Dunkirk, was pushed under the Thames in about thirty seconds in a collision with a dredger near Cannon Street Railway Bridge drowning fifty-one people. This was all too much for Stanley. When he heard that the hands of some of the victims had been cut off to help fingerprint identification he knew he had to get out. Policing had changed and he did not like it.

Stanley did not recognise post-traumatic stress syndrome. But he could not escape the seeds of trauma and its vision left planted in his brain, which often wrecked his sleep. The night-time silence shattered by his screams. He asked for a transfer, sold their Pepys Road house and moved to the country. He resented the gentrification of his part of London although he got more for his house. He objected to the way all those friendly students had been driven from the area.

They had had bread and cheese lunch, their usual, and then forty winks. Vera was still asleep when he came crashing in through the back door. He had obviously been keen to start his gardening instead of napping.

"Right, I'm at the end of my tether. How many times have I asked that groundsman not to light his fires when the wind is blowing in our direction?"

Vera sighed. Maybe she would kill him after all.

"I'm going round there to give him a piece of my mind."

"Be careful dear. He is a lot younger and more muscular than you."

There was a gate between the Lestrades' garden and the golf course. In addition to the clubhouse, there was a pavilion near the ninth green, used mainly, as far as Stanley knew, for storage of maintenance equipment. He had never seen anybody go in or out apart from the groundsman.

He was right. He could see smoke coming from the usual place, behind the pavilion. The wooden building blocked out a view of any fire from the direction Stanley approached. He marched across the course ignoring the shouts of 'fore' and the golf ball whizzing over his head, towards the smoke. But on turning the corner he did not see what he had expected to see. Nobody. No culprit. He had already rehearsed what he was going to say but had no opportunity. There was no groundsman. Stanley could see a fire, and a bigger one than usual.

The trauma of King's Cross fuelled his somewhat irrational anger. After watching the Grenfell Tower burning people alive he could not speak for two days. Vera got quite concerned but enjoyed the peace.

There was something very odd about this fire. It was a strange shape. As he got closer the last flames were fading out. There was a horrid smell and a fair bit of smoke. He first saw a pair of shoes, pointing up. He then realised the reason they were in that position was because they were attached to two legs. Then he clearly saw it was a body. He could tell it was male as it was bare from the waist up. He put a handkerchief over his nose and mouth and got as close as the heat would allow. It began to bring back that horrible time at King's Cross - that smell, which he would never forget. Fortunately he had not come across it again for over thirty years. Underneath the first body was another, this one smaller. This one had a jacket on.

His police training kicked in. He told himself not to panic but stay calm. His first thought was that he did not want to get involved but he could hardly ignore this. He cursed himself for wanting to confront a non-existent groundsman in the first place. So he had to work out what to do logically and rationally. He knew there was no chance they were alive. It must be a crime scene. He decided not to touch anything. There were no lives to save so there was no rush. He would have been trained to put the fire out to make sure it did not spread and to preserve evidence on the bodies, but it was dying down and it was not possible for it to spread anywhere. Crucially there was no means to dampen it down. No water. Nothing. He checked the time of discovery and walked from behind the pavilion towards the ninth green where he had heard voices.

There were four men, dressed in the loudest checked trousers Stanley had ever seen. He thought it must have been part of a dare or bet. No one would wear those if it were not for a forfeit. From the way they were talking he thought they might be businessmen. He thought should they not be working? Negotiating new deals abroad after Brexit?

"Excuse me gents, have any of you got a mobile phone? You see, there are two bodies behind that shed and I think the police should be informed."

Their banter stopped and they just stood there staring at Stanley for what was only a few seconds but seemed like minutes. One broke the silence.

"What? You having us on?"

"How do I know you won't run off with it?" said another.

Stanley stayed calm and replied in a way that made his accuser feel small.

"I think that is highly unlikely don't you? I'm a pensioner with a bad leg and there are four of you."

Stanley had broken his leg in the line of duty thirty years before when he slipped and fell off a gangplank trying to board a restaurant boat on the Embankment. The operation was botched at the private hospital the Met used. His young surgeon was a man called Carnicero. There was a good cover-up that protected the surgeon's career. Vera had told Stanley to stick to the NHS, they are the best at trauma.

"Your combined ages aren't much more than mine. If you can't outrun me you should be ashamed of yourselves."

Stanley suddenly realised he did not really need to stay calm or be polite now he was no longer in the force. There were two bodies on a bonfire and he found himself in an argument about a stupid mobile phone.

"See for yourselves, but give me your fucking phone you snivelling little prat."

Maybe over the top but it made him feel good and it was effective. The last time he had said something like that was before he retired. They got the message. Three of the quartet did not need another invitation or an order. They started to walk towards the pavilion. But their attitude and swagger was of young men who were determined to prove an old man a liar and nutter.

The fourth stayed on the green. He was not going to be talked to like that by an old codger.

"Too mean to get your own, eh?" was his parting shot.

Stanley ignored that swipe but there was some truth in that. Stanley resented giving money to a rip-off industry and so had never had one.

As they ventured around the other side of the pavilion the odour hit them all. They had never experienced such a putrid smell.

"Don't touch anything and stay back. It's a crime scene," Stanley ordered.

The one with the loudest trousers ignored him and moved forward towards the bodies. He was intrigued and not in the least horrified. The second in line was on his mobile calling the police. Stanley was pleased the job was done for him. 'Mr Loudtrousers', as Stanley thought of him, leant over the charring remains. Stanley spoke now with an air of superiority, condescension and authority.

"Which bit of stay back didn't you understand, you idiot? You're getting so close you'll end up as prime suspect and if you haven't already recognised it, that's a petrol can you are standing next to. It could ignite or explode anytime if there is anything left in it. It is hot."

'Loudtrousers' leapt back as though a snake had bitten him. It did the trick of preventing him interfering with evidence further. At this the fourth of the quartet walked around the corner of the pavilion from the green. He was not particularly curious but more inpatient.

"Come on boys, have you forgotten why we are here?"

He stopped suddenly.

"Crikey, are they really bodies?"

"Well it ain't the fifth of November, is it?" chipped in one of his mates.

"Will you hang around boys?" Stanley said, being practical again.

"Why?"

"Because the police will want statements from you."

"Is that right? Sorry old boy. I can't be seen here. I'm supposed to be in the office. My boss won't be impressed."

"Can't help that, I'm afraid, as you can't obstruct a police investigation, which this now is. What would you prefer? A statement now which your boss may not know about, or to become headlines of the local paper for obstructing the police in their work? Your choice, sonny."

56 - FLAMING AND BURNING

EVERYTHANG'S CORRUPT

For my birthday, buy me a politician
It's a shame that you got to dish your children
Everythang's corrupt

Everythang's a scam
Beat the next man, that's capitalism

Get ready, for the lynching brainwash media
And puppet politician

Ice Cube (2013)

"Did you see that goal Josh King scored for Bournemouth against Chelsea last night? Spectacular!"

The second policeman ignored the first.

"This one should be fairly easy to identify. It looks like his wallet in his back trouser pocket has survived and he has a tattoo on his upper arm."

"Everyone has tattoos now. That won't help," piped up the first policeman,

"He's Norwegian."

"How could you possibly know that? We've only just started looking."

"No, Josh King. Plays for Norway."

He was ignored again.

"This isn't the usual Love and Hate, or football crest, or something stupid in Chinese, but a face. Trying to place it. I know. It's the logo for Liverpool Airport. Looks to me like a John Lennon homage. Yes, it's him with, *Above us only sky* below it. And he is dark skinned."

"So would you be stupid if you'd just been barbecued."

The two on duty response officers did not want to be there. It was too near the end of their shift. They had entered the golf course through the main entrance and clubhouse and closed it down. The back-up they had called for refused to let anyone in or out.

"See their hands are bound together behind their backs? Poor bastards. Someone didn't like them."

"No shit."

"And look, the syringe and needle is still in him at his elbow. Melted, but definitely a syringe."

"And this other one is a schoolboy."

"How do you know that, Sherlock?"

"He has a blazer on. It has a crest on the front."

"So it does. Some writing in Spanish too, *Fas et Patria.*"

"That's Latin you wassock."

"Means speed and patriotism."

"No it doesn't. What sort of school did you go to? St Thicko's?"

"It means Faith and Fatherland."

"Very Nazi, I'm sure."

"Signed for Manchester United aged sixteen."

"Who did?"

"Josh King."

"Will you shut up about Josh King."

The camaraderie in the Dorset Police was, as elsewhere in the force, tainted by a competitive spirit that relied on piss taking. Although they were not allowed to call it a Police Force anymore, it is a Police Service. The false macho bollocks had died down a little since Stanley Lestrade's day but you still needed a thick skin to survive. This team did not really like each other. 'Sherlock', real name Tom Barton, was brighter than the 'Wassock', Charlie Barlow. But what the 'Wassock' lacked in brains he made up in aggression. They had had a long busy shift. They were both feeling irritable because of the inevitability of getting home late.

Tom Barton's dad had promised him life in the police would be better than this. DCI Richard Barton was of the era before even

Stanley Lestrade. He ruled his town. Instead of arresting youths he would just give them a bit of a beating down a dark alley. He was convinced it was more effective. No one could persuade him it was the wrong thing to do. He enjoyed a good punch-up and told Tom he would have women falling over themselves to get to him. He ruled the nightclubs, never had to buy himself a drink, and was never short of a party to go to after a shift. Strippers were a given. His children got police discipline. When Tom was late home one night, his father threw him in a police cell for twenty-four hours. His sister was escorted out of a pub on suspicion of soliciting when their dad was planning to meet another woman there. It was a good life. Tom was yet to be convinced.

"Looks a clear case of a double murder, doesn't it? Two bound bodies set on fire, petrol can nearby," said Charlie.

"One who had been injected with something. What else could it be?" replied Tom scornfully.

Charlie ignored the attempted put down as you had to if you wanted to survive in the police.

"Whoever dumped these bodies obviously didn't care about hiding the murders. It's like they wanted them found. Like a warning to others."

Knowing this was at the least a suspicious death they had taped off the area, started a crime scene log to record everyone coming in and out and decided on a common approach path. Charlie said he hated dealing with body parts to which Tom responded that the beef of his Sunday lunch and the bacon in last night's burger was one hundred per cent dead body parts. Tom then knew he had to get a doctor along to confirm life extinct and the Scenes of Crimes Officer to inspect the site. He had just dialled the number when they both saw two other squad cars approaching down the dirty track along the perimeter of the golf course. They had to weave in and out of a few trees to clear a route.

"These guys don't believe in walking a step further than they have to do they?" Tom said.

Barton and Barlow had parked at the end of the track.

701

"They are driving all over and away from my common approach path!" said Charlie, who then shouted.

"Oi, you, get off there before you…"

Out jumped four detectives, two from each car.

"Something troubling you, sonny?"

"Oh, er, no sir."

"Right boys, you'll be pleased to hear we take over from now on. Go home. One warning though, if you value your career, don't mention this to anyone."

"Smells like a fucking barbecue," said his colleague.

"I've got chicken drumsticks when I eventually get home, my mouth is watering already," added the third.

Sherlock and the 'Wassock' did not have to wait to be told twice, and the second part about not talking about the incident did not even register. After they had walked far enough down the track to be out of earshot Chief Superintendent Stevenson spoke.

"Right, pay attention. We are all answerable directly to Sir John, so you'd better get this right, 'cause my head's on the block too. I will not be pleased if you fuckwits mess up. Double-check everything you do and then with each other. Once you are certain, check it again. I want your report by six pm tonight. You know the story. Make sure the evidence fits it. We will then publish some facts for our friends in the media."

Stevenson had already tipped off his contacts. They were told where to leave the money, the drop off points were changed every pay off.

By the time they had finished all the evidence fitted nicely. They cleared the site of anything odd and put the petrol can in the car for disposal. The burnt bindings fell easily from the victims' wrists and the bodies were repositioned for the photographs. The contents of a charred envelope found in the tattooed man's jacket pocket did not make any sense to them, so to avoid confusion and a longer inquest than necessary, they destroyed it. On a damaged sheet of paper they could just make out these words:

Dearest Rob, keep on fighting the bastards and remember and ponder what Antonio Gramsci wrote whenever you think of me, *I'm a pessimist because of intelligence, but an optimist because of will.* With love, Rosa.

One of the officers joked.
"Who does Antonio Gramsci play for?"
"A. C. Milan of course," came the swift reply.

Commissioner Sir John Varken knew what he had to do, and the message had gone down the ranks to Stevenson. This case was no more than a pervert killing an innocent schoolboy and then, in remorse, ending his own sad, warped, depraved and twisted life - an increasing problem in today's society. Good riddance to the evil git. The first inclination was to pin this on Poison to discredit them but that was too convoluted.

He saw the first report at 6.10 p.m. Stevenson had done a good job. He needed to alter little and forwarded it as directed to Hammond, Sir James' manservant who passed it on to Sir James half an hour ahead of his deadline. They were all conscious that too hasty a conclusion may smack of conspiracy to frame so they left a more respectable time than the two hours within which Oswald was blamed for Kennedy's shooting. Police knocked on the doors of the Thackeray and Baigent households simultaneously at precisely 7.00 pm. The media had had their briefing before 8.00 p.m.

"*BBC Radio News*, this is Frank Phillips.
Police investigating the discovery of two bodies on a golf course in Dorset have issued a statement that they believe a man killed a schoolboy then took his own life. They are not looking for anyone else in connection with the crime. The adult male has been identified as Dr Robert Baigent, believed to be in his early fifties, a general practitioner from Kent. It is thought Baigent killed schoolboy Jeremy Thackeray before lethally injecting himself with a yet

unidentified substance and then, before it had rendered him unconscious, igniting the petrol he had poured over both of them."

"This is *Sky News at Six* with Stuart Hibberd.
Police investigating the murder of schoolboy Jeremy Thackeray and the suicide of the GP thought to have killed him, have told *Sky News* that hundreds of pornographic images were found on Baigent's computer. It was thought Baigent had faked a burglary to dispose of his computers when he became suspicious the police were about to mount a raid."

The Sun
- HOW MANY MORE PERVERT GPs ARE OUT THERE? We trust our lives to these monsters and they need exposing, writes John Snagge. We call for regular and random inspections of all NHS doctors' computers and we believe surgery inspections should be extended to take in their home as well. Turn to page 5 for the results of our investigation into gynaecologists. How many doctors go into this specialty just for the thrills? Have you been assaulted by your specialist?
- Donald Trump cameo in *Home Alone 2*. Win the DVD.
- New competition: Win doctors and nurses uniform to spice up your sex life. 100 must be won!

Kent Times report by Vernon Bartlett.
Why does Kent have more than its share of pervert doctors? First Ledward. Then Ayling. Now Baigent. It is almost an epidemic. What is wrong with their training? Are the wrong people being selected for medical school? Would it be better if all medical schools were private? These are the questions that now need to be asked and we demand answers. We have been told that Dr Baigent hid his mental illness from the authorities, and covered up his perversions and attraction for small children for years, possibly decades, and the images found on his computer dated back to the 1970s. He was in the media in recent years as a critic of government health policy,

704

alleging, despite little evidence, that the Secretary of State for Health was privatising the NHS. We now know he was a professional liar as well as depraved.

"*BBC Radio Kent* this is Alvar Riddell.
We managed to get an interview with Dr Lister, who was in partnership with Baigent.

"I am totally shocked and devastated. I, and I think I speak for all those who worked with him at the surgery, had no idea what he was up to. I feel so sorry for his poor wife and children who must be in pain, but also ashamed. We need to pick up the pieces now. I would like to repeat the sound advice of the General Medical Council and police. Anyone who feels they were a victim of Dr Baigent, or can offer any evidence that might help in their investigations, is urged to come forward.

Looking back, I now recognise certain things that were not quite right. Dr Baigent had been acting a little strangely recently. I was at a meeting with him a few days ago and witnessed a totally unexpected and unjustified public outburst of rage. There was at least one outstanding complaint that had not been resolved and the practice finances were in a bit of a mess. I blame myself for not being more alert but you know it's human nature to trust colleagues. I think I've said enough now though."

We also spoke to several ex-patients.

"I've only just learnt what has happened. I'm shocked. How can someone with those problems be allowed to practise? I feel violated now as he examined me on several occasions. And I now hear he was so left wing he was almost a communist. He had a picture of a nude woman on his wall you know. I'm not racist but we have never had a dark-skinned doctor in this village before."

And a lady who only wanted to be known as Saskia told us she put in a complaint about Baigent's sexual advances, but was then threatened. She does not know who was behind it, but she was told to 'withdraw it or else'. There was not universal condemnation however. We managed to find an Indian lady who says Baigent saved her life only last month by diagnosing bowel cancer and getting her treated."

"*TalkSport* the world's biggest sports radio station. The Headlines read by me, Frederick Grisewood.
- Rooney recalled to England squad to face Lithuania.
- *I'm A Celebrity* contestant Jordan Moffatt drops out after sex scandal. We give you the details.
- Prince Harry and Meghan stick up for the ginger brigade.
- And two bodies found on golf course in Dorset linked to paedophile ring.
- Plus we report from the sex doll factory, which made a grieving man an exact replica of his wife."

"*KMFM Radio* headlines every hour on the hour with Wilfred Pickles.
- Another Kent GP found dead. Suicide the likely cause yet again. This time though was he also a murderer and pervert? The statement issued by the police seems to imply so. Boy from Dorset found dead at same site.
- Migrant jobs squeeze alarms Kent fruit farmers; county councillor says it's all the fault of the French.
- Support for death penalty on the rise.
- Is your smart phone making you stupid?
- And 'possessed' salad curse strikes again.

Sir James was at his club. On a Friday morning he was rarely anywhere else. He had a day with relatively few appointments. He promised himself a leisurely morning reading *The Times* then after seeing Sir John Varken, had lunch with Gerry and Lyndon at Marcus in Knightsbridge. Gerry was late as usual. This time it was because he went to the wrong restaurant and had had an argument with the owner insisting his friends must be there somewhere.

Sir James followed this with a visit to Sonia his mistress in Pimlico. He had installed her in an apartment in Grosvenor Road overlooking the Thames. She often sat in Pimlico Garden and Shrubbery, near the statue of William Huskisson MP from where she could see Dolphin Square. Sonia had no idea who he was so in an idle moment looked him up on the Internet. She actually found it quite funny that he was the first railway fatality being killed by George Stephenson's *Rocket* in 1830.

Jim felt he was neglecting Dorothy somewhat and put a note in his diary to visit her the next day. Sonia and Dorothy were unaware of each other despite her flat being one of the Bessborough Gardens apartments, only a stone's throw away. Jim thought these were a good investment when built in the 1980s. The security barriers, the twenty-eight surveillance cameras, nor the regular patrols that knew him by name, never bothered him. He could walk between the two but was past the days of dealing with both mistresses on one day. He was chuffed he could still perform at eighty and the little blue pills would make sure two days in a row was not too much. Hammond was in charge of his supplies.

On page seven there was a short report about two bodies being found on a golf course in Dorset.

Madison Moodey felt the wave of nausea rise up. She was at the Yoga centre, but this time decided to spend time in the attached gym. She was on the cross-trainer listening to the *BBC News* through headphones. It was like being struck on the head with a brick.

"… has been identified as Dr Robert Baigent believed to be in his early fifties, a general practitioner from Kent. It is thought Baigent killed schoolboy Jeremy Thackeray before lethally injecting himself…"

She knew she was going to vomit. She jumped off the machine, not bothering with the headphones, which flew off and crashed to the ground. Chantelle, who was running on the treadmill across the other side of the gym, saw her rushing off to the toilet. She executed a more cautious withdrawal from her equipment and followed Madison. By the time Chantelle got to the 'ladies', Madison was throwing up in the toilet.

"Are you okay?"

"No. That GP, who saw our broadcast that we met, he's dead. The *BBC* says he committed suicide after killing a young boy. I don't know how much more of this I can take."

"Putain de merde."

Stanley Lestrade finally got around to spraying his tomato plant leaves with fungicide albeit a day after he had intended. Septoria lycopersici had ruined his Thursday more than his later discovery. The smell of the chlorothalonil was preferable to the barbecue odour he could not get out of his nostrils - King's Cross 1987.

From his garden he could see the lone bobby walking up and down near the pavilion and ninth green, guarding the crime scene. How boring. He could remember similar duties and wondered if he should take him a cup of tea. Then he found out Vera had beaten him to it. She had been listening to the news and came to tell Stanley about the bulletins.

"Filthy pervert," she had commented.

The day before he had watched the forensic team at work. This took him back too, but he still did not miss it. Stanley was a little surprised how quickly the police had solved this crime, or at least come to such concrete conclusions, and how swiftly it was all over the media. Perhaps privatising forensics had made them more efficient as they had claimed. But he doubted it. He estimated it was only six hours from his discovery to the media reports naming the victims. Something was not quite right.

At the last local meeting of the National Association of Retired Police Officers Stanley had met up for a few drinks with old friends and colleagues. He liked to keep in touch but avoided all the moaners who revelled in chat about 'it's not like it was in our day'. Most accepted that the way they used to police would have got them thrown out nowadays, but they defended themselves, saying it was far more effective. Where he did agree however was when he listened to his mates from forensics. According to them that area of investigation was now a disaster.

The Forensic Science Service had been privatised and thousands of test results had been tampered with or falsified. Several people at the private company called Efficient Testing Services had been found guilty of perverting the course of justice. Every force - or rather service - across the country had had to review hundreds of criminal investigations. They had had no option but to outsource their forensics to just one particular company.

"Strange that, a former cabinet minister is being paid nearly five grand a month as a consultant to them?" joked one of his old mates.

But nobody laughed.

"Yes, who'd have guessed that the Government forcing the privatisation of the nation's forensic service would lead to corruption, eh?" added another.

"By all accounts, bungs and bribes are now commonplace. The rich get off by having their samples altered in exchange for a fat brown envelope with a wad in it. I wish I had the money to buy a puppet politician. Perhaps I'll get one for my birthday. Everything's corrupt."

Stanley listened with sadness. Things really are going downhill. Perverts on bonfires and others perverting justice.

Jim Auger was near the end of his morning's deliveries. He still found it hard to believe he had exchanged ward rounds for a postman's round but he took great satisfaction in writing FUCK OFF across his GMC summons and sending it back. There were compensations. He felt free of all the stress and hassle. It was great to walk in the Fife countryside. Occasionally he took his dogs, Venus and Aphrodite with him. But he was still glad he only had one more early start before a full weekend off. Since privatisation he now had to work three weekends out of four for no extra pay.

Jim had a bit of a sore head after a night drinking with his new pal Reg Dwight. They got to know each other as fellow Sassenachs sharing a passion for *Caledonian Deuchars IPA*. They talked about its husky bready malt flavour and football - English football, not Scottish. Their new sport was winding up the locals about the

Scottish team's World Cup record. Reg told whoever would listen that he had named his son after Geoff Hurst, although spelt differently. They shared the same birthday. The two Englishmen lamented the demise of yet another 1966 hero, goalkeeper Gordon Banks - four of the wonderful eleven now dead, and two with dementia.

The Westport Tavern had mended its television and showed the Bournemouth vs. Chelsea cup game the night before. Although Reg was quite a bit older they got on well. They never talked about anything serious. Jim never mentioned why he came to Scotland and never let on he was medically qualified, and certainly not his specialty. A cryptic crossword expert might work it out from the names of his dogs. Venereal was derived from Venus the Goddess of love, sex, beauty and fertility, and aphrodisiac from Aphrodite her Greek counterpart. But banter was best.

Jim was listening to the latest podcast instalment towards his law degree through the headset on his phone when it started to pour with rain. The next cottage on his delivery round belonged to Mrs Cameron. She was in her eighties and wanted to mother Jim. She always offered tea and biscuits, a warm fire in the winter, a towel in the wet and a decent Christmas bonus. She saw him coming up the drive and opened the door.

"Yer aywis at the coo's tail, wee laddie. Get inside and dry off or a clean shirt'll do ye."

"Thank you Mrs Cameron, I will for a few minutes."

"It's a sair ficht for half a loaf."

Luckily for Jim the old lady always greeted him the same way so he had now found out from his mates in the Westport Tavern what she was on about. Reg was no use though with the interpretation but he said it would make a good Elton John lyric. Roughly translated it was, 'hurry up, you're dragging your heels or you're not long for this world' and 'life is hard work and you only get half of what you want'.

Mrs Cameron had lived alone since her husband died nearly fifty years before in the Ibrox Park disaster. Sixty-six football fans were crushed to death at an Old Firm game. The last thing he ever will have known was Colin Stein's equalizer for Rangers before he died from compressive asphyxia. She was clearly lonely, but she preferred this to being a burden on anyone. She had just heard on her radio that loneliness was as dangerous as smoking, but she would not add this to her list of worries. If it were not for Jim she would be adding to that statistic of one in ten old people not having any contact with other humans.

On a previous wet morning she told him that she was distantly related by marriage to the man that pretended to be Prime Minister a few years back.

"All his eggs are double-yoakit and his bum's oot the windae. The worst PM since Lord North. Just when the world needed to unite and live more harmoniously as a family, the idiot took us out of Europe and segregated, split and divided us, and set us all against each other, fuelled xenophobia, nationalism, jingoism and manufactured scapegoats. But we should have expected no less from a slave-owning dynasty, eh laddie?"

Jim gathered from this she thought her distant relative a boastful windbag who talked nonsense and of whom she did not approve. To Jim it was good to hear someone else condemn the man he felt was partly responsible for the death of his friend Alex Ephialtes. In the background *BBC Radio Scotland* was reporting on the death of a schoolboy and another English doctor.

Mrs Cameron commented.

"Whit's fur ye'll no go by ye."

Jim was not surprised but the news hardly registered.

"Haste ye back," she said, and Jim continued his round.

In the Westport Tavern Reg was reading the *Central Fife Times and Advertiser* at the bar. He did not pick up on the connection with the radio report. Not immediately anyway. His new partner hit him with it when he returned home. Amongst the mail was an invitation from Suzy inviting them down to see Reg's son and her brother Jeff, who was expected from California.

57 - ACHIEVEMENTS AND PRIDE

HEROES

We can be heroes, just for one day

We can be heroes forever and ever

David Bowie (1977)

Maximilien Rutherford was not dead. But he felt he might as well be - from time to time he even wished it. Aged seventy-seven and he had not seen natural daylight for, he guessed, over two years probably three. Only removed from his cell for torture sessions.

Guantanamo Bay Detention Camp detained people indefinitely without trial and severely tortured some, including Max. One of George Bush's legacies and a major breach of human rights, but nobody told the land of the free what they could or could not do. So that he could justify it all in the name of Christ, he re-defined torture to be only that that caused permanent organ failure or death.

Guantanamo, Max thought, was the twenty-first century's Devil's Island. We are no more civilised than we were then. Donald Rumsfeld said that the detainees were not entitled to the protection of the Geneva Convention. He knew the majority of detainees were innocent but kept them there for reasons of political expedience. Bush's successor as President said he would close the camp, but he never did. The new President wanted more camps built but would dump some detainees and terrorists back onto Europe to deal with. They could not get back into the States over his new wall.

Max was in solitary confinement, exposed to temperature extremes, beaten up, subjected to loud noise, sleep deprivation, prolonged constraint in painful positions, and waterboarding. Sexual assaults were left as threats but to Max's surprise not carried out - just the threat was a torture in itself. Max had no idea if anyone knew he was at Guantanamo. He felt more sorry for his family than himself. He always knew this would happen - that they would catch up with him. That was one reason he never had children.

There was one guard who was a little friendlier than the others. It turned out this was as random as Max having the same birthday as his mother - so he had an empathetic, if illogical attachment. Max had been told of the new influx of detainees courtesy of the President who wanted to load it up with bad dudes. He did not think waterboarding is tough enough, even though it was good enough for the Spanish Inquisition.

Places like Guantanamo were what the new language was invented for. Hunger strikes were now non-religious fasts and suicides acts of asymmetrical warfare. The Americans filled the place up by offering $5000 for any bearded foreign dude people did not like the look of. Another Mohammed ended up there this way, despite being just a student from Saudi Arabia studying English in Karachi. The translator at his interrogation was Yemeni where the word zalat means money. In a Saudi dialect it means salad, so Mohammed could not quite get why the Americans were so keen to know where he got his salad. So when he told them he could get his zalat from wherever he wanted and was freshest, the CIA decided he must be an al-Qaida financier and demanded to know his sources. The vegetable stalls near his boarding house did not seem that credible to his interrogators so they kept him there. It was as sad and pathetic as the mob that beat up a children's doctor because they did not know the difference between a paediatrician and a paedophile.

So many prisoners were at the detention camp because of mistaken identity but this was not true for Max. They really did know what he had been up to over several decades but he had remained too quick for them - until 2015 when the Special Operations Team finally caught up with him. He was suspicious that a Dutchman called Lars had betrayed him. Up until now, as far as Max was concerned, all they had managed to get out of him at the torture sessions was the truth. It was a strange form of information gathering. What his tormentors wanted to find out was how much did Max know about their own wrongdoings and illegal actions, and who had he told. Their number one aim was to stop the truth

713

getting out. They knew his sympathies and for these alone his captors thought he should die. But first they had to find out who else could damage them - who else was working with Rutherford?

Max drip-fed them information he thought they would already know and told them about contacts they would already be aware of. Recent activity in the Middle East involved the International Solidarity Movement. He had witnessed Rachel Corrie, a peace activist, being crushed to death by an Israeli armoured bulldozer in their efforts to prevent the Israeli army's demolition of Palestinian houses. Being an American her death attracted more attention than the other nine Palestinians, including a four-year-old girl killed the same night. He told them about North Korea's nuclear programme and the Iranian links. He warned them about a man called Rodrigo Duterte who was Mayor of Davao City who would fix the next Philippines election to become President. Max knew him to be a nasty piece of work and a murderer. If he got into power the Western world should worry. Max was not to know he had become President during his time at Guantanamo.

Max had background knowledge on Turkey's Erdogan, who had just become President when the Special Operations Team burst into Max's hideaway in Syria in the middle of one night and handed him over to the US. Max had arrived in Syria via Turkey. He had predicted Erdogan would become a dictator, no less powerful than Hitler in Germany. He would turn his back on Europe and introduce censorship, take over the judiciary and the media, ban opposition parties and imprison thousands. The re-aligning of powers in that region would threaten world security. Max told them everything he thought they wanted to know that fitted with his terrorist credentials - because like everyone who disagreed with the new world order, if you were not with them, you were against them and by definition a terrorist.

Max was fairly satisfied with his life's work. He knew he would be forgotten but was pleased he did not just moan about what a terrible state the world was in and hoped he had contributed something to stop it getting worse. He was annoyed his secrets and knowledge would die with him. He was sure he knew more about the conspiracies and corruption in the world than anybody else and had done his best to educate the next generation and group of fighters. In his time in solitary he often reflected on what his father had told him about Oppenheimer. He had learnt Sanskrit and read the Gita in the original language. What an intellect. *Kalo'smi loka-ksaya-krt pravrddho lokan samahartum iha pravrttah*, which he translated as *I am become Death, the destroyer of worlds*. He also reflected on the two vendettas that satisfied him most. Although insignificant in terms of the greater project, they were important to the family.

In February 1975 he had gone to the Hetherington Park Estate and confronted Charles Morrison. Morrison was by this time in his seventies and in a wheelchair after his stroke. Some speech had returned but not enough to make him understood easily. What Max wanted to achieve was made easy as Baron Willingdon, to give him his full title, had been put outside onto the veranda by his nurse and was alone. So Max did not bother the staff, but just drew up a chair and started talking to the old man. Arthur Rutherford would not have wanted his nemesis killed, after all Arthur was a pacifist. Max never discussed any violence he found himself engaging in, and to his regret he would respect his father's wishes.

So Max could only frighten Morrison and he certainly did that. He talked to him for a full half hour, never letting on he was not going to kill him. Like all bullies, Morrison was really a coward and started sweating profusely. After ten minutes his nurse came out to check on him and was surprised to find Max talking to her boss. Max introduced himself as the son of an old friend Morrison went to school with and that he would not be staying long. He did not want to tire the old man in the wheelchair. She offered him coffee, which he declined.

Max talked slowly and calmly leaving Morrison with lots of doubts about his own safety and that of his family, and how Max's team had the power to ruin him and they were going to. Psychological warfare. He said he knew about the crimes Morrison had committed that he was going to expose. These included the Guyanese war hero he helped kick to death on the streets of

715

Cambridge in 1919. Max left knowing that he had instilled enough fear in Morrison that would not allow him to relax until the day he died. He would ruin him. He made it appear that Morrison's whole life had been a failure, and that his father had sent his regards.

The paper in front of the disabled man ran the headline of Thatcher's election as leader of the Conservative Party. He had woken that morning feeling quite pleased. He never woke up with that feeling again. Morrison sacked his nurse for lax security and replaced her with one that allowed his whisky and sodas. Max drove away listening to Steve Harley and Cockney Rebel's *Make Me Smile*. He was smiling with satisfaction at a job done well. He could not wait to tell his father.

The second vendetta was nearly twenty years later. Through Guy at Poison, the Rutherfords learnt all about Dolphin Square and the associated atrocities. Max was given the job of seeking out Douglas. This he did with delight. He was living in luxury in Albert Hall Mansions. Keeping him tied up and in fear of his life, he got hold of all of Douglas's photos and blackmail material, then when he was satisfied he had all he wanted, threw Douglas out of his fourth floor window. He landed under the blue plaque to Sir Malcolm Sargent.

Max killed this time with a clear conscience knowing he did not have to tell his father as Arthur had died seven years earlier. But he hoped he would be proud of him. He could beat them, even if just for one day. He felt like a hero, even if just for one day.

58 - GONE AND LOST

ART OF DYING

There'll come a time when all our hopes are fading
When things that seemed so very plain
Become an awful pain
Searching for the truth among the lying
And answered when you've learned the art of dying

George Harrison (1970)

"We are just an advanced breed of monkeys on a minor planet of a very average star. This is one of the gems Dr Robert Baigent passed onto me in The Hung Drawn and Quartered pub after one of our masochistic games of squash. But only Rob would split hairs with the great Stephen Hawking who said this. Rob surmised that, we are not descended from monkeys though, but share common extinct ancestors with them."

They had all gathered in Rob and Suzy's garden, from now on to be referred to only as Suzy's garden. It was a bright, sunny and warm day with a slight breeze that made it perfect. Stephen was asked by Suzy to say a few words about her husband. She had telephoned Jenny to ask if she was in agreement. It was the first time they had ever spoken. Suzy was surprised how bold she felt and Jenny was shocked to get the call, but it began the thawing out process between them.

"Rob wanted us all to wake up to the truth that we just share this planet, and to stop thinking it is our right to rule it and so destroy it. Because we will destroy it, as we are not as clever as we think. Some people are but they are generally ignored. And like Stephen Hawking he felt we would need to find another planet to live on eventually, but take our NHS with us. It's the only really civilised achievement of man.

He had a theory that the more people in a room, the accumulative intelligence and common sense levels went down. So

717

in a crowd mob-rule would take over as they were guided by the stupidest. That was the only explanation he could give for the state of the world today. Speak to an individual and you might get somewhere. Speak to a large group, no chance. It was a conflict between the tenderness of the individual against the cruelty of the crowd. The cruelty is winning.

As a species we are not special. We think we are because we have culture, language and feelings. But we are not alone. Other species do too. Ours are probably just more advanced. With that comes arrogance."

Despite saying what he knew Rob would approve of, Stephen sensed he was losing his audience so put his notes aside. When discussing the early death of a mutual friend some years before Rob had made a throw away comment that 'at my funeral I don't want crap about what a jolly good fellow - I want lessons to be learnt from my time alive, or what's the point of having existed?'

"Why am I telling you this?" he said after a pause, "Because Rob believed that is proving to be our own undoing. We are using our so-called intelligence to be less advanced as caring creatures."

Stephen was quite used to public speaking but he knew he was not doing well. It was not flowing. He castigated himself for not preparing better. No choice though but to continue but he thought he should throw in a little more humour.

"We played squash regularly and it was a tradition to end with a bit of trivia, or to catch each other out with a rare syndrome. Neither of us would admit it but we looked up something before each game. I've two that will now never be delivered, so I know Rob would have appreciated hearing about foreign accent syndrome, which is self-explanatory, and genital retraction syndrome where, believe it or not, sufferers believe their genitals or nipples are retracting and will disappear. So glad I could mention genitals at Rob's funeral. He'd be proud."

Stephen went back to his script.

"Rob thought even in his lifetime we had become desensitised as a society. He truly believed a generation ago we would not just have shrugged our shoulders at hundreds of children drowning in the

Mediterranean, starving in Yemen, at the massacres, the abandonment of refugees, the homeless freezing to death and the abuse of children."

This had to be confronted head on.

"Yes, I said it. The abuse of children. I don't believe for a moment my old friend did the things said by the police and the media. And I don't believe anyone else here does either."

With that out of the way Stephen went back to his notes and determined to lighten up.

"I'm pretty sure I knew Rob longer than anyone here. We shared a flat as students in Brockley and often bumped into Kate Bush in the local Co-op."

That in-joke got only a weak reception from two others who understood. The joke was that the old flatmates used to kid each other they had bumped into their pin-up and were chatted up by her. She was brought up near Brockley. Not true of course. Pippa's sister from the Brick Lane flat, who was at the funeral as an old friend and to support Pippa, got the joke but the loudest snigger came from Rob and Stephen's old flatmate who was visiting from Australia - he no longer stalked Jimmy Page.

"Together we went to that torture chamber called Guy's Hospital Medical School run by the English Inquisition. Whilst most of our fellow students were born with silver spoons up their arses, Rob was from a family of builders in Margate who got their spoons from Woolworth's. Neither of us could believe the posh accents of some, but accepted that if Brian Epstein hadn't spoken the way he did no one at EMI would have listened to him and there might have been no Beatles. According to them, it was not posh but termed upper received pronunciation. They told us their clipped phrases and lengthened vowels were a sign of good breeding, and we were just cockneys who were allowed into Guys to help them qualify for more funding. Like an allowance for disabled people. A big mistake, we were told, as it diluted the quality of the profession. But it was only partly a class snobbery problem. What it is really is racism.

We all know that Rob had a Barbadian mother and was proud of that. But it was something the medical establishment then couldn't stomach. If we went back half a dozen generations in the families of some of our classmates, they were probably slave owners. Perhaps the owners of Rob's ancestors. Or at least they benefitted from money from the slave trade. And they flaunted their prejudice at Rob's expense, just like their right wing credentials. They were the next generation down from those in our so-called caring profession who fought against foreign dilution before the war. They lobbied MPs about the dangers of letting in Czech Jewish doctors. This is the sort of thing Rob hated and challenged all his life.

But one thing he wouldn't tolerate, his hometown being slagged off. He would defend Margate by saying if it were good enough for J.M.W. Turner and Tracey Emin it was good enough for anybody. So far from a detrimental effect, doctors like Rob helped raise the standard and countered the toxic effect of many of our embarrassing colleagues. They were the ones who diluted the quality towards homeopathic levels."

Stephen was beginning to win his audience back but was going on too long. He put aside the last two pages although he could not resist referring to several of Rob's weird personality traits.

"He was a good mate, a great doctor, and a devoted father. We shared a hero in John Lennon. But he was terrible at squash and had a warped sense of humour. He will be missed."

For Jenny's sake he left out the loving husband bit. Stephen finished by saying that Rob had requested music that said it all about him. He asked that everyone stood quietly while they absorbed the lyrics of the first track, but then mingled after that. John Lennon's *Imagine* started and nobody moved or spoke. During the second verse Suzy started to cry.

Imagine there's no countries
It isn't hard to do
Nothing to kill or die for
And no religion too
Imagine all the people living life in peace…

Her sister, Leila put an arm around her.

"That's exactly what Rob believed," she sobbed, "This was his favourite album."

Rob had been cremated earlier without ceremony. After he had been found dead she had to do the essentials like look for a will and the insurance policies, and found a note from Rob in the same file, dated the day after Rosa's funeral. Headed just AFTER MY DEATH, it said no proper funeral, certainly no religious content, a wicker coffin and a few drinks in our garden. It listed a few pieces of music. What was next sent shivers down Suzy's spine:

'If I die within the next year, treat my death as suspicious. Get some help, as there will be a cover-up.'

But he ended with a paragraph that produced the tears again.

'Suzy, as we met over Tennyson (as well as *Lassie*) I'd like to leave with some thoughts inspired by Lord Alfred. As I'm obviously dead, and prematurely, or you wouldn't be reading this, let no one try to claim I died not fighting for what I believe. I'm sorry Suzy, but I had to do what I did, *I must lose myself in action, lest I wither in despair.* Tell them all at my send off, *'Tis not too late to seek a newer world*, but above all Suzy, *Love is the only gold.*'

There was not a large attendance. Mainly family and very close friends. Rob's parents were both dead. Michael and Eileen were the first to talk to Suzy. Michael told her about the football game that was to be a surprise, but they now could not face going. Although trivial in comparison this let Stephen off the hook. He could now be at Ellie's dinner party and pretend there was never a conflict. He told Michael not to mention it. That was to go ahead as Ellie said that would be what Rob would have wanted. Stephen knew she was wrong but said nothing. He would have wanted them to go to the football.

Jenny had brought the three girls, now nineteen, seventeen and fourteen. Not only deeply traumatised by their father's death, they had to endure shouts from classmates about how their father was a dirty pervert. Individually they showed some sympathy, but when they got together as a group it was like *Lord of the Flies*. The eldest had had years of taunts about her port wine stain too. The father of a school friend who was old enough to remember Mikhail Gorbachev was insensitive enough to nickname her 'Gorby'. Rob had tried to help by saying tell them it's a naevus flammeus, that will shut them up. Of course it did not work.

As well as Leila, Suzy's brother Jeff was also there in support. He had moved to the USA, and although he had fallen out with his best man Clifford Wessel, he wondered if he would be there. He was not tactless enough to ask Suzy.

Only Giselle attended from the practice, as well as Celeste the practice nurse. No Clive though, which upset Suzy - but she had been told what he had said to the media. Snivelling creep. After all Rob had done for him. What could possibly have driven such a betrayal? She was also informed he had done a deal with the local paper but she did not want to believe that.

Rebel Rebel by Bowie began. Stephen turned the volume up. This was a Brockley memory. Ellie and Stephen were standing alone. A woman who they had never met introduced herself. Madison Moodey. Standing next to her, and obviously accompanying her was Chantelle. She was feeling awkward and beginning to wish she had been stronger and refused Madison's suggestion about coming. It was more than a suggestion though - it appeared almost like an order. She realised on the journey it was because Madison wanted to find out what she could and needed her support. Also, if Chantelle could witness this at first hand she might continue her professional interest - that was not necessary though to keep Chantelle on the case.

Madison apologised for gate-crashing as she had only met Rob once, but she had heard about his death on *BBC News 24* and just could not believe what was being said. She admitted she came partly out of curiosity, but felt the need to question the official narrative and that this seemed the obvious place to start.

Freddie Mercury was blasting out *too much love will kill you*. This was when Jenny had tears rolling down her cheeks. The lyrics were too close for comfort, but a conscious choice of Rob's to say sorry to Jenny. Her daughters comforted her.

Two people Suzy did not expect to see were Pippa and Dave. They had all been told about their respective losses on the same day, that terrible Thursday, and actually strangely enough, at the same time. Although Rob and Jeremy's bodies were found together none of them believed the police version. They had all decided to meet the next day on the Friday. They were not sure why.

Probably initially they found comfort in each other and something to occupy their time. But it soon became clear to them they had to stick together. They were all frightened as well as devastated and shocked. They had lost a child and a husband respectively. None of them knew what was happening and they were all feeling out of their depth. The decision was made not to speak to anyone about the tragedy until the dust had settled and they could think straight. It was at the time, when they were leaving to go home, that Pippa and Dave told Suzy they would not be able to face Rob's funeral. But that had been a week ago and they had come after all. The three of them hugged each other without saying a word.

It was a few minutes into the eulogy before Pippa realised who was giving it. She then remembered who Stephen was from his visits to Brick Lane but she had not seen him for years. She was not really keen to really talk to anyone but, after a little hesitation she approached him, and after he had offered his condolences they got chatting.

"You were what we called the Brick Lane lot weren't you?" Stephen recalled, "I visited with Rob a few times, but regret never joining you on any of those holidays."

He remembered how easy it was to talk to her.

"Yes, and I claim that I knew Rob longer than you!"

"Not sure about that but if you did we are talking of a few weeks. Whatever, it's well over thirty years. You remember Anthony Cairns who was often with us?"

"Vaguely," replied Pippa.

"'Afro Ant'?" prompted Stephen.

A faint degree of recognition appeared on Pippa's face.

"Well he is over there at the drinks table talking to Suzy's brother Jeff. I didn't recognise him at first either. He used to have almost an Afro of red hair - now none!" Stephen smirked.

"My sister, who you also would have met all those years ago, is here somewhere too," said Pippa. "Penny. It was her flat in Brick

Lane if you remember. She brought us here today as neither Dave nor I are really in a fit state to drive."

"Yes, I can fully understand that," sympathised Stephen.

Then after a pause.

"I'm grateful to her as she almost laughed at my in-joke."

"You must have come to some of our famous Brockley parties then too?"

"Yes, I certainly did, but could never let my hair down like the rest of you as I was usually with the bloke who ended up as my first husband."

"Oh yes, I remember," Stephen replied, subtly as ever, "We used to call him 'John the prat'. We never could work out what you saw in him."

Stephen thought he had better get off that subject and introduced Dave to Madison and more condolences were exchanged. He waited until they had got into a conversation before quietly saying to Pippa.

"Do you know why he used to call John that? Jealousy. He used to fancy you like mad."

This was another shock for Pippa. She did not know what to say.

"He told me once he dreamt about you," teased Stephen. "I won't tell you what happened in the dream, not at a funeral."

Now it was Pippa's turn to cry. It was all too much and made worse by the Beatles' *In My Life* soundtrack reaching her favourite baroque-style piano solo. Lennon's lyrics always got to her. It was Rob who gave her the Lennon education. Funerals were a time of reflection, but Pippa did not predict she would be reflecting on a missed opportunity. Why did I not pick up those vibes, she thought. She would almost certainly have dumped John the Prat for him although it seems clearer in hindsight. History could have been so different, but then I would not have had my Dave, she thought rather guiltily.

Stephen thought, oh shit, big mistake, me and my fucking big mouth.

"I'm sorry. Inappropriate," he said.

Actually don't apologise. It was good to hear something nice. For a nanosecond I actually was deflected away from the fact that I will never see my son again."

Stephen thought he should move quickly onto safer ground.

"At our last squash session Rob told me about Brandolini's Law, brilliant and typical Rob. Do you know about it?"

"Don't tell me. It's some law where you find out someone fancied you after they are dead?"

Clearly not safer ground, Stephen thought, but it seems she is not too bothered by my crass blabbermouth.

"Otherwise known as the Bullshit Asymmetry Principle. It's the amount of energy necessary to refute bullshit is an order of magnitude bigger than to produce it."

"Why are you telling me this, Stephen?"

"Because it was the last rant Rob had over a pint with me so I cherish it. And because I just babble when I'm nervous and feel awkward and funerals make me feel nervous and awkward. He went on about fact free, celeb-based medicine and the damage it does and how much time he used to spend in surgery persuading people that it was crap. How one Hollywood star said, *having a PSA test saved my life*, and a chat show host told people, *if you can pee two feet against a wall you don't have prostate cancer.* The only people, for whom that is true, are women. And then there was the MMR scandal. Apparently Trump believes that crap which has caused so many deaths because people were conned into fearing vaccinating their kids."

"Quite a few otherwise intelligent parents of children in Jeremy's class fell for buying separate vaccines. Someone made a killing. Literally," contributed Pippa.

"My favourite was the patient of Rob's who had heard Gwyneth Paltrow talk about vaginal steam cleaning and wanted to know if it was available yet on the NHS. And if not, why not?"

Then Pippa completely wrong-footed Stephen.

"What's wrong with that? I get it done once a week at the local car wash?"

But now she was weeping with a mixture of laughter and sorrow. Dave returned to see his wife smiling for the first time since the day that changed their lives forever. He brought Madison with him to introduce her to Pippa. The four of them got serious again.

"Rob was obviously onto something and I'm sure Stephen is right. There is no way Rob did those things or killed himself. We know he was not responsible for Jeremy's death. That was my fault for getting mixed up in all this."

Although suffering badly himself Dave had been Pippa's rock through all this and repeated, as he had done every day, that she must not blame herself.

"Do you know about the files we discovered and went through?" said Pippa, "Suzy, Rob and I sat up half the night with our mouths hanging open."

Stephen looked a little puzzled but Madison jumped in.

"Yes, we met in London and he told me all about them. They tied in with what my husband Pete was investigating. You know about him, I assume?" said Madison.

Again Stephen felt out of the loop.

"Pippa spent an entire evening searching for a French programme that you featured in Madison," said Dave.

Then the penny dropped for Stephen.

"Ah, yes, I saw that in an effort to improve my French and told Rob about it. You are the lady featured. Of course, I remembered you were from Texas and your French interviewer was called Chantelle, lovely looking lady. I told Rob at the time I wouldn't mind meeting her down a dark alley to practise my French."

"Well you can. Not quite a dark alley though. She is over there helping herself to another drink," smiled Madison, "You won't get anywhere though," she added, "unless you are much more than a man."

Stephen did not understand that last remark. He hoped it was not her opinion on his attractiveness to women.

Giselle was at the far end of the table and appeared quite uncomfortable. As if to avoid conversation she turned and started talking to Lars, Rob's Dutch cousin and Geert Wilders supporter.

Madison continued.

"Suzy told me that one on the left was her husband's practice manager. I think she introduced us to get shot of me. Despite their common nationality they seem to not want to talk to each other that much. The only word I understood was Debussy! I'll have to tease Chantelle about that when she returns."

Stephen made his excuses to get a drink and find Ellie. Suzy came over and stood in his spot. She realised she had been a little abrupt with Madison so tried to compensate.

"I know this is Rob's funeral but all four of us are suffering losses. I just hope your loss Madison, doesn't turn into a bereavement like ours?"

Then turning more to Pippa.

"When is Jeremy's funeral?"

"Next Tuesday. Tomorrow Bournemouth Football Club is observing a minute's silence before the game. Jeremy's cousins will go onto the pitch representing us. They are Penny's children. Rob used to get confused between the Poppies and the Cherries. They used to rib each other a lot about football. Rob was going to tease him about Poole FC. He went to the trouble of researching it. That shows what a nice man he was."

Pippa started to cry again. The sublime quiet nocturne second movement of Beethoven's *Emperor Concerto* was playing softly in the background. Rob had specified Vladimir Ashkenazy with Sir Georg Solti and the Chicago Symphony Orchestra.

"We have all been warned off in the worst possible way," said Dave, "This thing is much bigger than any of us. We are powerless and have to accept that. We cannot fight them, whoever they are, without risking another tragedy or death. But we must keep searching for the truth among the lying."

"I sympathise with what you say but I'm going to pursue this. I owe it to Pete. Until I met him I could not see where X marks the spot, because I was standing on it. I hope Chantelle will be helping me although she is working hard on a follow-up to her documentary about England's use of forced adoption. Then I know she wants to tackle the Grenfell Tower scandal. She thinks the British will do their, I mean our, usual cover-up," said Madison, "But I've lost the man I loved and don't care about myself any more. All hope has faded and what once seemed so very plain now gives me so much pain."

At that point Giselle walked past them all towards the front door. She felt out of place and seemed to be trying to leave when Judge Denning's daughter caught her.

"I'm here to represent my parents who are indisposed. We just wanted to show our respects. I am personally very grateful to Dr Baigent. He dealt with my miscarriage in the most kind and sympathetic manner."

Dave was in the process of drowning his sorrows. Life would never be the same. Willing himself through drunken thoughts and words, he wanted to turn an awful occasion into something more worthwhile. He wanted to say something about death. He was a proud atheist but needed some comfort. He used his interest in quantum mechanics to manufacture a comfort blanket from Schrodinger's cat.

"This thought experiment presents a scenario, where a cat may be simultaneously alive and dead as a result of being linked to a random subatomic event that may or may not occur."

"Dave, how strong is that beer your are drinking? What are you talking about?" said Suzy, recognising his attempts at making people feel a little better.

"It just so happens Rob had a supply of both the *Silent Slasher* and *Cocky Hop* beers in the kitchen."

"Not your Fritz Zwicky story again please, Dave," pleaded Pippa.

"No. He was an astronomer, my dear confused love. Erwin Schrodinger was a physicist and he posed the question, *when does a quantum system stop existing as a superposition of states and become one or the other?*"

Pippa could not stop herself.

"You can see where Jeremy gets it from, can't you?"

She then realised she was using the present tense.

"You English. This sounds just like something out of *Monty Python*," contributed Madison, who spoke on behalf of all wondering what Dave was talking about.

"It's just that Schrodinger's cat can be alive or dead at the same time. I wonder about Jeremy and Rob."

There was silence. Dave was remarkably articulate considering how much he had drunk.

"You remember, Pippa my love. You remember Jeremy telling us of his discovery of the multiverse? How there are an infinite number of parallel universes out there? And so an infinite number of alternatives, one in which Rob and Jeremy are still alive?"

"I know you are trying your hardest to ease my pain, but Dave, in this universe they are alive in our memories but dead as people," said Pippa.

"Sorry to interrupt," came a voice from behind Suzy, but also with a gentle hand on the shoulder. Suzy turned. It was Jenny.

"We haven't had a chance to talk and I'd like to, if you are okay with that?"

"Of course. I'd be pleased."

"Can I call you for a coffee, or even lunch in the next few days?"

"Please do."

Jenny who appeared nervous and shaky thanked Suzy and said goodbye to everyone. She rounded up her three daughters and then left. In the background Peter Cook and Dudley Moore were singing goodbye. Rob Baigent's indomitable sense of humour.

Now is the time to say goodbye.
Now is the time to yield a sigh.
Now is the time to wend our waaaayeeeeee.
Until we meet again some sunny day.

59 - SADNESS AND REVELATIONS

LULLABYE (GOODNIGHT, MY ANGEL)

Goodnight my angel, time to close your eyes
And save these questions for another day
I think I know what you've been asking me
I think you know what I've been trying to say
I promised I would never leave you
Then you should always know
Wherever you may go, no matter where you are
I never will be far away

Billy Joel (1994)

"I never thought when I bought my tickets to visit you it'd be for such a terrible event. I can't believe what's happened and I am so sad for you, sis. Rob and you seemed so happy."

That did not need a reply.

Jeff was quiet for him. He was really heartbroken for his sister, although surprised how tough she was appearing - externally at least. He had said he planned to visit some old friends on this rare trip to the UK but decided his sister was a priority.

He could still squeeze in a short visit to their mother and father - in Wales and Scotland respectively - despite the distance. Neither was well enough to travel for Rob's funeral, or so they said. He understood from Leila, their younger sister, that their Dad spent most of his life in the Westport Tavern in Cupar trying to convince the locals he was the real Elton John and telling the Scots their football was rubbish. Leila visited both parents more regularly than her sibs. Their mum was still working in her new partner's fish and chip shop in Tenby.

Suzy really wanted Jeff to stay with her as much as he could. She dreaded the first night on her own so was trying to put it off as long as possible. Jeff had been the typical older brother - bossy, mostly absent but protective. The five-year age gap, which seemed enormous in her teens and when he was at university was not important anymore. Now he was more sensitive, less bossy but still sure of himself. She worried about him. They decided to go for a walk. A circuit around the village.

"Everyone is dying, Jeff," Suzy said.

This startled Jeff. He did not quite understand what she was getting at.

"The very foundations of our lives are disappearing. Bowie, Hawking, Lou Reed, Bruce Forsyth, Tony Benn, June Whitfield, now Rob and Jeremy."

"Odd to lump them together but I know what you mean."

"The Queen won't be long," continued Jeff.

He instantaneously realised that remark just made things worse and was crass.

"Oh Jeff, that will be another rock gone. Our generation has known no other."

"She's Elizabeth the first if you are Scottish, not Elizabeth the second," he jumped in, trying to rescue the situation.

"And I'll miss Ray Wilkins, Ray Galton and that great campaigner Harry Leslie Smith," he added.

"On a day like today, comedy does help. It is not disrespectful. Do you remember that classic Galton and Simpson jury sketch delivered so brilliantly by Tony Hancock?"

"Remind me," said Suzy, appreciating her brother's attempts of support.

"Okay. This is my best Hancock impersonation, *Does Magna Carta mean nothing to you? Did she die in vain? A brave Hungarian peasant girl who forced King John to sign the pledge at Runnymede and close the boozers at half past ten?*"

"Very good, yes, I remember watching that with Dad."

Then Jeff decided this was the moment.

"We must talk. Leila said she'd keep an eye on the place. So now most of the others have gone, is this a good time?"

"As good as any Jeff," replied Suzy.

"There are a few things you need to know."

Suzy gave him a glare.

"Not least, Jeff, why you are travelling with a passport under the name Frank Gale?"

"Ah, yes, um. That was a bit careless of me. That's one thing I will explain. It's the name I use in the US."

"Why on earth do you need an alias?"

"Aliases, actually. But I have less than I used to, if that makes you feel any better? Chosen from our father's Elton John obsession. Follow carefully. *Goodbye Yellow Brick Road. The Wonderful Wizard of Oz* by Frank Baum. Dorothy Gale, the Judy Garland character in the 1939 MGM movie. Convoluted, but my other aliases are Elton John connections too. Ray Cooper his one time percussionist, and Guy Burnett remember *Song for Guy*? Another is Bennie… oh, you don't need to know any more."

"I didn't ask why you chose certain names, Jeff, but why you need them at all?" said Suzy.

She was exasperated after a tiring and very emotional day and just hoping he was not going to add to her worries.

"I feel after all these years and now you have got tragically caught up in it, I should give you a full explanation. It will only make sense if I go back to the beginning. It will take a while, are you prepared?"

"Yes, but before you start it's fewer."

He looked at her puzzled.

"You should say you have fewer aliases than you used to. Not less. Less is right for quantities like less sugar. Fewer correct for comparing numbers like fewer people."

"Thanks for that, Suzy."

They were passing through the King George V playing fields. A group of teenagers were playing football using their coats as goalposts. Nothing unusual in that, except they were all girls. They sat on the seat looking straight at them.

"Do you remember when I left university and went to work at Conservative Central Office?"

"Do I! It was such a shock. Dad calling you a fucking Tory and Mum refusing to speak to you for weeks. So out of character. We wondered what had happened to you at uni."

"Well, something did happen. I was recruited. I became a mole. I was never a Tory but I could not tell anyone that. It would have blown my cover. It was one of the trickiest things I have ever had to do. Defend the right-wingers and pretend to argue their case. Especially the Poll Tax."

"Recruited by what, who?"

"Who do you think? The anti-elite, anti-Establishment revolutionaries. When I left home, I met people saying exactly what I'd been thinking for years. It was a breath of fresh air, but after being recruited, I couldn't say so. I was seduced into thinking I was following in the tradition of Burgess, Maclean, Philby and Blunt, but not by the Russians of course. By an underground network of agitators committed to exposing the truth of what's really going on in this dreadful country we inhabit. Then I realised it was the world. They had the nickname of Poison. You will not have heard of them."

"I remember that era in our lives. That's where you met Wessel and Humphrey. Much to my cost."

"And Witney briefly. You have to know I always hated Wessel. I asked him to be my best man to help keep my credibility under cover. If you think he is horrible you should have met his German father! I tried to bash Cliff as hard as I could on the rugby pitch."

"So, then what? What else did you get up to?"

"All low key stuff for a while. My work in IT was an asset to my contacts. I took my instructions from a man called Guy who headed up the Investigative Unit. I helped accumulate a huge amount of data. I got quite expert at hacking into computer systems. The work became a little more dangerous when we uncovered several infiltrators. One of them was a Lewisham lab technician called Robin, who years later I worked out had known Rob. He disappeared about the turn of the century. Pretty sure he was disposed of for his double-dealing. From here on I realised I was at the point of no return. So I made life more interesting with a few trips to the US to teach our contacts in America how to hack and what to do with the information they came across. It was through this that eventually I came across Anonymous and built up links with WikiLeaks, which was founded just before Philip died. My dealings with Edward Snowden and Bradley Manning, before she became Chelsea, came much later."

"Bloody hell. This is all astonishing. You aren't just winding me up are you Jeff? It is getting quite worrying."

"I'm afraid you haven't heard the worst yet. To continue the story in chronological order so I don't forget anything important. I'd been sitting on a top-secret file I hacked from Whitehall about Thatcher's privatisation plans. Under her, a conference was held in 1988 and led by the top civil servant called Sir Roland Henderson. You will have heard of him. He eventually became Cabinet Secretary, now of course in the Lords and on numerous company Boards. This was dynamite as it proved the whole Government was telling the public barefaced lies. Taking a great risk and knowing Philip for a few years, through you of course, one Christmas family do, I showed it to him and asked him if he knew anything about it and what should I do with it?"

"How did he react?"

"Much to my surprise he hardly batted an eyelid. I was relieved of course he didn't think my place was in a police cell. He told me he was in a similar position being in possession, he said, of material a lot worse than that. So he turned it round and asked me to take what he had and do something useful with it. It turned out that amongst his files was the Westminster paedophile dossier."

"I was afraid you were going to say that," said Suzy.

"He had found out some terrible things through his contacts in his job, one being a mole called Mike who I now know is in the States, and realised his life could be in danger. He didn't want you to know as he thought it might endanger you too. But he needed to tell someone and put the info into someone else's hands. He knew I was planning to go to the States and thought it best out of the country and to possibly work from there. I told him nothing about Poison. Oddly he didn't ask where I got the files. The next thing I hear is that he has been killed in a road accident. I knew it was no accident."

"Oh, shit. Oh, shit. So Rob was right. So I now have two dead husbands, both murdered."

"Philip was right not to involve you wasn't he? I couldn't tell you anything either, as you can now see, sis."

Suzy just nodded.

"The next thing I knew a few years later is that you and Rob were an item. You came over to have a Californian holiday at my house, which was lovely. Do you remember I'd just taken delivery of that hot tub? I know you both got up to no good in it. You must have still been within the eighteen months period that you told me about."

Suzy actually blushed - this did not seem right coming from her brother.

"You remember I got the cash for that tub from a small inheritance from an old girlfriend. So as a tribute I named it after her, Daphne. Being in Daphne was always great."

"Please Jeff, spare me those details."

Suzy was serious. She did not appreciate her brother's crude humour.

"What?" Jeff feigned shock, "I am referring to being in my hot tub."

He continued.

"Anyway, Leila visited too with her children. It was nice. The age difference between me and our kid sister evaporated and didn't seem to matter anymore."

Then he threw in an after-thought.

"Daphne was murdered by the CIA."

Jeff thought he had better get back on track.

"What you didn't know was that at a late night drinking session when you and that girlfriend of mine, the one I ditched soon after you returned home…"

"Mia?"

"Yes, Mia. You have a better memory than me. Well, you two couldn't handle it and sloped off to bed, then Rob and I really got to know each other. We had both had marriage breakups that we hadn't properly recovered from. He said his guilt was still on his mind twenty-three hours a day. So we drowned our sorrows. We debated who had the most corrupt Government, then who had the most arrogant bastards. Then the fattest… well, in the arrogant bastard section, the medical profession didn't come away smelling of roses, especially in the States, and the name Wessel came up. You had told him he was my best man and he knew him from BMA conferences. He also knew you had slept with him. Top marks for honesty!"

"I told him about Neville Gideon too."

"What about him?"

"Well…"

"Oh Sis! You didn't! Not that nasty old Etonian git?"

"Somebody had to."

After a few seconds of reflection.

"Mia and me didn't even last the eighteen months. She got fed up after a year. Hated giving head, that's why she had to go!"

"Jeff, please. Too much detail!"

Suzy's blushing had spread but this was her chance to ask her big brother things she had not had the nerve to ask before.

"Have you a partner now?"

"No, I'm taking a break after Mia and Daphne, plus one or two others. I've never told anyone what happened with my marriage to Angela. After nearly fifteen years she went off with another woman! It was such a shock to me as she lived by the maxim that 'to keep a man happy, keep his stomach full and his balls empty'. So I was happy. But now they are happy, somewhere in Yorkshire. I still get Christmas cards. I'm glad now we didn't have children. Sorry I'm getting sidetracked.

The reason I mentioned Wessel was because Rob was convinced he was involved with the privatisation of the NHS, and he wanted to play his part in exposing and stopping it. For my part I was keen to find out how far Sir Roland Henderson's plan had progressed since 1988. Don't forget I was six thousand miles away and so a bit cut off. So Rob became my source for what was actually happening, not just the theory or plots. I sent him a document that Philip had stolen, still covered by the thirty year rule at that time, which exposed Thatcher and her Chancellor Geoffrey Howe, of their planning charging for state schools and to introduce compulsory private health insurance, which would mean the end of the NHS. Nothing less than the breakup of the Welfare State. The proposals had been drawn up by Henderson's old boss, a man called Alan Bailey from the Central Policy Review Staff."

"That's when he started going on about the NHS privatisation conspiracy. I thought him almost paranoid and too one-tracked and told him to consider the bigger picture. His hatred of corruption went onto a new and higher level at this point. I feel guilty now I didn't take him more seriously or follow what he was saying more diligently."

"The frequency of our communications increased and I knew he was getting more and more concerned, but the stream of material he sent me was mainly his own theories without much evidence. But Rob was thinking just like Philip. Some of the more recent information was safer out of the country however. So you see, Rob and I have been in contact over several years. We knew we had to keep you out of it as much as possible. Do you remember when I rang you in India on your honeymoon, and I had to pretend I'd dialled you by mistake? I hadn't of course but I'd got a bit lazy about security and didn't think you would be in earshot."

They sat in silence for a few moments. Suzy reached out to hold Jeff's hand. A flock of Canada geese flew overhead.

"Do you know they are monogamous?" said Suzy, "They seem to have life worked out. The front position of their V-shaped flight formation is rotated as flying in front consumes more energy."

"What if they are really in control?" said Jeff

"Not another conspiracy theory, surely Jeff? Are you going to tell me that Canada geese brought down the Twin Towers?"

"Not quite. They did bring down that plane into the Hudson though didn't they? And they did sell WMDs to Saddam Hussain."

Suzy appreciated Jeff's attempts to make her laugh when she thought she would never laugh again.

"No, what I mean is, what if we are really the pets of the animal kingdom? We think we keep cats, but perhaps they keep us. Who is more sensible? The cat that just does exactly what it wants, lies around all day, and gets fed? No job to go to, gets up when it feels like, no household chores and no real worries. No money worries, and as Lennon said, *no countries, no religion, no possessions.* Which is the stupidest species? I rest my case."

The two siblings got up from the bench to stroll home after Jeff had moved to return the football to one of the goalkeepers.

"That one is tasty."

"Jeff, she is probably only about fifteen."

"I'm only joking."

"Not funny in the circumstances."

"Sorry. He sent me some really damning and dangerous material before he died."

"What sort of stuff?

"A memory stick, with some awful stuff on it. If it had been intercepted we'd have all ended up in jail. There was a video made by a man called Sean who described how he'd been kept prisoner, basically as a sex slave, for a decade or so. Bad, but not earth-shattering on its own. What makes it dynamite is the photos backing up what he said. Lots of recognisable faces performing all sorts of, what do they call them now, lewd acts? Politicians, stars, Establishment figures, from all walks of life."

Suzy thought she would make it easier for him.

"He told me about meeting this bloke at Chartwell, I assume the same man. Pippa went with him. It was at this time he copied and posted memory sticks to a load of news outlets, only to have them all returned. I assume this is what he also sent you. So one at least got to where he had intended then? Slipped through their fishing net, presumably as it was addressed to a named person, out of the country, and using one of his sticky labels he had made for Christmas cards, rather than his unmistakably appalling handwriting. Not that he mentioned to me he was sending you a copy, but I see why now. I still don't really understand what he thought you would do with it?"

"He looked at me as a safe storage place. Out of the country, and unlikely to lose things. He knew he could trust me. Rob sent me copies of the files Pippa stole from that ex-Attorney General."

"You know about them?"

"It must have taken him ages to copy them, then put them on the disc that I have. We exchanged a few emails about these, but were fairly cryptic in our language. He thought he was being monitored. I haven't read them all yet, but there is some amazing dynamite there too."

"Amazing but not amazing enough to get our media interested. They are obviously still all in it together. Rob was trying to get the French media involved though."

"Yes, I know. He put me in contact with Madison, who we both met today for the first time. It was as though Rob wanted a few back-ups in case something happened to him. He didn't want all this effort and risk being for nothing. After all of this though, his main concern was still the NHS! Still one-tracked. He regularly wanted to learn about the healthcare scandals in the USA, and, believe me I'm not short of material there. The main reason for the Madison contact though was he wanted to help her in her search for what happened to her journalist husband Pete. He thought I might be able to help with my contacts, and I did manage to find out a few things."

"What did happen?" asked Suzy

"Well this is off the point a bit and I don't want to get side-tracked but he ended up in Guantanamo."

"Is he still there? Is he still alive?"

"The answer to both questions is, I don't think so. I'll tell you more about that later, but my main concern is how can you trust me knowing I kept a terrible secret from you all these last ten years or so? Now you have to believe me that I've agonised over this and came to the conclusion it wouldn't help you at all to know the truth about Philip. But what has happened to Rob changes everything. I've got no doubt he was murdered."

"Oh, no. This is all too much to hear it straight like that," she stopped dead in her tracks.

"Did Rob know that?"

"Yes. We are both responsible for keeping this from you. We wanted to protect you. But more recently he decided to drop a few hints to you."

"It seems everyone wanted to keep me in the fucking dark," she said angrily, "But now I remember him asking me if I thought Philip's car crash was really an accident. I think my reply was along the lines of, don't be a fucking idiot. I told him it's as likely as our Prime Minister being a lady-boy from Bangkok. So he was really trying to tell me something. It must partly have been in an effort to get me to take him more seriously. I was always telling him he was a paranoid jerk."

"Well, you now know the truth. Our PM is a lady-boy from Bangkok," said Jeff trying to keep a straight face.

That put Jeff onto another track.

"Did you know there have been thirteen coups in Thailand since 1932? There is still a General in charge."

They carried on walking and were nearly home.

"If you are going to ask me what do we do now? What next? Then save your breath, as I don't know," said Jeff, "I know the CIA, or someone is chasing me. That's why I have a few identities. I've even got my doubts about whether that new ignorant President we have will let me back in the country even though they haven't joined the dots yet about who I really am. Ray Cooper, me again over in the States, nearly got caught. I've had to move from Lucerne Avenue, not sure if I told you that.

Anyway we knew nothing would change if an Establishment figure like Clinton were elected. You know it doesn't really matter who is President, it's the system that controls everything and the so-called Chief Executive does what he or she is told. It was and still is a high-risk strategy but we recognised one possible road back to proper democracy was to cause a crisis. You are living that crisis now. The plan was to get a complete donkey in the White House who would be so obviously a complete corrupt dipstick, as opposed to the corrupt boneheads we have had up to now who have covered up and conned enough people to let things carry on as normal, under orders as I said. This man was to become a laughing stock. So extreme it could threaten the system. He and his whole administration would be so discredited that in the end everyone would be crying out for a better, cleaner, corrupt-free system. In other words cause a massive backlash.

So we hacked accounts, fed the FBI emails, leaked things to the Russians, all to get Trump elected. We gave him some of his best lines. 'Draining the swamp' wasn't new. It was *drenare la palude* in the original Mussolini Italian. And we got him to copy Stalin who talked about the press being the enemy of the people. He was too dim to realise where we were taking him. We knew he would implode, but we didn't realise he would make it so easy for us. Doing stupid things like sacking the FBI chief because he was onto him, giving secrets to the Russians, you couldn't make it up! Then tearing children away from their parents at the border. Inhumane acts like that. Terrible, but we couldn't believe our luck. Even we couldn't dream up a more unpopular policy. He declares exercise is bad, asbestos could have saved the World Trade Centre, environmentally friendly light bulbs cause cancer and wind power kills birds. Global warming is rubbish as it snowed in New York in October.

In my guise as Ray Cooper, the CIA got very close. Uncomfortably close. There were similar plans to get a robot elected in the UK... well, that's been done now. The problem is that may have backfired as the dim-witted UK electorate have kept her in power. That wasn't the plan! Let's hope our USA policy doesn't have the same fate.

Mike, the mole I mentioned, is trying to help Madison further and he has to be careful. He is over there now snooping around again and it's not for the first time. Years ago he got quite involved with Daphne, after I split from her. I don't blame him for her murder but I think he inadvertently led the CIA to her. I must warn him off. To him I'm Guy Burnett, but he knows my true identity. He worked in the same department as Philip in Whitehall and was Pete Moodey's source. I'm still not sure if Philip and Mike were working independently, or cooperating, or if they were actually working for someone. We don't talk about that."

"*Oh, what a tangled web we weave when first we practise to deceive*, eh?" said Suzy.

"That's Walter Scott, isn't it? First time I've ever heard you get a quote right."

"How dare you," she smiled for the first time that day.

"I'm the wrong side of fifty now for all this Jason Bourne stuff but I'm up to my neck in it, Suzy, as you can now tell. Don't forget I've been in the States for more than a decade. I have been living in what's coming your way in this country. In that sense I've seen the future. I can sum their society up in one example. Take prisons. Privately run and the more prisoners the more money they make. Why do you think they lock up people at a rate five times most other comparable countries? Money and control. It allows them to control the population. And black men are incarcerated at thirty times our rate. Thirty times! Astonishing."

"I need a drink. What a fucking awful day. It's made me quite scared and I was already before you started. Anything else you have to tell me?"

"I'm sorry. When I went over to California I was about forty. Not too old to start a new life I thought. I had to get out of the UK, as I was worried I'd be locked up as a hacker. The job I got with Sony was perfect for access to all the computers I wanted and worked well as a cover. I have contact with a load of geeks who are all working on making our desktops and tablets spy on us but that's another subject. But I promise you I had no plans to have this sort of new life. I certainly didn't want to involve others, especially you or Rob."

Suzy reached to hold his hand again.

"You have nothing to apologise for. It seems Rob was working in parallel to you, not following you."

"When I left the UK I sensed the country we were born in was having an identity crisis and a nervous breakdown. I could see the two pillars on which Britain built its foreign policy, Europe and the transatlantic relationship, collapsing. As a result, since the UK left the EU, no one cares what we think, we have no influence in the world, and all this is self-inflicted. We used to punch above our weight. Now the British have taken to punching each other in a polarised and uncertain country. Brexit rolled over a log and we all are seeing what crawled out."

"Wow. That is profound," said Suzy.

"In the US they not only think we are an irrelevance, but many yanks couldn't even pinpoint us on the map. It won't be long before the others move to take away our permanent status as a member of the United Nations Security Council. France wants that now we are no longer part of Europe. It would help Macron in his attempt to establish French as the dominant world language."

They were in sight of Suzy's house.

"We should have had this conversation along time ago."

"I had to protect you, Suzy. But now at least I think you know what I've been trying to say, and I think I know what you've been asking me."

As they were approaching Suzy's front door, she searched for her keys. Jeff stopped and looked straight at his sister.

"You are wrong, sis. I have got something to apologise for. There is one more thing. When you were little, I killed your pet budgie by mistake. Well, it wasn't exactly by mistake. I wondered what would happen it I squeezed it. I found out. It went all limp. I told you I just found it in the bottom of its cage. Sorry."

"Oh well, makes me feel less guilty about what I did. You know that girlfriend who suddenly dumped you and you couldn't work out why? I told her you were gay and had sent me to tell her as you were too scared."

"Oh well, at least I now know. I didn't really fancy her anyway," said Jeff without the least bit of concern.

"Let's get back. Leila should still be there. It'll be nice if we three could spend a few hours together alone. That hasn't happened since before you left home for uni."

"Why don't you come over to Culver City with me for a break? Get away from all this. You can spend your days sitting in Daphne, by yourself though. The Royal Academy will understand, surely?"

"Wouldn't that be just running away?"

"No. *Wherever you may go, no matter where you are, I never will be far away.*"

60 - ORDERS AND CENSORSHIP

THE CENTRAL SCRUTINIZER

This is the Central Scrutinizer…
It is my responsibility to enforce all the laws
That haven't been passed yet
It is also my responsibility to alert each and every one of you
To the potential consequences
Of various ordinary everyday activities
You might be performing which could eventually lead to
The death penalty –

Frank Zappa (1979)

MEMORANDUM
CONFIDENTIAL

To: all agents
From: the Central Scrutinizer

Subject: Dr Paul Hobday

Topic: Unlawful distribution and creation of fake news

Aim: To end the propaganda

Action and Method: By any means

Background

The Special Operations Team has been monitoring all communications involving a Dr Paul Hobday from Kent. We now know the source of some annoying stories that are too close for comfort, but still fake news and fictional untruths. His file runs to over two hundred pages. It was opened in 1983 when he joined the

Labour Party to save the NHS, as he put it in a letter to the press. MI5 monitoring began before that when he declared his opposition to the Falklands War. His activities bordered on treachery, but not enough evidence was collected for a prosecution. At that time it was not worth manufacturing evidence against him.

His membership of subversive organisations like CND, Amnesty International, and Greenpeace, together with his support for degenerate groups like the Greenham Common Women's Peace Camp, meant surveillance had to be increased. He supported the miners' strike and several other unpatriotic industrial disputes, including the failed strike by print workers at Wapping. He opposed Section 28 of the Local Government Act prohibiting authorities promoting gay activities, and spoke in favour of a united Ireland. His general opposition to the Thatcher Government led to raids on his home in the guise of burglaries and a smear campaign against his character.

He was active in medical politics for many years but realised he was 'bashing his head against a brick wall' as one of his emails put it. He was called once to give evidence to the House of Commons Select Committee on Health and the opportunity was used then to warn him off. I think our hints were too subtle for him.

He claims that he became disillusioned with orthodox protests and attempts to influence policy by persuasion. He left the Labour Party when he realised they were following Thatcherite policies and could not be coaxed into abandoning their privatisation policies, in particular of the NHS. Both the medical and political arenas were controlled by the people he despised most - privatisers who pretended not to be.

He has been a member of a number of other subversive organisations. He is certainly a dissident agitator, but we have yet to link him to any terrorist group. Some of his intercepted communications have appeared to imply he would be happy to see revolution and an armed struggle with violence to promote his cause. He started to be more of a nuisance to Government when the Health and Social Care Bill was published in 2010.

His profile was raised when he stood as a candidate in the 2015 general election for the National Health Action Party and became its leader in 2016. We took action. By that time we had infiltrated the party as he was becoming more dangerous and too close to the truth. He was ousted thanks to the work of one of our agents (CC).

Problem

The reason for passing this on is that we believe he has written a book about what he terms the plot against the NHS. That alone is not a problem. It has been done before and has not even come near derailing us in our goals - especially now that the public believes our accusations that people have been saying the NHS is being destroyed for years and yet it is still there - or it appears to be. Saying they are crying wolf has kept the public off the scent.

The problem is that he has seen the link with all the other policies and may upset the corruption applecart, as he knows too much about cover-ups, paedophile rings and all the conspiracies. He is determined to expose the fake news and the fictional truth that we use.

More worrying are his attempts to produce an understanding in the minds of the public as to what is actually happening. He is not that far away from exposing reality. Of course no one will believe him but we cannot even take a small risk.

We will naturally deploy all the dirty tricks we have at our disposal to discredit him. Denials, ridicule, character assassination, framing, mental illness including paranoid delusions and gullibility as starters, then threats to his family.

One of his contacts in the USA, and sources, goes by the name of Ray Cooper. He has been evading the American Security Services for more than a decade. The CIA are very frustrated and we must help them. We are still not sure whether Frank Gale is the same man. Bennie Jetsong may be another alias, or just a contact of Cooper's. Hobday has been known to communicate with Jetsong. The closest we have got to him was when we caught up with Peter Moodey, who you all know about, but Dwight - his code name - slipped through the net yet again.

Our allies across the Atlantic have got the name Emptage out of Moodey using their very persuasive methods but little else of value. We believe Emptage is the man who escaped when we neutralised Daphne. Apparently he continues to snoop around the States but we are not sure of his agenda.

It is believed Hobday has links to Poison but they remain elusive too. This is the terrorist link we are trying to get evidence for, so that Hobday can be locked up. We have silenced the French connection now that Chantelle Levesque is in HM Prison Bronzefield, a Category A private prison in Surrey, awaiting extradition to the USA. He sees himself as on a mission to warn the world. Fortunately he is no author and it is badly written. We must stop him getting the help he is fishing for to get it up to a readable and perhaps even credible standard. Unknown to him he will be guided towards one of our on-side editors.

Some of his so-called exposes include investigations into the Haut De La Garenne, the Jersey Home for Boys, where he is too close to unveiling the guilt of important members of society who we need to protect.

The US links to the successful Brexit vote are in danger of being exposed too.

He is backing a new film called *The Great NHS Heist*. We are aiming to infiltrate the group behind this propaganda, before neutralising them. They are worryingly effective. The film will not see the light of day.

The Grenfell Tower disaster is on his radar and we cannot afford further trouble over that.

We understand he has evidence that the Manchester bombing, during the 2017 Election campaign, was a Russian attempt to influence the vote.

Our friends at ASIS, the Australian Secret Intelligence Service, want him silenced over the fuss he is making about their Nauru Detention Processing Centre and their violations of the 1951 United Nations Refugee Convention.

All of this needs rubbishing if it emerges into the public domain. We are seeing to it that it does not.

He will be looking for a publisher. Make sure that does not happen. You are to report to Lars.

As is the compulsory practice, now destroy this communication. Failure to do so within one hour will lead to disciplinary action.

The Central Scrutinizer.

End

61 - WAR AND PEACE

PARIS SERA TOUJOURS PARIS

Paris sera toujours Paris !
La plus belle ville du monde
Malgré l'obscurité profonde
Son éclat ne peut être assombri
Paris sera toujours Paris !
Plus on réduit son éclairage
Plus on voit briller son courage
Plus on voit briller son esprit
Paris sera toujours Paris !

Maurice Chevalier (1939)

2028

"Merci beaucoup, Jean-Louis."

"C'est mon plaisir, ma Cherie."

Chantelle exchanged a smile with the café owner as he carefully placed her caffè macchiato in front of her but not close enough to interfere with her newspaper reading. He did not have to ask and she did not have to say. He knew what she wanted. Chantelle found it hard to get her favourite coffee in Paris and when she did discover a café that could produce it for her it was never as good as Jean-Louis's.

She had been a regular ever since she moved into the apartment four floors above six years earlier. Her smile was less forthcoming than usual. She was still saddened by the assassination of Noam Chomsky the American philosopher, even though he was well into his nineties. It seems his criticism of the US President Sarah Palin, had gone too far. Chantelle was not shocked though. Political opponents regularly disappeared, met mysterious deaths, or were victims of brazen murder. Everyone knew that the previous

President was behind the death of Michael Moore but he seemed untouchable.

In the last few years many former leaders had been imprisoned or murdered. Radovan Karadzic may have deserved it but what about Luiz da Silva of Brazil, Najib Razak from Malaysia, Park Geun-Hye of South Korea, Jacob Zuma of South Africa, or Ehud Olmert of Israel? And what about Blair, Angela Merkel, Trudeau and Obama?

Chantelle regarded herself as very lucky. She should have been amongst the victims. She had avoided extradition to the USA by bluffing her way out of the Category A prison in England and escaping to France. It was the one time she was thankful for privatisation. The company operating the largest female private prison in Europe just could not cope and Chantelle was released in error. She was amongst seventy others the Ministry of Justice admitted to releasing by mistake that year. The true figure was a lot higher.

She lost all her material about the Grenfell Tower disaster she had been investigating and was warned off even mentioning it again. Madison had given her what Pete had found out before the inferno just prior to his disappearance. It was a subject close to Madison's heart. A work colleague, Rashida Ahmed and her two children Aisha and Usman had been burnt to death in their home on the eighteenth floor. Madison remembered how scared Rashida was and that conversation on the Jubilee Line that will haunt her forever.

Chomsky had predicted that the American administration's climate change denial and massive increase in the use of fossil fuels would lead to millions having to flee the low lying plains of Bangladesh because of the sea-level rise and more severe weather. When proved correct and it happened, no American heard about it - it would have been too embarrassing. Even when the migrant crisis had reached thirty million people the US media, under right wing control, refused to report the story.

They certainly did not know that Bangladesh's leading climate scientist had claimed that migrants should have had the right to move to the countries from where all the greenhouse gases originated. He had said millions should be able to go to the United States, but the ruling Republican Party, which Chomsky called *the most dangerous organisation in world history*, had refused entry to migrants for over a decade now and actually expelled millions. They delighted in splitting children from their parents. Many of those children were never seen again. Quite a number were abused and offered to paedophiles.

Chomsky had also warned about the catastrophic decline in wildlife from the policies of homo sapiens and the resulting ecological apocalypse. Pollution, habitat changes, overuse of pesticides and global warming resulted in large tracts of land becoming inhospitable to most forms of life. Chantelle rarely saw birds in Paris nowadays. There were no seasons anymore.

In India lack of drinking water from temperature rises and Himalayan glacier melting was now killing millions. Forty per cent of the US population did not see this as a problem as Christ would be returning in a few decades.

The obituary ended with Chomsky's thought that one of the great achievements of the doctrinal system had been to divert anger away from the corporate sector, to the Government that implemented the programs, which the corporate sector had designed in the first place. Very clever. The highly protectionist corporate deals that are uniformly misdescribed as free trade agreements are a good example. The business world had to drive out of people's minds that Government could and should become an instrument of popular will - a Government of, by and for the people. But they had gone further. The business world was the Government now. And in convincing the public of this nonsense, they were more sophisticated in their approach than Hitler, Stalin or Mao - they had learnt from their mistakes.

President Palin called Chomsky a traitor and declared that the world was a sweeter place without him. But very little was said in the US media about him. His death was blamed on an escaped Muslim.

Chantelle had found an obituary in *Le Monde* and had devoured it whilst sipping her caffè macchiato. But there was no mention of

751

Chomsky or his death in *Le Figaro*, which had become even more right wing since President Marion Marechal-Le Pen had taken over control of its editorial staff. This was at least consistent. *Le Figaro* relegated the murders of Macron and Fillon to the deep inside pages and there was little mention of the suicide of the President's grandfather Jean-Marie Le Pen.

"Is Simone joining you this morning, mon bebe?" enquired Jean-Louis whilst clearing the cups and croissant crumbs from a neighbouring table.

"Yes, she will be here when she has locked up the shop for the day. We are going to visit Hotel Drouot this afternoon."

"The auction house? What are you wanting to bid for, mon chaton?"

Chantelle rummaged under *Le Monde* to retrieve her tablet, which had the *Gazette de l'Hotel Drouot* on it. She flicked to a bookmarked page to show Jean-Louis.

"We are hoping to buy some fine art or an antique to celebrate our tenth anniversary. This takes my fancy," said Chantelle proudly pointing to an unknown sketch by Toulouse-Lautrec.

"If my eyes don't deceive me it says the starting price is thirty thousand euro. I'd claim they obviously pay you journalists too well if I didn't know you worked for *Charlie Hebdo,* ma poussinette!"

"You are quite right about that, Jean-Louis! But my book *England's Stolen Children* did quite well, except in England where it was banned. And that was before all diplomatic relations were severed."

"What are you working on now, ma cherie?"

"I'm revisiting the Oradour-sur-Glane atrocity. You know that no one was really held to account for the massacre of six hundred and forty-two of our compatriots. I have a new lead. I was sent some anonymous information from London about a man who goes under the name of Hammond but is actually Gunther Niemand's grandson. Niemand was a Nazi war criminal, second in command to Adolf Diekmann who was in charge of the Das Reich regiment responsible for the massacre. The Americans helped him flee to South America after the war. I think he may know something useful, even if they are all dead now, and won't face justice. Rumour has it he, or the family, are hiding incriminating documents. Maybe I'll be visiting South America! My main problem is getting to talk or meet with Hammond now I can't go to England, and Anglo-French relations are not too far off a war footing."

"Good luck, I wish you well, mon ange, and look forward to watching it on TV or reading about it," said Jean-Louis.

"We have to be at Drouot-Richelieu by two pm so if Simone doesn't hurry she won't get any lunch."

Her father named Simone after Simone de Beauvoir, who Chantelle once said was the French Chomsky. He had just read *The Second Sex*, calling it the mothership of feminist philosophy. De Beauvoir echoed Wollstonecraft's theory that women are made not born. They met soon after Chantelle's escape to Paris. *Franceinfo* let her go, as she was too much of an embarrassment even for them. In her early days of unemployment, she was late for a party and had nothing as a gift and fortuitously passed a beer shop called La Moustache Blanche in Rue Des Tournelles. This was a street away from the gathering, not far from the Bastille. It turned out that Simone owned and ran it. Chantelle was surprised to come across the new shop, as last time she walked down that road it was a tobacconists-cum-newsagents. Simone was wearing a T-shirt with Marlene Dietrich holding a *Je suis Charlie* sign, which was a good talking point as Chantelle had just applied for a new job at *Charlie Hebdo*. Chantelle was instantly attracted to Simone and her bubbly character and was encouraged by the gay icon she was displaying. Simone instantly fell in love with Chantelle's amber eyes. They chatted about the different beers which Chantelle had learnt about in Marylebone, some stocked by Le Moustache Blanche.

"Do you want to come to a party?" Chantelle had said boldly.

Simone did not need to be asked twice. Within a few minutes she had locked up the shop and they were walking down towards the Bastille.

They both got drunk at the party after finding out they had so much in common. Their politics were the same. They were both driven by outrage about what was happening in the world. Simone thought the story of Chantelle's escape from England inspirational. They discovered that both their families originated from Alsace. They actually grew up only a few miles apart - Chantelle in the centre of Colmar and Simone in the village of Hirtzfelden about fifteen miles south. When the area was German before the First World War both had relatives who were drafted into both the French and German armies and ended up fighting against each other.

Some of Chantelle's family saw the writing on the wall in 1912 and emigrated from France to Canada. She could read the names of those who stayed behind on the war memorials in the villages of Lautenbach and Linthal as well as in Colmar. Chantelle still had relatives in Canada. The two families had entirely different pedigrees. Chantelle's family moved back to Colmar when her father got a job with the air taxi company Societe Air Alsace, which was based at the aerodrome. This was after leaving the French Air Force that took the family away from Alsace soon after Chantelle was born. The family had a spell in London where she learnt her fluent English.

Simone however had been there all her life and her family's roots went back generations. She was descended from the Jecker family, who dominated the graveyard on the outskirts of the village and had at least nine names on the 1914-18 War memorial by the Église Saint-Laurent. They claimed to have been in the area for several hundred years and spoke German. Her mother had a small house on Rue de la Republique. The village was only a few miles from the Upper Rhine, which had had its course changed by Louis XIV to gain land - moving it up to a mile to the east - and straightened by Johann Gottfried Tulla in the nineteenth century. The plains had often flooded.

As children they had both regularly visited Hartmannswillerkopf, a pyramidal rocky spur in the Vosges Mountains with spectacular views over the Rhine valley for picnics under the National Monument of World War One. They would play in the craters on the hill left by shelling although their families insisted on respect when walking amongst the hundreds of white crosses.

Both wondered how often they had been there at the same time, unaware that their futures would be entwined. They ended a glorious night in bed together at Chantelle's apartment back above the Le Barricou Bistro in Boulevard Du Temple opposite Cirque D'Hiver.

"Jean-Louis, as there is no sign of Simone, could I order Bruschetta de flageolets, and a demi-carafe of *Chateau Marsau*?"

"A great choice, mon ange."

Chantelle abandoned her *Le Monde* and picked up her tablet again for the *Gazette* so she could see what else she might like at the auction.

Owning a tablet, or any form of computer now meant total surveillance. An ordinary member of the public was only allowed to purchase one by signing the Terms and Conditions, which nowadays included clauses that insisted on access to all data and a microphone. So it was no surprise when she was checking out the *Gazette* that new adverts and suggestions had appeared for all her activity over the previous few hours - caffè macchiato suppliers, Chomsky's books, political murders, Islam, links to people called Niemand and Hammond, Oradour-sur-Glane, Toulouse-Lautrec, Hotel Drouot and even her own book. They really did know everything the citizen was up to. She was looking for the reserve price on a small decorative Louis XIV Boulle inlaid bracket clock circa 1710 when a man raising his voice declaring in English interrupted her concentration.

"What? You are kidding? After all we have been through."

She had not seen the couple come in even though they were only two tables away. She had been too engrossed in her *Gazette*. Chantelle could tell from the look on the woman's face he was being reprimanded for talking too loudly and drawing attention to them. She was facing Chantelle, and the man had his back to her. They appeared to be sharing a bottle of red wine, which was already nearly empty. Her face seemed familiar but Chantelle could not place her.

The reserve price was E25000. It was signed Dumont Freres a Besancon and at sixty-eight centimetres high perfect for their French gilt, metal-mounted, bijouterie table which they had bought a few years before at the same Drouot Auctions. They thought that it expensive at the time at E4000 as neither was on good wages. Le Moustache Blanche made a small profit and Chantelle's wages from journalism were not much better, but Chantelle had some money after she sold her parents' house and Simone was expecting to inherit her mother's place in Hirtzfelden eventually.

The couple caught her attention again. They were clearly arguing. The man had the typical approach of an arrogant Englishman who thought he could say what he wanted as no one would understand him.

"It's too late now to let your guilt get the better of you. You should have thought about that," he said too loudly.

The woman, who was speaking English with a French accent, attempted to calm him down and looked around to see who might have heard. Giselle caught Chantelle's eye but quickly looked away. That was it. Chantelle did recognise her. She was at Rob Baigent's funeral. She still could not remember who she was exactly but she remembered Madison teasing her about two French women not talking to each other except a brief exchange about Debussy. That was ten years ago. Jean-Louis appeared from behind with her wine and Bruschetta de flageolets.

"Bon appetit , mon tresor."

Chantelle seized her chance.

"Jean-Louis, I don't want to embarrass your client confidentiality, but do you know that couple over there? It's just that I recognise her and wonder if I'm correct before I make a fool of myself."

"That could never happen, mon oisillon," he coughed and gestured towards the bar.

He clearly had something interesting to tell her.

"Come to the bar to see the variety I have, ma biche," he said, trying to cover up an attempt at a clandestine chat.

Jean-Louis went behind the bar and waved his hand so that Chantelle leant over towards him. He began to whisper.

"They've been living close by in an apartment in Rue De Crussol and come in here about once a month. They moved over from England about five years ago. She is French and her lover an

English doctor. Her name is Giselle but I don't know what he is called. She is nice but he is an arsehole."

Chantelle realised it must be Rob Baigent's practice manager and if Jean-Louis was right about him being a doctor the man could possibly be his GP partner Rob had mentioned.

"But there is something suspicious about them, ma caille," continued Jean-Louis, "A few months ago they were having dinner and clearly both drank too much. A row developed. We couldn't help hearing what they should have been more discreet about, ma cocotte."

"Go on, tell me all you know, mon amie."

"She was going on about how guilty she felt about what they had done. He had no patience with this saying that's just Catholic crap, which upset some of our other customers. I had to tell them to calm down or leave. You know Florian, the caretaker of the Cirque d'Hiver opposite? Well Florian was at the next table with his lovely wife and heard more than I did. He told me the next day what he had heard as he was wondering whether they should be reported to the police.

Florian told me the man had been a GP in England, but was forced out of his practice when his patients and staff turned against him for what the woman said was ratting on his partner, but more troublesome of course was that apparently he was never qualified, forged his qualifications and bluffed his way through his medical career. Then, even worse, they absconded with a load of practice money and fled the country when the police in the UK decided to open enquiries.

Florian and I decided to let it all go as he admitted he had deduced all this from scraps of conversation. He certainly didn't get the whole picture and why should it interest the French police? Knowing Florian's reputation as an exaggerator I persuaded him to forget it. Nevertheless we didn't want to take the chance of ending up involved with the police and have to go to court as witnesses. Besides we have both heard a lot worse in Le Barricou before, mon caneton."

"Wow. Thank you Jean-Louis. That will all take a great deal of absorbing. But it makes sense and does fit with what I know. You see, I've met her before when we were all living in England. You remember? I was in London working for *Franceinfo*."

Chantelle returned to her Bruschetta de flageolets. She took a large gulp of her red wine. As she sat down Simone walked in.

"Sorry I'm late darling, but as it is such a nice day I thought I'd walk up the Boulevard Beaumarchais instead of taking the metro. I'd got about half way and my mother rang. She is not well and needs some help. I'll fill you in later and I promise I'll make it up to you. Have you found anything you'd like at the auction?"

Chantelle was always puzzled as to why Simone could not talk on the phone and walk at the same time. It often delayed them. However one look at those hazel eyes and all was forgiven as usual. Her sparkle could not be dulled. Before Chantelle could answer, Jean-Louis approached and greeted Simone with kisses.

"Bonjour, ma poulette."

"Your wonderful Moules et frites, s'il vous plait, Jean-Louis and a glass of Chateauneuf Du Pape. Merci."

"We have time don't we lover?" she said, turning towards Chantelle.

Without waiting for an answer she asked again about the auction. Chantelle was in a relaxed mood.

"What do you think about a nice Louis XIV clock? Three hundred years old. Le Roi Soleil is one of your favourites."

"Sounds good. I suppose I had better eat faster."

With that Simone took a huge mouthful, which stopped her talking. She had this odd habit of extracting the mussels from their shells then putting several in her mouth at the same time. When the frites were added Chantelle knew she would be quiet for a while.

"About my mother," she said after a fair bit of chewing, "I'm going to have to go to see her after the auction. Her carer didn't turn up this morning and she thinks the occupying forces might have arrested her. Mum hinted she was worried about her. Thinks she is working with the resistance."

"Are you sure it's safe? And it's a five-hour drive. I know the Germans are pretending to be nice, as nice as any occupying army can be, but at the *Charlie* office we hear of acts of sabotage by the resistance and reprisals, not much different from the Second World War."

"I'll be okay."

Chantelle could see her courage shine.

"Besides I have no real choice. She is worried about her diabetes and I think her insulin needs sorting out. I've made an appointment with her doctor in the morning. I've got all the right documents and the roadblocks at the new border aren't patrolled as diligently as they were two years ago. They seem more relaxed in the countryside than the city. Hirtzfelden will be safe. I'll avoid Colmar. I've already told her I'll be there by ten tonight."

Then after a pause the obvious.

"I suppose we should have learnt from history and cleared out of Alsace completely while we had the chance. It really is a nightmare. I could not have begun to imagine when I was young this sort of thing could happen. Taleb's black swan theory has come to life."

Simone smiled.

"I met Nassim Taleb once when he gave a talk whilst at the Sorbonne. He foresaw Le Pen getting elected, although not this particular one, and France following England and the Netherlands out of the European Union, but even he would have been amazed that the Germans would want Alsace back yet again, and by force. We saw the warnings when the right wing AfD did so well in the elections a decade or so back. Who would have thought history would repeat itself? It does when it has been forgotten. It was all over when the far right ultranationalist NPD grabbed power. Bismarck only annexed ninety per cent of Alsace after the Franco-Prussian war, but this NPD Leader Frank Franz has exceeded even that. Perhaps the Germans will never give up their Lebensraum policy, but this time they expanded west again, not east."

"How long before they go east again?"

"Well, they've infiltrated Greece well enough."

They both sat in silence for a few minutes reflecting on the terrible situation Europe was in, and while Simone finished her moules. Chantelle broke the silence. She was in reflective mood.

"I suppose we have to accept that the united Europe designed to keep the peace is no more and we are falling back to our default state, war and conflict for stupid reasons fuelled by nationalism, jingoism, racism and isolationism. American presidents said that was their aim. We are Government by mob rule now and the lowest common denominator of ignorance. Did you know a French Prime Minister before we were born, I think his name was Mollet, actually proposed a union between France and England. Franglaterre! That came to light only about twenty years ago. Some of our fellow countrymen said he was a traitor. Now we are further apart than ever. There were all those alliances with English Kings marrying French Queens. Edward I and II, Henry III, Richard II, Charles I, even Henry V. What a history we share too. The Battle of Hastings, the Norman influence that is still obvious in Britain today."

"Well we were at war a lot. Aquitaine and other areas English for so long. And we are French so we don't mention Agincourt or Waterloo! Hardly a time to be nostalgic about."

"Yes, but I naively really thought we were through all that and it was finished with. A union wasn't as daft as it sounded to prevent wars."

Another silence. Simone was as depressed as Chantelle about international relations.

Another period of silence, then.

"Such a lot has happened since we met, hasn't it? Our bond is about the only good thing I can think of in the last decade or so. Do you remember that first party I dragged you to?"

"Hardly dragged. I wanted to get you into bed as soon as you walked into my shop."

"Suppose I had already got a bottle to take along to the party. I wouldn't have come into Le Moustache Blanche and we wouldn't have met or be sitting here now. You have made me very happy."

"And you me, ma cherie. I don't want to believe in a multi-verse where we are living in a parallel world and you didn't come into my shop."

Laughing Simone asked Chantelle if she thought Jean-Louis had any other terms of affection he used. He was on about his tenth today. Her wit sparkled.

Then Chantelle, almost as if talking to herself, returned to a more gloomy tone.

"I've never said this before or thanked you properly but I don't know if I could have got through my parents' killing by those bastards if it wasn't for your support. You saved me."

"No, you are very strong. You escaped from England. You have stuck your neck out as a journalist. But more significantly, most people would have fallen completely to pieces walking into their house and seeing such a blood bath. Like I said, both our families should have left Alsace while we could. They'd be alive now. But they were so stubborn like most old people. And no one really predicted the re-invasion. No one in their worst nightmares could have predicted the massacres. No one could have predicted how Europe would fall apart so quickly and become bitter enemies again. So sad and so unnecessary."

"Started by those fucking populist ignorant isolationist liars who live in the past. And all fuelled by the USA and Russia. It's as though they were nostalgic for wars and conflicts and missed Europe tearing itself apart. Nostalgic for the thirty thousand troops killed in 1915 at Hartmannswillerkopf and wanted a replay."

"And some made their fortunes from it," added Chantelle.

Chantelle's parents, along with many other Colmar residents had been murdered five years before and she had not returned since that day when she walked into her childhood home and discovered them. They were just in the way of looting soldiers.

She was born in the house in Rue Des Marchands just a few doors from the Musee Bartholdi. Chantelle returned to look for her parents after the fighting had ended. She feared the worst when peering through the large wooden 17th century doors down the tunnel towards the entrance she saw that the museum, set up to honour Frederic Auguste Bartholdi, which was also his birthplace, had been burnt out and was still smouldering. The tricolor, which was prominently displayed over the entrance throughout her childhood, had been replaced by the newly designed German flag. The large bronze *Statue des grands soutiens du monde*, by the front door in the centre of the forecourt, of three figures supporting the world representing justice, labour, and the motherland, had been toppled from its plinth.

Bartholdi's most famous sculpture *Liberty Enlightening the World*, commonly known as the *Statue of Liberty*, had met a similar fate when President Palin destroyed the colossal neoclassical monument on Liberty Island in New York Harbour. This was in retaliation for France expelling American businesses and citizens, when they found out the US supported German's take-over of Alsace and its threatened expansion east into Poland. Palin deliberately added insult to injury by giving the copper Gustave Eiffel used to make the statue to France's new old enemy. The Germans used it in their wire, cable and motor industries. They were in an era of petty politics, which led to not so petty violence and wars. Chantelle had visited the museum often as a child. She found it ironic that Bartholdi had modelled the face on his mother. So it was the stern, unyielding features of a bigoted, virulently anti-Semitic woman that greeted every emigrant in America through the port of New York.

Her family home just a few metres down the cobbled street had all the shutters closed except one. Her father had had it painted green between the wooden supports and remembered how her mother complained about the colour for years. The upright figure of a bearded man on the corner of the house at first floor level had been smashed. The café opposite was boarded up. A cat startled her by jumping out of the window. At first Chantelle could not understand why the animal had left red paw-prints on the windowsill. She turned her key and called out, but no answer. There were more red paw prints around the house. Then she saw them, on the stone floor with their arms around each other in a large pool of blood. She never returned and sold the house for much less than its worth. The new rulers would only allow sales to German nationals.

"It's such a nice day, and our part of the auction doesn't start for two hours, so why don't we walk to Drouot-Richelieu?"

"I thought you said it started at two pm? You mean I rushed for nothing and bolted down my moules?"

"Sorry. I was wrong. I didn't realise until just now on checking the programme on the website that the time had changed. So can we divert past my *Charlie Hebdo* room? I realise I forgot an article I'm working on and the research material. We can soak up the atmosphere of our favourite city. Hopefully Paris will always be Paris."

Just as Simone was getting ready to stand up, Chantelle leant forward and held her forearm. She said in low tones.

"That couple behind you. Don't say anything but have a good look at them both as you leave."

Simone, puzzled, decided to ask her what this was all about after they had left the bistro. They said their farewell to Jean-Louis and thanked him for his splendid hospitality as always. As one of the very few privileged regular customers they had an account at Le Barricou that they settled every month. As they walked out it was clear the couple at the table that were speaking English did not want to catch their eye, but they did overhear one snippet of French.

"Va te faire foutre. Fais pas le con."

62 - EXPLOITATION AND EXTRADITION

THE RICH MAN AND THE POOR MAN

Oh, the rich man steals a million from the bank that he controls,
While the poor man steals a loaf of bread or a penny's worth of rolls.
They take them to the courthouse, one is laughing, one's in tears;
Oh, the rich man gets an apology while the poor man gets ten years!

Bob Miller (1932)

"Thank God they 'ave gone. I was dead scared they'd recognise and approach us."

"Nothing to do with God, Giselle. Just good luck. It's about time we had some."

"Yes, your good luck. You are the one they will deport as an illegal alien if you are caught. I know that pathetic tit-for-tat game the French and the English played was crazy but it is real. It affects ordinary lives and ours in particular. We live in a crazy world now. It would be worse for you if caught, if the extradition treaty with them 'adn't broken down. You would end up in a British jail. Being deported at least means you can avoid England. We'd be in prison in England now if Celeste 'adn't tipped us off and lied on our behalf. She was great."

"She had her price did old Mogadon. She cost us a lot of money," said Clive.

"Remember it wasn't ours to begin with," Giselle said, as she sipped her Lobodis coffee. The best.

"If I were to be arrested as a criminal, so would you my dear. It's just that I'd probably still somehow end up in an English G4S jail and you'd be in a French one. I still can't believe our two countries are enemies not allies, as was the case when we were born. I admit it's all the fault of my country. We have always been too weak in our dealings with the Americans. To give in to that threat from President Palin that, *if you aren't with us you are against us*, was cringe-making. To abandon all our European neighbours and kowtow to an ex-colony was cowardly and wrong."

"Well, it ended up with all my fellow countrymen and women who 'ad settled and made their lives there in the UK being expelled. Ridiculous. You realise since the *Secure Borders Act* even if you weren't on the run you will never be able to leave France?"

"Don't use that phrase. It makes me sound like a fugitive, Giselle."

"You are!"

"They won't be able to keep that up for long. Putting all people who want to cross the border into quarantine for four days, like we treated animals when we were afraid of importing rabies, just isn't practical and won't be tolerated."

"That just shows 'ow naive you are, Clive, I'm afraid. The elite won't 'ave to do that. They will always slip through the back door. It's just ordinary people like us 'oo will pay that price and there is nothing we can do about it."

There was a gloomy silence. Then Giselle continued.

"You'd better wake up to Britannia being like a big black 'ole now. It's only because of the fight and determination of my countrymen that France isn't similarly run by a despotic totalitarian regime of big business. The spirit of the revolution of 1789 had to be revived to save us from an authoritarian dictatorial tyranny. If you end up back there, you are dead. The terrible things 'appening in your former country make it sound like 'ell on earth."

"Well, Shakespeare had it right, *hell is empty and all the devils are here*, Ariel in *The Tempest*."

"I didn't think you knew 'oo Shakespeare was, Clive?"

"Oh, cutting. I learnt that through Sylvia Plath's book."

"Anyway," continued Giselle, "what we 'ave to hope is that France doesn't go the same way. Do you know the suicide rate amongst teenagers in Britannia is twenty per cent? Your Mr Shakespeare has been banned. There are tales of ghettos and concentration camps, which I firmly believe. Habeas Corpus went ages ago and there is not even pretence of a democracy. The fundamentalists have taken over to such an extent that a young girl gets twice the prison sentence compared to the man who raped her if she aborts the foetus, plus lashes."

The atmosphere between Giselle and Clive had been tense for weeks. Mostly this was generated by fear and guilt, although there was little guilt on the part of Clive. Both were surprised how long they had managed to live in Giselle's apartment in Rue de Crussol without suspicion, but when Giselle heard about a similar apartment on the opposite side of the street being available, she jumped at it. She had to play safe - something she could not rely on Clive doing. The position was excellent when they were free to travel where they wanted and for the frequent trips back to the UK - only four stops from Oberkampf on line 5 to the Gard du Nord, then two hours to London on the Eurostar. Even if they were not fugitives it was now no longer an option, since the borders were closed and the Eurostar was classified as an elite only train.

One favourite outing was still open to them. Two stops down line 9 to Voltaire and a walk along Rue de la Roquette, then south down Boulevard de Menilmontant to the main entrance, which brought them to Cimetiere du Pere Lachaise where, for some odd reason they could never fathom, they always felt safe and at peace. They usually broke the walk with a drink in La Grande Roquette. Giselle always marvelled at the smell of joss sticks around Jim Morrison's grave. It took them a while to find out what the Greek inscription meant. Apparently it conveyed the sentiment *True to Himself* put there by his father.

Following an odd-shaped circular route they always trod via the graves of Callas, Wilde, Piaf, Moliere, Morrison, Chopin and Proust, which they stuck to each time to avoid getting lost. One grave always fascinated Giselle and that was of a man called Henri Curiel who was assassinated in 1978. Giselle did her research and found out he was the co-founder of the Egyptian Communist Party and a cousin of the spy George Blake – a big influence. No one knew who murdered him.

Her father first took Giselle to the cemetery with her sister Francoise when they were children. It was near closing, on one occasion, and Monsieur Arouet went fifty metres outside the gates to buy them an ice cream to reward their patience with his indulgence. As he was paying, to his horror he saw the caretaker pushing the large gates closed with his daughters still inside. No amount of shouting and eventually threats to kill could persuade the official to let him in, or them out. A sympathetic local heard the commotion and told him that often happened with this particular caretaker. He told him all was not lost. There was another gate on the other side of the cemetery that was closed later on. How much later simply depended on how long it took the caretaker to walk across the cemetery. If he could run around the outside quicker than the caretaker could walk across he would get in to rescue his daughters. Giselle had never forgotten how frightening the episode was and had hated officials ever since.

"Exactly who was that woman anyway? You said she was at Rob's funeral, but didn't say how she was connected?"

"I wasn't properly introduced but gathered from Suzy she was a journalist Rob enticed into investigating some of 'is crazy conspiracy theories. They don't sound so crazy now, do they? She came with an American woman that Rob had met 'oo's husband had disappeared. 'E was also up to 'is neck in plots, secrets, scheming and machinations. I'm really not sure why they were there. As far as I know they were peripheral to Rob's life. Your absence was certainly remarked on though."

"I sort of half believed what I said to the media. It isn't out of the question Rob was guilty, is it?"

"Do you really mean that? I think you just saw your chance to take over the practice. I already knew you were capable of a degree of skulduggery, we both proved that, but to me that statement to the press put you in a different league. I still don't understand what drove you to betray Rob, and 'urt Suzy when she probably thought she couldn't be 'urt any further."

Clive at least and at last looked a little guilty and remorseful about that.

"My father said it is always necessary to speak the truth, but not always necessary to speak."

Clive thought that if she referred to her ascetic, godly father one more time, he'd flip. But thought better of it. Giselle frowned as Clive put butter and jam onto his croissant.

"You peasant."

"What?"

"Do you do that just to annoy me?"

"What?"

"You know what. Croissants fait maison are buttery enough and are just to dunk in your coffee. Making 'em extra sweet with jam is disgusting. I'm not surprised you 'ad to fake your qualifications if you don't know you will end up diabetic."

As soon as she had said that, Giselle realised she had gone a little too far. It was below the belt.

"Oh fuck off."

Giselle sipped her coffee and Clive continued to smear two more large spoonfuls of jam on what remained of his third croissant - in silence. But it had been building up in Giselle. This was the time.

"I can't believe we 'ave ended up like this. Up until I began working for you I'd never done anything remotely criminal. My father was a good guy. He taught me to be 'onest, and passed on worthy values and good morals and ethics. I've let 'im down and I feel very guilty."

Clive's knee-jerk reaction was not helpful. He repeated what he had said earlier when he had attracted too much attention in the bistro.

"Oh, not all that guilty Catholic crap again."

"It would be appropriate if your sense of conscience and guilt was a little more developed, no? You misled me Clive. Do you really think I would 'ave left Tower Hamlets for a job with you if I 'ad known you weren't even a doctor? Just faking it. I 'ave to admit you were very good at it. But then by seducing my mind and body you dragged me into stealing money from the practice. You don't realise 'ow out of character that is for me. I feel so foolish now as I ignored the most important concept my father taught me. I allowed the relationship piece of life's cake to grow bigger than the other parts of my life and it engulfed the others, including the moral, ethical and justice slices which are just as important but were relegated from my attention. I regretted it from the onset and should 'ave gone straight to Rob."

"This is nonsense. And I don't understand what you are on about, what piece of cake? What's cake got to do with this? The idea that an intelligent, sensible and strong woman like you could be fooled or pressurised into doing things against her will is complete bollocks. You saw we could get rich without being found out, and the fact that it was with me and we saw our future together was the icing on the cake, as you seem so obsessed with cake analogies."

"Well I've lost my sweet tooth and ought to listen to my Dad. 'E says I should leave you and make a fresh start. So does my sister Francoise. It's the old story. I can't be with someone who is capable of doing the things we 'ave."

"Now you sound like Groucho Marx," Clive said, in an attempt to lighten things up, but she just stared straight through him.

Giselle looked at him with disdain. It was time she was honest with herself and Clive.

"Actually, what I really mean is I can't be with someone who 'as done the things you 'ave."

"I had no idea they would kill Rob," he pleaded, "and you are still a couple of miracles short of sainthood yourself, Giselle."

It was a key point to be interrupted. Jean-Louis suddenly appeared to clear away what he could of Clive's mess, but only managed to repatriate the empty bottle of red wine.

"Can I get you another coffee, Mademoiselle?"

"Yes please," Giselle smiled, but behind the smile was pain.

Without an interruption Clive would have been his usual impetuous self and fired back 'well go ahead then, bugger off', but he was forced to count to ten and stayed silent, as he really did not want to lose her.

"You know Derek 'as been in contact with 'im and is pressurizing 'im to say where we are? I worry as Derek has important contacts in the City who seem to be running the country now. 'E 'as even threatened Francoise. Switching flats in the same street was un bordel, but necessary or 'e would have found us and reported us by now. My Dad is playing ignorant. 'Is concern is for me and 'is two grandsons. And you know my mother's attitude. She won't speak to me again until I reunite the family. 'Er strict Catholicism won't tolerate divorce for a second. And don't sound off against religion again, Clive. I know what you think and it's not 'elpful."

Clive desperately did not want to lose Giselle. He would rather do exactly as she wanted to make sure they stayed together. Time to cut the aggression he thought. He had put all his eggs in one basket with Giselle.

"Giselle, I'm sorry I got you into this mess. But we are where we are. Let's sum up. The English police would love to put me away for stealing money from the practice and impersonating a doctor. The tabloids would love it too. Well the ones that are left anyway. I couldn't possibly show my face anywhere in England, let alone near the practice or ex-patients. I've lost my family and am now hiding in France, but it's probably only a matter of time before they catch up with me, unless we really go for it and buy false identities and live a life in seclusion away from here. You are as guilty as me of stealing, but if I took the rap you'd get off quite lightly. But what seems more important to you is your family and children, and of course I understand that. All my problems are intertwined, but you could go back to your family and play very innocent as far as crimes are concerned and may get away with it. So the sixty-four thousand dollar question is, do we stay together and fight for a future together, or do we give up?"

"You will never understand the way I was brought up will you? You will never see that I don't want to get away with it, as you put it. It's time I paid the price for what I 'ave done. That could be the loss of my family and to continue a life with you, or it could be jail. I can't decide which will allow me to ease my conscience. The problem with punishing myself with a loss of family is that they suffer too. But they do if I get locked up. But at least I will feel that I would 'ave taken my punishment and then can start again."

"I do understand. I love you and will understand whatever you do, but even if you serve your time, I doubt you will exorcise your guilt and feel free again."

Clive was showing his desperation.

"How about finding a little cottage in the Dordogne where we can disappear and lead the simple life? We have enough money."

"L'addition s'il vous plait" Giselle shouted at Jean-Louis who was behind the bar washing glasses and pretending not to listen.

"Oui, mademoiselle."

Chantelle took Simone's arm as they passed the Metro entrance outside Le Barricou and crossed the road. They both reached for their shades as the sun was directly ahead as they turned in front of the Cirque D'Hiver. The caretaker came out of the glare and said good morning as he headed to the bistro for his break.

"Good morning, Fabian. Enjoy your Courvoisier."

"Do you know I've never been in there," said Chantelle, "what's it like?"

"It stages circuses, dressage events and concerts. Outside I don't know any other building that's an oval polygon of twenty sides with Corinthian columns, do you? It was opened by Emperor Napoleon III in 1852."

"Ah, the man who led us to defeat by Bismarck in the Franco-Prussian War the consequence of which meant Alsace was German, just like it is now. When I was working in England I visited the crypt in Hampshire where he is buried. He is with his son who strangely was an officer in the British army and was killed fighting the Zulus in South Africa."

"How do you remember all this weird stuff, my love?"

"Same as you remember Fabian always has a Cognac in his rest period."

"Courvoisier is known as *Le Cognac de Napoleon*. Napoleon III made them the official supplier to the Imperial Court. It is produced in Jarnac where Mitterand was born and buried."

They continued a gentle stroll in the pleasant sunshine down Rue Amelot to the junction with Passage Saint-Pierre Amelot. They stopped and stared down the passage and imagined the desperate scramble out of the windows of the Bataclan at the far end that night in November 2015 when eighty-nine people were massacred.

"Well, who were they?" said Simone, as they continued south.

"Who were who?"

"That couple you wanted me to look at in Le Barricou."

"Ah, yes, I almost forgot. This goes back to my time working in London for *Franceinfo*. You remember I told you about a British journalist who disappeared. He was married to an American called Madison who I met in my gym. I helped her look for him, as he was investigating all sorts of nasty stuff and we think the establishment silenced him. Well, a doctor in the UK contacted me having seen my programme and provided me with a lot of supporting evidence. Then he too was killed. I went to his funeral with Madison, the American I told you about, to sniff around, and that woman in the Bistro was his practice manager. I recognised her from the funeral. What I've also just found out is that the guy with her was the doctor's partner. From what Jean-Louis told me they live here now having fled the UK. Our caretaker friend Florian apparently overheard that they'd stolen money and that he wasn't a proper doctor. At least that's what he deduced from his amateur spying. He put two and two together from the snippets he eavesdropped but could have made five of course. We don't know how much Cognac he had drunk. However it all makes sense, but I don't know if it's just because I want to believe it."

"Small world. But what are you going to do with this new dilemma in your life, darling, if it is a dilemma, that is?"

"I've no idea, yet. I'll have to think about it, but probably nothing."

"That's unlike you and I'm surprised. It'll make a good story. You once told me one reason you went into investigative journalism is to expose corruption and get those who deserve it locked up. Surely those two deserve that sort of fate?"

"You might think differently if you know what else happened. I've already risked so much. I'm not keen to get that 3.00 a.m. police raid."

"Is it really that bad?"

Simone's worried look made her hazel eyes appear bigger.

"You just don't know who you can trust. The last I heard from Madison she was suspicious it had been her old friend from Texas, a girl called Cheryl, who had shopped Pete. She couldn't prove this and had never confronted her. Madison thought that by keeping her cards close to her chest Cheryl might give something away. She thought Cheryl did it out of envy and jealousy, not patriotism. It was a case of careless talk costs lives. Pete's mate, Mike, was in the States on holiday and he thought he'd look up Cheryl for old times sake, although Madison was pretty sure what he was really after. He was reckless enough to blab to Cheryl about what Pete had been up to and the sort of things he had found out. Cheryl decided that Madison was a traitor mixing with, as she saw them subversives, revolutionaries and commies, so she reported them to the authorities that eventually involved the FBI and the CIA. They jumped on Pete during his next visit to Washington. So as Madison put it to me Mike was to blame because he was stupid, but Cheryl because she was vindictive.

Mike wanted to make it up to Madison, so after Pete's disappearance went back to the US to try to find him. This too was stupid and naive. He did make contact with an organisation called Poison and was quite pleased with himself, but was being watched and led the CIA straight to a few operatives who were eliminated as a result. The CIA didn't pick him up because he was more valuable to them inadvertently exposing others.

At the time of the GP's funeral he was still snooping around supposedly to help Madison find Pete but actually doing more damage than anyone could imagine. Eventually, when he had led them to all he was going to, and was no longer any value, he was deported and dropped into the hands of the UK authorities who were glad to get their hands on him. He confessed to leaking documents from Whitehall over quite a few years and served a jail sentence. None of this was in the media. Last time I heard from Madison she was still in contact with him, but neither want to know Cheryl obviously."

They eventually reached Rue Nicolas-Appert and one of Chantelle's old places of work, although she still used it occasionally. It was her retreat when home was too noisy, and she hid her sensitive material there, rather than at home. But it was only a room kept on by *Charlie Hebdo* temporarily after the massacre for overflow storage. Simone stayed outside the fawn building with ugly aluminium windows whilst Chantelle dashed in to get her research material. Simone looked up at the memorial to the twelve killed in the offices by Islamic gunmen earlier in 2015 and could not believe that was well over a decade before. Chantelle told her the original brown plaque, the size of a small coffee table, spelt one of the victim's names incorrectly. The main offices were moved to a secret location in Southern Paris nine months after the attack. They had been planning to close this down for years so she would soon have to find a new hiding place. Much of *Charlie Hebdo's* work was done on-line. Chantelle reappeared quickly clutching a folder and a memory stick. They walked up Boulevard Richard Lenoir towards the St Ambroise metro station and chatted.

"What's the research?"

"About Oradour-sur-Glane mainly and another old story about the Butcher of Lyon, Klaus Barbie. But I do have a new one about sugar workers dying in Nicaragua."

"I'm full of admiration for where you get all this stuff."

"I've been in the game long enough to have loads of sources and contacts. A lot comes from the UK from underground former journalists too scared and intimidated by their Government's new laws, which are as close to a ban on free speech as you can get. Ever since England became almost a one party state, the Government can and does do what it likes. It's almost a dictatorship now. Their female leader has a vice-like grip on the press, media, security forces and the police. The opposition leaders are in jail on trumped up charges. So I've got a lot of material from them I have to sieve through. The stuff I got about Oradour was sent anonymously though."

"So what's new about Barbie?"

"Nothing new about him. It's US Intelligence. They employed him after the war, like they did many Nazis, to play a part in their pseudo-fight against Marxism. They helped him escape to South America. There he worked with the CIA to get Che Guevara and assisted Luis Tejada to orchestrate the 1980 Bolivian Coup d'etat. He worked for West German Intelligence too. This is the man who tortured our fellow Frenchmen while prisoners of the Gestapo. And children. He personally broke legs, used electric shocks and sexually assaulted them, including, believe it or not, with dogs. I don't understand how that one works but that's the testimony of victims I have on file. The estimate is that he was directly responsible for fourteen thousand deaths."

"So the story is more about the protection he got from our so-called American and German friends?"

"That's the line I will take. It's not really that new, but what is new is the actual scale of how so many top Nazi war criminals ended up working for the victors and their crimes conveniently forgotten. The Oradour story is connected this way too. I've been given the name of the grandson of the SS Officer who was second in command. He also ended up in South America. So many ended up working in Germany too."

"Didn't Barbie capture and kill Jean Moulin? How could his murderer be allowed to get away with it?"

To all French people, Jean Moulin was the most famous resistance fighter. Everyone recognised his photo with the scarf and fedora hat. This heroic emblem of the resistance overshadowed all the other martyrs of the clandestine fight.

"How do so many get away with so much? He was initially buried over there too, in Le Pere Lachaise Cemetery, the place just a kilometre east of here, but his ashes were transferred to the Pantheon in 1964."

As Chantelle spoke she gesticulated to their left, as though she was pointing out the cemetery, which of course they could not see.

"Do you remember our afternoon stroll around the Cimetiere de Passy, you know, the one in the shadow of the Eiffel Tower?" continued Chantelle.

She loved cemeteries, home and abroad. When in London she had spent hours at Highgate and Kensal Green visiting Karl Marx, Malcolm McLaren and another hero, Claudia Jones. She was surprised to see that Alexander Litvinenko was buried there too. She thought he would still be radioactive with Polonium-210. She had heard recently that Marx's grave had been destroyed.

"We visited it after going around the Jardins du Trocadero on a beautiful spring morning about two years ago. That other resistance fighter is there, Georges Mandel. We didn't see his grave as I hadn't heard of him then, but read about his opposition to Petain's armistice and execution afterwards."

"You should have known about him. The road next to the cemetery is named after him," teased Simone, "apparently Churchill preferred him to Charles de Gaulle as the leader of Free French Forces. His family was also from Alsace. They were brighter than ours. They moved into France after the annexation by the Germans at the end of the Franco-Prussian war."

"I do remember seeing the graves of Debussy and Faure," said Chantelle, "It was that Giselle who told me at the English doctor's funeral that Debussy had died of rectal cancer during the German spring offensive bombardment of Paris in World War One. Isn't it odd what is retained in the memory banks, but it has stuck as that's about the only thing she said to me, I suppose prompted by his *Clair de Lune* in the background. Odd what is discussed at a funeral."

"Yes, odd that I remember the grave of Princess Natalia Brasova who married the younger brother of the last Czar, Nicholas II," Simone added, "His sister Xenia is buried in France also."

"It solved one puzzle for me," Chantelle batted back, "The English have an expression when they are startled about something, or find something incredulous. They exclaim 'Gordon Bennett'. A bit like our Mon Dieu except not religious. It became popular after a man called Gordon Bennett, the publisher of the *New York Herald*, who became notorious for his scandalous behaviour. He turned up to a party drunk one day and pissed in the host's fireplace. He also sponsored Stanley's trip to Africa to find David Livingstone. He is buried there, and I saw this postcard of him next to the Café Kleber where you treated me to a caffè crèma."

"We only went there to pay homage to Edouard Manet, didn't we?"

"And you bought a postcard of *Le dejeuner sur l'herbe* in the same shop and sent it to Madison. I was quite jealous and wondered if you fancied her."

"Don't be daft," Chantelle fired back, but embarrassingly remembering her faux pas in the yoga centre in Marylebone.

"And of course we searched for the grave of Simone de Beauvoir, we had to didn't we? Only to realise we were in the wrong cemetery," said Simone.

"Yes, so we walked the four or five kilometres over the Seine on Pont d'Iéna, under the Tour Eiffel, across Champ de Mars to eventually find Cimetière du Montparnasse," replied Chantelle excitedly.

"It took a while to find the grave. Together with Jean-Paul Sartre of course. A real highlight," said Simone.

"But do you remember who else we found?" asked Chantelle mischievously.

"You know very well! Jean Seberg. You teased me as I said I fancied her, especially in Jean-Luc Godard's *Breathless* with her short hair."

They chatted like they had no troubles. They basked in the warm glow of how free and safe they felt in France compared with most other countries, but worried about how long that would last. By now they were on Line 9, just six stops to Richelieu-Drouot.

"So what's the Nicaraguan sugar workers scandal, Chantelle?"

"Thirty thousand sugar cane workers have died of kidney disease in the last three decades and it's not clear why they get it. But they die because the only treatment is dialysis and that isn't available to most. There is growing evidence it's due to harsh working conditions though, particularly long hours exposed to sun without sufficient shade, rest and water. There's absolutely no doubt it's an occupational disease. One day of sugar cane cutting can be compared to running half a marathon. The cutters are paid less than a dollar per ton, and they harvest between four and eight tons a day. So boycott Flor de Cana rum!"

The noise of the train meant they had to speak louder than they really wanted.

"Give up sugar altogether!" replied Simone, "Sugar is addictive and can be compared to crack cocaine. I read about a study by French scientists who showed rats chose sugar over cocaine, even when they were addicted to cocaine. It's as dangerous as addiction to tobacco and alcohol. Trouble is they stick it in everything. Orange juice, cereal, sandwiches, a large chai latte has about twenty teaspoons in it. Then there's the high fructose corn syrup, which the industry loves as it's cheaper and sweeter. Its completely unnatural, goes through a terrible production process that leaves it riddled with heavy metals like mercury, and causes obesity, diabetes and liver damage."

"What I'm investigating in parallel is the hiring of so-called crave-ability experts by the food industry whose job it is to get us all addicted to their processed foods. They are paid to invent addictive hyper-palatable junk foods. The industry spends millions on misinformation campaigns. As Harry Truman said, *if you can't convince them, confuse them.* But all the consumer really needs to know is that HFCS is a marker for poor quality, nutrient-poor, disease creating industrial food products."

"That would help but they need to know a lot more than that, I'm afraid. Don't forget I've had to become quite an expert on diabetes. I was only five when I found my mother unconscious in a diabetic keto-acidotic coma. Anyway you know the shop was part-newsagent before I took it over? Well, I was sorting out a load of rubbish the previous retiring shopkeeper had kindly left in the cellar for me, when I came across a suitcase full of old newspapers. It seems he collected editions announcing landmark events from all the years he ran the place going right back to the moon landings. I found de Gaulle's and Coco Chanel's deaths, the Maastricht treaty, France winning the World Cup, the introduction of the Euro, the

Nice terrorist attack. All fascinating. I tried contacting him to see if he wanted them back. Found out he died two months after retiring. His widow, who wasn't interested, said she'd only just got rid of all his junk, why would she want more? Oh, and the stuff about Coco Chanel was fascinating. She had been a collaborator in the war. Tried to meet Churchill for peace talks."

"Very interesting but is this leading anywhere?" queried Chantelle.

"Oh of course. I almost forgot my point. It's those wonderful amber eyes of yours. Puts me off. It can get a little boring in Le Moustache Blanche in the quiet spells so I've been ploughing through them. It was good to find Simone de Beauvoir's obituary. I can see why I'm named after her. But in a paper declaring Macron's election I found an article called *The Diabetes Payroll*. Old news I know but this was with a sinister twist. Do you know who Frederick Banting was?"

"No, but you are going to tell me," replied Chantelle, wondering where this was going.

"He was a Canadian and co-discoverer of insulin in 1921, a life saver for type one diabetics. Too important he thought to have a patent. It should be readily available to all who needed it. Big Pharma didn't think so though, too good a business opportunity. Now only three companies in the US manufacture insulin: Eli-Lilley, Sanofi and Novo Nordisk. Lantus alone made over seven point five billion dollars. Tweaking the insulin molecule allows for additional patents and cheaper generics to be kept at bay. With collusion between the companies, prices of newer insulins went up over three hundred per cent in the last five years."

"Well we know Big Pharma is corrupt, but they are too powerful now and not even governments can challenge them. There's nothing that can be done, is there?"

The latter was a rhetorical statement from Chantelle, not a question.

"The story gets a lot worse," said Simone, "The bit I'm sure you do know is that in 1977, US dietary guidelines made fat the public enemy number one. The subsequent high carbohydrate intake led to obesity which has led to the diabetes epidemic."

"Known to me, yes, as I've written about it, but sadly still not common knowledge."

"What you might not know is that to get more victims into the treatment net, they altered the definition of type two diabetes, instantly rendering one point nine million more Americans diabetic. Getting greedy, they invented this pre-diabetic state, and then changed the definition of that too, pulling in another twenty-five million Americans. This now means if you add the number of diabetics to those with pre-diabetes we are at over half the population. In other words it's more common to have these conditions than a normal blood sugar. Suddenly every company wanted a diabetes drug. Thirty appeared in the decade up to 2013, and by 2015 sales of diabetic drugs had reached twenty-three billion dollars."

"All right, so big business may be culpable in producing more diabetics, but aren't they also treating them?" said Chantelle, trying to find the flaw in Simone's conspiracy theories and playing devil's advocate.

"Three points. One. The majority of those on the panels changing the definitions had links to the companies set to benefit. Two. The American Diabetes Association reaped more than seven million dollars from its pharmaceutical partners. Three. All these drugs do is reduce high blood sugars instead of helping patients. Clinically important outcomes like heart attacks, strokes, blindness, kidney failure and deaths are not being improved. Symptoms are being treated, not the disease. Diabetes is a disease of high insulin resistance. All we are doing is pushing sugar from where it can be seen, that is the blood, and into the body where it's invisible and pretending things are improved. Lifestyle changes clearly improve health whereas drugs don't but this inconvenient fact hardly matters to the big pharmaceuticals."

"So they create a problem then sell the treatment. A bit like the makers of oxycontin. Declare there is a pool of untreated pain, then get people hooked. This is the root of the opioid crisis in the USA killing thousands. I need the references for all this. Who is the author? I can feel an article coming on," said Chantelle.

"This is why I'm telling you all this, but there are deeper reasons," said Simone with a worried look.

"The article had the name Dr Jason Fung at the bottom. But when I tried to find out more about him, nothing. None of the search engines even mention him. His article, which must have been online too, even in those days, was nowhere to be found. A complete blank, as though he hasn't existed for the last decade or so since he wrote the piece."

"Implying he was silenced?" said Chantelle.

"Precisely. Except more than that, air-brushed from history."

There was a period of silence as they reached their stop. They looked at each other with concern and went up the stairs.

Chantelle broke the silence.

"Trouble is the best hope we had of sorting out such corrupt and dangerous industries, mandatory regulation and targeted taxation, has gone now that big business runs most countries and governments are just their impotent puppets. They have won. You can tell that, as they don't even bother to trot out their crap about personal freedom and the nanny state any more. They just had to ride it out with completely ineffective voluntary agreements until they gained the power they now have."

By now they were emerging into the sunshine from the Richelieu-Drouot metro station.

"We allowed the fox to guard the hen house. Now the fox is in control of everything and rules the world," Simone finished.

"And the rich steal millions and get an apology, while a poor man steal a loaf of bread and gets ten years. The world is unfair and corrupt."

It was a short pleasant walk past antique shops to the Hotel Drouot auction house. Simone commented that the streets were much cleaner since Paris banned all dogs because of their large contribution to the ecological footprint. Chantelle, although a dog lover, had to agree.

They pushed through the large glass doors, went up the escalator and collected their bid number from the man who had just started to let people into the room.

"You realise we are bucking the trend?" Simone said.

"How so?"

"Well, we are spending money and we are very happy. A few years ago a Harvard psychologist published a study that showed that sad people not only buy more, they pay more, because they want to change things and this is how they can do it, or so they think."

Chantelle looked intrigued.

"The sinister side of this is that they don't want us to be happy. They want us to be sad. They want us to be fearful. They manipulate us for their own interests and against our own. It boosts control and capitalism. Why do you think shops like to pipe out mournful music, or why Walmart plays Celine Dion on a loop?"

"Some years ago, Simone," said Chantelle, "I would have accused you of paranoid fantasies. Now I'm wiser. I know that is the kind of thing that is happening."

They were happy to get such a lot off their chests. They had the illusion of feeling free even in this deteriorating world.

Chantelle asked a question as they walked out after the auction.

"Don't you think we should grass those two up to the authorities?"

Simone thought they probably should.

"By the way, where did you get those beautiful amber eyes? Has anyone else in the family got them?" Simone said, as they said goodbye to each other and hugged.

Chantelle said she did not know. She knew they were rare but most common in Asia and South America, but sometimes Spain.

"My mother was very friendly with a Spanish musician the year before I was born. My father was away with the French Air Force. Need I say more?"

As Simone drove to Alsace she started to worry whether it was just asking for trouble. She spent two days sorting her mother out. Her mother's carer had indeed been arrested. On her return to their apartment in Boulevard Du Temple, Chantelle was nowhere to be seen.

63 - DOMINATION AND RULES

DIAMOND DOGS
Bowie (1974)

~ PERMISSION TO QUOTE LYRICS REFUSED ~

"Music is everybody's possession.
It's only publishers who think that people own it."
John Lennon

2030

Suzy felt her palms getting sweaty. Her heart was thumping.

She was aware she got more anxious than she used to. But that's what happens to old people. What she would have dismissed as day-to-day trivia when with Rob all those years ago sometimes ruined her day now. Molehills became mountains.

Rob always said everyone has a worry box in his or her brain, which had to be kept topped up. There was always something that had to be found to put in it. When young it was worries about careers and major life problems like relationships, children and Manchester United's league position. When old it became where to park the car, why the cat had not eaten his food or arriving late at places that really did not matter. Although now approaching sixty Suzy could not accept she was ageing but this reaction told her otherwise. The box had to be full and if there was little that was serious to worry about something would emerge to fill the vacuum, hence the sweaty hands and palpitations. With the malfunctioning of the synapses with age, however, the worries seeped out of the box short-circuiting the other brain functions causing accidents, other faults, failures and impairments. The computer would crash and need re-booting.

Suzy was worried about her status. She would not be able to relax until she had inserted her Tier One card into the compliance slot on Francine's central monitoring panel. Suzy's most recent synapse malfunction happened as she swiped her card the wrong way round against Francine's gate. She got it right the third time. The gate opened and with that she could feel herself relaxing again. She walked through. She had five minutes to spare before the deadline. She thought she had allowed plenty of time for the journey from her apartment in her tower block on the new Romney Marshes Camp to her stepdaughter's house.

However, there was no public transport nowadays. Public was a dirty word. Private was the only way. She could only travel, like most without cars, by asking for help from friends or, like she had to today, going back to the old risky days of hitching. Not least for this reason she had to dress smartly. Nobody would pick up anyone who looked dodgy. A short skirt helped a few years ago. Now nearly sixty she thought she should dress her age. But it worked both ways of course. Suzy never knew what type of character was offering her a lift. She had had to fight off groping men on several occasions.

For a few years after Rob died, she thought the tide had turned with a backlash against sexual abuse. But that was short-lived. A few famous names like Harvey Weinstein and Kevin Spacey were exposed and they did not work for a while. Their reputations were temporarily dented, but then the backlash prompted a reactionary backlash. The Establishment feared where this would lead, so they orchestrated a campaign of ridicule. It was not a laughing matter. Attacks and smear campaigns on the accusers built up to a crescendo. Soon people like Spacey were heroes again. It legitimised abuse once more as locker-room banter. Now it was almost expected.

A woman offered her a lift this time, which was a relief. But one of the five automatic registration plate recognisers had failed and the security forces were logging everyone's movements manually and causing hold-ups. The roads around the Marshes were fairly unreliable now sea levels had risen. Malaria, which was last seen at the turn of the nineteenth century, had returned. A neighbour of

Suzy's in the opposite flat died of plasmodium falciparum cerebral complications only a few months back. Malaria and malnutrition were now the top two causes of death in the area. Netting was too expensive for most on the Marshes.

Despite the mosquitos there was very little other wildlife. The bird population had declined markedly along with the decline in bees, ladybirds, moths, butterflies and beetles. The planet was now in real trouble from the lack of pollination. There was frequent flooding, which often required detours. Most of the Walland and Romney Marshes had become tidal again for the first time in nearly two thousand years. Appledore was on the coast again, whilst villages like Brenzett and Lydd had disappeared and the Roman Portus Lemanis could anchor the yachts of the elite again. The French company running the old nuclear power station at Dungeness had abandoned it when relations broke down. EDF did not mind too much as access was only possible by boat. As the sea had receded from the seventeenth century onward the lighthouses had to be rebuilt nearer to the water's edge, but in the last fifty years the reverse was happening as the coastline had moved inland.

The climate change deniers of the last few decades had won. Along with paying senile old ex-Chancellors to promote their cause, they had funded as a false flag operation those who claimed the sea level would rise by just a few centimetres. This served several purposes. It gave the impression both sides of the argument were being aired whilst at the same time being smothered, sometimes literally. The genuine scientists, who measured the rise in metres not centimetres, were silenced. By the time the floods occurred it was of course too late. The deniers had continued to profit for longer than they could have dreamt from their involvement with industries like energy, agriculture, transport and deforestation. And companies like Exxon were now in charge.

The block housing Suzy frequently had a foot of water around it. Today though the road was reasonably dry and she arrived with those vital five minutes left. Francine heard her walking up the gravel path and greeted her warmly. She hugged her as well as she could whilst holding a ten-month-old baby in her arms. The birthday girl, Roberta, ran out behind her.

"Hello, Nana," she squealed.

There was an acrid smell in the air, so they all dashed inside as quickly as possible. A diffuse smoke was making their eyes sting and Suzy's were redder having been exposed for longer. It seemed to be coming from the direction of the Civic Centre about a mile away. No one commented on it.

Suzy gave Roberta the usual over the top grandma greeting.

"If you don't mind I had better register. The broadcast is on in a few minutes?"

It was evident to Francine that Suzy was still anxious but this would solve it. Francine made way for Suzy, who dropped her bags and walked briskly past the birthday banners with *4 YEARS OLD TODAY* on them and inserted the card into the communications gateway. It sat along side all the other cards for the household, already inserted in preparation. With the monitor on, registration accepted and the broadcast being received, she could now enjoy the birthday party. The four year old was jumping with excitement on the sofa next to Nana.

"Oh, silly me. I've left your present in the hallway."

It had been over a decade since Rob's death. So much had changed. Jenny had brought Suzy into her children's lives from the very beginning. She initially found it difficult to admit even to herself but she quite liked Suzy. Yes, Suzy stole her husband when the three girls were at a very vulnerable age, but to be nineteen, seventeen and fourteen when their father died was worse.

The abuse from their friends at school who told them their father was a pervert and that death was too good for him made the trauma unbearable. They had known Suzy for only a few years and irritated Jenny by bringing home reports of how nice she was. With her three most prized achievements needing as much comfort as possible, Jenny's calculation was that Suzy was necessary for them and had to be brought into the fold whatever her personal grudges. She had to put the girls' wellbeing above everything.

Jenny was business-like about the care of her three. She organised a meeting with Suzy just a few days after the funeral to map out the way forward. There was a deal to be struck. Jenny would be civil, cooperative and even friendly, as long as Suzy would do the same and never do anything other than recognise Jenny as number one in their lives. She also expected help with them during difficult adolescent years. They were to stand solid together. They had their love for Rob in common, even if shaken by what was said about him and the sullying of his reputation. The character assassination was relentless and persistent.

Suzy was surprised and only too delighted to agree. She told herself she would do more than Jenny asked to show goodwill. It also helped to explain to Jenny that she really wanted children but it never happened. That volunteered an advantage to Jenny to demonstrate some humility. Her past was just two dead husbands.

After an hour they were chatting freely and had a laugh at Rob's expense about his strange habits. Laying out his Weetabix the night before - or the Shredded Wheat in Suzy's time - his habit of labelling everything, his Beatles obsession. How all the waste bins had to be kept empty. They reminisced about Stephen's funny eulogy when he alluded to these weird personality traits - sadly very few went to his funeral.

Suzy kept the conversation firmly on Jenny's territory asking about the children's names. Why friends chose particular names for their children fascinated her. Jenny warmed to Suzy more as she had the chance to explain that Francine was because Rob was a Francophile and the first girlfriend to cause unexplained and surprising stirrings in the groin area aged twelve, was a blonde called Francine, the daughter of the village bobby. Leona and Barrett were more her choices, Leona meaning lion and derived from Latin - animals and the dead language were passions of Jenny's. Barrett was after Elizabeth Barrett Browning. Persuading Rob took some effort, until he remembered the John Lennon song and one of his hero's last *Grow Old With Me* was inspired by Robert Browning's poem.

Despite the two Bs, to them Barrett Baigent had quite a sophisticated ring to it. After all, the poet had two Bs too. So did her husband Bobby Browning, Rob would tease.

Jenny told Suzy that Rob had gone on several occasions to the National Portrait Gallery to admire Michele Gordigiani's oils on canvas of the Brownings. Suzy thought it wise to keep quiet that she knew only too well about that. They wondered if they had compounded the error by giving her the middle name Elizabeth but did not care. It was Jenny's mother's name and a good fall back if, when she grew up, their third daughter rejected Barrett. There will not be many of them in the phone book, Rob used to say - nobody in 2030 knew what a phone book was.

From then on, their relationship got closer and the girls benefitted as a result. Both enjoyed talking about Rob and they did freely in front of the children to keep his memory alive. They were quite alone with that. Suzy was looking forward to seeing Jenny who was due to turn up to her own grandchild's birthday party later on. She had not seen her since Jenny's own sixtieth party a month before, which was an unusually long gap for the two of them not to have some social engagement. Jenny was known as Granny to make the blood link more obvious to others.

The King's speech had just started and all the adults in the house got the routine necessity of corneal recognition out of the way. Every year the monarch would deliver new policy and law announcements. Everyone was expected to watch, listen and take note. This was monitored by card insertion into the compliance slot on the home central monitoring panel as they had all done, and then corneal recognition to prove the person whose card had been inserted actually was there and was watching. This is why Suzy had sweaty palms and could not relax until the process was complete. This was only King William V's second annual statement. He had inherited the throne after the rather unexpected death of his father, King Charles III who, having had to wait until the age of seventy-four, only held the crown for five years. Gossips said he died of a broken heart only six months after Camilla succumbed to cancer of the bowel.

Sometime towards the very end of the second Elizabethan age, a small elite Establishment group - descendants of the original members of the Right Club from nearly a century before - decided on a solution to overpopulation and immigration. They had grabbed absolute power but continued to struggle with what they regarded as an unhealthy dilution of English stock. Eugenics was fashionable again. The former Prime Minister Hubert Witney had been successful in lobbying for a statue of his great grandfather, Sir Edward Vaughan-Warner who had championed Francis Galton and the Eugenics Educational Society. A new fifth plinth appeared in Trafalgar Square. For years they knew there was not enough room for all - at least not enough room for all to have a comfortable and privileged life. So some, in fact the majority, had to be sidelined and discarded. They divided the population into two, not including themselves of course who were the cream on top. For them the name the elite stuck.

The two very large groups consisting of the rest of humanity were the privileged Tier One, and the ordinary Tier Two, soon to be more commonly known as the desirables and undesirables. The privileged or desirable citizens were granted rights as long as they were compliant, loyal, unquestioning and upheld British values. Within that subsection, some had more rights and privileges than others. All rights had to be earned and were accessed through the Citizen's Loyalty Card or CLC as it became known. This held identity data too and was really regarded as a privilege. There were gold, silver and bronze CLCs.

The other far larger group comprised the ordinary, the less worthy. The undesirables. This population group was split into two. At the very bottom the dregs, that is, non-English, immigrants, less intelligent, disabled, and criminals. The other group above the dregs of society, and by far the largest contingent, were all those ex-manual workers who, since automation, robotisation, advanced technology, and artificial intelligence were now redundant and of no use to society. As undesirables - a name that had stuck - they would be used but not generally seen. It seemed society worked quite well and most were grateful for their lot, as long as the undesirables were ignored. Everyone feared being relegated to that group. There was never promotion again. People disappeared forever. Out of sight, out of mind became the mantra.

This division of society began as a small-scale experiment back in the days when governments existed. There was a deliberate policy to set group against group - the old against the young, the educated against the uneducated, the rich against the poor. Benefits were only given to scroungers and became known as Universal Benefits, but the shame of collecting it put people off. They often had to run the gauntlet of two rows of disapproving public who would insult them, spit at them and strike out and attack them on their way into the Department of Disgrace.

But as soon as big business took over, the system became more widespread. With control of the media who did not mention the more difficult areas of policy, such as destroying popular institutions like the NHS and the *BBC*, the general public did not notice, or at least it never reached conscience levels. They were too busy watching *Strictly Come Dancing*.

Both groups - the privileged and the undesirables - received a basic universal income, which was enough to just keep the bottom tier who could not work alive. The top tier - the desirables, as the privileged were also known, were quite comfortable as they were always capable of adding to this basic income by working, and always did. One of the big businesses was responsible for this allocation and population control. It was cheap and profitable. No means testing was necessary. The digital cryptocurrencies, which had a brief moment of dominance a decade before, had been banned. Bitcoin threatened the power and control of the elite and banks began to be sidelined. That was stamped on.

It was at King Charles's third proclamation in 2026 that the new order and control of society was brought into being and he explained how it would be.

"Britain was class-ridden and had been a two tier society for too long and this would end for the benefit of all," the King announced.

Naturally the anonymous elite was excluded - not even mentioned. All deserving hard-working loyal citizens would have a good life. Those showing outstanding devotion to the country would get the CLC. But others would not be tolerated. It was not necessary for the King to go into more detail. It was just presumed they were taken off to live in the ghettos for the undesirables.

To keep within the desirable class meant being compliant and loyal, for example listening to and agreeing with the King's speech. This is why Suzy was so worried about logging in and registering her corneal image.

To most it appeared everyone was in the desirable group as the rest were never mentioned. Certainly everyone they knew and socialised with were at the same level. Straying across boundaries just did not happen. They were all part of a fair and equal society, or so they were told repeatedly to the point of brainwashing.

In reality the elite ran the world and the undesirables were the cannon fodder and slaves who were herded into ghettos far from sight. Their living conditions were poor but nobody cared. Amongst other jobs they were the toxic waste cleaners, and often disappeared to die on their own of radiation poisoning. As the undesirables' camps got too crowded thousands at a time were shipped abroad. The Australians had developed an expertise in trafficking, processing and looking after the unwanted.

It was ironic that two hundred years after Australia was used as a penal colony this role was re-introduced on a much larger scale. One hundred and sixty-two thousand convicts, including the Tolpuddle Martyrs, Chartists and Sean McColl's great-great-grandfather Patrick McBride, were transported between 1788 and 1868. Modern day deportations were in a different league. At least this number was disposed of from Britannia every year.

The Australian Government had built numerous offshore immigration detention and processing centres on South Pacific Islands like Nauru, Manus and Christmas Island, run by G4S Security. Australia's answer to Guantanamo Bay, they had been described as like concentration camps where sexual abuse occurred and deaths due to inadequate medical care - a clear breach of the

1951 United Nations' Refugee Convention. And when the numbers got a little out of control Australia did deals with other countries like Cambodia and Papua New Guinea to host refugees.

So human processing occurred across the world. The Right Club worked with big business to develop control over all humans. Monopoly providers could insist on conditions before letting consumers have their goods. Phone companies would not sell a phone unless its purchaser agreed to GPS surveillance and monitoring of calls. Even then they had to pass a loyal citizen's test to become eligible. Computer companies insisted on similar scrutiny and supervision. Cars became a special right that needed to be earned. The elite had flying cars. Citizens, now just called consumers, needed the Gold Citizen's Loyalty card in order to get a car. Gold was the best they would ever achieve but needed to be fought for and guarded carefully. There were incentives within this system. The three types - gold, silver, and bronze - opened doors to a better life. Few had Gold Cards. With this access was granted to the better food stores and better food, to more exclusive parks and areas of cities, to certain forms of entertainment and, of course, better types of healthcare.

The public had a completely free choice. The choice was to agree with the conditions or go without, lose points on the card and eventually have it taken away. Citizens were relegated down the social ladder until they eventually ended up joining the undesirables. If a citizen gained enough points on his or her card, their Bronze or Silver Card could be ungraded. That might allow qualification for luxuries such as a People's Car. Suzy only earned her Silver Card four years ago. She had had points deducted for being associated with an undesirable - Rob - retrospectively applied, and in the last decade, traitors such as Pippa and Dave. And of course King Charles told every citizen that to have a chip inserted was of great benefit, necessary for your own safety, and thoroughly recommended by the monarchy. In fact the King would take it as a personal insult and affront if anyone voiced objections to this further leap in progress. So the CLC was the most cherished possession in any family. They were vital for survival. The only person they knew with a Gold Card was Jenny.

Nana had returned from the lobby with Roberta's present. Gifts to children were carefully regulated. At four years old they could still be given toys but this had to be accompanied by the *History Of The World*, written in simple terms. There were fifty-two chapters, one was expected to be read each week. The whole family had experience of this as Barrett, Rob and Jenny's youngest, was the first to produce a grandson, Kesha. By this generation the children's skin had lost Rob's tan, which was a relief with the new wave of racial prejudice and segregation. He was now six and had progressed onto other compulsory volumes. So they had all seen his *History Of The World*.

Books were rare nowadays, but this was kept in book form to emphasise its importance and to ensure it was always accessible in anyone's house. There were a limited number of novels available on the communications gateway, but the Internet was only available to the elite. Social media had been wiped out after the trouble it caused twenty or so years before. It had been used for dissident groups to communicate and election results were not as they were supposed to be. So the Internet disappeared. And so did elections. Suzy was at first delighted. No more drivel of people spending all day typing what they had for breakfast and how much they all loved each other.

The special treat, before a large tea party and cake, was to be the trip to the Park. They had to wait until the end of the King's speech but then all put their shoes on. The heat of the day was settling to make it possible to stay out for longer. Global warming had made such a difference. Coats were never needed at any time of year, and few were really bothered by the ban on women wearing trousers. In France it had been illegal for women to wear trousers from 1800 until it was finally rescinded in 2013 – but unlike in France where it was never enforced, in 2030 in Britannia it was, and females were punished severely.

Since the melting of Greenland, sea levels had risen six metres, not only affecting the Marshes but also covering Norfolk and much of what used to be called Holland. Some of the London basin had to be evacuated. The Isle of Thanet became a true island again for the first time since the Romans with the Wantsum Channel opening up to be two miles wide. The Wash extended to make Cambridge and Peterborough coastal cities. The rise in temperature accelerated the extinction of many more species upsetting the ecosystems and food chains. This was all kept a secret.

They checked out of Francine's premises with their cards and started to stroll up the hill.

"Thank goodness that smoke has nearly cleared. I've never experienced such a putrid smell," said Francine and immediately regretted it because it encouraged discussion.

"What was that coming from?" asked Kesha, living up to his Russian name meaning innocence.

Aiming her reply towards her chip in her upper left arm Francine said clearly.

"I expect it's just from the undesirables, darling. The bad people. Nothing to worry about."

"Something was very flammable," he kept on.

Suzy glanced at her and knew she needed help, so chipped in with a pedantic point that she would have loved to use on Rob. But he was no longer there to educate, so it fell on the next generation.

"Kesha should it be flammable or inflammable?"

He looked at her bewildered.

"Actually they both mean the same. The prefix 'in' in this case means 'into' not 'non'. Does that make sense?"

"So are capable and incapable the same, Nana? I hope so as my teacher says I'm incapable."

Suzy thought she had better move on.

"So, Roberta, do you want to go on the swing, the slide or the roundabout?"

"All of them!" she shouted.

They gained entrance with Suzy's Silver card, which gave her access to certain parks and walked slowly through security imaging which held them up temporarily in the shadow of two massive sculptured masses of granite. Diana Mosley was correct when she stated seventy years earlier that the statues of Hitler and Goebbels would adorn the main squares of the capitals of Europe. They did, and they were copied for the parks too. She died bitter at the turn of the century because her husband, Sir Oswald, was not next to them. Now all parks were in private hands, their cards automatically took payment too. This also committed the visitors to agree to all terms and conditions.

After a further walk they reached the children's pods. These were shaped like caskets but with cartoon characters on the outside. Both Kesha and Roberta jumped in and the lid was closed. The front was transparent so the child could be seen, and a microphone system allowed them to communicate. Kesha had selected 'shoot' on his and went through the virtual reality and sensations of descending down a giant slide. Francine pressed 'swing' for Roberta who after only thirty seconds told her Mum to stop, as she felt sick. She unsteadily got out of the pod.

Sitting on the grass but hidden by the trees, high on the hill were Jerry and Ian. They were each vaping - this had totally replaced cigarettes, becoming more profitable for the companies - and were looking down on the park, pleased with their day's work of burning down the Civic Centre. Beside them were their CVDS, or Camera View Detector Systems, that allowed them to move about dodging the CCTVs.

Ian was now very skilful checking his phone with one hand. He had lost the left hand in a car accident about twelve years before when pushed off the road and left for dead by MI5. He crawled out of his Daewoo on his hands and knees over the dead body of his colleague. The police had not got the message in time, so they took him to hospital. Those officers never worked again. He was tough. He went straight from being on oxygen in Intensive care to the latest party.

They could see three women, one with a baby, taking two children from the play pods and then begin their stroll down the Avenue of Heroes. Each park had an Avenue of Heroes. This one had the usual memorials to Robert Mugabe, Benito Mussolini, Hendrik Verwoerd and Eugene Terre'Blanche, the leader of the Afrikaner Weerstandsbeweging. Next to these African heroes was the memorial to the late Queen Elizabeth II's consort Philip of Mountbatten. Great pride was taken in restoring his full and proper surname, Schleswig-Holstein-Sonderburg-Glucksburg. The bust of Horst Wessel stood on a grand plinth and was to be found in every park. The storm trooper was made into a martyr for the Nazi cause by Joseph Goebbels, and a Horst Day to celebrate his life was held on 23rd February that year to mark the centenary of his murder. Recently erected were the new ones to honour David Irving, Oliver Letwin, David Icke and Sir Francis Galton.

Suzy moved towards the last as she really did not recognise the name but could not admit that out loud. Below was a quote:

Could not the race of men be improved? Could not the undesirables be got rid of and the desirables multiplied?

Next to this promoter of eugenics were two others, Sir James Crichton-Browne and Bertrand Russell. The latter, Suzy knew, had proposed the issuing of colour-coded procreation tickets to prevent the gene pool of the elite being diluted by inferior human beings. Those who tried to have children with holders of different coloured tickets would be punished, usually by compulsory sterilisation. The King had talked about this in his first address.

They decided to stroll back to Francine's house in time to meet Jenny. On the other side of the Avenue they passed the statues to Robert Relf, the founder of the British Ku Klux Klan and John Colin Campbell Jordan with his quote underneath:

Jesus was counterfeit. Hitler was the real Messiah and his resurrection will make him the spiritual conqueror of the future.

Jerry and Ian were still proud of Poison. It was their life and the only thing they knew now. They gave up blowing up statues years ago as just futile gestures. Targets now had to fulfil the criteria 'would this delay or sabotage the execution of the Establishment's evil ideology?' It got approval only if the answer was yes. Neither Charles Morrison nor Douglas fulfilled the criteria. They were only revenge targets. That is why Max had dealt with them himself. He would not put his troops at risk unless it achieved something that helped their cause.

Years before other terrorist groups had realised that killing civilians was a waste of effort - the Establishment did not care. Those deaths did not change anything except to allow those in control to introduce more surveillance. It was only when they changed tactics and hit the infrastructure that it began to hurt. Hitler had made the same mistake. He might have won the Battle of Britain ninety years before if he had carried on bombing the airfields rather than changing direction and bombing London. However the re-written history told the new generation otherwise. Poison now preferred the more difficult targets that people could not fail to notice. Both Ian and Jerry were both resigned to dying in one of their attacks.

Ian's phone rang. Vilma's face appeared on the screen. New orders.

64 - HISTORY AND TRUTH

THE TRUTH, THE WHOLE TRUTH, NUTHIN'
BUT THE TRUTH

Lonely days lonely night

The truth, the whole truth, nothing but the truth
Don't need your lies I got my proof

I know you ain't for me

Ian Hunter (1979)

When Suzy, Francine and the baby, Barrett, Kesha and Roberta arrived back, Jenny was already there. She had arrived with the quality food bought with her CLC Gold card, unavailable to the others.

It was agreed as a family that Jenny should denounce her dead estranged husband in the strongest possible terms, that was the minimum necessary, to help her get the top card. All knew she was not being genuine. It meant little and it benefitted them all. Those who knew he was innocent and murdered felt slightly better getting some payback. Those who thought Rob a nasty evil paedophile would probably not notice. There was a danger it would be seen as sour grapes from a jilted wife but it was a statement to get her a card, not to get comments from people she knew. However it did not run smoothly. After the denunciation things got worse at first. She was forced from her work as a nurse and told the card was never a possibility. She had to sell up and downgrade as a result. But with the family's backing she continued to collaborate.

After two years in a flat on the site of the former Dungeness Nuclear Power Station, Jenny was surprised to be told a card had been issued after all. That allowed her to apply for a better flat in her present block further inland. This was just in time. The Dungeness site became almost uninhabitable with the rising sea level. Others were not as lucky. Jenny never knew who had pulled strings for her but someone clearly had. These things never happened without a reason. They all guessed it could have been Lars but Leona was more likely.

The relationship between Suzy and Rob's second daughter Leona seemed to change dramatically after Rob's death. It was not true that the tragedy had hit her harder than the others but she certainly had reacted differently. Seventeen is a very vulnerable age and Leona's relationship with the rest of the family was very strained over the next few years. When Jenny suspected she had fallen in with the wrong crowd she was more worried about drug taking than anything else. It was Suzy who found out that the wrong crowd was actually a group of right wing extremists who seemed to have connections with the Establishment. Ignoring, or perhaps just naively not realising the possibility of the Establishment having anything to do with her father's death, Leona embraced their values of exclusivity and superiority. For some reason Leona felt it easier to confide in Suzy about her new friends, which to her were a breath of fresh air and possessed values she had not been exposed to before. Suzy was horrified to hear her talk about eugenics as a right of the ruling elite and the deserved fate of the undesirables, before they were even labelled that. How ironic that Leona had the lightest skin of Rob's children. How ironic, considering her grandmother's Barbadian origin. Suzy kept quiet and went along with what Leona was saying, coaxing as much out of her as possible. When Suzy told Jenny all about it she clumsily made it sound like she had got in with an evil nasty version of the *Made In Chelsea* cast. The battle to save Leona was one of the first common problems that helped draw Rob's two wives close.

In the following decade, Leona kept her views closer to her chest and refused to talk about her friends, connections or work. She did eventually come back into the family fold and matured into a lovely person but they all suspected she still had dealings with the dark side. Only a few years ago they discovered she was still communicating with the AfD in Germany, the Partij voor de Vrijheid in the

Netherlands and the Lega Nord in Italy. That was before all the boundary and frontier changes.

So getting a card was a turning point in Jenny's fortune. The years crept by, the girls left home, and she managed to secure a People's Car. Eventually with more collaboration she was upgraded to a top of the range version. The superior model allowed her to ignore all speed limits and of course was only available to Gold cardholders. The children loved the rides with Grandma as they could go over three times the permitted twenty miles an hour strict limit. Jenny was a bit of a maniac according to her daughters. Only dark windowed large limousines carrying anonymous VIPs still powered by internal combustion engines ever overtook her. They all knew only one other person with a Gold Card besides Jenny. He was a neighbour and they suspected him of being an informer so most people steered clear. Leona had been spotted talking to him sternly one day on a visit.

What turned out to be the most rewarding perk was the Gold Card Holder's Club, which met once a month officially to discuss and promote the King's message but provided like-minded contacts at any time. It took Jenny some time to realise - at least a year's worth of meetings - that the members mainly used the club to further their own ends, make their own lives easier and to make connections. She knew that that was pretty slow and dumb of her but it encouraged her to keep attending just at a time when she was on the point of giving up. A smooth talking Aryan-looking pompous banker in his sixties eyed her up. He clearly fancied himself and thought he could get into her knickers. To help him in his quest, although it had the opposite effect, he bragged and boasted too much and said probably more than he ought to have done. He let slip that many had blocking chips that stopped their conversations being picked up by their own upper arm insertions. To Jenny this explained why he had moaned about issues in some conversation groups yet appeared very reverential in others.

"Come to dinner and I'll show you my glorious status symbol," he had said with a smirk.

With a little bit of prodding Jenny established more about them and how to obtain one. They could only be activated for short periods to avoid arousing suspicion. The surveillance signal pick-up was patchy just like in the old days when ordinary people were freely allowed mobile phones. When the blocking chip was activated, they had to claim that they were in a black spot if investigated. After a few liaisons she managed to charm one out of the SS Gruppenfuhrer Reinhard Heydrich look-alike without having to succumb to his desires. He was too old and could not move fast enough to catch her.

"You aren't right for me," she said, having to be blunt.

Jenny had been browsing through Roberta's new *History Of The World* as they came through the door. She greeted the family group.

"I see more history has been re-written. The truth, the whole truth and nothing but the truth. Have you looked at this yet?"

The others stared at her with alarm.

"It's okay, we are blocked 'til five twenty-three, so say what you wish."

"Hello, Grandma!" Roberta shouted, ignoring all the worried adults.

"They have another new version of the twentieth century. Communism isn't mentioned. There was no Russian Revolution. Czar Nicholas II didn't end up down a mineshaft but ruled 'til after the Second World War. His sister Xenia took over 'til her death in 1960. Hitler claimed total victory after a stunning Blitzkrieg winning the Battle of Britain in just two weeks. After the successful invasion of Britain, Nazi HQ was set up at Blenheim Palace and Hitler's country retreat was in Shropshire. The Americans stayed isolationist as the planned attack on Pearl Harbour was thwarted by intelligence provided by a hero called Tyler Kent who was intercepting Churchill's secret communications. Unbelievable. But let's not allow that to spoil the party."

At that, there was a knock on the door and three other four-year-olds arrived for tea and cake. Kesha being two years older decided he would pull rank and be in charge. He shepherded the three girls and one other boy towards the children's room where they had the virtual reality equipment.

Children did not have their surveillance chips inserted until they were ten years old. It had developed into a landmark ceremony of celebration, a bit like inauguration into the Hitler Youth - the Jugendbekenntnis or Lebenswende - a religious confirmation, or Jewish Bar Mitzvah before these were banned and then air-brushed from history. Like in Nazi Germany, the elite ran a totalitarian society integrating their own ideology into every aspect of life. Like under Hitler religion was a problem since the church wanted to do the same. The Youth Consecration, as it was originally called replaced all other rituals. As a mark of respect for the Third Reich showing the way forward, the German term was preferred, Jugendweihe.

Kesha wanted to play tennis but allowed the girls one game of netball first. Children's parties had changed their nature since the banning of cameras and all recording devices. No longer were parents clicking away for a photo album. If one wanted a photo of anything this was arranged by applying for an official to attend, having given reasons why it was necessary. At first when the ban was introduced to heritage sites and national landmarks some people welcomed it, as tourists obsessed with taking photos and not appreciating what they were seeing annoyed a lot of citizens. However, it soon became clear this was commercial. Since most historic buildings, national parks, and famous landmarks had been taken over by multi-nationals pre-prepared images had to be purchased. With no photos to take the adults then took advantage of the small window of opportunity before the birthday tea while the children were occupied, to chat - all before 5.23 p.m. however.

"I know I'll find out when I read the book to Roberta, but what else does it say?" enquired Francine.

"The experiment with the European Union has been airbrushed from history too. It was never formed. The worrying part of this are the paragraphs devoted to what seems to be a new aim, setting country against country, almost as if the Establishment want to recreate war in Europe."

"I suppose that's consistent. If Hitler had won the war there would have been no European Union," said Barrett with her first contribution.

"It goes further and we see the destruction and dismantling of countries. Catalonia, Andalusia, and the Basque regions gained their independence from Spain. The Balearic Islands split off too. Transylvania from Romania, Upper Silesia from Poland, Frisia from the Netherlands, Sardinia and Sicily from Italy, Bavaria and Schleswig-Holstein from Germany, Corsica and Normandy from France and Wallonia from Belgium. No mention of Alsace being amalgamated back into Germany though."

"The idea is to reduce the size and therefore strength of Nation States so that the large companies are more powerful and can dictate," said Suzy, "Another of Rob's predictions coming true."

Jenny could sense her audience was interested.

"That is why we are told the Nordic countries are our enemy. They stuck together against the rest of the world and its Americanisation and globalisation. Those eight states combined form the seventh largest nation on earth. That's a threat we are told, just because they aren't compliant. The Old Norse language is now a rival to English. Their culture has been suppressed here. No Grieg, Lindberg or Sibelius, no Ibsen, Hans Christian Andersen, no Munch."

"I think it must be great to be a Scandinavian. So civilised. So sensible. All the right values. I'd love to live in their free society," said Francine.

"But according to this, they are the new enemy. They are the new Islamic State. An enemy is always necessary. They were blamed for the destruction of that new US Embassy at Nine Elms in London. We all remember the huge explosions wrecking what was supposed to be a fortress. It was a cube-shaped glass-facaded monstrosity and I'm glad it is no more. But we all know it wasn't them, despite this new book proving it with evidence. Bollocks."

Jenny continued.

"The few decades of majority rule in South Africa isn't mentioned either and apartheid continues. I say apartheid, but there only appear to be whites left. Blacks are not mentioned at all in that country, which is probably ethnic cleansing on the biggest scale ever - an example of the extermination of an indigenous people nearly matched by the rout of the aboriginal Australians. All the military dictatorships in South America have been reinstated and are praised as patriotic heroes. There was no Vietnam War."

Suzy picked the book up from the table and started flicking through the pages. She went quiet for a while whilst absorbing some of the new facts from this edition. Francine was given some of the priceless tea from Jenny's bag and went off to make some for all.

"Hitler won the battles of Stalingrad and Kursk and ended up in Moscow. They even have pictures of him in Red Square. But he did a deal with Halifax, the British Prime Minister, to peacefully co-exist. A chap called Ramsey succeeded Halifax and was PM for a record fourteen years."

"Have they a photo of Stalin and Hitler having tea on the moon too?" said Francine, not without a large slice of sarcasm.

"The new edition makes a big thing of the kidnapping by the SS of the Duke of Windsor in 1940 in what was called Operation Willi. He was re-installed on the throne after George VI was shot, along with the others on the Sonderfahndungsliste GB or Gestapo Special Search List For Great Britain. What a triumph it was to get a hero back where he rightly should have been! His state funeral in 1972 was the biggest since Hitler's, they say."

"I know the truth about Operation Willi. I studied that era when I was younger," said Jenny, "It was unsuccessful, and the Duke got away to the Bahamas. The aim was for Edward to sort out a peace settlement. He was not trusted, nor was his pro-German wife, who was at one time supposed to be von Ribbentrop's lover. When word got back about Edward slagging off the Royal family for the way they treated Wallis, and his disparaging remarks about Churchill's wartime policies, Churchill threatened to have him court-martialled unless he obeyed orders!"

"So Hitler had an ordinary funeral did he? What happened to him in the end according to the new history?" asked Francine, as she came back with the tea.

"Hardly ordinary, but I know what you mean. Better than having your corpse covered in petrol and burnt, then stuck in the ground. Apparently he died peacefully in his bed at the Berghof in Berchtesgaden aged seventy-five in 1964. Heading up the mourners at his grand three-day funeral in Berlin was President John Kennedy. We seem to remember him being assassinated in Texas the year before, but that's been re-written. In fact he served two terms followed by his brothers Bobby and Ted. Then his son. Then straight to Reagan. LBJ, Nixon, Ford and Carter, there were no presidents by those names! Joseph Kennedy was declared a hero. A dynasty had been created until discredited by Trump and Palin. Shows what power some families can have but then easily forgotten. We always knew that their father Joseph, who was American Ambassador to the Court of St James's until a year into the Second World War which Hitler now apparently won, had a reputation of an appeaser who wanted to negotiate with Hitler. This has been turned around from being a slur to being praised. They now celebrate his Nazi sympathies."

"Okay, so I suppose they also celebrate his anti-Semitism and support for McCarthy, not to mention forcing his daughter to have a lobotomy," added Suzy.

"They have expanded the chapter on the Second World War greatly, and reduced that about the Third World War. In fact they don't call it that anymore. Now it's just a clash between the US, Australia, Russia and China. Europe isn't mentioned and the sacrifices by the citizens of Britannia and Germania ignored. They seem to want to make examples of what happens to traitors to deter others I suppose. There was a famous Special Operations Executive agent called Noor Inayat Khan, who went under the other names of Madeleine, Nora Baker and Jeanne-Marie Rennier. She was Britain's first Muslim war heroine. She was sent to aid the French Resistance as a radio operator. Their life expectancy was six weeks. The section on her seems to delight in details of her interrogation at the Gestapo

HQ at 84 Avenue Foch and how she was dealt with under Hitler's 1941 Directive Nacht und Nebel, or Night and Fog, and then beaten and shot in Dachau. The new edition implied that this was to be expected for a Muslim, and patriots destroyed her memorial statue in Gordon Square.

"If you know your Wagner you will recognise the alliterative hendiadys Nacht und Nebel was first used in Das Rheingold in 1869. That's why Hitler liked it, I suppose," said Francine.

Jenny thought she would lighten the mood.

"1964, that was the year your father was born so maybe Hitler was resurrected and re-born after all!"

"That's not funny, mother."

"No, I'm sorry. Totally unwarranted and undeserved but I have to rekindle my reputation as a denouncer from time to time."

"Save it for when they can hear you," said Francine.

"What really worries me is that from time to time I can't really remember what is truth and what is fiction anymore," said Suzy, "Take those Hitler diaries. Now we are told they are genuine. I remember as an eleven year old the *Sunday Times* being conned, or so it was believed, by forgeries. It damaged the reputation of a historian called Trevor-Roper who declared them genuine, but now they say he was right. Hitler was worried when Eva said he had bad breath! Who to believe, eh?"

After a pause Jenny said quietly.

"Hugh Trevor-Roper married 'butcher' Haig's daughter."

But it was a detail nobody was interested in. Then, being unclear whether she wanted anyone else to hear.

"I can't believe he has been dead fourteen years."

Then louder so all could hear.

"He quoted Tennyson to me, *'Tis not too late to seek a newer world.* We have to believe that, or what's the point?"

It was well over a decade in which so much had changed. Although the European Union according to the new version of history had never existed, the adults remembered the Referendum in Britain to leave what never had existed. That then led to a break-up of the United Kingdom. Scotland went independent and after that the banning of all religion except one version. Ireland was re-united as there was no reason not to. England and Wales were too small on their own so borders were abolished and in an Anschluss one country was formed called Britannia. The Welsh people approved this in a referendum where ninety-nine point nine, nine, nine per cent said yes. They also voted to ban the Welsh language. Eventually all other languages were banned. The American language was all that was necessary. This alienated the French even more, to the point of a total breakdown of relations. There was quite an exodus to Scotland and Ireland. Britannia sank from the fifth richest economy in the world, to twenty-fifth below Belgium.

Corbyn and the military coup organised by the Right Club, which got rid of him as soon as he won that election to No. 10 Downing Street, are not mentioned at all. Airbrushed. Same time as Habeas Corpus was suspended.

The population was told by King Charles in his last broadcast that there was now irrefutable proof of the existence of a God. One God. The scientists were now certain. This was why it was ruled that only one form of religion was necessary and allowed. It was tolerated by the Establishment rather than welcomed. This was a pragmatic approach as they saw from history that driving it underground would be more damaging. All other forms were banned and then extinguished from the memory banks. No youngster would grow up knowing anything about Islam, Judaism, Hinduism, Buddhism, Sikhism and the many others - they had never existed. The chapter about Henry VIII had to be changed and other reasons had to be found to explain wars. The Pope was removed from the Vatican, which was destroyed in the war between Italy and Germania. He and most cardinals were never seen again. There had been plans to make the Catholic Church a proscribed organisation under the Terrorism Act, but this became unnecessary as it withered away in any case. The pro-abortion vote in Ireland made it an irrelevance and the sex scandals finally saw the end of it.

It was not intentional, but the religion became known as One God. Corporates fell over themselves to get attached to the new faith with Walmart being the first sponsor. Over the years other corporate sponsors included Exxon Mobil, Apple and Toyota. Creationism was reintroduced into schools and scientists were re-educated about their mistake that the earth and the universe were older than six thousand years. School trips were organised to the Creation Museum in Kentucky where the scientific proof was laid out for all to see. Almost half of Americans already believed God created everything so they had a head start over the citizens of Britannia. One God took over from fundamentalism when it was realised the profits would be greater.

Policy was changed as good business practice had been stifled. All children, with the exception of those in the ghettos and camps, received a basic education up until the age of eleven, but children were then split, streaming those with potential to serve society to the grammar schools. Children were encouraged to leave school as early as they desired. The structure was designed to segregate, divide and support the class system, which had served the elite and the Establishment well for centuries. Britannia almost invented class and nowhere else exploited it as much. They were convinced that this is what had made the country great. Their opponents knew this was a cancer destroying civilized society.

The schools were run according to the needs of the businesses sponsoring them. They wrote the curriculum and syllabus. The core subjects were history, business, chemistry, maths and English. Art, music, biology and other languages were thought not necessary and out of date. Health education informed the children about the importance of sugar in their lives and the need for processed food. The biggest schools sponsor was the arms trade who won the contract to write the history lessons. The shareholders could vote out disruptive pupils, or those thought to be a bad influence. Higher education was just for the elite. It was expensive for the individual but students with potential could get the first six hours free. The only permissible subjects were those that led to work that had been proven to improve the country's GDP.

They were told there was now proof that the best healthcare is based on competition between doctors and hospitals run by big business. The NHS was a distant memory, but never mentioned anywhere. It was as though it never existed either. The doctors worked to strict protocols and guidelines. Their status had been reduced significantly to the same level as a machine operator. Training now took just one year and was sponsored by Toshiba Medical and Hitachi. Before any human contact any potential patient had to have a mandatory full body CT or MRI scan. Toshiba Medical and Hitachi made the scanners.

It was celebrated that business had eliminated hunger in the world. There were no more food scarcities or crop failures as competition farming, pesticides and the market was so efficient. The term famine was replaced by acute food insecurity many years before, but nowadays even this is not mentioned – nor was the elimination of bees.

The moon landings were re-branded as a corporate success. No one at Roberta's 4th birthday party was born when Neil Armstrong set foot on the moon in 1969, and Sir James Morrison was sitting in his club reading about it, but Jenny and Suzy clearly remembered seeing the photos and film clips at school. Neither could recall Armstrong having the logo LUCKY STRIKE on his helmet or the letters AT&T on the side of the Apollo 11 capsule, but maybe they were too young. Jenny knew someone had been busy with some photo-shop software when she saw Apple and its icon on Buzz Aldrin's back. Apple only came into existence seven years later. She dared not say anything however. Now American big business had taken over space. The US companies of Lockheed Martin, Boeing, Raytheon and United Technologies Corporation had got together to exclude the British BAE Systems and push out Airbus. They controlled access to space, satellites and exploration. In effect they had privatised the reachable and exploitable universe.

One failure blamed on the old system of government was the development of driverless cars. It was soon realised that a stream of cars following the same route, bumper to bumper, was actually what they used to call in the old days a train. The train owners did a good job of ridiculing those manufacturing the driverless cars until they went out of business. But cars had developed. The internal combustion engine had become a victim of its own success. Their contribution to global warming increased the baseline temperature of the planet and so led to the development of solar panel roads, which became the energy source of the People's Car. So the elite, who wanted to travel faster, banned the internal combustion engine except for their use. A familiar sight were teams of undesirables laying these new roads. Many died of kidney disease for the same reason as sugar workers, mainly dehydration, exhaustion and malnutrition. But there was a plentiful supply of workers that would not run out. The forty per cent partial eclipse of January 2028 caused the first breakdown of this new road system, and lead to more of the elite keeping their internal combustion engine cars to escape the consequences of the fifty per cent eclipse due in June of this year. All roads charged a toll payable by all except the elite and Tier One Gold cardholders.

Huge arsenals of weapons of mass destruction were at long last supposedly found in Iraq, so the USA, the UK and its partners were not only justified in invading and toppling Saddam Hussein but they had prevented the possible destruction of the planet. Illustrated with photographs, this was a whole new chapter in *The History Of The World*. The Chinese had sold Hussein the weapons - it was a lie, they came from the US and British arms dealers everyone was told. But Britannia remained the second biggest arms dealer in the world, proudly selling arms to Saudi Arabia to help them maintain their enviable human rights violations record. The war in Yemen was won with nuclear and chemical weapons turning the area into a wasteland.

There were other parallels where mass destruction was prevented. The assassination of Kim Jong-un's successor and the warning nuclear explosions over Pyongyang brought the world back from the brink according to this new edition. This became inevitable after North Korea invaded the South to achieve the supreme family's ambition of uniting the Korean peninsula. The US demonstrated it would not put up with the threats to Guam either - its military base in the western Pacific Ocean. The new Russia-USA alliance and friendship was responsible for that operation. No trace could be found of the killing of half a million civilians on any website. There was no mention of the destruction of Tokyo.

The USA had achieved what it wanted in the Ukraine. The CIA had orchestrated a coup in Kiev. It had installed a regime rotten with Nazis. Prominent parliamentary figures were the political descendants of the notorious Organisation of Ukrainian Nationalists and Ukrainian Insurgent Army (UPA) fascists. When Aung San Suu Kyi was assassinated by the CIA and replaced by the military again in Myanmar, the genocide of the Rohingya people was completed with great efficiency. Most that had escaped to Bangladesh over the previous few years drowned in the floods.

The new enemy was China and its overseas allies and organisations. Most terrorist incidents throughout the world were blamed on the Chinese in the 2020s. They had their proof. No need for lies. This justified the counter-insurgency activities of the new expanded NATO, which was renamed the World Peace Organisation as it now included Russia. The USA had been keen to revive the Russian economy with its corporate businesses taking over the country in its efforts at world domination of economies. Just as important, the deal was that the Russians were to leave Ukraine as it was, and thus allow the USA to build up its military forces on the border with China. Economically the Russians were in no position to refuse - and the Americans would have done it anyway. Having already established bases in the Gobi Desert in Mongolia, and in Kazakhstan, and with the US bases on Jeju Island off to the South and with the thirty-two bases on the Japanese Island of Okinawa, the Chinese were surrounded. This cemented US military domination of the world.

All this was presented to the people in a sanitised version of *The History Of The World*, which was careful to justify all actions. But the over-arching world domination plan was top secret and known by only the elite who had been planning this for decades. The official counter-truth argument was that China was a threat to the world by building military bases and runways on its artificial offshore islands. Nobody believed, as the Chinese claimed, that this was in self-defence - this was ridiculed. The Americans were really defending their business interests. They controlled the trade routes in the Indian and Pacific oceans and were not going to let anyone threaten them. Browsing through the book there was no mention of Gandhi, Martin Luther King, Mandela or even Alan Turing. They had disappeared from history.

It was 5.23 p.m. so any subversive discussion had stopped. Roberta blew out the four candles on the birthday cake. The children were all tired and Barrett decided to take Kesha home. They did not live far away.

Of the invited children, the boy, Hendrik had made the others cry - it was not clear why or how. Francine decided he would not be invited again. He seemed quite nasty. She did not like his parents anyway after they appeared delighted to get good tickets for the next public executions. These took place in every region once a month. In Francine's area they took place in the Joseph De Maistre Stadium, named after a key figure of the Counter-Enlightenment who regarded monarchy as both a divinely sanctioned institution and the only stable form of government. He declared the most important official was le bourreau, the executioner.

Leona rang on the communications gateway and wished Roberta a happy birthday. As all these communications were monitored the others just exchanged a few pleasantries. Jenny and Suzy, who both lived alone also made their way out of Francine's door, but a lot slower as both were reluctant to spend the evening alone - too many lonely days and lonely nights. Francine saved the day by inviting them both for coffee the next morning. Neither hesitated to agree and they set the time.

Jenny offered Suzy a lift home. They had grown very close.

65 - DISPOSAL AND SILENCE

CALIGULA SYNDROME

Is this what true power feels like?
Racing round my veins

My Caligula syndrome

Have I become just a little deranged?

Soft Cell (2002)

It was unusual to see a limousine in the area and certainly rare to see two outside an Old People's Home. But Suzy the passenger pointed it out to Jenny the driver as they drove past along the solar panels on their way home. She clearly saw a man in the back of one and the two chauffeurs standing together twenty yards away chatting and smoking. Another man prowling around the cars had all the demeanour and swagger of a bodyguard cum bouncer. Ex-police and firearms Tom Barton moved to self-employed status when all law enforcement was privatised.

"Not a sight one sees every day. Some VIP I suppose, from the elite. Not using their flying cars today."

"But what would an elite be doing in our area and using our sort of home?" puzzled Jenny, "We all know their care, whether health, social, pampering or servants, is in a different league altogether."

"Maybe whoever they are visiting has fallen out of favour!" said Suzy.

Not quite out of favour, but certainly in the way of a risk to security and a revenge target.

Inside the rundown building Sir James Morrison was suffering a visit from his son on his birthday. Ninety years older than Roberta, but sharing the same day. His son did not want to be there either. He disliked his father and always had. He had come to check up on how gaga he had become. Is he blurting out too much to the nursing staff?

As usual, father and son reverted immediately to father and son roles. The father did the talking. The son was expected to listen and, still at fifty-nine, do what he was told. But the son had already got some revenge on the past. That was why Sir James was in a people's Old People's Home. That is why he no longer could call himself Sir. It was as though his knighthood had never existed. He had been bed-bound since a second stroke six months before. He was helpless for the first time in his life. It was history repeating itself. Sir James, or to give him the title he did not use, and now could not, Baron Willingdon, had seen his father, Charles, from whom he inherited the title, become helpless after his second stroke.

"Get me out of here and into the sort of establishment I deserve," he demanded, "I'm a Baron for fuck's sake. My Club arranges these sorts of things. See to it!"

His voice got louder towards the end of his sentence.

"And get Sir Laurence Glover here to see me. He's the only decent doctor around."

His son ignored this and just stared at him.

"And where's Hammond? You owe me everything. I made you what you are and I helped make the sort of society we have now. You are rich, powerful and in the top tier due to me. Without my help and influence you'd be nothing."

His son just smirked with enjoyment.

"More powerful than you. You should remember that."

"Yes, you are and you are with the elite. The group, the cream, who are smarter, healthier, wealthier and live longer."

Then he thundered.

"Thanks to me!"

Then more quietly.

"And most important of all, in control. You owe me everything."

He repeated.

"You could have so easily ended up in the underclass of biologically run-of-the-mill humans, like the lot looking after me here. I demand again, get me out of here!"

A response was needed to stop the rant.

"Well, I'm a bastard because you are. You are right. It's in the genes. I learnt from you how to tread on people and destroy anyone in my way. We are creating people who are superior to others and the previous generation and that includes being more superior than you. An unpalatable fact as far as you are concerned is that we can no longer support hangers-on. Those, like you, who were all-powerful now reduced to a pathetic useless lump of decaying flesh."

The son wanted to hurt but he knew his father was made of a very thick skin.

"The gene editing tools we've developed allow our scientists to cut, paste and delete single letters of the genome with unprecedented precision to override abnormal genes. Even normal ones are being replaced now with enhanced versions. You realise father, all of those evil characteristics you've got could be abolished! But your evil was necessary to get where we are now. You have served your purpose. You are finished."

The last sentence was his main point and why he brought this up.

"I don't know what you are on about. We ethnically cleansed without the need of the laboratory. This genetics is just a fashionable passing fad. We revived, adopted and adapted Himmler's 1940 SS Eindeutschung programme, the Generalplan Ost, to our means and it worked well. He kidnapped over four hundred thousand racially valuable children. We hit the million mark. He germanised them. We anglicised them."

He started to say something else, but had lost his train of thought.

"Without me you'd be nothing," he repeated yet again, but then more quietly, "I'll admit you have certainly changed things. Now governments don't exist we are in total control. Doesn't do you any good though does it?" he added with cruelty and delight.

"As well as the bespoke gene editing, we are now controlling the Artificial Intelligence and the robotics. The power is in our hands. We are creating clones to supply us with organs if they fail but it's too late for you father."

Gideon was showing his inherited sadistic streak.

"We now have donor T-cell infusions available in every pharmacy. This breakthrough cures a lot of things. It would probably help you but you aren't going to get it. Chisholm has control over all pharmaceuticals and decides on the worthy candidates. You are not one of them. Those who do qualify still only get it if they can afford it, which most can't. Because of this we don't really need antibiotics any more."

Sir James was not really interpreting what his son was saying but he felt the need to impress on him yet again his own importance.

"We brought Thatcher to power and got the neo-liberal policies enacted. We abolished the welfare state. By the time we had finished there were no public employees at all. We got rid of manufacturing and the unions. We had the idea of Operation Epeios and the Blair project. We promoted eugenics and launched the economic confidence trick on the public. We got rid of the NHS, which everyone said was impossible. We airbrushed socialism from the history books. We..."

He had lost his train of thought again.

"Your achievements were good and necessary to get us onto the next step. But your real achievement was to control the truth. You told me once that Goebbels was a practice run. That although he had your admiration he'd made elementary mistakes and you had learnt from them. You thought he was a weak womaniser whose dick distracted him from being fully effective. Well the same could be said about you. I remember you saying that through cerebral activity, not brute force, you could be more in control of the world than Hitler, Stalin, Mao, or Pol Pot ever were. But you had to use your testosterone properly."

A nurse entered the room to check on Sir James and do some of the standard observations.

"Go way!" He barked. "No. Get me Sir Laurence Glover... now!"

The nurse looked at Neville for help, puzzled.

"Ignore him," Gideon said to the nurse who then left. There was a spell of quiet when neither man said anything. After some tranquillity the old man spoke.

"Adela was here earlier. As beautiful as ever. Still very blonde. I'm so proud she did her bit for the Fatherland."

"If you are referring to grandfather's cousin, the Nazi spy, I don't think so. She'd be at least one hundred and fifteen by now. You must have been hallucinating."

"She seduced me you know. We were at home watching the Queen's coronation on our new television set and she was visiting. I was only seventeen when she took me upstairs. She was about twenty years older and very experienced."

Gideon was content to let him reminisce. Whether what he was saying was true or just fantasy hardly mattered. He hoped it was not true though as he knew his grandfather had had a two-year affair with Adela. But it all helped to calm him down and avoid another injection into those withered buttocks.

"She came to see me with John, you know."

"John who?"

"John Amery, Leo's son. You know his brother Julian was an MP and married Macmillan's daughter Catherine? Shagged her too, I did."

Neville was losing his patience.

"I doubt that, you stupid old man. And John was hanged for treason in 1945, so I think it unlikely he was in this room either."

But the older man was now quite peaceful - for him at least.

"John was a good man. Served us well. Made good connections with the French fascists and Jacques Doriot in particular. His broadcasts from Germany in the war were excellent according to my father. Right on the money. If only more had listened."

He then seemed to turn on some rare affection for his son.

"Neville, you were the youngest Chancellor of the Exchequer since Randolph Churchill. As Bullingdon Club members, you both smashed up places and drank too much champagne. You both fell out with your Prime Ministers, Randolph with Lord Salisbury, and you with that son of Gerry's, Hubert Witney. But you did okay. We have grown further apart since then, but I have to say I'm pleased that you carry our torch further down the road for us. It was always part of the plan."

"Whatever happened to Witney?" he said after a pause, "He only used the office of PM as a stepping stone to greater power and wealth. A generation or two back, what greater ambition could one have but to be PM or President? You changed all that. To give you some credit you knew we could go much higher.

"The real power lies in the industrial and digital world, you once told me. Good advice. He was right to get out as he saw that governments were to be a thing of the past. He is now on the boards of several multi-nationals, like me father. I still see him from time to time. Things are a little frosty. When the ice is broken between us, there is still freezing cold water underneath. We both still play our part in the Right Club. He is sixty-six now and looks eighty-six."

"I do miss Gerry. He was a buffoon, but loyal."

"Dead isn't he? What happened?"

"The smoking and drinking caught up with him. Lung cancer, shortly after his masterful work fixing the 2010 election for us. At the end he fell out of bed and broke his neck. He invented all the good catch phrases. He wouldn't have been impressed with 'strong and stable' though would he? Witney got a statue put up to his grandfather, Sir Edward, for his promotion of eugenics."

This produced the first shared smile of the day.

Even the Establishment was surprised as to how quickly the state fell apart and unravelled once they started to pull at the thread. First the welfare state. Then local government services - although there were actually few services left after the outsourcing campaign. Citizens had to dispose of garbage themselves. It had to be transported to the private site, which had an entrance fee. Failure to do so led to steep fines.

Education and health had been completely privatised and there was no role in either for the state. Private companies who dictated the curriculum ran all schools. They were sponsored and taught creationism. They had an easier job once it was decided not to allow the undesirables to be educated. Silly idea of Blair's trying to get as many to university as possible. His masters lost control of him for a moment. Much better now that policy had been reversed and only the top five per cent were eligible. Simpler to control too as only the four universities Oxford, Cambridge, London and Durham remained. All the others were sold off, knocked down and developed.

There were far fewer schools needed because even some of the desirables could not afford to pay for their children's education. It was helped by that decision to let pupils leave when they felt like it.

Each citizen who had the money paid his or her own doctor direct for what was required. The consumer had usually decided on the Internet what they wanted, before any consultation. It was now no more of a consultation than taking a car in for a new set of tyres was a consultation - straight into the scanner before blinking. All hospitals had been closed down. Care was all 'in the community'.

A few corporate operating theatres were still needed of course. However the ones open to those other than the elite were few and far between. Many died before they got there but from the state's point of view that solved the problem. Two or three tier healthcare was a deliberate policy.

The conversion of the public to the idea that good care had to be earned and deserved did not take too long after several decades of blaming the people for their illnesses. It started with 'fat people bring it on themselves so why should I pay' - this soon progressed to denial of care. All insurance companies now had a clause that if an individual contributed towards his or her illness in any way, even to a small degree, claims were rejected. This meant a denial rate of seventy-six per cent with no appeal.

The death rate rose amongst the undesirables and life expectancy dropped. This justified the closure of more of the care centres for the poor due to lack of demand and a vicious downward spiral of less care needed, less care provided.

Inconvenient evidence had to be suppressed and destroyed. This meant research studies, that proved people became fat only as a result of the food industry profit seeking, big business, and the addictive drugs secretly put into their foods, failed to get published and the scientists discredited to the point of ending their careers.

The Vice President of the United States says diabetes is a punishment for not going to church enough and can be cured by prayer.

No one in 2030 could really remember newspapers or what purpose they served. They had all been closed down as soon as the profit margin was too small to make billionaires. They had lost their influence on the electorate well before that, when social media pushed them out of the way. Quite a few editors went to jail or disappeared when certain victims sought revenge for their poison.

News channels went bust due to lack of consumer interest. The *BBC* was eventually abolished after being dismantled and delivered into the hands of a few media moguls by dying governments in their last twitches to stay alive and relevant. The decline accelerated when the American President who was in the end diagnosed with Wilson's disease attacked the media and legalised fake news, and abolished libel and slander laws. His attitude was anybody should be allowed to say or write whatever he or she wanted, true or false. This was true freedom. The result was that no one knew what was true or untrue. All that was broadcast was devalued to such an extent that nobody tuned in any more.

As a consequence the President's diagnosis was questioned too, despite there being no doubt. He turned out to have a genetic mutation where copper builds up in his body and is, as in his case, responsible for frontal lobe dysfunction and subcortical dementia. The disease in the right side of his pre-frontal cortex was more advanced and so exaggerated the worst and more pessimistic of his emotions. The President had to be removed from office.

The first signs of his illness were impulsivity, impaired judgement and promiscuity. The American public were getting used to him insulting the disabled but many of his own supporters were shocked when he grabbed the breasts of a female reporter whilst live on air at *ABC* and asked if she was wearing any underwear. Soon his dementia and psychosis became evident. The public got used to his fantasy statements like, *the Inauguration crowd was the biggest in history, period*, despite all the evidence proving otherwise. Then, *I saw one thousand Muslims dancing in Jersey City on the night of 9/11. Fact.* People started to ignore him.

Dementia had been the biggest killer for many years but it still took some time for the President's diagnosis to be correctly made, much to the cost of the world. He had ordered a nuclear attack on Sydney because the Australian Prime Minister cancelled a state visit when the President said it was his diplomatic duty to have sex with the PM's wife and children. The public then realised even old Soviet spies like George Blake were talking more sense than some western leaders. Aged ninety-five he warned of the self-destruction of humankind having been put back on the agenda by irresponsible politicians. A true battle between good and evil.

At a press conference, he was noticeably more orange which was actually jaundice. He produced a spectacular haematemesis all over the Secretary of State when his oesophageal varices ruptured. On admission to hospital he was discovered to have ascites from his acute liver failure, cardiomyopathy, hypoparathyroidism, and died of hepatic encephalopathy. His Kayser-Fleischer rings were noticed in his eyes. He entered the Guinness book of records as the oldest newly diagnosed patient with Wilson's disease but in retrospect it should have been diagnosed at least a decade earlier.

The Goldwater Rule delayed his removal from office. This was one of the Principles of Medical Ethics of the American Psychiatric Association introduced after the Republican Presidential candidate in 1964 - Barry Goldwater, was said to be psychologically unfit to be President by 1,189 psychiatrists in a survey for *FACT* magazine. It became unethical to express an opinion without examination or consent. So many held back from stating the obvious. The irony was that the President was protected from a law that went against his free speech policy. Unfortunately, the Vice-President who took over was not much better. He too was mentally unstable. Part of the American dream was that anyone could become President. Now Americans were beginning to believe it. Anyone can.

The elite realised that the dissemination of news too widely had been a mistake, as had the distribution of mobile phones and the spread of social media. With more people in sub-Saharan Africa having phones than access to clean water the lives of the richest people in the most prosperous parts of the world became agonisingly visible to everyone. As a result the rural poor fled to the cities and, when they found nirvana did not exist there they joined the ever-greater numbers of economic migrants in search of a better life overseas. This was caused by globalisation and it had to be stopped by those in control of globalisation. There was a backlash by the less tolerant population so those in control pulled up the drawbridge and cut off the supply of communication devices of all sorts. That was when the restrictions on mobile phone ownership were brought in.

The barriers built up within and between nations stopped their cooperation and the working together that was necessary to tackle the awesome environmental problems such as climate change, food production, overpopulation, the decimation of other species, epidemic disease, and the acidification of the oceans. It was easier, more convenient, and better for business to pretend and deny any of this was happening.

There was no need for the police as private armies were now in control. They patrolled the streets to 'keep everyone safe' and were funded by big business. G4S was one of the biggest employers in the world. Defence was the responsibility of the individual. In one of the Government's last acts before it was abolished in 2025, the arms manufacturers and gun lobbyists had won with a law ending up in the Statute Book making gun ownership compulsory. It was the ultimate in disseminating the nation's defence policy down to the individual, giving them the 'responsibility and freedom' and completely privatising the armoury. Those voting this through had made sure beforehand that they had bought as many shares in the industry as they could afford. With their fortune made they happily then voted themselves out of a job. The claim was that all necessary laws were in place so the Statute Book had been finalised. They could not foresee any more new laws being necessary and, more importantly, there was nothing left for any form of government to run. Everything, literally everything, was in corporate hands. The elite who had the best interests of the citizen at heart would make any future decisions.

Neville Gideon got up and locked the door. Sir James did not notice.

"The future is in your hands. I have made us one of the controlling dynasties. But it is up to your generation and that of your children now. On the other side of the pond Nelson Woodward seems in control. Is that right? I wonder if he still likes soccer?"

Nelson was now sixty-two and Secretary of State in the US administration of President Sarah Palin. In America power had always been in corporate hands so the citizens noticed little change. These official titles were mainly ceremonial positions as they always had been, although the public did not understand how weak the President and Secretary of State really were. The change was more dramatic in Britannia as the transfer of power to corporate hands really was a transfer of might.

"I don't know if you heard but his father Lyndon died the year before last. He was ninety. There were many nice things said about his patriotism and success in rolling back the state. He did a great job as Secretary of State in the Haig Presidency in the late nineteen eighties according to President Palin's tribute."

This news did not seem to register. It was clear to Neville his father was getting sleepy. What he did not add was that Lyndon Woodward was regarded as a security risk. He knew too much and the truth could not be allowed to get out. It could risk the entire project, which was now in its tenth decade. So he had to die. Nelson was in full agreement. It was seen to that he died peacefully in his sleep.

It was now Morrison's turn.

Gideon picked up the cushion on the chair he had been sitting on. He made sure he got eye contact with his father, as he wanted him to know what was going to happen, and to make sure he knew he was hated. He had never seen fear in his father's eyes before. He was pleased. With no emotion at all he placed it over his father's face.

After five seconds there was a little struggle but it soon stopped. Sir James was dead. It seemed he did not even want to put up a fight.

Is this what true power feels like? Racing round my veins. My Caligula syndrome. Have I become just a little deranged? All this flashed through Gideon's mind in a second, but dismissed. Gideon put the cushion back and started to search through Sir James's possessions. He found nothing incriminating. He forced some welling-up of tears, unlocked the door and walked slowly to the nurses' station.

"Nurse. I think my father has just died. Could you come to check?"

After a respectable delay and pause, he told the administration office of the home that his people would be in contact to make the necessary funeral arrangements. What had slipped his mind was that only the elite were now allowed to have funerals. The Body Disposal Company dealt with the rest of the population. This he should have remembered. Six years ago he was intimately involved in the drawing up of the contract with them and was drawing profits regularly.

He walked down the grubby corridor, past the door with a sticker with Felix Denning written on it, to the entrance. Penetrating through the door was what seemed like a 1950s radio announcer's voice telling someone to treat the nurses with more respect. After walking down the steps towards the two limousines he told his chauffeur he was ready to depart but just needed a word with the occupant of the other limousine. He got in the back seat to sit alongside Sir Ivan Humphrey.

"Well. Is it done, Neville?"

"Yes, Sir James Morrison died peacefully in his sleep, nineteen thirty-six to twenty thirty. He had a good innings, as they say."

"Good work. It was necessary. We cannot take chances. He remembered too much and was likely to blurt out more as the senility set in. A small but real risk to our plans."

"No need to justify it or to make me feel any better. I'm relieved to get shot of the old bugger."

"I assure you nothing was further from my mind than trying to make you feel better. I don't care about your feelings any more than you care about mine. Let's go though. Nelson and the others will be waiting."

Without another word Neville Gideon, orphan, got out of one limo and into his own, followed by his bodyguard Tom Barton. They both needed to get to the monthly meeting of the Right Club.

66 - BUSINESS AND TRICKERY

BIG BROTHER
Bowie (1974)
~ PERMISSION TO QUOTE LYRICS REFUSED ~

"The music business is a cruel and shallow money trench, a long plastic
hallway where thieves and pimps run free, and good men die like dogs.
There's also a negative side" - Attributed to Hunter S. Thompson

---

Suzy was waiting at the bottom of her tower block on the Marshes when Jenny pulled up.

Wellingtons were needed that week as the water level had risen again. Jenny could only get within one hundred metres so Suzy waded towards her. Hers was in the shadow of two others. They now were burned out shells after fires. The residents knew the cladding was dangerous but had no one to complain to. They were on their own and had been for years. The fifty-two storeys each had four flats. All had been destroyed or rendered uninhabitable. There were few to re-house, as there had not been more than a handful of survivors. No one knew the total number of dead but it was certainly in four figures. Most of the bodies were still inside the blackened tombs.

The landscape had been like that for six years. The residents in four other towers - including Suzy - had got used to living in fear. They took it upon themselves to put buckets of water on each landing and to buy ropes so if necessary they could attempt to abseil down the side of the building. Some had pulled the cladding off themselves but that left the flats exposed and cold. They had been abandoned.

These two single women with one thing in common, the same deceased husband, had developed strong bonds. It was as though they both realised the emotions of envy, bitterness, anger and guilt were just negative, destructive and useless and further increased their pain. Life was short. They were both just either side of sixty and they wanted to make what remained of their lives as pleasant as possible.

"Hi Suzy, jump in. The chip is blocked while we are travelling so it's okay to talk."

For the last few years this was always the first thing that was mentioned. If not made clear in the early exchanges, all would assume that surveillance was probably taking place - safer that way. In the early days they were told that a limited amount of surveillance was necessary as an anti-terrorist measure. Few saw anything wrong with that but this really was a typical politicians con - where the thin end of the wedge became very thick and intrusive. They had been deceived, but now it was too late.

Neither woman was working. Both had been forced out of their jobs because of their association with Rob. Travel restrictions were put on both of them the day after Rob's funeral. Jenny was still nursing when Rob died and with the three girls at home she had to earn. That was one reason she felt she had no choice but to denounce her ex-husband. However, her work colleagues made it clear she was not welcome and hounded her out. Association with a pervert and a murderer not only tainted her, but he had been a man who questioned the values of British society - a troublemaker, a man who rocked the boat and got everybody wet.

Suzy was dismissed two days after Rob's funeral during a visit by a man from the Government, who threatened that her life would be made intolerable if she even went near the Royal Academy of Arts or the people there again. She was certainly not to communicate with them. She should not doubt the sincerity of the British Government's motives if she valued her life and should be grateful her punishment was so lenient.

So both women shared another common link. Short of money, they both had to sell their houses and move to small flats. Suzy had been on the Marshes for ten years, and Jenny nearby for nine. Both had to keep their heads down.

"Nice day yesterday. I'm looking forward to this. It's great to get together. I know I've said this before but I'm still so grateful to you being so forgiving and integrating me into the family. I really think life would have turned out so miserable without the girls in my life," said Suzy, surprising herself with unexpected emotion.

Jenny just touched Suzy's arm in recognition, and while the surveillance was blocked she turned off one of the authorised composers from the car communications centre, and started playing Bowie who had been declared decadent by the King in one of his recent broadcasts.

"Reminds me of my childhood and gives me such a warm feeling despite the material!" said Jenny.

Diamond Dogs was based on Orwell's *1984* and Bowie's vision of a post-apocalyptic world. How did he know? Suzy knew the album well despite being only a two-year-old when it appeared. Her Dad played every new Bowie album from its release date until he almost wore the vinyl out. He was at the Hammersmith Odeon gig when Bowie shocked by retiring Ziggy Stardust. He was lucky to be admitted, having arrived late after going to the wrong venue. What made him go to the Fulham Odeon he still could not work it out? So all of Bowie's work was ingrained in her DNA - and of course both remembered that Rob had insisted *Rebel Rebel* be played at his funeral thirteen years earlier. Discussing the album *Low* had been responsible for creating an early bond between the two women.

Now the most authorised and approved of music was American. The Americanisation of Britannia was almost complete. Cage, Barber, Berlin, Joplin, Porter and Sousa rotated around the clock. Gershwin and Bernstein got airtime despite their faith, as they were so popular. Wagner was probably still the most played foreign composer and there was some Beethoven and Mozart, but music from undesirable composers like Mendelssohn, Glass and Mahler for being Jewish and Tchaikovsky for being gay was banned. Copeland was beyond the pale for being both Jewish and gay. Many other favourites from their younger years had disappeared from history. Selected Beatles tracks were still available, but many of Lennon's more awkward compositions had not been heard for years. The lyrics of *Imagine, Revolution, Sunday Bloody Sunday, Woman Is The Nigger Of The World* were not acceptable. They were not exactly banned but those heard playing them often got a visit and it jeopardised their chances of getting a card.

Jenny turned the music off as they went through the first of five tolls on the route.

"I didn't ask Francine yesterday, but has her baby fully recovered? I know it upsets her greatly so didn't want to spoil the birthday party?" asked Suzy.

"It was a terrible problem but a sign of the times. Yes, luckily he seems to have suffered no long term effects."

"What exactly happened?"

"Well, you probably know it was to do with his asthma. The atmosphere was particularly bad that day, due to another arson attack. When the smoke wafted over towards Francine's house he rapidly began struggling to breathe. She rushed him down to the People's Clinic, which is now manned by Health Assistants working on protocols, but in the rush she forgot her credit card so they refused to even let her and her baby into the building. G4S now stand guard. Obviously he deteriorated and by the time she got home again, collected the credit card, which then had to be approved, and identity card authorised he was almost moribund.

He was on a ventilator for three days and in the nearest hospital which is now eighty-five miles away for a further six. Of course there was no one qualified enough or with the skills to intubate, but they can bag patients. So some teenager who had never done it before bagged the baby the whole eighty-five miles. She didn't qualify for an ambulance so they went by the state-approved taxi scheme. It is a miracle he survived. They are thinking they might have to sell the house, as there was an outstanding loan for her maternity care and a bill from when Roberta cut her hand. That hasn't been paid yet. I only found that out myself the other day. I wish I could help but I have nothing spare."

Jenny slowed as was mandatory for the vehicle registration check.

"When Rob was trying to warn us that this would happen, even I thought he was exaggerating. Very few in his profession paid any attention as, despite apparently being bright, they really didn't understand. The ones who can't be forgiven are those who did understand but did nothing. Rob always said they were blasé because their logic was that even if the worst happened they were well off enough to save themselves. They certainly got a rude awakening. Many certainly took a while to wake up to the fact that a greedy few were determined to become mega-rich at the expense of the many. To survive, no one could be trusted. The first question you had to ask of anyone was, is he after my money, and what new way is he intending to filch it from me?"

"That is why they privatised all health and social care, and Rob told me that too. I thought he was taking it all too far," said Suzy, "but if you think about it what better way of robbing every single person and legally? Everyone gets ill and everyone needs healthcare. Make everyone buy it from us. And because we have a monopoly we can charge what we like. Who cares how many bankruptcies there are? It's the system the Americans have always had. Now it's universal. The Americans have won and deliberately spread their cancer to us."

Jenny had said this before in another way but thought it worth emphasising.

"Attitudes have changed dramatically in our time. Compassion has been driven out of formerly decent people. It's the I'm-all-right-Jack approach. Most people's first thought is how will this affect me, nothing about the wider consequences and how things affect those who cannot look after themselves? It's worse than a fuck-you approach, it's a you-don't-exist-in-my-thoughts world. They are ruthless. Take that rumour we heard about the oxygen supply to those hospitals being cut off. I've no doubt it is true, but all covered up."

"What was that?" enquired Suzy.

"Several hospitals west of here didn't pay the private oxygen company money they owed. After just one warning they cut the supply without further notice. It is said about thirty people dependent on oxygen died and pretty well the whole occupancy of the intensive care neo-natal unit perished in one. The CEO of the oxygen supplier apparently said, 'now they won't do that again. They will pay on time when we ask'. Worst of all, people accept this attitude nowadays. The indoctrination of the masses to be convinced you get all you deserve if you don't pay your bills to the corporations. It's as though our species has had a new evil gene inserted. But it's taking survival of the fittest to an extreme that makes me feel we don't deserve to survive. If all that is left is a monster race, then roll on that collision between our Milky Way and the Andromeda Galaxy. Only four billion years of suffering left."

Appropriately, in the background Bowie had just finished the track *1984* and was about to start *Big Brother* which reflected on Winston Smith's brainwashing to be complete and that he now loves the leader. Jenny, in resigned sorrow, summed up both their feelings.

"Looking back on those times, we had had such a civilised spell after the Second War that none of us believed it could go so wrong, did we? Who would have believed no Europe, no governments, no state, no NHS, no public services, no transport system, no free media and very little culture. And just American to speak?"

"And no compassion, altruism, or care for our fellow man. All aided by the professions that we grew up with being deliberately destroyed," added Suzy.

It was refreshing to be able to let off steam like this knowing no one was listening, and they were not endangering themselves but now it was more in sorrow than anger.

Jenny agreed.

"We seem to have peaked as a species in our attempts at civilisation. There was just that tiny window in our history and development on this planet when we were heading in the right direction. We were lucky enough to witness it and benefit from it. A simple life, universal education and healthcare for all paid for collectively. Public services that looked after everyone all in an atmosphere of altruism, caring for the vulnerable, and working well despite being starved of funds deliberately by those who opposed helping others."

They passed through the last of the tolls.

"And freedom to read whatever books, see whatever films or plays you wanted to."

"Who, except us oldies, remember or even have heard of trade unions?"

"The world was shocked into that more civilised era and dragged to its senses by depression and two world wars which now nobody remembers," Jenny explained, "They are in the books our children are forced to read and learn, but to them it might as well be fiction. And the wars were supposedly good."

"You're right. Apart from a few battalions of cannon fodder in the military, most Americans have no idea what war is really like. The last one on their mainland was the Civil War one hundred and seventy years ago. So war is something the US does to others. They glorify it. It's a sanitised movie. Ultimately they won," said Suzy, "Altruism is a dirty word. Survival of the fittest has been hijacked."

Just in the last few years she felt confident enough with Jenny to talk freely about Rob.

"Our husband told me once this was called 'catch twenty-four', when greed overcame selflessness."

"Oh, he bored you with that too, did he?" Jenny laughed.

"In that case you know 'catch twenty-two' was one of his favourite books and he also had a definition of 'catch twenty-three', which I can't remember. Did he make all these up do you think?"

"Probably. More than likely he invented 'catch one to twenty-one' as well to satisfy his OCD, as it wouldn't have suited his personality to start anything at number twenty-two. It would have stopped him sleeping."

They had arrived at Francine's house. It was a sunny day so the solar panels worked more efficiently. Jenny inserted her card to gain access. Francine walked towards them.

"We are here for coffee as planned, darling," said Jenny.

"I've a surprise for you," said Francine, as a greeting.

Jenny and Suzy walked into the kitchen to the smell of coffee left over from Jenny's supply of yesterday to see a couple who disappeared out of both their lives over ten years before. Pippa and Dave were sitting at the table. They had not set eyes on each other since their shared tragedy. Everyone froze. This was a real shock.

They all spent a few moments just looking at one another. They were thinking things none of them would say. They all looked much older. Dave had lost most of his hair and a lot of weight. Pippa for the first time in her life had very short hair but it was still dark. Her arm was in a sling. The view of those at the kitchen table was of overweight Suzy and a haggard Jenny.

Then the realisation, the greetings, the hugging, the tears, and the relief – no one knew where to start, so much to catch up on, the good, the bad and the ugly.

"It's okay, our chips are blocked. We can speak freely," said Jenny.

Dave and Pippa explained how shortly after the funeral they were both arrested. Police turned up on the doorstep and insisted they accompanied them to the station. They were charged with burglary and a new law, which criminalised possession of files. They were taken to London and questioned for two days by the security forces before being released on bail. That was only the beginning of it. Only the next night their house was raided at 4.00 a.m. and they were tied up, blindfolded and bundled into a van. They were driven for miles then taken into a warehouse. They had no idea where they were. But it turned out not quite as bad as they feared.

After Jeremy, they thought they would be killed. They had instead been rescued by Poison who knew the authorities were coming back for them the next morning with new charges and this time they were to be remanded in custody. They were told by Poison that most in their predicament ended up being extradited to Guantanamo. The motive for rescuing them was simple - to save the files and gain more recruits to their cause. Somehow their leader knew Rob and all about the files that Pippa had acquired. They actually had little choice about their recruitment and the part they were to play. They both were offered the protection of the unit for a little bit of subversion. So for the next few years they were on the run but helping with sabotage operations, information spreading, burglaries and kidnappings. Their new enforced life was frightening and yet exciting. They were spurred on to get some revenge for what happened to Jeremy. Dave said it was not a good idea for them to know about the details.

Four years ago they slipped up. Although in disguise, they were out simply buying some provisions from their secret lodgings in London when they were stopped, quite randomly, for routine questioning and for the checking of passes. But Pippa had forgotten hers, which was an offence. They were passed over to the Special Operations Team where iris recognition was compatible with a couple that had not reported for their compulsory quarterly registration appointments, but worse had skipped bail. When questioned about why they had not attended as required they claimed they were protesting against the system. They knew they had owned up to a crime that attracted a minimum of three years in prison, but this was better than being questioned about what they had really been up to.

Since the privatisation of the police, each area had their own security force. They were in competition, often tendering for the same contract, so never cooperated. That is why the police failed to recognise where Pippa and Dave's old house was. They just did not coordinate nor join the dots together - one police force not aware that another force was searching for them for more serious crimes. The security forces, mainly G4S, had had so many personnel changes that they got away with it.

Pippa and Dave did not see or hear of each other for their whole three-year term. In the last week of incarceration a female guard, who had taken a dislike to her, deliberately broke Pippa's arm. She received no medical attention. A cellmate splinted it for her. They knew that some day they might end up separated and had planned what to do if that did happen, and a way of getting back together on release. For some reason Dave got out one month before Pippa and spent an agonising few weeks just waiting for her, hoping she would turn up. He did not even know if she was still alive.

They had been free for nearly six months. They travelled back to Dorset to find their house occupied by someone else. They had no possessions or money so they were living in a nearby camp for undesirables. Friends pretended not to know them. They had never felt so isolated. They eventually traced Pippa's sister, Penny, who thought they were both dead and had a very emotional reunion. That took a while as Penny, unbeknown to them, had been working for Poison from about a year after the funerals and went under the name of Thérèse Defarge. Then they had their first bit of luck when they heard the name Baigent while in the People's Clinic getting help for Pippa's broken arm.

Jenny had been advised to change her name and that of the girls to avoid the Baigent stigma soon after Rob's death. But the three girls decided to keep Baigent despite being married. They now knew the truth about their father and thought that cooperating in disassociating them from him would be a further betrayal of his memory. Suzy had reverted back to Dwight. Every little helped in the effort to get a card.

Francine was collecting her baby's asthma inhaler that morning. Despite the medication only lasting two weeks she could only afford one inhaler a month. Dave needed the loo and had left Pippa in the waiting area where the sign was constantly flashing:

'Current wait five hours at a cost of £100
Two hours £200 - Immediate help £400'

As he walked past the Pharmacy he heard a woman in a white coat with Chisholm Chemists on the front calling out.

"Mrs Baigent?"

Dave only knew one family with that name, but it was a name that originated from the southeast so he did not think anything of it, until he looked at the lady's face as she approached the counter and saw the port-wine stain. Francine had inherited only a very diluted version of Rob's skin colour so the birthmark always stood out.

Francine recognised Dave despite his weight loss. They had not seen each other since Rob's funeral but Dave had been in Rob and Jenny's three daughters' lives from their births. They were so pleased to see each other, and so shocked. She invited them back, even though she was expecting her mum and stepmother, but especially as she was expecting them.

Suzy summed up her life since losing Rob as pretty shit and Jenny just explained she lived her life through her children. This was a phrase she regretted as soon as she had said it, remembering Pippa and Dave's loss, but they seemed to let it go.

"Jeremy would have been twenty-seven. We often wonder what he would have been doing, don't we Dave?"

"He could have been an astronaut or Stephen Hawking's successor as Lucasian Professor of Mathematics at Cambridge," said Jenny, helping out with a tear as she spoke.

"Or manager of Bournemouth Football Club," added Dave.

"And Rob would have been sixty-six and probably enjoying retirement," said Suzy careful not to add with me for Jenny's sake.

"But he'd have been insufferable, saying I told you so every few hours," said Jenny.

Jenny was anxious to tell them why they had not been able to come to Jeremy's funeral due to the travel ban. Pippa said she had wondered why.

"Was prison really awful? And who or what is Poison who you say initially rescued you?" Francine asked Dave.

"The re-education that we had to sit through every day was certainly awful. Propaganda and absolute crap continually. What was alarming was that I think the teachers actually believed what they were saying, as though they'd been programmed. They became someone to claim us, someone to follow, someone to fool us. Big brother. Many exposed to it eventually seemed convinced. An Edward Bernays master class. Pippa says she had exactly the same experience so it obviously is a national curriculum."

"It actually was counterproductive," said Pippa. "It made me more convinced to continue to help Poison on release."

Dave told Francine about Poison. Jenny and Suzy seemed to know about it. Dave also took the opportunity to say that he was against them getting involved again.

"Was there anything positive?" asked Jenny.

"Well, we learnt a lot from other undesirables who had sinned. Most were in the detention centres for what we used to call political differences, which aren't allowed now of course. We were detained, as most were, under an Imprisonment for Public Protection sentence, which was part of Blair's *Criminal Justice Act* of 2003. It was abolished for a while when thought to be unfair and unjust, as in effect people seemed to be detained indefinitely, but then reintroduced quietly when no one was looking. We met all sorts. There was many an hour whiled away in intelligent conversation with bright people who half a century ago would have been candidates to run the country. Private companies run all these centres and prisons, so they were understaffed with poor quality couldn't-care-less wardens. They couldn't keep on top of where we were let alone us exchanging information."

Francine was listening intently as she poured more coffee. Dave clearly wanted to offload. He knew he could trust his audience, although he had no evidence for that assumption.

"Rob was spot on with his fears. Everyone took for granted that it had all started with the US-designed globalisation, which was imposed through the twin methods of commercial dominance and military supremacy. They have benefitted massively from it and have now conquered all. It's easier actually looking back on it to see what they were up to. We couldn't see the wood for the trees back then. There were so many clues that we failed to see. New universities with the curriculum created by the likes of McKinsey and Virgin. Total privatisation policy failures that were clung to at all costs destroying transport, water and energy services. Even probation services and prisons as we also know to our cost. Little things like the CEO of United Health earning sixty-six million dollars in 2014. Why would anyone need that? Was he really worth two thousand times more than his nurses? Talk about syphoning off all the money. Big brother. Many exposed to it eventually seemed convinced. An Edward Bernays master class."

Pippa thought that was a weak example so she tried her own – the one she too had first heard from Rob.

"Do you remember how few of us could explain Britain, as we were then, and the extraordinary decision to leave the European Union? Made no sense at all then, but now I can explain. It was US-backed. The Atlantic Bridge think tank linked the extreme right in

Britain and the US. It was set up to defend people from European integrationists and to allow the Americans to get their hands on all that untapped wealth in our NHS, schools, colleges, security forces and jails to name just a few. They were the real instigators of Brexit with the very specific task of bringing home a hostile corporate takeover of the UK as it was then. Don't you remember all those cosy photos of the Brexiteers with the US President?"

Francine poured more drinks.

"Take the NHS. And they did. At that time it had a relatively small budget, or rather market, of a hundred and twenty billion pounds. But they saw the potential. If they applied their system they could make it cost four hundred billion pounds within ten years and pocket most of that. Their market practices and mantra were that two procedures are better than one whether you need them or not, that hundreds of billions of dollars are spent on unnecessary care, that the private insurance industry siphons off an equal sum for overheads, profit and administration.

They initially thought their best bet was a good trade deal through the EU, as they couldn't see the EU going away. They could get access to the NHS that indirect way. They couldn't believe their luck when the right wing in Britain started to make progress and so they decided to help destroy the Union completely. They always wished for that anyway, as they didn't like the competition, but had thought it unachievable. But Brexit opened the direct route to the English NHS.

Don't forget how desperate the UK Government was at that time to creep around the new idiot of a US President. But it was more to save face rather than for the good of the country. That woman Prime Minister at that time would have traded her own grandmother. The cabinet then was what the word kakistocracy was coined for - Government by the truly incompetent. She needed the appearance of a good trade deal, whatever the cost, to try to prove the Brexiteers right. So she gave our NHS to the Americans instead and we all started eating chlorinated chicken, beef treated with growth hormone and pork laced with ractopamine.

Why am I so confident about this? Well first where's the NHS now? Gone. Who do you get your crap healthcare from now and at an enormous price? Yes, the Americans. Third. How did they get Britain to leave the EU? They got in an American PR company who had already done a great hatchet job on climate change and for the food and drinks industry and right wing politicians and they conned the Brexiteers. The basic line was 'facts don't work'. But the Establishment elite learnt a lot from this, to broaden it out and develop a political system that abandons facts, and a media ecosystem that does not filter for truth. And this explains a little of how we got here today in 2030. I met several people who worked for them who they banged up to silence."

"Makes sense," said Jenny.

But Francine seemed less concerned.

"I've never known anything different really. I was about eighteen when we left the European Union and in my mid twenties when the whole thing disintegrated. And I never was conscious of using a free healthcare system, as I was never ill. I've always had to pay or go without and I've never known any different. Was it really as great as you say or are you all just full of nostalgia?"

"I think the fact that your son nearly died through neglect as you didn't have your credit card on you answers that one, Francine," said her rather irritated mother.

Suzy was in deep thought. She managed to remember something Rob had told her.

"The great irony is that all those right-wingers who admired Churchill so much didn't realise they were going directly against his philosophy and advice. In a 1944 House of Commons speech he said we have three alternative paths to consider. Draw closer to Europe, concentrate on our own Imperial and Commonwealth organisations, or depend upon our fraternal association with the US. With the second and third options we would have to rely on the English Channel to protect us with our air and sea power. So he decided the first was the way forward as that famous poster said. But they decided to walk into the lion's mouth instead, and we have been eaten by that American big cat."

"Very well put," said Dave, "When in detention we were denied any means of recording what we had learnt. All writings were inspected and censored, so we will have to try to remember it now, but log it secretly. The more people we tell though the better. The thoughts and plots randomly spring to mind. I wake up in the night remembering different tales. So the stories come out piecemeal and not in order of importance. Some of the most worrying slip from our minds, I think you can tell this from our incoherent ramblings today."

The others disagreed. They were spellbound and said so. Dave was encouraged and carried on.

"For instance, Shipman. Remember the GP who murdered a load of elderly patients? Hundreds. He was caught around the year two thousand, jailed, but then hung himself in 2004."

"Sorry Dave," Suzy interrupted, "You mean hanged not hung. A picture is hung, a person suspended by a rope around the neck until dead is hanged."

"Okay Suzy. Thank you for that."

But Dave was not going to be sidetracked.

"Guess what? Shipman never existed. All made up."

"But hanged is for people only. If an inanimate object is suspended from the gallows the correct term is hung."

"How often are inanimate objects hung from gallows?" asked Pippa, in an attempt to deliberately tease Dave and encourage Suzy's pernicketiness.

"Quiet, Pippa. The Shipman plot was a means of discrediting GPs, weakening the trust between them and their patients, and introducing controls on their use of potent drugs in the community. It got palliative care taken away from family doctors so it could be commercialised and run by private companies. So many had unnecessary agonising deaths as a result. Even the name was an anagram. Harold Frederick Shipman is 'dark morphine acrid flesh'. Harold Shipman is 'morph had slain'. At the time I remember Rob saying that no matter how good a doctor you are there will be people who think you are crap, and no matter how bad, there will be people who think you are brilliant.

Another bit of fiction. The Twin Towers, nothing at all to do with al-Qaeda or Osama bin Laden. They were set up by the CIA to provide a pretext for invasions of Afghanistan and Iraq. And the US Government created al-Qaeda and ISIS to fight the Soviet Union."

"You know what President Harry Truman said about the CIA, don't you?" Jenny intervened, "*I would have never agreed to it if I had known it would become the American Gestapo.*"

Pippa decided to get serious again and told how they had been so cut off and totally unaware of some of the changes in the last few years of their incarceration. They knew about the attitude announcements when, about once a month, a new view of society was promoted. This was broadcast to the prisoners.

Much of what Dave went on to tell them was not new to his audience. Public executions were one of the first. Portrayed as normal, ethical and right, but also always a potential punishment. That short period without capital punishment was written out of history. They even held another referendum, not about whether the death penalty was right, but which method to adopt - hanging, electrocution, lethal injection, or firing squad. Quite a few ticked the disembowelling box. The public had not been softened up enough. The pharmaceutical industry won that one - highly profitable. If it had been important then the result of the referendum would have been decided in advance. As it was not, it gave an opportunity to demonstrate that democracy was alive. G4S were granted a torture licence having won the first contract. They knew less about how it came to be that democracy was not necessary, and in fact an outdated concept that just held progress and development back.

Following on from that was the commercialisation and expansion of the brothel industry. It was called the fourth sexual revolution and this was used to explain the change. The first phase for homo sapiens lasted the previous few thousand years when sex was just sex and a pleasure. No big deal - part of life. Not in any way an embarrassment.

So the first revolution was when women saw they had a power to get money big time. In eighteenth century London theft rather than sex was the main object of the trade of prostitution. Women would steal from their clients or potential clients. Prostitutes played key roles in the criminal underworld. It was not about the exploitation of women, but of men. The women moved back and forth between different types of respectable labour and went into prostitution again when times were hard - the trade was controlled by women. As many as one in five women - sixty-two thousand, five hundred - were prostitutes in eighteenth century London. English society expected, even encouraged, men to pay for sex. The culture was rich with its low-class flash mollishers, theatre-dwelling spells, bagnio-owning bawds, or Covent Garden nuns. There was even an annual directory called *Harris's List of Covent Garden Ladies* describing the appearance and sexual specialties of the women. The money transformed Georgian London and fed a construction boom. But women were getting too powerful.

The second revolution was the backlash. The attitudes of the Regency period were replaced by a new order of puritan control and repression lasting well into the twentieth century. Men felt threatened by the economic and personal independence enjoyed by women and so men regained authority and domination by introducing a moral panic. Early Victorian moralists proposed masculine self-control. So it was driven underground into a secret world accompanied by the inevitable hypocrisy. Rather than run the risks of the solitary vice or contamination from illicit acts with questionable lovers, men could purchase a femme de voyage or inflatable sex aid.

The pendulum swung the other way with the more minor third revolution of the swinging sixties. It was thought for a long time that women were liberated once more with effective, available contraception and to a certain extent this was true, but the real reason was the more widespread use of another pill, penicillin, not 'the pill'. People were much more careful when syphilis was a killer, but when a cure became available everyone felt liberated. Penicillin brought syphilis rates down by ninety-five per cent. So the real increase in risky sexual behaviour actually began in the so-called prudish fifties. The result was that men panicked again as women took more control. The reaction was get them back in the kitchen as domestic goddesses.

So the potential of vast profits produced this fourth revolution. They could trouser the same wads of cash as the Georgians if the commodity of sex became industrial. Attitudes had to be manipulated. So men were weak and unpatriotic if they did not visit a brothel at least once a week and were to be held up to ridicule. Women could be let off the hook of their men's unequal appetites. A win, win with improved harmony at home. The elephant in the room of sexual frustration gone for the first time since all those men in Victorian times went to brothels. So-called sex scandals did not happen any more. There was a backlash against the clampdown on sexual assaults of a few decades before. It was decriminalised, de-stigmatised and became nothing more than a joke again. Although in his seventies Harvey Weinstein was welcomed back into the movie industry.

There was little point in trying to use sex to sell commodities when anyone could just have the real thing. It dominated the media less. The more mature citizens did not have to cringe and bite their lips as their kids talked like they were the first generation to discover sex. The profits of the new industry began to rival Apple and Google within two years. These companies retaliated with the production of their sex robots that began to alter human behaviour. Men used porn and large virtual reality visors strapped to their eyes. The separation rate increased, as men preferred this to their partners. The decline was first noticed twenty years before when a study revealed over forty per cent of single people below thirty-five in Japan had never had sex with another person. It was a good way of getting the Universal Citizen's Income back off the population.

Pippa added that sex was used in prison to help control the aggression and continued by telling them about another new attitude, the legalisation and encouragement of the use of drugs.

Drugs were a good thing to be promoted. They were free in prison. They were harmless and a boost to life enhancement. Although profit-making they were subsidised to encourage use. Royal Palaces accepted sponsorship from Big Pharma - Bayer

Buckingham Palace, Sanofi Sandringham, Johnson & Johnson Balmoral, and Novartis Windsor Castle. The opium of the people really did become the opium of the people and was a means of control.

So was control by denial. This was a new policy and the modern equivalent of that box that had to be ticked or no further progress could be made - 'I accept the Terms and Conditions' - if no agreement to what was said, then no access to anything, and so denied. A phone was only available to card holders and only if the box was ticked 'I agree to all my calls being monitored'. A television, now known as a monitoring station, was only installed as long as all the King's broadcasts were viewed. A bank account was only available if there was an agreement that all transactions went through that bank and the private company monitoring the people's money had access - but nothing could be done without a bank account.

If you were lucky enough to get a People's Car then that was on the condition it was fitted with a monitoring device. To own a computer, agreement had to be given for all information on it to be downloaded to the surveillance company - a private multi-national company called The Counter-Terrorist and Protection Agency.

The corporate world had found a way of controlling the population through denial of what was essential if the customer was not fully compliant and cooperative. The free speech attitude was that we should all be grateful for the right to talk openly but to show that gratitude by not exercising that freedom.

Although very little surprised them after all that they had been through, Pippa and Dave were still quite shocked at the legalisation and acceptance of paedophilia. It was a huge money-spinner. Centres had been set up for those that way inclined and it became an offence to discriminate against paedophiles.

They all had noticed the tendency for scapegoating or allocating the blame, as it was officially known. Scapegoats were a very useful mechanism for deflecting blame from those really at fault and for unifying against an enemy. Jews had been used for centuries for this, more recently Muslims and other religions. Football fans, strikers, immigrants, the obese, the sick, the disabled, all used at one time. In the new era it was the undesirables.

Jenny was alarmed that Francine seemed against them. It was as though the younger generation had begun to swallow the propaganda. She tried to counter her daughter's prejudice by telling her about McCarthyism, even though it was well before they were all born, eighty years ago and not mentioned in the history.

"Suzy mentioned that word McCarthy yesterday. I did mean to ask her what it was," said Francine, "but you went on and on about the Second World War, Mum and I lost my chance."

"It was the practice of making false accusations of subversion or even treason without proper regard for evidence," said Dave, "Unfair allegations were used to restrict dissent or political criticism. You won't have heard of Arthur Miller as he has been airbrushed from culture as a dissident playwright, but he wrote *The Crucible* about the Salem witch trials as a metaphor for McCarthyism. Its theme was that, once accused, a person has little chance of exoneration given the irrational and circular reasoning of the public and the courts. Joe McCarthy was a US Senator who became the most visible public face of a period in which Cold War tensions fuelled fears of widespread communist subversion. Victims included Robert Oppenheimer, Charlie Chaplin, Leonard Bernstein, Albert Einstein and, of course Miller. In this country over one hundred years ago Admiral Jellicoe was scapegoated for the Battle of Jutland. But there are plenty of examples of soldiers being blamed for the errors of others, especially politicians. Tragic was the shooting of the Columbian footballer Andreas Escobar for scoring an own goal against the USA in the 1994 World Cup. Apparently it caused the drug barons to lose a lot of money on a betting scam. So poor old Escobar became the scapegoat and was blamed."

"Trust you to bring football into it, Dave," laughed Suzy, "It's true what you say about anti-immigrant stories, though, that's gone on since time began. The 1871 great Chicago fire, according to the *Tribune*, was started when Catherine O'Leary, an Irish immigrant knocked over a lantern while milking her cow. It was not true but a good story and she was vilified for the rest of her life."

"That won't be in today's history books, will it?" countered Jenny.

Pippa was in pain with her arm. She realised without proper medical care that pain would continue for some time. She did not want to stop the conversation however. She wondered about the others from the past.

"Whatever happened to that friend of Rob's, Stephen, the friend who said a few garbled words at his funeral?"

"Oh, I'm still in contact," said Suzy.

Pippa was curious about him as she remembered that it was he who crushed her by telling her Rob fancied her, but she obviously kept this to herself.

"The year after Rob died his wife Ellie was tragically killed when she fell from her horse and it rolled over on top of her. Well at least that's what the coroner said. She was on her own so we will never know. What was odd is that she never rode solo. Stephen and I got quite close for a while after that. But before you ask, no, not that close. I could have fallen for him, he was quite a hunk, but there was something about his attitude that put me off him. I don't blame him for playing safe after and not wanting anything to do with conspiracy theories after what happened to Rob, but I was still quite keen for a while to try to find out the truth. He refused to help me in any way. There's nothing like cowardice as a turn off. This was a huge mistake on my part. I did eventually find out he had made quite a nuisance of himself, complaining about corruption and clandestine privatisation, but quietly and behind the scenes. He got sacked for his troubles. At the same time Ellie was killed."

"Crikey. Do you think that was connected to his whistleblowing?"

"Who knows? I wouldn't be at all surprised after all we have seen," replied Suzy.

"What about that snivelling little toad of a partner of his and that practice manager?" asked Pippa.

"Rumour has it they scarpered to France and went on the run with practice money. They kept a low profile for a while and thought they were safe until that journalist Rob had met in Marylebone just before he died saw them in Paris. Her name was Chantelle Levesque. I know this, as out of the blue a few years ago a lovely French lady called Simone, who said she was her partner, contacted me. Chantelle had suddenly disappeared and she was naturally desperate to find her. She told me that just before Chantelle vanished she was considering informing the police about the two fugitives which turned out to be that nasty couple. She suspected the couple beat her to it by telling the security forces about Chantelle's prying and probably made up a few things about her and about what she was investigating. Too close for comfort. That would have explained her disappearance.

Just last year Jeff, my brother, snooped around for us and discovered that Chantelle was in Guantanamo Bay. About the same time as this a story hit the French papers of a crime of passion in the Dordogne. Giselle's husband Derek and his father caught up with them both. They went there apparently just to scare him but things got out of hand. Derek's father who had just been released from prison after another conviction for GBH stabbed the fraudulent doctor to death. The GP's wife and children in England hadn't seen him for over ten years so the loss to them wasn't as great as it could have been."

"Wow," said Jenny, "You never told me about this."

"It's all too painful. I've buried it in my subconscious, but," she continued, "I remember Giselle served a short sentence for her embezzlement and lived with her widowed father Francois immediately on release. The British wanted her extradited but the French stuck two fingers up. She got her children back because their father Derek was an accomplice to the murder of Lister and is still in Clairvaux prison. His father, who actually used the knife, is in the same prison. Having been convicted of manslaughter he will be there for some time. They both share the jail with Carlos the Jackal.

Simone has stayed in touch, still not giving up on Chantelle, and keeps me in the picture. She blames Giselle for the fate of her lover and watches her with an unhealthy obsession. Last thing she told me Giselle had shacked up with an economics teacher called Felt who had to flee Britannia when chased by the Security Services for sedition and insurrection."

Giselle had got her life back into equal boxes.

"Please stay a little longer while I pick Roberta up from her history class," said Francine

"Thank you. We'd love to if we are not too much of an intrusion."

"And what about that American who, I thought quite rudely, barged into Rob's memorial day? Her excuse was her journalist husband had disappeared."

"Oh, I think you mean Madison, Dave?"

"Yes, that's right. Madison. Any news of her fate? Did she ever find her husband?"

"Nobody really knows," said Suzy, thinking out loud, "Chantelle was the only one who might, but she couldn't tell them from Guantanamo Bay."

"Simone did mention an old friend called Mike who had been making enquiries in the States about Madison's husband, but she thought he had been picked up by the CIA."

They could have sat around chatting for hours but the chip blocking was about to time out and they could not risk a further period without arousing suspicion. So they moved on to natter about Jenny's other children and grandchildren - safe areas. They agreed not to lose contact and to see each other again.

It was not to be. Pippa and Dave were both killed the following month. A vehicle four times the size of her old deux chevaux-vapeur detoured onto the sidewalk (as they had all learnt to call the pavement) giving them no chance. The last conscious thought Pippa had before she became different molecules was that the driver looked familiar. Lars had done his job.

67 - PUBLISH AND DIE

EVERY DAY I WRITE THE BOOK

When your dreamboat turns out to be a footnote
I'm a man with a mission in two or three editions

All your compliments and your cutting remarks
Are captured here in my quotation marks

Elvis Costello (1983)

"Thank you for seeing me. I'm Paul Hobday and I've written a book. Obviously or I wouldn't be sitting in a publisher's office. I've never done anything like this before. I'm in no sense an author really as you will tell immediately you open it from the poor structure and grammar. I probably use the Oxford comma too frequently, and get my apostrophes wrong too. I'm not even a storyteller. But at least I don't start every sentence with so. I don't know any publishers or anything about the publishing world. I've not let anyone interfere with the contents or look at it as I didn't want to end up writing by committee but the downside of that is of course I haven't had any feedback. So I'm not clear whether it is even worth considering?"

"What is it about? You are supposed to give a sales pitch in a few paragraphs to interest someone. Include in that something original and eye-catching. That's my first tip if you want to be taken seriously."

"It's difficult to sum up. I suppose it's about the future and the way the world is going. Initially it centres on a GP in the present time. He starts to get a political awakening concerning his main field of interest, which is healthcare and the NHS. It dawns on him he is witnessing the deliberate destruction of what he cherishes the most. He is forced to no longer believe in a cock-up, which everyone has joked about for decades, but conspiracy, which is not in any sense funny. But what shocks him is the eventual realisation that there is a common theme running through the way the country is run. Every day patients come in and tell him how their lives are being wrecked. As an experienced GP he has noticed a significant increase in the pathology that comes through his door, which he believes is a direct result of government policy. It threatens everything he finds comfortable in his life."

"Is that it? Hardly original is it? Would send me to sleep quite quickly."

"No. I broaden it out and go back to tell the tale of all the earlier coordinated plots from before the War that began the whole process and set the trend. How they gather momentum and became established over the next few decades. It's about how the way the world is run and is hardly ever questioned, and any dissenters that do exist are outcasts. It's about how Rob, the GP, and a few others who begin to poke at the behind-the-scenes ruling Establishment to find out what is really going on, and he gets caught up in trouble that finds him out of his depth. It explains the connection to all the scandals of the modern age and why certain things happened. It attempts to join up all the dots, which people have gone to great lengths to prevent. Things that seemed inexplicable at the time, as each was just one piece of a jigsaw then begin to link together. Few saw the complete picture. There are quite a few characters but in one way or another their lives are all linked by their pursuit of the truth."

"Not quite John le Carré or Ray Bradbury is it? And where does it lead?"

"Murder, other evil acts and a world that even Orwell or Atwood would not have predicted".

"So it's dystopian fiction?"

"But it's all quite chilling as it is true."

"What do you mean, true? It's a novel you said?"

"It is all becoming true and quite frighteningly so. My belief is that I've seen the future and it's very, very distressing. So I've written about it as a warning. My hope is that people will read it, realise it is quite credible and do something to prevent it actually happening. I don't want my grandchildren to have to live in such a terrible world."

The publisher did not respond.

"I've tried to make it believable, unlike *Fahrenheit 451* or Zamyatin's *We*."

"Don't repeat that 'I've seen the future' phrase to anyone else will you? They will think you are a nutter or David Icke. Have you got a title?"

"Well, I've thought of a few options but I can't say I'm happy with them, The Truth And Nothing But The Truth."

"I'm sure that's already been done. Perhaps stick the whole truth in the middle?"

"The Evil Amongst Us."

"Sounds too much like Stephen King. Too satanic. Work to be done on that then."

"Perhaps Modern Times, although I don't want to get mixed up with Charlie Chaplin."

"Then on the way here I thought of The Deceit Disease but that hardly rolls off the tongue, so perhaps The Deception Syndrome? I'm told titles with a 'y' in the title often sell better, which is another example of the strange world we live in."

"Hmm. We will have to help you out here I can see."

"There's another that might get people's attention. 'CATCH 69'?"

"Been done. You've got the number wrong."

"No, let me explain. The world is controlled by the rules of catch twenty-two, catch twenty-three, and catch twenty-four. All of these add up to catch sixty-nine."

"You have lost me. The only one I know is Heller's *Catch-22* and that was written nearly sixty years ago."

"Yes, and I bet you wish you had published that one? Anyway, everyone knows what catch twenty-two means. Well almost everyone. Catch twenty-three is when trying to solve a problem you create an even bigger one. Like bringing management consultants in to advise on running the NHS. And catch twenty-four is what I'm trying to expose, hidden agendas ruling the world, stupidity, evil and greed dominating, the ultimate in capitalism. Catch sixty-nine is when they all operate together. Add them up."

"It might work as a title I suppose."

"So with that in mind I've also used the book as a platform to get over messages about certain philosophies and ideologies. There are a fair number of economic arguments in it. I'm attacking conventional so-called wisdom."

"Sounds a bundle of laughs. A lot of that will have to go."

"Anyway, thank you Mr Hobday. Leave it with me and I'll give it some consideration. I assume you have copies? Oh, I'm sorry. I see you made the appointment in the name of Dr Hobday. Are you medical?"

"Well, I was. I was a GP for thirty years."

"What made you change tack?"

"A nightmare I had. I saw it all happening. I'm convinced it is happening. I began to have too many sleepless nights and had to get this off my chest."

The editor appeared quite unimpressed.

"Consider using a female pseudonym or nom de plume. Worked for George Eliot as well as Ellis, Currer and Acton Bell and nowadays books by female authors sell better."

"Who?"

"Oh dear. Anne, Charlotte and Emily Bronte."

Hobday thought he was beginning to lose credibility in the eyes of the man behind the desk. He wanted to avoid appearing too desperate but started to talk faster.

"I'm afraid there are holes in the story and many inconsistences, but that is the nature of the beast. There is no way the full picture can be painted as of course what is going on is secret and people trying to expose this evil world have died for their troubles. We will never get the full truth and so will never be able to convincingly tell the whole tale. I'm painting by numbers with the numbers altered and colours missing. I suppose ultimately it's a condemnation of our species and the realisation that we are fundamentally flawed."

The man behind the desk stood up, signalling the end of the interview.

"I came to you as I was told you have a reputation for open-mindedness, and were not one of the Establishment keen to prevent debate and quash anything that rocks the boat?"

"I'd like to think so, now…"

"Interesting you used the term nutter earlier. You know about the 1967 CIA memo about conspiracy theorists?"

The publisher gave nothing away with a frozen face.

"They weaponised the term to make it an insult, and to discredit and shut down anyone who didn't push the official narrative out to the public. They started on those doubting the official *Warren Report* on the assassination of President Kennedy. The same theme runs through all their attacks on what they call nutters. They say they are wedded to their fantastic theories before considering the evidence, of which they say, there is nothing new and they are politically and or financially motivated. They used to be accused of being communists but, nowadays, Russian propagandists. And now it's called fake news."

"Why are you telling me all this?"

"Because it backs up my story. It partly explains one of the Establishment's tactics."

"Do you think I am part of the Establishment, and if I reject your work you will think that gives you more evidence that you are right?"

"I hope you aren't, and even if you personally are full of scepticism you might at least find it an interesting read. People didn't have to believe *1984* to find it troubling and heed the warning, and Orwell didn't have to convince publishers it was true to get it into print. Don't forget through the years *1984* has been banned or legally challenged as subversive or ideologically corrupting, just like Huxley's *Brave New World*."

The man moved from behind his desk towards the door.

"By the way, you didn't tell me how long it is, Mr Orwell, sorry, Mr Hobday?"

Hobday ignored the clumsy, sarcastic attempt at a put down.

"About three hundred and eleven thousand words."

"Oh dear. You really are a naive first time author, aren't you? Far too long even, for a fantasy thriller. You'll need to get it down to one hundred and thirty thousand or so."

"Then you won't like my added lyrics at the top of each chapter either?"

"What? What for? That'll be a real copyright headache."

"To give a flavour of what the next part of the book, or more specifically that chapter is all about. Besides I like them. They are favourites of mine."

"You might get away with a line or two or even a verse perhaps, but you will still have to convince me they are not just a waste of print space."

There was an awkward pause.

"Any good sex in it? That sells, even if it has won the Auberon Waugh 'Bad Sex Award'. Perhaps especially if it has."

"I'm not E. L. James."

"Pity."

"If you slash the word count to half and leave out the lyrics the work will be emasculated. It would mean leaving out important arguments. That will take away its purpose. It probably wouldn't be worth reading."

"Suit yourself but you risk it not being published at all."

With that response it flashed through Hobday's mind that this character he was facing was not going to allow his theories into the public domain. He had picked the wrong man. Maybe those who suggested him were also part of the Establishment? Or was he really getting a little paranoid? His wife and friends thought so. They certainly were not buying the line that the world was as bad as he was suggesting. In the book the wife of the GP often accused him of paranoia. Who could he trust now? Was he paranoid too? What was real life and what was fiction? Was he too much like Rob? All those compliments and cutting remarks captured in quotation marks. Was it Rob, or really him?

"If it's not published then you won't make any money, will you? Your dreamboat will turn out to be a footnote."

"I think you miss the point. This is not to make money. It's also a one off. I'm not writing any more and there won't be a sequel. This is my one attempt to get an important message across and for it to be a warning to everyone about the way the world is spiralling down a big black hole. I'm a man with a mission. And to prove it, if the book does make money I intend to donate any royalties to campaigning groups to fight for justice and for democracy."

"Oh dear. That's also very naive. You'd better keep that one quiet too. You are making a good case for it being binned right now. The thing is we are book publishers and of course we want good quality stuff. Every publisher wants to find the next le Carré, Stephen King or Beatrix Potter. But at the end of the day we are all in it to make money. The more the better."

"Do you know who Dick Rowe was? I'm sure you've heard of fellow publishers Constable and Robinson?"

"The publisher I'm familiar with, but Dick Rowe? Where is this leading, Mr Hobday?"

"Rowe worked for Decca and turned down The Beatles, and Constable and Robinson rejected J. K. Rowling. Now I'm a million miles from that league but you seem like a nice bloke. I'd hate you to be remembered for the wrong reasons."

"Goodbye, Mr… I mean Dr Hobday."

"Hello. Yes. It's me. Yes, of course he turned up. He thinks he is onto something. He believes it's original and he's the first! Yes. He thinks he's seen the future. Yes. It's a one off. He says there won't be a sequel! Surprised he didn't ask about film rights! I know. I'll deal with it. There won't even be a first, so don't concern yourself. He tells me no one else has seen or read it, no one at all. Yes. He's made it easy for us. The boys will go through the manuscript to see what he has found out, then we will deal with it and him."

A pause.

"Do you know, he even said he thought judgement without knowledge should be a crime?"

68 - MEGALOMANIA AND DESTRUCTION

THE END

This is the end
Beautiful friend

Of our elaborate plans, the end
Of everything that stands the end
No safety or surprise, the end
I'll never look into your eyes again

Doors (1967)

Wessel was staring up at the Sir Peter Paul Rubens' ceiling canvases wondering how he could acquire them for his country estate in Arbroath. If they could be transported from Antwerp, they surely could travel again? His parents had told him they had been to the Banqueting House in Whitehall a few weeks after he was born to attend, by Royal Command, the celebration of the Queen's Silver Wedding Anniversary to Phil the Greek, as his German father called the Consort. Then his daydreaming was interrupted.

"Cliff, are you still practising?" enquired Neville Gideon.

"Of course old boy. But practice is not the word. I'm perfect already. Still the best in the business. I can rake in a fortune every few weeks with my eyes closed and my hands tied behind my back now the NHS is long forgotten. It's money for old rope, as they used to say. I don't need the money of course so profits go to the next generation to keep up the momentum of our good work. We all knew that socialist experiment was a terrible mistake as it by definition caused a dip in our fortunes. Very overrated that silly idea of looking after the poor too.

I admit a little of the growing pile also helps me keep my women in the lifestyle they demand. Did you know I bought Kelly Castle in Arbroath out of small change? I know Scotland counts as a foreign land now but I couldn't resist it. It used to belong to one of our founder members, the late great Sir Archibald Ramsey. Don't you think these Rubens would look good there? According to the new *History Of The World* updated by Charlotte over there, Ramsey was PM for a record fourteen years. Not that the new generation know what a PM is, or was, eh?"

At which point he laughed so loud everyone in the room turned around. Gideon wanted to stop this self-praising monologue. Having asked him one simple question and got a speech back in return.

"I was told by Humphrey your area of expertise is cataract surgery? Is that correct? It's just that I think I need one done."

"I'm expert in pretty well anything. This ophthalmology business is easy. Don't have to think much but you will have to like Wagner as I always have either *Götterdämmerung* or *The Ride Of The Valkyries* blasting out as I operate. Never have got over Bayreuth's *Festspielhaus* being destroyed by those terrorists. Hanging was too good for them. That idea of Stanek's to re-introduce disembowelling really should be put back on the agenda. We should have taken the referendum more seriously, by which I mean the result should have gone our way. It's no good letting anybody but us make the decisions, you know."

Then almost unable to control his laughter.

"My dog Horst would love a good feast on viscera."

Others in the room turned again. Gideon turned pale at the thought.

"Talking of Horst, you do know busts of my famous distant relative are being placed in all parks now? I won my battle. Not that I've ever lost one."

He looked around the room in the expectation that others were listening.

"Seriously though, I'm damned annoyed those Rutherfords are still on the loose. Frampton isn't doing his job properly. Anyway back to your eyes. Make an appointment and come to see me. If you can afford me, that is? One eye or can I double my money with two?"

"Only one. It's a traumatic cataract caused by that attack on me a few years ago by Poison."

Neville Gideon wasn't quite sure whether Sir Clifford Wessel actually meant it about the money but he was fairly certain. Then Wessel went further to demonstrate his personality defect and that it probably was meant to be a joke.

"All those years as Chancellor of the Exchequer, when those State appointments actually existed, and you can't tell me you didn't stuff quite a few Lady Godivas in your back pocket, eh?"

He roared with laughter yet again. He thought his jokes were always the best.

"But fifty pound notes are small change nowadays aren't they? Ever seen one Gideon? You'll need a thick wad for my bill," this time with a smirk.

Gideon was beginning to wonder if he really was deranged or had some drug habit. Maybe he should seek help for his cataract elsewhere.

"I'm off to Welchtown House for a few weeks, so I won't come to see you yet. I've taken it over now my father is dead and I want to see what state it is in. Barbados isn't my favourite place."

"It'll be more than a few weeks. The demand to see me is high. You might have to wait a while."

Even when it came down to business Wessel could not resist putting down whosoever he spoke to.

"This Welchtown House. Part of a plantation isn't it? I'll take it off your hands and add it to my property portfolio if you wish. I'm well on my way to owning most of the island anyway."

Adam Stanek was in the Chair as usual and called the meeting to order. He thought himself the most powerful man in the land, but that was not because of the role he was playing today, but his control of so many large multi-national companies, some with turnovers larger than medium sized countries. Being chair of the Right Club was really no more than a little bit of fun allowing him to keep his finger on the pulse. Just as important he could keep an eye on any dissents.

For more than a decade, political positions were dead-end jobs. They came with no power, just pretence of democracy. In fact those

858

in the elite did not even bother pretending any more that they had a value or served democracy in any way. The rich and powerful were those in charge of the major corporations. This slow transition was first evident in the early 2000s and 2010s when the role of Prime Minister became just a stepping-stone to a fortune. It was a means to an end, not an ambition in itself.

The same small executive committee had remained constant for several years but a few powerful figures with influence pushed their way in, like Lord Frampton and Sir Roland Henderson. They were very disciplined with their attendance and punctuality. Around the table with them were as usual Hubert Witney, Simon Chisholm, William Hartman, Ivan Humphrey, and Charlotte Corday. Their special guest today was Nelson Woodward. Another invited guest to give a presentation on up-to-date public relations techniques was Leni Kahrnl. Anyone else who had been through the revolving door as often as she had would have not been able to count all the money she had stashed away from health privatisation because they would experience bad vertigo. Kahrnl was as tough as they come however.

Wessel and Gideon finished their exchange and joined them.

Somehow Hartman had managed to survive in power despite being generally loathed by all. Stanek, from the Sudetenland, had particular reasons to hate him when he found out about his family's Nazi background. Both had come a long way since being just Party dogsbodies then junior government ministers in the 1990s, but they were both feeling their age now. Witney had been seeking revenge on Stanek ever since being totally humiliated and abused by him in the grounds of Sir James Morrison's mansion thirty-four years before. It was a long time ago but it was difficult to outmanoeuvre one of the most powerful men in the land. His acquiescence and creeping had paid off with a spell as Prime Minister, but he knew that role held little power - he was just a puppet. Being PM was like winning the FA Cup - a temporary period of figurehead powerless fame just like a television celeb.

Likewise Ivan Humphrey. His two terms as London Mayor were just a stepping stone to greater things. He first cut his teeth with the

Freedom Association. His younger stepbrother, Clifford Wessel, was feared by all however. He decided from early days to build up a power-base and support team of thugs. It was well known he did not flinch at the murders, torturing and blackmail that went on in his name. One of his henchmen, Simon Chisholm was rewarded with a place at the top table. Between them they controlled the healthcare industry. Chisholm knew he had to be nothing other than a loyal ally although he had total control of the pharmaceutical arm. They had travelled far since the BMA.

Sir Roland Henderson left the Treasury when it was abolished to make his fortune and insisted on having control of an industrial giant as a reward for his successful privatisation projects of everything that moved. He was an old warrior from the Thatcher era. Many looked back on his seminars of 1988 with affection, knowing they had been part of history. He knew too much to be disobeyed. But that also made him vulnerable. More than once Wessel had considered whacking him, as his friends in the mafia put it.

Lord Frampton, a descendant of the Tolpuddle martyrs' foe, still living on his Dorset estate, forced his way in and was feared like Himmler, as owner of all the private security firms. This industry was the first to have half a billion workers and a turnover in the trillions.

And then there was Neville Gideon. Born into privilege. A former Chancellor of the Exchequer, promoted above his intelligence for his ability to be manipulated and controlled. Known as a cad from a long line of bastards.

Charlotte Corday was the only woman. Known as the chameleon because she was the master of disguise and could blend in with any environment. One of her first infiltrations was into a group who set themselves up to Save The NHS. She fooled them all and managed to destroy a potential threat to privatisation. She moved through other organisations with the slickness and speed of a cheetah. Her colours changed to suit her moods and allegiances to the point where no one thought it safe to trust her. By being slippery she progressed. She slid up the pole like magic. Absolutely ruthless - author of *The History Of The World*.

All understood the omerta - the code of honour that places importance on silence and the non-interference in the illegal activities of the others.

Nelson Woodward was invited and was to be wooed to help companies in Britannia get support and business. Now sixty-eight, he was in semi-retirement in the ceremonial position as President Palin's Secretary of State. The American giants were crushing the few remaining Britannia companies. He was due to appear after some tea.

As was the custom they toasted King William as the first item but now it never went ahead without the usual under-the-breath mutterings of 'as long as he does what he is told'. All parties knew he was a dispensable figurehead, a vehicle used to get messages across to the masses so that the Establishment could keep a low profile. They were never seen in public. In fact no one really knew who they were and security made sure it stayed that way. When the Royals had outlived their usefulness Charlotte would write them out of history and Frampton's men would find a suitable mineshaft. This was a reference to what really happened to the Russian Tsar and his family, not the Corday version, which had him ruling another twenty years, to be succeeded by his sister Xenia.

Although the Right Club meetings were every fortnight they were all aware that was not really necessary. Most things ticked over and worked to plan like clockwork. If the club had a role, it was really just to make sure nothing blew them or their plans off track. They all knew the club was an anachronism - almost a nostalgia fix. They liked to pretend they were important but they all knew deep down the real power lay with the secret inner circle. Stanek, Frampton, Wessel, Corday and Henderson were thought to belong, but no one knew for sure. These were amongst the corporate emperors. The secret inner circle consisted of the bosses and owners of the ten most powerful and wealthy corporations: Nestle, Disney, Monsanto, ICBC, Lockheed Martin, Inbev, Pearson, Pfizer, and Alphabet Inc who own Google and YouTube - the faces of corporate evil.

But the members enjoyed their meetings. It was wonderful to be regularly reminded how far they had travelled. Most of their objectives had been achieved. No State, no government, no society, just dictatorship in its purest form, corporately run. Plato and Hobbes might have approved. There were times when they worried their plan would fail. If the voices against them had been louder and not silenced it would have been a more difficult struggle.

Few in control now remember a Marxist academic called Ralph Miliband but their fathers talked about the danger he posed. He wrote a book called *The State in Capitalist Society* in 1969 in which he predicted the future. He warned that failure to tame the markets would lead to the increasing domination of key sectors by a relatively small number of giant firms and that equality would never be achieved with a ruling class dominant across society. Absolutely correct - it was exactly what they wanted. Now they had achieved it. Miliband's nightmare was their dream, and his voice had to be drowned out in order to get there. They could not afford for his concerns to become the concerns of many.

They had had to be devious. The new world could not have been built for them without their deceit. Deceit was the key. An identifiable pattern of deceit. A complex of concurrent deceit. A pattern of deceit producing a particular social condition. A predictable characteristic pattern of deceit. A syndrome. The deceit syndrome.

They were the elite, separate from the masses. They avoided the term super race but they all thought they were part of it. *Power tends to corrupt, and absolute power corrupts absolutely. Great men are almost always bad men*, wrote the impressively hirsute Victorian politician and historian Lord Acton in 1887. Never was the phrase more appropriate than now. But power, they thought, still brought responsibility. Responsibility to keep the new order functioning and to pass it down the generations. Their generations.

Everyone around the table had responsibility for one area, and was in charge of an administrative team. The biggest area by far was security as nothing else was needed in the new world. There was no state apparatus, just Britannia by name. The change over twenty years had been dramatic. Hundreds of thousands of civil servants, local government officials and politicians totally abolished and replaced by just a handful of the Establishment elite. There were no ministries. Even the contracts were organised by private companies. Never has the phrase 'jobs for the boys' been more appropriate. Between them they awarded, distributed and supervised the deals for health, food, energy, war, trade, transport, justice, private armies, housing, culture and truth. But in reality, they were awarding themselves presents every day. Contracts were not scrutinised properly - they were just for show but most thought why do we even need to pretend?

Since the introduction of the UCI or Universal Citizen's Income no economic portfolio was needed. This was an idea stolen from the Nordic countries. They used it to raise the living standards of their people. Britannia used it to keep the poor under control. There was a time when two-tier Britain was used as a condemnation of an unequal society and frowned upon. Since convincing the masses that two-tier Britannia was a good thing and necessary however, the introductions of two levels of UCI were accepted. The desirables of course got the higher level, known as the Deluxe UCI and the undesirables the very basic UCI, known as the Generous UCI.

The basic level did not need to include an allowance for food as the undesirables were fed from communal food banks, which worked out cheaper. For years the elite had patted themselves on the back, claiming that food banks were 'rather uplifting as it shows what a compassionate society we are'. They needed nothing for housing as they were put into ghettos. Education did not happen, and only emergency health care was provided. The economic department planned to abolish the Generous UCI completely soon as they could not see that such life forms really needed any money. This was the result of automation making redundant all the low-skilled jobs, meaning the low skilled were not needed. In fact they were nothing but a nuisance. The toxic waste workers still had a place despite the new industry of waste colonialisation but the turnover was high as the average life expectancy was twelve months - radiation sickness usually set in within ten months. Human worth had become just economics. In fact everything was economics. Waste colonialisation started with old tyres being dumped in India, but because it was so cheap rapidly expanded to other poor areas of the planet.

The new attitude toward art was also economic. Art was not there for its aesthetic value, rather what it translated to in terms of pounds, shillings and pence, which had been re-introduced. Abandoning the sixty-year-old decimalisation project was a deliberate policy to push nostalgia. Farthings, florins, crowns and sovereigns came back. Nostalgia for the past was useful to deflect the gaze from all the more unpalatable things that needed to be forced on to the population. For the same reason the metric system was made illegal. No longer kilograms or centimetres, but good old British pounds, ounces, and stones, feet and inches, yards and furlongs. Wessel lead the cheers in the Lord's enclosure at the reintroduction of chains - the distance between the two wickets on a cricket pitch.

Those undesirables in the ghettos knew nothing of the outside. Rumours always circulated about the better living conditions of some others but the contrast was never understood. Many of the elite had third or fourth homes in the old Foreign and Commonwealth Offices that had been converted into luxury apartments. The grand staircase was preserved and the imaginative conversion of the rooms of the Locarno Suite, producing perfect accommodation, was the main prize for those at the top of the tree, namely Stanek, Frampton and Corday. The Treasury and other grand Victorian buildings received a similar fate. The few offices required were now located in Milton Keynes.

Some of the Establishment now lived in the new mansions built on Hyde Park. The Houses of Parliament and the Palace of Westminster was mysteriously burnt to the ground, strangely enough on the ninetieth anniversary of the Reichstag fire, 27th February 2023. The parallels did not end there. A young communist was blamed and emergency decrees to suspend civil liberties were passed. Mass arrests of opposition groups took place. Another false flag operation.

The regular meeting place of what they still called the Right Club was now the Banqueting House, the only remaining part of the Palace of Whitehall, destroyed by fire in 1698. Inigo Jones's masterpiece, with its Rubens ceiling, was one of Charles I's last sights before he lost his head just outside. Ironically, the paintings portrayed the divine right of Kings.

There were several standing items on the fixed agenda. The King's next broadcast was one. That was for new announcements and policies. Security and Control was another. This was since the H incident, as it became known for short, eleven years before. Although a relatively minor event the name stuck as it was the first example of a possible spilling of the beans and could have been a very serious threat to the cause. H stood for Harm - referring to any harm that could befall the project. Originally some thought it was for Hobday, a misguided extremist who uncovered a few inconvenient truths but all records of him, the events surrounding his activities and several people associated with him, including a traitor called Baigent, were liquidated. It was quickly and savagely quashed and was really only a threat in their imaginations, but they shuddered at what could have been. Left to grow and with the truth spreading to the masses via social media, this potentially could have derailed their mission. Fortunately lessons learnt from that had ensured security was tight and no one could actually remember the last time this particular item took more than a couple of minutes. It was however always accompanied by a list of recent dissident executions. Over the last few years they had had success with a few accidents and assassinations. It was Humphrey's job to always read out the list.

"I have great pleasure in announcing the following are no longer a threat: Aung San Suu Kyi's allies, Oscar Denning, Noam Chomsky's relatives, Bernie Saunders, Jeremy Corbyn, Chelsea Manning, John Pilger, Edward Snowden, Recep Tayyip Erdogan, Ken Loach, Kim Jong-un, Marine Le Pen, Dilma Rousseff, Park Geun-hye, Rodrigo Duterte, Prayuth Chan-ocha, Thérèse Defarge, Pablo Iglesias, Yanis Varoufakis, Juan Guaidó and Alexis Tsipras.

Please submit your suggestions and recommendations for the forthcoming month."

"Guaidó?" queried Witney, "We spent years grooming him as a puppet to orchestrate that coup in Venezuela for the oil grab. What went wrong?"

"Got too big for his boots. Hubris. We picked up signals he was thinking of turning on us," replied Humphrey.

His job was done.

War was a third item as this was perpetual. The nuclear fall-out after the destruction of Southern Australia, Columbia, Uganda, all of the Korean peninsular and Myanmar over the last ten years was still kept secret. Wars now however were not between nations, but large companies that had their own armies. Sabotage was commonplace especially cyber warfare and espionage. Edward Snowden's activities and whistleblowing was why he ended up on the list. Company computer systems, their power supplies, satellites and telecommunication systems were all targets.

The inner circles of the ten most powerful multinationals were in the first division and cooperated for control and mutual benefit. They eyed each other with great suspicion but would not engage in open warfare. All knew they played a game of subtle sabotage but would not admit it. The wars were between those trying to build their power to gain entry into the inner sanctum - that is to get a promotion into the first division inner circle. Companies like JP Morgan Chase, ExxonMobil, Amazon, Apple, Facebook, General Electric, Berkshire Hathaway, United Health, Walmart, Disney and Royal Dutch Shell knew the rewards were great.

Population controls were another standing item. When the club was first formed the world population was just over two billion. Now it was eight billion. In fifteen years it will be nine billion, and by 2150 two hundred and fifty-six billion. Ruthless measures were being drawn up to keep it below one hundred billion. Measures that made the Final Solution seem tame and small scale. Hubert Witney, who delivered an update, reported that the numbers of undesirables continues to fall dramatically, more from neglect than active extermination. The lack of basic public health measures, individual healthcare, education, nutrition and law and order in the ghettos had driven life expectancy down, a trend that started with neo-liberalism. This had accelerated since all immunisations in that group had been withdrawn. This was welcomed in the camps as the undesirables had been repeatedly and deliberately exposed to the old Trump/ Wakefield propaganda that vaccines were a dangerous mistake and killed more than they saved. One epidemic followed another. The elite were fully immunised.

They broke for tea very satisfied with themselves as usual - although several went for something stronger. They were waiting for Woodward to show up which he did, only ten minutes late which was quite prompt for him.

They reconvened with a tribute to Nelson Woodward's father, Lyndon who had recently died peacefully in his sleep. It did not go unnoticed that the same fate had just taken off Gideon's father, Sir James Morrison, too. Both had served their countries well and were both in their nineties.

The tribute did nothing to soften Woodward however. He launched straight in without any introductory pleasantries and told them the companies that they were seeking help for were not going to get it. They were on their own and they should not be surprised. What was this project all about if it was not dog-eat-dog? Had they learnt nothing? He was quite sure the American lion would eat them up, to mix his metaphors, and he did not care either. In fact he emphasised it was best for capitalism. It was capitalism. No favours for anyone. No attempted manipulation of the market.

"If you think there is still a special relationship you are deluded."

Woodward made sure there was no misunderstanding.

"Your country has served its purpose. You should have got that message from our attitude over the Malvinas Islands. Galtieri, whom I met, was a great leader and my regret is that the US didn't support him more."

Woodward knew this would anger them, especially calling the Falklands the Malvinas.

"The USA is now world dominant and we've a few areas still to tidy up but Britannia is an irrelevance now. You showed how weak you are when we took Gibraltar, the Caymans, Bermuda and Pitcairn off you adding to our nine hundred overseas military bases. You've isolated yourselves through stupidity. You were so stupid you evicted your own citizens from the Chagos Archipelago so we could build our US military base on Diego Garcia. Fat lot of good that creeping did you. Nixon couldn't believe how gullible you Limeys were. Gave us a good base for our CIA to torture suspects on their way to Guantanamo though, so thanks for that. Your family owned slaves on the coconut plantations there, eh Witney?"

Hubert Witney's jaw just dropped.

"Nobody is interested in your has-been country anymore, but I speak in old fashioned imperialist terms, gentlemen."

Woodward was enjoying himself.

"Take consolation in that the few of your companies you have left after putting all your eggs into the service and financial sector and destroying your manufacturing still continue to make those of you around this table rich, for now anyway. But if it needs to be spelled out, you are subservient to us and our power grab will continue. We will take Cyprus, Anguilla and Ascension Island next."

His bluntness shocked even an audience of ruthless despots and tyrants but nobody glanced at anybody else.

"Resistance is futile. Who was that King of yours who tried to order the tide to turn? King Canute? Even he was a foreign invader. You couldn't even keep a Dane out. I see he was more accurately CNUT the Great. Cnut the spelling mistake, more like it."

He was really enjoying himself.

"Let me give you an example of continued decline, and our superiority. Some of you know my love of your soccer. My first World Cup was in Mexico in 1986. I saw Diego Maradona knock you lot out with the 'hand of God' goal. It was then I realised the potential of the sport, a multi-trillion dollar goldmine, too valuable to be left in the hands of knucklehead sportsmen. Not quite the goldmine your defunct NHS has turned out to be, better than we thought, but still another area for us to control. So it gives me a hard-on just to let you know that my company will be buying the last English-owned Premier League club while I'm over here, giving us total control of the sport. We plan to amalgamate it with our football. Total commercialisation."

They were all in position.

Vilma Rutherford set the crosshairs of her .22LR sniper rifle at the entrance to the Banqueting House. She was at the small round window to the side of the clock over the arch opposite in the old Admiralty building. Behind her was where the Trooping the Colour was once held in Horse Guards Parade until King Charles was instructed to stop all ceremonies. Vilma also remembered it as the site of the launch of their mortar attack on 10 Downing Street in 1991. Mary, her sister, felt her extra two years as she crouched down with her rifle taking up her position at a window of the Household Cavalry Museum.

They were all aware of dozens of G4S security personnel walking up and down Whitehall, but few seemed to be paying any attention to what was going on around them. People had got used to patrols of the streets by the paramilitary.

Ian sat in the southwest tower of the old War Office looking down onto the same entrance. His job was to oversee and coordinate the assassinations. With only one hand he was too disabled to now play an active part, even though he itched to do so. He surveyed the area. He could see Florence loitering near the statue of Earl Haig. It still amused him that she was given the name Nightingale to wheel McColl around Chartwell. She was another lookout and stood out in her yellow coat. He checked on the positions of the other snipers on the roof of the old Scotland Office, in the side windows of what used to be the Cabinet Office, but had now been converted into luxury flats for the elite.

The other windows of the Old Admiralty Building, to the north of Mary and Vilma, where Nelson's body rested the night before his grand funeral, were also occupied. They were all ready and they knew their victims would be coming out of the main door - but when? How long would they have to wait? He then told Jerry who had set up the main communications system on the roof of the old Cabinet Office.

"All ready, boss."

Jerry could see others in his team placed near the statues of Monty, Alanbrooke and Slim. They were to move north towards the Banqueting House entrance when he gave the signal. Guy was by the black memorial to the Women of World War Two further down Whitehall. These memorials did not quite fit with the re-writing of history, but no matter - all references to the generals had been eradicated so no one could find out what they did or who they were anyway, but they were still covered in graffiti with words like coward and loser being prominent.

Ian felt alert and all prepared for this mission but he wondered if he was getting a bit old now for active duty. Perhaps this should be his swan song. He always hated the waiting. Although obviously a necessary part of the operation he just wanted to get on with the job. But he could be there for several hours. His mind wandered.

He studied the statue of the Eighth Duke of Devonshire directly below him - the only man to lead three political parties. One of the Rutherfords told him that the Duke had expected to succeed Lord Salisbury when he resigned as Prime Minister in 1902 but his nephew Arthur Balfour was favoured. 'Bob's your uncle' they laughed.

He was the Duke whose descendants included the husband of JFK's sister Kathleen, the husband of Unity and Diana Mitford's sister Deborah, the husband of Fred Astaire's sister, and the wife of PM Harold Macmillan. Devonshire's your relative, he thought. The tenth Duke died in 1950 unexpectedly in the presence of Dr John Bodkin Adams, the GP and suspected serial killer. The death was not investigated, as it should have been. Ian had read this was to avoid drawing attention to the sham marriage between his sister and Macmillan, who tolerated her long affair with Lord Boothby. It would have damaged his political career. Another Establishment cover up he wondered. Bodkin Adams was linked to one hundred and sixty-three suspicious deaths and inspired the invention of Harold Shipman.

Ian had in his field of vision the equestrian statue of the Duke of Cambridge, a German head of the British Army who worked with his cousin, Queen Victoria to fight all reforms. In the opposite direction was Earl Haig 'the butcher of the Somme'. He chuckled to himself as he remembered Blackadder saying Haig was about to make another gargantuan effort to move his drinks cabinet six inches closer to Berlin. This was just a memory. This sort of entertainment had been banned for about twenty years. Neither of those bastards should have statues, he thought. Pity we cannot destroy them too. But enough daydreaming, Ian reprimanded himself.

Nelson Woodward had passed on the message he wanted to, although it was not really necessary. It just gave him immense satisfaction. It was not at all important, as he knew in approximately fifteen minutes all in the great Banqueting House would be dead.

"Well, Gentleman, I will leave you. I doubt we will ever see each other again."

"Surely that's a little dramatic and unlikely Nelson?" said Stanek.

"We go back a long way," added Gideon.

"Our relationship has burnt out and it's time you realised your place in the world."

With that he got up and left.

At last the Poison team saw people emerging. Ian recognised Nelson Woodward and his American contingent, but they all knew he was not their target. He instructed his snipers to be patient.

"Wait for the large group which should follow shortly," he told them, as rehearsed, over his radio, "and wait for my command."

Ian watched as Woodward walked very briskly - almost a slow trot - towards Trafalgar Square. He wondered why the rush?

Stanek told the others they needed a few minutes break after that unexpected and ungrateful outburst. On reconvening they summed up their feelings.

"It shouldn't be a surprise," said Wessel, "The Americans put themselves first whatever. It's not new. 'America First' was Woodrow Wilson's slogan in 1914. They took control after World War Two and tried to quash our Empire by deliberately bankrupting us."

Gideon told them his father always wanted revenge on Lyndon Woodward for something that happened at his 60th birthday party, but he never found out what. He was not surprised that the shit had a shit son.

Charlotte Corday had a contribution.

"We still have our infiltration into his State Department and President Palin's office, so we should have anticipated this. I'll investigate. Our intelligence is so much more advanced than theirs, especially after all their leaks and the previous President's indiscretions. They get caught. We don't."

"Perhaps he ought to be put onto our list," added Chisholm.

"That would only attract more revenge. You know what they are like," retorted the Chair, wanting to prevent any knee-jerk reaction and to get the meeting over and done with.

William Hartman helped his foe by changing the subject as he had something important to sort out before they dispersed.

"Chairman. I did give you notice of an item under Any Other Business."

Stanek gave him permission to go ahead but in the manner of a headmaster addressing a pupil told him to be brief.

"I want to take control of Porton Down. It should not be in Frampton's portfolio. I'm the weapons expert and the manufacture of the nerve agents is abysmally slow. Too slow. I'm the one to sort that out."

Frampton was jolted from his doze.

"I say. Steady on. If we go faster we will end up with more deaths just like Ronald Maddison's from that sarin disaster. We have it going at the right pace and furthermore, it's our territory, Hartman."

"The Maddison incident was nearly eighty years ago. Hardly relevant, and have you lost your mind? What do a few guinea pigs matter?" chipped in Chisholm.

"You obviously don't know about all the other hush ups, do you? So-called accidents on a massive scale."

Frampton was getting flustered.

"Since the Salisbury fiasco twelve years ago we have now managed to reduce them to a minimum and stopped all leaks. And I'm not saying the deaths of any guinea pig matters at all. The point is, for the sake of efficiency and profit maximisation we have to get the science right. So as I said, that means proceeding at the correct pace."

Hartman was not going to give up.

"Frampton has messed up over and over again. He only got away with Salisbury because the Russians at that time were a plausible and convenient scapegoat to blame it on."

Whilst Frampton was talking Stanek could not help but stare at Hartman. He hated him. He could certainly believe the Nazi Konrad Henlein was a distant cousin. The resemblance was astonishing, even from photos. Hubert Witney decided he had had enough. This was not going to be a short dispute.

"Gentlemen, I bid you farewell as I have an important engagement tonight back at Houghton Hall. See you in two weeks…"

Witney had not finished when it happened. A huge explosion. The Predator drone had successfully hit its target with four AGM-114 Hellfire missiles. Nelson Woodward turned from his vantage point on the steps of the National Gallery in Trafalgar Square to see the effects. He was careful to position himself behind a column under the portico to avoid glass and other flying debris. They had been there from ten minutes before zero hour.

"Bullseye," he congratulated himself.

The whole of the Banqueting House was hidden behind dense grey smoke. Rubble fell out of the sky as from a volcano. It was landing all over Trafalgar Square. Windows had been blown out in every building that could be seen.

"That lasted precisely four hundred and eight years. It'll cost more than the fifteen thousand six hundred and eighteen pounds it cost to build to replace that one."

The blast knocked Sir Henry Havelock off his plinth in Trafalgar Square, but Adolf Hitler on the fourth plinth survived. Of the memorials to Jellicoe and Beatty, the latter was totally destroyed but Jellicoe's remained undamaged. Justice at last. Woodward knew none of the Right Club could have survived. Nor did Tom Barton, Neville Gideon's bodyguard, who had only just recognised the interior of the Banqueting Hall from the cover of his Dad's ELO album of 1971, and was just thinking of this when he was crushed to death.

The end of an era, he thought. Now a fresh new generation can carry on the project.

"Good riddance to bad rubbish. Great to have a good clear out," he told his new Dutch aide Lars, "Like a frigging mega-laxative. Come on, let's get some grub and pig out. I could bite the arse off a low-flying duck I'm so hungry. Killing makes me that way."

Lars told Woodward that Leona would be waiting for them.

"What the fuck was that?" radioed Jerry to Ian. The window had crashed into the room he was in at the old Cabinet Office but he was crouched behind some new rich occupant's large antique chaise longue so was unhurt. When the dust had settled he brushed it off and looked outside. He saw bodies and debris everywhere - a scene of utter devastation. His first thoughts were for his troops but it was clear the Banqueting House was the target and it was an amazingly accurate hit. Someone had done their job for them in a not too subtle manner. Amongst the bodies he thought he could see Florence or at least a torso in her yellow coat. No legs were attached. Earl Haig was on her head.

"So this is the end, my beautiful friend," he said to himself, "I'll never look into your eyes again."

The Duke of Devonshire and the Duke of Cambridge had been toppled.

He tried Ian again. No answer. Then to his relief from his vantage point high up he saw them down on Whitehall, in the middle of the road amongst the rubble. A man with one hand standing by the remains of the statue of the Duke of Cambridge's horse, appeared to be talking urgently to two women he recognised as Vilma and Mary. He worried they were taking a risk being in such an open place, but he guessed they thought in the general chaos and panic no one would notice them. It seemed they had just assembled but very quickly they started to scurry off down Great Scotland Yard towards the embankment on their way to Watergate Walk.

Jerry thought it wiser and less risky to catch up with them later as planned. They would regroup, if safe, at York Watergate, in Victoria Embankment Gardens. Ian chose that spot just so he could tell the others it was built by Inigo Jones in 1626 just after he finished the Banqueting House and was the gateway to the Thames until the Embankment, built in the 1860s, pushed the river back 150 yards. If that seemed unsafe with too many G4S security staff and paramilitary around, a second rendezvous point would be Arthur Sullivan's memorial further into the gardens.

The Rutherford women had at last seen their grandfather's nemesis punished. The grandson of Charles Morrison - the man who over a century before had slashed his face at school - had been killed. But the vendetta against all the Morrisons and their type was really for what they stood for and their poisoning of human society and positive progress, not just because of an incident on the playing fields of Eton in the last century. That was not the reason for them targeting the Right Club either. Morrison's grandson was just a bonus.

Silas at eighty-eight had outlived his dad by a year and his twin, Maximilien, who had died after six years in Guantanamo Bay, by ten. The family learnt of Max's fate some years later from Mike Emptage who had been released from the detention camp as not worth bothering with. Vilma and Mary got a message to their father about the latest events via Vilma's son. It was now up to that generation.

Jerry pondered on who was responsible for this massacre and why? He was unaware of any other dissident group - Poison had the field to themselves he thought. It was either the inner circle or those vying to enter that inner sanctum. Whoever it was he feared they were determined to move that tenet of normal public opinion and what was acceptable further to the right of the field. Surely it could not be his worst nightmare? The present, but now deceased, group of utter bastards aren't or weren't bastard enough - too feeble in their ruthlessness, selfishness, arrogance and megalomania? Is there a bigger war going on amongst the top zero point zero one per cent for control of everything? Three yacht battles had now grown into three mega-company wars. It used to be one yacht was not enough. Now one empire is not enough. Where is the human race going? They will never find out for sure. If it follows the pattern of previous assassinations and coups this will not be reported anywhere. Then Guy their long-term and trusted coordinator radioed in.

"It's finally happened. Our elaborate plans, the end. That private security firm has just announced they have taken over. They've announced the deaths of five inner circle company chiefs and moved in for the kill, of everything that stands. The end."

Thinking he wished he had stayed in Purley, Jerry screamed.

"Oh, for fucks sake!"

EPILOGUE

EVERYDAY LIFE

Maybe this world is a broken mirror
Reality in reverse
Maybe it's just a shadow of a parallel universe
I don't know
Why do I want to go there?
Why do I really care?
Why should I climb a mountain?
Find a way - if you dare

Robert Miles (1997)

In a parallel universe Jeremy refused to get into that red van and ran off as his Mum said he should if approached by strangers. So he did not get a smoothie from the lady driver, and she did not get to hear about the infinite parallel universes Jeremy loved to tell people about, or Schrodinger's cat. Instead he lived and grew up to play in goal for Bournemouth Football Club - the Poppies not the Cherries.

In another universe at only nineteen years of age he became the first Green MP for the constituency of South East Dorset, beating the incumbent who had a quadruple-barrelled name and a slave trader ancestor. One of his slaves was Rob Baigent's three times great-grandfather. The people of Dorset no longer wanted as their representative a Harrow educated Lord of the Manor who voted against Alan Turing being pardoned, against private landlords being required to make their homes fit for human habitation, and against making female genital mutilation a crime.

Clive Lister's O.J. Simpson-class barrister was knocked over on his way to court by a taxi carrying a fellow Judge the one and a half miles to his club, Brook's in St James's Street. His replacement turned out not to be as good so he was found guilty of inappropriate sexual conduct with a patient in Hackney and struck off the General Medical Council register he was never actually on. Rob Baigent and Lister's paths never crossed in this other universe so Rob appointed a disillusioned gastroenterologist as a partner in his practice called Alexei Ephialtes instead. Alexei retrained as a GP when he got fed up with his daily routine of instrumentation of orifices. They made a good campaigning team to fight for the renationalisation of the NHS and it never occurred to Alexei that he should put a noose around his neck.

In another universe Rob married Pippa his fantasy woman, retired early and travelled the world. He still felt passionate about the NHS. At the risk of being called a champagne socialist he sent bottles of the French sparkling wine to the investigative reporters who exposed the ignorance and corruption of the Kent MPs who supported the closure of vital stroke units. They were jailed for bribing those responsible for trying to decimate the pathology service down to one private company in which they had a financial interest. Sadly for those MPs they suffered at the hands of the private security firm in the prison they voted to privatise. A prison they shared with the crooks and cheats who lied to discredit the Keep Our St Helier Hospital campaign.

Jenny was very happy with Robin. They both worked at Lewisham Hospital their entire lives, as did their children.

Philip Hobbs did have an awful car accident in 2007, the cause of which was never discovered, but survived thanks to a passing medic called Nigel Carnicero who went on to become President of the Royal College of Surgeons. Philip and Suzy had three daughters. Her first husband, an RAF pilot, underwent gender reassignment surgery soon after their divorce, but sadly his vaginoplasty was complicated by clitoral necrosis.

Philip did well in the civil service, finally succeeding Sir Roland Henderson in the top job after photographs exposing his zoophilia found their way onto the Internet. Henderson fled and became involved with the German support group *Interessengemeinschaft Zoophiler Menschen* through which he was reacquainted with Clifford Wessel. Simon Chisholm was meant to join them but died in a fracking related earthquake that destroyed Blackpool where he was opening up another chemist shop. Philip turned down the automatic knighthood, suggesting his deputy Mike Emptage would be a worthy recipient.

There is another universe where Rosa was at home cooking and the phone did not ring. If it had, Rosa would have rushed to it and in the process burnt herself, albeit in a minor way on the stove. The resulting blister on her hand got infected with staph aureus. This entered her system and set up the spinal abscess that caused her cauda equina syndrome. Because the phone did not ring as the man from the local Labour Party decided he would be seeing her that evening anyway, she remained healthy and finished her teaching career twenty-two years later.

1991 and Jerry Dolan joined the 27 Club. He had just seen an eighteen-year-old Ryan Giggs play a blinder at Selhurst Park where Palace lost to Manchester United 3-1. He thought he would cheer himself up reading *Marxism Today* in his bath and died after miscalculating his drug dose.

Hubert Witney won a popular vote as the most useless Prime Minister ever. The competition was fierce.

Cheryl married the President of the United States but sadly her first child died of measles and her second was autistic.

Lyndon B. Woodward served in Vietnam and was executed for his part in the My Lai Massacre when US Army soldiers murdered about five hundred unarmed civilians.

Pete Moodey deleted the email from Madison and could not retrieve it so they never re-united at the Landmark Hotel in Paddington. So Madison stayed in the USA working for the Republican Party. She supported the President's Federal Government shutdown provoked by Congress refusing to agree an appropriations bill to fund the Anschluss with Canada and Mexico. Eight years later the Government shutdown became permanent.

Rashida Ahmed and her two children Aisha and Usman were not killed in the Grenfell Tower fire disaster - nor were seventy other people as it did not happen in this universe. It did not happen because the woman who had Madison's job at the Department of the Environment was divorcing the man on the Finance Committee of Kensington and Chelsea Council following his affair with a woman from the housing department. She wanted revenge. Several years before her husband had dropped hints about the refurbishment of the Tower, the cost cutting and the warnings the Council had had about the fire risk. Now she told the press. An investigative journalist experimented by setting fire to cladding like that lining Grenfell live on television. The Council had no option but to evacuate and rehouse the residents. But in a neighbouring universe press barons Maxwell, Dacre, Berlusconi and Black had sacked all investigative journalists, the cladding problem was not exposed and so they did burn to death.

Sean McColl did run away to London where, when down on his luck, he met Craig sleeping rough. The shiny polished car driven by the predatory Douglas took a different route that fateful night and missed the two boys. They found a squat at King's Cross and washed glasses in The Flying Scotsman in the Caledonian Road. An audio engineer from Trident Studios in St Anne's Court, Soho was a regular at after hours lock-ins at the pub, got to know the two lads and offered them work at the Studios where they bumped into the likes of Elton John, Bowie and Genesis. Craig's Liverpudlian accent and Sean's adventurous, almost reckless spirit had them rising through the ranks of the music industry until they were both quite wealthy and well connected. Sean escaped motor neurone disease however. He noticed the first purple skin lesion of Kaposi's sarcoma in his early forties and eventually succumbed to acquired immune deficiency syndrome at home in Mayfair.

Chantelle Levesque and her partner Simone never left France and joined the *Mouvement des gilets jaunes*. So did Giselle Arouet who watched Philippe Garrel's *Regular Lovers* again with her father Francoise to get her in the mood for protest. They all marched down the Avenue des Champs-Élysées together initially full of optimism but thinking back to 1968 they were conscious of someone saying, *The only thing we learn from history is that we don't learn from history*. Simone opened branches of her *La Moustache Blanche* in several major cities. Florian the caretaker of the Cirque d'Hiver left that job to work for her in the original Rue Des Tournelles branch. She lived a long happy life with her lover. Francoise Arouet went on to teach Humanities at the École Normale Supérieure de Lyon.

Arthur Rutherford did well in a parallel universe. He still had a clubfoot but avoided Morrison's scar when he hit him over the head with his Walsham and Hughes leg brace. He realised early on after attending one of Goebbel's rallies the power of the media. With Soviet money he moved in quickly to buy and get control of *The Daily Herald* and *The Daily Worker*. He started up *The Daily Citizen* again. The *Daily Express*, *Mail* and *Telegraph* each went out of business. Lords Rothermere and Beaverbrook were jailed for printing lies. Trotsky was the democratically elected leader of the Soviet Union having outmanoeuvred Stalin. A bad universe for pick-axes, the right wing press and dictators. It became the first genuinely truly altruistic communist state working for the people free of corruption.

Alicia D'Avignor-Goldsmid did go to Spain with her Welshman Robert Owen Davies and assassinated Francisco Franco Bahamond. Her son Brigadier Gerald Vaughan-Warner was killed in 1971 in Northern Ireland by his own troops. His right eye failed him. He stepped out in front of an armoured personnel carrier, but just to make sure his second lieutenant reversed back over him. The republicans won the civil war and joined Britain against Hitler ending the Second World War in 1943 - something else knocking two years off the war.

An Australian called Rupert Murdoch had his attempts to influence political leaders across the world halted in 1969 when his wife was kidnapped and murdered with the wife of his deputy Muriel McKay. He gave up his attempts to buy *The Sun* newspaper and became a missionary in the newly formed state of Zaire.

With the help of Rutherford's media Attlee won the 1950 election with an increased majority and forced Churchill into retirement to Chartwell for good. Bevan as Housing Minister achieved his ambition to house every family and guided through Parliament the Bedroom Tax Act, which stated all citizens were entitled to one good bedroom each. Nobody needed more than one so all stately homes had to be given over to the homeless.

Charles Morrison and wife were evicted from their Hetherington Park estate and the *Anti-Privilege Act*, which forbad the wealth buying advantage, meant that their son James ended up working for the local Council. His son Neville benefitted from the standard uniform excellent state education, which evolved after all private schools were taken over for the good of all and paying for education became an offence. He managed the local vegan supermarket but was sacked for refusing to give up his leather shoes.

Slave owner compensation was confiscated from the Vaughan-Warner and Cumberbatch families and sent back to Barbados. Amongst others who benefitted from trickled-down Government pay outs when their families had to release their slaves were at least two Prime Ministers - Gladstone and Cameron - and Graham Greene, George Orwell and Elizabeth Barrett Browning. Because of this Rob Baigent rejected his wife Jenny's suggestion that their third daughter be called Barrett. Quintin Hogg's family had to return £101 million (the equivalent of what £129,464 was worth in 1833) to the families of the slaves they owned in British Guiana used as indentured labour on plantations.

When everyone had a home and the housing crisis was a footnote in history Vilma Rutherford ran the House Transfer Association, which meant estate agents became as extinct as dinosaurs. Mary Rutherford was head of the Legal Association giving out free advice once lawyers had been outlawed.

The nextdoor universe had Bevan defeat the right-wingers in the 1950 Labour Government and no charges were introduced for dental care and spectacles. The NHS principles remained pure and were extended. Once leader he outlawed immoral private practice and the NHS became truly safe. It was universally accepted as the best of man's creations.

A universe not far from that one had a united Palestinian Israeli state free of any weapons where peaceful coexistence was the norm. The same happened in India where on liberation from the British Empire Hindus and Muslins agreed to respect each other and live in harmony. A Pakistani State was unnecessary. The United Nations had real power and segregation was banned across the world. Ireland was united, as there was no reason for it not to be.

Just like if enough monkeys were put to work on enough typewriters one would eventually produce the works of Shakespeare, if the search was thorough enough a universe would be found where everyone lived peacefully together, no weapons existed, there were no national boundaries, good healthy food was plentiful, everyone had a job properly rewarded, education, healthcare and housing were rights freely obtained with equal opportunity, broadcasting was fair and truthful, energy was all clean and renewable and global warming was not a threat. And democracy worked.

Mr Albert survived his aortic aneurysm because a re-born National Health Service won against its enemies, adversaries and detractors, and Max Rutherford died without fuss in his bed aged ninety-nine. Mrs Sharma saw all of her three children produce their own grandchildren. None of them were allowed to eat processed meat. She married her partner Marko Visnjic and eventually the threats to deport him ceased.

Nobody had ever heard of a book called *The Deceit Syndrome*. It did not exist. It was not necessary.

Rob Baigent's molecules were scattered in peace.

Imagine there's no heaven
It's easy if you try
No hell below us
Above us, only sky
Imagine all the people living for today
Imagine there's no countries
It isn't hard to do
Nothing to kill or die for
And no religion too.
Imagine all the people living life in peace
Imagine no possessions
I wonder if you can
No need for greed or hunger
A brotherhood of man
Imagine all the people sharing all the world

ABOUT THE AUTHOR

Paul Hobday qualified as a doctor at Guy's in London in 1979 and after a few terrifying hospital jobs - scary for him but probably more so for his patients - settled as a GP in the Kent village of Sutton Valence and stayed for over thirty years. He felt very privileged to be trusted to care for sometimes four generations of the same family practising real family medicine but apologises for his mistakes.

Throughout that time he fought a seemingly losing battle to help protect the founding principles of the NHS against ignorant politicians, the medical establishment, a gullible media and a bewildered public.

In desperation and anger he stood for Parliament on a Save the NHS platform in 2015, but having been left speechless by events, thought he would write it all down instead and detonate a book on the unsuspecting public.

Despite all that, he feels his proudest achievements are his daughters whom he desperately wants not to have to get their future healthcare from an American-style moneymaking system.

He is thinking of getting a Nye Bevan tattoo. This is his first and last book. One-finger typing takes its toll.

THE LAST WORD

On behalf of all workers in the NHS who risk the sack by speaking the truth, I would like to stick two fingers up at all the snivelling, self-serving, hypocritical, sanctimonious politicians past, present and future, who say how wonderful the NHS is when his or her child falls through a plate-glass door and needs the NHS, whilst at the same time being responsible for cutting, privatising and destroying the service and denying the workers who may have saved their child's life a living wage. These are usually the same creeps who have to pretend to oppose the closure of their local hospital, whilst defending their Government's policy, which is to do just that!

Dr Paul Hobday

"Those who formally rule take their signals and commands not from the electorate as a body, but from a small group of men. This group will be called the Establishment. It exists even though that existence is stoutly denied. It is one of the secrets of the American social order... A second secret is the fact that the existence of the Establishment - the ruling class - is not supposed to be discussed."

Arthur S. Miller

AVAILABLE FROM
STRAND PUBLISHING UK LTD

The Strand Book Of Memorable Maxims - ISBN 9781907340000
The First Casualty by J Adam & MA Akbar - ISBN 9781907340031
The Challenge of Reality by Bashir Mahmood - ISBN 9781907340048
The Path Of The Gods by Joseph Geraci - ISBN 9781907340055
The Strand Book of International Poets 2010 – ISBN 9781907340062
The Assassins Code 1 by Christopher Chance -ISBN 9781907340123
Tragedy Of Deception by Humayun Niaz – ISBN 9781907340130
Marie Antoinette, Diana & Alexandra: The Third I by Alexandra Levin –
ISBN 9781907340161
The Box by Clive Parker-Sharp – ISBN 9781907340154
Storm Over Kabul by Imran Hanif – ISBN 9781907340208
Rhubarb And Aliens by Paul Hutchens – ISBN 9781907340215
The Deceit Syndrome by Dr Paul Hobday – ISBN 9781907340222

All books are available to order online from Amazon.co.uk and
Amazon.com, Kalahari.com, Play.com, Tesco.com, WH Smiths,
Waterstones, Blackwells, Ingrams, Gardeners, from all good booksellers
and direct from Strand quoting the ISBN number.

Follow #strandpublishuk on Facebook and Twitter
Strand Publishing UK Ltd on Pinterest
Youtube: http://www.youtube.com/watch?v=xCa6XrkePNE

For more information about our books and services, visit:
http://www.strandpublishing.co.uk
email: info@strandpublishing.co.uk

Visit the Lightning Source website or read the link below for further
information on our Environmental Responsibilities.
https://help.lightningsource.com/hc/en-us/articles/115001410043-
Environmental-Responsibility

Lightning Source UK Ltd.
Milton Keynes UK
UKHW010706080222
398335UK00001B/53